BY ALEXANDER GORDON SMITH

ESCAPE FROM FURNACE
Lockdown
Solitary
Death Sentence
Fugitives
Execution

The Night Children
An Escape from Furnace Story

The Fury

ALEXANDER GORDON SMITH

the
FURY

FARRAR STRAUS GIROUX
NEW YORK

This one's for Ariana Winter Edwards-Smith.
Thanks for making me an uncle!

Farrar Straus Giroux Books for Young Readers
175 Fifth Avenue, New York 10010

Copyright © 2013 by Alexander Gordon Smith
All rights reserved
First published in Great Britain, in different form,
by Faber and Faber Limited, 2012
Printed in the United States of America
Designed by Jay Colvin
First American edition, 2013
1 3 5 7 9 10 8 6 4 2

macteenbooks.com

Library of Congress Cataloging-in-Publication Data
Smith, Alexander Gordon, 1979–
    The Fury / Alexander Gordon Smith. — First American
edition.
        p.   cm.
    "First published in Great Britain, in different form,
by Faber and Faber Limited, 2012"—Copyright page.
    Summary: To defend themselves, a ragtag group of teens
bands together at an abandoned amusement park after one day
when, without warning, the entire human race turns against
them—Provided by publisher.
    ISBN 978-0-374-32495-7 (hardcover)
    ISBN 978-0-374-32497-1 (e-book)
    [1. Supernatural—Fiction.   2. Survival—Fiction.
3. Horror stories.]   I. Title.

PZ7.S6423Fv 2013
[Fic]—dc23

                                                2012032621

Farrar Straus Giroux Books for Young Readers may be
purchased for business or promotional use. For information on
bulk purchases please contact Macmillan Corporate and
Premium Sales Department at (800) 221-7945 x5442 or by email
at specialmarkets@macmillan.com.

CONTENTS

Wednesday.. 1

Thursday 13

The Other (1) 55

Friday.. 63

The Other (2) 173

Saturday 179

The Other (3) 261

Sunday 277

The Other (4)... 387

Early Monday Morning 395

The Other (5) 449

Late Monday Morning... 463

The Other (6)... 501

Monday Midday 511

The Other (7) 549

Monday Afternoon 559

Monday Evening... 663

WEDNESDAY

What are we but kings of dust and shadow? Lords of ruin,
Who watch empires rise and believe they will stand for all time;
Who tell each other that the end will never come,
That the night will never fall, that the abyss will stay forever closed.

What are we but mindless fools? For the end will come,
The night will fall, the abyss will open.
Soon or late the Fury will rise in all mankind;
And in its light the whole world will burn.

—Ancient Prophecy

IT WAS AN ORDINARY WEDNESDAY AFTERNOON IN JUNE when the world came to kill Benny Millston.

It was his birthday. His fifteenth. Not that anyone would have noticed. He sat in the corner of the living room in the tiny box of a house that he'd called home ever since his parents had split up three years earlier. His mum lay on the sofa, idly picking foam out of the holes the dog had made in the ancient fabric. She was staring at the TV over her huge stomach and between two sets of freshly painted toenails, her mouth open in an expression of awe and wonder, as if she were watching the Rapture, not *Deal or No Deal*.

On the other side of the room, slouched in a wicker bucket chair, sat his sister Claire. She had once been his baby sister, until his *actual* baby sister, Alison, had arrived a year ago. The youngest Millston shuffled in her high chair in the door between the living room and the kitchen, smacking her dinner tray with a plastic spoon. Their dog, an elderly Jack Russell that he had named Crapper when he was a kid, sat under her, snapping half-heartedly at the spoon whenever it came close but too old and too lazy to make a proper effort.

Not one person had said happy birthday to him all day.

This wasn't what was bugging Benny, though. What was really starting to scare him was that nobody had even *spoken* to him all day.

And it wasn't just today, either. Strange things had been going on since last week. He couldn't put his finger on it, exactly; he just knew that something was wrong. People had been treating him differently. He wasn't the most popular kid at school, not by a long shot, but in the last couple of days even the guys he'd called friends—Declan, Ollie, Jamie—had been ignoring him. No, ignoring was the wrong word. They had talked to him, but it had almost been as if he wasn't really there, as if they were looking *through* him. And the stuff they said—*We don't need any more players, Benny. We're busy now, Benny. Goodbye, Benny*—had been downright nasty. They'd been treating him like they *hated* him.

Things were no better at home, either. His mum's vocabulary was usually limited to about twenty words, of which "Do it now," "Don't argue with me," and "I'm busy" were the most common. But this week he'd heard worse. Much worse. Yesterday she'd actually told him to piss off, which had come so far out of left field that he'd almost burst into tears on the spot. Claire too was acting weird. She'd not said anything, but it was the way she glanced at him when she thought he wasn't watching—the way kids looked at strangers, at people they thought might be dangerous.

She was doing it right now, he realized, staring at him, her eyes dark, lined with suspicion, or maybe fear. As soon as he met them she turned back to the television, pulling her legs up beneath her, crossing her arms across her chest. Benny felt the goose bumps erupt on his arms, his cheeks hot but a cold current running through him.

What the hell was going on?

Benny reached up and rubbed his temples. His head was banging. It hadn't been right for a couple of days now, but what had started off as an irritating ringing in his ears now felt like somebody pounding the flesh of his brain with a meat tenderizer. And there was a definite rhythm to it, syncopated like a pulse: *Thump-thump . . . Thump-thump . . . Thump-thump . . .*

Only it wasn't his pulse, it didn't match. If anything, it reminded him of somebody banging at a door, demanding to be let in. He'd taken a couple of aspirin when he'd gotten home from school an hour ago, but they'd barely made a difference. It was literally doing his head in.

He realized Claire was glaring at him again. He pushed himself out of the armchair and his sister actually flinched, as if he'd been coming at her with a cricket bat. He opened his mouth to tell her it was okay, but nothing came out. The only sound in the room was that thumping pulse inside his head, like some giant turbine between his ears.

Benny walked toward the kitchen, Claire's eyes on him. His mum was watching him too, her head still pointing at the TV but her eyes swiveled so far around that the red-flecked whites resembled crescent moons. He turned his back on them, squeezing past Alison's high chair. His baby sister stopped banging her spoon, her face twisting up in alarm.

"Don't cry," Benny whispered, reaching out to her, and the way she pushed back against her seat, her chubby fingers blanched with effort, broke his heart. She wasn't crying. She was too frightened to cry.

That's when he felt it, something in his head, an instinctive command that cut through the thunder of his migraine—*Get out of here!*—surging up from a part of his brain that lay far beneath the surface. *Run!*

It was so powerful that he almost obeyed, his hand straying toward the back door. Then Crapper shuffled out from under Alison's high chair and limped over to him. The dog peered up with such kindness and trust that Benny couldn't help but smile. "There you go, boy," Benny said, tickling the dog under his belly. "You don't hate me, do you?"

And all of a sudden the voice in his head was gone, even the pounding roar slightly muted. Nothing was wrong. He was just having a bad week, that was all.

Benny poked Crapper tenderly on his wet nose then stood up, a head rush making the room cartwheel. He opened up the kitchen cabinet, searching the dusty shelf for a glass.

It wasn't like normal was even a good thing, he thought as he filled the glass with water. Normal sucked. He took a deep swig, letting his eyes wander. Something on top of one the cupboards hooked them, a scrap of color peeking out from the shadows. Benny frowned and placed the glass on the counter. He scraped a chair across the floor and hoisted himself up, coming face-to-face with a rectangular box in crimson gift wrap. A ribbon had been carefully tied around it, topped with a bow.

With a soft laugh he reached out and scooped up the package. It was big, and it was heavy. About the same kind of heavy as an Xbox might have been. And that's when the excitement really hit him, knotting up his guts. His mum had never, ever bought him a console—not a PlayStation, not a Wii, not even so much as a DS. But she'd always said he could have one when he was old enough. He'd never known just how old he'd have to be to be "old enough," but now he did: fifteen!

He leaped down from the chair, bundling the box into the living room, almost knocking Alison out of her high chair in the process. So that's what this had all been about: his mum and his sister teasing him, pretending they'd forgotten his birthday before surprising him with the sickest present ever, probably a 360 with *Modern Warfare 3*.

"Thanks, Mum!" Benny yelled, thumping back down in his chair with the box on his lap. There was a gift card under the loop of the bow, and he fumbled with it, his fingers numb with excitement. *To Benny, at long last, maybe now you'll stop nagging us about it! Wishing you a really happy birthday. Lots and lots of love, Mum, Claire, and Alison.*

"This is so cool!" he said. "I knew you were just kidding."

His headache had gone too, he realized, that generator pulse now silent, obliterated by the unexpected turn the afternoon had taken. He tore at the thin paper, one rip causing it to slough to the floor. Beneath was a green and white box, the Xbox logo plastered all over it, like some beautiful butterfly emerging from its chrysalis. His mum had hefted her bulk from the sofa and was waddling toward him, arms out, and he waited for the hug.

The slap made fireworks explode inside the living room, raging spots of color that seemed to burn through his vision. He was rocked back into the chair, so shocked that the box tumbled off his lap, crunching onto the carpet.

You'll break it! was the first thought that rifled through his head. Then the pain caught up, a flash of heat as if he'd been standing too close to the fire. There was no time for anything else before the second slap caught him on the other cheek, setting off a high-pitched ringing in his ears and making it feel as though his whole face were alight. He looked up, tears turning the room liquid. His mum was there, at least a blurred silhouette the same shape as his mum, one arm held high, swooping down.

Crack! This time it wasn't a slap, it was a punch. Benny's mind went black, nothing there but the need to get away. He could taste something coppery and warm on his tongue.

Blood.

Panic catapulted him from the chair, and he pushed past his

mum hard enough to shunt her backward. She windmilled across the tiny patch of floor, striking the sofa, looking for a moment like she was about to do a top-heavy tumble, only just managing to catch herself. She grunted, the kind of noise a startled boar might make, and Benny looked into her piggy black eyes and saw absolutely nothing human there at all.

"Mum," he tried to say, but the word wouldn't fit in his throat. She teetered, her bare feet doing a weird, silent tap dance until she found her balance, then she threw herself at him. The air was full of noise, the heavy, wet rasps of his mum's breathing and something else: a rising pitch, like a kettle coming to boil. It took Benny a split second to understand that his sister Claire was screaming. She climbed out of the chair so fast that he couldn't get out of her way, her body flapping into his, skinny arms locked around his neck. Then his mum hit them both, her momentum knocking them to the floor.

Benny smacked his head on the carpet, seeing his mum falling on top of him, cutting out the light. Her weight was impossible, pinning him to the floor, refusing to let him breathe. He was enveloped in her smell—body odor and shampoo and the stench of nail polish. He lashed out, throwing everything at her, but he couldn't get any force behind his blows. And she was hitting him back, fleshy fists bouncing off his temple, his neck, his forehead.

Something white-hot burrowed into his shoulder but he couldn't turn his head to see what. This time the pain made him shriek, the cries muffled by the heft of his mother's chest.

It isn't real it isn't real it isn't real.

But he knew it was; he could see sparks flashing in the edges of his vision as his oxygen-starved brain misfired. And worse, so much worse, he could sense death here, *his* death, somewhere in the dark recesses of the shape on top of him.

The thought gave him strength, so much adrenaline flooding his system that this time when he punched upward he caught his mum in the jaw. Her head snapped back and she spat out a blood-soaked grunt, her body weight shifting to the side as she flopped off him. He pulled himself out like someone escaping quicksand, his nails gouging tracks in the carpet. Halfway out he saw that Claire's teeth were lodged in his upper arm, a scrap of flesh caught between them. Then he saw her eyes, so full of rage, and his fist flew automatically, catching her on the nose. With a cry she let go, tumbling away.

Somehow, Benny made it to his feet, careening wildly. He saw that Crapper's jaws were locked around his mum's ankles, aware even in the chaos that his dog was trying to save his life. His mum was rolling like a beached whale, her groans ugly, awful. She was trying to get up, he could see the determination in her eyes as they burned into him. She was trying to get up so she could finish the job.

Claire was already on her feet, lurching at him like a zombie. Benny stabbed both hands in her direction, pushing her into the wall. She bounced off, came at him again, and this time it was Crapper who stopped her, leaping over the floundering body of his mum and latching onto Claire's thigh, bringing her down like a snapped sapling.

Benny crossed the living room in two strides, the kitchen door right ahead of him, the back door visible beyond that. He could make it, get out into the light. He *could* make it.

He sensed a shape at his side and turned to the window in time to see it implode. A hail of glass blasted into the room and he ducked to his knees, his arms rising to protect his face. Something crashed into him and he almost went over again, slamming a hand down onto the carpet to stop himself toppling. He pushed himself up, a sprinter's start, but a hand grabbed his ankle, yanking it hard, causing him to drop onto his face. He kicked out, turning to see his new attacker: a stranger dressed in jeans and a green T-shirt. He had both hands around Benny's leg, and his face—bleeding heavily and flecked with sparkling shards of glass—was a mask of pure fury.

The man pulled again, reeling Benny in like a hooked fish. Claire had managed to prize Crapper loose and now the dog was running in circles howling, the whites of his eyes the brightest things in the room. His mum was on her feet again. There was someone else clambering in through the window as well—their neighbor, Mr. Porter, a man in his seventies, cataract-dulled eyes seething. His hands were balled into white-knuckled fists.

Benny tried to spin around, but the strange man was holding him too tight, his fingers like metal rods in his flesh. He hauled Benny closer, his fingers working their way up to his knees.

"Mum!" he screamed. "Stop it! Stop it!"

They threw themselves onto him, all of them, so heavy and so dark that he felt like a body being lowered into a grave. He thrashed, but he couldn't move his legs, and now something heavy was sitting on his back. Fat fingers were tight around his neck, squeezing his windpipe so hard that his throat whistled every time he managed to snatch a breath. He snapped his head around, trying to shake them loose, seeing two more people climbing through the shattered window, nothing but silhouettes against the sun. They crowded into the tiny room, trying to punch, claw, kick, bite—no sound but their hoarse, ragged breathing and tinny laughter from the television.

Something too hard to be a fist made contact with the back of his head and a seed of darkness blossomed into full-blown night. He could still hear the sound of each blow, but he could no longer feel them. He closed his eyes, happy to let himself sink into this comforting numbness, happy to leave the pain and the confusion behind . . .

It stopped as suddenly as it had started. When Benny tried to breathe in he found that he couldn't. In the last seconds before his life ended, Benny heard the back door opening and the wet patter of footsteps leaving the house, the crunch of the wicker chair as his sister sat back down, a soft whine from the dog.

Then, incredibly, he heard the sound of his mum filling the kettle in the kitchen.

And it was that noise, so familiar, one that he had heard every single day of his life, that ushered him out of the world. Then that too was erased by the immense, unfathomable cloud of cold darkness that had settled inside his head.

His heart juddered, stalled, and he felt something burn up from inside him, a surge of cold blue fire that burst free with a silent howl. Then Benny Millston died on his living-room carpet while his mum made herself tea.

THURSDAY

Heav'n has no rage, like love to hatred turn'd.
—*William Congreve*, The Mourning Bride

EVERYBODY LOVED CALLUM MORRISSEY.

Captain of his class's football team. A gifted student but cool with it, not a try-hard. All-around nice guy. Right now he was belting up the right wing of the school pitch, the ball at his feet, running so fast that the roar of the wind almost drowned out the noise of the crowd. The opposition fullback, Truman, was dead ahead, big but slow. Cal feigned left, tapping the ball through the kid's tree-trunk legs before spinning to his right and cutting toward the goal.

In the eighteen-yard box were two of his best friends, Dan and Abdus, both of them with their hands in the air yelling out for a cross. Cal ducked around another defender, thought about trying to put it in the back of the net himself. But he wasn't greedy. He'd scored once already, a free kick taking the game to 3–1 in their favor. It was better when they all had something to celebrate after the match.

He took a deep breath, enjoying the way time seemed to slow down. The clock mounted on the single stand of tiered seats to his right read 2:32—thirteen minutes left, then it would be over, one step closer to the end-of-year Inter-class Trophy. They'd be paraded through their classes like they were already champions, and maybe this time even Georgia would look up from her book for long enough to congratulate him. She couldn't ignore him forever, not when he was playing this well.

He drew back his foot, ready to launch a high, looping pass

into the center of the box. And that's when something ripped across his ankle.

He dropped to the ground, agonizing heat biting into his leg. He blinked the tears away, gritting his teeth, rocking back and forth with his ankle between his hands until his vision cleared.

Incredibly, the game was still going on. Truman, the one who had tackled him, was back on his feet punting the ball down the pitch. Everyone else was chasing after it like Cal didn't even exist, including Mr. Platt, the PE teacher, who was acting as referee.

"Hey!" Cal yelled, lifting his hand to try to get the man's attention. It wasn't like he'd dived or anything—he could see the blood soaking through his sock, five lines raked over his ankle from Truman's cleats. He called out again, but there was nobody left in earshot.

Up ahead the ball was at the feet of an opposition midfielder. Cal ignored the game, jogging toward Truman. The arse had his hands on his knees, bent double, trying to get his breath back.

"Hey," Cal said, increasing his speed. Truman turned in time to see Cal's fist heading for his cheek. There was a soft thud and the kid's head wobbled like a punching bag. It seemed for a moment like he was going down but he managed to stay on his feet, his plug-ugly mug creased with annoyance.

No, it wasn't annoyance. The look he shot Cal was *way* beyond that. For a second his eyes seemed depthless, full of a hatred that Cal had never before encountered. His face was so dark with anger that it seemed bloated, poisoned. It was the look of somebody who wanted to kill him.

He backed off instinctively, hearing the whistle blow again and again, its shrill pitch gaining volume as Mr. Platt ran their way. Truman lunged, fists balled into boulders.

Someone grabbed Cal from behind, arms locked around his chest. Someone else was at his side, shoving him, shouting at him. In no more than a heartbeat he was being bulldozed by a crowd, their hands and arms like pistons, the sensation like being trapped inside an engine.

"Get off," he yelled. One of the opposition team shoved him hard and he nearly fell, his legs tangled up in those of whoever stood behind him. Then the jowly face of Mr. Platt rose into view. The teacher reached out and grabbed Cal's shoulder.

"That's enough!" he bellowed, his whistle dropping to his chest. "I said stop that, right now."

"Let it go, Cal," said a voice in his ear, and he recognized Joe McGowan, their right-winger, the kid who was holding him.

"Fine, it's over," he said, his voice lost in the roar of the crowd. "But look what that loser did to my leg, almost took it clean off." He reached into his sock, then held up fingers stained with blood, waving them at Truman. "See that?"

"I said enough!" Mr. Platt barked. He blew his whistle again, waving everybody away and reaching into his pocket. He flashed the red card at Cal's face with the enthusiasm of a priest waving a crucifix at a vampire. "You're off, Morrissey, and you're in trouble too. Get moving."

Truman lunged again, but without conviction, happy to let his teammates hold him back. His face had softened and the expression it wore now was one of confusion, almost as though he couldn't quite remember where he was. Maybe Cal had punched him harder than he thought. Mr. Platt turned to the bully, the red card hovering to his side.

"Don't push it, Truman," he said. "Or you're off too. You're lucky I didn't see that tackle."

Gradually the players were drifting away, a series of boos and jeers drifting down from the stands. Cal ran a hand down his football shirt, straightening the creases, and when he looked up Joe was staring at him, one eyebrow raised.

"You okay?" he asked. Cal nodded, and Joe's face broke into a grin. "Almost knocked him on his ass."

Joe's smile was contagious, and Cal found himself laughing. The adrenaline had dulled the pain in his ankle, and there were perks to missing out on the last ten minutes of the match—one in particular sitting in the front row of the stands. Joe held his hand out and Cal gripped it in a surfer's handshake.

"Stick one in for me, yeah?" he said.

"You betcha," Joe replied, running off. Mr. Platt had put the ball down about ten yards from where Cal had thumped Truman, and once again he blew on his whistle, waving at Cal to get off the pitch.

"Yeah, yeah, I'm going," Cal muttered, walking as slowly as he dared. He raised his hands to the crowd, shadowboxing like Rocky, and milked a cheer from them that he rode all the way to the sidelines. He made his way over to his classmates in the first line of folding seats, grateful to be in the shade of the stand. Eddie Ardagh clapped him on the back.

"Douche bag had it coming," he said.

"Shouldn't have hit him, Cal," said Megan Rao, shaking her head. One of her crimson-dyed curls popped loose and she tucked it back behind her ear. "He's gonna be after you for that. You know Truman's crazy."

"Let him come," Cal said, flopping down on the empty seat between Megan and Georgia. Georgia Cole. She had her perfectly petite snub nose in a novel, the way she always did, and when he lightly elbowed her she gave him the merest flicker of attention. Cal didn't press the matter—it didn't look good when you were the one doing the chasing. Instead he turned back to the daylight-drenched field as his team once again fought their way up front. He saw Truman waddling around by himself outside the opposition eighteen-yard box, gently nursing his cheek.

Cal had never been scared of him, even though he was a year older and a hell of a lot bigger. Cal didn't feel scared of anyone, not really. He'd studied Choy Li Fut kung fu since he was eight and although he'd never had to use it in a proper scrap, he knew he could if he needed to.

In his mind's eye he could still see Truman's face after he'd hit him, that primeval hate in his expression, a blood-boiling rage. Megan was right, everyone knew that Truman was crazy. But this was the first time that Cal had thought that maybe he actually *was* crazy.

"Thirsty?" Eddie said, offering Cal a bottle of water.

"You know I don't drink that stuff," he said, pulling a can of Dr Pepper out of Megan's rucksack. He opened the can, taking a deep swig before unleashing a burp that almost blew his head off. "DP. Pure rehydration."

"Don't know how you're still alive," muttered Eddie. "Your insides must be glued together with sugar."

"Go on!" Megan screamed, jumping about a meter into the air, and Cal saw that Ab had dribbled the ball into the box. He shot and the keeper dived for it, meeting it with about half a fingertip but enough to send it wide. Cal was on his feet, hands on his head.

"Man, that was close," he said, collapsing back down hard enough to nudge Georgia's book. This time she looked up at him with a forced scowl, peering at him from beneath her blond bangs. He grinned at her. "Sorry, George, but this ain't no place for a nerd."

"I was dragged here against my will," she replied, and somehow her deepening glower made her look even more gorgeous. Cal felt his stomach fold into itself, his whole body suddenly too heavy, like gravity had just doubled.

"Your leg okay?" Georgia asked, smiling coyly.

"Dunno," he said. "Feels like it could be fatal. Might need some mouth-to-mouth resuscitation in a moment."

"Ew!" Georgia protested, slapping him gently with her book. "Get Eddie to do it."

"*I'll* do it," Megan chimed in, blowing Cal a kiss.

"Thank God," muttered Eddie.

Cal laughed gently, lacing his hands behind his head and resting back in his seat. There was a worm of discomfort nuzzling at his temples, but that was nothing unusual after a match, especially one like this. It was part adrenaline hangover, part dehydration. He knew he should drink more water but he just hated the stuff. Dr Pepper, that was all the liquid he needed.

"That guy is a total donkey," said Megan as Steven Abelard, their slowest midfielder, trotted up the pitch.

Cal took a deep breath, the pressure in his head softening. Then he exhaled and the pain returned, that and a faint pulse that seemed to echo around the front of his skull, no louder than the whisper of distant bird wings.

Thump-thump . . . Thump-thump . . . Thump-thump . . .

"YOU'RE SCARING ME . . ."

Daisy Brien retreated, the ice-cold wall against her back making her jump. Her two best friends, Kim and Chloe, were moving toward her, their hair in identical braids, both wearing old-fashioned puffy dresses that hid their feet and made them look as though they were gliding. Their eyes were wide, unblinking. Ghost eyes.

"Guys, stop it!"

They had boxed her in, the overpacked clothes racks to her right and left like the walls of a hedge maze, too thick to escape through. There was only one door here, invisible in the gloom, but Daisy could make out the green emergency exit light. It seemed a million miles away. Kim and Chloe were close enough to touch, and Kim reached out deliberately slowly with a hand draped in white lace. She ran a cool finger over Daisy's face.

"Stop it!"

"See how she leans her cheek upon my hand," said Kim in a low, phantom groan. "Oh, that Fred were a glove upon my hand, that he might touch her cheek!"

Chloe raised both hands, fluttering them in front of Daisy's chest.

"One, two, and the third in your bosom," she moaned. "Which is where Fred wants to be!"

"Oh, Fredeo," added Kim. "Fredeo, wherefore artest thou, Fredeo!"

"Where fartest thou?" said Chloe. And that did it, the three of them cracking up in peals of laughter that filled the dressing room like sunlight.

"I told you, I don't like him!" Daisy said when her air-starved lungs began to function again. She slapped Kim playfully on her arm, the blow cushioned by an enormous shoulder pad.

"But he's your Fredeo," said Chloe, holding out her hands. Kim grabbed one and Daisy took the other, hauling her back onto her feet. "Fredeo and Daisiet, the world's most romantic love story."

"He's like so not interested in me," she said.

"The lady doth protest too much, methinks," said Kim, wiping the tears from her eyes.

"Wrong play, dingbat," Daisy shot back. She pushed past them, escaping the labyrinth of the theater wardrobe and walking to the huge mirror on the left-hand side of the room. It was ringed by bulbs, just like in a Broadway dressing room, and they painted her reflection in sickly yellow light. Even so, she couldn't help but approve of the way she looked, with her long brown hair trussed up in an elaborate plaited bun. The dress she wore was so white and so elaborate that she could have been a bride, the high, narrow collar making her look taller and more slender than she actually was. It made her look older too, maybe fifteen instead of almost thirteen.

Just about the right age for Fred . . .

She felt the heat in her cheeks and she was glad that she was already wearing her makeup, thick rouge concealing her embarrassment. She busied herself with her gloves, elbow-length strips of cobweb-thin silk that were a nightmare to put on.

At first, three months or so ago, when they'd discovered their roles in the school play, she'd been mortified that the Romeo to her Juliet was going to be so much older. But she'd bitten back her fear and soldiered on, the way her parents had taught her to. And despite her protests, she'd actually liked the attention. She had to keep telling herself that he was just acting, that this fifteen-year-old Adonis who already had a girlfriend wouldn't be interested in the real Daisy Brien in a million years.

"I still can't remember my lines," said Chloe, her reflection joining Daisy's, half a foot taller even though she was a month or two younger.

"You've only got about three," said Daisy as she pulled the first glove on. Chloe was playing Lady Montague, Romeo's mother, and even though she appeared in only two scenes she always managed to get her words in a muddle. Kim was Tybalt, Juliet's cousin, who, their drama teacher had decided, was going to be a girl in this version of the play. She stood to the side, leaning against the makeup shelf, idly waving a cardboard sword back and forth.

"I wonder if you could actually kill anyone with this," Kim said. "Mrs. Jackson, maybe."

All three girls looked at the way the bent sword flopped back and forth and once again they were laughing. The moment was cut short by the snap and creak of the dressing-room door opening, a round, bespectacled face peering inside.

"Did I hear my name?" Mrs. Jackson asked. "Do you need me, girls?"

"It's okay, Mrs. Jackson," said Kim, jabbing the sword in the teacher's direction and breathing *die die die* in between her words. "We were just practicing our lines."

"Good, good," Mrs. Jackson said. "Well, hurry up and get

ready. Dress rehearsal starts in"—she checked her watch for what felt like an eternity—"seven minutes."

She hung on for a second more, as if waiting to be dismissed, then ducked back out of the dressing room.

"I can't be bothered with this," said Daisy, feeling an unwelcome pressure in her chest. She knew it wasn't that she couldn't be bothered. It was nerves. She felt them every time she went onstage, but it was definitely getting worse. "Does someone want to take my place?"

"And fake-snog Freddy? No way!" said Chloe. "I'd rather kiss Mrs. Jackson."

"Liar," said Daisy with a smile. She'd finally managed to pull on her other glove, straightening out the silk around the crook of her elbow. "Ready?"

She turned from the mirror to Kim. Her friend was still waving her sword back and forth, harder now, faster. It was difficult to tell in the murk of the windowless room, but she seemed to be staring right back at Daisy, her eyes impossibly dark. And each time the tinfoil-coated blade swooshed through the quiet air her mouth breathed that same whispered word.

Die. Die. Die. Die. Die. Die. Die.

"Um . . . Kim?" Daisy said. Kim cut back and forth once more, then seemed to stir, as if emerging from a hypnotic trance.

"Huh?" She blinked heavily a couple of times.

"Nothing," said Daisy, walking toward the door. "Come on, let's get this over and done with."

BRICK THOMAS HATED EVERYBODY.

He hated his dad, he hated his stepmum, he hated his real mum too for dying when he was a red-haired brat in nursery school; he hated his brother, who'd left home two years back to join the army; he really hated his teachers, who had told him not to even bother turning up for his college-placement exams, and he really, *really* hated the school counselor who'd informed his dad he had behavioral difficulties; he hated his friends, if you could even call them that when they didn't bother talking to him anymore; and if he was totally honest there were times when he hated his girlfriend—although he wasn't sure about this one because sometimes love and hate felt so similar he couldn't tell the difference between them.

He hated himself too, his brain, the way it made him feel perfectly happy one minute then as miserable as a graveyard the next. He hated it for whispering things to him—*You're no good. You can't do that. You're too thick. No one likes you because you're a head case*—not all the time or anything, but often enough for him to feel like there was something living up there, something that detested him. Most of all, though, he just hated the hate. It was exhausting.

He sat on the raised concrete footpath that looked down over the beach, idly tossing stones at the calm, quiet surf. The tide was out, but even so there were only about twenty meters of shore between the water and the massive dune behind him. On the other side of that lay Fursville, a vast shipwreck of shorn metal and rotting wood and rubbish and rat droppings that had once been north Norfolk's biggest and most popular amusement park.

Back when Brick was a kid he'd come here all the time with his folks. There had been a roller coaster, one of the old wooden ones, no loop-the-loop or anything but still pretty fast. Loads of arcades too, so many that they'd stretched all the way up from the plaza to a pier that had caught fire in 1999, on the eve of a massive Millennium celebration, and which was now a broken, skeletal limb all but buried by sand and surf.

His favorite thing about Fursville, though, had been the water flume, because you had to squeeze into this tiny little longboat that was ratcheted up Everest-high slopes before being slingshot-ted through freezing puddles of water. He'd liked it because it was the only time he'd ever gotten a hug from his dad. The old man didn't have a choice in the matter—you had to grab hold of the person in front of you or risk flying out of the boat on the downward bends. He'd loved that feeling of being held in place, the weight of those tattooed arms on his shoulders, like his dad and gravity were one and the same, stopping him from bouncing right off the planet into the cold, infinite darkness of space.

Not that he ever would have admitted to those feelings, even if he'd been able to put them into any kind of words back then. If nothing else, his pop would have thumped him. Brick was eighteen now, and he didn't care what his dad thought.

He glanced at the sky, a vast expanse of pale blue, the sun so bright that it made his retinas sting. There was no sound but the whisper of the knee-high waves as they cruised onto the stones and the distant chatter of birds. A decade ago he'd loved it here because there were so many people, their constant motion and sound the exact opposite of the cold vacuum at home that his mum had once filled so effortlessly. Now he appreciated it precisely because of the quiet, the stillness. Here, in the mangled guts of Fursville, there was nobody to hate.

Brick's backside was getting numb and he stood up, lobbing a last fist-size rock into the sea. His phone informed him it was after three. Lisa would be leaving school any second now and he'd told her he'd be waiting by the gates. Fat chance, it would take him an hour or so to get back into the city and by that time he expected she'd be home, sending him angry texts.

He groaned, feeling the delicate equilibrium of his mood start to slide. He closed his eyes, the spotlight sun leaving the faintest flutter of pain against his skull.

He walked down the path, the back of his neck stinging where the sun had caught it. He tanned about as well as an albino vampire, his freckled skin veering wildly between extremes of milk white and tomato red throughout the year. His hair color was to blame, about as bright a shade of orange as you could imagine.

About a dozen meters from where he had been sitting was one of the many breaches in the Fursville fence. Most had been caused by nothing more than neglect, the metal simply rusting into oblivion. This one he'd made himself about three years ago when he and a couple of mates had first explored the abandoned park. They'd brought a pair of wire cutters and a flashlight and a rucksack, and they'd spent the night looking for treasures.

In the end they'd not found much apart from a couple of tubs of moldy-looking taffy and a stack of plastic-wrapped urinal-disinfectant blocks that Brick's friend Derek Frinton had claimed they could use to make their own vodka. But they'd had a hell of a night exploring the place. Although the outside areas of Fursville were derelict and dangerous, the inside—once you got past the chains and the locked doors—was in pretty decent shape. Brick had even spent the night there once after a massive dust-up with his dad, sleeping in the old restaurant curled up under a couple of tablecloths that had been left behind.

He pushed his way in through the hole, making sure to tuck the fence back behind him and cover it with a massive square of plywood. Not that he really needed to. Nobody ever came out this way anymore.

It was always like running an obstacle course, getting from the beach into the central plaza, but he negotiated the rubble, the broken glass, and the faded grins of the kids' mini merry-go-round characters with practiced ease. His 50cc motorbike was where he'd left it, propped up against a fountain overflowing with algae. He'd been riding it illegally for a year now but he had no intention of ever going for his driver's test. Not until he was rich enough for a Ducati, anyway.

He pulled the helmet on. It pinned his ears back uncomfortably but at least it hid his hair. Then he clambered on board, the bike far too small for his six-foot-five frame. It took six kicks before the motor decided to wake up, the bike accelerating slowly across the plaza. He ignored the signs for the exit—the front gates were boarded up and chain-bound, Alcatraz-style. Instead he cut toward the southwest quadrant of the park, the engine whining like a bloated fly. He followed his own tire tracks in the dust around the corner and down past the medical shack— the words "Boo Boo Station" just about still visible on the pebble-dashed wall. Right ahead was a gap in the fence, just the right size for his bike. He slowed as he squeezed through, gunning the engine to make sure it didn't stall, then edged between the two enormous laurel bushes that grew up right outside it.

The wide road beyond was deserted. On the other side of it was an abandoned auto showroom that had been forsaken for almost as long as the fairground. Past the empty expanse of concrete and dirt Brick could make out the smoking chimneys and blinking lights of the fertilizer factory that lay half a mile inland. That was the closest anyone really came to Fursville nowadays.

He paused for a minute, enjoying the stillness, the way time seemed to stop here. Even with the nasal whine of his bike it seemed quieter and more peaceful than back in the city. But Lisa was waiting, and the sad fact of it was that she was scary enough even when she wasn't screaming at him.

Sighing, Brick gunned the engine and took off for town.

"So . . . it's BRICK, RIGHT?"

Brick nodded, trying not to smile at the sight of Lisa's mum and dad—staring out at him from the safety of their front porch. He'd avoided meeting them until now. Mr. Dawlish, who was in his early fifties but who looked twice that, was gripping the door with both hands as if he thought he might have to slam it shut at a moment's warning. His wife, who had all Lisa's bad features and none of her attractive ones, was on tiptoes peeking over his shoulder. Both weren't so much smiling as grimacing. He was used to it. Big and broad, he made people wary. And he had one of *those* faces, so he'd been told—whatever that meant. It was just his lot. Everybody hated Brick Thomas.

"She knows you're here," said Mr. Dawlish.

Mrs. Dawlish peered at the helmet clasped in Brick's hands. "I hope you're not planning to take her anywhere on that?"

"No, Mrs. Dawlish," Brick lied. Lisa always rode pillion. It wasn't like anything bad could happen to her—the bike's top speed was just shy of forty when there were two people on it. Despite his answer, Mrs. Dawlish frowned.

"Why Brick?" Mr. Dawlish asked after an uncomfortable silence.

"Just another brick in the Thomas family wall, I guess," Brick said. "My mum and dad have always called me it. It says John on my birth certificate." That was a lie too, his real name was Harry, but he liked to see the look on people's faces when they thought his name was John Thomas. It took Mr. Dawlish a second or two to get the joke, and when he did his forehead creased like an accordion. There were another few strokes of awkwardness before Brick heard footsteps from inside the house. Her parents both turned as Lisa appeared.

"Four o'clock?" she said, tapping the bare patch on her arm where a watch might have been. She was pretty, there was no doubt about that, but she did a good job of hiding it behind too much makeup and hair that was constantly straightened and dyed before being scraped back into a ponytail. She had a stud in her nose and a ring in her eyebrow—both of which he knew her parents had blamed Brick for, even though he hated piercings. She looked at him now from behind false lashes that had been badly fixed. There was something in her eyes, in the way she looked at him. For some reason it made his skin crawl. She must have been *really* angry.

"Sorry," Brick said. "I got caught up at work; there was a late delivery."

"Trouble on-site?" Mr. Dawlish asked. Brick had told Lisa that he worked for the same scaffolding company as his dad. Which was true, strictly speaking, although he hadn't helped out for weeks now.

"Nothing we couldn't handle," Brick replied. "You just can't get the staff these days."

For some reason that seemed to relax the old couple. Mr. Dawlish nodded, a glimmer of a smile appearing in the folds of his face.

"You're not wrong there, son." He turned to his daughter. "Come on, love, are you going or not? You're letting all this heat in."

Lisa locked eyes with Brick for a good seven seconds, then uttered a mini-scream of frustration, barging past her parents and out the door.

"You better make this up to me, Brick," she muttered, that expression demolishing the foot of height difference between them and making him feel like the smaller of the two.

"Easy, tiger," he said, holding his arms up in surrender.

"Have fun," Mr. Dawlish said as they walked down the path. Brick waved, hearing Mrs. Dawlish's shrill cry follow them all the way to the gate.

"Be back by ten, please. And don't you go anywhere on that bike!"

He smiled, but it was short-lived. He glanced at Lisa again, trying to work out what was making him uneasy and wishing that he'd stayed on the beach.

"UM, 'TIS HE, THAT VILLAIN ROMEO," said Kim without enthusiasm, still thrusting her sword but this time at Fred.

"More venom, dear," said Mrs. Jackson from the wings, interrupting the same way she had done with pretty much every single line so far. "You hate his guts."

"I hate *your* guts, you old bag," muttered Kim, the acoustics of the school hall carrying her voice farther than she had intended. Daisy would have laughed except she was exhausted. They'd been here for well over three hours and they were still on Act I. At this rate they wouldn't be home till the weekend, even though they were only doing a cut-down version of the play.

"'Tis *he*," Kim spat, thrusting her weapon, giving all the venom she could manage. "That *villain*, Romeo!"

"Content thee, gentle cuz, leave him alone," said Ethan, the fat kid from Daisy's year who was playing her dad. He was wearing a toga, and he'd drawn a goatee on himself with eyeliner that made him look ridiculous. "I would not for all the wealth of all the . . . town, um, here in my house do him . . .'"

"Disparagement, Ethan," said Mrs. Jackson without needing to look at the script in her hand.

"Yeah, disparagement. So be patient, take no note of him, it is my will."

"It fits, when such a villain is a guest," Kim went on. "I'll not endure him."

"You'll make a mutiny among my guests!" roared Ethan, shaking his fists. "You will set cock-a-hoop!"

Everybody giggled—they always did at that line.

"Romeo?" said Mrs. Jackson. "Romeo, wherefore art thou, Romeo?"

"Huh?" Fred said, obviously perplexed. He stood on the other side of a large canteen table, and he must have sensed Daisy looking because he glanced up, catching her eye.

"It's your line, Fred dear."

"Oh, er." He put both hands on the table and stared at Daisy. "If I profane with my unworthiest hand this holy shrine, the gentle fine is this: my lips, two blushing pilgrims, ready stand to smooth that rough touch with a tender kiss."

In the corner of her eye Daisy could see Kim cracking up, and it took all her strength to stop from joining her.

"Good pilgrim," she said, her voice trembling.

"Too soft, dear, they won't be able to hear you at the back."

Daisy cleared her throat, speaking louder, talking not quite to Fred's eyes but to his chin. "Good pilgrim, you do wrong your hand too much, which mannerly devotion shows in this; for saints have hands that pilgrims' hands do touch, and palm to palm is holy palmers' kiss."

"Good, Daisy," said Mrs. Jackson, doing a perfect job of ruining the dramatic tension.

"Have not saints lips, and holy palmers too?" asked Fred.

"Ay pilgrim, lips that they must use in prayer."

"O, then, dear saint, let lips do what hands do; they pray, grantest, lest love turn to, uh . . . despair?"

"Close enough," said their drama teacher.

"Saints do not move, though grant for prayer's sake," said Daisy. Her pulse was quickening. Three more lines, then it was her favorite—and least favorite—part of the whole play. She took a sideways step to her left, Fred mirroring her.

"Then move not, while my prayer's effect I take," he said, using a fingernail to scratch a mark from the surface of the table. His cheeks were starting to glow as well. "Thus from my lips, by yours, my sin is purged."

They both took another step to the side, converging on the narrow end of the table.

"Then have my slips the sin that they have took," she said, her tongue not working properly.

"Sin from thy lips?" Fred said, his voice a mumble. He stepped around the side of the table and Daisy moved with him so that they were facing each other, almost touching. Daisy's head was pounding—not really painful, just a pressure there, like it might pop clean off. The theater had never seemed so quiet. "Oh, trespass sweetly urged, give me my sin again."

Fred leaned forward. Daisy craned up, standing on tiptoes, falling toward him. Her head was screaming now, a kettle coming to boil between her temples. Daisy's eyes rose, she couldn't stop them—up from Fred's chin, past his lips, his nose, meeting his eyes as their lips converged.

She froze, suddenly breaking into a cold sweat, as if the temperature in the hall had dropped below zero. Fred's eyes were empty, the unseeing, unfeeling black beads of a doll. They looked as if they might just roll out of their sockets as he angled in toward her. She recoiled, but Fred kept on coming, towering over her, his teeth clenched.

Then his mouth opened, and he spat in her face.

Daisy could feel his warm saliva on her top lip—not much, just foam really, hot against her cool skin, but she couldn't seem to lift her arm to wipe it away. She couldn't move a single muscle.

Fred started to laugh, those dead eyes still boring into her.

And then somebody else joined him. Daisy saw Kim pointing at her and screeching with delight. It was taken up by somebody else, and another, then another, until the hall reverberated with the sound of it.

"You kiss by the book," said Mrs. Jackson in between soft chuckles of her own.

"What?" Daisy asked, staggering back, wiping her gloved forearm over her face.

"Your line, dear. You kiss by the book."

It was all too much, the hall starting to spin. She turned and ran, thumping down the wooden steps and barging through the double doors, Mrs. Jackson's voice shrieking out behind her.

"By the book, Daisy, *by the book*!"

CAL / *Oakminster, 6:34 p.m.*

"STILL CAN'T BELIEVE WE THRASHED THEM," said Abdus, breathless as he paddled past on his skateboard. He reached the steps that led to the small plaza outside the library, ollieing down them but bailing before he hit the tiles. He recovered his balance, chasing after the rogue board before turning back to Cal. "Three–one!"

Cal raised both hands in a rock-star salute. He was sitting at one of the metal tables outside the milk shake café that had become their favorite place to hang out, especially after a match. Udderz let you pick your favorite chocolate bar then blended it with ice cream and milk to make just about the best shakes on the planet. Cal was on his third of the afternoon, this one made up of Boost bars. It was making him feel a little queasy, but he wouldn't let that stop him from finishing.

The place was mobbed. Sharing his table were Megan, Eddie, Dan, and the keeper, Jack, who was perched on the edge providing a nice bit of shade from the evening sun. The other two tables had been occupied by the rest of the team, all except Steven Abelard, who lived out in the sticks and always had to leave early. Several other kids from his year were scattered around, including Georgia, who sat just inside the large front window, behind the huge stenciled "e" of Udderz, absorbed in whatever it was she was reading.

Someone else flashed past on a board, a kid from the year below, Cal thought. He ollied onto the handrail that dropped down into the plaza, doing a sketchy grind then a trey flip, landing with nothing more than a wobble. He swooped around in an arc back to where a bunch of his mates were looking up at the occupied tables, like they were planning an invasion.

"So, fancy our chances tomorrow?" Eddie asked, pushing his glasses up onto his nose. Eddie was asthmatic, he had it pretty bad, which meant he couldn't play for the team. That was a shame, because whenever they kicked the ball about at lunch he was actually pretty decent.

"Those guys are tough," said Jack without looking around. "They won it last year. They got that tall kid, Nasim, the one everyone said was being scouted by Arsenal."

Cal snorted, pretending to be unimpressed. Truth was that Nas, a midfielder, *was* good enough to be signed. Last time they'd been in a match together Nas had run rings around Cal. But Cal was a hell of a lot better on the pitch now.

"We'll take them," he said. "Nas or no Nas."

"Well, if you can't outrun him you can always punch him in the face," said Megan, and everyone laughed.

One of the skateboarders took a tumble on the plaza, doing an impressive forward roll before lying flat and staring at the sky. Everybody cheered and clapped. Cal leaned back in his chair, taking another sip of his supersweet shake. It was so warm here, and peaceful.

The only thing that was dragging on the mood was his stupid head, still pulsing. It didn't hurt, not the way a proper headache did. It was just uncomfortable—*thump-thump, thump-thump, thump-thump*—like there was something inside there, a dying bird slowly flapping broken wings, trying to lift off . . .

Christ, where had *that* come from? Cal shuddered, the image making his stomach churn even harder than before. Dan had reappeared, slamming back down into his seat and sucking on a brand-new shake. The sound he was making seemed too loud, and it was a second or two before Cal realized that it was because the chatter in the plaza had softened. People were still talking, but in whispers. It was almost like one of those weird silences, the kind where everyone stops speaking because they think everyone else has, and they all look at each other for a minute wondering what's going on, then laugh and carry on.

Only nobody was laughing. The younger kids below were still looking up at the café like they wanted the tables. The skaters had stopped and were all staring at them too.

"Creeeeeepy," Cal said, doing his best to smile. Eddie was observing him with an expression of intense confusion, as if Cal had suddenly sprouted a pig snout or panda ears or something. It wasn't just Eddie, either. Megan was frowning his way, her nose wrinkled up. Cal's head swung left and then right to see that pretty much everyone on the plaza seemed to be glowering at him. Even Georgia had finally looked up. It might have been the reflection of the evening light on the window, but Cal could swear her lips were pulled back, distorting her flawless face into a grimace.

He scraped back his chair, getting to his feet, running a hand through his hair.

"Ha ha, very funny, guys," he said, his lonely voice echoing across the plaza. The three pints of milk shake he'd consumed that afternoon were now rioting in his stomach.

Nobody replied, they were all just staring at him, their faces bent with the same stupefied expression. Cal pushed himself through the wide-eyed crowd, trying not to run as he made his way toward the steps. His throat tickled, the way it always did when he was about to hurl. The shake bar didn't have a toilet, but the library did.

He crossed the plaza in a dozen strides, dashing through the automatic doors. He stopped for long enough to look back, relief flooding through him when he saw that one of the skateboarders was moving again, that Eddie and Megan and the rest of his mates seemed to be back to normal, chatting away.

They've had you good and proper, he thought as he walked toward the bathroom. *Psst, at quarter past seven tonight everyone stare at Cal, see if we can freak him out, pass it on.*

And the worst thing was it *had* freaked him out.

He slammed open the outer door, pushed his way through the inner door and straight into the only empty stall. The second he opened the lid he thought his last shake was coming back, boiling up from his stomach. But after a couple of dry heaves he felt it settle. He stood hunched over the bowl for a minute more just to be sure, then put the lid down.

Cal walked out of the stall, splashing some water on his face and staring at his reflection in the graffitied mirror. He did look a little pale—*peaky*, as his mum always said.

Feeling a little steadier, Cal made his way out of the toilet. He'd suck it up, let his friends have their victory. Girls liked a guy who could laugh at himself. Georgia was always saying that he took things too seriously.

He walked over to the plaza, keeping his head down in mock shame, dodging the skateboarders who crisscrossed the tiles, waiting for the catcalls, the whoops, the jeers. They didn't come, and it was only when Cal had jogged up the steps that he realized the kids who were sitting there weren't his mates at all. The younger kids had occupied every single table, laughing and shouting at each other, a few of them eyeballing him warily.

What the hell? he said beneath his breath, scanning the inside of the café. Georgia had gone, *everyone* had gone. He swiveled, seeing no trace of them anywhere in the plaza or the two footpaths that led out toward the street. He looked at the nearest kid, a girl with green hair and a Linkin Park T-shirt. "You see where they all went?"

"No," she spat, like it was the stupidest question in the world.

They were still here, somewhere, Cal was sure of it. Probably wetting themselves laughing. Well the hell with them, he wasn't going to stand around like an idiot waiting for them to show their faces. He moved away from the café, his head banging as he walked alone into the hot, heavy summer evening.

BY THE TIME BRICK ARRIVED BACK AT FURSVILLE the sun was well on its way toward the white heat of the horizon. It was no cooler, though, the coast flattened by an invisible muggy fist.

"OMG, Brick, you've crippled me," Lisa said as she clambered off the pillion seat, nursing her backside with both hands. "When are you gonna get a car?"

"When I can afford it," he said, waiting for her to stand clear before swinging his leg over. He stretched, hearing his spine pop, then weaseled off his helmet. The pain of his pinned-back ears began to ebb, leaving the strains of an approaching headache. He recognized the discomfort, like the first rolls of thunder from a distant storm.

Why on earth had he brought Lisa here?

It had been a spur-of-the-moment thing, a *stupid* spur-of-the-moment thing. After he'd picked her up they'd ridden over to Riverside Cinema, stopping at his house for a spare helmet. She'd demanded that he take her to the movies to make up for being so late, and he'd reluctantly agreed, even when the only thing about to start had been some awful romantic comedy with Jennifer Aniston and some dude he half recognized from a comedy show on TV.

After the film, Brick had been so relieved to be out in the sunshine again that he'd had a sudden rush of euphoric happiness. The only other place he'd ever really been this happy was Fursville, and in some bizarre and flawed twist of neural logic he'd decided there and then to let Lisa in on his secret.

"You wanna see something cool?" he'd said as they made their way back to the parking lot. "Come on, it won't take long."

She'd protested and grumbled and moaned, and it only took about five minutes of riding out toward the coast with her voice in his ear for Brick's mood to plummet.

"What the hell is this place?" she asked, pulling off her own helmet, shaking out her curls. For a second, as she did so, she looked unbearably pretty to Brick. Then her face crumpled up into that all-too-familiar mask of misery and disappointment. "Fursville? Didn't this used to be an amusement park or something?"

Duh, thought Brick, glancing up at the big Ferris wheel, or what was left of it. With only a few of its gondolas remaining and its broken spokes bent out at all angles it resembled some leprous, anorexic giant.

"Please tell me you didn't drag me out to see *this* crapyard," she spat. He didn't say anything. He didn't dare. He felt ridiculously protective of the place. Hearing her talk about it this way made his blood boil.

"Let's just get inside," he said. "I don't want people to know I come here."

"I'm not surprised. Why *do* you come here?" Lisa said as he wheeled the bike into the laurel hedge. It was cooler there, like he'd stepped into a fridge, and darker too. Just being out of the sun calmed him down a little. He could hear Lisa stepping after him, swearing as the branches snagged her hair, as the fat, cool leaves slapped against her face. Then they were out, pinned between the shrubbery and the fence. The gap was dead ahead and he maneuvered himself and the bike through it, hefting it over the rubble and the rubbish.

Home sweet home.

They emerged out onto the plaza, the whole place drenched in silence. The big wheel stretched overhead, and behind it was the rotting wooden track of the roller coaster.

"Bloody hell, Brick, you really know how to impress a lady, don't you."

"You're no lady," he said.

"Oi!" She tried to clip him around the head but he dodged out of the way, jogging backward as she came after him. "You stand still and take your punishment, Brick Thomas."

She charged again, and this time when he wheeled beneath her hand she was laughing. He turned, running to the left of the big wheel, past a boarded-up kiosk crowned with a huge plastic hot dog, making for the biggest building in the park. It was a squat, ugly box about the size of the hall back at his school, with a turquoise plastic façade that was supposed to make the roof look like rolling waves. A few of the three-meter-high letters above the main door had fallen off, leaving the gap-toothed word PAV L IO . Lisa caught up with him under the decaying awning of the veranda, grabbing his elbow and spinning him around.

"I told you to take your punishment." She grinned, then leaned up and kissed him. He closed his eyes and opened his mouth, feeling her tongue flick against his. He didn't know how much later it was when she pulled away, and it took him a moment to remember where he was. The kiss had helped his headache too, that relentless *thump-thump* quieter now, like distant waves.

He turned and walked along the side of the building. Lisa sneaked up beside him, lacing her hand through his.

"You seriously come out here by yourself?" she asked as they came around the corner. The path here was cracked and uneven, the nine mini-golf holes to the side overgrown almost beyond recognition. A giant squirrel with half its concrete face missing watched them go from behind a thorned veil of brambles.

"All the time," he said. "The only place I can get any peace and quiet."

"It's majorly creepy."

Halfway down the pavilion's side wall was a fire exit, the two doors connected by a chain the size of a boa constrictor. Brick took hold of one and pulled, the doors opening a couple of feet before the chain stopped them. He ducked underneath it, squeezing into the darkness.

"No way, Brick, it's filthy in there," Lisa said, her voice muted by the sheer weight of silence inside. Tendrils of light oozed down from algae-slicked skylights, barely enough to see by.

"It's fine, I promise," he said, pushing the doors out as far as they would go. Eventually Lisa squatted down, worming through the gap, doing her best not to touch anything. She stood, looking around the gloomy corridor, brushing her palms over her jeans.

"It's pretty run-down," Brick explained, turning right toward the front of the building.

Lisa was quick to follow, the click of her heels echoing into the swamp of shadows that stretched the length of the corridor.

"But the basement's still in decent shape."

"The *basement*?" Lisa said, pulling herself closer to him.

Brick passed two doors on the left but opened the third. What lay beyond resembled a tar pit, so pitch-black that it seemed to bleed darkness out into the corridor.

"No way am I going in there, Brick," she said, and the tone of her voice had changed, her anxiety now genuine.

He reached in, fumbling in the shadows until he found what

he was looking for. With a click the flashlight he'd picked up came to life, banishing the artificial night to reveal a staircase leading down toward a short corridor packed tight with junk. Even with the light it looked pretty sinister.

"Gets better down there," he said. He held Lisa's hand tight, pulling her gently but insistently after him. "Come on."

She stumbled in his distorted shadow as he wove through the junk and pushed open another door, leading her into the basement. He hadn't been lying, it *was* better down here. For some reason the smell of damp and rot that infested the entire park, especially the pavilion, was less potent belowground. It had been cleared as well, the large, open space free of clutter. He propped the flashlight against the wall, its soft glow illuminating a moth-eaten pink sofa against the far wall, a coffee table in front of it. Other than a boiler that sat cold and quiet in the corner, and a bunch of electrical boxes on the walls, that was about it.

"Moved everything else upstairs," he said, walking to the table and picking up a box of matches. There were a couple of candles there he'd swiped from home and he lit them both, the shifting light on the walls making it feel like they were underwater. "Kind of cozy down here, yeah?"

"I guess so," she replied. "If you're Dracula."

"Shut up," he said without malice. He let go of her hand, walking to the sofa and perching there. His laptop sat open on the coffee table and a pay-as-you-go Internet dongle poked out of one of the USB ports, the tip flashing. He got a better signal upstairs, but he preferred it down here, especially in the evening, and it wasn't like he ever needed to hurry. That's what he loved about this place, there was no rush. Time just didn't seem to matter.

His headache was back with a vengeance and he used both

hands to massage his temples, willing it away as Lisa sat down next to him.

"Okay, you've got me down here," she said. "What do you want to do?" She smiled, tilting her head and chewing her bottom lip.

The flashlight threw her face into sharp relief, picking out the woodchip-like spots beneath her makeup, but her eyes flashed with excitement and something else too, something that made her just about the most desirable woman Brick had ever seen in his life. She leaned in, and he met her, the world peeling away around them, forgotten.

DAISY / *Boxwood St. Mary, 7:07 p.m.*

DAISY SAT ON THE STEPS outside the school's main entrance, waiting for her mum to show up and trying not to think about what had happened back in the theater. She was hurt and angry and sad, but the emotions were so evenly matched that all she really felt was numb. She couldn't believe that Fred had spit on her, that he'd *spit right in her face*. It wasn't that which had really stunned her, though, it was the laughter that had followed. It was like something from a nightmare, one of the ones where you've done something stupid and everyone turns on you and you can't understand why.

Except this was no nightmare. Everyone had turned on her, *everyone* had laughed.

She could still see Kim's face, twisted by some kind of sick glee. And Mrs. Jackson too. She at least should have known better. Why hadn't she said anything?

A car pulled into the parking lot, circling the memorial flower bed at its center, and Daisy straightened. It was blue though, not white, and she slumped back down, clamping her rucksack to her chest. She'd hoped her mum would arrive before everyone started to leave; she didn't want to see anyone else that night. She didn't want to see them ever again. She just wanted to go home and watch TV and draw and try to forget about everything.

The main door clicked behind her, making her jump. There was a thunder of footsteps, a gang of kids running down the steps. They looked at her curiously, as if they couldn't quite remember who she was. Better that than them still laughing, though. Daisy shrank into her rucksack, peering over the top of it.

Come on, Mum, hurry up.

Click, more footsteps, and this time Daisy felt a hand on her shoulder. She looked up to see Chloe there. She'd taken off her costume and was wearing her school uniform again, her hair still done up in old-fashioned plaits.

"What happened to you?" she asked.

"What do you mean, what happened?" Daisy asked, the anger quickening her tongue. "You were there, I saw you laughing."

"That thing with Fred?" Chloe said, sitting on the step next to her. More kids barreled out, streaming into the parking lot. "The *sneeze?*"

Daisy frowned, shaking her head. She quickly glanced over her shoulder to make sure the coast was clear before leaning in toward Chloe.

"What do you mean, 'sneeze'? He spit in my face."

Chloe grinned, but there was nothing nasty in it.

"He sneezed," she said. "Then you went running off before he could say sorry."

Daisy was still shaking her head. She could still see his eyes, devoid of anything nice, anything kind. He'd spit on her, and it had been deliberate.

Hadn't it?

"He said sorry?" she asked after a moment.

"No, not in so many words. He would have done, though, obvs, if you hadn't run off like your knickers were on fire."

"You were all laughing," Daisy said, quieter now, staring down the steps. "I saw you."

Chloe leaned in, putting an arm around Daisy's shoulder.

"Sorry, but it *was* funny, you've got to admit that. I bet you anything you'd have been laughing if it was me."

"Or me," said a voice behind them. Kim jogged down the stairs, gave Daisy a quick hug from behind, then carried on, heading for the blue car. "That's my dad. Sorry, Daisy, but it was quite funny. Don't be sad; I'm sure Fred still loves you."

She clambered into the passenger seat, blowing Daisy a kiss through the window as the car pulled away. Cars were spilling through the gates now, drivers doing their best not to run over the small army of pupils that had assembled at the foot of the steps.

"See, it's all fine," said Chloe, removing her arm and using it to gently nudge Daisy. "You're coming to rehearsal tomorrow, right? The last one, you have to."

Daisy didn't answer. Her shoulders felt a little lighter, her head clearer. Maybe Chloe was right. Maybe it had all been a misunderstanding.

"That's me," said Chloe, giving Daisy a hug. "Love you."

Daisy nodded, managing a ghost of a smile, then Chloe was gone, climbing into the back of her dad's four-wheel-drive. It drove up to the gate, pulling out at the same time as a familiar battered white Spacewagon entered. Daisy got to her feet. She didn't think she'd ever been so relieved to see her mum. She ran to the car, opening the door so hard it bounced on its hinges, almost swinging closed again. She fought her way into the passenger seat, still clutching her rucksack to her chest like a life jacket.

"How'd it go?" her mum asked, tucking a wisp of white hair into her headscarf.

Daisy opened her mouth to answer, then froze. Mrs. Jackson stood at the open door of the school, a lump of shadow. Her half-moon glasses seemed to burn across the parking lot, right into Daisy.

"Fine," Daisy lied, shuddering. "It went fine."

Her mum drove through the gates. Behind them, Mrs. Jackson stood in the doorway, unmoving, unblinking as she watched them go.

BRICK / *Fursville, 8:01 p.m.*

"Ow!"

Brick snapped his head back, almost leaving part of his bottom lip between Lisa's teeth. He sucked it into his mouth, feeling it start to swell.

"What the hell, Lisa!" he said. "That really hurt."

Lisa didn't reply, she just stared at his mouth. Brick wasn't sure how long they'd been kissing but it felt like forever—in a good way. The basement was still coming into focus around him, the real world slowly reassembling itself, like it hadn't existed at all for the last hour or so.

"You gonna try and eat me again?" Brick asked, feeling his mood wobble. Lisa shook her head, looking as dazed as he felt. Her eyelids were heavy, half-closed, and most of her makeup had rubbed off against his cheek, revealing the blush underneath. She had a red patch on her chin where his uneven stubble had scraped against it. She leaned toward him again and he wrapped his arms around her, pulling her close. Everything felt like it was in slow motion, the silence more of a physical pressure in his ears than an absence of sound, and Brick once again had the absurd notion that they were underwater. He kissed her, their tongues dancing, reality spinning away once again.

More pain, this time so sudden that he saw it as a bright flash of light. He pushed Lisa back, putting his hand to his mouth. The tips of his fingers came away red. She'd bitten him in exactly the same place as before, a knot already forming beneath the skin of his lip.

"Jesus, Lisa, stop it." He could taste blood against the words, coppery and sharp. "I'm serious."

Still she didn't speak, sitting back against the sofa and licking her lips. She seemed half-asleep, and beneath her drooping lids her eyes were darkened with something that Brick couldn't quite identify. For the first time he wondered if the air was safe down here.

"Lisa? Baby?" He'd never called her "baby" before, but she was seriously starting to freak him out. "You want to go? Get some fresh air?"

After what felt like a solid minute she shook her head again. She reached out and grabbed Brick by the scruff of his shirt, reeling herself toward him with a wide-open mouth. Brick recoiled, his lip throbbing, but the thought of another kiss snuffed out everything else. He pushed his mouth against hers, working his hand back underneath her T-shirt where it had spent the last half hour hovering with nervous impatience around her lower rib, uncertain about which direction to take so taking neither. Her skin was so hot she might have had a furnace under there. Brick's heart was like the beat-up engine on his bike, going so fast and so hard he was worried it might stall.

Lisa's hand was still wrapped around the collar of his shirt and she used it to push him back into the sofa, clambering onto his lap, their lips never parting. The change of position, his neck wedged at an awkward angle, made his headache worse, that pulse so loud it was like a hand inside his skull.

Lisa's kisses were furious now, so hard that their teeth were clashing. She banged her nose against his and he tried to tilt his head so it wouldn't happen again, a lance of discomfort spearing his neck. She didn't let up, bearing down on him, covering his mouth with her own so that he couldn't get a breath in, her tongue trying to worm down his windpipe.

He attempted to shove her away but she felt heavier than he would have believed possible. The angle his body was locked in—bent into the crook of the old sofa—made it impossible for him to find leverage. He pushed forward with his head and she moved with him, locked onto his lips like a leech. He did it again, butting her with more force. Her head swung back.

It wasn't Lisa.

It looked like her but there was something wrong with her

face, like it had melted. All of her muscles had gone slack, reminding him of his gran when she'd had a stroke.

"Lisa?" Brick said, the words half eaten by fear as he squirmed beneath her. "What's wrong? Baby, tell me what's wrong."

She came for him again, that sunken face closing in, her mouth so wide that Brick almost screamed at the sight of it. He grabbed her shoulders, keeping her at arm's length, trying to maneuver himself toward the edge of the sofa.

He shook her, her head lolling back on her shoulders like a rag doll before snapping back, dropping toward him again.

"Brick," she slurred, and he could see that the paper bag of her mouth was almost smiling.

And just like that the pounding in his head stopped, the pain vanishing with such speed that its absence was almost as frightening.

"No way," he said. Lisa had stopped trying to kiss him, her head tucked into her chest, swaying gently. He still had her by the shoulders and he could feel the muscles beneath her T-shirt, small but tense. He wondered if maybe his headache and her weirdness were related. Maybe he shouldn't have lit the candles without proper ventilation. "You okay? Let's get—"

Lisa screamed, the noise like nothing Brick had heard. It was raw, it was savage, it was hate-filled, and it seemed to go on forever. The scream died out with a hideous rattle, flecks of spit popping from her lips. Lisa lowered her head, her eyes so dark they looked black; insect eyes, fixed on Brick with a look of undiluted fury. He tried to call her name but he never got a chance.

She went for him, her head darting forward like a cobra's. Her teeth scraped down his forehead, locking onto the flesh of his eyebrow and biting hard. Brick found his voice, shrieking. Blood gushed into his eye, trickling into his mouth, choking him. She was chewing, working his face like a tough lump of lamb, her breath coming in short, meaty gasps. She was punching him too, he realized, the blows lost in the supernova of agony that burned in his face.

He cried out again, catapulting off the sofa. Lisa clung on, wrapping her legs around his waist, her fists slapping against his shoulders, his ears, his throat.

Brick staggered, tripping on the coffee table, both of them toppling. She hit first, grunting as he crushed her, his weight rolling them both off the other side onto the floor. She landed on top of him, her teeth ripped from his eyebrow. She lunged again, going for his cheek, and he only just managed to get a hand up under her chin before her jaw snapped shut. He noticed she'd lost one of her teeth, but she didn't seem to care. Her eyes blazed only hatred. She was rabid, feral.

And she was going to kill him.

He drew back his arm and punched her, catching her in the nose, showering himself with warm blood. Then he brought his knee into her ribs, twisting the same way so that she tumbled off him.

He grabbed the table, hauling himself to his feet. Lisa was quick, though, uncoiling and sinking her teeth into his heel. The pain almost sent him sprawling to the floor again. He wrenched his foot loose, limping toward the basement door. He could hear Lisa scrabbling and looked back over his shoulder to see her squirming on her back. Her ankle looked wrong, bent at a strange angle. She rolled, jerking up onto her feet like she didn't even notice her foot was broken, coming after him with long, clumsy strides.

Brick threw himself forward, hearing her gaining, hearing that animal groan spilling from her lips. He careened into the door, falling through it face-first into the wall beyond. He thrashed in the darkness, turning, seeing Lisa tear toward him, foam spilling from her jaw, blood trailing out of her nose.

He kicked the door shut, and the whole corridor seemed to tremble as Lisa hit the other side. The door started to open and he braced his back against the wall, keeping his legs tense, grateful for once to be six-five, tall enough to keep his feet against the metal fire plate. There was a patter of footsteps then another spine-snapping crunch, more like a rhino charging at the door than a sixteen-year-old girl.

More steps, another attempt. Brick didn't move, just kept his whole body tense as the door bulged then clicked shut, bulged then clicked shut, some awful heartbeat as she charged again and again and again. Only now did he notice that he was bawling like a baby, his face wet with tears and blood and snot. But he couldn't stop, those sobs too big to be kept inside. He lay there crying, screaming into the boundless darkness of the corridor, while Lisa bayed for his blood.

THE OTHER (1)

Heed the breath of the Beast;
in death he rises,
and in our darkest days
he will devour us all.
            —*The Book of Hebron*

MIDNIGHT, ON ONE OF THE HOTTEST, muggiest nights of the year, and here he was buried alive in the morgue of Scotland Yard.

And it wasn't even his shift.

Inspector Alan Murdoch traipsed down the last flight of stairs and along the green-tiled corridor. There was nobody at the reception desk, which wasn't surprising given the time, but he knew the way all too well. The morgue was his second home, he spent more time in this crypt than he did at home with his wife—not to mention the baby he'd seen maybe a dozen times in twice as many days since it had been born.

Murdoch sighed, wiping a hand over the thick stubble he hadn't had a chance to shave since beginning his own shift twelve hours ago, Thursday noon. Then he leaned on the door, almost falling through it into the waiting area. He was expecting it to be deserted as well—during the graveyard run people tended to avoid coming down here—but it wasn't. He did a quick head count: eight people crammed into the small room. His good friend and the force's chief pathologist, Dr. Sven Jorgensen, was in the middle, a blond beanpole in a white surgical suit who towered over the similarly dressed assistants to his side. Even through the biohazard mask his face was creased into a deeper frown than usual. He caught sight of Murdoch and looked over, the reflection of the harsh halogen lights exploding on his visor.

"Good to see you, Alan," he said, his voice muffled. He waved a hand and scattered his assistants as Murdoch walked over. "You're not going to want to miss this."

"Miss what?" Murdoch asked. "Why the suit? Terrorists?"

The last time he'd seen the pathologist in a biohazard suit had been when the antiterrorist squad had brought in three jihadis who'd poisoned themselves with the ricin they'd been planning to use on the subway.

"Uh-uh," Jorgensen said, shaking his head. "This is . . . this is something different. I can't explain it."

Something had rattled him, that truth was in the waxy color of his cheeks and a sheen of sweat on his forehead that had absolutely nothing to do with the close confines of the biohazard suit.

"Sorry to call you out so late," Jorgensen went on. "I wanted to show you. I don't know how much longer I'll have."

"What?" Murdoch asked. "Why?"

"I had to call this one in," he said, brushing his gloved hands down his overalls. "MI5. This is something new."

"The national security goons?" Murdoch said, raising an eyebrow.

"You'll understand when you see it." Jorgensen paused, and in that hesitation Murdoch saw that the man didn't want to go back inside the morgue. Jorgensen not wanting to go to work was like a kid not wanting to go out to play at break—something was seriously wrong. The man seemed to snap out of his trance, turning a pair of bloodshot eyes toward the door. "You'll need a mask."

Murdoch looked at the pathologist for a moment longer, then turned and walked to the steel lockers against the far wall of the waiting room. The one marked "Hazardous" was already open, a couple of full-face masks left near the bottom. He slipped one over his head, switching it on and making sure the rubber seal was tight around his neck. He hated these things, the air inside them was like breathing from a dead man's lungs. Still, better this than inhaling whatever was inside the morgue, whatever had unsettled Jorgensen so much.

"This way," said the pathologist, as if Murdoch hadn't been here a hundred times before. One of the morgue assistants held open the waiting-room door for them and Murdoch followed Jorgensen through. The main entrance to the morgue was a few paces farther down, and yet more white-suited staff were clustered outside it. One of them pushed the door, holding it for them as they passed through.

"No change, sir," the woman said. She had to shout over the rumble of the air-conditioning units, which were working overtime to cope with the heat.

Jorgensen nodded at her, leading the way across the huge room toward an area sectioned off with hospital-style privacy curtains. He stopped next to them.

"This is top secret, Alan, okay?" he said. "Until we know what this is, nobody can find out about it. I brought you in because you're a friend, because I trust you. But nobody else can know. Okay?"

Murdoch nodded. A bolt of pure white anxiety exploded in his gut and he took a couple of long, deep breaths that misted his visor. He was grateful for it, because the mist obscured his vision as Jorgensen reached out and pulled the curtain to one side.

He didn't want to see what lay in the corner of this room. He could hear it, a sound that rose up over the rattle and clank of the overworked air conditioners. It was a scream, a wretched, terrible, strangled scream gargled through a wet throat—not one thrown out but one clawed *inward*, like a desperate asthmatic breath. He could almost feel that breath on his skin, breaking out a blanket of goose bumps that clung to him like a disease. It made him want to run from the room and throw himself into a bath of disinfectant, to hurl himself into the sun just so it could burn the touch from him.

The mist on his visor was clearing, and through the plastic he saw a naked body lying on a stainless steel surgical table. It was a young man. And it was a corpse. Of this there could be no doubt because its chest had been opened up like a birthday present, torn flaps of wrapping-paper-red skin pulled to the side to reveal a gift basket of withered organs. Its body was blackened on the underside where the blood had pooled in postmortem lividity.

Don't look at its face, his brain told him. Yet he could no more turn away than he could sprout wings and fly out of the morgue. His eyes drifted up from the feast of its stomach, past its pulseless throat, to a face that was still alive.

No, not alive. Animated, yes—its mouth hung open, too wide, wide enough for Murdoch to get his whole fist into if he could ever bring himself to move again. It was this that was making the noise, that gurgling wheeze. Even though the body was dead, even though it wasn't moving, he could sense life inside it. It was as if something lay just beneath the surface of that parchment-thin skin, something writhing and twisting and breathing in that endless inverted scream.

It was its eyes, he realized. They were white marbles in puckered sockets, shrouded with death, and yet they could *still see*. He understood that instinctively, that these two pinprick pupils that stared at the tiled ceiling of the morgue were seeing something; they were watching.

"It's been like this for an hour now," said Jorgensen from his side. "Since the ambulance brought it in. There's no pulse, no blood pressure. It's one hundred percent dead."

"It's not," Murdoch said. "It's breathing."

Jorgensen turned back to the corpse, shaking his head.

"Not quite," he said. "It's inhaling. But its lungs are flat, we opened them up to see where all that air was going."

"Where is it going?" Murdoch asked, shouting over the same grating, unchanging, unending breath from that dislocated jaw.

Jorgensen shrugged, opening a bottle of talcum powder that was lying on the tray next to the table. He took out a pinch and flicked it over the corpse's mouth, watching as the dead man sucked it in like a vacuum cleaner.

Murdoch managed a step forward, peering down into the gaping maw to see that the powder had vanished down the black pit of its throat.

Jorgensen put the cap back on the bottle as he spoke. "That's why I called MI5. That's what I don't understand. That air, it's not going anywhere; nowhere we can find, anyway."

Behind them, one of the assistants appeared at the door.

"Sir," he said. "I think the agents are here."

"I'll be right there," Jorgensen said. He turned to Murdoch. "Whatever this thing is, wherever that air is going, it's not here."

"Not here?" Murdoch asked. He looked at the corpse—its open chest gaping, its mouth inhaling, those pale eyes burning into the ceiling. "Sven, what do you mean *not here?*"

Jorgensen sighed, a noise that sounded more like a sob.

"I mean exactly that," he said. "I mean it's going somewhere else."

FRIDAY

Turning and turning in the widening gyre
The falcon cannot hear the falconer;
Things fall apart; the centre cannot hold;
Mere anarchy is loosed upon the world,
The blood-dimmed tide is loosed, and everywhere
The ceremony of innocence is drowned.
                    —*W. B. Yeats, "The Second Coming"*

BRICK SAT AT THE TOP OF THE BASEMENT STEPS, his head in his hands, flinching every time he thought he heard a noise from below.

He felt empty, completely and utterly drained. It had taken all his strength just to make it up the stairs. Shortly after getting out of the basement he'd found a steel rod in the pavilion—it looked like one of the electrical poles from a bumper car—and had managed to wedge it tight between the door and the wall. He'd packed everything he could find around it to lock it in place, praying that it would hold up against the onslaught from the other side. It had, so far. Lisa had spent the best part of three hours battering the door, each attempt growing weaker and feebler until the sound of her body hitting the wood and metal was no louder than a gentle slap.

Worst of all were the groans and snarls, noises that could have come from a wounded animal in a trap if it wasn't for the half-words buried in the mess. The only one he could recognize was his name, shouted again and again in panting, wretched screams until he had to clamp his hands over his ears and blot them out with cries of his own.

At 10:53 the attack on the door had stopped. Brick had pressed his ear against it, hearing jagged, even breathing. Lisa was asleep, or unconscious. That's when he'd made his way up the stairs. He knew that was the exact time because he'd had his crappy Nokia on his lap ever since. He'd been on the verge of calling for an ambulance about a hundred times, but something had stopped him—the thought of what the paramedics would say when they got here, them and the cops. They'd see a girl beaten half to death, a broken nose, a snapped ankle, and God only knew what else; a girl who'd almost killed herself trying to break out of a locked basement in an abandoned amusement park. And when Brick showed them his single injury, the teeth marks in his eyebrow, they'd just say she'd done it in self-defense.

He looked down into the pool of liquid darkness that sat at the bottom of the steps. There was a fine silver gauze hanging from the skylights but it didn't have the guts to go anywhere near the basement. He could just about make out the slit of candlelight under the door, unbroken ever since Lisa had stopped moving. He'd thought about going back down, seeing if she was okay, but his body had mutinied, refusing to obey a single command from his brain.

What *was* his plan? He didn't know. He just wanted to curl up and sleep, to wake the next morning in his own bed with a text from Lisa saying *soz, wn't hpen agn.* But he was too wired to sleep, his body aching all over from the fight.

There was a soft noise from below. Brick cocked his head, his heart once again in overdrive. At first he thought he'd imagined it, but sure enough there was another sliding sound, then a scrape that could have been fingernails on wood.

She was awake.

Brick didn't move, afraid that if he so much as breathed too loudly it might set her off again. The stripe of golden light split into two, then into four, then disappeared altogether as Lisa pressed herself against the door. He could hear breathing now, wheezed, desperate. There was a rattle as she tried the handle, the metal pole holding.

"Brick."

Her voice was an old woman's, his name misshapen, the "B" barely there and the "r" now a "w." It was spoken not with malice but with fear.

"Hel . . . hel me."

His stomach dropped into his feet, his heart following. He stood, swaying.

"Help me."

"Lisa?" he said, his own voice high and broken. The shuffling noises grew louder. He could hear her scraping the door.

"Let me go, Brick," she said. "Please, I'm hurt."

Brick ran a hand through his hair, feeling the tears coming again, echoing Lisa's, which rose from the basement. He took a step down, gripping the railing like he was descending Everest.

"Please, Brick," Lisa cried. "I'm scared, why are you doing this?"

"I'm not," he croaked, taking another step. "You attacked me, you *bit* me."

"I didn't," came her reply, choked almost beyond recognition. "I didn't do anything, just let me go, Brick. I won't tell anyone, I promise."

Tell anyone *what*? What did she think had happened? What if she didn't remember? What if she honestly believed he'd attacked her? He realized he was halfway to the next step, his leg hovering. He pulled it back.

"Brick!" she screamed, rattling the handle harder now. "I'm bleeding!"

That did it, breaking through his need for self-preservation.

"Okay, I'm coming, just hang on," he said as he walked unsteadily down the steps.

"Brick, hurry up!"

He dropped down the last two, careful not to trip in the darkness. Lisa's sobs grew louder as he neared, the scrape of her nails on the door setting his teeth on edge.

He reached the corridor below, crouching down to try to locate the metal brace. From behind the door Lisa's words were getting weaker. There was a grunt, a desperate breath.

"Brick . . . let . . . e . . . o . . ."

"Hang on," he said, grabbing hold of the bar with both hands. "I'll be there in a minute."

Her words were now meaningless clumps of sound pinned between piglike snorts. Brick paused, angling his head again. That short delay probably saved his life.

Lisa threw herself at the door, so hard that the top corner pinged open a crack despite the bar. She screamed, then again, pounding relentlessly, driving Brick up the stairs on all fours. This time he didn't stop at the top. He ran blind down the pavilion corridor, her bansheelike shrieks giving chase.

CAL / Oakminster, 7:02 a.m.

CAL WAS WOKEN BY HIS PHONE, the machine-gun sound effect calling him up from a dream about Georgia and prison cells. It spun apart before he could catch hold of it, dissolving into the warm morning light. He reached out groggily, fishing on his bedside table until he found it. The text was from Megan.

What happened 2 u yesterday?!?!?!

It took him a second to remember yesterday, and when he did he sat up in bed frowning. They'd left him, all of them, run off and deserted him at the library. He'd ended up walking home, even though it took about forty-five minutes rather than ten on the bus, getting more and more annoyed with them the later it got. By the time he'd stormed in the front door, ignoring his mother and going straight to his room, he'd been properly pissed off.

He yawned, then wiped the sleep from his eyes, blinking the phone back into focus.

You all left me, he started writing, then after a moment's consideration he wiped the screen clear and replaced it with *Got bored, went home.* He wouldn't let them have the satisfaction of knowing they'd gotten to him.

He dropped the phone onto the table, folding himself back under the duvet. He couldn't be bothered with the thought of school today.

His mum would let him skip, no problem. She was a big softie, all he had to do was give her his best puppy-dog expression and she'd give in to him. His dad—the only potential obstacle to his plan—was away on one of his endless business trips in Spain.

To be honest he wasn't actually feeling all that well anyway. His head was weird, like it was stuffed with cotton wool, that faint *thump-thump* of a headache still breathing against his skull.

He rolled over, stretching his legs and looking at the window. The light that seeped in past his curtains was thick and honey-colored and he could already feel the heat of the morning pressing in from outside. It was going to be another flawless day. Too good to spend in bed, he decided, headache or no headache. Better to stockpile his sick-day points, use them later in the year when it was hammering down outside and the streets were ice rinks.

He checked his phone again to make sure Megan hadn't texted back, then clambered out of bed. He got changed then headed downstairs, making a brief detour to the bathroom before strolling into the kitchen.

"Morning, Mum," he said, yawning again, slumping down on one of the stools around the breakfast bar. His mum stood in the corner by their huge double range, a pan bubbling on the burner. She made him an egg every morning whether he wanted it or not.

She didn't reply. Cal left her to her cooking, turning to the paper on the table and idly scanning the TV guide. Behind him, the pan rattled and clanked like an old car.

The machine-gun noise went again from inside his pocket and he whipped it out. Megan again: *A-hole, we didn't no where ud gone.*

What was she playing at? They were the ones who had left.

Something popped from the stove, the smell of burning filled the kitchen. Cal got up, walking over.

The pan on the stove had boiled dry, two eggs inside oozing out of their blackening shells, the whole thing shaking so much it looked ready to take off. Cal grabbed the handle and lifted it from the gas, slamming it down onto another burner.

"Earth to Mum, you're burning the house down," he said, turning to her. She still hadn't moved, her bleached-blond hair concealing her face. And she smelled funny, older somehow. *Oh Jesus, she's had a stroke* was Cal's first, heart-stopping thought. He reached out, pulling her hair back so he could see her face, and the touch made her jump—not just flinch, she literally jolted so hard her whole body came off the floor, like she'd had an electric shock.

"Mum?" Cal asked. "What's wrong?"

She turned her head slowly, her eyes taking a moment to find him. They were bloodshot and streaked with yellow.

"Mum?" Cal asked, taking a step back, suddenly cold.

"Yes?" she said. A phantom smile danced over her lips.

"Are you okay?"

She nodded like a puppet on a string. Then she seemed to remember where she was, picking up the saucepan with the eggs in it and giving it a shake.

"Oh, these are no good, shall I make you another?"

The way Cal's stomach was churning he didn't think he'd ever eat again.

"I'm okay," he said, retreating toward the kitchen door. For some reason he didn't want to turn his back on her. "I'll get something at school."

"Your lunch is on the table," she said, opening the metal trash can and hammering the upside-down saucepan against it like she was chopping firewood. The noise was deafening.

Cal grabbed the brown bag, almost tripping over his feet in his hurry to get out of the room. His mum watched him go, beating the pan against the can's side in purposeful, even strokes that he could hear long after he'd closed the front door behind him.

BRICK WOKE BENEATH A BLANKET OF SUNSHINE, and it was only when he tried to move—a hundred tiny blades worrying into his muscles—that he remembered where he was. He sat up, Fursville shimmering into focus around him, drenched in fresh morning light. He was lying next to the Boo Boo Station, a stone's throw from his bike, a patch of thick sea grass for a mattress and his T-shirt for a pillow. He leaned back against the wood, brushing ants from his face and neck, knowing there was a reason he felt so sore—*Lisa . . . we had a fight, she tried to kill me, she's still down there.*

That thought sucked all the warmth from the day, leaving the park as cold as December. Brick shivered and pulled his T-shirt back on, wrapping his hands around his knees and hugging them tight against his chest. He rocked gently back and forth.

He'd made it this far last night after Lisa had started hammering on the door again. With nowhere else to go, and unable to leave her, despite the fact that she'd turned into a raging psycho, he'd collapsed on the spot and drifted into an uneasy sleep. His dreams that night had been full of Lisa's screams, and he wondered if they'd been real, if they'd cut up from the basement full of fury, searching for him.

He dug his phone from his pocket. There were no missed calls. Lisa's mum and dad must have been absolutely bricking it. Literally *Bricking* it, he thought with a bitter snort of laughter. He'd promised to get her home by ten at the latest. They'd be out there looking for him, the police too by now. Luckily they didn't have his number: his phone was a cheap prepaid burner.

And nobody, apart from him and now Lisa, knew about this place.

He froze. *Lisa* had a phone. What if *she* called the police? That would look even worse; it would make it seem like he really *was* keeping her prisoner.

But wait, no, if she'd been able to use her phone then she'd have done it by now. The place would be crawling and Brick would be inside a cell at Norwich Station, cops pounding him with questions. Maybe she was too far gone to remember how to work it. Maybe she'd messed up her hands so badly trying to get out that she couldn't press the buttons. Or maybe she couldn't get a signal down there. That would be it. Not all networks reached this far out of the city.

Brick started to rock again, feeling guilty at the relief that soothed his knotted stomach. He slapped his forehead, twice, three times, opening up the wound in his eyebrow, feeling the tears start to swell again. What the hell was he going to do?

His dad. Maybe he should just tell his dad everything. He'd probably get a smack for it, but his dad would know what to do. If they went to the police together, then it mightn't look so bad. His dad was a waste of space, no doubt about it, but at least he was an adult; they'd listen to him, they'd believe him.

Brick pushed himself up the wall of the Boo Boo Station, his whole body trembling, hollow. Over the caved-in roof of the ticket gate to his left he could see the highest peak of the log flume, not quite as tall as the roller coaster or the big wheel but still pretty impressive. He could see himself in the plastic canoe, racing downhill, his dad's arms rooting him in place. Gravity.

His mind made up, Brick walked to his bike, flipped up the kickstand, and climbed onto the saddle. His helmet made his face sting but it did a good job of covering the wound. It took even longer than usual to get the bike going, seven or eight attempts before the engine buzzed to life and he was out through the fence. He had fought his way through the laurel before he noticed that his fuel gauge was in the red. *Dammit*, he'd meant to fill up on the way over—two people on the back made the bike guzzle fuel—but he'd decided not to because he couldn't face the thought of stopping long enough for Lisa to start moaning at him again.

It was okay. There was a station about a mile west. He'd fill up and be back in Norwich by nine. His dad would be at work but Brick knew which site he was on, the same one he'd been on for eighteen months—the massive housing development next to the old paper mill. He checked both ways, the coast clear, then he wobbled left, accelerating down the road and taking the first right toward the fertilizer factory.

It felt good to be moving, even though something in him balked at the idea of leaving Lisa behind. The thought of running, of never coming back, ghosted at the back of his head, but it vanished almost as soon as it had appeared. He kept at a steady forty, not wanting to draw attention to himself even though he felt as if he had a giant arrow over his head, labeled GIRLFRIEND KILLER.

But she isn't dead, he kept telling himself. *She's going to be okay.*

He turned off the main road into the station forecourt, pulling up at the nearest pump and cutting the engine. There was a five and change in his wallet, which would get him back to the city. Through the window of the shop he could make out the cashier. He'd dealt with him dozens of times before on the way out to Hemmingway, a right miserable old git. But the way he was looking at Brick now was different. Brick felt his cheeks light up and lowered his head. The man probably just thought he was going to skip as soon as he'd fueled up.

He looked again and the cashier had gone. He glanced at the pump—watching the meter. Maybe he needed to find a hideout that was closer to home, he thought, before realizing that he might never be able to go back to Fursville. Strangely, that thought filled him with more grief than anything else.

There was a squeal of tires behind him and he turned in time to see a small red hatchback slam into the back of a battered taxi across the road from the station. The cars rocked together, steaming, then lay still.

Least I'm not the only one having a bad day, he thought. The driver of the taxi was getting out. He looked mega-pissed. The woman behind the wheel of the car was opening her door too, her hair a mess, her face white. From the look of it they were about to have an almighty screaming match.

A bell rang from the other direction and the shop door opened. Brick swung around to see the cashier walking through it, probably to make sure everyone was all right. There was still something wrong with the man's face, it was twisted up into a kind of snarl, his eyes burning—

He looks like Lisa, exactly like her, Brick thought, and some kind of instinctive alarm began to ring in the center of his brain. The cashier was coming right at him, walking fast, grunting with each step.

"I'm going to pay!" said Brick, his voice broken into a thousand pieces.

The cashier didn't seem to care, his pace quickening. There were noises from the other direction too, a ragged shriek. Brick swung around to see the taxi driver coming across the street, breaking into a run, heading straight for him. The woman was right behind, her face so bent by fury that it looked painted on. She was the one who was screaming.

Brick ripped out the nozzle, throwing it to the ground. He jumped back onto the bike, fear turning his bones to liquid. He slammed his foot on the starter, the bike wheezing then falling silent. The cashier had reached the pumps, his old face mottled, jowls swinging. He was a small man, too fat and too old to ever have scared Brick. But that expression . . . There was nothing in it but murder.

The cashier threw himself at Brick and unleashed a punch. Brick ducked, the bike almost toppling between his legs and bringing him down with it. Only fear kept him upright. The man grabbed hold of his helmet, wrenching his head down.

Footsteps behind him, more howls from the woman.

"No!" The word forced up past the choke hold on Brick's neck. "No!"

He let go of the handlebar, unclipping the helmet and freeing it. The cashier stumbled backward, hitting the curb around the pump and falling on his backside, the helmet still grasped in his hands. Brick didn't look back, just leaped onto the starter pedal again, throwing all his weight down on it.

The engine wheezed, popped, then sparked to life. He revved, the bike moving impossibly slowly. Something grabbed the back of his T-shirt, pinching his flesh, and he shunted himself forward on the seat. He caught sight of his reflection in the shop window, an ecstasy of terror, white-eyed and openmouthed, the taxi driver and the woman bearing down on him.

He wrenched the accelerator so hard the rubber grip tore, the bike guttering, on the verge of stalling. He swept around between the pumps and the shop, his feet on the ground propelling the bike forward, skidding on the oil-slicked tarmac, the woman still clutching his T-shirt. There were more people on the street now, swarming from their cars, all of them glaring—*Just like Lisa, they're just like Lisa*—all of them running toward him, a stampede. He recovered his balance, accelerating out of the station, the woman's hand ripping loose. He ducked beneath the arms of a man on the sidewalk, thumping into another woman hard enough to send her sprawling. Someone in a car veered toward him, clipping his rear wheel. But he clung on for his life, weaving left, right, the swelling crowd surging after him like rats after the piper as he fled into the sun.

DAISY / *Boxwood St. Mary, 9:38 a.m.*

DAISY WAS LATE, REALLY LATE. School had started an hour ago and she was only just now scrambling out of her pajamas, trying to find a clean polo shirt and socks while staring in disbelief at the clock by her bed.

Why hadn't her parents woken her up? They pulled her kicking and screaming out of bed every morning without fail, which was why she never bothered to set her alarm anymore.

She pulled a ball of socks from her drawer, doing her best to put them on while walking briskly down the landing toward the stairs.

She had clattered down the first four when she heard something moving in her parents' bedroom. She stopped, cocking her head over her shoulder. In the silence she became aware that her head was aching, a pulse—not hers—swelling and ebbing in her ears, the same as it had been yesterday but worse now. *Thump-thump, thump-thump, thump-thump.*

Frowning, Daisy made her way slowly back onto the landing.

"Mum?" she called out. "Dad?"

She walked to the door, only now noticing that it was closed. Her parents never closed their door, even at night. When she was much younger Daisy had demanded it always be left open, and it had stayed that way ever since, even though she was nearly thirteen now and knew things she hadn't back then and would almost *prefer* it if they kept it shut. She reached out, her knuckles hovering next to the wood but not making contact.

What was she scared of?

She knew exactly what she was scared of. She was scared of walking in and seeing her mum puking into the basin, her hair coming out in clumps, her skin the color of dishwater. She was scared of having to go through it all again, even though they'd told her that the chances of it reappearing in her mother's brain were extremely low. She was scared of other things too, worse things, but she'd trained herself to stop thinking about them because just having those things in your head might make them come true.

She swallowed, even though her mouth was as dry as sandpaper. Then she knocked.

There was another thump from inside. Then a thin, reedy voice. Daisy couldn't make out what it said, so she knocked again, her ear almost touching the wood. That voice again. Was it calling her name?

Her heart lodged in her throat, Daisy twisted the handle and pushed the door open. Darkness and a dusty, almost sour smell seeped out into the hallway. The curtains had been pulled shut—thick, double-lined velvet ones that her dad had hung so that her mum could sleep when she'd been really ill. It looked like 3 a.m. in there.

"Hello?" she said, the room swallowing her voice.

"Daisy?"

She took a step inside, her eyes taking a moment to adjust. Her parents were two lumps beneath the duvet, their upper bodies black smudges on the cushioned headboard. For some reason the sight made her think of gravestones side by side in a cemetery, and she actually heard herself gasp.

She saw her dad move, leaning forward then throwing himself back, making the headboard crunch against the wall.

"Dad, what's wrong?" she asked, walking toward the bed, trying not to breathe in. The air was thick with the stench of old people—not old like her mum and dad, but *old* old.

"Come here," said her mum, her voice like a breeze kicking leaves down the street. Daisy waited for the "we need to talk" but it never came, the only sound the click of her dad's throat as he breathed. She walked around her mum's side of the bed, her hand on the footboard to steady herself. She wanted to rip the curtains open, the window too, but she didn't dare. She didn't want to find out who was lying in that bed.

My parents, obviously, she told herself. *Who else could it be?*

The wolf, something in her brain said. *It's the wolf, and it's dressed like your mum and dad. Look closely and you'll see it, Daisy. And you'd better, because if you don't, then the wolf will get you.*

Shut up, she shouted to her brain. It always played tricks on her when she was scared. As if to prove to it that she was brave,

Daisy sat on the edge of the mattress, her hand smoothing the duvet until it found her mum's. She clasped it, holding it tight.

"Are you okay?" she asked. Her mother's fingers were damp stalks. They made no effort to tighten around Daisy's. "What's wrong?"

"Nothing," said her mum. A little light was trickling in from the hall, tentatively exploring her parents' faces. It hung in their eyes as a bright spark, but it wasn't strong enough to illuminate their expressions. She was pretty sure she could make out her dad's teeth, though, clenched together between pulled-back lips. He sat slowly forward then lurched back again, the thump making the whole bed tremble. For the first time it occurred to her that she might be dreaming. Her mum turned her head until those sparks found Daisy. "Come, lie with us."

Don't, said her brain. But once again she shushed it. She climbed onto the bed, trying to avoid trampling her mum as she wedged herself into the middle. It was the safest place she could ever imagine being, sandwiched between her mum and dad in their room. It was the place she'd weathered a thousand nightmares. And yet she didn't tuck her legs beneath the duvet.

"What's wrong?" she said again, looking from her mum to her dad and back. "Are you ill again?"

Her mum's head slid around, her body completely motionless. In the gloom the smile she gave Daisy belonged to a china doll.

"I'm fine," she said. "I'm as right as rain."

"Right as rain," said her dad, making Daisy jump. She looked at him and he stared back. He smiled too, but it slid off his face like water from a raincoat. There was a clack as he snapped his teeth closed.

"We just wanted a cuddle," said her mum.

"A hug," added her dad.

They moved together, their bodies shifting, their arms rising—too long, too spindly in the dark. Her mum looped both hands over Daisy's shoulders, pulling her close, nuzzling her lips against her hair. Her dad followed, wrapping his arms around them both, his chest against her back. They were breathing perfectly in time, and when they inhaled Daisy felt her bones creak as the space between them shrank. She tried to shift her arms to return the hug but there was no room.

"We love you, Daisy," said her mum. "Whatever happens, never forget that."

Daisy couldn't twist her head around to see her mum, the kisses on her forehead were too fierce. They were battering her, like hail, making her headache sing.

"What do you mean?" she asked. "What's going to happen?"

No answer, her parents tightening their grip, ratcheting her in like a snake with its prey. The smell seemed worse here and a tickle of fear crept into Daisy's stomach. Once again she could hear that voice in her head: *They're not who you think they are, it's the wolf and it's wearing your parents for pajamas.* It was such a ridiculous, terrifying image that she couldn't decide whether to laugh or scream.

"What's going to happen?" she asked again. "I don't want anything to happen."

"Everything will be okay," said her mum, her words muffled by Daisy's hair. "We love you so much. Nothing will hurt you. *We* won't hurt you."

Hurt her? What was that supposed to mean? She began to squirm, the tickle fast blossoming into full-blown panic. But they weren't letting her go, their grip so tight now that it was twisting her neck.

"Mum, it hurts."

She could see her legs kicking on the bed, pushing the duvet down in rumpled folds. The old people smell was like something solid over her mouth.

"Mum!"

The hug began to loosen, her dad's arms relaxing as he rolled onto his back. Her mum unlocked her wrists, letting Daisy push herself up. She massaged her neck, looking at her parents, only just managing to keep the tears from flowing. Her mum smiled at her, using cool fingers to brush a strand of hair from Daisy's face. Her eyes were dark, but that firefly of light buzzed freely in them. It made her look happy, but far away. She stroked her hand down Daisy's cheek, gently holding her head.

"Whatever happens, whatever happens, always always remember that we do love you. Always remember. We love you so much, Daisy."

"I love you too," Daisy said. Then she threw herself at her mum, hugging her with the same force that she had been held by, pressing her forehead against her mum's cheek so hard she could see spots of color bloom in her vision. "I love you more than anything."

Her mum breathed in, the noise almost a snort, and Daisy could feel her body tense up. She let go, worried that she was hurting her.

"You're late for school," her mum said, the warmth stripped from her words. She was facing forward again, her arms by her sides. "You should go."

"But, Mum, I don't want to le—"

"Go!" The word shot from her mum's mouth like a bullet.

Daisy crawled off the duvet, feeling like something was about to explode from her chest. She stood at the foot of the bed for a moment, looking at the dark lumps of shadow there, then she retreated through the bedroom door.

Her mum called out after her, her voice as flat as a recording. "We'll see you soon."

But somehow, Daisy knew that was a lie. Somehow, so deep down that she wasn't even truly aware of it, she understood that they'd never see her again.

BRICK / *Fursville, 11:55 a.m.*

BRICK SAT ON THE WOODEN STEPS that led up to the log flume in Fursville, shaking so much that his elbows kept slipping off his knees. He'd ridden straight back to the park after the incident at the gas station—*They tried to kill me, they* all *wanted to kill me.*

The crowd had followed him down the road, their faces twisted and contorted in his single rearview mirror, their eyes angry white blisters. They'd actually *trampled* each other trying to get to him. The car that had almost knocked him off his bike had tried to come after him too, but it had veered off the road into a garden after a dozen yards or so, the driver kicking his way out of the broken windshield and pursuing on foot.

By the time they faded out of sight there had been twenty people there, men, women, kids, grandparents. Brick had seen all this with absolute clarity—every bared tooth, every clenched jaw, every snatching, greedy finger.

He was paying the price for his escape now. He felt the same way he did when he was really ill, the light too bright, his whole body trembling.

The worst of it was that somewhere en route he'd lost his phone and his wallet. They had probably slipped from his pocket when he'd almost come off the bike, or maybe it had happened during the attack at the gas station. The phone he didn't mind so much, but dropping his wallet could be bad—it meant the police would know he'd been in Hemmingway. From there it didn't take a genius to think of searching the old amusement park. He was shaking so much he felt like a pneumatic drill, like he was about to hammer himself into the ground, and he pushed himself to his feet, pacing.

What the hell was going on?

There was an explanation banging on the door of his head, yelling at him, but he was refusing to pay it any attention. He was refusing because it was stupid, even though he'd seen stuff like this in a million movies—people turning feral, ripping into their loved ones. Usually it happened when the dead came back to life, but not always.

Zombies, great thinking, Brick. You're a genius.

But that was exactly it: zombies were something from the TV, from video games. They didn't exist in real life, they *couldn't* exist, it was impossible.

Then what was it? What had turned Lisa against him and then invited the whole goddamned world to take a shot?

As far as he could tell, there were three ways of finding out. First, he could call his dad, ask him what was going on, see if it was happening in the city too. Of course that was no longer an option because his mobile was gone and the nearest pay phone was—*Ha-ha, Brick, try not to laugh at the irony*—back in the station he'd just fled from. Second, he could get back on his bike and head somewhere else, back into Norwich maybe. This wasn't really an attractive option either, because if a stationful of people had almost managed to kill him, then a whole cityful would certainly succeed. It felt a bit like diving into a shark-infested ocean to see whether there was a great white hiding beneath your boat.

That left door number three: the *basement* door. His laptop was in there. It had been on the table when he and Lisa had cartwheeled over it, so he didn't even know if it was still okay—the fact that she obviously hadn't used it to e-mail anyone for help wasn't a great sign. But maybe she just hadn't thought of it. Or maybe the dongle had come loose and she couldn't get it to work again.

Either way, if he could get in and snatch his computer then he'd be able to search the news sites, see what was going on. He had a store of food and drink in there too; not much, but enough to keep him going for a day or two.

The thought of opening that door, of seeing what was inside, made him shudder harder. If he was going to do this, he had to do it now.

He set off toward the pavilion, both hands clenched in his tangled hair like he was a prisoner being marched at gunpoint. He reached the fire door, thinking *Please God, don't let this be the last time I see the sun* as he squeezed under the chain. He didn't let himself stop, knowing that if he paused for so much as a second he'd never get moving again. He'd end up like one of the statues outside, the grinning squirrels in the mini-golf, frozen until the end of time.

He jogged to the door at the top of the basement staircase and peered down into that throat of darkness. The bottom corner of the lower door had been bent out from the wall, but it was still closed, the metal bar firmly in place. No light crept through it now. He couldn't hear anything as he stepped softly downward.

He put his ear to the door, his breath locked tight. It was silent in there, as if he had his ear against a coffin lid.

Lisa? he said, realizing only after a moment or two that he hadn't spoken out loud. He struggled to unblock his windpipe. "Lisa?" He barked the word out this time, making himself jump. It sounded like it had been loud enough to bring the roof down. He held his breath again, listening.

Something moved inside the basement, the noise like a heavy object being dragged across the ground. *A torso,* Brick thought. *It sounds like somebody moving a corpse.* There was a quiet cry, a kitten's mewl, followed by silence.

At least she was still alive. The knowledge filled Brick with equal amounts of relief and terror. Alive but weak, perhaps. He might be able to open the door, run in, grab what he needed and get out before she even really noticed he was there.

He went to call her name again, then thought better of it. In his head he counted down, *three . . . two . . .* and without waiting for *one* he kicked out at the bar, sending it clattering to the floor. He wrenched open the door, uttering a short, desperate cry of his own. Then, fists clenched so hard his nails were like scalpels in his palms, he stepped into the basement.

CAL CROUCHED ON THE GRASS, the sun trying to peel open his head, the heat drumming on his skull—*thump-thump . . . thump-thump . . . thump-thump*—wondering why the pain had gotten so bad in the space of a couple of hours.

The shrill call of the whistle made him wince, and he squinted up to see Mr. Platt jogging onto the pitch. Both teams were waiting for the game to start, eyeballing each other over the halfway line. Cal had gone to the changing rooms as normal, wondering if anyone would mention what had happened yesterday on the plaza. Nobody had, but the way his mates wouldn't meet his eye, gazing at the floor as they walked outside, was evidence enough that they were ashamed or embarrassed.

Cal reached down and grabbed the bottle of Dr Pepper by his foot, finished it off and tossed it to the nearby sideline. Behind it was the pitch's only stand, and it was packed—two hundred kids, waiting for the match to begin. The usual suspects were once again in the front row, Eddie sitting in between Megan and Georgia. For once, Georgia didn't have her book with her and was joining in with the chants. The noise was exhilarating.

He looked at the clock. Noon. Tim did a few keepy-uppies before placing the ball on the center spot. Platt blew for the game to start and Cal charged into the opposition side of the pitch. It didn't take long for the ball to find him, a clever volley from Steven. Cal controlled it, knocking it ahead and chasing, feeling like he was running at the speed of sound. He heard someone yell "man on" and stopped abruptly, trapping the ball as the defender flew past. Then he turned and scanned the pitch for white shirts, lobbing the ball in toward the box.

It wasn't his best pass, granted, and one of the other team intercepted, heading it clear. Still it was pretty obvious that it was going to be a good game. An *easy* game.

The other team was pressing forward and Cal jogged after them, happy to let the defense handle it. Jack, the keeper, caught a shot and booted the ball upfield. The crowd was less noisy now, nothing more than a handful of chants and insults hurled onto the pitch. Cal glanced over as he ran, waving at Eddie and Megan and Georgia. They were looking right at him but none of them returned the gesture.

Actually, *everyone* in the stands seemed to be looking right at him. They were facing the sun, so their eyes were narrow slits in their faces.

Up the other end of the pitch Nas was closing in on the goal, Jack trying to make himself as big as possible to stop the shot. His two center-backs should have been closing in but they were just standing there, like they didn't quite know what to do with themselves.

They were both staring at Cal.

Thump-thump . . . *Thump-thump* . . . *Thump-thump* . . .

Confusion was making the engine in his head rev even harder, battering against the soft flesh of his brain.

"Go on," Cal yelled. "Tackle him!"

More of the players were turning to face him now. Nas had actually frozen outside the six-yard box even though it was just him and the keeper, even though nothing was stopping him taking the shot. The kid's head was twisted around too far as he fixed his eyes on Cal. Even Mr. Platt was looking his way, his whistle clamped between his teeth. It was quiet enough in the stands for Cal to be able to hear the whistle warble softly every time the teacher exhaled.

Jack took a couple of steps toward the ball then stumbled to a halt, as if his batteries had just run out. He raised his head, his eyes dark despite the sunlight on his face. Jack was the last. Now every single person was looking at Cal. The only sound was the soft whisper of the whistle, almost lost behind the hammer blows inside his head.

He turned to the crowd. People were standing, pushing themselves out of their seats. The way they moved reminded Cal of a flock of birds, how they all seemed to do the same thing at the same time without being told. Two hundred or so people swayed as one, their gaze so intense it seemed to push Cal down into the warm soil.

Something in his head, something buried deeper than the ache, was screaming at him. It was just about the oldest, simplest, most instinctive message the body was capable of sending.

Run.

And Cal would have too, if the pulse of agony in his head hadn't vanished—*thump-thump, thump-thump, thump*—gone so suddenly that it was as if somebody had thrown a switch. He'd had the headache for so long that for a second or two its absence was almost worse, like not having it there meant there was something missing in his brain. But there was no denying the relief.

It didn't last. Mr. Platt staggered forward, running toward him—not jogging, *sprinting*—his face knuckled into a fist of rage. Others followed, as if the teacher pulled them behind him. A peal of thunder rose up from the other direction and Cal swung around to see the crowd surging from the stands, a tidal wave that crashed and spat down the aisles, spilling over the seats. There was so much movement that the ground was shaking.

That voice inside him, that raging, desperate animal cry, screamed, *RUN! RUN! RUN!* And Cal understood with absolute clarity that if he didn't obey that voice then he was going to die.

He lurched so hard that he almost tripped on his own feet, bolting up the middle of the pitch as the crowd surged onto it. He saw a couple of kids from the front row fall beneath the weight of the mob, lost in the surging mass of feet.

Cal ran faster than he thought possible, his arms and legs pistoning him across the school field. He risked a look over his shoulder to see Nas right behind him, spit hanging from his too-wide mouth, his eyes two hate-filled sores in his face as he gained ground. Behind him churned the crowd, a tsunami of flesh.

The main school building was in sight. If he could just get inside then somebody would stop this, one of the teachers or the headmaster. But even as the thought crossed his mind he saw a group of kids sitting outside the doors lift their heads, sniffing the air like lions scenting a gazelle. As one they scrambled to their feet, charging toward him, that same look of lunatic rage turning their faces into crude Halloween masks.

Cal angled off to the left, toward the bike sheds, his mind a hissing mess of white noise. There were more kids converging on him from the school doors. One of them screamed, a brittle shriek that was picked up by somebody in the crowd behind him, and Cal only realized how quiet they had been when they all started to cry out, the sound almost a physical force against his ears.

He heard rasping, jagged breaths right behind him, then

something brushed his shoulder. Cal forced himself to think. He'd been studying martial arts for years now, but every single thing he'd learned had somehow been sucked from his brain, dissolved by terror.

Nas reached again, and this time he snagged Cal's shirt, yanking him so hard that he missed his footing. Cal fell, skidding on his knees, almost managing to push himself back up again before Nas thumped into him, sending them both sprawling. Nas pinned him and threw a punch that glanced off his jaw, not hard enough to hurt.

Cal bent and spread his legs beneath Nas's weight, planting his feet firmly on the ground. Then he punched up with both arms, knocking Nas's hands loose and trapping them beneath his own. At the same time he rolled his hip, pushing up with a grunt. Nas tumbled off, the murder never leaving his eyes. Cal lashed out, hitting him square in the throat as he jumped up.

Someone else was right there, reaching out for him, and Cal shoved the kid as hard as he could. He ducked under another pair of hands, plunged into shade as the crowd tried to surround him. It was like running into a forest of limbs: rootlike feet tripped him, torsos like trunks blocked his way.

Cal threw himself at the only shard of sunlight that remained, breaking free, his whole body numb as he started to run again. He was right next to the school building now. One of the windows exploded outward, a bloodied face squirming through teeth of broken glass, reaching for him. Cal shot past it, scrambling beyond the bike sheds and up the narrow path along the side of the school. Straight ahead were the closed gates, and past them Rochester Street with its cars and its crowds.

To his side was a fence, and past that a strip of woodland. The trees there were spindly, too few to provide any cover. But what choice did he have?

He threw himself at the fence, grateful that there was no barbed wire as he flopped clumsily over the top. Through the mesh he could see the crowd flood the passageway, a thrashing river that pushed itself against the wire, causing the posts to bend into the woodland. Megan was there, or something demonic that had once been Megan, her hands twisted into talons, straining for him.

Cal gulped down air, slipping and tripping over the rough ground. Somehow he ran, using the trees to push himself on until he hit the fence that backed onto Rochester Street. He climbed, slipped, climbed again, rolling headfirst over it.

Hands reached through the wire, pinching his shirt, his flesh, driving him to his feet again. He heard an engine gun, looked up in time to see a car veer across the street straight at him. Through the sunlight-dazzled windshield he could make out a face identical to the ones behind him, and it was the sight of this twisted mask rather than two solid tons of silver SUV that made him leap to the side.

The car slammed into the fence, piling right through it into the crowd. Cal looked back to see that people were pulling themselves over a mound of ruined bodies, twitching limbs, their eyes still blazing. One girl was crawling after him even though her left arm was no longer properly attached. She pulled it along like a baby dragging a toy.

Cal scanned the street as he limped onward. People were streaming from the Tesco supermarket opposite the school. More cars were accelerating up the hill, veering wildly from side to side. One smashed into a lamppost, bending it at a forty-five-degree angle. The driver, a middle-aged man, had opened the door and was stumble-running across the road, shrieking.

The car. It was his only chance.

Cal threw himself toward the man, waiting until he was close enough before unleashing a powerful Choy Li Fut side kick. His football cleats sank into the man's face, almost making him do a full backward flip. Cal raced for the car, throwing himself into the driver's seat and closing the door just as the first of the Tesco shoppers reached him.

The engine had stalled. Cal pushed in the clutch and twisted the key the way he'd been taught in his driving lessons, and the engine roared to life. A woman was swinging her basket at the window, the glass already cracking. More shapes threw themselves at the doors and Cal engaged the central locking just in time. Someone had climbed onto the hood and was kicking at the windshield.

Cal tried to wrestle the gear stick into reverse. It wouldn't go. He felt it with both hands, finding a ring on the shift, pulling it up and allowing the stick to slot into place. He revved and let the clutch out.

The engine stuttered, then cut out. The passenger window exploded, hands reaching in. There was no sunlight left inside the car, three more people now on the hood, so many on the roof that it was bowing inward, the metal creaking. He twisted the key again, forgetting to push in the clutch. The car juddered, people falling from it into the surging crowd.

Cal swore, pushing in the clutch, trying the ignition, revving it hard with his right foot. The whole car was rocking now as the people outside attempted to roll it over.

He let the clutch rise slowly. It bit, groaned, then the car jolted backward. It didn't get far, the sea of bodies behind it blocking the way. Cal stomped on the accelerator, shunting his way through them. The car growled, flattening anything behind it as it gained speed.

Cal slammed on the brakes, remembering to push the clutch in as well. He wrestled it into first, spinning the wheel all the way around as he pulled away, not caring that people were bouncing off the bumper, not caring that he drove right into a kid that he'd played football against yesterday, not caring that the car was bucking wildly because of the countless squirming bodies beneath the wheels.

He just drove down the hill as fast as he could, screaming silently through the sun-drenched, ruby-red-stained glass of his windshield.

BRICK / *Fursville, 12:17 p.m.*

THE FLASHLIGHT LAY JUST INSIDE THE DOOR, on its side. Brick turned it on and it spat out a weak beam, hardly enough to illuminate the gloom.

The first thing he saw was his computer, lying facedown on the floor. He scanned the room, waiting for a shape to come flying at him, for teeth to lock into his face, his throat. But it was strangely still in here, like he'd stepped into a painting, the quiet broken only by the thrashing beat of his pulse.

Then a portion of the darkness moved, smoke against shadow near the far wall. From here it looked like a burlap sack, a lump of cloth bundled into itself. A groan escaped it, followed by a soft sob and a clump of unintelligible words.

"Lisa?" he asked. He couldn't stop himself.

She raised her head, tilting it first one way, then the other. She attempted to crawl toward him, but her left wrist was bent back at an impossible angle, the tips of her fingers almost lodged in the crook of her elbow. It couldn't hold her weight, and she crashed down.

Lisa had done this trying to hurt him. She had *broken* herself. Even now she was trying to get to him, using her legs to shunt herself forward, her face sliding wetly. It was this that spurred Brick on. The longer he stayed here, the more damage she'd do to herself.

He walked to the table, never taking his eyes off her. He picked up the laptop, folding it closed, feeling for the dongle and finding it in the USB port. Lisa had raised her head again, studying him. The change of angle meant that he could see her eyes. One of them was completely red, swimming in blood. In spite of her injuries they burned. She looked possessed.

Brick walked to the corner, to the pile of shopping bags that sat there. They had been emptied over the floor, a bottle of water half drunk and lying on its side and three or four bags of candy. Still keeping his eyes on Lisa and one hand on the wall, he edged around the room, crouching down and loading the sweets back into a shopping bag. There were five bottles of water left in the multipack and he snatched them too, then changed his mind and left three. He could always drink from the taps in the kitchen, and he didn't know how long Lisa would be down here.

He put everything, even the laptop, into the bag, holding it in one clenched fist as he retreated. Lisa watched him move for as long as she could hold her head up, then it dropped once more. She uttered another moan, full of frustration, full of confusion. He waited until the open door was at his back before speaking.

"I'm sorry, Lisa, I don't . . . I don't know what to do. There's water, and I left you some candy." The sound of his voice was making her lurch, a hand sliding toward him. He took a step back, stumbling over the junk in the corridor, hitting the wall hard enough to have his breath snatched away. He clutched the bag to his chest. "I'll find a way to help you," he said.

She made one last effort to look at him. There was nothing in that face, it was a half-melted mask that seemed to be sliding loose. Her mouth fell open, something bubbling from it, but Brick reached out and slammed the door shut before he could hear what it was.

HE SECURED THE METAL POLE BETWEEN THE DOOR and the wall again, not that he thought Lisa would be going anywhere. Then he walked up the stairs and turned left, heading down the corridor away from the fire door. He reached a double door on which a faded sticker read: "To all Pavilion staff. Remember to SMILE!" And for some reason he obeyed that advice as he pushed his way through, his mouth peeling open into a corpselike grin.

Yeah, no doubt about it, he was going nuts.

He was in the front foyer of the pavilion, the box office a small window in the wall to his right, and past that the main doors, sealed tight with more chains.

He collapsed against a wall among plastic jungle plants, next to a glass-eyed leopard, taking one of the water bottles from his bag and quenching a thirst that had raged unnoticed until now.

He pulled out his laptop, expecting to see the screen cracked and useless. When the machine warmed up, however, he saw that it was just as he had left it, apart from a dark, inky blotch on the top right corner of the screen. The battery sat at a little under half full, which was worrying because out here there was no power. A little box told him that he had been logged out because of inactivity, and he quickly logged back in.

The little blue light on the dongle flashed furiously as the screen reported *Waiting for network . . . Connecting . . . Authenticating . . . You are online!* Then the box disappeared, leaving the browser window. He went to BBC news, the page loading up faster than it would have downstairs but still painfully slow.

Brick scanned the text as it appeared. NORTH KOREA NUCLEAR TESTS CONDEMNED. ROYAL DIVORCE TO GO AHEAD. And a whole raft of sports news. Not a single mention of savage mob attacks or unprovoked violence. Brick frowned. Maybe it was a local thing. He went to the *Eastern Daily Press* home page and found reports about broken council pledges and a bit about some guy who collected antique mailboxes. He found the date and time of the latest article. It had been posted eight minutes ago.

This didn't make any sense. Brick rested his head against the wall, chewing on his thoughts. When an old lady was so much as knocked over in the street the *EDP* gave it a six-page feature, how the hell could it have missed this? That gas station must have been swarming with cops and paramedics all morning, juicy photos of bloody tarmac and shattered windshields just begging to be taken. He typed "gas station, Hemmingway" into Google, finding nothing but an address for the station and a load of stuff about the famous writer, even though the names were spelled differently.

Something hit the main doors hard enough to make the chain rattle. A white shape bounced up past the filthy glass, squawking, another one joining it. Two seagulls. There was a flash of yellow as the birds fought. One flew off, the other in pursuit. Brick tried to swallow his heart back down into his chest, waiting for his hands to stop shaking before hitting the keys again.

"Why does everyone hate me?" he typed, scanning the list of results. They were all from Q&A and self-help sites. He clicked one, Yahoo Answers, reading a few lines about some kid who didn't have any friends.

"I'm sorry to hear that," Brick said as he clicked the Back button. "But I think my problem is worse than yours."

He wiped his hands on his jeans then tapped the keys gently, trying to decide what to do next. After a minute or two he loaded up the Yahoo Answers page again, logging in with his ID. He chose the "ask" option, typing in "Why is everybody trying to kill me." Then he filled in the next box:

This isn't a joke. My girlfriend just tried to kill me, for no reason. REALLY tried, she bit my face. Then I went to fill up my motorbike at the gas station and suddenly there was a crowd of people coming after me. Someone tried to run me over and they would honestly have killed me. They chased me up the road. I'm serious. This ISN'T a put-on, I'm really scared. Has anyone else had the same thing happen? If you have, please answer.

He read it through, making sure it didn't give anything away about his location. He couldn't do much about his identity—he had to use his Yahoo ID to post the question. But as long as nobody knew *where* he was, it would probably be okay. He selected the Post option, waiting for the new page to load up. Looking it over again, the question seemed absurd, so ridiculous that it made him doubt the whole thing.

He closed the laptop to conserve the battery, folding his legs up to his chest and resting his head on his knees. All he could do now was wait.

DAISY / *Boxwood St. Mary, 3:17 p.m.*

DAISY STARED AT THE POSTER ON THE DOOR of the school theater, a lump in her throat the size of a house. It was the ad for the play, and where her name had once proudly stood was now a big black smudge. Underneath it somebody had scribbled "Emily Horton as Juliet."

Daisy rubbed her temples, that same *thump-thump* drumming inside her skull. For a moment she just decided she was going to go home. Let them do the stupid play without her. But something stopped her—the thought of her parents side by side in the bed, lying there like dolls in the dark. Instead, she walked into the theater, a couple of lanky older kids nearly bowling her over on their way out. Hoisting her rucksack onto her shoulder, she made her way down the short corridor that led to the second set of doors. She pushed through them into a maelstrom of movement and noise, a hundred or more kids running around the auditorium, leaping over the folding chairs, throwing balls of paper at each other. On the stage were a couple of girls from her class who'd been appointed scenery managers. They were trying to move a wooden picnic bench—Juliet's balcony—into the wings.

Emily Horton was there too. She was on the other side of the boards, chatting with Kim and Fred. And she was wearing the Juliet dress. *Her* dress.

Daisy hesitated, the theater suddenly huge, the stage boundless. In her whole life she didn't think she'd ever felt so small. She walked up the steps toward the back of the stage, stepping through the curtain. Then she inhaled deeply and marched across the stage until she was standing next to Emily. The girl was taller than her by about half a foot. So was Kim. Fred towered over them all, looking at Emily and smiling. Daisy didn't think she'd ever seen him smile like that before.

"Excuse me," Daisy said. Nothing. She reached out, grabbing Emily's collar. Emily looked down. They all looked down, their smiles vanishing like mice beneath a hawk's shadow. Daisy's voice was a whisper: "There's been a mistake," she said, her eyes burning. *Don't cry, be strong.* "I . . . You're still the understudy."

She glanced at Fred, hoping that maybe he'd say something, stick up for her.

Wrong. Fred was standing there checking his nails, as if he couldn't bring himself to look at her. This was all *his* fault. Everybody had seen what had happened yesterday, when he'd spat in her face, and now they all thought she wasn't even worth talking to.

"But you don't even know the lines," she said to Emily, brushing a hot, fat tear away furiously. "You haven't been to rehearsals."

Emily still didn't reply, grabbing the sleeves of her dress—too short, the ruffles only reaching the middle of her forearms—and tugging hard to try to make them longer. Daisy shook her head, tasting salt as the tears flowed freely again. That dress had been made for her, her mum had taken in the sleeves especially, and she'd hemmed it too so that it fell right to her ankles and wouldn't trip her up. Emily was too big for it, packed in like a sausage in a casing. One sudden move and the dress would split.

There was a call from behind the curtain, the whole thing billowing before Mrs. Jackson's face popped out. She saw the turmoil in the stands and trotted onto the stage, calling to the kids who rioted there.

"Right. Right! Everybody, this is no way to behave in a theater. I want you all to take your seats, straightaway please. Anyone who doesn't want to be here had better leave right now."

Gradually the noise levels ebbed as the audience took their seats, a few people drifting out the back.

Mrs. Jackson looked at Emily. "Are you ready?" Emily nodded. "Good girl, now off the stage so we can get started. You too, Fred, Kimberly."

"Mrs. Jackson," said Daisy. "What about me?"

Mrs. Jackson had already vanished back into the dressing room.

Daisy stood there, hugging her backpack strap with both hands. She had the terrifying idea that she was actually dead, that she had choked in her sleep or something. How else could she explain what was going on?

The lights in the hall went out, the stage spotlights blazing overhead, blasting away Daisy's shadow and making her feel even more like a phantom. Once again the curtain opened, Mrs. Jackson reappearing. She walked to the center of the stage, about three meters from where Daisy was standing, and held out her hands.

"Thank you all for coming," she said, her voice trembling with nerves. "It's lovely to see so many of you here. Um, as you all

know this is technically a dress rehearsal, not a finished perfor-
mance, so please forgive any slips of the tongue or prompts from
myself or occasional retakes."

Daisy couldn't move, her cheeks burning more fiercely than
the lights.

"Please, please, please remember to turn off your mobile
phones, children," Mrs. Jackson continued. "And, yes, just enjoy
the show. Ladies and gentlemen, I give you *Romeo and Juliet*, a
tragedy by William Shakespeare."

Mrs. Jackson turned around to go, and Daisy managed to
break her paralysis.

"Please, Mrs. Jackson," she whispered as softly as she could,
sensing the weight of the audience in the shadows. "I need to talk
to you."

"You shouldn't be on the stage," Mrs. Jackson replied. The
harsh lighting turned her face into a leather mask. "Get off."

"But—"

"You're going to ruin it," Mrs. Jackson snapped, waving at
Daisy like she was a fly on her dinner. "Now shoo."

Daisy stood there in the middle of the stage, her mouth
hanging open in disbelief. The crowd was silent, an audience of
glass-eyed dolls.

"Get off," said Mrs. Jackson, and this time she took a step toward Daisy.

Daisy stumbled, looking for the stairs. She saw them too late,
missed her footing and tumbled down. Pain grabbed her left leg
like a clawed fist as she landed on her hands and knees, her heavy
rucksack swinging over her shoulder. She waited for the laughter,
but the theater was deathly quiet.

Daisy struggled to her feet. From here, out of the glare, she could see the kids in the crowd. Nobody was looking at her. On-stage Mrs. Jackson was holding the curtain open, ushering out the girl who was playing the narrator. She gave her a thumbs-up then sank into the black depths. The girl took her position then started to speak.

"Er, two households, both alike in dignity . . ."

Daisy backed away, heading for the doors, wishing that everybody *was* laughing at her. This was worse, so much worse. By the time she was at the doors she was running, bursting through them, barreling out the main exit into the sun. She tore across the parking lot. Eventually she crashed against a hedge, snatching breaths in between fits of sobs.

Only when she felt like she had wrung out every last tear did she look up, using her sleeve to clean her face. Compared with what had just happened, home seemed like the best possible thing she could imagine—even if her parents were tucked up in bed, even if her mum, God forbid, was getting ill again. At least they still acknowledged she was there.

The short walk home helped clear her head. She reached her front gate, feeling a little better. So what if everyone at her school was a total jerk. She had more important things to worry about. Maybe that's why she'd had such a rubbish week—maybe life was preparing her for a tough few months, maybe it was trying to make the thought of staying at home and caring for her mother easier. Yes, that was it. For the first time in what seemed like the whole day she remembered to breathe in.

She was halfway down the path before she realized there was another piece of good news.

Somewhere between leaving the school and arriving at her front door, her headache had gone.

• • •

DAISY OPENED THE DOOR, the gloom inside her house like a solid, living thing. She stepped in, pulling the Yale key free and wiping her feet on the big doormat. The silence was immense, as if it had wrapped itself around her head, pulling her in. In spite of the fact that her headache had gone—or maybe because of it—she felt weird. Lighter, somehow, as if part of her wasn't there.

The house was empty. She could always tell. A house without people had a different sort of atmosphere, as though it was waiting for something.

Daisy slung her rucksack on the floor beneath the coat stand, massaging her shoulder where the strap had dug in. It was brighter in here now that the imprint of the sun had ebbed from her retinas, but even so she flicked the hall light on, and the kitchen light too, as she walked to the back of the house. Her dad would be at work—he was an accountant at a firm in Colchester. Her mum hadn't gone back to her teaching job after her illness, but she often popped out for shopping, or to see friends, or just to get a little fresh air.

Or maybe they're at the hospital? Mum back in the cancer ward, Dad pretending that his eyes are red raw because of the pollen, or the exhaustion.

She shushed the thoughts, going to the sink and filling a glass from the filter tap. She finished the water and walked back through the kitchen, heading for the living room. It would do her good to sit down and watch a little TV, it would help calm her. Already the events at school seemed vague and distant, as if she'd imagined them. It probably hadn't been as bad as it had seemed at the time. It wasn't as if this was the first time that people had ignored her.

She was through the kitchen door when she realized that something was wrong. She ducked back inside, looking at the key hooks over the radiator. Hanging on those hooks were three sets—the spare one, her mum's, and her dad's. Daisy frowned, prodding them as if to make sure they were actually there. The little "Best Mum Ever" and "Dad's Taxi (and Cash Machine)" key fobs she'd bought them last Christmas jingled. That didn't make any sense. If the keys were here it meant—*They're still in the house, they're still upstairs . . .*

She told herself it was no great shock that her parents were still in bed. She already knew—or as good as knew—that her mum was ill, so it made sense that she'd be up there, under the covers, resting, her dad keeping watch over her.

So why didn't she want to go and look?

Daisy took a step forward, and another, her momentum building as she walked to the stairs. She was halfway up when she understood what had happened. It hit her like a fist to the gut, making her slump onto her hands and knees on the steps.

It was the smell. She knew it from the time a cat had been hit and killed by a taxi outside their house. None of the neighbors had known who it belonged to so her mum had brought it in and put it into a cardboard box in the garden shed. Daisy—she'd been seven or eight, she couldn't remember—had opened that box and the smell had clawed its way down her throat right to her stomach. It wasn't a rotten smell, not like when the trash can needed emptying. It was hardly even there at all, yet somehow it was everywhere. And even though she was only seven or eight Daisy had known exactly what that smell was. It was death, plain and simple. It was the smell that death left behind when it had been inside your house.

It was here now. It clung to everything—the stairway carpet, the walls with the framed photographs. It was on her skin too, so pungent that she thought at first that *she* was the one who stank, that death had come for her.

Only it hadn't. It had been here, but it wasn't Daisy it had taken.

She forced herself to climb the last few steps. Hunched over, she crossed the landing to her parents' room. The door was closed, and on it was a sheet of paper on which her mum's haphazard script read: *Daisy, do not open this door. Call the police, darling. Please don't come in.*

She reached up, a puppet, unable to stop herself. The handle popped, the door creaked, and a fresh wave of the smell washed over her, settling into her nostrils. The heavy curtains were still pulled tight and it seemed that there was no air in the dark room, just death.

There were two figures in the bed, the same as before. Only this time they didn't stir. They sat propped against the headboard, leaning on each other, two shadows that reminded Daisy of the pictures she'd seen at school of the victims of the nuclear bombs in Japan, their shapes burned onto the pavements by the heat of the explosion. She wanted to call out to them, but she didn't. She didn't want to fall into the silence where their response should have been.

Instead, she moved to the window and grabbed hold of the heavy velvet, yanking the right-hand curtain first, almost hard enough to jar the pole loose from its mounts. The light that flushed in from outside was less golden than umber, burned and sticky. She wrestled with the left, jigging it along. It got stuck halfway and she had to tuck the end behind the mirror on the

sideboard. She stared into the glass, seeing her parents asleep on
the bed. Only they weren't asleep. She turned to face them. Her
mum's head was resting on her dad's shoulder, and they looked
more peaceful than she'd seen them in years. Their faces were pale,
except for a spot of color on each cheek. Their eyes were closed.
They looked like plastic models of her parents, like the waxwork
people she'd seen once at Madame Tussaud's—so close to human
and yet so obviously not.

Daisy felt a scream building in her head, her mind reeling as if
reality had slipped off the tracks and was now plowing in a new
and frightening direction. She no longer felt like crying, she
wasn't entirely sure if she could remember how. She looked at her
mum's hand, cupped in her dad's, both of them as still as a photograph. Next to this was another sheet of paper, folded in half, her
name printed on the front. Daisy reached over and lifted it, opening it up. It was her mum's handwriting—scratched and scribbled
in big, frightening, insane letters—and there was a lot of it. She
scanned the lines, unable to make sense of it, as if it had been
written in a foreign language. Only the final paragraph was clear,
inscribed in letters twice as big as the rest:

PLEASE FORGIVE ME, DAISY. DIDN'T YOU FEEL IT?
SOMETHING IS COMING, SWEETHEART, SOME-
THING BAD, AND IT WOULD HAVE MADE US HURT
YOU. I FELT IT ALREADY, SOMETHING INSIDE ME,
SOMETHING PLEADING WITH ME TO DO TERRIBLE
THINGS TO MY LITTLE DAISY, TO MY SWEET BEAU-
TIFUL DAUGHTER. I DON'T THINK IT'S THE DIS-
EASE. NO, IT'S DEFINITELY NOT THE DISEASE. I
HAVE TAKEN CARE OF YOUR FATHER FOR YOU. I

DON'T KNOW FOR SURE IF HE WOULD HAVE HURT YOU BUT I THINK SO. WE BOTH WOULD HAVE. BE SAFE, BE STRONG. WE LOVE YOU, DAISY. WE HAD NO CHOICE. WE COULDN'T BRING OURSELVES TO HURT YOU. WE COULDN'T DO ANYTHING TO HURT YOU. WE <u>WOULD</u> HAVE HURT YOU.

That last "would" was underlined so hard that the pen had been pushed through the paper. Daisy didn't read it again. She carefully folded it and laid it on the bed. She made her way calmly downstairs and back into the kitchen, pulling the cordless phone from its cradle and dialing. Somebody picked up on the third ring.

"Emergency, which service do you require?" said a woman.

"An ambulance, please," said Daisy, like she was ordering a pizza. "My parents are dead. My mum killed herself. She killed my dad too."

There was a pause, then the woman said: "Oh my saints." It was, thought Daisy, a stupid thing to say. "You hold on now." There was a click, then Daisy was talking to somebody else, a man. She answered his questions without really thinking, just staring out into the garden, not seeing the flowers or the grass or the skies, not seeing anything at all.

"The ambulance will be with you in a couple of minutes," the man said. "I'm going to stay on the line with you until it arrives."

"No, it's all right," Daisy replied, her voice not her own. She dropped the phone, her thumb going for the Off button, the man's faint, muffled voice cut off mid-sentence.

CAL SAT IN HIS LIVING ROOM, waiting for images of himself to appear on the television, waiting to see his own screaming face as he ran from the hunt. The house was empty, as it always was at this time of day. His dad, a businessman who never liked to talk about what kind of business he did, was abroad, and his mum volunteered at the charity shop around the corner in the afternoons, Tuesday to Friday. He was glad that they weren't here. As much as he wanted to talk to them, to hear them say that everything would be okay, he didn't know what would happen when they saw him—*They might come after you too, Cal. They might chase you and kick you and stamp you into the pavement just like everybody else wants to*—and he needed to find out what was going on before they came home. He needed to work out what to do.

His whole body shook. The last few hours didn't seem real. These kinds of things didn't happen, except in the movies. And yet ugly purple flowers were blossoming on his arms, his chest, his neck, and his back where they had grabbed and beaten him. He had a bite mark on his hand that he couldn't even remember getting.

He almost hadn't made it home. The car had seemed to pull people off the sidewalks like a magnet, random strangers throwing themselves at it, bouncing off like bags of meat, squirming in his rearview mirror. He'd expected to see the police behind him, had *wanted* to see the police there just so they could make sense of it all. But there were no police, no ambulances, just an army trying to batter its way inside.

The crowds dwindled the farther from school he had gotten, disappearing altogether when he reached his street fifteen minutes later. He'd parked the gore-encrusted car inside the double garage so that nobody would see it and then staggered into the house. He hadn't quite made it to the sofa, collapsing onto his knees beside the television where he still sat.

The twenty-four-hour news channel had pretty much run its headlines and there was nothing there about a savage mob attack on a seventeen-year-old boy in East London. He left the TV on, pushing himself up, forcing his numb legs to navigate across the living room to the computer desk by the French doors. He slumped in the chair, switching the machine on and closing his eyes while he waited for it to boot up.

After loading his Yahoo home page he scanned the links down the left-hand side, not quite knowing what to do. He was clicking through the news items when his pocket started to vibrate, making him jump so hard that his knees cracked against the bottom of the desk. He pulled out his phone. It was Megan. He stared at her pixelated name, laid over a photo of her with two pens in her mouth pretending to be a vampire, for what felt like hours. Then he answered.

Silence. His mouth felt too dry to form words.

"Cal?" she said eventually, and he was relieved at how far away her voice sounded. "Did you hear what happened?"

That you all tried to kill me? But all that came out was a grunt.

"Georgia's in the hospital, she got trampled. Where did you go, Cal? We needed you."

Cal lowered the phone, rubbing his eyes, then looking at her picture again to make sure the call was real. He heard Megan shouting his name and he put it to his ear.

"Are you okay?" she asked. "Things got a little weird at school. They think there was a problem with the stands, that the kids at the back thought it was collapsing or something. So they stampeded."

"Megan," he managed eventually. "What are you talking about?"

"Today, during the match," she said. "You must have seen it. We thought that's why you'd run off. Thanks very much for that, by the way, *my hero.*"

Did she not remember chasing him? Did she not see what happened? She was talking fast, the way she always did when she was emotional.

"You tried to kill me," he interrupted. Megan must have said two dozen more words before it sank in.

"What?" she said after a moment's pause. "Be serious, Cal, this isn't a joke. Georgia's got a broken leg and a fractured collarbone or something and I've . . . well I sprained my finger, which isn't much but it still hurts, and it was scary, Cal, all those people."

You think? he almost spat.

"Cal, please, will you meet us at the hospital?"

There was no dishonesty in her voice, no sense that she was trying to lure him out so they could attack again. There was just Megan, scared and hurt but the same girl he'd known for nearly eleven years now. Even though he could see her running after him, teeth clenched, her face a mask of pure fury, he couldn't work out how to be angry with her.

"I'll be there," he said softly. It was a lie, but it seemed to calm her down. "Just give me a little while, okay?"

Megan laughed.

"Thanks, Cal. Love you."

He didn't reply, and after a second or two she hung up. He sat there with the phone against his ear, unable to make sense of the conversation. Why didn't she remember? Had she blocked it out from shock or something? It was crazy, and he threw the phone onto the desk with a grunt of frustration.

Think, Cal, he said to himself, rocking back on his chair. *What do you do?*

There were rules to surviving a natural disaster, he'd read about them. They were designed for earthquakes and volcanoes and hurricanes, stuff like that, but he guessed they'd work for this too. Rule one, find a safe place. He'd done that, he was safe here, for the moment anyway. Rule two was to check for injuries and do the utmost to ensure your own survival. Well, he was pretty beaten up but he wasn't going to die from bruises and bites. Rule three was to look for other survivors, to make sure nobody was trapped under the rubble or cut off by lava or stuck on the roof of their house. Rule three, essentially, was to find out whether anyone else was in the same situation.

Cal leaned forward, clicking in the Yahoo search box. He paused for a moment, trying to work out the best way to phrase his question, then wrote: "Why is everyone trying to kill me?"

DAISY / *Boxwood St. Mary, 4:13 p.m.*

"HOW DID IT EVER GET IN SUCH A STATE?"

Daisy spoke the words beneath her breath as she brushed her mum's hair. It was easier than usual because her neck was really stiff, almost locked in place, which meant her head didn't jiggle. She worked it into a ponytail, trying not to notice how cold her mum's skin was.

Daisy felt like she should be crying but she was still numb all over, inside and out. The only thing she could really feel was a great big pressure in her chest, like something was sitting on her.

The room was shifting, and Daisy looked up to see waves of thin blue light flicker across the window, like she was underwater. She went to kiss her mum on the cheek but froze halfway at the thought of that damp, waxy skin against her lips. Instead she blew one, climbing off the bed as much to hide her guilty expression as to look out of the window.

"They'll look after you," she said, pulling back the net curtain to see an ambulance outside, parked right behind their car, two wheels on the pavement. One man in green overalls climbed out, arching his back. The other was inside. Daisy couldn't make out his face because of the glare of the sun on the windshield. The blue lights flashed, and Daisy suddenly realized that these strange men would be taking her parents away inside that thing, away to be buried or burned.

That awful weight on her chest seemed to double and she had to rest her forehead against the cool glass to stop from keeling over. The man in the street looked up. He squinted into the sunshine, putting a hand up to shield his eyes. Daisy waved. Her face felt as tough and plasticky as her mum's and dad's. He glanced back inside the ambulance then started walking toward the house, carrying a bag with him. He didn't seem in much of a hurry.

Daisy made her way to the top of the stairs. She'd left the front door off the latch so the ambulance people could come in, but the man rang the bell anyway, turning the handle as the chimes of Big Ben filled the house. From where she was standing she could only see the bottom of the door, a pair of black shoes trampling over the mat.

"Hello," Daisy said. The man replied, but she couldn't quite make out what he'd said. It had started off like a word—hello, she thought—but by the time it had reached the "ll"s it was stretched out of shape, becoming more like a groan, a weird, throaty purr that seemed to fill the hallway below. He took a lurching step forward, his legs coming into view, then snorted.

"Hello?" she said again, uncertainty turning the word into a question.

The man took another step, then another, his chest appearing and then his shoulders and then his . . .

It wasn't the same guy. Somebody else had come into her house. No, not somebody but *something*, something wearing the man's clothes and his hair and carrying his bag but something that wasn't here to be friendly and helpful. This was something bad, something using the man's face as a mask, its mouth drooping open, like a horse's mouth, the teeth huge and blunt and yellow.

He lumbered up the steps, so fast that he tripped on one and banged his forehead on the wood. He didn't seem to notice, just crawled up them on all fours, his limbs too long for the treads. The noise was deafening.

He was halfway up before the part of her brain that was saying *Don't worry, he's here to help* was completely and utterly consumed by the part that screamed *GET OUT OF HERE! YOU HAVE TO RUN! HE'S A BAD MAN!* She backed away down the landing, unable to take her eyes off him. He reached the top of the steps, trails of foam hanging from his lips, the whites of his eyes blazing. He used the banister to pull himself up, wrenching it so hard that the rail splintered free from the post.

Daisy screamed, spinning around and running for the back room, the man's animal grunts right behind her. She made it, slamming the door closed and leaning against it. The man struck it a second later, the wood making a sound like a pistol shot. All the doors in the house had tiny privacy locks, and she flicked it across just as the handle turned. The man threw himself at the door, a jagged crack running down the side. Daisy staggered back. This was the guest room, barely big enough for the single bed against the wall and the piles of old clothes that slept on it, and by the time she'd taken three steps she'd hit the window.

The door crunched again, specks of plaster drifting down from the ceiling. She could hear more footsteps too, hammering down the hallway. Fists and feet pounded the door. Why were they doing this? Did they think she'd killed her parents?

"I didn't do it!" she shouted, her voice lost in the thunder.

The door flew open so hard it ripped a chunk out of the wall. The man seemed to take up the entire room, a giant whose braying horse's mouth looked big enough to swallow her whole. Daisy's legs gave out, but before she hit the floor his massive hands connected with her chest, shoving her through the window.

Glass exploded, the universe shattered into a thousand sparkling shards as Daisy fell. She hit the roof of the kitchen extension, pain like fire in every part of her body. She rolled, tumbling over the gutters, in midair once again until the rhododendron bush broke her fall.

Even past the agony, past the roar of blood in her ears, Daisy could hear the screams of the men above her. She sat up, seeing nothing but fizzing silver light for a second before the garden popped back into view. She rolled out of the flower bed, not trusting her balance enough to stand up, crawling sideways down the garden like a crab. Only when she was past the sprawling bulk of the laurel hedge did she dare look back.

The window was empty.

The shed sat at the bottom of the garden. It wasn't locked because it was falling apart, the roof all but caved in. She wrenched open the door and tumbled into the far corner. A fog of damp wood and slushy grass from the mower washed over her but it was so much better than the stench in the house. She breathed it in, hearing the familiar squeak of the back door.

Footsteps rose up from the other end of the garden. Daisy pulled her knees to her chest, trying to make herself as small as possible, even smaller than she actually was, as small as the wood lice that scuttled into her shoes and under her pant legs. *Please God don't let them know where I am, I'm begging you.*

The noises grew quiet. Still Daisy didn't dare move, even though her skin burned and she could see a blade of glass glinting in her arm, even though her shoulder and ankle throbbed.

Voices. She could hear them, although not well enough to make out what they were saying. One of them she recognized. It was the old Scottish lady who lived next door, Mrs. Baird. The other voice was a man's, just a deep rumble. Incredibly, they were laughing.

She couldn't bear it anymore, not knowing what was going on. She eased herself up from the corner, skirting around the walls of the shed, careful not to trip on any loose firewood. Taking a deep breath, she peered through the grime-covered window.

The ambulance men were there, both of them. Only the

second one was a woman, not a man. They were standing next to the fence in a puddle of broken glass. Mrs. Baird was leaning over from the other side, pointing up at the guest-room window. The man shrugged, looking at the garden. Daisy ducked, but she couldn't stop herself from peeking out again.

The lady paramedic walked into the house through the back door. The man was shaking hands with Mrs. Baird, both of them laughing again. Then he followed the woman inside.

Daisy watched the door swing shut, half relieved that, for some reason she didn't understand, they seemed to have given up looking for her but half wishing that they would stay outside, because she knew that they were going to take her parents now, knew that they weren't going to let her say goodbye. She sat back down beneath the window, put her head in her hands, and started to cry.

BRICK / *Fursville, 4:30 p.m.*

REFRESH. NO CHANGE. Refresh. No change. Refresh. No change. Brick felt like taking the laptop and hurling it into the ocean. It was driving him crazy. He'd been sitting in the foyer for four hours now, and for the last forty-five minutes or so he'd had the computer on his lap repeatedly loading up his Yahoo page. Apart from the ads there was nothing new every time the page displayed. Just his desperate question and some tosser's idea of a funny reply.

Dear weirdo: Either you are a total nutjob who has imagined all this BS and needs to seek professional help for your brain *problems, or you are a total nutjob who has p****d a lot of people off and done some crazy stuff and needs to seek professional help for your psycho problems. Hope this helps.*

Brick wished he could find the guy—PWN_U13—so he could throw him down in the basement with Lisa and watch her claw his throat out. Let's see who had *psycho problems* after that. Refresh. No change. Refresh. No change. Refresh. No change. "Come on, you piece of junk," Brick shouted, grabbing the laptop by its screen and shaking it. The battery was dipping toward quarter full now. If it died . . . well, he didn't want to think about that. He should be conserving it, but the longer he sat here the more anxious and angry he got.

Refresh. No change. Refresh. No change. Refresh. No change.

This time he actually smashed his fist down on the keys, writing "kjhhjuk" in the question box. He deleted it, replacing it with "How would you like it if I smashed you on the floor and stamped on your stupid electronic guts?" He poked Return, unsurprised when Yahoo couldn't find him an answer. He clicked back onto his page. No change. Refresh. No change. Refresh. No change. Refresh. No change.

Even though it wasn't yet five o'clock, it seemed to be growing darker in the foyer, colder too. The thought of that blanket of night unfolding across the planet, ready to bury him and Lisa together in its lightless folds, was terrifying. In the dark he'd have no idea if she'd gotten out, if she was stalking the corridors, if she was standing right next to him . . .

Refresh. No change. Refresh. No change. Refresh. No change.

His anger was like something living inside him, tendrils worming up his throat into his brain, making it scream. His temper had never been very stable. There had been times when he'd shouted at Lisa, when she'd gotten on his nerves so much that he'd almost lifted his hands to her. Almost. As for hurting the laptop, though. He wouldn't have a problem with that if his temper reached a thousand degrees again.

Refresh. No change. Refresh. No change. Refresh. No—

He'd gotten so used to the routine that it took him a few seconds to realize that something *had* changed. There was another answer below the first, and the shock that rocked Brick's system almost meant that he couldn't read it. He took a deep, shuddering breath and closed his eyes for a second, feeling a little calmer when he opened them again. The response was from somebody called CalMessiRonaldo.

WTF man? Are you serious? This has jst happened to me too. i was at school and everybody attacked me for no reason, chased me onto the street and i had to steel a car to get away. i think i ran some people over. Why is it happening? What do i do?

Brick leaned into the screen, reading the message again, then again, then again, trying to work out if it was real or if it was another idiot who thought he was a comedian. There was nothing in it to suggest it was a joke. Although it was hard to get a sense of somebody through a written message, Brick got the feeling that this guy—this *kid*, if he was attacked at school—was scared.

He typed a response beneath the kid's answer.

Look, I'm not messing around, this really happened to me. If you're being serious then I need to talk to you.

He paused, reading back over what he'd written and then deleting it, starting again.

I need to talk to you. I'll start a forum. I'll call it

He stopped again, trying to think.

Hated, okay? It means we can talk where nobody will see it. Be quick, though.

He posted it, checking the battery life of the laptop, then set up a new forum.

Tell me what happened? Are you on your own? Has it happened to anyone else? I don't know what to do.

He thought about writing more, telling the kid about Lisa, but something was holding him back. He'd wait to find out who he was, wait to see if he thought he could trust him. But he couldn't stop that calming blue wave of relief from damping the fire in his gut at the thought that maybe he wasn't in this alone after all.

"Come on, CalMessiRonaldo," he said to himself. "Don't keep me waiting."

He looked at the clock on the screen—4:42. Then he settled back against the wall.

Refresh. No change. Refresh. No change. Refresh. No change.

CAL PULLED ANOTHER SWEATSHIRT from the chaos of his wardrobe, stuffing it into the duffel bag on his bed. He'd already packed half a dozen T-shirts, all of his jeans and tracksuit trousers, and two more sweatshirts. He'd emptied his underwear drawer and wedged in a second pair of running shoes. The little pack with his toothbrush and other stuff from the bathroom sat on his pillow along with his mobile phone charger.

He pulled his coat from the hook on the back of the door. It was summer, hotter than he could ever remember it being. But he didn't know how long he might be out there.

Out where? he asked himself as he laid it into the bag. *Where are you gonna go, Cal?*

He had a quick check inside the wardrobe to make sure he hadn't missed anything, then he hefted the bag from the bed—it weighed a ton—and out into the upstairs hallway. He walked into his parents' room, an instinctive sense of guilt gripping him as he entered their walk-in closet. Tucked at the back of a bottom shelf was his dad's safe.

He got down onto his knees, pulling out the musty collection of old shirts and throwing them to the side. His dad didn't realize that Cal knew the combination. The fact was he'd known it for about three years now, and it had taken him almost that long to work it out. Pretty much every time his parents had gone out Cal had been in here trying out different sequences of numbers— birthdays, memorable dates, telephone numbers, mathematical equations he'd learned at school. Nothing had worked, but he'd never given up. He hadn't even known what was in the safe. His dad—whenever he was around, which wasn't often—had refused to tell him. It had become like a secret mission, like he was a spy and the safety of the world depended on him eventually cracking the secret. He'd grown obsessed with it.

Eventually, when he was fourteen, Cal had worked it out. He'd been talking to his mum and dad over dinner one night. They'd both been in a great mood, better than he'd seen them in ages. And they'd been telling Cal about how they first met, at a party in the West End.

You were gorgeous, his dad had said, flashing his mum a look that Cal hadn't really understood back then but which he knew all too well now. *You were my very own perfect little 36, 24, 36.*

The numbers had been a mystery, but the next day when he'd gotten home from school he'd given them a go, unable to stop giggling when he'd heard the safe click and the small, solid door swung open.

As it did so now, the memory was powerful enough to loose an insane surge of laughter up his throat. He choked it off, glancing into the bedroom to make sure he wasn't being watched before turning his attention to the safe. Inside were the same things he'd first seen three years ago. On the right-hand side was a pile of money—tens, twenties, and fifties all bound together in neat little bricks. The amount changed every time Cal looked, but he'd counted it once and it had totted up to over a hundred grand—more than enough for Cal to steal a few hundred every now and again and not be found out. Next to that was a small, flat black box containing his mum's most valuable jewelry, and resting on the box was a portable hard drive that he was pretty sure was just their family photos and things—he'd never bothered investigating.

There was one more thing in the safe, and it was this that Cal reached for. It was heavy, so much heavier than it had any right to be, so much heavier than they ever looked in the movies. The polished wooden grip fitted his damp palm perfectly, the dull silver barrel much longer than the toy Airsoft BB version Cal had in his bedside cabinet. He flicked out the chamber—six empty holes peering back at him—then shut it with a deft flick of his wrist. He cocked the hammer, the tendons in his hand biting with the effort, then he pulled the trigger. *Click*.

He'd played with this gun for three years, cocking it then firing in a thousand imaginary games. He'd even put bullets in it once, from the box marked .38s at the back of the safe, although he hadn't dared pull back the hammer on that occasion for fear he'd blow a hole in the wardrobe wall—or his own leg. Cal found it hard to imagine his dad—who was balding, wore glasses, and was usually mild-mannered and gentle—with the gun in his hand. His mum always described him as a "businessman," although it was a business that involved monthly trips to Spain and lots of dodgy characters turning up at the house after dark. Cal knew the truth in his heart, of course, although he never wanted to admit it. His dad was one of the bad guys.

Cal picked up two bundles of cash—a couple of grand, he reckoned—and the box of bullets. Then he elbowed the door closed and spun the dial back around, hearing it lock. He paused for only a second, doubt nagging at the back of his mind. If he got caught outside with a gun, a *real* gun, then he wasn't going to get a slap on the wrist and a lecture from the cops. He was looking at a long, long time behind bars.

But if he didn't take it . . .

He carried his stolen treasure back into the hall, placing the gun carefully in the bag, burying it in a nest of his clothes. He put one of the wads of cash in with it, then zipped the bag up tight.

He stuffed the other one into the pocket of the tracksuit pants he'd put on when he was packing, throwing the bag over one shoulder. He struggled downstairs, into the short corridor that led to the garage, leaving it by the door. Then he doubled back to the main lounge, stopping in the kitchen for a bottle of Dr Pepper from the fridge. The computer was on, the Yahoo answers page up where he had left it. It had been the first thing to appear on the search engine when Cal had typed "Why is everyone trying to kill me?" He took a swig from his drink, the sugar perking him up, then he clicked the Refresh button.

There was a comment beneath his answer, and Cal felt a mixture of relief and panic as he read it. Relief because he wasn't on his own. Panic because if this had happened to somebody else as well, it meant that things were *really* bad out there. He ran the mouse over the guy's screen name, Rick_B, then he clicked on the link to a private forum called Hated. The chances were that the man was nothing but an Internet creep who was trying to get kids to talk to him. It didn't matter if he was, Cal had the gun now, he could defend himself.

"Okay, Mr. B," he muttered to himself as the forum loaded. "Let's see what you've got to say for yourself."

CalMessiRonaldo: it's like i said, i was at school playing football and everyone started chasing me. not for a joke, i thought thats what it was at first, then they tried to stragle and punch me and they chased me right out the school onto the street and others came after me too, like shoppers. i only got away cos of the car. they would have killed me. what bout u?

Brick put another candy into his mouth, chewing slowly as he reread the post that had appeared below his own. He swallowed, then reached out and typed.

Rick_B: My girlfriend tried to kill me, she tried to bite my face off. Then she pretty much battered herself senseless trying to get to me through a door. I'm holed up somewhere safe, somewhere no one knows about, need to find out what's going on. Any ideas?

He posted it, then took another sweet from the packet. He adjusted his position on the hard floor, wondering whether he should go upstairs to the restaurant where there were comfy chairs and tables. He didn't dare move, though, in case somehow he lost the connection to the one person who might be able to help him. He wanted to refresh the page right away, but he forced himself to wait for five minutes—actually counting slowly to three hundred in his head—before he clicked.

CalMessiRonaldo: no idea, scarin the sh!t out of me, tho. i'm at home, my mums gonna be bck any minute. you think shell attack metoo? where are you?

Brick reached for another sweet, but the seven or eight he'd already eaten were boiling unpleasantly in his empty stomach. He belched acid, swallowing it back down with a grimace. What now? Should he tell him about Hemmingway, about Fursville, or would that be too risky? He needed some kind of proof that the kid had been through the same thing.

Rick_B: What happened after?

He posted the question, thinking about the way that Lisa had seemed to snap out of her fury, go back to being herself, the way she had forgotten what she had done.

CalMessiRonaldo: i sh!t myself, thats what happnd after. what do u mean?
CalMessiRonaldo: actually i got a call from my mate, one of the ones who attacked me if thats what you mean. she didnt re- member what shed done. where are u?

There was no way the police could know that, right?

Rick_B: I'm on the coast, a place called

Another thought crossed his mind. This guy had been attacked in the same way as him. But did that mean he wouldn't attack Brick—or vice versa—when they came face-to-face? The last thing he needed was another crazy trying to kill him.

Brick deleted what he'd written, starting again.

Rick_B: I'm in Norfolk, on the coast. I can tell you where to meet me. We need to be sure we can trust each other, that we won't try and kill each other, okay? Where are you?

He posted it. They didn't have to meet at Fursville. Pretty much the whole of Hemmingway was a ghost town, just the fertilizer factory inland, then the Sainsbury's about three miles to the north on the road over to Winterton. There were a few houses up that way, old people in bungalows mainly, but he'd never encountered any of them close to Fursville. He just couldn't see a bunch of old grannies climbing over the fence to sit on the rotting wooden horses of the carousel. He refreshed the forum.

CalMessiRonaldo: london, oakminster. i can prob get to u in a few hours if i can get out the city,. tell me where, i gotta get out here real soon

Brick's fingers hovered over the keys and he chewed his bottom lip like it was another sweet. He was better on his own, he always had been. He wasn't good with other people, they either picked on him or pissed him off. And this kid was a footballer, pretty much number one on Brick's list of people he hated, and people who hated him. If he told him about Fursville, then the chances were they'd end up killing each other anyway, even if they weren't affected by what was going on.

But the alternative was worse. The alternative was that he

stayed here by himself, Lisa dying in the basement—*if she isn't already dead*—him slowly going crazy in the creaking, rusting remains of his childhood paradise.

Rick_B: You need to head north, right up the coast. There's a village called Hemmingway, just up from Hemsby. It's deserted. About a quarter mile from the village sign there's a track going off to the right, to the beach. Loads of dunes and stuff. At the end of it is a parking lot, well overgrown, and an old restroom block that's boarded up. That's not where I'm staying, that's just a place we can meet without being seen. If you're leaving now you can get there by eight. If you're late, just wait there overnight and I'll try again tomorrow. DON'T BRING ANYONE ELSE. Okay? If you're not alone I won't even show myself.

He read it back through, feeling ridiculous, like he was doing a hostage negotiation or something. But it paid to be careful. He posted, read it through again, then typed something else into the text box.

Rick_B: Good luck.

He closed his eyes, letting his head drop. He felt exhausted, which wasn't a surprise considering what he'd been through. He didn't want to sleep, though. He didn't want to close his eyes now and wake up to find that darkness had fallen, that he was alone here with his nightmares.

He logged back on to his original message board, wondering whether he should wipe his original question, at least until he found out what happened when he met this guy. He clicked onto it, the mouse hovering over the "delete question" option, his thumb ready to tap the trackpad button, and he almost didn't notice them before it was too late.

He scrolled down the page, his eyes widening, his pulse quickening as he took in what he was seeing:

There are currently 8 answers to your question.

CAL / *Oakminster, 5:05 p.m.*

CAL SAT IN THE DRIVER'S SEAT of his mum's Freelander convertible, the engine purring quietly and the nose nudged out of the right-hand garage door. He'd put it in neutral so that he could rest his foot off the clutch, and his leg jiggled with nervous impatience as he kept watch on the gate. To his left was the car he'd escaped in, the blood now dried into veinlike rivulets along its sides and shattered windshield, its roof caved in like a fruit bowl. His bag was on the backseat of the four-by-four, along with three shopping bags stuffed with chips, sweets, and drink.

He didn't know yet what his plan was, if worst came to worst. The guy he'd talked to online sounded weird. Yet his message had seemed pretty genuine. And what option did Cal really have? He couldn't exactly head west into London. East was Southend and the ports, twenty-four-hour industrial hubbub. South was the endless traffic into Dartford Crossing, over the Thames. Sure, there were a few quiet places around here— hundreds of fields within driving distance, plus the local park where he could shelter in the trees. But what was he supposed to do? Live like a bum for the rest of his years? At least if he headed north he'd be moving away from the city into the ghost-lands of East Anglia.

Somebody walked past the garbage can outside the gate and Cal jumped, his twitchy right foot revving the engine. It was an old man shuffling along. Sunlight glinted off his specs. He didn't look in. On the other side of the street one of the neighbors was loading something into her car. The sound of the door slamming and her feet crunching across the gravel seemed to carry too far, too loud, on the heat.

Cal ducked down in the leather seat, keeping his head as low as possible.

There was a thump. Cal looked up to see the garbage can lid open. It slammed shut to reveal his mum behind it. She grabbed the handle and pulled it into the drive, that hollow rumble the loudest thing in the world.

What if she came at him like the others, tried to open the door and pull him out so she could stomp on his head with her Uggs? But it was his mum, for Christ's sake, his *mum*.

"Please be normal," Cal whispered.

She was halfway down the path when she heard the mutter of the car engine. She stopped, putting her hand up over her face, peering at him through a mask of shadow.

A car drove past on the street outside and his mum peeked over her shoulder. When she turned back to Cal she lifted her hands, her bright red nail polish like rubies in the sun, and shrugged dramatically.

"Cal, what the hell are you doing?" she said, her voice muted.

Cal let out a breath that he hadn't even realized he'd been holding. She was okay. She was normal.

His mum let go of the can and it rocked back on its wheels, rattling. She took a step toward him.

"Turn that engine off right now, young man," she said, walking toward the garage. Cal grinned at her, reaching for the key.

"It's okay," he shouted, wondering how the hell he was going to get the gun back into his dad's safe without her noticing. "I was just having a laugh."

"You're going to be in big truuuu, yumman," she said.

Cal froze. His mum's face had come loose. One side of her mouth was drooping. She took another step, swaying this time. "Get out the car, get out, Caaaaaaaa . . ."

His name stretched from her lips, horribly distorted, dripping out alongside strings of saliva. His mum lurched across the last ten meters of the drive, her face slipping even further like a mask that had been badly glued on. She hit the hood hard enough to jolt the car, her hands squeaking on the metal as she clawed her way toward his window, still groaning that guttural version of his name. This close, Cal could see that her eyes were like hot coals, full of darkness and yet blazing with heat.

Cal shook his head, unwilling to believe what he was seeing, even though deep down he had known this was what would happen, even though there was nothing left of his mum in the thing that pounded on his window with small, brittle fists, coating it with spittle as her voice grew into a banshee scream. "Mum, I'm sorry."

He put the Freelander in gear and pulled away slowly, so as not to hurt her. She ran alongside, thumping the windows hard enough to leave smudges of orangey blood there. He pulled out onto the pavement, not looking where he was going. His eyes were on the rearview mirror, on the figure that lumbered after him like a zombie, her face so familiar, and yet so alien. She lost her footing on the gravel and plunged from view, and it took everything he had not to stop the car and go to help her.

Goodbye, Cal tried to say. Then he floored the accelerator, lifted the clutch, and roared up the street.

BRICK / *Fursville, 6:07 p.m.*

BRICK COULDN'T BELIEVE WHAT HE WAS READING.

> *This is happening to me 2, got attackjed by my brother. :(((((((*
> *need help as I canb't walk.*

It was right at the bottom of the page, posted by somebody called EmoTwin3 literally two minutes ago. It was the twelfth answer. Above that was the eleventh, by JoeAbraham:

> *don't call the police they tried to kill me I AM NOT JOK-*
> *ING. Happened last night, Only got away by jumping in a river.*
> *mum was one of them thought she was gonna strangle me. i'm at*
> *my dad's place 'cause he's away for the summer but there's people*
> *all over and I ain't going outside again unless I got somewheres*
> *safe. where u at bruv?*

They'd both just appeared the last time he'd refreshed. Brick scrolled up the page, his hand trembling so much that he kept losing his place. He'd read the other entries over and over. Not all of them were serious, somebody had written "You guys are massively weird" for answer number seven. But the rest were so similar that they could have been left there by the same person.

. . . she broke my arm, she was trying to pull it right off . . .

. . . they all just came after me like they hated me . . .

. . . I went to the hospital and it was the same there, one tried to scalpel me . . .

. . . please help me I don't know what to do . . .

They pretty much all ended along those lines too—*please help*—like Brick was some messiah who could lead them all to salvation.

He put the laptop on the floor so he could stretch out his legs. Pins and needles radiated from his backside. He could just switch the computer off and ignore everything he'd read. He could delete his question and the answers would vanish alongside it. He might even be able to convince himself he'd never seen them.

No. He couldn't do that. He could no more leave a bunch of people to die than he could run over the ocean.

And they sounded so young too. His age and even younger. That was why the messages had all seemed so similar—the language, the spelling, the lack of grammar—they were written by kids.

The laptop sat open, the screen almost fully dark to conserve the battery but those messages still visible, staring up at him, imploring.

"Okay, okay," he muttered to them. "But not before I know you're not all gonna go psycho on me, okay?"

That was the best solution. He'd go out and meet CalMessi-

Ronaldo, and if they didn't end up tearing each other's throats out then maybe he'd send word to the rest of them. This other guy might have some better ideas too.

He checked the clock. It was only a twenty-minute walk to the parking lot from here. He pushed the lid closed with his foot, hearing the computer go to sleep. Then he set off back down the maintenance corridors, stopping at the top of the basement steps for no more than a second before it felt like his heart was about to slip from his throat and plop down the stairs like a slinky. And *was* it quiet down there? Wasn't that a gentle scraping he could hear? Nailless fingers on wood? He almost ran the last few meters to the fire door, crawling and kicking through the chains like a man pulling himself from his grave.

CAL / *M11 freeway, 6:10 p.m.*

THIS WAS BAD.

Really bad.

And it had been going so well, a clear path out of Oakminster, the main road free of traffic despite the fact that everybody was leaving work. He'd had to stop once, at the set of lights they'd just put in for the giant new big-box store, but no pedestrians had crossed the intersection. The woman in the car behind him had started to get out, but the lights had changed before she could stagger over.

The satnav had offered him a choice of routes: via Ipswich or Norwich. Some inner voice had drawn him irresistibly to the second option. Now he was wishing he'd ignored it. He'd taken the back roads onto the M11, happy keeping the Freelander at seventy in the middle lane, passing people too quickly for them to see him or *sense* him or whatever it was that was going on. Traffic had been fast on the freeway, and it was only about an hour after setting off, when he finally let himself think that he might actually be okay, that luck took a massive crap right on his head.

The electronic message boards were flashing a warning—AC-CIDENT, DELAYS BETWEEN JUNCTIONS 8 AND 9—and he could see the gridlocked traffic from half a mile away. The inside lane had been barricaded by a police van, its flashing blue lights multiplied a hundredfold in the windows of the cars that purred motionlessly alongside it. Farther down he could see a pillar of smoke rising almost perfectly straight into the calm blue sky. He slowed, keeping to the middle lane as the cars started to converge around him.

"Take the next exit," the satnav lady suddenly barked at him, making him jump.

"I'll try," he replied. "But it isn't going to be easy."

The brake lights from the car in front blazed and he slowed from forty to twenty-five. Something big trundled by on his left, hydraulic brakes hissing, plunging him into shade. Behind him an old Mercedes was pulling up fast, the driver a hunched shadow behind the wheel.

This was really, *really* bad.

The car in front reached the back of the line and stopped dead. Cal slammed on his brakes at the last minute, the Free-lander rocking to a halt. Another truck pulled up to his right, squealing, and it got even darker in the car, the steep-walled containers on either side making him feel like he was inside a grave.

Stay calm, just stay calm, he told himself. *They don't know who you are, they're not going to come after you.*

Then why was the guy in front climbing out of his ugly green

Fiat? It was a middle-aged man, dressed in sweats and running shoes like he was going to the gym. He stopped with one leg in the car and one leg on the freeway, stooped over, frozen. The Mercedes behind was closer now, the driver gunning the engine. Was he *speeding up?*

The Fiat man seemed to remember what he was doing, dragging his other leg out of the car. Then he turned to Cal.

"Oh no," Cal said as the man's face changed, his cheeks sagging like old cloth, his lower eyelids drooping to reveal the red-veined orbs of his eyes. He staggered forward like a marionette, throwing himself at the hood of the Freelander just as the Mercedes slammed into it from behind.

Cal's car lurched into the back of the Fiat, the man caught in a bear trap. There was a crack, a spurt of blood from his misshapen mouth, then he vanished between them. The impact threw Cal forward, his face hitting the center of the wheel hard enough to honk the horn. He crashed back, wondering why the airbag hadn't gone off, trying to make sense of the world through the supernovas that detonated in his vision.

Fiat guy had to be dead, Mercedes guy wasn't moving. But Cal could make out other people climbing from their cars farther down the line. There were seven or eight of them making their way toward him, all with looks of concern, some with phones out, others beckoning urgently to the police van in the inside lane. One by one, as they stepped past an Argos truck maybe twenty meters away, their expressions changed, their pace increasing as they lurched and stumbled toward his car.

Cal fumbled it into first gear, praying that the crash hadn't done any damage as he hit the gas. There was a deafening crunch, the squeal of metal against metal, but the Freelander didn't budge. He looked over his shoulder at the Mercedes crammed up against him, its hood crumpled and smoking. He was pinned tight. He swore, wrenching the stick into reverse, flooring the pedal and shunting the car back a meter or so.

A hand thumped his window, somebody trying the handle. Cal didn't look, just threw it into first again and rammed the back of the Fiat, freeing up another bit of space. Somebody was screaming, half-words buried in the noise as they battered the glass with their fists. One of the people from the line—a teenage girl—was trying to climb onto the hood, but Cal reversed again and sent her tumbling to the ground. He managed a little more momentum this time, knocking the Mercedes back far enough for him to break out.

He swung the wheel all the way to the left, nudging the wrecked Fiat out of the way. There was hardly any room between it and the truck to his side but he didn't let up, squeezing through, serenaded by more shrieking metal. Somebody was on the back of the car trying to tear through the canvas roof, two black blisters of eyes boiling through the hole he'd made.

More people were surging up the aisles between traffic, and for a second Cal thought they had him, that there was no way out. Then he squeezed past the truck to see that the car in front of it was a Smart car. He pulled hard to the left again and rammed it. He was only doing twenty but the weight of the Freelander pushed the tiny thing in front out of the way like it was a toy, rolling it onto its side and clearing a path onto the hard shoulder.

Cal accelerated onto it, passing the police van close enough to rip its bumper off, hitting fifty in five seconds. The man on his roof had gone. Up ahead he could see the source of the smoke he'd spotted earlier, a car that had come off the road, punched through the barrier and down the bank to the side. It sat in a field, surrounded by people, hundreds of them, swarming all over it the same way they had swarmed over him back at school. They didn't seem to care about the black clouds that billowed from the engine; they were just tearing and scratching and kicking and even biting at the metal like starving rats trying to get at the meat inside a trash can.

He eased his foot onto the brake as he drew level, slowing to about twenty before realizing what he was doing. Some of the people on the smoking car looked up, a couple of them tumbling free from the pack and starting to run up the slope toward the road. The crowd behind was catching up too, a tide of flesh filling his rearview mirror.

Then he heard it. Although *heard* was the wrong word because this had nothing to do with his ears. There was something in his head, something that wasn't him, a voice that at the same time wasn't a voice. It seemed to grab time and pull it to a halt, the people all around him running in slow motion. The voice seemed to be the opposite of noise, a profound silence that cushioned the world and yet still somehow communicated with him. And in that instant Cal knew exactly what was inside that car.

It was a person, somebody just like him.

And they needed help.

The screams from outside were deafening now, more people pounding and scraping at the Freelander. Past faces ravaged by hate Cal could make out the car below, bodies squirming all over it. He accelerated hard, swinging to his left, grinding past flesh and bone as he headed for the broken barrier. He didn't know what he was going to do when he got to the wreck, but he had to do something.

The lightning came before the thunder. The car in the field erupted in a ball of white heat that sent bodies spiraling out in all directions. Cal had time to see a fist of smoke punch up toward the heavens—and something *inside* that smoke, an impossible shape of blue flame that opened its mouth and howled—before the shock wave hit the Freelander, peeling away the people outside and blowing in the passenger windows. He shielded his face, poisoned air clawing into his lungs, the four-by-four bouncing on its wheels so hard he expected it to roll over.

By the time he lifted his head the worst of the explosion had passed. Smoke still gushed skyward like liquid from the blazing car, but there was nothing in it except darkness. The engine had stalled and Cal turned the key to bring it back to life. He swung the wheel to the right, onto the interchange to the A11, accelerating away from the carnage, away from the burning shapes that ran and howled and fell in his mirrors.

There was one more police car on the hard shoulder, and he passed it with plenty of room. The line continued up the freeway, faces peering out of car windows at the smoke-darkened skies, but the A11 was clear.

"Continue on the current road," ordered the woman inside the satnav. Cal wiped the ash from his stinging eyes, trying not to think about the people who had been on the car—twenty, thirty, maybe more, all dead; trying not to think about the person inside it, the wordless voice somehow begging him for help, which had vanished like a radio being turned off the moment the car had exploded; trying not to think about the shape in the smoke, that figure of flame that screamed as it rose.

He let the fresh air empty his head, and drove on.

DAISY CRAWLED THROUGH THE GARDEN ON ALL FOURS, making sure to always stay hidden in the overgrown bushes.

She hadn't seen anyone inside the house for a while. The ambulance man had last appeared maybe half an hour ago. It might have been less. He'd gone back inside after smoking a cigarette, chatted to some police in the kitchen, then they'd all filed out and that was the last she'd seen of them. Of course they might still be inside, hiding in the shadows, ready to jump out at her . . .

She twisted her hand in the long grass, locking herself to it, smelling the roses and the rhododendrons and the buddleias. It reminded her of her poor mum. It had come back and had been eating her brain, just like before. The tumor had made her act weird last time, but only twitches and tics and the occasional word that came out wrong. This was so much worse. She had killed Dad, she had killed herself.

It wasn't the cancer, though. She said it wasn't the disease. It was something else. She knew what was coming, that she was going to hurt you.

She pushed the thoughts away, untangling her hand and creeping toward the back door. There was a big, bald patch of lawn between the last bush and the house. If she crawled over that then anybody inside would be able to see her. She glanced right, the flower beds full of thorny things, and past them the passage up the side of the house. To the left, old Mrs. Baird's garden. Her apple trees hung over the low fence, a pool of shadow beneath them.

Daisy skirted toward them, grateful when she plunged into the shade. She could hear something on the other side of the fence. It might have been Pudding and Wolfie, Mrs. Baird's cats. She started forward again.

About ten meters or so from the bush where she'd landed after her fall from the guest-room window Daisy saw the first shard of glass—about the size and shape of one of the steak knives in the kitchen. It was nestled in the dirt, a line of blood down one side. Sunlight shone through it, painting the grass a vivid shade of red, making Daisy think of cathedral windows until she remembered it was *her* blood.

She stood up, not wanting to cut her knees and elbows on the twinkling scalpels of glass between here and the house, squatting to stay below the fence. It was hard walking like this but there wasn't far to go. The noises to her left were louder now, but she could definitely hear the familiar "briiiow" of the cats. It was the noise they made when Daisy sneaked out some prawns or tuna for them after dinner, the noise they made when they were being fed.

But if *Daisy* wasn't feeding them . . .

She glanced over her shoulder to see a figure half hidden behind the knotted trunk of one of the apple trees. It was wearing an ancient brown dressing gown, and smoky puffs of thin white hair billowed out from the pink scalp beneath. One small black eye peeked out from the shade, looking right at her.

"Mrs. Baird?" Daisy asked, coming to a halt, still on her haunches.

The old lady was breathing hard, almost grunting, still staring at her with that one dead eye.

Daisy straightened, taking a few steps toward the back door.

And she'd just grabbed the handle when the old lady threw back her head and screamed.

Mrs. Baird hurled herself against the fence, the wooden panels bowing under her weight. She lost her grip, disappearing with a sickening snap. *That's a broken bone,* Daisy thought as her neighbor reappeared, her whole body trembling, great trails of saliva hanging from her pale lips. She was still grunting, the noise a pig might make. Daisy turned the handle, pushing the door, almost banging her head on it when it wouldn't open. She tried again, using both hands this time.

It was locked.

There was another gut-wrenching noise, then something thudded to the ground. Daisy looked to see that Mrs. Baird had managed to flop over the fence and was now lying in a heap trying to get up. Her arms and legs wriggled in the air, like a beetle on its back, her dressing gown open to reveal the velour tracksuit underneath. One of her slippers was gone, and there was something wrong with that bare ankle. It was pointing the wrong way.

Daisy turned back to the door, wrenching the handle, kicking the bottom hard enough to make the glass rattle.

"Come on!" she screamed at it, suddenly wishing that the police were still inside, that *anybody* was still inside. Mrs. Baird was no longer trying to get to her feet. She had flipped herself over and was scuttling across the garden on all fours the same way Daisy had been earlier, her wrinkled fingers pulling out clods of dirt as she clawed forward.

Daisy kicked the door once more then backed away, heading for the side passage that led to the street. Mrs. Baird was gaining, her sagging face filled with exhaustion but those piggy eyes

focused, more alive than Daisy had ever seen them. Her glistening mouth gaped wide, breathing in the same short, piercing
double-shriek cries that might have been her name—*Day-seee,
Day-see, Day-see*—broken and clogged with spit. She plowed
across the grass, her arms and legs moving too fast for an old
woman, like there was a horrible clockwork machine under her
skin.

Daisy turned and fled into the passage, not knowing where
she was going, not caring about the voices she could hear from
the street outside, just wanting to get away from the thing that
crawled after her, that called her name with each wheezing
breath.

CAL / *Boxwood St. Mary, 7:07 p.m.*

"TURN AROUND WHEN IT IS SAFE TO DO SO."

Cal really wished he could take the satnav lady's advice. He
wanted nothing more than to be able to swing the Freelander
one-eighty, get the hell out of this weird little town and back on
the highway.

Only he couldn't. Something had made him pull off the rela-
tively empty A11 just after Mildenhall—that same weird voiceless
voice inside his head, making him ignore the instructions from
the console, flick his indicator on, and pull the car off the main
street down a narrow road packed with houses.

There were people here. A delivery driver was unpacking
crates from a van a few cars down, and a bunch of teenage skateboarders were messing around on the corner, one riding on the

back of another, all of them laughing. They could have been Cal and his mates outside the library back in Oakminster.

The delivery driver started to sniff the air as Cal pulled closer. The crate tumbled from his hands and a plastic carton of milk burst. He ran at the Freelander and Cal pressed his foot down a little harder, accelerating. The skateboarders had caught wind of him too. With a row of parked cars on each side there wasn't any room to maneuver, so Cal kept his speed at a constant twenty-five, hoping they'd get out of the way.

They didn't, the first kid meeting the four-by-four head-on like a charging bull, bouncing almost straight backward. The others were bumped aside by the hood, knocked into the gaps between the cars. Cal didn't stop, even when the Freelander ran over something big and soft. He steered around the corner, guided by that strange radar in his head, a silence that seemed vast and unbroken even though he could hear the monkeylike shrieks from behind him, the slam of doors opening, the thunder of footsteps. There was a turn to the left and he took it, increasing his speed so that the little kids with the garden sale wouldn't sense him until it was too late.

The road went down a hill, curving to the right then rising steeply again. Whatever it was inside his head was louder now, but still utterly silent, a perfect, pitchless peace. Even though he could see the crowd running after him in his rearview mirror, even though he had no idea what lay ahead, it made him feel safe. It made him feel that he was doing the right thing.

He swung around another corner, the Freelander clattering over a bicycle that had been abandoned in the road. There was movement up ahead, a man running in the opposite direction, toward a small mob clustered outside a house on the left. There were four or five of them, men and women and even a little boy who didn't look any older than five. The ones he could see wore the same expression of utter fury, so fierce that it turned their faces into demon masks. He sped up, somehow knowing the exact same thing he had known back on the freeway—that there was somebody close by who was just like him.

There was no time for a plan. Cal reached the mob in seconds and slammed on the brakes, the Freelander skidding into a woman. She staggered and came at him, howling as she tried to worm in through the broken passenger windows. Cal reached for his bag but couldn't get it, the woman's fingers pinching the flesh around his throat, her breath hot on his face. He grabbed the first thing he could find, a two-liter bottle of Dr Pepper, using it to batter her hands away. He opened his door and tumbled away from her onto the street.

Another woman reached for Cal with bloodied fingers. He screamed, swinging the bottle like a baseball bat. It made a ridiculous *boing* sound as it hit her head, spinning her onto the tarmac. The first woman was crawling out of the car and Cal slammed the door in her face, twice, then legged it around the back of the Freelander.

One of the adults in the garden charged at Cal, stumbling on the broken wall and giving him enough time to see that the others were clustered around a gated passage that led down the side of the house. Past the bars of the gate he could see a girl. She looked maybe eleven or twelve and she was screaming, but it was a different sound from the one the people on the other side of the gate were making. It was filled not with hate but with terror.

He lifted the bottle over his shoulder, waiting until the man was almost on him before swinging hard again. It clipped his nose, a brittle crack echoing around the street. The man didn't seem to notice, grabbing Cal around the neck and squeezing, flecks of blood spraying from his face with each snorting breath.

Cal thrust the bottle into the soft spot beneath the man's chin, pushing up until the hands around his throat loosened. He swung the bottle at him. It hit, but exploded, the drink fizzing out. The man gnashed at it, distracted, and Cal punched him in the face.

Something was biting him in the leg and he looked down to see the little boy there. He knocked him away as gently as he dared, kicking the woman who followed in the face. The last guy was big, but Cal remembered his Choy Li Fut training. He stepped behind him, locking his right leg around the man's knee then shunting hard. The guy tripped, dropping like a felled tree, his head cracking on the concrete path.

Cal glanced up the street to see people hammering down it. He had maybe thirty seconds before he was swamped. He ran to the gate, ignoring the fire that burned in his muscles and lungs. There were actually two people inside, the second a white-haired old lady with crooked fingers coiled around the girl's legs. The girl was kicking out at her, her face twisted by fear and blunted by shadow, her screams amplified by the narrow passageway. Cal tried the gate but the handle wouldn't budge.

"Hey!" he yelled. "Let me in!"

The girl ignored him, her cries reaching a crescendo as the old woman sank her teeth into her leg. Cal glanced up the road again. Fifteen seconds. He swore, took a step back, then kicked out. A jarring pain tore up his leg and his back but the gate didn't budge. He paused, breathing in through his nose, taking up a guarding stance then kicking out again with every ounce of strength he had.

The rusted lock snapped, something metal clanging down the passageway as the gate swung open. Cal ran through it, booting the old lady like he was taking a penalty. He grabbed the girl under her arms, ignoring her screams and her punches.

"It's okay, trust me, I'm not going to hurt you," he said, the words only half-formed in his breathless panic. He clamped her to him as he sprinted out into the garden, dodging one of the mob who was back on her feet then tearing open the Freelander door. The woman who had climbed inside the car was unconscious—or dead—and Cal grabbed her by the hair and tried to pull her free. She wouldn't budge, her limbs locked between the seats. The hail of footsteps was deafening now, each panted breath audible.

"Don't run," he said, putting the girl down and grabbing the woman with both hands. Her body slid from the car like a bag of meat, slopping to the ground. The girl took a few steps away from him but stopped when she saw the crowd pounding down the street—maybe twenty people now, all howling. She looked up at him, her eyes wide with shock.

"You can trust me, I promise," he said. The kid at the head of the crowd—one of the skateboarders, Cal thought—had almost reached them. "We need to go."

He held out a hand and she took it, letting him help her into the driver's seat. He climbed in next to her, slamming the door just as the skateboarder drew level. Momentum carried the kid past and he slipped on the gravel, disappearing with a yelp. The girl shuffled into the passenger seat as Cal slung the car in gear and floored it, barreling down the street, the chaos and the carnage once again safely contained in the cracked glass of his rearview mirror.

• • •

THE ONLY ONE WHO SPOKE WAS THE SATNAV LADY, and even she seemed relieved to Cal as he happily followed her directions out of Boxwood St. Mary back toward the A11. He didn't take his foot off the gas, finally remembering to breathe when he hit the ramp that led back onto the divided highway. Only when he was doing seventy in the outside lane did he notice that his entire body was as rigid as stone. He let himself relax, tremors taking the place of the tension.

"Continue on the current road," said the lady.

Cal glanced over at the girl. She was curled up in the passenger seat, making it look huge. Her face was ashen, like she'd been completely drained through the cuts on her arms and neck. Her long hair swayed like seaweed in the gale from the broken windows. She stared out of the windshield, but Cal knew she wasn't seeing anything except maybe a replay of whatever it was she'd been through.

"This lady's name is Miss Naggy," he said, his voice too loud despite the howl of the wind and the heavy thrum of tires. "She lives in the car and tells me where to go."

The girl didn't budge. At least she wasn't trying to attack him; that could only be a good thing. A car was coming up fast behind him and Cal braced himself, indicating left and sliding into the inside lane. The BMW wobbled a little as it blasted past but it didn't stop. Cal checked his mirrors then pulled out again to overtake a truck. If he moved past people quickly enough they seemed to go back to normal before anything bad happened.

"When I go the wrong way she tells me off," he went on. "Well, she usually tells my mum off, that's why she called her Miss Naggy. It's her name, not mine."

Smooth, Cal, he thought. *You're so great with kids.*

"What's your name?" he asked. She didn't reply. He thought about leaving her alone. Maybe she was in shock or something, and he wasn't sure what you were supposed to do with people like that. Wasn't there a rule about not letting them go to sleep? Or was that for something else? Constipation or something.

Concussion, idiot, his brain said, and he snorted a laugh. The noise made the girl jump. She snapped out of whatever trance she'd been in and gazed fearfully at Cal. He saw her fingers stray toward the door handle and he held up his left hand to show that he wasn't going to hurt her.

"It's okay, please don't be scared." The road ahead looked clearer and he pulled back into the left-hand lane, slowing down so that the noise inside the car was more a summer storm than a full-blown hurricane. "My name is Cal, you can trust me, I promise you."

She shuffled farther back into her seat, curled up like a hedgehog.

"Where are we going?" she said. Or at least that's what he thought she said, her voice a whisper bound up and carried off by the wind.

"Somewhere safe," he replied. "At least, I think so."

The girl seemed to relax. She rested her chin on her knees, those huge eyes never blinking.

"Miss Naggy wants you to put on your seat belt," Cal said, realizing that neither of them was wearing one. He clipped on his own. "She'll tell us off if you don't."

The girl looked at him, then at the built-in console where the voice came from. She reached up and pulled the belt over her curled-up legs, clicking it into the socket. They'd driven another half mile before she spoke, her voice so soft and so full of sadness that Cal felt a lump rise inside his throat.

"Everyone hates me."

"They don't," he said before he'd thought about what he could follow it with. "There's just, I don't know, something wrong with people. It's making them do things they don't want to do. Like zombies, you know?"

She didn't respond.

"Everyone has been attacking me too. It started at school, all my friends, they tried to . . ." he faltered, the words scared of being heard. He coughed them out. "They tried to kill me. Then people from the street, people I'd never seen before in my life." He'd wiped a tear away before he even noticed he was crying. "Then my mum."

The girl looked back at him, her mouth hanging open, and a jarring blast of fear tore through Cal as he thought she was about to throw herself over the seat and sink her teeth into his throat.

"Your mum tried to hurt you?" she said. Cal nodded. She stared at something a million miles away, deep in thought. There was a moment of revelation there, some awful understanding. Then she lowered her head to her raised knees and began to sob, great heaving cries. Cal's hand hovered over her for a second or two before landing on her shoulder. Her whole body jolted at the touch but other than that she didn't acknowledge it. He gently stroked his thumb back and forth, the way his mum had always done with him when he was upset.

"It's okay," he said, keeping his voice low, soothing. "It's all going to be okay, I promise. We'll find out what's going on and then we'll know how to stop it, we'll fix it, then our mums will be okay, they won't be angry with us anymore. I promise."

He was making a lot of promises for a guy who knew nothing about what was happening, but what else could he do? It didn't seem to be working anyway. If anything, he'd made the girl cry even harder. He put his hand back on the wheel, seeing a huge green sign advertising Norwich in fifteen miles and Yarmouth in thirty-five. The satnav said they'd be there within an hour. They would be late, but he was pretty sure Rick_B, whoever he was, would hang around.

He drove in silence for the next few minutes, the satnav lady chirping up and navigating him around a series of roundabouts onto the Norwich bypass. It was a while later that the girl stopped sobbing, her face rising from behind her kneecaps. Cal smiled at her as gently as he could, not wanting to say anything else in case he set her off again. But she seemed like she was cried out, wrung dry. She looked up at him, wiping her nose with the back of her hand.

"You really think there's a way to make things normal again?"

The look she gave him, suddenly so full of hope, of trust, meant there was only one answer he could give.

"Yeah," he nodded. "I really do. Whatever this is, we'll work it out together. I promise."

She wiped her nose again, sniffing. Cal leaned over and popped the glove box, a half-empty pack of tissues inside. He gestured at them and she took one, patting her eyes dry then scrunching it up and tucking it in her sleeve. She took a deep, juddering breath that seemed to shake some color back into her cheeks.

"Thanks," she said, a ghost of a smile on her thin lips, in her pale eyes. "My name's Daisy."

CALMESSIRONALDO WAS LATE.

Either that or he was dead. Where had he said he was coming from? London? If things were as bad as Brick thought, that was one hell of a journey, literally—a gantlet of ten million psychotic people trying to slaughter you on the street. Maybe the guy had decided not to come. Brick hadn't exactly been a charmer in his messages. He tried to think back to what he'd written, unable to recall a single word other than to come alone. Why did he always have to be so unfriendly?

Blame it on stress, he thought, twisting a long strand of grass between his fingers. *Blame it on shock, on fear.* But the truth was much simpler than that. He *was* unfriendly. He promised himself he'd make an effort to be nice as soon as the guy showed up.

If he showed up.

He wished he had a watch, or the phone he'd dropped when he was riding away from the gas station. Norfolk was as flat as a pancake, which meant the daylight stretched right out into the evening, but once it hit ten it would get dark. Really dark. He'd have to be back at Fursville by then or he'd end up spending all night on the beach.

An ant struggled past right under his nose, its feet moving so fast they were just a blur as it attempted to negotiate the crumbling sand. He lowered a piece of grass in front of it, watching it climb on board before gently letting go. The ant scuttled off along the grass, vanishing into the tangled web.

"You're welcome," he said, sitting up to stretch his spine, trying to shake the blood back into his legs. The knees of his jeans were wet. How did sand always manage to stay moist even on a day like today? He was brushing the blotchy stains with his hands when he heard a car, distant but unmistakable.

He ducked back down, peering through the mess of sea grass, his heartbeat rising along with the pitch of the engine. It seemed to take an eternity before it finally showed itself, the thing that trundled from the tree line not a car but one of those baby Land Rovers. There was something spattered all over the crumpled hood, as bright as paint. The passenger windows were wound down, or broken, and a massive crack stretched diagonally across the windshield, making it difficult for him to see inside. The car limped over the concrete and pulled up next to the toilet block.

Nothing happened. Nobody got out.

"Come on," Brick whispered. The car was pointing straight at him and he got the feeling that whoever was inside was watching him, waiting for him to make his move.

He looked to his left and right, scanning the beach. What if the guy hadn't come alone? What if there was more than one of them? His friends might have spread out, flanking the parking lot, ready to attack him from all angles. He swore. Why hadn't he brought a weapon? Fursville was full of metal bars and old tools; there were even knives left in the restaurant. All he had here were his own two fists. It wasn't too late to retreat. If he slid down the dune, he could walk back along the shore.

Calm down. You're panicking like an old woman.

He wiped a hand across his forehead, sand sticking to the sheen of sweat that had broken out there. He felt a weird pressure in his head, a silence that was almost a sound. He squinted, trying to make out the shape behind the steering wheel. There was definitely somebody there, but was that somebody in the passenger seat too?

The car horn blared and Brick almost screamed, his rasping cry lost in the flap of a dozen birds that took flight from the trees.

"Get out of the car," he hissed into the dune.

His words were too quiet to carry, but they worked anyway. There was a loud clack, then the driver's door swung open with a painful squeal. It was a kid dressed in gray tracksuit pants and a T-shirt, looking maybe sixteen or seventeen.

"Hello?" the boy called out, the tremors audible in his voice even from where Brick was lying. Again that instinctive need to get away almost ripped him from the dune, numbed by the weird, calm silence inside his head.

"Is anyone there?" the boy called out again, his words drifting effortlessly over the hot ground. "Rick?"

Rick? Brick wondered, before remembering his log-in name. He felt an answer surging up from inside him of its own accord when he heard the sound of the passenger door opening. He clamped his mouth shut as the boy shouted something at the car, gesturing at whoever was inside. Brick couldn't hear the reply but it didn't matter. The kid had broken the rules.

He began to retreat. This wasn't worth the risk. One teenage boy he could handle, but if there were two or maybe more in there then he was in trouble—especially if they started to attack him the same way as everyone else. The car was almost out of sight when the passenger climbed out, dropping to the ground. Brick paused, shuffling back to the top of the dune. The other person was a little girl, tiny next to the car. She was wearing black trousers and a burgundy polo with what might have been a school badge.

A boy and a kid, maybe brother and sister. Even if they did go crazy, Brick thought he'd be able to handle them—so long as he took out the guy first he could easily outrun the girl.

I guess we're about to find out, he thought. Then he ran his hand over his forehead once more and got to his feet.

CAL / *Hemmingway, 8:55 p.m.*

"THERE'S NOBODY HERE," CAL SAID TO DAISY.

"Yes there is," she replied, looking up at him. "Don't you . . . don't you *feel* them?"

Cal shook his head, but there was something there, that same strange, ebbing sense of peace ringing around his skull. The gun was tucked into the waistband of his trousers, and every time he nudged it back into place he worried he would set it off and blast away half of his backside. He should have left it in the car.

"See," Daisy said.

He followed her line of sight to the dunes that hid the sea from the parking lot. Somebody was walking down them, a tall guy with hair so red that it glinted like copper in the fading sun. He was wearing jeans and a filthy white T-shirt, and his long, gangly arms were held out from his sides, fingers spread.

"Is he going to hurt us?" Daisy asked, running to his side. Cal didn't reply, holding her tight with one hand. He felt the gun, cold and sharp against his back.

The guy—it was difficult to tell how old he was—stopped at

the bottom of the dune, about ten or fifteen meters away. This close Cal could see the bloodstains on his T-shirt, looking more like chocolate in the growing pool of shadow. Dried blood pocked his face as well, an ugly-looking wound above one eye. There was something about the guy that made Cal instantly suspicious, something in the bluntness of his cheekbones, the narrowness of his eyes. And yet there was something inside his own head— more the absence of something, really; a feeling that was telling him it was okay, that the red-haired man was one of them.

All the same, for a good minute or so nobody moved, everybody wary of the same thing—that someone was about to start screaming, to charge across the parking lot fists flailing and teeth biting and eyes boiling. Those sixty-odd seconds seemed to stretch out forever, only the quiet lull of the unseen waves and the crack of the trees letting Cal know that time hadn't frozen.

"He isn't attacking us," Daisy whispered, looking up. The guy must have heard her because he snorted a laugh. His hands lowered to his sides, but he was still visibly tense.

"Are you Rick?" Cal asked. "I'm Cal."

Rick squinted, holding up a hand to shield his eyes. The sun was over Cal's shoulders, nesting in the treetops, lighting the guy from the chest up. "What do you think?" he said, his brow crinkling. "I thought I told you to come alone."

"Um, this is Daisy," Cal said. "I found her on the way. She's like—" He almost said *us*, but it was too soon for that. "Like me. She got attacked too."

Daisy lifted her hand and gave a flick of a wave.

The man watched warily, his eyes dodging back and forth between Cal and Daisy.

"CalMessiRonaldo," he said. "You like football, then?"

It was spoken more like an insult than a question, so Cal didn't answer. He could feel his hackles rising. The silence that followed was just about as awkward as silences could be.

"I'm Brick," the guy said eventually.

"Brick?" asked Daisy. The man smiled, just a slight twitch of his lips but a smile nonetheless. It seemed to make his face more human.

"Because of my hair," he said to her. "It's the same color as a brick."

"No it's not," she replied. "Bricks are sort of dark pink and your hair is bright orange."

Brick's smile grew, finally reaching his eyes. Cal could see that, despite his height, Brick wasn't much more than a boy himself.

"You can call me Carrot if you like," he said. He looked back at Cal and the smile vanished. Seconds of silence ticked away, the gulls circling overhead like vultures. "What's going on out there?"

"It's bad," Cal said. "You're the first person I've seen other than Daisy who hasn't tried to rip my head off."

Brick nodded. He glanced to his right, then back at Cal.

"Yeah, it's really hit the fan all right." He was chewing on something, but after a moment or two he spat it out. "Gonna get dark soon. I've got a place, a safe place I think. It's about twenty minutes from here. No food or lights or anything—"

"We've got food," interrupted Daisy. "Got loads of stuff in the car. It's Cal's, not mine."

"That's good," Brick went on. "It's not ideal but nobody knows about it. You can come if you want."

Duh, thought Cal. *We just drove all this way to say hi but now we're gonna hit the road again.* But instead he said: "Sure, okay, can we bring the car?"

Brick looked at the Freelander as if it was another unwelcome stranger. Cal shifted his weight, and as he did so he felt the heavy knuckle of metal slip from his waistband and down his legs. It hit the concrete with a crack. Brick's eyes widened as he saw the gun there. Then, before Cal could say anything, he turned and ran.

"Wait!" Cal yelled. The guy was bolting with impressive speed, his arms and legs pistoning him back up the dune. "Wait! It was just in case, I wasn't going to use it!"

Brick wasn't listening, practically vaulting over the dune in a shroud of kicked-up sand. Cal swore, then bent down and snatched the gun.

"Wait here!" he said to Daisy, legging it across the parking lot. He jumped onto the dune, his feet sinking as he charged upward. He reached the top in time to see Brick sprinting down the beach.

"Brick, wait!" he shouted. The older boy didn't stop, didn't even slow. Cal started down the slope, making it four or five paces before realizing that, as fast as he was, he was never going to catch up with him. Instead he lifted the gun, pointed it straight up, and pulled the trigger.

The recoil juddered down his arm into his shoulder, ending up as a painful cramp beneath his ribs. Brick missed his footing and sprawled onto his face. He spun around, crawling backward like a crab.

Cal kept the gun high, pointing toward the skies, half thinking that the bullet was going to come right back down and cave in his own head. He took a deep breath, gunpowder like firework smoke in his lungs.

"I'm not going to shoot you!" he yelled. "I only brought the gun in case you were crazy. Look." He lobbed the pistol toward Brick. It landed halfway between them, burrowing itself into the sand. "It's yours, take it, just don't leave us here, okay?"

Very slowly, Brick got to his feet. He was stooped over, hunched into himself like he was expecting another shot to come from somewhere else. He walked back through the craters of his own footsteps, picking up the gun by its barrel and holding it away from him. He reminded Cal of a kid carrying scissors.

There was a frantic puff of breath and Daisy appeared by Cal's side, grabbing his right hand with both of hers. They looked at Brick, who stood statuelike, the gun still held out before him.

"Please don't leave us," Daisy said. "We weren't going to hurt you."

It seemed to take an age for Brick to nod at her. "We'd better go. The sound of that shot must have carried for miles." He turned and walked slowly along the shore, keeping close to the water. "Leave the car here. We don't want tire tracks. Just grab your stuff and follow me."

DAISY / *Hemmingway, 9:13 p.m.*

DAISY WALKED BETWEEN THE TWO BOYS, breaking into a trot every few seconds to keep up with their giant strides. She was exhausted, her legs aching from the sand and her hands from the two shopping bags she held.

She should have been more nervous about following these two strangers, but that usual horrid feeling in her chest and stomach she got when she was scared—like there were living things crawling around inside her—just wasn't there. It might have still been the shock of what had happened. It might have been the fact that in the last few hours everything in her life, everything she knew about the world, had changed.

But there was something else too.

"So, where are you from?" she heard Cal ask.

He was a few paces in front of her, a huge black duffel over his shoulder and the last bag gripped in one hand. The other boy was a few paces in front of him and he wasn't carrying anything except the gun. They were almost walking in line. The sea was still to their right, huge and shiny like a big bit of silver foil. The dunes rose to their left. The sun had dipped below them now, making the sand look more like wet cement. She jogged forward a few steps until she was by Cal's side again.

"Around here someplace?"

He's from the Larkman, Daisy thought idly, skirting around a clump of dried seaweed that looked like a dead tarantula. Which was weird because she'd never heard of the Larkman before.

"Norwich," Brick grunted without looking back.

Oh, thought Daisy.

"A place called the Larkman, actually," he went on. "You won't have heard of it."

"Cool," said Cal. He smiled down at Daisy and she smiled back without having to think about it. Cal was nice, and she could trust him. Even if he hadn't saved her life, she'd have known that. He wasn't from Norwich, he was from a place called Oak Minster or something. It made her think of a church built of wood. That little piece of knowledge floated in her brain like an ice cube in a glass of water, kind of see-through and almost invisible but definitely there. It made her head feel cold, not in a bad way.

"You okay?" Cal asked her. "You want me to take those bags?"

"I'm fine," she replied, not wanting to look even more like a kid than she felt. She looked up at Brick's back. Even in the dark the bigger boy's hair seemed to glow orange. *He hates it,* she thought. *Not because of the color, or because people tease him, but because it reminds him of his dad.* Her head was full of ice cubes, each one different, all of them clinking little bits of knowledge over her thoughts.

"Who did you say attacked you?" Cal asked. "Your girlfriend, was it?"

Brick shot a look over his shoulder that was easy enough to read—*Don't go there*—but it softened after a moment. He bent down and picked up one of the little stones that littered the beach, lobbing it out into the sea. It went a long way. Daisy felt sorry for it, because it would be stuck in the cold, dark water for ages. Maybe forever.

"That's how it started, yeah," he said as he walked. "We were making out, y'know? Then she just went mental. She bit me." He turned again and pointed at the filthy wound above his eye. "Wasn't just that, though, she was proper psycho, tried to claw me to pieces. No reason, I didn't do anything. Then I went to the gas station to get help, and a load of people came after me. They wanted to kill me."

He's not saying something, thought Daisy. And another ice cube floated by inside her mind: a dark corridor and some steps, a locked door at the bottom of them. This thought gave her a bad feeling, an unpleasant tickling in her stomach, and she pushed it away by focusing on the gulls that bobbed on the sea. They peered back at her, and their little eyes reminded her of the people who had attacked her—the ambulance man and Mrs. Baird and all the neighbors and people she'd never seen before—because there was nothing at all in those eyes. They were hollow black marbles.

"You call the police or anything?" Cal asked.

Brick shook his head. "They'd have come after me too. Don't know how I know that but I do." He looked at Cal. "You know it too."

So did Daisy. Everyone would come after them, no matter where they went or what they did. Until they found a way to fix this, the whole world would have the fury. This wasn't another ice cube thought, this was a big flashing light in her head, impossible to ignore or push away.

"The fury," said Brick, nodding as if Daisy had spoken it aloud. "Question is why. Why us?"

The only answer to this was the whisper of the sea as it lapped the beach with its foamy tongue, that and the gentle cries of the gulls settling into bed. Did they sleep on the water? That was odd. How did they not capsize in the middle of the night?

They walked in silence for a few more minutes, Daisy falling farther and farther behind as the soft, uneven ground took its toll on her legs. She tried to make sense of the other ice cubes. She could see one with a pretty girl reading a book. That was Cal's. There was another of a pier full of arcade machines that was too see-through to make any sense of. There were nasty ones too—people screaming and biting and punching and kicking and chasing—that belonged to both of the boys. Daisy clicked through them like someone channel surfing, not really understanding how these things could be in her head, unless she was imagining them.

After a while Brick moved off to the left, toward the dunes. Up ahead the beach narrowed, and she could make out a weird wooden thing—like a huge collapsed rope bridge—stretching over the sand into the sea. She jogged to catch up, almost stumbling. Cal waited for her at the bottom of the dune, Brick already halfway up.

"You sure you don't want me to take your bags?" he asked, hiking his load up over his shoulder. "I don't mind."

"It's okay," she said. "I think we're almost there."

How did she know that? She wasn't quite sure, she just did. Just like she knew she'd see a big wheel even before it rose over the top of the dune like a rusty metal sun.

Brick flapped gracelessly down the other side of the dune, toward a huge fence. Daisy saw that there wasn't just a Ferris wheel ahead but a whole theme park—there were two roller coasters, by the looks of things, and one of those rides that whizzed up and down and made you feel sick just looking at it, and a large square building with a roof like waves. Her heart lifted when she saw a carousel too, although she could only make out the painted, cone-shaped roof over the fence. She loved carousels! It was the closest she'd ever really come to riding a horse.

"It's an amusement park," she said.

Brick turned and somehow a smile managed to land on his sour face again.

"It used to be," he said. "Don't get excited, though. Nothing works anymore. But it's safe, nobody ever comes here apart from me."

It didn't matter if nothing worked, there still might be horses. In fact couldn't she see them now, like another one of those weird half-invisible thoughts that made her brain feel cold? She could see their kind eyes and their long noses and that horrible dark corridor and the steps going down and the locked door and something behind it that moaned.

Her skin went prickly and she ran to Cal, walking by his side as they followed Brick down the dune onto a concrete walkway. It ran alongside the fence, and about halfway down Brick squeezed through a gap and disappeared. He was waiting for them on the other side when they caught up.

"Watch you don't scratch yourself," he said to Daisy. "The wire is pretty sharp."

Cal grabbed the fence and pulled it open and she looked at the gap. She searched inside herself for warning signs, for those little electric currents that told her something bad might happen. But they weren't there. Other than that corridor and the locked door—*which might not even be real, which might just be in your head*—she felt absolutely safe.

She crawled through the gap on her hands and knees, standing and dusting herself off as Cal followed. Brick shushed them out of the way, grabbing a huge piece of wood. He rested it against the fence, giving it a shove to make sure it was firmly in place. Even with the exit blocked Daisy couldn't feel the slightest trace of fear. In fact she couldn't remember ever being anywhere before where she'd felt quite as much like she was *supposed* to be there.

Brick turned and stretched out his long, freckled arms. This time his smile was nervous, almost bashful.

"Cal, Daisy, welcome to Fursville."

IT COULD HAVE BEEN A ROMANTIC DINNER, if it weren't for the fact that he was eating a packet of shrimp-flavored chips and the person sitting opposite him, on the other side of the candlelit table, was an ugly redheaded guy called Brick.

They were on the first floor of the pavilion, in the small restaurant called Waves. One side of the room was made up of floor-to-ceiling windows, but there was no sea view anymore. The windows had been boarded over from the outside, much of the glass cracked and stained so that the stuttering candle was reflected in it several times, making it seem like the room was alight. The whole place was an inch deep in dust and cobwebs, and the stench of sea rot hung in the air along with the smoke.

His discomfort must have shown because Brick snorted out another one of his not-quite-laughs.

"It's not the Four Seasons or anything," he said.

"It's fine," said Cal, funneling the crumbs into his mouth then flattening the chips packet against the moldering tablecloth. Daisy lay on a small, damp chaise longue to their side. She'd climbed on it about five minutes ago and she was already fast asleep, her snores as soft as velvet. "It's safe."

"It's definitely safe. Nobody's ever here. Ever."

That wasn't a surprise, from what they'd seen in the last half hour. Brick had given them a guided tour, acting like he worked here as he showed them the roller coaster and the log flume and the carousel and the bumper cars and the overgrown miniature golf course. What he really should have been doing, Cal thought, was showing them the emergency exits, the safest hideaways, the supplies, the weak points, the lookout areas. At the very least he could have pointed the way to the facilities. But no, he'd walked around muttering about arcade machines and doughnuts and which was the best seat to take on the flume if you didn't want to get wet—even though none of it even worked anymore.

Cal hadn't said anything, though. It did seem quiet here and, from what he and Daisy had seen in the car on the drive up, this part of the coast was as good as deserted. There would be plenty of time to shore the park up in case people came looking.

He sighed, hard enough to make the candlelight flutter. It was the first time he'd admitted to himself that this might not go away overnight. It might not go away at all.

"What?" Brick asked.

"Nothing. This whole thing, it doesn't seem real."

"I know. Feels like another lifetime that I was riding out here with Lisa, that we were fine."

Another lifetime, thought Cal. It really did. How long had it been since he was back at school playing football? Maybe ten hours. Ten hours for the rules of the universe to unravel around him, for everything he knew to turn to rot. It reminded him of a poem they'd done in English, but he couldn't remember how it went. Something about things falling apart. They sat in silence, both of them chewing their own thoughts as the candle guttered like a chesty breath, a death rattle.

"Your girlfriend," said Cal. "Lisa? What . . . I mean, er, is she—"

"You don't have to worry about her," said Brick sharply, with a look that told Cal it would be better not to pursue the subject any further.

"You have any idea what might be causing this?" Cal asked, quickly changing tack. "I mean I can't think of anything. Except genetics maybe."

"Huh?" Brick grunted.

"Like cats. You know how some cats are, they just need to see another cat and they go for it. They fight to the death sometimes. Dogs too, I guess."

Brick nodded, deep in thought.

"But something like that doesn't just happen," he said eventually. "You don't just flick a switch and everyone hates you."

"It wasn't just that with me," Cal said. Daisy stirred, snuffling and pressing her face into the chaise longue. He waited for her breathing to even out again before continuing. "Things have been strange for a few days now. People were ignoring me, acting weird. I thought they were just playing games but . . ."

He didn't need to finish. Brick drew patterns in the dust on the table, the nail on his forefinger a crescent moon of dirt and blood. When he lifted his arm Cal saw a circle with two x's for eyes, angry slanted eyebrows, and a downturned mouth. A smiley without the smile. Somehow, without properly acknowledging the thought, he'd known that was what Brick was going to draw.

"The fury," Brick mumbled, looking at his creation. "Good name for it, right?"

"Certainly fits," Cal said. "Why us, though? And why now?"

Brick leaned down and rummaged in a shopping bag—one that he'd picked up from the foyer as they were passing through. He hefted a laptop from it and laid it carefully on the table, covering up his dust drawing.

"I need to show you something," he said as he opened the lid.

Cal heard the whine of the hard drive coming to life, and the boy's face was suddenly bathed in a sickly white glow. Cal got up, wiping the dirt from his palms as he walked around the table. Brick was online, the browser showing the same Yahoo Answers page that Cal had seen back at home. He could see Rick_B's original message, and below that his own panicked response. Brick peered up, looking half his age from this angle. "It's not just us," he said.

"I know," Cal replied, watching Brick's eyes widen. "I saw it happen on the freeway, a ton of people on top of a car attacking somebody inside. It was someone like us. I'm not sure how, I just know it."

He choked as the memory burned back, the flames from the explosion seeming to sear the flesh of his brain. Brick turned back to the screen. When he raised his dust-blackened finger to the trackpad it was shaking.

"It's not just that," he said. "You weren't the only person to reply. Look."

He scrolled down the page slowly enough for Cal to read the eleven answers that followed his, all of them but two almost a carbon copy of his own. By the time he'd reached the last he felt like he'd been punched hard in the gut.

"That's from four hours ago," Brick said, moving the pointer over the time of the last entry, 6:05 p.m. "I haven't checked since then."

He led the arrow up toward the Refresh button and Cal almost screamed for him not to press it. He didn't want to see. He didn't want to know.

Brick clicked. The page loaded up painfully slowly. The Yahoo header, then the ads, then the frame, then Brick's message. The answers followed, all together like they were being vomited onto the page.

All forty-eight of them.

"Jesus," said Cal, and this time he had to take a seat on the chair to the left of Brick's. "Please tell me they're not all real."

Brick was scrolling down again, and his ghostly pallor had nothing to do with the light from the screen. Cal watched the boy's face crumple into itself a little further with each new answer he read. It seemed like an age later when he finally turned his red, swimming eyes up. They looked at each other properly for the first time, and despite their differences they could have been mirror images.

"Brick?" Cal asked. "What do they say?"

"The same thing," he breathed, breaking away to the screen again. "They're all exactly the same."

"What do we do?"

Brick looked up, and this time when their eyes met Cal knew exactly what Brick was thinking.

"We tell them," Cal said. "We tell them about this place."

"We have to," Brick confirmed. "I don't want to but we have to. Look, you and me, we haven't killed each other, or Daisy. If we're . . ."

"Different," Cal said when he saw him struggling.

"If we're different, if there's something about us that's different from the others, from the Fury—"

He's given it a capital "F," Cal realized, *it's more than just a word now.*

"—then we have to get together, as many of us as we can. It's the only way we can be safe, we can figure it out."

"But you can't tell them where we are," Cal said. "Not on

there, what if the others find us? Brick, we need to think about this."

"We don't have time," he replied, tapping his finger on the top of the screen. Cal noticed the battery icon there, red and flashing. "It's about to shut down and there's no power here."

Cal swore, loud enough to stir Daisy again. She wriggled over, opening her eyes and seeing him. By the time her distant, dreamer's smile had faded she was asleep again.

"Look," said Brick quietly. "I won't tell them about Fursville. There's a secondhand car showroom just over the road, it's empty. I'll tell them to go there and wait for someone to come to them. We can keep watch on the place, and if anything looks suspicious we just won't show ourselves. Yeah?"

Cal shook his head.

"Yeah?" Brick repeated.

"Okay," Cal said, throwing his hands in the air. "Okay, whatever."

Brick was already typing: "You're not alone. We have a safe place, there's a few of us here and we're not attacking each other. If you can get to us, we're in a town called Hemmingway, in Norfolk, right on the beach, up from Hemsby. On the main coast road there's an abandoned car showroom called Soapy's. Go there and wait, we'll check it at noon every day." He stopped, running both hands through his hair.

"Will that do?" he asked. Cal didn't reply. Brick read it through once more, the pointer hovering over the Post Reply button. "I guess it will have to."

He clicked, and five seconds later the post appeared on the refreshed page.

"You know it's not gonna take a genius to work out that if

we're not in the showroom we're gonna be in the bloody great big empty amusement park next door," Cal said, slumping back. "We should have met them at the parking lot."

"It's too far away," Brick said. "We'd have to make that slog every day. It's not safe."

"*This* isn't safe," Cal snapped back. Brick closed the laptop, tapping his fingers on it. "We need to make extra sure this place is secure," Cal went on. "Seal up the fence, have an emergency plan, just in case."

It took Brick a moment to look up. He stared at Cal, but it seemed that he was peering through him, at something much deeper.

"Things fall apart," he said, his voice as low as the guttering candle. Cal shook his head as the poem he couldn't remember, the one he'd learned at school, tumbled from Brick's lips. "The centre cannot hold. Mere anarchy is loosed upon the world."

Brick looked away, firelight burning in his eyes as he finished.

"The blood-dimmed tide is loosed. And goddamned everywhere the ceremony of innocence is drowned."

THE OTHER (2)

In his presence the mountains quake,
and the hills melt away;
the earth trembles, and its people are destroyed.
Who can stand before his fierce anger?
Who can survive his burning fury?
His rage blazes forth like fire,
and the mountains crumble to dust in his presence.

—*Nahum 1:5–6*

"LOOK, I JUST WANT TO KNOW WHAT'S GOING ON."

Detective Inspector Alan Murdoch had been speaking the same words to the same locked door for the better part of three hours. And it was nearly twenty-four hours now since he'd been bundled into a car along with Jorgensen and his assistants from the morgue and taken to the massive MI5 headquarters by the Thames. He was being treated like a terrorist, as though somehow he was responsible for the freak corpse and its endless breath. When he'd first arrived they'd strapped him with diodes and sensors and asked him question after question, blatantly refusing to answer any of his. And after that he'd been thrown into this windowless basement room to rot.

He hadn't even been allowed to call his wife. His phone and police radio had been confiscated, and so had his warrant card. He was supposed to have been home this time yesterday; she'd be worried sick.

"I really am sorry," said Jorgensen for what must have been the hundredth time that day. He sat on the other side of the small room—no, the *cell*—looking a hundred years old. "I never should have called you in, Alan."

No, you bloody well shouldn't have, Murdoch thought, saying: "This isn't your fault, Sven. You were just doing your job."

The pathologist gave him a weary smile, then planted his head back in his hands. Murdoch slammed his fist against the door, hard enough to hurt.

"You've got no right to keep us in here, dammit," he roared. They'd been given water and a sandwich each but that had been hours ago. Murdoch's hunger was lost behind the rage inside his gut. "I'm a police officer, I have a right to know what's going on."

Rights. Murdoch laughed bitterly. He had no rights, not here, not in the heart of the government's secret service. They could hold him forever and make sure nobody ever asked any questions. But *why?*

There was a metallic clang from outside the door, then footsteps. A key turned, then the door swung out to reveal a man and a woman in orderly uniforms. The man was holding a tray with more sandwiches and two bottles of water. He started to walk in but Murdoch barred his way.

"You can't keep us here," he said. "I demand to see your commanding officer."

"I'm sorry, sir," said the woman. "I'm afraid nobody is available to speak to you right now."

"Please wait inside the room," added the man, and there was a definite *or else* that he left unvoiced.

Murdoch bit his tongue, looking past the orderlies to see a long, windowless corridor. At the end of it was a reinforced metal door, guarded by armed men. Murdoch knew that's where it was, the living corpse. The thought of it there, so close, made him shudder. Even as he watched, the door opened and a group of people walked out. They wore a mix of uniforms—some military top brass, some white surgical coats—but they all wore the same expression of fear. They strode down the corridor and turned out of sight.

"Look," said Murdoch, forcing himself to stay calm. "I don't want to cause any trouble, I just want to go home. My wife, she doesn't know where I am. Can you at least tell me how long you're going to keep us here?"

The orderlies must have seen the desperation in his gaunt face, because their expressions softened.

"The truth is, we don't know," said the woman. "There's something . . . they're saying it's something bad, really bad. They're keeping anyone who's had any contact with it. Did you see it?"

"Yeah," said Murdoch, sighing. "And they're right, it's bad."

"Take this," said the man, passing the tray to Murdoch. "It might be over soon, they're bringing in some kind of expert. With any luck they'll be able to work out what's going on and get you guys out of here."

"An expert?" said Jorgensen, walking over. "What kind of expert?"

The man shrugged, saying, "Just somebody who might know what this thing is."

And what it wants, Murdoch's mind added.

The sound of voices rose up, a group of soldiers walking out of the same corridor the others had left by. They headed up toward the guarded door and Murdoch saw somebody else with them, somebody dressed in black robes. The woman looked over her shoulder.

"That's him now," she said.

"The *expert?*" Jorgensen asked. The man and woman nodded.

"No way," Murdoch said, scarcely able to believe what he was seeing. The soldiers reached the door and the man turned, revealing the white collar around his neck, the heavy crucifix that hung over his chest. The expert wasn't a scientist or a doctor or a general.

He was a priest.

SATURDAY

*The fiend in his own shape is less hideous than when he rages
in the breast of man.*
  —Nathaniel Hawthorne, *"Young Goodman Brown"*

"WE SHOULDN'T BE DOING THIS."

Rilke Bastion ignored her brother the way she had learned to do through years of practice. He trotted along by her side as if he were a dog, not her fifteen-year-old twin, his sad little face turned up to her with those puppy-moist eyes. If Schiller had a tail, it would be permanently fixed between his legs.

"Rilke, please, Mother will be angry."

Their mother wouldn't even know. She was cocooned in the same musty, tea-stained sheets she spent half her life in. She spent the other half in the old-fashioned wooden bath chair that sat wheel-locked beside the huge windows in her bedroom suite, her eyes watching over the estate but her mind rotted, unthinking.

"Please, Rilke, I don't want to go."

His canine whine was a knifepoint in her ears, making the headache she'd had for at least two days now infinitely worse. She stopped, spinning around and grabbing Schiller by the collar. Looking into his face was so like looking at her own reflection, and yet utterly different. She could see the same high cheekbones, the same icy blue eyes, the same narrow nose. And yet it was as though she were staring into a trick mirror, one of the ones that distorted your image, making her chin too weak, her jowls too loose, her eyes too watery. She glared at Schiller until he looked away, as he always did. Only then did she release him.

"Go on, then," she said as he brushed his hands down his polo shirt, trying to get the creases out. "Go home."

Schiller peered down the street where the vast bulk of St. Peter's Church sat like a mountain in the dark. A mile or so past that lay home, the crumbling manor house entombed in the shadows of its endless grounds.

"Go on," she snapped. "What are you waiting for? If you're going back, then go. I'm finding this party with or without you."

"But I don't feel too good," Schiller replied, rubbing his left temple. His eyes darted up, meeting hers for a fraction of a second. The truth was that she wasn't feeling too good either. But she ignored the throb, glaring at her brother until his hand dropped in submission. "Okay, but I don't want to stay all night. Please, Rilke."

Good boy, she thought. *Good dog.* She patted him on the head, hard enough to make him flinch. Then she turned and carried on down the street. She'd heard about the party from a cleaner called Millie who worked part-time at the estate. Not that Millie had told her to her face—none of the staff dared talk to Rilke. She'd overheard the girl chatting to one of her friends when they were dusting the library. An illegal rave, she'd called it, and they'd giggled at the word "illegal." *It'll be cool, just music and stuff, come along, it's not far out of town, you know the Logan farm up by the coast.*

"Not all night, though?" Schiller said to her back. "Please?"

"All night, little brother," she said. She always called him that, even though he was technically a few minutes older. "Till the birds start singing."

Farlen wasn't a big town. Some people didn't even call it a town at all, more like a village with an ego. It had grown up around their own house, centuries ago, back when the Bastion family was rich and influential. Over the last couple of generations the estate had crumbled under its own weight, the huge house disintegrating, rats gnawing at its foundations and pigeon droppings eating through its rafters. And the town seemed to be under the same curse.

Good riddance to it, Rilke thought as they reached the end of the main street and the boarded-up shops that sat there. The line of lights ended, a pool of bottomless black beyond looking like the edge of the world. The stars were out, the moon too, but the cool silver glow they emitted was reluctant.

A pang of something nestled uncomfortably in her stomach. She slowed, opening her arm and letting Schiller slide his own through the loop. He hugged it tight, and she could feel his gratitude ebbing off him in great golden waves.

"I love you, little brother," she said. "You know I won't let anything happen to you."

"I know," he whispered as they stepped out of the light. Rilke slid the flashlight from her jacket pocket, flicking on the beam and carving a channel through the night like Moses with the Red Sea. She pulled Schiller closer, picking up the pace and practically dragging him along by her side.

"Come on," she said. "It's not far."

THE MUSIC HIT HER AT THE SAME TIME as the stench of the ocean.

She hated that smell. What did they say? That in Britain you were never more than seventy miles from the sea. And every year it seemed to creep in a little closer, eroding the beach and the cliffs, rotting the land away a few meters at a time. It was the vast weight of it that scared her, not just its width—spanning the gulf between continents—but its unthinkable depth. There was just so much of it, and if one day it decided to swell, to spill its lightless guts onto the land, it could wipe the world clean without a second thought. A frightening thought, if not necessarily a bad one. There wasn't much in this world that made Rilke smile.

She breathed through her mouth, focusing on the glow ahead. Spotlights rose from a stubbled field maybe half a mile away, throwing light right back at the stars and the pale grinning face of the moon. The music was nothing more than a pulse that she could feel in her feet, as if the very ground were alive. The truth was she hated this kind of party, the people you got there, all high on something or drunk off their faces. All stupid, the same way most people were stupid. But it had to be better than another night of unrelenting boredom at home. Rilke had never been a big sleeper.

She shone her beam on the short, grassy bank then stumbled up it, Schiller's arm still limpet-tight around hers. It was tough going on the uneven ground but the earth was hard and she kept her pace steady, sticking to the same plowed furrow. The heartbeat grew more powerful the closer they got, popping in her ears, brushing against her skin. It found an echo in the pain between her temples—*thump-thump* . . . *thump-thump* . . . *thump-thump*—like something was stuck inside her skull and trying to beat its way out. She picked up her pace, the rave pulling itself out of the distance like a cathedral of light.

They were halfway across the field when Schiller stopped, planting his feet into the dry earth like an anchor. She turned, shining the light into his face.

"I don't want to go," he moaned, squinting in the harsh beam. "I'm scared."

"You're such a baby, Schill," she replied, wrenching him forward. He dug in, fighting.

"Something bad is going to happen," he went on.

"Don't be stupid." And yet even as she said the words she felt something inside her, something in her gut, scream out—*He's right, he's right, he's right*—a wordless, instinctive jolt. The rave was close enough for her to see the ring of vans and cars that circled the party like wagons, and past them the heaving mass of flesh that seemed to breathe in and out with that bone-shaking heartbeat.

Rilke swallowed, suddenly cold. She almost retreated right there, ready to lead the way back across the field toward home. But once again that stubborn streak stopped her in her tracks, made her bury that instinctive warning. The Bastion family had always been driven by its women. They were the ones to lead.

She clenched her arm, trapping Schiller's tight and pulling him across the field. *He needs a leash,* she thought. They walked for another minute or so, the crowd ahead coalescing into individuals—guys and girls in their teens and twenties pretty much all wearing glow sticks. Most were inside the ring of vehicles, but others were loitering in the shadows around the party, talking or kissing or lost in their own private drug-induced dances. There was nothing to be scared of here. She'd stay for an hour or so, just to see what it was like, just to have had the experience, then they'd go. She'd pretend to be leaving for Schiller's sake, that way he would owe her.

He was resisting again. Rilke looked over her shoulder, not slowing. He said something, his words lost in the deafening bass thump that seemed to rise from the earth. *What?* she mouthed, shrugging her shoulders, waiting for him to start moaning again. But he wasn't.

"My head," he yelled, leaning in close. "It doesn't hurt anymore."

She was halfway through a reply when she realized that the ache in her own brain had gone, so swiftly and so suddenly that she hadn't even noticed. She put a hand against the side of Schiller's head, stroking his temple with her thumb.

"See, little brother," she shouted, smiling. "What did I tell you? Everything is fine."

He couldn't have heard what she said over the noise but he smiled back, the reflected spotlights making his eyes twinkle.

It didn't last.

She knew what he was looking at before she could even turn around, like she'd seen it with her own eyes—two people, a man and a teenage girl, stumbling toward them. And there was more—a flash of something else, something that smelled of rot, a girl and two boys asleep in an old restaurant, someone else walking through a forest, someone else driving a car, then a dozen more, two dozen maybe. The images were so strong that she was gripped by vertigo, as though she'd been wrenched out of her own body and thrown into a lightning-fast orbit.

Schiller called out her name and she spun around. The man and the girl were sprinting toward her, *fast*, uttering pig grunts as they gained ground. There were others too, the kids that had been loitering outside the party, charging across the field.

They all had the same expression, silhouetted against the lights but unmistakable. They were furious. These people meant to kill them both, Rilke understood—the knowledge absolute and unquestionable. They meant to trample them into the field, to make mud of them.

She gave Schiller a shove, yelling at him: "Run!"

HE SWAM UP FROM AN OCEAN OF ICE, breaching it like a swimmer who has gone too deep, expecting to feel warmth and daylight on his face but instead rising into an endless, heatless night. He tried to take a breath, couldn't remember how, his lungs screaming at him.

He could see the new kid, Cal, right there, giving off a weird light like some deep-sea jellyfish. The boy was struggling in the torrent of darkness, his eyes bulging, his mouth gasping like a fish. And behind him, visible over his shoulder, a tiny form that could only be Daisy, her twig-thin limbs clawing at the water, trying to find the surface.

He reached out, noticing that his own skin seemed to be glowing, as though he were radioactive. He stretched, trying to grab hold of Cal, willing the kid to grab hold of the girl, all of them kicking upward.

Brick woke, his screams more like barks as he coughed up darkness. He pushed himself to his feet, his chair toppling over behind him. There was still no light, but he could feel the ground under him, could feel the pain in his cheek where he'd been sleeping on his laptop. There was something else too, a ringing in his ears that was also profoundly silent, inverted cathedral bells whose peals were each a gaping absence inside his head.

Daisy cried out, her voice pinched by fear. Brick screwed his eyes shut, even though there was no light, trying to remember where she was.

"Daisy," he called out, edging around the table, feeling for the matches. "Don't worry, we're here."

She began to cry even harder, and he heard a thump as she rolled off the chaise longue.

"Daisy, don't move, you'll hurt yourself, just hang on."

He found the candle, burned down to the stick, and beside it—bingo, a box of matches. He carefully pulled one out, striking it on the box, the tiny flame filling the huge restaurant with soft light. Daisy stood by the sofa, her arms out, her sobs muted as she studied the burning match.

"Here," said another voice, and Brick turned to see Cal walking over from the far side of the room. He held a candle out to Brick and he lit it, placing it on the table. Daisy saw Cal and came running over, hugging him tight, her eyes still full of sleep. "You okay?" Cal asked her. "You have a bad dream?"

"We were drowning," she said into his T-shirt. "You were there, and the other boy too."

"Brick," reminded Brick. Cal looked at him, and when their eyes met Brick realized the boy had been locked inside exactly the same nightmare. Not only that, but he knew that if he'd waved in his dream, the others would have seen it. That ringing in his head seemed to grow louder, and yet infinitely quieter, and he worked his jaw to try to unblock his ears. It was a second or two before he noticed that Cal was doing the same thing.

"You hear that too?" he asked.

"Bells," Cal replied.

Daisy pulled her head from his chest and jammed a finger in her ear.

"They're too loud," she said. "But not loud. I can't really hear them. I don't like it."

"I've had this before," Cal said to Brick, his hand gently smoothing back Daisy's ruffled hair. "My head was . . . I don't know, like full of sound but empty at the same time. It led me to Daisy."

And just like that Brick knew exactly what he was hearing. They all did, a moment of understanding that passed between them as easily as the reflection of the candlelight in their eyes.

"It's one of us," said Brick.

Cal nodded, saying, "And they need help."

RILKE / Farlen, 12:37 a.m.

THE FIRST OF THE CROWD, the man, was nearly on them. Rilke bent down, scrabbling on the field until her hand closed over a stone the size of a tangerine. She waited until he was close—his animal grimace a jagged, toothy chasm that split his face in two—then she lobbed the stone at him with every ounce of strength she had.

It struck his nose with the sound that a milk bottle makes when it's dropped on a stone floor, and the man fell. Rilke bent down, looking for another missile, but it was too late. The teenage girl slammed into her, sending them both tumbling over the field. Cornstalks dug into her arms and legs, the wind punched from her as the girl's elbow hit her solar plexus. By the time she'd worked out which way was up the girl was on her chest, knees gouging her ribs and claws raking down her cheeks.

Rilke shrieked, the gargled sound that spilled from her own lips somehow more terrifying than the assault. There was no pain, just the roar of her blood. She lashed out, thumping her attacker in the cheek then grabbing a handful of soil, rubbing it into the girl's eyes and forcing her back.

Another howl. Rilke looked up in time to see some dreadlocked guy about to take a punt at her head. She rolled, the girl spilling from her, the man's foot swinging wide and sending him tumbling off balance. She scrambled to her feet, each breath a shriek. There were more people coming now, maybe ten or twenty of them.

"Schiller!" she yelled, ducking as another girl swung a punch. She kicked, her foot connecting with the girl's knee and unleashing a pistol crack. Where was he? There was only the crowd, tearing relentlessly forward. If she couldn't find him then they were both dead.

There, fifteen meters or so away, a bundle of shadow that had too many arms and legs. It had to be him.

Rilke ran, slipping on the loose soil and nearly going over. The tremors she felt beneath her feet were now nothing to do with the music that still played. She didn't look back, knowing that to do so would kill her. The only thing that mattered was reaching Schiller.

She could hear him now, his brittle cries. He was lying on the ground, a man sitting on his stomach choking him with hands in fluorescent orange fingerless gloves. Schiller's eyes were the size of pickled eggs, looking like they were about to pop right out of his head, his own hands batting pathetically at his attacker.

"GET OFF HIM!" Rilke screamed. She was a dozen steps away now, her fist bunched and held over her head ready to cave the bastard's face in.

Someone behind her clipped her foot and she went flying,

momentum flipping her body over in a clumsy somersault. A weight dropped on her back and this time there was pain, a buckle of white heat that burned up her spine. A fist connected with the back of her head, pushing her face into the dirt. Then another, like a sledgehammer. She tried to breathe but found only soil and wormstench. Somebody had hold of her right hand, bending it backward.

She was going to die. They were going to kill her in this very field, a mile from where she lived. They would bury her here, and nobody would ever find her. It was an impossible thought, too crazy to be real. Too insane to believe.

They're going to kill Schiller too. Those screams of his will be the last thing you ever hear. And *that* wasn't impossible. *That* wasn't crazy. That was all too real. They would kill her brother, stomp him into the ground.

No. She wouldn't let them. They couldn't have him.

Rilke wrenched her head up so hard she thought her neck would snap. She reached behind with her left hand, grabbing a fistful of flesh and squeezing hard. There was another grunt, this one laced with pain. The weight on her back shifted—not much but enough for her to slide her way forward. Schiller was ahead, almost close enough to touch. There were four or five people over him now, each one different and yet each one wearing that same fury-filled expression. Their hands and feet rose and fell, rose and fell, like pistons, like some horrific machine. Yet Schiller was still alive. She could see him through the gaps in the crowd, a hand held out to her.

Something told her that if she could just reach him . . . *What? You can die here holding hands?* No, it was something more than that.

A knuckled weight crunched down on her leg, another on her shoulder. She didn't stop, crawling forward with everything she had. She reached for Schiller, the distance between them mere centimeters now but at the same time a vast, abysmal chasm.

"Schill," she spoke his name through blood, but he heard her, turning his red, disbelieving eyes her way.

"Rilke." He stretched, his fingers crawling over the soil. She grasped for him, the gap shrinking from five centimeters to four, to three, to two.

Their fingertips touched and the world burst into cold, dark fire.

DAISY / *Fursville, 12:44 a.m.*

"DID IT WORK?" ASKED CAL.

"Did what work?" said Brick. "Standing here like a bunch of idiots holding hands?"

They were doing exactly that, huddled in a circle in the flickering light of the restaurant. Daisy wasn't sure why. She couldn't remember whose idea it had been. It had just happened, the same instinct that makes you flinch when somebody throws a punch, that makes you seek shelter when you hear thunder.

"It worked," said Daisy, freeing herself from Brick's huge, clammy palm. Brick pulled his other hand out of Cal's, both boys wiping their hands on their clothes as though they had poison on them. Cal held on to Daisy for a moment longer, giving her a gentle squeeze before letting go.

"How do you know?" he asked.

"I just do," she replied. And she did. She'd seen it in her head, inside one of those little ice cubes. Although "seen" was the wrong word. She hadn't really seen anything, she'd just felt it. But what exactly had she felt? Two people, or maybe just one, they were so similar she couldn't be sure. They'd been scared, they'd been in pain. They'd been about to die.

But then what?

Daisy didn't know for sure, but she understood that the three of them—she, Cal, and Brick—had helped. They'd done *something*. She could still sense the person, or the two people—the *twins*, she realized with a sharp intake of breath. Only there was something different about them, something she couldn't quite put her finger on.

They were coming here, though. That much was clear. Daisy frowned, trying to remember more, trying to see inside those transparent, clinking movies that played inside her mind. There was something there that frightened her, something that burned, but she couldn't work out what it was.

"What now?" asked Brick. "We light some incense sticks and sing 'Kumbaya'?"

Daisy didn't reply, she just stared at the fire inside her head, trying to work out what was wrong, and why she felt so scared.

RILKE / *Farlen, 12:45 a.m.*

RILKE'S FIRST THOUGHT WAS THAT SHE'D DIED.

The thought that followed was that she couldn't have died, because she was still thinking. Then came the realization that she couldn't have died because she was in *pain*.

She opened her eyes, the lids sticky as if she'd been asleep for a week. The stars were moving, spiraling across the infinite black canvas of the sky. Her ears were humming. Her whole body seemed to be locked tight with a muted, throbbing ache. Smoke clawed its way into her nose. It filled her head too, draping heavy shadows over her thoughts, her memories.

Why was she here?

Schiller, her brain told her, and at once her paralysis snapped free. She sat up, a jet of milk-white vomit erupting from her mouth without warning. She held her stomach with one hand, wiping spit away with the other. Stars drifted down from the night, landing on her face and the field beside her, glowing fiercely. She held out her hand, letting one drift onto it. The spark guttered then died. *We knocked the stars from the sky,* she said to herself. *Our fingers touched and we knocked loose the stars.*

Only they weren't stars. How could they be? They were ashes, like the flickering embers from a bonfire. They filled the air, dancing on their own heat. She looked through them, the world gradually coming into focus. Schiller was there, lying next to her. His face was a mosaic of bruises, blood running freely from his nose and his mouth. But he was alive. Seeing him like that brought everything back, and Rilke staggered to her feet, ready to defend herself from another attack.

There was nobody there.

Not only was there nobody there, she didn't know exactly where "there" was. They were in a field, a *different* field. This one had something growing in it—a carpet of fat leaves painted silver by the moon. There was a glow against the horizon, and it took her a minute to understand that she was looking at the party, the rave. The distant crowd danced in the weak glow as if nothing had happened. She looked back at her brother, her brain desperately trying to put the pieces together, trying to make some kind of sense of what had just happened.

"Schill?" she asked.

He didn't reply, didn't show any sign that he'd heard her. Rilke crouched down beside him, pressing two fingers against his throat and feeling the pulse there, faint but steady. But he was cold, he was *freezing*. Touching him was like picking up a glass of ice water, and Rilke had to pull her hand away after a minute or so as the numbing chill crept through it.

"Schiller," she said again, shaking the blood back down her arm. "Talk to me. Please."

He was in shock. He had to be. He'd taken a pretty bad beating, they both had. But how had they gotten from over there, getting the life stamped out of them by a bunch of stoned strangers, to right here? *I fought them,* her brain argued, picking strands of logic from the confusion. She looked down at her hands, stained pink like she'd been cutting up beetroot. *I fought them, and we ran, and it was so terrifying that I've already blocked it out.* That had to be it, didn't it? She wished she had a watch, or a phone, so she could check the time.

And so you can call an ambulance, right?

No. She wasn't going to do that. There was no precise reason why not, only that she knew it would be the wrong thing to do. There was an image in her head, a picture, a memory that she had no actual memory of—a paramedic in his green overalls, his face somehow a horse's face as he threw himself at her, as he pushed her through a window.

Somebody cried out from the direction of the party, a word she couldn't make any sense of. She tapped her pocket, feeling for the flashlight but not finding it. It was probably better this way. If they saw the light then they might come after her again. They might be coming after her now, feet pounding through the darkness, fists clenched, that same depthless rage burning through their faces.

The Fury.

"We need to go," she said, lifting one of her brother's arms and looping it around her shoulders. She braced herself, pushing up with her legs, his body rag-doll loose against hers. "Schiller," she snapped, his name seeming to echo against the night. "Pull it together. We need to get out of here."

His head lolled against his chest, swinging from side to side like a nodding plastic dog on a car's dashboard. She looked over her shoulder to the party, trying to get her bearings in the dark. If she was where she thought she was then the road back into town was way off to her right. But that's not where she was headed.

"Fursville," she whispered, the word ridiculous, meaningless, and yet somehow the only thing she could think of. She caught a glimpse of a roller coaster, the wood rotting, a deserted restaurant. This was where she was supposed to go. And somehow she knew how to get there too, something pulling at her, leading her.

You're crazy, her head told her. *Go to the hospital, get Schiller some help. He'll die if you don't.*

Only she wasn't crazy. This was something else. The swarm of ashes had calmed, but they were still falling, darting like fireflies. She held out her free hand and caught another one, a fragment of charred pink leather that flickered and died in her palm. Another followed, this one a burning scrap of fluorescent orange— *Like the man's gloves, those fingerless gloves around Schiller's throat, choking the life from him*—that took flight again after a second or two, rising back into the night.

Yes, this was definitely something else.

She hoisted Schiller up and started walking. He didn't give her any help but she hauled him after her step after step after step. The cold that was coming off him was unbelievable, like she was walking through the middle of a blizzard. This wasn't something a doctor could sling a bandage on or temper with antibiotics. Schiller didn't need a hospital, he needed whatever lay inside the place in her head, that abandoned amusement park called Fursville.

Right?

She pushed the questions away, locking onto those instincts, to her absolute gut belief that what she was doing was okay. The sea wasn't far from here, and the little boatyard that belonged to the neighboring village. She could hot-wire one of the old dinghies. She'd done it before. It was a clear night, no wind, they could be there—wherever *there* was—before dawn. All she had to do was follow that feeling in her head, that guide rope tugging gently on her thoughts.

Shivering, her teeth chattering so hard she was worried the ravers might hear them, Rilke kicked her way through the ash and the dirt, heading for the sea, heading for Fursville, heading for answers.

BRICK / *Fursville, 5:59 a.m.*

WAKING WAS EASIER THIS TIME. Brick sat up, rubbing both hands through his hair and yawning so hard his jaw popped. Beads of light pearled through the cracks in the boards over the windows, hanging on the dust and revealing Daisy on the sofa, Cal lying on the floor beside her, both still fast asleep.

What had happened last night? They'd sensed something, or someone. It had been Daisy's idea to try to send them a message, a mental picture of Fursville. It had seemed like a good idea in the dead of night, but daylight had a habit of bringing reality with it, common sense. Brick felt his cheeks burn at the thought of the three of them standing hand in hand in the middle of the restaurant beaming psychic baloney out across time and space.

He made his way to the door, careful not to nudge any of the chairs or tables. He increased his speed once he was out in the corridor, hurrying past the peeling menus and special-deal posters—*Upgrade to a large haddock or cod for an extra 30p!*—and down the steps into the foyer. The light here was brighter, making his eyes sting, and he was almost glad to be back in the service corridor that led toward the fire exit.

Until he reached the basement steps.

He stopped, his heart jackhammering in his throat. If Lisa was alive, then this was about as close to her as he could get without her going nuts again. Without her getting the Fury.

He cleared his throat, then he called out her name. The word was a sigh, deafening to Brick but too soft to carry. He looked right and left, trying not to think about what might have happened if she'd gotten out, if she was loose inside the building. He imagined her hands reaching from the shadows, those broken fingernails scraping down his face.

Something moved behind the oil-black darkness at the bottom of the steps, a shuffling thump.

"Brick?" Her faint voice almost knocked him to his knees. His eyes burned again, tears flowing before he even knew he was crying, and he put his hand against the wall, hoping that somehow his touch might travel down into the basement, warm against her cheek. "Please let me out." It sounded like she was speaking through a mouthful of toffee, but she seemed stronger than she had yesterday. "Brick? It's not too late."

"It's okay, Lisa," he called back. "There are more of us now, we'll think of something together, okay?"

"Please, Brick, just let me out and we can talk about this, I'm not . . . I'm not angry at you."

"I know," he said. "I know you're not. I know you don't understand. I don't either, but . . ."

But what?

"I will," he answered. "I will fix you, Lisa. I . . ."

I love you, the words were there, but his mouth didn't know how to shape them.

"I'll make it so things are like they were," he went on, those three unspoken words burning a hole in his throat. "I swear I will. Just hang on, remember to drink, I'm right here, I won't leave you."

There was another thump, a crash this time, and at first Brick thought Lisa was throwing herself at the door again. He took a step back, trying to get out of her radar, or whatever it was that set off the Fury. It was only when he heard it again—a pounding, like fists on wood—that he realized it wasn't coming from the basement.

It was coming from outside.

It's the police, they've come for you.

He moved down the corridor and crept under the chains of the fire exit, his whole body on alert, ready to bolt at the first sign of a flashing blue light. He was fast, he could outrun them. *Can you outrun the dogs too? The helicopters?* But there were no sirens, no bullhorned demands, no thunder of chopper blades. There was just that same rattling thump.

Brick swallowed, realizing that his head was filled with the same muted numbness as the previous night—that weird inverted silence. With that realization the fear sloughed away. Whoever was out there, it wasn't the police. He started across the overgrown path, walking past the mini-golf and the one-eyed giant squirrel, heading for the seaward side of the park. By the time he'd reached the storage sheds that ran along the back of the pavilion he could hear a voice too. The sound of the sea disguised the words but he was pretty sure it was a girl.

"Hello?" he called out. Maybe he should go back, wake the others. He could get the gun too, just in case. But despite his nagging worries he didn't feel in any danger. He walked alongside the nine-foot-tall fence, boarded with the park's old ride signs and billboards. The one with the "Hook-a-duck" picture on was rattling hard, and when he stopped beside it the girl's voice was clear.

"Is anyone there? Let us in."

Us? Brick thought, wondering again about the gun.

"Hello?" he said. The pounding stopped, leaving the park eerily quiet. For some reason it was colder here too, like he was standing next to an open fridge. "Who are you?"

"We need help," the girl said. He could hear her shivering. "My brother is hurt."

The girl, whoever she was, hadn't gone rabid. She wasn't snarling at him through the fence. That had to be a good thing.

"There's a way in," he said. "Go left. About fifty meters or so down there's a break in the fence. I'll meet you there."

He set off without waiting for a reply, jogging until he reached the engineering workshops. He ducked down the alley between them, moving the board and squeezing between the wire. The sun was just lifting up over the horizon, already dazzling, and he capped a hand to his forehead, peering through the shadow to see two people walking down the beach. The girl was a little younger than him, dark-haired and pretty, her face so pale it was blue. She was almost carrying a boy, his arm around her shoulder, and as they got closer he saw that they had the same face.

"You maybe want to help?" she snapped.

Brick grunted, trotting toward them. He was maybe a dozen yards away when the cold hit him, like he was running into a winter storm. Goose bumps broke out over his arms and he could see his own breath, ghostlike, in front of him. He stopped, wrapping his arms around himself.

"What the . . ." Then he saw the dusting of ice that covered the boy's face, crystals hanging from his lips and his eyelashes. His skin was gray, and although his eyes were open they had been frosted over.

"Hurry up," said the girl. Brick started forward again, slower this time. His whole body was shuddering, the cold actually burning him. He maneuvered himself around the side of the boy, ducking under his free arm and taking his weight. It felt as though he'd just buried himself in a snowdrift. The girl eased herself out, standing away and rubbing flecks of ice from the side of her face. "We need to get him inside," she said.

"What's wrong with him?" Brick asked through his clicking teeth. The girl fixed him with a look as cold as her brother.

"That's exactly what you need to tell me. Because I want an explanation, and I want it now."

DAISY COULDN'T WORK OUT how the boy could be so cold and yet still be alive. Brick had carried him into the restaurant a few minutes ago, waking her. He'd shooed her off the sofa she'd spent the night on and laid the boy there, running off to find something to put over him.

"It's going to be okay, Schiller," said the girl who had walked in with him. She knelt beside the boy. She was wearing just a short skirt and a top. No wonder she looked so frozen. Her face was very pretty, but there was something in it that made Daisy feel uneasy. It was probably just because she was a stranger.

"I've found a couple more," said Cal, walking over with a handful of candles. He placed them on the coffee table beside the sofa, lighting them from one that was already burning and using the wax to stick them to the wood. The flames seemed reluctant and Daisy didn't blame them—the air was so cold that even fire had to feel it. It would be easier to take the boards off the windows and let the sun in, but Brick had told them they couldn't do it in case people noticed and came snooping.

"Who are you people?" the girl asked.

"You were attacked, right?" Cal said. "By complete strangers."

The girl stared at Cal and even though half a dozen candles burned, her eyes stayed dark. Daisy felt some of those strange, translucent ice cube images clinking in her brain. She tried to get a better look at them but they bobbled just out of reach.

"Right?" Cal said when she didn't reply.

"And you saw our message online?" added Brick as he staggered back into the room, peering over a mountain of linen. He dumped it all at the head of the sofa and the girl began to sort through it, shaking out each tablecloth before layering them over the boy, tucking them under his motionless body. His cold had turned the damp inside the sofa to a sheen of ice that glittered like diamonds. Daisy blew out puffs of cotton wool breath, watching them dissolve into the air for the few minutes it took for the girl to finish.

"Schill, can you hear me?" she said, getting to her feet and blowing on her blue fingers. The boy didn't respond, his glazed, frozen eyes staring at the ceiling. He was wrapped up tight, like a mummy. She put her hand to his forehead, then turned and glared at Brick as if this was somehow his fault. "Message?" she said after a moment.

Brick looked at Cal, then at Daisy, and when nobody else spoke he finally turned back to the girl.

"We left a message, on an online forum, saying for people to come to Hemmingway if they'd been attacked." He floundered, running his hands through his hair. "You didn't get it?"

More clinking ice cubes in her head. Daisy saw a field, and the heavens falling—burning flecks of stars. The boy was there, the girl too. And she could sense *herself* in the picture, her voice weird, like she was listening to it on a badly tuned radio.

"You heard us," she said. "Last night, we told you to come here and you did."

The girl looked down at her, scowling. She took a deep, shuddering breath that appeared like a thought bubble. Daisy could almost read it, the emotions there packed tight—fear and anger and a great deal of confusion. She felt sorry for her.

"Look," said Cal. "The truth is we don't know any more than you. I don't think so anyway. Let's go outside, get some air, some sun. We can talk about it there. Yeah?"

They all shivered through another moment of awkward silence, and in it Daisy saw an ice cube vision float through her brain, the same one she'd seen last night only now much clearer. This one was full of fire, so real that she felt like putting her hands to it, thawing them out on its heat. But there was something bad about it, something she didn't quite understand. The image shifted, melting, and Daisy thought she saw the park, Fursville, lost inside the flames. And the girl too, in the center of the inferno. Then the images split apart, fading into the guttering candlelight of the restaurant.

"Okay," said the girl. She tucked the tablecloths around her brother's neck and whispered something into his ear before looking at Cal. "Lead the way."

Cal walked from the room, the girl following, then Brick. Daisy trotted after them, wondering if it was safe to leave the boy here swaddled in cloth next to half a dozen candles. It wasn't that which was making her uneasy, though. The ice cubes had gone but they'd left something unpleasant in her head, a feeling that she couldn't quite shake even as she left the darkness of the restaurant and stepped into the brightness of the foyer.

The new girl was dangerous.

THEY SAT ON THE ROOF OF THE PAVILION, eating chips and bread and taking turns to tell their stories.

The tall redheaded boy went first, stuttering through his tale involving a psychotic girlfriend and an attack in a nearby gas station. He was the one who had found this place, Fursville, and he was reluctant to share it. That didn't come across so much in his words as in the pauses between his words, slight hesitations in which Rilke seemed to be able to peer inside that copper dome of his and get a sense of what he was really thinking. Of course it was probably a hallucination brought on by exhaustion—she'd been awake for well over twenty-four hours now. If that was the case, then what was it that made her lean forward when he had finished speaking and say:

"Your girlfriend, she's still here."

The boy's mouth dropped open, his cheeks blazing, his fist crumpling up the slice of bread he was holding.

"Don't be stupid," he muttered. "Of course she's not."

She didn't have to read his thoughts to know that was a lie.

The sun had hauled its lazy bulk up from the horizon and daylight splashed across the roof, giving the four of them long, thin shadows that spilled over the edge. It was filthy up here, the spaces between the ventilation stacks and air-conditioning units and aerials covered in bird mess and rotting debris. But there were comfy moth-eaten director's chairs that the park's staff had long ago dragged up here and the view wasn't bad. If you looked to the left, that was, over the crests of the fake waves and across the flat, featureless land all the way to a distant factory. In the other direction lay the sea, the same one Rilke had spent all night on. She didn't want to look at it ever again.

Still, at least it was warm, and getting hotter by the minute. It occurred to her that they should fetch Schiller and leave him out in the sun, but it would be safer inside, at least until they knew what was going on. Out here the world seemed too big. Anything could happen.

"What's your story, anyway?" the red-haired one asked, aggression in his voice.

"Hang on," said the other kid. He was conventionally good-looking, but beneath his messy hair his face was featureless and bland. *He's soft,* thought Rilke. *He's a pushover.* He wiped crumbs from his lips, saying, "Let's stay friendly, okay? My name is Cal, Callum. This is Daisy. She's, what, eleven?"

"Nearly thirteen," corrected Daisy. "I just look younger, that's all." The girl offered a nervous smile and Rilke returned it.

"And that's Brick," Cal went on, nodding at him.

"Why Brick?" Rilke asked. She took another piece of bread from the open bag, tearing off a sliver and putting it in her mouth. She felt like she was literally starving, but she didn't want to show weakness by scarfing down half a loaf.

"Because my dad's motto was never hit anyone with your fist when you've got a brick," he growled.

"Nice," she said. *Neanderthal.*

"What's your name?" asked Daisy.

"Rilke," she said. "Rilke Bastion. The boy in there is my brother, Schiller."

"Your parents liked poetry, then," said Brick, which threw her. How did a caveman like him know that they were both named after German poets? He smiled smugly. A smile that said, *Didn't expect that now, did you?* Daisy coughed politely, diffusing the tension.

"My parents, they . . ." the smaller girl started, and in that pause Rilke's brain filled in the gaps. She didn't see it so much as just feel it, the weight, the awful gravity, of two dead people in a bed. Daisy's face had crumpled like a paper bag left out in the rain and Rilke had an urge to go to her, to wrap her arms around her. Girls had to look after one another. But Cal beat her to it, and Daisy seemed to find strength in his arms.

"My mum, she didn't want to hurt me," Daisy went on. "She was ill anyway, she had . . . cancer in her head. It made her act strange. She . . . she took my dad, then herself, so they wouldn't hurt me. Then the ambulance people tried to kill me, pushed me out the window." The girl looked at the boy who held her. "Cal found me. He saved me."

"Nearly didn't," said Cal, giving Daisy a squeeze then letting her go. He told his story more smoothly than the others, as if he'd rehearsed it in his head. When he'd finished he looked at Rilke. They all did. "Now you."

What could she say? She didn't have a clue what had happened. The only reason she was so calm about it all, so logical, was that the full force of it hadn't sunk in yet. None of it felt real. Maybe none of it *was* real. Maybe they'd gotten to the party and someone had slipped her some acid, ecstasy. Maybe all this was just a bad trip. She finished her bread then shrugged, more to herself than to the others.

"We got attacked at a party, a rave. Then suddenly we moved, we were in another . . . I don't know. Anyway, we managed to get away. I heard . . . no, *felt* you guys speaking to me so I brought my brother here. I thought you would know what was happening. I thought you'd have answers. I thought you'd be able to help us."

Out of nowhere it hit her, a tidal wave of panic and fear and utter helplessness that sluiced through her brain. She clamped her teeth together until the feeling washed away. She couldn't afford to look weak in front of these people. Not now, not ever. *It's too late,* she realized, seeing the way Daisy stared at her, as though her thoughts were flashing across her forehead. She got to her feet, turning her back on them. It was starting to get hot, ridiculously so.

"We know what you know," said Cal behind her, and for a second she thought he was admitting to the ridiculous notion that they could read minds. "That people are going crazy. That they're filled with . . ."

"The Fury," added Brick.

"Yeah, the Fury. It doesn't seem to affect them unless one of us is close. Then they just go mental, try to kill us. They seriously try to rip us to pieces."

"But afterward they just go back to doing whatever they were doing," said Brick. "They go back to their lives, like nothing has happened. They totally forget that they went psycho. If you can get away from them, if you get out of their radar, then they'll leave you alone. I think so, anyway."

A couple of squabbling gulls flapped onto the roof, ogling the strangers warily before taking off again. Rilke turned back to the others.

"What about Schill?" she asked. "Why is he so cold? What's happened to him?"

They looked at each other, and she could sense the vast black gulfs in each of their thoughts. They didn't have a clue. She shook her head, disgusted.

"So why bring me here?"

"Because we're safer when we're together," said Daisy.

That's it? She had to bite her tongue to stop from saying it out loud.

"It's the only way we'll find out what's going on," said Cal. "The more of us there are, the quicker we'll find answers."

"Well I'm here now," Rilke snapped back. "There are five of us, where are the answers?"

A memory from the previous night swam back into her thoughts, images of somebody driving a car, somebody else running through the woods. She shook her head, knocking them loose.

"It's not just us, is it?" she said. "There are others coming."

Brick smiled without humor, leaning forward in his chair and resting his head in his hands.

"You have no idea."

CAL / *Fursville, 10:54 a.m.*

"THERE'S A GAP," SAID CAL. He pointed at a battered stretch of fence in the front right-hand corner of the park, almost hidden behind the bulk of the log flume. There were piles and piles of scaffolding back here, rusted poles propped up against the wilting barricade. It reminded him of a bamboo forest, like in all the old martial arts movies, and he could even see a scraggly bird nest sitting precariously on the top of one.

"Where?" Brick asked. The two of them had been scouting the perimeter for the past few hours to make sure the park was secure. It had been Cal's idea, and when he'd suggested it to Brick the boy had seemed to take it as a personal insult, as though Cal had said, *Hey, man, you're ugly, shall we see what we can do about it?* Daisy and the new girl, Rilke, were keeping an eye on Schiller.

"There," Cal said, stamping down a clutch of vicious-looking brambles in order to take a step closer to the fence. One corner had come loose from the ground leaving a flap of steel. Behind it was the towering bulk of the laurel hedge that shielded the park from the street. Brick snorted.

"That's not a gap, who's going to get through there? A midget?"

"It's still a problem," said Cal. "This place needs to be as tight as we can make it. You never know what's gonna happen."

"Fine, put it on the list," Brick said, waving him away like a bad smell.

Cal lifted his notebook—a restaurant order pad—and added "log flume, loose panel" to the two other breaches they'd found.

"I don't know what your problem is, mate," Cal said, running to catch up with the bigger boy. "Haven't you ever seen zombie films? Once one gets in, they all get in, and if you're overrun then you're finished, dead meat."

"These aren't zombies," Brick replied. "They're not dead for one thing."

"I know they're not real zombies," Cal said as they walked past a couple of carnival stalls, both of which had rotted in the sea air. "Duh. But you know what I mean. They swarm. If one comes after you, they all do."

Brick grunted, shrugging his shoulders.

"Anyway, at least we're doing something, right?" Cal went on as they walked up to the small, squat ticket office. "Better this than sitting around in the dark twiddling our thumbs."

"Specially with that girl in there," Brick added, whispering even though there was no way she could have heard them. "She scares me more than the ferals out there."

Cal laughed, the sound floating on the warm air, seeming to fill the whole park for a second, bringing it to life the way laughter had once kept its heart beating.

"You're not kidding," he said, keeping his own voice low and casting a secretive look back at the pavilion. "I'm not going to sleep in the same room as her, she might kill me in the middle of the night."

Then they were both sniggering into their hands. It felt good. It seemed like years since he'd laughed. *It wasn't years. It was yesterday, remember? Yesterday when things were still almost normal.* But yesterday was gone. There was just before and after, and before was a million years ago.

"So how well do you know this place?" Cal asked, walking to the window of the ticket office and peering through the filthy glass. There was light inside, spilling through the massive hole in the roof and revealing a cash register with its tray open and empty, a couple of waterlogged magazines, and a lot of dust.

"Spent more time here than I have at home this year," Brick replied. Cal could see him reflected in the window, his hair like fire. He was picking his nose. "I've pretty much been in every building. There's nothing left but junk."

Cal walked down the side of the office, the main gates towering over him. A chain the size of a fire hose was looped around the ornate ironwork and they'd been boarded up to hide the park from the street. There was a brick tower on each side, maybe ten meters tall. A turquoise ladder ran up the left-hand one to the massive sign that straddled the entrance. There were half a dozen bird nests lodged in the back-to-front letters.

"That's a good lookout post," Cal said. "You can probably see half a mile inland from up there."

"Yeah, if you want to sit around all day in bird crap," Brick said. "What do we need a lookout for, anyway? Nobody ever comes out here, I told you."

Cal didn't reply, just jotted it down in his notepad. Brick had a way of talking that instantly got his hackles up, but surely it was because of the situation they were in. There was a chance the guy might have always been an asshole, but Cal was willing to give him the benefit of the doubt. It was important that they get on— God only knew how long they'd be living here together.

"Gift shop," said Brick, nodding toward the building on the other side of the gate. "Lost and found too. It's empty, pretty much."

Cal walked to it. The windows were boarded over, but one sheet of plywood had been pulled off to reveal a single square, glassless eye. He checked the gap between the building and the fence to make sure it was secure.

"So, you used to work out here or something?" he asked as he joined Brick again.

"Me? Hell no, this place was in ruins when I was, like, seven or something. How old you think I am?"

"I just thought, with you being so tall and everything . . ." Cal said, shrugging. "Twenty-one maybe?"

Brick snorted out a laugh. "I'm eighteen," he said. "Same as you, I wouldn't be surprised. Just had to grow up a bit faster, that's all."

Cal studied him properly for the first time, seeing the freckles, the loose covering of fine red stubble. And his eyes—they were squinty and unwelcoming but they were still those of a kid.

"You want to kiss me or something?" Brick said, taking a step back and holding out his hands. "You're giving me a weird look."

"Gross," said Cal, his cheeks heating. "You wish. Plus, I'm seventeen."

There was an awkward moment, then they both started laughing again.

"I'm glad we got *that* out of the way," Brick said. They walked along the side of the gift shop, entering a pool of jagged shadow thrown by the huge roller coaster on the southeast side of the park. "There's another way in just here. It's the one I usually use. There's a gap in the fence that's hidden by the hedge, easy to sneak in and out of. It's—"

Cal froze, grabbing hold of Brick's arm. The bigger boy carried on speaking for a few more seconds before the words dried up in his throat. Then they both stared in silence at the path that led down between the toilets and the Boo Boo Station, peering into the gloom at the blond-haired, bloodstained boy who stood there.

He was young, he looked even younger than Daisy. He was wearing a pair of Adidas tracksuit trousers and a Batman T-shirt, both of which were coated with plum-colored grime. His feet were bare and filthy. His near-white hair had been stained pink in places, his face too—the dried blood making his skin look like parchment. He had no expression whatsoever. He looked like a shop-window dummy, his eyes empty pockets.

"It's one of *them*," Brick hissed, taking a step back. Cal still had him by the arm, refusing to let go when Brick tried to pull away. "Cal, come on!"

"Wait," Cal said. "I think he's okay. Don't you feel it?"

There was something in Cal's head, that same deafening silence as before. It reminded him of the ocean on a calm day, when the sea was as flat as glass but you could still sense the vast, churning weight of water beneath the surface. Brick relaxed and Cal let him go.

"Hey," Cal said, talking to the boy. He took a step toward him, his hands held up to show he didn't mean any harm.

How had he gotten here? The boy didn't look like he could punch his way out of a wet paper bag, let alone travel to the armpit of Norfolk. Something definitely wasn't right with this picture.

"We're not going to hurt you," Cal said, edging closer. He got down on one knee beside him. "Just let us know your name, or anything. Just say something so we know you're not one of them. Yeah?"

"You won't get the little git to talk." The voice came from the hedge, followed by the snapping of branches and the crunch of footsteps. Cal felt his skin grow cold as a double-barreled shotgun emerged through the broken fence. The guy who was holding it was in his late teens, maybe early twenties, his thin face concealed by a scraggly beard. He was wearing a green farmer's jacket over a white shirt. He lifted the gun to his shoulder, aiming it right at Cal. "Don't move, or I'll blow your head off."

Cal lifted his hands, backing away. At his side, Brick looked ready to bolt, his body tensing up, then he obviously thought better of it. The man approached, swinging the gun from side to side. He drew level with the young boy, giving him a look that sent him scuttling away.

"Get in here," the gunman shouted. There was more rustling, then a girl appeared, her hair almost as red as the rings around her eyes. She stepped out and another boy squeezed through the fence. He looked the same age as Cal, tall but slightly overweight. They both wore the same expression: *Help us.*

"You better tell me what I'm doing here," the man said, jabbing the gun like it was a spear. "Why everybody in the goddamned world is trying to kill me. Why you're inside my head screwing with my thoughts."

Cal took another step back, slipping on the rubble-strewn ground.

"I said, *DON'T MOVE!*" the man barked. His finger was on the trigger, and it was tense. Even from here Cal could see where the joint had blanched. If the guy so much as sneezed then their brains would be splattered all over the Boo Boo Station.

"There's no need for that, mate," said Cal, more tremor than voice. "We're not going to do anything."

"Got that right," said the man, still walking toward them. The barrel of the shotgun was like two dark, unblinking eyes. "How many of you are here?"

Brick and Cal glanced at each other.

"How many?" the man demanded.

"Five," blurted Cal. "One of us is injured."

"Where?"

"Back there," said Cal, tilting his head over his shoulder. "In the pavilion. We're just kids."

"Fatty, go check they're not armed." The big kid didn't budge. "Do it!" the man yelled, making the boy jump so hard his flesh wobbled beneath his shirt. He trotted over, apologizing beneath his breath as he patted down Cal then Brick. His eyes didn't rise above their kneecaps. He scampered out of the way as soon as he'd finished.

"Nothing," he whispered.

"Right, turn and start walking," said the gunman. "Take me to where the others are, hands on your heads."

"What do you want?" asked Cal, obeying. He didn't really want his back to the guy but he didn't see how he had a choice.

"I want answers," said the man. "Shift, or I swear you'll be dead before you hit the floor."

Cal started back the way they'd come, his hands clamped in his hair. Brick walked by his side, his face pale and downturned.

This is going to get nasty. The thought hit Cal hard. It wasn't just a fear, it was a premonition. *Someone is going to get hurt.*

And those words were still ringing in his mind when he stepped out of the shadows and the gun went off.

RILKE / *Fursville, 11:22 a.m.*

"SOMETHING'S WRONG."

Rilke looked up from her brother when Daisy spoke. The younger girl was sitting on a chair beside the sofa, huddled into herself and shivering. They'd been here for hours now, throwing more blankets on cold, unresponsive Schiller and sorting out the food into piles. Daisy had tried to start a few conversations but Rilke had been too tired to throw back more than a couple of words. This time, though, there was an urgency in her voice.

"What?" Rilke asked. There were plenty of things wrong,

Schiller for one, his skin like marble, radiating cold. And the world. Right now the whole world was wrong.

"It's Cal," said Daisy, getting to her feet and standing there trembling. In the flickering candlelight there was something not quite real about her, something fairylike in her saucer-shaped eyes and her ghosted skin. "He's going to die."

"What?" Rilke said again, frowning. "Cal? Why?"

"I don't know *why*. I . . . I just know."

Rilke used the sofa to pull herself up off her knees, brushing the dust from her skirt. Her pulse was fast, and in its rhythm she understood that Daisy wasn't being hysterical, she wasn't making it up. Cal was in danger.

"Is it Brick?" she asked. There was something about the tall boy Rilke didn't trust, something in his face, and in the way he'd avoided answering her when she'd asked about his girlfriend. He'd looked guilty. Daisy shook her head, her eyes on the floor and yet also somewhere else, somewhere far away.

"It's not Brick, he's in danger too. We all are."

"Come on," said Rilke, holding out her hand. Daisy took it, her skin fever-hot compared to Schiller's. They began to walk toward the door but Daisy stopped, shaking herself free and running to the far side of the restaurant. She slid a grocery bag out from beneath a table, rummaging inside it and pulling out something big. She ran back across the room and held it out to Rilke.

It was a gun.

"Where did you get this?" Rilke asked as she took the weapon. It was heavier than it looked. She'd used guns before, shotguns mainly. Schiller loved to shoot the pigeons and the rats for target practice and she'd often gone out with him, mainly because there wasn't much else to do.

"It's Cal's," Daisy said, her tone more urgent now. She kept glancing at the door. "Brick hid it, but I found it when we were going through the bags. Come on, *please*."

They linked hands again, Daisy practically dragging her out of the restaurant, down the stairs and out through the chained-up fire exit.

"Wait," said Rilke, her heart jackhammering now. "Daisy, hang on."

Daisy's only reply was to increase her speed, racing past the pavilion's main doors toward the front of the park. Rilke trotted to keep up, and she was about to call out again when she saw them at the other end of the overgrown path.

Cal and Brick emerged first, their hands on their heads like prisoners of war. Then came the long, steel barrel of a shotgun, followed by a man, a teenager maybe, in a green jacket.

"Do it," Daisy said, skidding to a halt. *Do what?* Rilke thought. *Shoot him?* And, incredibly, Daisy screamed: "Yes! Shoot him now!"

There was no time to question it. Rilke lifted the pistol, using both thumbs to pull back the stubborn hammer. She aimed past the notch on the barrel until she found the man's face. He had a dark beard, his eyes squinting against the morning sun. She pressed both her forefingers against the trigger, a storm of thoughts all shrieking at once inside her head—*You can't do this, you can't shoot a man!* Then, as if they had been vacuumed up, they vanished, leaving only one, leaving only Daisy: *Do it.*

She squeezed. The gun resisted, then the trigger clicked. The shot was deafening, almost jolting the pistol out of her hands. She managed to cling on to it, peering through the smoke to see that Brick and Cal were on the ground.

Oh God, I hit one of them, she thought. Then she saw them both squirming in the dirt, trying to crawl away. The guy with the shotgun was still standing, but there was a crimson tear down the left side of his face, stretching from his cheek to his ear. She'd grazed him. His expression of shock was so extreme it was almost comical. It seemed to take him an age to see Rilke, and as he started to swing his shotgun around she took a step forward, aiming her weapon at his head.

"The next one won't miss," she said, staring at him dead-on. "I swear to God."

The shotgun stayed down, pointed at Cal's back. Both boys looked up at her, their faces distorted by fear. The gunman's shock was fast becoming anger; even from where she was standing Rilke could feel it burning off him. But there was something else too, the same weird, clanging silence she'd felt just before meeting Daisy and the others. This guy was one of them.

He is, but he's a bad man. Please, Rilke, do it, I don't want Cal to die.

Had Daisy said that or was it just in her head? Either way the little girl's voice blasted everything else away.

"Drop it," she shouted, her finger tensing. Was she supposed to cock the gun again? "Do it right now. *Right now.*"

Blood was trickling from the man's wound, but he still wasn't letting go of his weapon. She thumbed back the hammer, the click barely audible over the feedback-like whine in her ears.

Please, Rilke, Daisy's voice again, right in the flesh of her brain. *I know you don't believe me but—*

"He's going to kill him," Daisy said out loud, the switch making Rilke reel. The little girl was sobbing now, her words fractured. "He's going to die."

The gunman tensed, his face screwed into a wicked grimace.

He raised the gun slightly, so that the barrel was pointing right at Cal's head. Cal was on his back now, his arms up in front of him, frozen like one of the sculptures in the White Witch's palace. The bearded guy never took his eyes from Rilke.

"Yeah?" he sneered. "What if I—"

Rilke pulled the trigger, bracing herself this time. The gun barked but she let her arms absorb the recoil, watching as the man staggered back, a perfectly round hole punched into his forehead. Even though he was dead—he *had* to be dead—he still stared at her, something keeping his body rigid, upright, something stopping him from crashing to the—

White heat, burning like phosphorus.

The man exploded, like a bomb detonating in the middle of the park. A shock wave tore outward, crumpling the food booths on either side of the path. Rilke didn't even have time to scream as she saw it hurricane toward her, ripping her from the ground and sending her spinning backward into the wall of the pavilion.

It could have been a fraction of a second or a million years later that she remembered how to open her eyes. Debris still flew from the impact of the shock, moving in slow motion as if time had been knocked off its axis. Metal poles were falling ridiculously slowly from the big wheel, thudding into the ground like giant javelins. Brick and Cal were in midair, rolling like rag dolls as they were hurled away from the source of the detonation.

The man, the gunman, was suspended over the path, his arms out to his sides like he was being crucified. His whole body shimmered, red-hot. Suddenly his head snapped back, his spine arching, and his body seemed to split, like two ropes on either side had just been pulled taut. Inside him was an inferno, almost too bright to look at, but Rilke didn't turn away, she didn't blink. She *couldn't*.

Because something was coming out of the man. It could have been *another* man except this one was too big, and this one was made of fire—ferocious blue-white flames. Its distended jaw hung open in a silent scream, and the fire stretched outward from its back, unfurling like twin sails. Its eyes blazed, and in those broken seconds the thing looked at Rilke, burning right into the fabric of her soul. Then another shockwave ripped outward, atomizing the man's body and the thing that clawed its way out of it, blowing the hot-dog stand to ash before slamming into her.

She dropped into darkness.

DAISY / *Fursville, 11:48 a.m.*

DAISY WAS BURNING.

She sat up, noticing that her pants were smoldering gently, slapping at them until the dull embers died out. Smoke hung in the air all around her, a silvery gauze like morning mist. It smelled bad, like when her mum sometimes pulled hair from the brush and threw it on the fire. She was lying in the middle of the weed-littered path that led past the pavilion up to the sea. She clambered to her feet, staring through the smoke to see that one of the food places, the one with the big soft drink on the roof, was on fire.

The whole park was a mess. The little shack on the other side of the path, the one with the hot dog, was totally gone. Farther down was a huge crater in the concrete, so charred that it looked like a vast hole in the ground. The kind a giant spider might suddenly crawl out of. There was no sign of the man, but his gun was a bent and buckled ruin.

The man. She'd seen something in her head, like a badly filmed home movie of Cal being shot. She'd told Rilke, and they'd come out here with the gun.

Rilke. Daisy couldn't sense her, the way she'd been sensing people recently, those little ice cubes in her mind. She couldn't see Cal or Brick up there in her head either. There *was* an ice cube, though, one with a room that looked like a dentist's place, with the big chair. She could see a poster with a kitten on the ceiling, but there were no people in the ice cube.

What had happened? Rilke had shot the man, hadn't she? And it was okay, because he had been nasty, really nasty. He was the one who had been going to kill Cal. He'd deserved it. But then what? Daisy had seen something inside the man, a fire that howled, that tried to pull itself loose. She must have passed out and seen those things in a dream.

She started down the path, feeling woozy. Great big metal needles stuck out of the ground, like hedgehog bristles. Daisy looked up, wondering if they'd fallen from the big wheel. It was lucky nobody had been spiked. There was a pile of rags up against the pavilion doors, and she almost dismissed it until she realized who it was.

"Rilke!" Daisy yelled, stumbling over the cracked ground. The girl's face was covered with soot, and there was no sign of life.

What were you supposed to do if someone was unconscious? They'd done it at school with a plastic dummy, the ABC rule. "A" was for . . . *A heartbeat?* It didn't sound right, but Daisy pressed her fingers against Rilke's neck, praying to feel something there.

Pulse-pulse-pulse-pulse, rapid, like a rabbit's. Daisy almost cried with relief, stroking Rilke's long, dark hair away from her face.

"Is anyone here?" Daisy called out again. Then, more softly, "I'll be right back, Rilke, I'm going to find help."

She set off again, heading for the front of the park and that gaping crater.

"Hello? Cal? I need you!"

"Daisy?" It wasn't so much a shout as a groan, uttered from somewhere to her right. She walked toward the splintered remains of the hot-dog stand, treading carefully over the rubble. There were a few crates beyond, and half a cinder-block wall that was covered in scribbled writing. Past it she could see a pair of feet, one in a running shoe and the other in just a sock. They were moving.

"Cal?" She ran around the wall to see Cal sitting on the path. He was a mess too, and some of his hair was missing, giving him a funny bald patch just above his right ear. He saw her coming and tried to get up, collapsing onto his rear. Daisy crouched down beside him, putting a hand on his shoulder. There was a big rip across the front of his T-shirt. "Are you hurt?"

"Not really," he said, patting his hands over his body. He smiled, but it obviously caused him quite a bit of pain. "Help me up, yeah?"

Daisy grabbed his arm and he used it to pull himself to his feet. He stood for a moment, his hands on his knees, his eyes scrunched shut.

"I feel like I was hit by a truck."

"Guys?" Brick was limping toward them down the same path. He had coal-dark rings around his eyes, like a raccoon, and there was blood dripping from his left arm.

"I'm okay, but Rilke is hurt. She's not waking up. She needs help."

"She breathing?" Brick asked. Daisy nodded. If she had a heartbeat then she had to be breathing, didn't she? "Got to get the fire out first. If people see it they'll call the fire department or send for the police."

"Got any water?" Cal said.

"No time," Brick replied, jogging toward the burning stall. Cal ran after him, hobbling in his one shoe.

Daisy followed, still not wanting to get too close to the crater. By the time she had skirted around the edge Brick and Cal were pulling the front wall of the soda stand free, releasing a plume of smoke. The fire flared up as it gorged on the fresh supply of air but Brick didn't hesitate, stamping and kicking on the flames until they began to wither and die. He stumbled away, coughing so much that Daisy didn't know how he could manage a breath.

"Where are the rest of them?" he said when he had finished, clutching his wounded arm. Tears painted black stripes down his face. "You see them?"

The rest of who? she thought as Brick and Cal set off again. She ran after them as they wove through the spikes in the ground, trying to keep up, not wanting to be left on her own.

"There," she heard Brick yell. He turned the corner by the carousel, vanishing behind more debris by the side of the path. Daisy heard a voice, a panicked shout, and suddenly there were more ice cubes sliding around in her brain. Even before she turned the corner she knew she was going to see three people there, two boys and a girl.

"We weren't with him!" the girl was shouting, holding her

hands up in surrender as Brick stormed toward her. Her hair was red, almost the same color as his, and her face was streaked with dirt and smoke. "We didn't know him!"

"Brick, hold up," said Cal. "I think they're telling the truth."

Brick stopped, taking a deep, rattling breath. The little boy in the Batman T-shirt edged cautiously around him, sidestepping toward Cal and casting quick glances at Daisy. The dentist ice cube was his, she realized, and she could see more now—a woman in a white suit screaming through a face mask and reaching for him over the chair.

"Adam," she said, seeing his name in the ice. He turned at the sound of it, his bloodstained brow creasing. She held out her hand. "Come on, you're safe here now."

He walked to her straightaway, not looking back, and she took his hand.

"Do you want to come inside? We've got some food."

He didn't smile, but he didn't let go either. Daisy looked back at Brick, who was pacing from one side of the path to the other like a caged tiger. Cal was just behind him. The girl and the other boy were terrified. Daisy could feel their fear inside her, like the ice cubes were melting, bleeding their emotions into hers.

"Who was he?" Brick said. "Christ, he must have been carrying a bomb or something."

"I picked him up," the overweight boy was saying. "The same way as the others, only he had the gun and he . . ."

"It's okay," said Cal. "Right, Brick? It's okay. We can trust them. Everyone just calm down."

Brick snapped his hands up in an angry shrug. More blood dripped over his fingers, pattering on the ground.

"It's just the three of you?" he asked. "Nobody else?"

The boy and the girl looked at each other, but it was the little kid by her side, Adam, who gave it away. Daisy saw a silver car inside his ice cube, a big one, and something thumping and shrieking in the trunk, something with blood on its breath.

"There's one more," said the girl, looking up the path that led out of the park.

The plump boy finished for her. "But it isn't one of us."

BRICK / *Fursville, 12:09 p.m.*

THE REDHEAD'S NAME WAS JADE. The fat kid was Chris. They told Brick this as they walked back down the side of the Boo Boo Station and out through the gap in the laurel hedge. Daisy had taken the little boy inside and Cal had gone to check on Rilke. Brick kind of wished he'd had their job and they had his, but he didn't trust them to be able to deal with the situation.

He certainly didn't trust the boy and the girl beside him. Whatever they said, they'd brought the gunman here, they'd led him to the park. He looked at his arm, an ugly gash above his elbow. At least the blood had slowed to a trickle, he wasn't going to bleed out. He'd been lucky. They all had. Who the hell carried a bomb on them?

And yet there was a memory scratching at the back of his head that told him it wasn't a bomb. He'd been looking right at the man when he'd exploded; hadn't there been something there, something crawling out of him with a body of fire?

"It's just there," said Chris. He nodded at a silver car parked at an angle on the curb. It was a snob's car, a Jag or something, huge. There were bloodstains on the hood. Brick could already hear the fragile thumps from the trunk, and a weak, groaning cry.

"We didn't have a choice," said Jade. "That guy, the one with the gun, he knocked him out and stuck him in the trunk. Woke up, I don't know, half an hour before we got here and he's been trying to beat his way out ever since."

"Weird thing is, when we're not anywhere near him he acts normal," said Chris. "Like now, shout something to him and he'll probably shout back."

They both looked at Brick expectantly. He shook his head.

"I know. They're all doing that." He sighed, swearing under his breath. They couldn't leave the car out here, the first person who saw it would call the police. They couldn't bring it into Fursville either, there was nowhere big enough to get it through the fence. They could take it to the parking lot where he'd met Cal and Daisy last night, but he didn't fancy a ten-minute drive with a feral in the trunk. Fursville had a parking lot of its own. It was locked up but they could probably find a way in.

Whoever was inside must have heard them, because the voice got louder, still muffled but now audible. "Please, let me out, I promise I won't tell."

And suddenly it was *Lisa* inside that car, clawing for oxygen in the heat, scraping at the lock with her nails. Brick clamped his eyes shut until the image disappeared.

"You got the keys?" he asked.

"They're in the ignition," Chris said.

"We can park it in there," he said, pointing at the Fursville lot. "You'll have to ram the fence. We'll hide the car, work out what to do with him later."

Chris nodded. He wobbled over to it, taking a deep breath before sliding into the driver's seat. Jade stayed by Brick's side.

"Ain't getting back in there," she said when he looked at her. She didn't offer an explanation, just folded her hands over her chest as if she were cold.

Brick walked across the pavement, hearing the trunk-man's voice deteriorate into a series of howling barks. The thumps got louder, the metal trunk lid shaking as he pounded it from inside. Fifty meters down was the entrance to the Fursville parking lot, the main gates bolted shut. The fence at this spot wasn't so big.

Chris swung the car out then lurched back onto the curb, plowing into the fence with a sound like fingernails running down a blackboard. The engine growled but he didn't let up, revving hard until the wire snapped and the car jolted through.

"Over there!" Brick shouted, pointing toward the huge hedge that separated the parking lot from Fursville. There was a small wooden office—a garden shed, really—where you'd once had to pay a fee. "Drive in as far as you can, the other side of that building."

Chris obeyed, steering the car over the rough dirt until the hood disappeared into the hedge. It penetrated as far as the middle of the roof before hitting something and crunching to a halt. There was a cacophony of rustling snaps and grunts before Chris appeared, batting branches away from his face. He stepped gingerly away, looking forlornly at the battered Jag.

"Dude, my dad's gonna murder me when he sees his car," he said, blanching when he realized what he'd said. He bared his teeth in a bitter, humorless smile. "Again."

The voice from the trunk was even louder now, the snarls of a caged animal. But the car was pretty well hidden, Brick thought, the small office concealing it from the road. He'd grab some boards from the park and cover it up properly once they'd decided what to do about the man inside.

"Come on," he said, turning and heading back toward the ruined fence. "Let's get back. Something tells me we need to talk."

CAL / *Fursville, 12:33 p.m.*

CAL LACED UP HIS SPARE SNEAKERS, grateful that he'd thought to pack some before leaving the house. He removed his smoke-blackened sweatpants and pulled on a clean pair before joining the others.

They all sat in the restaurant, huddled around a table on the far side of the room from where Schiller still lay like an ice sculpture on the sofa. Outside it was warm and sunny; inside, behind the boarded-over windows, it was freezing even with the dozen candles that sputtered and spat. But it felt safe here. It felt quiet. It felt hidden.

Cal cast another look at Rilke. He'd carried her here. She was curled up on the floor in the corner, covered with a tablecloth, her head resting on a bundle of clothes he'd taken from his duffel bag. She'd had a pretty bad knock on the head, the lump there like someone had sewn an egg beneath her skin. He didn't think it was too serious. He'd gotten lumps like that before and they went away after a day or two.

"What's wrong with him?" Jade said, nodding at Schiller. "Why is he so cold?"

"Tell us about you first," Brick said. "I want to—"

"Do you want some food?" Daisy interrupted, earning a glare from Brick. "Or some chocolate, or a drink?"

"We haven't got much," Brick said. "We should be conserving it."

Daisy looked at the table, obviously contemplating something. Then she scraped back her chair and pulled two packets of chips from the stash behind her. She walked to the new kids and handed them over, flicking a defiant look at Brick. Cal smiled, everybody waiting for Daisy to pour some soda into a couple of glasses they'd found in the kitchen. The big bottle was too heavy for her and quite a bit of it fizzed out onto the tablecloth, hissing like acid.

"Thank you," said Jade, downing the drink in one, then burping into her hand. "God that's good. I haven't had anything to eat or drink since yesterday."

"So what happened, then?" Brick snapped. "Why are you here?"

"You told us to come here, didn't you?" Chris answered, speaking through a mouthful of chips. "Who was it that left the message online?"

Brick pulled a face, shrugging. He glanced at Cal as if it were his fault.

"I saw it," Chris went on. "Look, this is what happened. I was at home, playing Fallout, it was about nine maybe, nine-thirty. Next thing I know my mum has snapped, she's coming at me with a knife." He sat back in his chair, tugging on his shirt. "And she trips, right, she's so . . . I don't know, so savage, so mad, that she doesn't look where she's going." He stopped again, holding up his hands, his eyes locked in a thousand-yard stare. "So I called an ambulance. But before they arrive someone comes into the house, some guy I've never seen before, and he starts punching me, strangling me. Only he falls over my mum, smashing his head on the table. I swear, it was like something from *The Three Stooges*."

"Then what?" asked Brick when the boy didn't continue.

"To be honest, I don't remember," Chris said. "I left the house, got in the car. My dad's car. He came after me in the garage, but he's like on crutches because of a toe operation, and he falls. So the ambulance people arrive and even before they get up the road I know what they're going to do. They start tearing at the car along with my dad. They looked like animals. I just drove, found somewhere quiet, used my phone to check the Internet, which is where I found your message."

"You still got your phone?" Brick asked. Chris fished it from his pocket.

"No signal," he said, putting it back.

"What about the others?" Brick said. "What about that man?"

"Well, that's the strange thing," said Chris. He grunted out a laugh. "Well, *one* of them. I . . ." He looked at Jade, and for some reason his cheeks flushed. "I . . . we . . . just knew where they were."

"I'm from Whitehaven," said Jade, filling the pause before it got awkward. "But I was staying with my friend Heather who's moved down to Grantham, yeah? Anyway, we were in the taxi on the way to a gig in town, and I didn't even want to go 'cause of my head, it was really bad." She felt her temples automatically, as if trying to find the pain that had been there. *We had that too*, thought Cal, sharing a look with Brick, *the headache, it's part of this*. "And the night's just getting worse and worse because

Heather isn't even talking to me and I don't know why and then the taxi driver crashes the bloody thing into a tree. Like, a proper crash and everything and we rolled over onto the side in this ditch." She wrapped her arms around herself again, pulling her legs up onto the chair for a moment before lowering them. "And Heather is kicking me and scratching, but I just think she's trying to get out because she's underneath me, yeah? So I pull myself out the window then lean back in but she takes a *bite* out of me. I mean really." She held out her hand, a purple half-moon on her wrist. "And the next thing I know the taxi driver is going at me, even though . . ."

She stopped, looking like she was going to barf.

"His arm," she said, her eyes filling. She put her hand to her mouth. "His wrist was broken, his hand almost coming off, but he was still . . ."

She looked at Chris. He lifted an arm as if to comfort her then chickened out, resting it back on his knee.

"I got there a while later," he said. "I didn't even know where I was going, I just *had* to go that way. And I see the taxi on its side and an ambulance and a police car, and I know she's not there, but she's somewhere close, so I park farther up and go into the woods and she's just sitting by a tree. And it's like we've known each other forever, you know?"

Cal did know. He was feeling it now, as if he'd grown up with these guys, spent every waking hour of his life with them.

"So we get into the car and drive a bit farther until I'm just too tired to go anymore, and we sleep in the car in this clearing. Then the next morning we both start feeling this thing in our heads, like . . . like I can't even explain it."

"Like a silence," said Cal. "But a silence you can hear."

"Yeah, that's just like it. So we both had that silence and we know we only have to drive and we'll get to where we need to be."

"Him," said Jade, nodding at Adam. The boy wasn't listening. He was chewing chips, but the slow, mechanical movements of his jaw were the only sign he was alive. "Man, we almost died. He was at the dentist's, yeah? In this house on this normal kind of street. Where was it? Peterborough?"

"Ely," said Chris. "Well, near there, anyway."

"He'd managed to hide in the attic, God knows how long he'd been there. This dentist, she went for us, but . . ."

She looked at Chris again and in that look Cal saw what they'd done. What they'd had to do.

"He doesn't talk," she went on. "We got his name from the label in his shirt. Poor little dude."

"And the guy with the gun," said Brick. "What about him?"

"He was the last," said Chris. "We were on the way here, following your message to come to the sea. Not that we'd have needed it, I mean something was pulling us out this way anyway, that same . . . *thing* that led me to Jade, then to Adam, then to that guy."

"Never told us his name," said Jade. "We show up at this farm, it's not even that far from here, an hour maybe. And I knew it was a bad idea, 'cause there was blood everywhere, like *loads* of it." She shuddered. "So this guy comes up to the car and he's just insane. Not like the others, not like the *feral* people. He was with it, just *crazy* with it, you know?"

"He dumps an unconscious man in the trunk, gets in and says he'll shoot us unless we do what he says," said Chris. "So we drive up here, all of us, and we didn't even need the satnav. We just knew you were at the park."

There was silence when he finished. Cal took a sip of his own soda, ignoring the dirt on the glass. It felt good, crackling on his tongue.

"I'm glad you killed him," spat Jade.

"You see any explosives?" Brick asked. Both Chris and Jade shrugged. "He had to have been wired with something, an explosion like that. Sounds like he was crazy, so he had to have wired himself, yeah?"

"I guess so," said Chris, although he didn't look sure.

Cal thought back to the exploding car on the highway, the shape that had risen from it on wings of fire, screaming.

"We'll never know now, I guess," Chris went on. "Guy's splattered all over the place."

"You said your head hurt," said Cal. "Right before everything happened."

Chris and Jade nodded.

"And mine," said Daisy. "It was really sore for days. And I could hear it too, like a pulse."

"*Thump-thump*, *thump-thump*," said Brick.

Daisy nodded, her eyes widening. "That's it," she said, sitting up straight in her chair. "It was *just* like that!"

Cal's skin tightened into knots of goose bumps, his scalp tickling like someone was breathing on it.

"Things went bad right after my headache stopped," said Chris. "Like, *right* afterward, within seconds."

"Yeah, me too," said Jade. "I even remember thinking *Maybe this night isn't gonna be so bad* because my headache had gone, and then three seconds later or whatever we were in the ditch."

It had been exactly like that, hadn't it? Cal thought back, remembering the football pitch, the sunlight. The pounding ache between his temples had gone, like it had just been switched off. Then the whole world had come after him.

"My headache was definitely gone when the ambulance man came," said Daisy.

More silence. They all looked at each other, and in their eyes they saw themselves, they saw their own confusion and fear.

"What does it mean?" asked Jade.

"It was like something banging on my skull," said Brick. *"Thump-thump, thump-thump, thump-thump, thump-thump."*

The sound seemed to shake Adam from his trance. The kid looked up at Brick, his jaw frozen mid-chew.

"Thump-thump, thump-thump." Brick was slapping himself on the head now. "It's like something was trying to get in there, trying to break down the door. *Thump-thump."*

Adam was fully awake now, his eyes like saucers.

"Thump-thump," Brick went on. *"Thump-thump*, just like that. *Thump-thump, thump-thump."*

"Brick," said Cal. "Just—"

And that's when Adam opened his mouth, uttering a cry so shrill and so loud that Cal had to slap his hands to his ears, a cry that caused his glass to shatter into shrapnel, that swept across the room and extinguished every single one of the candles, plunging them into night.

BRICK FUMBLED FOR THE MATCHES, SPARKING ONE UP.

"Give him some air," said Daisy, who had her arm around Adam's shoulder. "He's scared."

"We're all scared," said Jade. "What the hell was that?"

"He just didn't like the noise," said Daisy, glowering at Brick.

He felt a perverse impulse to do it again, to start shouting *thump-thump* at the top of his voice, but he resisted it.

"He's fine, he just needs to get out of this place, it's too dark and scary in here," Daisy said.

"Yeah," said Cal. He pocketed the matches, then walked to the restaurant door, holding it open and letting faint, dusty light into the room. "Come on, it's too cold anyway."

Rilke was still unconscious beside her brother. Brick left her there and followed the others down the corridor—grateful that there was no noise from the basement—and out through the fire exit. The heat held him like a golden hug and he wished it was possible to pull yourself out of your skin and soar up over the tinfoil brilliance of the ocean, to just follow the sun around the world for the rest of time and never have to be imprisoned by flesh and gravity and darkness ever again.

"What's going on?" He recognized his own tone—aggressive, like he thought they were all hiding something.

"How should I know?" Cal snapped back.

"This isn't normal."

"Really?" said Cal.

Brick bit back his first response and went with his second.

"We need to really think about this," he said. "Because it's seriously messed up, Cal. And . . ." *I'm scared,* he wanted to say, but something stopped him. He coughed, looking out across the mini-golf course. The one-eyed giant squirrel stared back, grinning insanely.

"I'm scared too," said Daisy, as though she'd read his mind. She had sat down between Jade and Adam on the low wall that surrounded the mini-golf. The little boy seemed to have calmed down, but his doll-like expression creeped the hell out of Brick.

"We need to work out exactly what we know," said Cal. "Everything. Like, logically."

"People are trying to kill us," said Chris.

"It's not just that, is it?" Cal pushed himself up from the wall, pacing. "They only want to kill us when we're close to them, when we're, what did you say, in their radar?"

"Yeah," said Jade. "It's like they sense us and they go mental, like a dog senses another dog."

"And if we get away, get far enough away, they go back to normal," Cal went on. "They totally forget what they've done. But why? What would make them do that?"

The only thing to answer was the lapping of the waves.

"Okay, we need to start from the beginning," said Cal. "The headache, the thumping. Maybe it was some kind of, I don't know . . . some kind of psychological change."

"Physiological," corrected Jade. "It would have to be chemical. Maybe we're producing a new kind of pheromone, some kind of mutant gene that makes people hate us."

"Makes sense," said Cal, his shoes scuffing the dry ground as he walked back and forth. Each step was treading on Brick's temper but he swallowed it back down, the anger boiling in his stomach. "Until you think about Schiller. And Adam. I've never heard a scream like that before in my life."

"Daisy too," said Brick. Cal stopped, and Daisy looked up, frowning.

"What about me?"

"You knew that kid's name," he said. "After the explosion. I heard you call it out, before anyone said anything. How did you know that?"

Daisy just shrugged.

"You wanna hear something weird?" Cal said, running his hands through his hair. "I've been doing it too, like I can sometimes see things that you guys are thinking. It's nothing bad or anything. It's probably nothing at all. All it is, is that some of the thoughts in my head aren't mine, you know?"

Brick hawked up a ball of spit and launched it toward the mini-golf. It tasted of ash. "You serious?"

"And what about the explosion?" Cal said. "Brick, me and you were lying right next to that guy, I mean just feet away. We get thrown halfway across the park, but we're *okay*? That blast demolished the hot-dog stand, it cut loose bits of metal from the big wheel, but we're *okay*? You think about that?"

Brick hadn't thought about it, not until now. But Cal was right, if the man had been carrying explosives then they'd have been blown to pulp, bits of them would still be raining down on Fursville. He'd just assumed that they'd been lucky, but that in itself was a long stretch. Luck, after all, was used to giving Brick a wide, wide berth. So maybe the man hadn't been carrying a bomb, maybe it was something else . . .

But it was, remember, you saw it, something crawling from his belly.

Brick shook his head, the image dissolving like salt in water, forgotten. They'd been lucky, that's all, lucky, lucky, lucky. *Keep saying it, Brick, and you'll believe it eventually.*

"What does that mean, that we're invincible?" asked Chris, leaning against the wall, his expression a portrait of desperation.

"I have no idea," Cal went on. "We have absolutely no idea."

Brick felt the sun on his face, burning his fair, freckled skin. And suddenly something hit him. "Not yet, we don't," he said. "But I think I might know how to find out."

"Dude, this is a *seriously* bad idea."

They were in the parking lot, close enough to the trunk of the Jag to hear the feeble moans but far enough away not to trigger the guy inside, not to make him feral. It was about twenty meters, Brick had worked out, maybe a handful more. That's how far their radar stretched, whether they could see or not. He held a burlap sack in his hands, a big one he'd found inside the kitchen next door to the restaurant. It was filthy, but hopefully it would do the job. Cal, Jade, and Chris were beside him. Daisy had volunteered to look after Adam back in Fursville—it was better that they didn't see this.

"Seriously, dude," Chris said again. "This won't end well."

"Gotta say I agree with him, mate," said Cal. He was holding several long strips of fabric they'd torn from another sack. "You don't know who's in there or what he's capable of."

"We never saw him," said Jade. "He was unconscious when that farmer guy put him in. Could be anyone."

"Doesn't matter who it is," said Brick, gripping the bag. "Right now he's the only one who can explain what's going on."

And Lisa, right? She's down there, in the basement, you could always tell them about her?

No. Not yet. He didn't know what to do about Lisa, he needed more time to work out how to help her.

"Everybody set on what they have to do?" he asked, psyching himself up. "Remember, he's been in there for a day, in the sun, with nothing to eat or drink. He's going to be weak. Just remember that."

"Christ," muttered Chris. "This is insane."

"Pop it," said Brick, opening the sack.

Chris held out the remote lock and thumbed the trunk key. There was a soft click as the metal lid popped up an inch. The moans inside stopped, as if in disbelief.

"Go!" Brick yelled, charging forward, hearing Cal's feet thundering along beside him.

The lid was lifting, darkness peeling away from a pale face. The man saw them coming, his frightened pleas lasting maybe five or six words before they got close enough to do whatever it was they did. His face creased up like someone having an electric shock, his lips pulled back, his eyes bulged, and he started to scramble out of the trunk.

Brick screamed, plunging the burlap bag over the man's head. The guy was fast, swiping his hand across Brick's cheek. He ignored the pain, yanking the bag down hard until it covered the guy down to his waist.

"Quick!" he panted. The man crunched into Brick and butted him to the ground. He hit hard, forgetting to tuck in his head, fireworks gouging chunks out of his sight. The feral landed on him, knees working into his ribs. Savage, guttural howls blasted out from behind the cloth, the man's jaw flexing in the burlap, like he was trying to chew his way through it and straight into Brick.

There was a crunch as Cal kicked out, sending the feral rolling to the side. The man managed to find his feet, just a pair of legs and a sack that ran in wild circles. Cal lashed out, an impressive punch that knocked the man on his backside. He pinned him to the ground, calling out for help as he tried to wrap the canvas strips around him.

Chris got there first, sitting on the man's legs. Jade was quick to follow, pressing both her hands on his head until Cal had looped the first strip around and tied it tight. He wrapped another around the guy's waist, then used the last one to bind his feet. When he was done he fell backward, wiping the sweat from his brow and spitting out a couple of choice swears. Chris and Jade retreated too, leaving a burlap mummy squirming on the grass.

"Yeah, *real* weak," Cal said, his chest heaving.

"Now what?" asked Jade.

"We get him inside," said Brick. "Then we make him spill his guts."

RILKE / *Fursville, 1:33 p.m.*

RILKE SWAM UP FROM FIRE INTO ICE, the inferno of her dream extinguished by the immense cold of the room.

She curled into herself, shivering, knowing that Schiller was close by because nothing else could be pumping out that chill. She lay there, trying to hang on to her nightmare, remembering only that she had been falling through a storm of fire, a tornado of heat and light and noise; falling toward a churning ocean made up not of water but of long limbs and twisted jaws and eyes of burning pitch. The image was so real that she was sweating despite the temperature in the restaurant, her skin burning.

Rilke was suddenly aware of how quiet the room was. She couldn't even hear the sea anymore, just her brother's soft, rapid breathing, no louder than a heartbeat. Where was everybody?

Outside, she knew. She could almost see them there, an image that hung in the corner of her vision, something she could sense but couldn't quite make sense of.

"You okay, Schill?" she asked, not expecting a response. The pattern of his breathing remained unbroken. She shuffled across the room, heading for the soft glow of a candle. She used it to light a fresh one, the dancing flame bringing back more memories from her dream—a man on fire, something clawing its way free from his belly.

She collapsed into a chair. What had happened out there, before she blacked out?

An explosion, a shock, from the guy you shot in the head.

She had *killed* somebody. She'd pulled the trigger and taken his life. She rested her elbows on the table, cradling her head in her hands. It had been Daisy, it had been the little girl's fault. She'd made her do it, she'd whined and cried and screamed until Rilke hadn't been able to think straight. Had the man been about to kill Cal? There was no way of knowing; she'd shot him before he even had a chance. And worse still, it hadn't even been one of the ferals, it had been one of *them*.

Her thoughts blazed and guttered like the candle. She'd killed a man, but it wasn't just that, she'd killed something else too. She closed her eyes, dragging herself back, seeing the thing that had unzipped the man's body like a sleeping bag, that had torn and ripped and raged its way free, had opened the abyss of its mouth and howled at her, spread impossible wings of fire. It couldn't have been real, and yet this thing, this creature, was more real than anything she'd ever known.

Her body shook with the force of a pneumatic drill, her teeth chattering.

Think, you stupid girl, she shouted at herself, slapping her forehead. What had it been, this thing? What was it doing disguised as a man?

Or maybe it hadn't been disguised. Maybe it had been *hiding.*

She pictured its face, those eyes that blazed—not with emotion, but with power. The heat from them seemed to burrow into her mind. What was it? And more important, if it had been hiding inside the man then was something like that hiding inside her too? Was there one inside all of them? Was this what made them different? Had they all been . . .

The word "chosen" was what popped into Rilke's head. *That's right, isn't it? We're special, we've been chosen.*

She curled up against the table, shivering, feverish. She was strong, like all the Bastion women. When she put her mind to something then she always got it done, whatever the cost. It was no surprise that she'd been chosen.

But chosen for what? She wiped a hand over her brow, the skin cool and damp with sweat. It was as cold as a church in here, and the thought brought back memories of St. Peter's in the village. She'd been forced there for mass every week for as long as she could remember. But maybe all those hours hadn't been wasted.

Because in the stories she heard in church people were always being chosen.

For good things, and for bad.

"Why are we here, little brother?" she asked Schiller. "Can you see it, from where you are? Are there answers there?"

Maybe it was some kind of test. Maybe she'd been supposed to shoot that guy, proof that she was strong enough to do whatever it was that she was here to do. Maybe his role in all this was a sacrificial one, a pawn to be slaughtered so that she could be pointed in the right direction. There were plenty of slaughtered pawns in those church stories too.

She had killed. But was it really a bad thing? Was it truly any different from the times she'd gone out with Schiller and taken potshots at the rats in the grain barrels? Or sniped the pigeons on the telephone wires and the rooftop? She'd shot a cat once too, although it had been about to die anyway, stuck in a fox trap for God knew how long. Dead rat, dead cat, dead bird, dead human. What did it matter to her?

Because she was none of those things.

The restaurant reeled, vertigo making her grip the table before she lost her balance. Her body shook, the truth suddenly as bright and as golden as sunrise. It was almost too much to take in, too much to think about. She closed her eyes, her lips peeling open into a shuddering grin.

And just like that, she knew exactly what she had to do.

"DO YOU MISS YOUR MUM AND DAD?" DAISY ASKED THE BOY.

She sat on the carousel, on one of the three horses that remained. It had lost most of its paint, but she didn't mind—its plain gray coat made it look more like a real pony. It still had parts of its face, its frightened eyes and its big teeth. It reminded her a bit of the ambulance man but she tried not to think about him. This was Angie—her mum's name—Angie her beautiful white Lipizzaner. She leaned against the pole, swinging her legs absently, gazing at the horse beside hers. Adam was sitting on it, his arms wrapped around its neck, his cheek resting on the colorless plastic mane. His eyes blinked every few minutes, but that was about all he seemed capable of. She'd had to lift him up there because he was so limp.

Truth be told, she was a little scared of him now. The noise he'd made, back in the restaurant, that scream. It had come from the little boy's mouth, but it hadn't been him. She was sure of it.

"I miss my parents," she went on, then stopped. "What shall we call your horse?"

The ice cubes in her head clinked. She was learning to make sense of them, of the different layers they formed. The ones down deep were always dark, cloudy. She could see things in them but she couldn't see what those things were exactly. The middle ones were better, they had some sounds too, muffled voices or piano music, things like that. But every now and then one would bobble to the surface and it would be just like she was living inside it, as though she were really there. She didn't always like these particular ones because sometimes they were too real. And sometimes, very occasionally, they were full of fire. She saw things in the flames, things with burning faces, things that scared her.

"Geoffrey," she said, reading an ice cube, seeing a dog there, a small one with big ears and a goofy dog grin. The boy's eyes met hers as she said the word, and she thought she saw a smile in them, gone before she could be sure. "Was that your dog? Geoffrey? Okay, your horse is Geoffrey, mine is Angie. What about that one? It will feel left out. How about . . ." She giggled. "How about Wonky-Butt the Wonder Horse."

Adam opened his mouth and Daisy leaned toward him, almost sliding off her horse. He was going to speak! He never got the chance, as more voices bubbled up from close by, angry, panicked shouts.

Daisy turned to see the others traipsing into Fursville. Then she noticed what they were carrying, and she didn't need the ice cubes to tell her that there was someone inside the sack. It wriggled and shook and screamed and bucked, the four of them struggling to hold it. Cal was at the front, his arms locked around the man's head. Brick had the middle and Chris and Jade the legs.

The sack lurched hard and Cal dropped it, the man's head thumping to the ground where it continued to shake wildly. She heard Cal swear. He hefted the man's head up again and they all waddled off toward the pavilion like some weird caterpillar. Daisy sat up straight, wondering what to do. She had an idea where they were taking the man, and what they were going to do with him.

"Do you want to have a walk?" she said. Adam shook his head

and hugged his horse even tighter than before. Daisy nodded. It was probably better that he didn't see. "Well, shall I leave you here for five minutes? Will you be okay?"

Adam didn't reply. His eyes had taken on that glassy, lifeless sheen. Daisy grabbed the pole and swung herself carefully off the horse, walking over to him.

"I won't be long," she said, stretching on her tiptoes so she could run her hand up and down his back. "Don't move, okay? You're safe here, but stay on your horse. And if you need me, just call out in your head, okay? I'll hear you."

It seemed a strange thing to say, and yet perfectly natural at the same time. He didn't respond. Daisy stood there for a moment more, then clambered off the carousel and ran after the others. By the time she caught up with them they were shoving the frenzied sack-man through the chained fire exit. He was writhing so much that it seemed likely he'd pull the doors off their hinges.

The man howled. There was no pain in that noise though, or fear. There was nothing but fury. Jade threw herself down onto the man's feet, hugging them as Cal pulled him into the pavilion.

"Little help?" yelled Cal from inside. Brick muttered as he ducked through, reeling back as the man kicked out then crawling awkwardly inside. Chris followed, struggling to get his bulk into the gap.

Daisy waited until the shouts had faded a little before entering. When her eyes had adjusted to the gloom she saw that Cal and Brick were dragging the man up the shadowed corridor.

"In here," Brick yelled, kicking open a door halfway down. Daisy followed them as they hurled the man inside, dumping him roughly against the far wall.

"Go!" yelled Cal, everyone stampeding from the room, almost tripping over one another. The sack-man was already clambering up, looking like a headless, limbless torso in the dark room. He bounced off a hatch in the wall and lumbered toward the corridor. Brick waited for everyone to scramble out before pulling the door shut. The man thumped against it, hard enough to shake the dust from the ceiling. His savage growls were barely muffled by the wood.

"Now what?" said Jade, panting. "How do we lock it?"

Brick glared at her, but he didn't answer.

"We can use more sack," said Cal, digging in his pockets. "Move."

The others stood to one side as he tied a strip of something around the door handle, then looped the other end around a pipe that ran down the side of the door, knotting it twice. It didn't look particularly secure to Daisy, but it seemed to make the others relax. They stood back, collapsing against the walls.

"You ready to tell us what your plan is yet?" Cal said, panting. "How're we supposed to get anything out of him when he's like that?"

"You see the hatch in there?" said Brick, wiping his hand over his face. "Dumbwaiter. There's a shaft leading from it right up to the kitchen. Come on."

He led the way through the lobby, up the stairs and past the entrance to the restaurant. It was freezing here, an icy draft blowing through the crack between the double doors of Waves like it was the middle of winter. Daisy shivered, pressing herself against Cal as they walked past the restaurant.

"You wanna check on the twins?" asked Cal.

"No," Brick grunted. The corridor up here was a small one,

with only one other door. Brick pushed through it into another dark hallway, then took the first opening on the right. Daisy had to squint against the blade of sunlight that cut through a broken board on the window, her eyes gradually adjusting.

The kitchen was huge, the metal surfaces and industrial ovens covered in grime—feathers and bird droppings everywhere. The tiled floor was cracked and, incredibly, little clusters of sea grass had planted themselves in the dirt, stretching tiny green fingers up toward the window. In a decade or so the whole park would probably be lost in a forest of green.

Brick made his way over to the far wall, to a small, square door that sat right in the middle of it—the other end of the dumbwaiter.

"You ready?" he asked nobody in particular. He opened the hatch, the rusted hinges putting up a fight but finally giving in. Inside was nothing but darkness, and Brick nervously stuck his head into it. Daisy expected to see a frenzied face emerging from the shaft below, jaws snapping shut around the boy's throat. He cleared his throat, speaking into the bottomless gloom of the dumbwaiter. "Hello? Can you hear me?"

A noise rose up from the room directly below, a rattling clank. Daisy guessed it was probably the guy trying to break out of the storeroom. Sound traveled perfectly up the dumbwaiter, as though the man were in this very kitchen.

"Hello?" Brick said again. "I know you can hear me, jackass, so say something."

"You want me to do this?" said Cal.

Brick held his ground for a second then stepped away, holding his hands up. "All yours."

"Listen," Cal called out, sticking his head through the door.

Daisy leaned in to better hear what he was saying. "We're not going to hurt you, we just want to talk."

More clattering, then the squeal of a door opening. At first Daisy thought the man had managed to get out. Then the sound of deep, rasping breaths ghosted up the shaft.

"Hello?" The voice was weak, and old. "Who's there? Why are you doing this?"

"There's water in the tap," said Cal, turning back to Brick. "Isn't there?"

Brick nodded. The rasping faded, replaced by the distant sound of pipes rattling. The man returned after a minute or so, panting hard as if he'd just downed six pints in one go.

"Thank you," he wheezed. "Look, please, whoever you are, I don't have anything, I'm not rich, I just have a farm, nothing else."

"We don't want anything from you," Cal shouted. "We only want to know why you tried to kill us."

Silence, even his breathing faded.

"What?" he said eventually. "I never tried to kill you, I don't even know who you are."

"You don't remember what just happened?" Cal went on. "You don't remember us locking you in the room?"

"I . . . I . . ." Daisy imagined him taking a good look around him, trying to work out where he was. "I don't know how I got here," he stuttered.

"What's the last thing you remember?" asked Cal.

"Being in the car," he answered hesitantly. "In the trunk."

"And before that?"

"Um, I was at home, working. It's Friday, isn't it?"

"Dude, he doesn't even know what day it is," said Chris. Cal hushed him with a hand.

"Then what?"

"I, er, I don't know. I don't know." He was sobbing now—big, gulping, metallic cries. "It's just black. You've drugged me."

"Ask him his name," said Daisy quietly. She couldn't read anything from this man, there was nothing of his life in the ice cubes in her head. *Because he isn't one of us,* she thought. "Tell him your name too."

"We haven't drugged you," said Cal. "We're trying to help you. I'm Cal, by the way. What's your name?"

"Maltby," said the man. "Edward Maltby. Ted."

"Okay, Ted. I need you to *really* think," said Cal, and there was something calming about his voice. "Who is the last person you remember seeing?"

More thumps, but this time it came from behind them, from the restaurant. Daisy glanced at the kitchen door, expecting to see Rilke stroll in. Instead she heard the girl walking down the stairs. At least she was back on her feet after the explosion. Daisy was relieved.

"I don't know," the man repeated, the shaft giving his voice a robotic quality. "Please just let me go, I have a son, he . . ."

Silence, everyone crowding around the dumbwaiter door to see what came next.

"Wait, I remember him, my son, coming back to the house. Is he here? He hasn't been well, he's had this headache . . ." Another pause. "That's right, he was shouting about how it had gone, and . . . and then I don't know, then there was nothing."

"So the douche bag with the gun was his son," muttered Brick. "Makes sense."

"You're sure there's nothing else, Ted?" asked Cal. "Nothing you can remember?"

"I . . . I think I must have been dreaming," said Maltby, still weeping. "I saw something, in the darkness. There was something bad there, I can't remember, but . . . it, was just bad, it needed to . . . I don't know, why are you doing this?"

"What was it?" asked Cal. "What did you see?"

The man replied but his words were garbled. Brick leaned in, shoulder to shoulder with Cal, both of them peering down into the darkness.

"What did he say?" Brick asked.

"Sssh," hissed Cal. Sure enough the man spoke again, his whimper like a dog's, curling up at the end into a snarl.

"Is he going feral again?" said Jade.

"It's Rilke," said Daisy. "She's with him."

The eerie haunted-house squeal of a door rose up the dumbwaiter. The man roared, a scream of rage that sent everyone skittering back from the wall. It was just as well, because the noise that followed would have deafened them—the unmistakable crack of a gunshot.

BRICK / *Fursville, 2:27 p.m.*

BRICK AND CAL LOOKED AT EACH OTHER as the gunshot echoed around the room. Then they turned and ran.

Brick got there first, his long legs giving him the advantage as he thundered down the stairs and across the lobby. He smashed through the door marked STAFF ONLY, skidding to a halt when he saw Rilke in the corridor.

She was holding the gun.

"What the hell have you done?" he yelled. Her eyes gleamed, the brightest things in the dusk. The barrel of the pistol was smoking, the air thick with the bitter scent of cordite. Brick started forward again, reaching the stockroom door and looking inside. He felt his stomach churn, his legs shaking so much he had to lean against the doorjamb or fall face-first onto the corpse that lay inside. A ragged hole had been sunk into the old man's chest and blood had pooled there.

Clattering feet, then Cal was by his side again. He made a noise that was halfway between a gulp and a dry heave, then whipped around.

"Don't look, Daisy," he said. "Stay there, stay there."

Chris barged between Cal and Brick. "You *killed* him," he said.

Brick looked at Rilke again, the girl's face set in stone.

"I said *what the hell have you done?*" he shouted. He took a step toward her, stopping only when she lifted the gun, pointing that smoking barrel right at his forehead.

"That's enough, Rilke," said Cal. "Christ, what do you think you're doing? Put that thing down."

"Answer, dammit," said Brick, the emotions stewing in his gut, ready to make him do something stupid. "Why did you do that? He was talking to us, he was about to tell us something."

"No," said Rilke. "He wasn't."

"How do you know?" Brick went on. "You weren't even there."

He felt a hand on his arm, Cal's fingers squeezing. He shrugged him away, taking another step toward Rilke. *How many shots have been fired? One on the beach, two outside, I think, then another one now. Two bullets left?* She'd only need one to put a hole in his brain.

"I reloaded," she answered his unspoken question for him,

offering him a smile as sharp and as dangerous as a scalpel blade. "Cal was kind enough to bring a big, big box of bullets with him."

"Rilke, I know you've been through a lot," said Cal in that infuriatingly calm tone of his. "I know how you must be feeling. We all feel it. But he was safe in there, we'd locked him in. He couldn't hurt us."

"I know," said Rilke, her entire body motionless except for her eyes, which slid around toward Cal. "That isn't why I did it."

"Why, then?" asked Cal.

"Because he wasn't one of us," she said. "And anyone who isn't one of us doesn't deserve to live."

"You don't know what you're talking about," said Jade.

"But I do," she said, lowering the gun but keeping her finger on the trigger. "I know exactly what I'm talking about. And you do too, Daisy."

Brick glanced back to where Daisy stood, wreathed in darkness by the door. He could see her silhouetted head shaking.

"Leave her out of this," said Cal. "Just give me the gun, okay, then we can talk about it."

He moved forward, his hand out, but Rilke took a step back, her trigger finger twitching.

"None of you understand what's going on," she said. "It's pathetic. But we know, don't we, Daisy? We know the truth."

"I don't know what you're talking about, Rilke," said Daisy. "I don't know anything."

"You *do* know," Rilke went on, still retreating down the corridor. "You've seen it. The fire inside them, inside *us*."

"Fire?" said Brick. "You're off your head."

"Please, Rilke," sobbed Daisy. "Please give Cal the gun, please. I don't want anyone to get hurt."

"They'll try to stop us," Rilke said. "We can't have them here."

Them? Brick felt a finger of ice run up his back, settling at the base of his skull.

Rilke stopped when she reached the door that led down to the basement. She reached out and turned the handle. Brick's entire body tensed, ready to fly at her.

"Don't you dare," he growled. "I'll kill you."

"Dare what?" asked Cal. "What's in there?"

Brick tuned him out, tuned them all out. His head was a furnace, nothing but white heat and noise. He started forward, not even stopping when Rilke raised the gun again, that unblinking black eye staring right at him. She was crazy but there was no way she'd shoot him, no way she'd pull that trigger.

Then the corridor flashed, the shot making his eardrums ring. It was like a cannon had gone off. He crashed to his knees, his hands up to his face, expecting blood. But everything was there, where it should be.

"The next one won't miss," said Rilke, the same thing she'd said right before blowing that guy's face off. She'd pushed open the door and was now treading carefully down the stairs, never taking her eyes off him.

"Please," Brick said, his voice breaking. He crawled to the top of the stairs on his hands and knees, hearing Lisa's panicked cries below, becoming less and less human as Rilke closed in. "Please don't do this, don't hurt her, she didn't do anything to you."

"Not yet," Rilke said. "But she will, if she gets the chance. They all will. It's us against them, now, but we're so much better than them." She laughed, a lunatic chuckle that rose from the darkness of the steps. "We're creatures of fire. And what does fire do best? It *purges*."

Brick was crying, everything that had been boiling inside him now escaping like steam. The tears dropped onto his hands, impossibly hot, and through the blur he saw Rilke kick away the pole he'd used to wedge the basement door closed. Lisa was thumping herself against it, howling, screeching.

They couldn't be the last sounds she'd ever make, they *couldn't* be. He wanted to hear her speak again, even if it was just to insult him; he wanted to hear that laugh, the one he'd always found so annoying but which made him smile when she wasn't looking; he wanted to feel her lips on his, the warmth of her body.

"Rilke," he sobbed. "I'm begging you."

"Don't," she called back up the stairs. "You're better than that now. You're *more* than that."

And with that she opened the basement door. Brick watched as a shape flew out of it on all fours, thumping headfirst into the wall. He watched as Rilke leveled the gun at Lisa's head. He watched as she pulled the trigger. Then he closed his eyes and let the grief consume him.

Past the racking sobs, past the thunder in his ears, he heard Rilke walk back up the stairs. She put a hand on his shoulder.

"You'll thank me for this," she said.

Then she was gone.

DAISY WATCHED AS RILKE CAME BACK UP THE STAIRS and patted Brick's shoulder; watched as she walked calmly down the corridor toward her. Daisy wanted to flee before Rilke tried to shoot
her as well, but her legs were made of stone. She was fixed there,
in that dark corridor that stank of bullets and meat.

"Don't be scared, Daisy," said Rilke. She leaned in, her eyes
catching the light that seeped through from the foyer. It made
them look like alien eyes, as if they were radioactive or something. "You may not know it yet, but I had to do that," she said.

Rilke straightened up and walked through the door. Brick's
sobs filled the space where she had been, the noise so much
worse because it was coming from him, coming from someone
so strong. Bricks weren't supposed to cry, they could weather
anything.

"Brick?" Cal was stooped over the bigger boy, his hand where
Rilke's had been. Chris and Jade looked on like they were in the
audience at the theater, their jaws unhinged. "Brick, mate, what
just happened? Who was that?"

His girlfriend, of course. Lisa, thought Daisy. She'd been locked
down there, that's why the stairs had given Daisy the creeps. Her
head was full of ice cubes, all smashing against each other. She
could see her, a pretty girl who maybe wore a little too much
makeup, who swore a lot and who didn't always *get it.* Daisy wasn't
sure exactly *what* she didn't get, it was just what she could see,
and sense, from those little transparent movies. He'd loved her,

though. He'd loved her with everything he had, and now she was gone. Now he wouldn't be able to fix her. Not ever.

Those ice cubes were melting, and with them came anger—not hers, she understood, but his. She took a step toward Brick and Cal, then thought better of it, bolting through the door and chasing after Rilke.

"Daisy, wait!" Cal called out behind her. She ignored him, almost tripping up the sweeping stairs. Rilke was walking into Waves, but she must have heard Daisy's clattering footsteps because she turned around, a weird, false smile imprinted on her lips. The gun hung by her side.

"We don't have a choice," said Rilke. "This is happening for a reason."

"You can't just *kill* people."

"There are more important things at stake here," Rilke said. "Don't you see that? We have to survive. We *have* to. If we don't . . ."

For the first time the expression on Rilke's face wavered, her smile fading. It was like watching a ventriloquist's dummy, thought Daisy, as though she was speaking not for herself but was a mouthpiece for someone else; some*thing* else. The older girl looked down at the gun in her hands and swallowed hard, but when she looked back at Daisy the smile flickered on again—uncertain on her lips but bright and unshaken in her eyes.

"I need you to trust me," she said. "To trust that I'm telling you the truth. Those two down there, they would have killed us without a second thought. Don't you see? It's us against them, now, but there's more to it than that, it's . . ." She seemed to struggle again, her eyes flicking left and right. "Just trust me," she said, trancelike. "And trust *them*."

"Who?"

"Them," Rilke said. "You'll understand it, soon enough."

Daisy heard the STAFF ONLY door creak below, then the stomp of feet coming up the stairs. Rilke retreated farther into the darkness of the restaurant. Cal appeared by Daisy's side. His eyes were red, the dirt on his face tear-streaked.

"You shouldn't have done that," he croaked. "That was his girlfriend. He's going to kill you."

"No," said the shadow in the doorway. "He's not. He's going to do exactly what I tell him."

"What?" Cal spat. "What are you talking about, Rilke?"

"*Exactly* what I tell him," she said again, sinking deeper into the tar-pit dark. It didn't sound like Rilke speaking anymore, it sounded like something much older. "He doesn't have a choice."

Cal looked at Daisy. He was scared, it seemed to ooze from his every pore. Daisy reached out and took hold of his hand and he squeezed back, so hard she felt one of her finger joints pop. Rilke retreated even farther, letting the door swing shut.

"You all will come to me when you're ready," said Rilke, her voice muffled.

There was a click, a heavy thump, and it took Daisy a moment to realize she'd locked the door. Rilke laughed, a soft chuckle that set Daisy's teeth on edge.

"Because you'll die if you don't."

THE OTHER (3)

And when they shall have finished their testimony, the beast that ascendeth out of the bottomless pit shall make war against them, and shall overcome them, and kill them. —Revelations 11:7

THE CONVOY WAS MADE UP OF NINETEEN VEHICLES. Four police motorcycles took the lead, sweeping other cars out of the way, blocking the entrances onto the divided highway and letting the first three black government limousines move at high speed. Smack bang in the middle was a private ambulance, long, black, and windowless, which looked more like a hearse. Two more police motorcycles flanked it, their riders equipped with machine guns and dark-visored helmets. Another three limos rode in their wake.

Detective Inspector Alan Murdoch sat in the second of these, sandwiched in the rear between Dr. Sven Jorgensen, the Scotland Yard pathologist, and one of his assistants from the morgue. He glanced through the tinted glass of the rear window to see the two squad cars and four motorcycles that formed the tail of the convoy. Their blue lights turned the city around them into a constantly shifting ocean, the illusion so strong that Murdoch suddenly felt like he was drowning, like there was no oxygen left in the car.

He sat forward, sucking in air, the seat belt tight around his chest. The convoy thundered onto a roundabout, hardly slowing, then pulled onto the M1. Wide-eyed people watched them go from inside their cars.

If only they knew, he thought, peering through the vehicles in front to see the ambulance. Its single patient lay in a bed in the back. Not alive. Not dead either. Breathing in that one endless, howling breath. *If only they could see.*

He wanted to signal back at them. He wanted their help. He wanted them to know that he was a prisoner. Of course they'd never actually said that, the soldiers who had escorted him out of his Thames House cell. They'd invited him to come with them, but there had only been one answer he could give. This was MI5, this was national security. He may have been one of the top ranking detectives in the capital, but if he'd made a break for it—as he'd so desperately wanted to—they'd probably have shot him dead on the spot.

Murdoch was so tired that he wasn't sure if the muscles in his face worked anymore. His eyelids felt as though they were being pushed down, like those of a corpse that somebody was trying to close for the last time. He had to sit forward in his seat again, fists clenched, to stop the world from spinning. The guy to his left, one of Jorgensen's assistants, sat with his face against the window, sobbing gently. He'd been like that since they'd left MI5.

A police motorcycle accelerated past them, its siren squealing, vanishing past the side of the ambulance. *Please let us stop,* Murdoch prayed. *Let something distract them so I can get out of here.* But the convoy continued, blasting through the heavy evening air like a freight train. They were heading out of London, he realized, going northwest. The only place he could think of that lay out this way was Northwood, the military base.

He looked to his side, past Jorgensen's weary face, through the shaded window that turned the sunlight to toffee. He lived close to here, over in Finchley. Right now Alice would be putting John in the bath, maybe feeding him, trying to stay calm for the baby. She'd have called his work, his friends. She'd be desperate. Maybe government agents would already have spoken to her, told her he had been detained, but that would only make her more frantic.

He wished he could put his hand to the glass, somehow beam out a message to her. *It's going to be okay.* He realized he was doing it anyway. *I'll be back soon, I won't let them keep us apart. I promise. Please don't worry.*

It was as he was directing those words out of the car, willing them to fly home, that he heard the squeal of brakes in front and the unraveling of his world began.

"MICK, WHAT THE HELL IS IT DOING?"

Mick Rosen jumped at the sound of his partner's voice. He felt like he was lying on a knife-edge, the slightest movement or sound ready to slice him in two. After so many years as a medic, he thought he'd seen just about everything there was to see, every horror that man was capable of inflicting.

He'd thought wrong.

He glanced at the stretcher that lay in the center of the private ambulance. There were no machines there, no wires or drips. Why would there be? The man that lay on it, a sheet pulled up to his neck, was dead. He had no pulse, his blood wasn't flowing, he stank of rot the way any day-old corpse does in the middle of summer.

Yet his mouth hung open, too wide, a snake's just before it devours its prey. And it was still inhaling that single, unending breath, that hellish wheeze that had already made Mick throw up once that afternoon and was close to making it happen again. He was wearing a biohazard suit so he didn't have a choice but to hold it back. He swallowed a mouthful of bile, groaning without even knowing he was doing it.

Nobody knew for sure what this thing was, but there were rumors. They'd had a priest come in to look at it—not a doctor, not a surgeon but a *priest*. That had spooked Mick more than the corpse itself, that and the fact that he'd heard a few people whispering words like "Antichrist" and "Defiler." It was absurd, ludicrous—until he looked back at the corpse, heard that awful, unending breath.

"What do you mean?" he managed after a moment or two. His partner, sitting next to him in the soundproofed cabin in the back of the ambulance, was Alik Garro. They'd been working together for a couple of years now for MI5, mostly disposing of the bodies of terrorist suspects who had been subjected to overenthusiastic interrogation. They weren't exactly friends, but they got on okay, united by the knowledge that what they were doing was keeping the country safe, was keeping the bad guys out.

"I thought . . ." Alik started. He was staring at the corpse, and most of the color had drained from his face, leaving it ashen behind the plastic of his visor. He shook his head, sitting back. "Nothing. It's nothing."

The ambulance swung around a corner, hard enough to throw Mick against Alik. His seat wobbled, and for a second he thought he was going to end up face-first on the corpse.

Hurry up, he screamed in his head at the driver. They were only going to Northwood, why hadn't they arrived yet? He would give practically anything to get out of this metal coffin. He felt the ambulance slow, pulling left then accelerating again.

"Mick, there it was again!"

Alik was on his feet this time, one of his gloved hands gripping the back door handle. Mick stared at the corpse, those eyes so dead and so alive at the same time. He'd tried to close them, as had Alik, but they kept springing open. There was a darkness in those milky, lifeless pupils, a heavy black weight that seemed to fly back and forth, invisible but unmissable. It was like there was something in there that wanted out.

"Wha—" Mick started, then he saw it himself.

The corpse's mouth was widening. It wasn't *opening*, it was just getting bigger. Mick realized he was on his feet as well, his back pressed against the door of the ambulance. *Open it,* his brain screamed. *Open it and jump, because better to be dead on the freeway than to see this.* But he could no more turn the handle than he could force a word up the constricted passage of his throat.

A tooth dropped from the corpse's gums, vanishing into its throat with a dry click. Another followed, sucked in like it had been vacuumed up. And that noise, that relentless breath, was getting louder, increasing in pitch.

"No," Mick said, the fear like a suit of razor wire beneath his skin. Those gums were crumbling, dissolving into its expanding maw, slowly but inexorably. The dead man's lips, too, were coming apart, breaking into a million particles that defied gravity, circling the chasm of its mouth.

"Jesus, stop the ambulance!" Alik was screaming, the words misting up his visor. He was clawing at the door now, thumping on it, his eyes so wide they didn't look real. "Stop the ambulance! Let us out!"

The ambulance didn't slow, the screams lost in the turbine-howl of the corpse's breath. Its eyes had changed too. That spark of life inside them was brighter, full of rancid glee. Mick reached out and grabbed Alik's arm, holding it tight.

"Where's your radio?" he asked. Alik stared back like he didn't recognize him. "Your radio, Alik?"

Alik didn't reply, and Mick knew he'd lost him. He'd seen

what fear could do to a man. It could strip his mind in seconds and leave him nothing but a collection of broken, unconnected parts. Mick swore, scouring the ambulance for the radio. It was the only way of getting through to the driver.

Don't look at the corpse, his brain told him. He knew that his own mind was on the verge of cracking. He could feel the madness there, like an unscratchable itch right at the base of his brain. *Don't look, Mick.* And yet how could he not? His head seemed to swivel around by itself, his eyes focusing on the nightmare in the middle of the ambulance.

The corpse's face was a whirlwind of particles that circled a throat of utter darkness. That throat wasn't just lightless, it was devoid of *everything*. It was pure, absolute absence. It was still growing too, the flesh of the man's cheeks and nose crumbling into dust, circling that pool like debris around a black hole.

And those eyes. Those dead, all-seeing eyes. They were alive with laughter, a sick delight that seemed to scoop out Mick's insides. He collapsed against the door, the radio forgotten, all things forgotten. Nothing mattered anymore. How could it, when something like this existed?

The ambulance slowed and Mick felt himself being pulled toward the center of it. He managed to grab the door handle, to root himself in place, but Alik wasn't so lucky. His partner slid across the floor without a sound, hitting the end of the stretcher and doubling over it.

That whirlwind breath seemed to double in volume, an inward howl that detonated inside Mick's head, making him clamp his hands to his ears. Alik's face was dissolving into the whirlwind. His eyes were the first to go, melting into sherbet and spiraling down the churning hole. The rest followed, erased like an oil painting drenched in turpentine. Alik's body juddered and shook, suspended off the ground as if by invisible ropes.

There was something else too, something else coming out of Alik. Mick couldn't see it so much as feel it, an energy seeping from his partner, being pulled from every pore, sucked into the corpse.

It was eating Alik's soul.

The Antichrist, Mick thought. *The Defiler, the Beast.* Only somehow he knew that this thing was so much older than anything in the Bible, something ageless, and infinitely evil.

The itch inside his skull expanded, obliterating everything in a single, devastating short circuit. Mick no longer knew he had a wife, he couldn't remember the names of his children. Every second of his past was erased in that one fraction of a second.

The last few flecks of Alik circled the mouth, disappearing. The vortex growled, bigger now, hungrier. It wanted more. Mick could feel it reaching for him, invisible fingers seeking to pull him close, wanting to devour his soul too. But he wouldn't let it have him.

He turned away, opened the door of the speeding ambulance, and stepped into the evening.

A MAN FLEW FROM THE BACK OF THE AMBULANCE into the hood of the car in front, smashing the windshield and rolling over the roof like a rag doll. He dropped under the wheels of the limo in which Murdoch was riding, making it lurch so hard that everyone inside was jolted from their seats. Murdoch's head cracked against the ceiling but he didn't even notice. He watched the other car veer off onto the hard shoulder of the freeway, striking the barrier and cartwheeling into the field beyond.

"What the—" said Murdoch, looking out the rear window as they passed the wreckage, the air behind them already full of smoke. "What the hell are you doing? They need help."

"Convoy doesn't stop until we get to our destination," said the driver. And he said something else but the words tailed off, becoming a gasp as he looked at the ambulance.

"What *is* that?" Dr. Jorgensen said, pressing himself against Murdoch, pointing past the front seats. Murdoch followed his finger, and at first he couldn't work out what he was seeing. Something was happening inside the ambulance, a raging tornado of objects that surged and spiraled through the air. The lights were flashing on and off, the door flapping, making it impossible to see clearly what was going on.

"Get in touch with lead," said the driver. The front-seat passenger—another MI5 agent—put his hand to his ear and began murmuring into his mic.

In the back, nobody spoke. Murdoch squinted, peering into the flickering chaos. A noise had risen up over the thrum of tires on tarmac, a sound that grated down his spine. *It can't be,* he thought, but it was. It was the corpse, that same breath, only louder now. Much louder.

"Pull over," he said again, his voice a hiss. "Do it now."

"No, sir," said the driver. "Our orders—"

"Screw your orders," said Murdoch. "Stop the car *now*."

"I need you to calm down, sir," said the man in the passenger seat, turning. His right hand had strayed under his suit jacket and Murdoch knew what he had holstered there—a government-issue 9mm. It didn't matter. Whatever was happening inside that ambulance was a million times worse than any gun. "Sit back in your seat and do not speak."

Murdoch didn't obey. He reached to his side, past Jorgensen, grabbing the door handle and wrenching hard. It was locked. He tried the other side, the morgue assistant next to him no longer crying, just staring through the windshield making choking noises.

"Sir, if you do not sit back in your seat and calm down then I will be forced to subdue you."

The door didn't budge, and Murdoch sat forward, ready to shout back at the man, ready to take a swing at him if he had to. He never got the chance.

In front, the ambulance exploded—not into fire, but darkness. It seemed to happen in slow motion, a whipcrack of black lightning that buckled the metal walls, opening them like a flower; that lifted the wheels off the road, making the whole vehicle fly. A lightless wave pulsed from the ruined ambulance, so dark that it hurt Murdoch's eyes to look at it. It was as if that patch of existence had been erased, as if substance had been inverted, turned to absence. Through that gap, past that hole in reality, was something so vast, so infinite, so empty that his heart broke the moment he saw it. *That's the real universe,* he understood. *The truth behind the mask. That's all there is, and it's nothing.*

Another blast ripped the ambulance apart, sending pieces of wheel and engine and flesh in every direction—still in slow motion, like time had no power here. Its exhaust javelined backward, punching through the windshield of the car, impaling the driver, not stopping until it had passed right through Jorgensen in the backseat. Murdoch could hear the sizzle of blood on the hot metal, the air suddenly heavy with the stench of cooked meat. Jorgensen's hand gripped his arm, flexing once before falling still.

The car smashed into the center divider, sparks cascading from the doors as it ground to a halt.

The corpse was suspended above the road in a pocket of absolute night. Its mouth was a churning void. Its eyes blazed into the car, right into Murdoch's head.

It lifted its hands, and as it did so another rippling wave of shadow expanded across the freeway. Murdoch saw a motorcycle lifted into the air and pulled into pieces, its rider atomized into a sparkling crimson cloud that was sucked toward the corpse's raging mouth. He saw one of the limos in front peel apart like a kit model, its passengers disintegrating as they were dragged into the chasm. A storm of metal and emptied flesh ground around the living corpse like a tornado, more blinding black lightning firing wildly in the maelstrom.

There was another crack of thunder. Murdoch glanced around to see two young girls on the road, holding each other as a hail of burning embers drifted down around them.

I'm sorry. One of the girls spoke. He couldn't hear her, but he could read the words on her lips. *I can't save you.*

He reached out to them, his fingers pressed to the glass.

Don't be sorry, he thought. *It will devour you too. It will devour us all.*

"Alice," he said, thinking of his wife, of his son, knowing that he would never see them again—not in this life, not in any other.

The corpse gestured again with its fingers and more of the world disappeared beneath a blanket of darkness. Murdoch felt his car lift off the ground, then that shadow reached him and it was as if everyone he knew and loved had died—a grief so heavy, so impossible that it literally pulled him apart. He lifted his hands to his face, seeing his fingers begin to fragment into particles the size of sand grains. They funneled up toward the dead man, his hands vanishing, then his arms, his vision sparking as his brain turned to dust. And it was almost worse that there was no pain, because at least pain would be one final reminder that he had once lived.

But there was only the vast, roiling, infinite, silent darkness.

Then nothing.

THE FURY / *Fursville, 7:31 p.m.*

THEY ALL FELT IT.

Brick was drenched in sweat from toiling in the unforgiving sun, every muscle aching. He laid down the shovel, straightening his back, feeling as if night had fallen suddenly and without warning. Lisa lay beside him, in a patch of sun-drenched grass close to the back fence, covered with a tablecloth. He had carried her out here himself, her deadweight making her a hundred times heavier than she had been before. He hadn't yet looked at her face, because he knew that once he did there could be no more doubt, no more fooling himself that she'd be coming back. He blinked, the sunshine gradually returning. But that chill remained, keeping the gooseflesh on his arms. He picked up the shovel, stepped into her grave, and carried on digging.

CAL AND DAISY FELT IT. They were watching Brick from a distance, her hands wrapped tight around his arm the way she had always clung on to her mum. They turned to each other, both of them feeling that same sudden, crushing sadness, the knowledge that something in the world had gone terribly, irreversibly wrong. It was like animals sensing an earthquake, Cal thought, not knowing why they are scared, just understanding that they have to escape. *It's the Fury,* he realized. *Things are changing.* And even as the words crossed his mind Daisy hugged him tighter. He looked into her pale eyes and saw her voice there. *It's going to get bad, Cal. It's going to get a lot worse.* He gripped her tight, the same way he would grip a float if he was drowning. He didn't ever want to let go.

JADE FELT IT. She sat slumped in the hallway inside the pavilion, a dead man within spitting distance. She felt it as a pressure, one that grated down the corridor and forced itself into her head, blocking her ears like she'd dived too deep into a swimming pool. It sat there, an unwanted guest, making even the sadness seem obsolete, futile. It was so dreadful that she opened her mouth to scream, but she couldn't get the noise out. She sat there, silently howling, knowing that nothing would ever be the same, nothing could ever be *good* again.

CHRIS FELT IT. He stood on the beach, throwing stones into the sea. He watched one hurtle through the hot air, thinking that despite the Fury, despite the shootings, things weren't all that bad—at least the sun was shining. Then, in an instant, it was as if the ocean rose up, a solid wall of darkness that towered over him, that blocked out the light and dragged itself over the world, burying everything in silt and saltwater. He dropped to his knees, fighting to remember how to breathe, blinking reality back to life. But even with the sun on his face again he knew that the darkness was still there. It had been born.

• • •

ADAM FELT IT. He slept deeply in the pavilion foyer. His dreams of horses and fairgrounds were abruptly tainted, like ink dropped in water. Dark, bulging clouds mushroomed outward, their blue-black surface as dense as granite, polluting everything and leaving him alone inside a bottomless cavern. He cried out for the girl, Daisy, but all that existed in the night was him and a shapeless creature of boundless sorrow. His sleeping body shook, but he did not wake.

RILKE FELT IT. She shivered in the candlelit restaurant, still holding the revolver. She'd killed for a reason, because she had to, because they all had a more important job to do and they couldn't let anything stand in their way. But the faces of the man and the girl she had murdered hung before her, ghostlike against the gloom, not speaking, not moving, just watching her. They'd be there forever. They'd be there until she died. And the thought seemed like the worst possible thing she could imagine, until it hit her, a depthless, hopeless wave of utter nothingness. She dropped the gun, clamping her hands to her head, screaming *go away go away go away go away*.

EVEN SCHILLER FELT IT, locked inside the cold casket of his body. He groaned, his body twitching, shedding sparkling flakes of ice on the floor. Rilke shot up, running over to where he lay and collapsing to her knees beside him. She called his name, holding his head, stroking his cheek, waiting for his eyes to open. He moaned again, a nightmare noise, then he lay still. But she knew he'd sensed the same thing as she had, even from deep inside whatever fathomless sleep he was lost in. He understood what was happening.

"You have to get better soon, Schill," Rilke said, brushing

back strands of thin, dark hair from his eyes. "We need you. We all do."

She put her head on his chest, trying to ignore the bone-numbing chill, focusing on the shadow that had pulled itself over her mind, that had pulled itself over everything.

"Because it's here, little brother," she said. "It's here."

SUNDAY

Destroy the seed of evil,
Or it will grow up to be your ruin.
—Aesop

HE WOKE TO THE SENSATION OF NEEDLES IN HIS BACK, moving rapidly up and down his spine. It wasn't painful, it was almost relaxing, until something else began to jab into the flesh of his shoulder.

"Ow!" he said, rolling over, the world a blur. There was a flurry of noise, wings beating and a coarse caw. He blinked hard until he made out a seagull on the ground a few feet away. It stared at him with black-eyed curiosity, skipping closer as if about to begin another attack. Brick grabbed a handful of soil and lobbed it at the bird, watching it waddle clumsily then soar with perfect grace into the burgeoning dawn. "Yeah, you better run," he called after it, and he almost managed a smile before remembering where he was.

The sandy soil was from a mound next to him, a five-foot-five by three-foot outline in the grass. It had taken hours to dig, but only minutes to fill in—he'd desperately swept earth over Lisa's corpse and its checkered tablecloth shroud until no trace of it remained. She had been cold when he'd touched her, stiff. She hadn't felt real. Brick wasn't sure if that had made it easier or harder.

He'd walked onto the twilit beach when he'd finished. There he'd found a starfish, a dead one. He'd placed it on the head of her grave and told himself he was doing it as a mark of respect, so he wouldn't forget. In reality he'd done it because he worried that if he didn't weigh down the grave with something then her body would crawl free in the night. It would come after him. He'd followed the starfish with about a hundred stones.

And then he'd fallen asleep next to her. She had been cold, but the earth had been warm. It had spent the day soaking up the heat, and the touch of it on his skin was almost human. It could have been her lying next to him, keeping the night at bay.

But it wasn't, of course. He'd killed her. He hadn't pulled the trigger, but he hadn't stopped it from happening, and that made him as guilty as Rilke.

Brick struggled to his feet, his whole body aching. The effort made his head spin, a blood rush that caused the morning light to prickle like static. It brought back something else, a feeling he'd had when he was digging, a sensation that something really bad had happened. *It did, you moron,* his brain told him. *Lisa died.* Only it was more than that. He couldn't explain it, just that it had felt as if the entire world had lost someone it loved.

Had he seen something too? A shape amid the chaos? A man whose mouth was a storm and who bled endless darkness onto the world?

He snorted, feeling ridiculous for even thinking it. The shovel was lying on the other side of the mound and he picked it up. The dirt-encrusted wood cut into the blisters on his palm, making him wince.

Rilke. She'd shot Lisa dead. She'd pay for that, she and her comatose brother. She had the gun, but that wouldn't help her, not forever. Sooner or later she'd let her guard down. Brick gripped the handle, sweeping the shovel through the air. The blade caught the amber light of the morning, making him smile. Yeah, she'd pay.

Lisa's grave wouldn't be the last to be dug in Fursville.

DAISY DIDN'T RECOGNIZE THE VOICE, and it was this uncertainty that pulled her from her dream. By the time she'd opened her eyes she'd already forgotten what had been in her head, only that it had been bad, an echo of what she'd felt the previous evening with Cal.

She was lying in the staff room of the pavilion, on a bundle of cushions she had pulled off the stinky, damp sofa. They hadn't been very comfortable, but she'd still slept okay, considering everything that had happened yesterday. She sat up, looking around. Adam was curled up next to her. Chris was bundled in the far corner of the room, his face pressed against the dirty wall. Jade and Cal were gone. Brick had never been there.

Silky yellow light crept in through a crack in the boarded window. It seemed to shine through the ice in her head, and she could see another boy, skeleton-thin. She clambered off her makeshift bed, careful not to disturb Adam, then walked to the door. Her hand was on it before she remembered that there was a dead man outside, down the corridor.

Just don't look and it won't be there.

She opened it and turned left, walking purposefully toward the fire door, speeding up only when she thought she heard Edward Maltby's feet tap-tapping after her, his soft groans as he reached out with bloody fingers. She dived under the chains, squealing, kicking out at the illusion. When she stood, brushing herself down, she realized she wasn't alone.

"And that's Daisy," said Cal. He was talking to the boy she'd just seen in her thoughts and heard in her dream. Another teenager, maybe a year or two older than her. He was very skinny, his T-shirt fluttering like a sail on a mast. He smiled gently from beneath a mop of curly hair, then stretched out a hand. Daisy noticed that it had been wrapped with cloth, like a white boxing glove tinged with pink. He seemed to remember the bandage and slapped his hand to his side.

"Sorry," he said. "Hi."

"Marcus," said Daisy, plucking his name from her head. The boy frowned, looking at Cal for an explanation. Cal just shrugged.

"I told you things were weird here," he said. "Marcus saw the message we posted."

"Would have come anyway," said the boy. "You guys got this psychic brain pull thing going on. Couldn't have stayed away if I'd wanted to."

"Would you like some food?" Daisy asked.

As soon as she said it she remembered Rilke, and the fact that the girl had locked herself in the restaurant with all their supplies. Luckily, Marcus shook his head.

"Been in the old car showroom, over the road," he said. "Found a box of something that used to be crunchy in the office. Got there this morning, 'bout three or four, maybe. Didn't want to come over until I knew who was about, even though it felt safe, y'know?" He tapped his temple then paused, squinting at the brightening horizon over Daisy's shoulder. "Wasn't just me. There were four of us, till we got to a place called King's Lynn."

He looked at his hand, and more ice cubes bobbled to the surface of Daisy's head. She saw two girls and an older boy, floundering in a sea of raking fingers and blunt teeth and bulging eyes.

Their screams filled her mind, and for a terrible instant pain flared all over her, burning. She gasped like she'd fallen into a frozen pond, forcing the ice cubes down where she couldn't feel them anymore.

"We got ambushed trying to steal some gas," he went on, the words catching in his throat. "I had to leave them. I—They would have killed me too." He held up his bandaged hand like a half-hearted excuse. "Grabbed a bike and cycled the rest of the way. Could do with a rest, yeah?"

"You want to show him to the staff room?" asked Cal. Daisy shook her head. She didn't want to go back inside, back to where the dead man lay. Better to stay in the sunshine where ghosts couldn't get you. Cal gestured at the fire door and he and Marcus ducked under the chain, vanishing into the gloom.

Daisy looked left, toward the front of the park. She didn't want to go that way either. That way was the tail of the night, still sweeping over the land. That way was whatever she'd seen in her head last night. She set off to her right. It was brighter here, the sun already creeping over the fence, and she could hear the soft whisper of the waves. She slowed when she turned the corner, seeing the mound of soil that lay halfway across the patch of over-grown grass next to the miniature golf. She and Cal had watched Brick for what seemed like an eternity last night. He'd still been digging when they'd gone inside. The poor thing.

She approached the grave, her thoughts turning to her own parents. Would they be underground now? She wiped tears away furiously, but they kept coming.

She hurried away. There was a banging noise coming from somewhere nearby, and when she walked down the back of Furs-ville she realized it was coming from one of the small metal sheds against the fence. She passed UTILITY then SANITATION then DANGER: DO NOT ENTER before coming to an open door marked CARETAKER. She peeked around it to see Brick inside, rummaging through piles of junk.

"What are you doing?" she asked. He glanced at her, then went back to whatever the answer was, throwing sheets of corrugated iron against the wall of the shed. The clatter was deafening. Eventually he reached down and grabbed something, holding it up.

"Bingo," he said, tripping out of the shed into the light. He held up a hammer that was so rusted it looked like it had been dipped in bright orange gunk. It didn't have a handle anymore, just a short metal nubbin. He set off back the way Daisy had just walked. He didn't even look at the grave as he passed it, using the little hammer to hack through the jungle of the mini-golf course. Daisy followed, careful not to get scratched by the thorns that pinged back after him.

When she caught up she saw that he was hammering a big nail into the fence. It was awkward because he couldn't really get any strength behind it, but he was taking his time and making sure he hit the nail squarely on the head. Gradually, millimeter by millimeter, it disappeared into the soft wood.

"This bit was loose," Brick said, running his thumb over the sunken nail. "Whole fence could open up. No good if we want to keep the ferals out."

He pulled another nail from the pocket of his jeans.

"I'm sorry about Lisa," Daisy spluttered, the words out of her mouth before she could stop them. Brick tensed up, studying the nail in his hand as if it had the answer to everything written on it. Daisy stood there, hoping he wouldn't be mad. After a moment or two he looked at her through red-rimmed, exhausted eyes. He nodded, and she understood that it was a thank-you. He placed the nail against the flapping fence panel and began to hammer again.

"There's another boy here," she said. He paused, then carried on. "He's very thin. He said there were others but . . . but they didn't make it."

He finished the nail and started on a third. Daisy hopped from one foot to the other. She was hungry, thirsty too. She didn't want to ask Brick about food, though. She didn't want to give him any reason to go inside and see Rilke. Only bad things could come from that. But there was another matter she wanted to talk to him about.

"Brick," she started, talking over the hammer blows. "Did you feel it too? Yesterday."

He didn't even pause this time, tapping away at the nail until it vanished. He gave the fence a shake, the panel still flapping at the bottom, before reaching into his pocket again and squatting down.

"It was really horrible," she said. "Just this . . . a kind of feeling, like being numb, but being really sad too." He still didn't reply. Daisy chewed her thumbnail, wishing she was better at finding the right words. "It was like something had gone wrong with . . . with Life."

Tap. Tap. Tap. Brick hammered away, the nail going in at an angle. Daisy waited a moment more then turned to go. She didn't really need him to answer. She could see it in his head, in his thoughts.

She glanced back at Brick. He was looking at her, and as their eyes met an understanding clicked home.

This storm, this whirlwind, this bad thing, it wasn't a

something, it was a *nothing*. It was the absence of something, and that absence was spreading—deleting, erasing, canceling everything it touched. That's why it felt so sad, so horrible, because this thing was the very opposite of life, the opposite of death too, it was the opposite of everything.

Antimatter, the word that floated to the top of her thoughts, belonged to Brick, not her; she didn't even know what it meant. She knew that he was thinking the same thing, though. They both knew what it wanted, this *other*. It wanted to take everything and turn it into nothing, to devour it, to wipe it from existence.

And when it was done, reality would be nothing but a hole in time.

RILKE / *Fursville, 8:42 a.m.*

"**Please, Rilke, I just need to talk to you.**"

Rilke stood on the other side of the restaurant door listening to Cal rant and rave. He'd been out there for a while now, pacing back and forth like a wolf, first pleading, then threatening, then fuming.

"Rilke, we need our food, our drinks. It's not fair, that's *our stuff.*"

He banged on the door, flakes of ice drifting loose. Rilke's silent laugh came out as little puffs of breath. She clutched the gun, her hand so numb from the cold that she couldn't feel it, only its weight.

"Open the door!" Cal yelled. "Seriously, I'm getting really

pissed off. Are you gonna shoot us all? Tell me what you want or I swear to God I'm gonna break this door down and give you a slap, girl or no girl."

Rilke uttered a brittle chuckle that seemed colder than the breeze.

"I only want one thing," she said. "I want to talk to Daisy."

Cal protested, but after a while he gave up. She listened to him retreat down the stairs, his curses eventually fading into the immense quiet of the pavilion. She pressed her forehead against the frozen wood of the doors, wondering if he would give her what she had asked for.

He will. He has to if he wants to eat.

She straightened and walked over to the nearest table, laying the gun down beside a flickering candle.

The two people she had killed, the two *humans*, they hadn't deserved to live. None of them did. That's why she was here, why she had been chosen. And very soon she'd have weapons that would make this gun look like a plastic toy. Wasn't that what she'd felt last night? The knowledge that there was something out there, something terrible and yet wonderful. A force of pure, cleansing power.

Schiller lay in his pocket of ice, his body still radiating cold like an inverse sun. He hadn't so much as twitched since the previous evening, but she knew he wouldn't stay like that forever. She wasn't sure how she knew, she just did. He wasn't dying, he was changing, like a caterpillar in a cocoon.

"But into what, Schill?" she whispered. "What are you becoming?"

Daisy had the answers. The little girl didn't realize it, but they were locked away somewhere inside that pretty little head of hers. She just needed a bit of encouragement to get them out.

The candle was struggling, as if the darkness had weight, snuffing out the solitary flame. Rilke took another one from the pile she'd collected, lighting it from the first and planting it in a socket of melted wax. It too began to stutter against the heavy gloom. She smiled at the blatant metaphor. *We few are the flames,* she thought to herself, mesmerized by the dancing colors. *We are the light in the darkness.*

And what could the darkness be, other than humanity? This crushing, heaving mass of people who had no legitimate right to life. How many souls lived on earth now? Six billion? Seven? All of them like insects, crawling around on their hands and knees or slaughtering one another in pursuit of scraps. They were ignorant, they were cruel, they were the night that smothered the day. They did not deserve their existence.

That's why all this was happening. That's why she and Schiller had been attacked—why they'd *all* been attacked. The people sensed something different in them, something special. And they hated it, because it was *better* than them.

And what about the thing she had sensed last night? That wave of utter nothingness, that awful knowledge that what lay beneath the skin of the world was an infinite abyss of absence. She wasn't sure, but this creature, this force—whatever it was— might be here to show them the way. As dark as its image had been, it might be the light they needed to follow. Why else would she have seen it?

Footsteps, more than one set. Rilke cocked her head, feeling Daisy's presence outside even before Cal's voice came through the doors.

"She's here," he said. "She says she'll talk to you, but only if you let us have some food."

Rilke walked to the doors, then doubled back and picked up the gun. Cal was too pathetic to try anything, she was pretty sure about that, but she couldn't afford to take any chances, not when the truth was so close. She slid back the lock, then pulled open the door with her free hand. Daisy stood there, squinting. Cal was beside her.

"You don't have to go in," he said. "Whatever she has to say, she can say it right here."

"It's okay," said Daisy. "She isn't going to hurt me."

Daisy gave Cal a hug, then walked into the restaurant. Cal watched her go, then glared at Rilke.

"You'd better not," he hissed. "You'd better not lay a finger on her. I'll be right here, Rilke, I'm not going anywhere."

Rilke laughed at him and let the door swing shut in his face.

DAISY / *Fursville, 9:03 a.m.*

DAISY WALKED TO THE TABLE WITH THE CANDLES and sat down, putting her trembling hands between her knees so that Rilke wouldn't notice she was scared. She had lied to Cal, she didn't know if Rilke was going to hurt her or not. But she had to do something to get some food or they'd all starve. She glanced around as innocently as she could, but she couldn't see the shopping bags anywhere.

"I've got them somewhere safe," said Rilke, her eyes gleaming. She walked over, putting the gun down in the middle of the table before sitting opposite Daisy. Her face had the same crazy look as last night. She was dangerous. "Just until we've had a little talk."

"About what?" said Daisy, shivering. It was colder than ever in here, Schiller entombed in ice on the sofa.

"You *know* what," said Rilke, planting her elbows and stretching her hands across the table. The way her forearms uncurled made Daisy think of a praying mantis. She didn't offer her own hands. "About this, about everything."

"But I don't know anything," said Daisy. Where would the food be? In a corner somewhere. Or under a table.

"I think you do," said Rilke, her face splitting into a grin, her eyes burning. "I think it's all there, in your head, you just don't know how to read it."

Daisy didn't answer. Maybe Rilke was right. There had been all kinds of things happening in her brain that she couldn't make any sense of. The ice cubes, rattling and clinking around, showing her things she couldn't possibly know. They were doing it right now, but they were moving too fast, the way they seemed to do when she was frightened.

"I don't want you to be scared of me, Daisy," said Rilke, gentler now. "We're the same, you and I."

Except I don't murder people, Daisy thought but didn't say.

"I had no choice," Rilke went on. "You know how dangerous the ferals are. You can't have forgotten what happened to you already?"

Daisy shook her head, thinking of the ambulance man and his horse's teeth.

"Things are changing, Daisy. The world is changing. You felt it too, didn't you? Yesterday evening. All I want is to know what it was. Because I think something is trying to tell us what to do. It's trying to guide us, only we don't know how to listen."

That made a strange kind of sense. It did feel a bit like when she was at school sometimes and she didn't really understand what the teacher was saying.

Rilke stretched her hands out a bit farther, opening them to Daisy.

"I know things have been really bad. I've lost people too, I'm worried I'm going to lose my brother. The whole world has turned against us; we have to be there for each other. We're different now, different from the rest of them, all of us—me, you, Schill, Cal, Brick, and the others. We're a family, we have to trust each other."

Daisy liked the idea of a family. Cal already felt like her brother. In fact it was as if she'd been friends with all of them forever, even the new boy, Marcus, who, she knew without being told, liked loud music and hated football—she hoped Cal wouldn't mind this last fact. Rilke too was not a stranger. She never had been. She relaxed a little, her hands creeping toward Rilke's.

"Do you trust me?" Rilke asked. Daisy chewed her lip, then nodded. Rilke's smile widened even farther, revealing a row of perfect, small teeth. "Then take my hands."

This time, Daisy didn't hesitate. She threaded her fingers through Rilke's, the older girl's skin as cold as marble. Rilke held her tight, but not so hard that it was painful. The contact felt nice. She smiled back at her, forgetting why she'd been so worried before.

"You're a special girl, Daisy," said Rilke, her voice barely louder than the flutter of the candles. "You can do amazing things. I think we all can. Not yet, maybe, but soon. I think we all have a gift."

"What kind of gift?" Daisy asked.

"Think about it, Daisy. Why would the whole world turn against us? Why would they try to kill us?"

"Because they hate us, I suppose," Daisy replied, shrugging. Rilke shook her head.

"*Think*: Why would they hate us? What would make them behave that way?"

Daisy frowned, wishing that Rilke would just tell her. She hated being asked questions that she didn't know the answers to. Then, out of nowhere, she said: "Because they're *scared* of us."

Rilke nodded, obviously delighted, and Daisy felt some of the stress drain from her chest. It made a certain kind of sense, she realized. People did do silly things when they were really scared. Even so, they didn't usually go feral and start trying to pull your arms and legs and head off. They—

Don't they? said Rilke, interrupting her thoughts, and Daisy couldn't tell whether the other girl had spoken or not. "It's happened before, throughout history. The ones that are different, who rise above just being human. People get scared of them, they kill them. What if they are supposed to be scared of us, Daisy? What if they're *right* to be scared of us?"

"Why?" Daisy said, struggling. Rilke eased her grip, but she didn't let go.

"Don't be frightened. I'm not going to hurt you. I could never hurt you. Don't you see? Don't you remember that feeling from yesterday?"

Daisy shivered just thinking about it.

"It's a sign," Rilke said. "A sign that everything is going to change."

"But why?" Daisy asked, feeling her throat tighten. "People will get hurt, I don't want that. People are nice."

"Are they, Daisy?" Rilke said. "Think about it, *really* think about it."

She didn't want to but she did—thought of the times she'd been bullied, back in her old school when she'd had eczema on her arms and everyone had called her names; the little boy in her town who'd been murdered by the creep who'd delivered leaflets, whose head had never been found; all the riots on TV, people beating each other up for stupid things they didn't even need; and even her own mum, when the cancer had been bad, when it had made her say things that were really cruel. There was another memory too, but this one was Rilke's, a man with rough fingers and long, dirty nails and breath that smelled of coffee and alcohol, his huge face looming in. Daisy squirmed, pushing the thoughts away, so sick of having other people's hate and fear and confusion inside her head, ready to scream, *Leave me alone!*

"No," she said instead, choking on the word. "People are good, Rilke. They're nice, most of them. I don't want things to change."

"It's too late. I'm sorry, Daisy, but it is. What's happening to the world . . . it has already begun."

"But what *is* happening?" Daisy asked, catching her breath. Rilke squeezed her hands, pulling them closer to her.

"*We* are," she said. "We're happening. Don't you see? Isn't it clear what we have to do? We've been sent here to make things different. To clean things up. Look inside your head, Daisy, and tell me I'm wrong."

She didn't want to, not again. If she peered into those ice cubes then who knew what she might see? It would be bad, and there would be fire.

"Please, Daisy," Rilke said. "I can't do this without you. I need you, Schiller needs you, we all do. Just see for yourself."

Daisy glanced again at the boy in the corner. He would be so hungry now, and thirsty. He might die if they couldn't wake him up. As horrible as it might be, what if she could help? She tightened her grip on Rilke's hands, grateful at least that she wasn't on her own. Then she closed her eyes and let the images float to the surface . . .

IT WAS LIKE TAKING OFF A BIG COAT in the middle of winter, one that was drenched with snow and water and weighed a ton. She became as light as the dust that rose in the candlelight, free of everything and anything that could hold her down.

Even with her eyes closed she could see the others as if they were all standing in the same room. Only they weren't, they were scattered over the park—Adam and Chris and the new boy, Marcus, still sleeping (they were sharing a dream, she realized, one involving tortoises), Jade sitting on the log flume thinking about the friend who had tried to kill her, Brick still mending the fence, his thoughts full of revenge, and Cal just outside the restaurant door, his ear against it, shivering as he tried to work out what was happening.

There were loads more, boys and girls she didn't yet know but who she seemed to recognize. They were everywhere, maybe twenty of them, more even, and they were all flowing this way. The sight of them—although it wasn't quite sight, it was more than that, a *vision*—was dizzying, but it was comforting. These were members of her family. They were all welcome.

The same feeling from yesterday was there too, and this was certainly not welcome. It tainted everything, the way the world turns the color of old bruises when a storm is about to start, and it made her feel like crying even though it had been so good to soar through her thoughts. She wanted to be away from this thing, whatever it was, and she fought to claw her way back into her body.

It's okay, nothing can hurt us here. The voice was Rilke's, emanating from everywhere. *Just a little longer, Daisy. Just so we can see it.*

Why did she want to see it? It was horrid. But Rilke was right, it couldn't hurt them. Even though it felt like she was a million miles away in a million different places she knew she was still inside the restaurant in the little park by the sea. She focused on the dark cloud, trying to work out what it was and why it felt so unkind.

A picture began to emerge: a wide road with fields on either side of it. There were several big black cars there, and men in suits holding guns. Some of those men were screaming, others were pointing at . . .

What *was* that?

It was a man, but he was floating inside a whirlwind of chaos, and his mouth . . . Daisy groaned. *It isn't real, it isn't real,* she told herself. But it was; this was the thing they had all sensed last night. She tried to close her eyes but the pictures were in her head, the sounds coming from inside her. She could smell blood, and burning flesh, and smoke, she could taste the thick, oily air on her tongue. None of it mattered, though, because the man in the storm had left her empty. There was nothing left of her. She had never, ever felt this alone.

A blast of light, like an old-fashioned photographer's flash, then a raging fire bit into her skin, making her scream. It was as if the floor had given way, her stomach lurching up into her throat. She opened her eyes and the air was full of flames, flickering blue and yellow and red. Just as quickly they were extinguished, leaving the same wide road as before, only this time it was completely and utterly real. Rilke was there, her mouth open in a rictus of shock, her hair billowing around her shoulders. Both of them were standing now, their hands linked together, the wind roaring past them like a train. Hundreds of bright embers had been caught up in the gale, all being pulled in the same direction.

Daisy watched them go, seeing them dragged toward the man in the storm. He was raised over the ground like he'd been hanged, his eyes blazing black light, his face like a drain, sucking in clouds of darkness. The noise was terrible, an inward howl like someone with asthma taking their last, desperate breath. It went on forever. All around him the air was in upheaval, like a tornado. *He's a sorcerer,* she had time to think. *Or something worse.*

One of the cars was in the air, and Daisy looked through the windows to see five men inside, all of them screaming. One—the man sitting in the middle of the backseat—glanced at her, and she could read the horror in his bulging eyes, his bared teeth.

"I'm sorry," she said to him. "I can't help you." And somewhere in the chaos she realized that although she was here, actually *here* on this road, these events had already happened. She could almost hear the vast, groaning weight of broken time.

The man in the storm hurled out another whipcrack of black lightning, more of the world disintegrating. The car exploded into a million pieces, the bodies inside turning into sand and spinning into the corpse's mouth.

Daisy screamed, even her breath stolen by the storm. The man's lifeless eyes rolled toward her, the sensation like she'd been punched in the gut. And it knew who she was, because the raging storm seemed to call out her name—only, it *wasn't* her name. It wasn't even a word. The dead man flexed his fingers and Daisy felt herself rise from the ground. She gripped Rilke with everything she had, both of them swept up toward the vortex. And she knew that if they didn't get away, get away *right now*, then they'd be pulled inside it, that they would become nothing.

Even Rilke seemed to understand this.

Daisy screwed her eyes shut and suddenly she was falling again, the sensation so real that her whole body flailed. Another flash, more flames. She lurched backward, the chair spilling over behind her, making her topple. She scrabbled on the cold ground, expecting to see the storm man there, ready to suck her up. But there was just the restaurant and a blizzard of glowing embers that drifted lazily to the ground.

DAISY WAITED FOR THE REAL WORLD to feel solid again before sitting up. Rilke sat on the other side of the table, wearing that same lunatic grin. She looked at Daisy, then she started to laugh.

"I told you," she said. "I told you that things were about to change."

Daisy got to her feet, half running, half tripping toward the doors, no longer caring about the food. She flew into them, fumbling for the lock, spilling out into Cal's arms. He held her tight in the warm glow from the foyer, stroking her hair as the tears came.

"What happened? What did she do to you?"

Daisy clung to him, hearing the sound of footsteps then the crunch of the doors closing behind her, the snap of the lock.

"Rilke, what did you do? Daisy, look at me."

She tilted back her head and he ran his fingers over her cheek. They came away covered in fine red sand.

"What is this?" he asked, and there were tears in his eyes too. "Tell me."

Daisy hugged him again, his shirt soon stained red with powdered blood. It wasn't hers, though. It wasn't Rilke's either. No, it belonged to a man whose body had disintegrated miles and miles from here, in another place and time, who had been dragged into the vortex. He had been real, it had all been real.

And so had the man in the storm.

CAL / *Fursville, 10:23 a.m.*

CAL LUGGED THE HEAVY PAN OF WATER out the kitchen door, careful not to trip over the dead Edward Maltby, who still lay there covered by a tablecloth. Steam rose from the water that slopped inside it, welcome against his face. He'd warmed it on one of the industrial gas burners, which, incredibly, still worked. Chris was standing down the corridor, outside the bathrooms.

"Want me to take that for you?" he asked. Cal shook his head, even though his arms were trembling with the weight of the pan. He pushed into the left-hand bathroom, laying the pan down beside the small shower unit that sat beside the single cubicle. Then he ducked into the staff room next door. Daisy was sitting on the sofa, wrapped in Jade's arms. The other girl had wiped most of the weird red sand from Daisy's face but it was still stained pink, like she was sunburned.

"Sorry it took so long," Cal said as Chris walked in after him. "Took ages to heat up."

"Thanks," said Jade. Daisy glanced up, but she was looking at something far beyond Cal, something distant. He smiled at her, and she imitated him robotically. She hadn't said any more about what Rilke had done to her. She hadn't said much of anything at all since coming out of the restaurant.

"Come on, Daisy," said Jade, gently tugging on her hand and easing her from the sofa. "Let's get you cleaned up."

Cal waited until they'd walked from the room before turning to Chris.

"Brick?" he asked.

"Won't come, says he's fixing up the fence. That guy . . ." He scowled, but he didn't finish. Cal was glad. Brick was a douche, but he *had* just seen his girlfriend get murdered. Cal walked past the sleeping figure of Adam and over to Marcus, shaking him gently. The new kid snorted, but it took another couple of attempts before his eyes opened. He flinched when he saw Cal, struggling inside his cocoon of tablecloths before remembering where he was and relaxing.

"Sorry," said Cal. "I didn't want to wake you, but we need to know about Soapy's."

"The car place?" Marcus said, groaning as he sat up. "What about it?"

"Is there more food over there?"

He wiped the sleep from his eyes.

"Um . . . yeah, I think so. Not much, mind, a few cans, a couple of boxes of cereal maybe, that's what I had. Thought you had stuff here?"

"Long story," said Cal. "We don't. You up for a return trip?"

"Over the road?" said Marcus. "Sure, just gimme a minute, yeah?"

"Meet us outside," said Cal, standing. He turned to Chris. "We should take weapons, just in case."

Cal walked out into the corridor and through the fire door, blinking against the glaring sunshine. There wasn't a single cloud up there, the sky a vast, perfect blue. Any other weekend he'd be heading up to the park with his mates, or into town to sit outside the library, maybe even hopping the school fence to use the pitches for a kickaround. It seemed so long ago. He was already forgetting what they looked like, all of them except Georgia. But even when he thought of her he could only see her eyes, the rest of her face hidden behind a book.

What's the point? Why bother trying to find food, trying to survive, when everything you had is gone?

He sighed as Chris walked up to him, holding a couple of rotting wooden stakes.

"All I could find."

"Then let's hope we won't need to use them," said Cal.

Marcus appeared through the fire doors, rubbing the sleep from his eyes.

"Ready?" Cal asked.

Marcus nodded.

"Then lead the way."

BRICK / *Fursville, 11:02 a.m.*

HALF AN HOUR AFTER CAL AND THE TWO NEW BOYS had scuttled into the car showroom, like roaches, Brick watched them leave it. He was perched on his lookout post above the main gates. The world looked different from up here, like he'd literally risen above it, like he could just watch life go by and no longer be a part of it. Up here he was halfway to the sun, halfway to oblivion. It felt good.

It was bloody uncomfortable, though. He shuffled, holding on to the big plastic exclamation mark of FURSVILLE! to stop himself toppling off. It was only about two stories or so to the ground, but he'd probably still snap a leg or an arm or maybe a vertebra. Cal and the guys disappeared into the hedge in completely the wrong place, and he could hear them rustling about in there, whispering urgently, trying to find the opening in the fence.

They hadn't found much food, that was pretty clear. It didn't bother Brick too much. They had water and that was the main thing. They'd think of something.

He took a deep breath of salted air then swung off the top of the pillar onto the small access platform that ran beneath the park banner. It creaked under his weight but the rusted bolts held fast in the worn brick. When he'd been rooting around in the caretaker's shed he'd found a can of paint and a couple of brushes that had seen better days. The paint was black, for ironwork, but it would do the job.

He walked carefully down the ledge, stopping at the giant green "S." Using the handle to pop open the can, he gave the gloopy liquid inside a stir and slapped the dripping brush against the plastic. A few big strokes did the trick, and he stood back to admire his handiwork.

FURYVILLE.

He started back, then changed his mind and edged all the way to the end of the platform where a big, goofy animal smiled down at the world. It was another squirrel, the park mascot.

"Don't know what you're grinning at," Brick said, dunking the brush again and giving the creature a drooping, unhappy line for its mouth. He added two giant X's for its eyes, with sweeping angry brows—the same picture he'd drawn back in the restaurant when Cal and Daisy had first arrived. "Not so happy now, are you?"

He left the paint there, wiping his hands down his jeans. The fumes were making him light-headed, and he retreated to the ladder, clambering carefully back to solid ground. He could hear laughter from nearby and he trudged toward it, curious.

Daisy, Jade, and Adam were sitting on the carousel. Daisy was the one who was giggling, the sound like birdsong. She was pretending to ride her horse, as were the other two, like they were racing. Cal, Chris, and the new one were standing beside them, holding whatever they'd gotten from Soapy's and grinning as they watched the race. Brick turned to go. It was better for everyone if he wasn't around at the moment. He'd only taken a couple of steps, however, before Daisy called out his name.

He looked back to see her waving at him. Her face was spotless and glowing and seemed too tiny to hold that giant smile. She looked like an angel. The others glanced over as well, Cal holding up a hand. Brick hovered for a second, unsure, then swallowed his protests and joined them.

"We're having a race," said Daisy, jiggling up and down and kicking her legs. Adam was shaking an invisible pair of reins so hard he was in danger of falling off. Jade was going along with it, her head down and butt up like a jockey. None of their horses was actually moving, of course, although the whole carousel was rattling alarmingly.

"Yeah?" he said. "Who's winning?"

"We're all winning," Daisy said.

Brick considered telling her the definition of "race" then thought better of it. He turned to Cal.

"Any luck?"

"What you see is what you get," Cal said, holding out a box of cereal. "It's these and some dog biscuits, I'm afraid."

"We can feed the dog biscuits to the horses!" exclaimed Daisy, breathless. "They'll need something after all this running."

"That's a deal," said Cal. "Biscuits for the horses, Weetabix for the jockeys."

"Think I'd rather be a horse," said Chris. "Weetabix taste like soggy turds."

The new boy, a skinny runt of a kid, waved a bandaged hand.

"I'm Marcus."

"Brick."

"Brick? Kind of a name is that?"

"Because I'm built like a brick outhouse, obviously," he said. Marcus laughed.

"No you're not, you're almost as skinny as I am."

"Bollocks," said Brick, but the new kid's good humor was kind of contagious. He stuck his middle finger up at him, doing his best to scowl. "Welcome to Furyville anyway."

"*Fury*-ville?" said Cal. Brick held up his paint-stained hands but he couldn't be bothered to explain. The others looked at him, perplexed, but nobody pressed it. Brick turned back to the carousel, the three people there even more animated than before.

"Come on, Angie, we're nearly there!" cried Daisy. "Adam, you have to talk to your horse to make it feel good."

The little boy shook his head, glancing nervously at his audience but still tugging on those imaginary reins.

"You have to talk to it, Jade," Daisy screamed. "Remember it's called Wonky-Butt the Wonder Horse!"

"It's called Samson," Jade called back. "*You're* called Wonky-Butt."

The three of them rode hard, their horses wild-eyed and nostril-flared, so real despite the fact they were obviously plastic. And for an instant Brick was tearing over the ground, the wind rushing past his ears, the bulk of the animal beneath him—the sensation of movement so powerful that he was gripped by vertigo. He closed his eyes, staggering, thinking *That's what she's seeing, that's what's going through Daisy's head*. And it was so good to be moving. Then, just like that, the moment passed. He opened his eyes, grateful that nobody was watching him.

"So, anybody want one of these?" Cal asked, rummaging in the cereal box. "They're out of date, but . . ." He opened the bag and pulled out one of the blocks, sniffing it cautiously and shrugging. "I don't think they're too bad."

Cal nibbled the Weetabix. He pulled a face as he swallowed, then took a bigger bite.

"Gross," he said through a mouthful of mush. "But it's better than nothing."

He handed one to Chris, then another to Marcus. Brick shook his head when he was offered, then took one anyway. He didn't know when he'd get to eat again. He bit off half of it in one go, the biscuit like cardboard. It took him an age of chewing before it was small enough to force down his throat. Cal was up on the carousel handing out Weetabix to Daisy and the others.

"You don't think they'll be poisonous, do you?" asked Daisy, scrunching up her nose.

"Yeah," said Brick. "Eat them and you turn into a feral."

Daisy scowled at him, and as if to prove him wrong she nibbled at the biscuit.

"Nah," said Marcus, his mouth full. "This whole thing's got nothing to do with food. It's like . . . like possession, y'know?"

"Like *what*?" asked Brick.

"Possession. Demonic possession." Marcus coughed self-consciously, all eyes on him. "I don't know, was just a thought. 'Cause the, what do you call them, ferals? The ferals act like they're possessed, like they've got demons in them or something. You must have seen films like that."

Brick spat out a humorless laugh.

"Least I'm trying to think of things," Marcus said with a gangly shrug. Daisy was looking at him nervously, and Cal must have noticed this too because he patted her horse.

"You're falling behind, Dais," he said, and she started bouncing again. Adam was imitating her, and at least the little kid was kind of smiling. Jade was climbing down from her faded saddle. She looked exhausted.

"No, Jade!" Daisy yelled. "Not until the race is over."

"It's a relay," the other girl said. "I'm passing the baton. Who wants it?"

"Brick does," Daisy said. "Let him have a go."

"Uh-uh," he said, backing away. "No chance, give it to someone else."

"It's yours, Brick," said Jade, hopping down from the carousel and approaching him. "Come and get it."

She broke into a run, grinning, and a wild excitement broke in Brick's chest, one that made him swirl around and start to run too. He tripped, his arms wheeling, and Jade slapped him on the back.

"It! Brick's it!"

And before he even knew what he was doing he was tearing after Cal, the other boy kicking up dust as he spun out of the way, too fast to catch. Brick changed direction, darting after Chris, the bigger boy wobbling as he bolted.

"No fair, you can't get me, I'm big-boned!"

Brick tagged him, spinning off in a different direction as Chris jumped onto the carousel and chased Daisy and Adam from their horses. They ran in circles around the central joist, everyone overcome with laughter. Even Brick, sprinting as Daisy gave chase, laughing so hard he couldn't run straight, tears streaming, the wind roaring in his ears just like before, so good to be moving, moving, always moving.

RILKE / *Furyville, 12:43 p.m.*

EVEN THOUGH SHE COULDN'T SEE THEM, Rilke knew what they were doing.

She could feel it, a warmth that crept through the chilled air of the restaurant, a light that robbed the shadows of their strength. They were letting themselves laugh, they were letting themselves forget.

And it was *wrong*.

She was so cold now that she could no longer feel anything. Even the chills had subsided, her body too frozen to shake. There was no light to see her skin by, but she knew it would be the color of ivory, maybe even gunmetal blue, like the time she'd been locked out of the house for three hours in the middle of a blizzard. She could feel the dusting of ice on her but it no longer burned. She was beyond pain.

Schiller lay where he had been since they arrived, his breathing as steady and as slow and as constant as the ocean outside. He emanated the winter wind, and it was because of this that Rilke wasn't scared of it. Why would she be frightened of her brother? He had never hurt her, he idolized her.

More to the point, why should she be frightened of what he was *becoming*? If they had been chosen for a reason then surely they wouldn't be harmed in the process.

Rilke pulled her legs against her chest. The last candle she had lit had gone out a while ago—exactly how long she had no idea—and she couldn't quite make herself get up to light another. There were clothes strewn around the room, mainly Cal's. She wouldn't wear any extra layers, though. Whatever was doing this to them, maybe it was *testing* them. She didn't want to look weak.

Unlike the others. Their weakness rode into her head on a wave of light and warmth, nauseatingly pathetic. The world was changing, something incredible was happening, and yet all they could do for the past hour or more was run around outside like children, laughing. They had no idea, they had no respect for what they had become. And they would pay for it, they would be punished.

Her eyes were sore and she tried to blink, but her skin was too cold and her eyelids wouldn't obey. This didn't matter either. She got the feeling that soon she wouldn't need them. She wouldn't need any part of her body. She would never feel the cold again. Neither would Schiller, when he broke out of his icy chrysalis. That's why she had brought him in here rather than leave him out in the sun to thaw. It had all been part of his test, and surely he had passed.

She sat and she shivered and she thought. What had happened, when Daisy had been in the room? Rilke remembered the creature they had witnessed. It had towered over the world, a vortex of strength. It had been terrifying, yes, the same way death was terrifying. Because it was something pure, something ultimate. It was a force of good not because of any artificial sense of morality, but because it would strip away everything ugly, the tainted, the impure, the rotten, the broken. It promised oblivion, a beautiful, flawless nothing into which all the world would fall.

And she had been chosen to help it.

Are you sure? something inside her asked, a voice frozen in the core of her mind. *Are you really sure, Rilke? Because it doesn't seem right.*

But it *was* right. How could there be any other explanation? The human race had turned against her and Schiller, and the rest of them too. It had hunted them down the same way villagers hunt down a lion or a wolf that has been feeding on their livestock. The human race had turned on them because it was scared. *And it should be,* she thought, trying to work her frozen face into a smile. *It should be terrified.*

It had run its course, humankind. That much was clear. It had *always* been clear. Rilke despised church, and yet there had been a truth in the stories she heard while sitting on those cushionless pews. Warnings that humanity's place here was not to be taken for granted, and stories of a terrible vengeance that could be wreaked upon those who did. It had happened before, and now it would happen again—a tide of fire and wind and blood that would wipe the world clean.

And had they learned? No. Every day war and famine and pestilence and disease; every day murder and greed and fear and stupidity. Worse things too, things that had happened to her that she never, ever let herself think about. Yes, every day the human race became sicker, and this was the cure. Just like the stories.

Yet this thing, this man in a storm that she had seen, was older than anything written in the Bible. It was as old as time.

There were still so many questions, but Rilke had faith that answers would come in time. For now, she knew enough. Something had called on her and her brother to try to make the world right. Something had called upon them both to fight. They had all been chosen, even the idiots outside. If Cal and Brick and Daisy and the rest of them decided not to accept then they'd be punished just like the vermin who scurried through the streets in every single corner of this planet. Yes, everything was about to change, Rilke understood that better than she'd understood anything else in her life.

She was a soldier now. And there was a war coming.

DAISY / *Furyville, 3:02 p.m.*

"YOU OKAY?"

Daisy glanced up to see Cal looking at her, his face still flushed from their games. It had been so much fun. More fun than Daisy could remember having in *ages*.

Now she and Cal and Adam were sitting in the sun on the wooden walkway that led up to the log flume. It was absolutely baking. She couldn't bear to go back inside, though, not after what had happened with Rilke. "I'm okay," she said. "Just tired."

"You must be," Cal replied. "I don't think I've ever seen anyone run so fast for so long. You even managed to catch Brick, and his legs are like three miles long."

Daisy giggled. Brick had gone off somewhere with Marcus and Jade, and Chris had staggered off to the toilet a while back saying that all the running around had "knocked something loose." Daisy didn't care to think about what he meant. She shifted on her uncomfortable seat, putting an arm around Adam's shoulders.

"Are you thirsty?" she asked. He nodded. Cal had brought out another saucepan full of tap water, cold this time, and they'd taken turns drinking from it. But it was empty now.

"No probs," Cal said. "Come on."

They wandered slowly back toward the pavilion, Adam following and taking wild swipes at everything he passed with a stick that he'd found. When they reached the fire door, Daisy heard a scuffling coming from the back of the park.

"Wait here," said Cal.

He set off, but she didn't wait, chasing after him as he disappeared around the corner of the pavilion. When she peeked she saw him standing outside one of the little buildings, the one that said DANGER: DO NOT ENTER. The voices inside reverberated with an eerie metal twang.

Daisy pressed up against Cal, looking into the shed to see Marcus and Chris there. The walls were covered in weird boxes and big wires and yellow stickers that had skulls and crossbones on them.

"What are you guys doing?" she asked.

Chris turned and flashed them a grin from the dark. "Marcus here is an electrician, he reckons he can get the park up and running."

"No," Marcus said. "One, I'm not an electrician, I've just started my apprenticeship in plumbing, and we cover a bit of electrics too, for bathrooms and stuff. Two, this place hasn't had a feed in years, so there's maybe a zero point one percent chance that anything will work ever again."

"Like I said," Chris went on. "He's going to fix it."

Marcus sighed and turned back to whatever he was doing.

"Are you sure that's a good idea?" Cal asked. "If it does work and we start using electricity, won't people notice?"

But neither of the boys was listening; they were fighting over something that Chris was holding, which didn't seem like a great idea, given all the warning stickers.

"Come on," said Cal. "Let's leave them to blow themselves up."

They walked back the way they'd come, crawling in through the fire doors. Almost as soon as the cold darkness of the corridor gripped her Daisy felt the ice cubes start to return, clinking their way back to the surface of her brain. She tried to push them down again but they kept slipping loose and rising. She followed Cal into the kitchen, telling herself not to look at the dead man. He wasn't there, and at first she thought that maybe he'd gotten up and walked off. Then she saw the tracks, oil-black in the gloom, which led off toward the basement. Somebody finally must have moved him.

"Here you go," said Cal, picking a cracked, filthy tumbler from one of the shelves and filling it from the tap. "This should do it."

He handed it to Adam, who slurped noisily.

"Can we go back outside?" Daisy asked. Cal nodded, and she could see by his expression that he was scared in here. Scared of the dark, scared of Rilke. They retreated up the corridor, stopping only when they heard Brick behind them, slamming through the door from the foyer.

"She still isn't letting us in," he said. "I swear I'm going to light this whole place on fire and smoke her out."

"Calm down, Brick," said Cal as they waited for him to catch up. "We'll think of something else."

"See if she's so smug when she's burning," he said. "Her and her brother. See if she's so smug when she has to watch *him* die."

Daisy squeezed under the chains, holding them up so that Cal and then Brick could follow. Out in the sun the bigger boy seemed to lose some of his anger, but his fists were still clenched so hard that Daisy could see where his long nails dug into the flesh of his palms. It was so sad, because just an hour ago he'd been running around with the rest of them, his laugh a high-pitched giggle that had made him seem like an entirely different person.

"She wouldn't even answer me," he said. "After everything, after what she did, she wouldn't even answer me."

"Come on," said Cal, putting a hand on the other boy's shoulder. "Let's go and find the others. I think we need to make a plan."

CAL / *Furyville, 3:42 p.m.*

"WE HAVE TO DEAL WITH THE FOOD SITUATION FIRST," said Cal. "We can't do anything if we're starving to death."

They were back at the carousel, although nobody was sitting on the horses. Daisy and Adam were walking between Angie,

Geoffrey, and Wonky-Butt the Wonder Horse with piles of dog biscuits cupped in their hands. The rest of them—apart from Marcus, who was still messing around at the back of the park—were perched on the rusted metal steps, in the shade of the half-disintegrated canopy. The air smelled of sea salt and sweat.

"Amen to that," said Chris. "I'm gonna waste away if we don't get something soon."

"Yeah, somehow I don't see that happening," said Brick, nodding at the folds visible beneath Chris's T-shirt.

"It's water retention," he replied, blushing. "No, actually it's in my genes. Hang on, wait, it's *none of your bloody business.*"

"Seriously, guys," said Cal, feeling an uncomfortable tickle of impatience in the vast emptiness of his stomach. The Weetabix he'd eaten had done nothing to fill him up and the prospect of going all night without eating was making him nervous. "We need to think of something. Any ideas?"

"Yeah, I think maybe not running around like crazy people using up all our energy might be sensible," said Jade. Her eyes were red again, like she'd been crying, but she managed a gentle smile.

"Fair point," said Cal.

"We need to find a way to get Rilke out of her rat hole," said Brick. "I'm serious, we could light a fire outside the restaurant. She'd have to come out."

"Look, forget about her," said Cal. "You really don't want to make her angry. She's still got the gun."

"And who brought the gun, genius?"

"I'm not saying you can't get back at her, Brick," Cal said. "But we need to think about food first or none of us are going to be able to do anything."

Cal's gut gurgled, loud enough for Daisy to turn around.

She held out the dog biscuits.

"No thanks, Daisy, they might make me grow a tail."

She laughed and went back to her game, Adam following her around the carousel like a shadow.

"You leave any food in your car?" Brick asked. Cal shook his head.

"No, we brought it all. We got to think of something else. You know the area, Brick, can you think of anywhere we might be able to get supplies?"

"Well there's an ocean right there," he said. "If anyone knows how to fish."

Nobody responded, which was answer enough. Even if they managed to catch anything, Cal wouldn't have a clue how to take its scales off and pull its guts out or whatever you had to do to make sure they weren't poisonous.

"We could always eat Fatty," Brick said, looking at Chris. Cal had to stop himself leaping up the steps and thumping the guy square in the mouth. He waited for the anger to fizzle away before speaking.

"Is there a supermarket or anything nearby? A shop we could break into after dark?"

"There's a gas station about a mile inland," Brick mumbled, almost reluctantly. "But it's open twenty-four hours. That's where I nearly got it. There's a Sainsbury's too, but there are always people in there. They stack the shelves at night, my brother used to work at the one in Norwich, before he joined up."

"That it?"

"That's it."

Cal shook his head. He wasn't sure what he'd expected. It wasn't like he'd ever been in this situation before. He tried to remember the ride up, with Daisy in the car. They had to have passed something.

"Hang on," he said. "What about the factory, the one you can see from here?"

"That place? They make fertilizer or something. You gonna eat that?"

"They might have a café there," said Chris, shrugging.

"Yeah, they'll have a cafeteria, if it's a big place," Jade added. "My old man worked in a car plant, took me for lunch there sometimes if I wasn't at school."

Someone else's stomach rumbled.

"But there's no way we're getting in," said Brick. "There's a security guard, probably more than one."

Cal swore, dropping his head into his hands.

"I'm telling you," Brick went on. "We have to force Rilke to come outside; then we can get our supplies back."

"What, a few bags of chips?" Cal snapped back. "That will keep us going for a couple of months, yeah?"

"I really think the factory could work," said Jade. "Think about it, if there's, what, a couple of guys looking after the place at night then we could distract them while somebody goes in to look for food."

"Distract them?" said Chris. "How do we do that?"

"We just have to get close," said Cal. "Then we'll trigger them. They'll chase us."

"That does *not* sound like fun," said Chris.

"But we could take the car, stop outside the gates until we hook them, then drive fast enough to stay away but slow enough to pull them along." Cal stood up, already excited. "We could be in and out in a few minutes, if we can find the café or whatever."

He looked at Jade and she shrugged. Chris was shaking his

head but he was licking his lips too. Brick's face was as hard as his name, his eyes glowering.

"Brick?"

"Dangerous. We should give it a few days, think about it."

"We don't have a few days," said Cal. "Tomorrow, we should do it then. It's Sunday tomorrow, there will be nobody there."

"I hate to break it to you, Cal," said Jade. "But tomorrow is Monday. If we're going to do this, we need to do it now."

"Now?" he said, and suddenly the idea of leaving Fursville and breaking into a factory seemed utterly ridiculous, completely impossible. "Maybe you're right, Brick, maybe we should think about it some more."

"You think?" said Brick, flapping his arms and making chicken noises. "Not such a tough guy now, are you?"

Cal took a step toward the bigger boy, his fist bunched.

"Go—"

He never got the chance to finish as the top of the carousel exploded, sparks flying from the rows of broken bulbs. He ducked down, shrapnel slicing through the hot air, stinging his skin like mosquito bites. Daisy was screaming, crumpled in a heap as an electric rain dripped down on her. A screeching noise rose up from the battered ride, winding up into an old-fashioned song that was so out of tune it sounded like something from a nightmare. The horses were moving, lurching forward then halting, all the while a deafening, grinding roar emanating from the machinery beneath them.

"Daisy!" Cal ran for the steps but Brick was already there, hoisting the girl in one arm and Adam in the other. He almost fell as he clattered back down, his face twisted into a grimace. Jade was legging it, her hands over her head.

There was a second explosion, this time from overhead. Cal looked up to see the big Ferris wheel shake, unleashing a monsoon of dirt and dust and metal shavings so thick that it turned day into twilight. One of the few remaining carriages tore loose, crashing into the booth that sat below it and firing out another deadly barrage of broken glass. The structure juddered, squealing so loudly that Cal slammed his hands to his ears. Daisy squirmed free of Brick's grip and ran over to him, hugging him tight.

"What is it? What is it?" she sobbed.

From the other side of the park there was an almighty crunch, wood splintering. An ugly fist of smoke thrust up toward the sky. Cal could hear more music now, coming from everywhere, a hundred different tunes that clashed with each other. It was so loud, so confusing, that it was making him feel seasick. And there was laughter too, laughter and applause like in a game show, like there was a crowd watching them. This was what terrified him the most, because it was an impossible sound. It had no right to be here.

Chris was yelling at him, pointing at the pavilion, but the hurricane of noise swept his words away. The carousel was spinning faster now. The horses looked wild, like they were about to leap right off the platform and stampede through the park. They looked as if they were coming alive.

The whole park was coming alive.

Cal suddenly understood what Chris was yelling.

"Marcus," Cal said. He saw Brick's confusion and shouted, "It's Marcus. He must have got the electricity working."

"The *what*?" Brick called back, dropping Adam to the ground. He broke into a run, heading for the back of the park.

The big wheel shuddered hard, another wave of dark matter spiraling down from its skeletal frame along with half a dozen metal spikes that thudded into the path. A siren rose up, a blaring air-raid noise that was coming from the pavilion.

"It's okay, Daisy," Cal said. The girl was clinging on to him so hard it hurt. He could feel her whole body shaking. "It's just the electricity, it's come back on."

"They're going to hear it," she said. "They're going to hear it and come and kill us."

"They're not, they won't, there's no one close enough."

He prayed that he was right. If he wasn't, if people came to investigate, then they were all in serious trouble. Daisy looked up at him, her eyes like saucers.

"But I can *see* it, Cal, in my head. They're going to come."

The carousel lurched, the mirrors on the central post shattering. One of the horses jolted so much that its post snapped, the plastic animal bending out at an angle as it rotated. The pole caught on the pile of rubble next to it, peeling the horse from its mount and depositing it on the ground. Cal grabbed Daisy and pulled her away.

"It's going to be okay, Brick will sort it out."

Another shower of sparks ripped from the top of the carousel, dropping like a curtain, then the machine ground to a halt. The tune got slower and deeper before dying out completely. Gradually, the rest of the chaos passed, leaving the park quieter than it had ever been. Cal straightened, breathing a sigh of relief like a tornado had just passed overhead. His heart felt like it had received a sudden surge of electricity too, palpitating.

Adam had run over and was gripping Daisy with the same force she was using to hold Cal.

"You didn't get hit by glass or anything?" he asked them.

They both shook their heads. Daisy was looking at something that nobody else could see, her eyes flicking back and forth.

"I can *see* it," she said. "They're going to—"

And that's when the screaming started.

DAISY / *Furyville, 4:07 p.m.*

THEY WERE COMING FROM THE PAVILION—muffled screams that were somehow louder than the deafening chaos that had just faded. Daisy clung on to Cal's arm, her head a constantly churning madness of ice cubes.

"Who is that?" said Cal as another shriek tore through the air. Even the birds had stopped singing, as if they were afraid of what was to come.

The screams were desperate and broken and insane and weak and strong all at the same time. It made the inside of Daisy's skull tickle, the blood in her ears roaring like there was an ocean flowing through them. Adam was crying into her chest, his skinny arms locked around her. Cal swore, running his hands through his hair. Chris was beside them, ghostlike. None of the boys seemed to know what to do.

"Wait here," Cal said to him. "Make sure they're safe."

"No, man, we should stick together," Chris said. "If it's the ferals, we shouldn't split up."

Cal nodded, prying Daisy loose.

"Okay, stay with me, yeah? Stay close, and keep hold of Adam." He looked at Chris. "Grab a weapon, mate, we might need them."

Both the boys scrabbled in the rubble, picking up metal poles of different lengths. Cal tucked his beneath his arm, taking Daisy's hand and leading her toward the pavilion just as another awful screech pierced the walls. They ran past the chained front doors, almost bumping into Jade as they tore around the corner.

"Was it you?" Cal asked her.

She shook her head, turning her wide eyes to the fire door. Daisy heard a scuffling of feet, then Brick appeared from the other direction. He was holding Marcus by the scruff of the neck and he looked angrier than Daisy had ever seen him. They marched down the side of the pavilion, Brick giving Marcus a shove when they were right outside the entrance. The younger kid fell, sprawling in the dirt.

"That's Rilke," Brick said. The screams were louder here, squeezed from the fire door as if they were trying to escape whatever was inside. An ice cube clinked to the top of the pile in Daisy's head: the restaurant, and a shape that moved inside it—bright and dark at the same time. *Don't go in, please don't go in.*

"What's happening in there?" Jade asked.

"Whatever it is," Brick said, "I hope she's screaming in pain."

Marcus was on his feet again.

"It started when the electricity came on," he said. "Sorry, by the way. I didn't think all that would happen."

"We should—" Cal had to stop as more screams tore the air in two. "Come on."

"You serious?" Brick asked, moving in front of the fire door. "Let her suffer."

"We don't know what it is," Cal said, toe to toe with the taller guy. "For all we know it could be another one of us in there, someone who wandered in when we were out front. Rilke might be doing something to *them*. You think about that?"

Brick obviously hadn't, because after chewing on it for a second he stood to one side.

"We might even be able to grab some food while we're up there," Cal went on. "If she's distracted."

He looked at Chris, nodding. Chris nodded back, his metal bar raised, then the two of them ducked into the darkness. Brick swore, following them in on his hands and knees. Daisy looked down at Adam. He was shaking his head, still crying.

"Don't be scared," she said. "We're safer if we're all together. They'll look after us."

He resisted for a second, then let her lead him to the door. She crouched down, squeezing through the gap. After the blazing sunlight the corridor was extraordinarily dark. She couldn't breathe under the weight of the shadows, but when she turned to try to escape Adam was in the way, Jade already pushing through from outside.

A shriek echoed down the corridor, so much louder now, so much more real. Daisy opened her mouth, a scream of her own rising fast, cut off when she felt a hand on her shoulder.

"Come on," said Cal. "Stay with me."

They huddled together as they passed through the dust-thick light of the foyer and up the stairs. The restaurant was in sight when the next scream cannoned out, the doors rocking in their frames with the force of it, flakes of ice spiraling to the frozen floor.

"What the . . ." said Brick. "We should get out."

While we still can. Daisy realized they were all thinking it. There was a crunch from inside Waves. Something big slammed into the other side of the wall, a huge crack splitting the plasterwork and making them all stagger back—Marcus almost tumbling down the stairs. A cry, howled out with heartbreaking strength:

"Schiller!"

"Whatever's happening, she deserves it," said Brick, retreating. "She can go to hell for all I care."

Crunch. Dust rained down from the ceiling. Rilke called out her brother's name again.

"Ah, screw this," Cal said, taking a step back. Daisy thought he was going to leave, but he was just getting a run-up. He threw himself at the doors, yelling as he kicked out. The wood splintered but they didn't open. He did it again, and this time they flew apart to reveal a world turned inside out.

There was light in the restaurant, a flickering glow that was definitely fire, but too cold and too bright for a candle. In its uncertain grip Daisy could see that the restaurant had been trashed, every single table and chair upturned, most splintered into pieces. There was barely a patch of floor that wasn't covered in rubbish.

Rilke knelt in the middle of the room as though she were praying, her legs folded beneath her. The flames were reflected in her wide, unblinking eyes, and in the rivulets that ran down her cheeks, making her look like someone burning up from the inside. Her mouth gaped open. Without warning the scream came again—not from Rilke but from something else. It was like a needle sliding into Daisy's brain. Adam let go of her, collapsing to his knees with his fingers in his ears, and it took all her strength not to do the same.

The source of the light was moving, fast, the shadows in the room sweeping in wide arcs. A shape flew across the restaurant, bathed in weak flames. It thumped into the far wall and dropped to the floor, struggling like a dying bird. It wouldn't stay still, launching itself into the air again before Daisy could make any sense of it. It plowed through an upside-down table, blasting it into splinters before flailing out of sight.

"Rilke?" Cal yelled into the room. "Get out of there!"

Her head swiveled around, staring right at them. Daisy understood that Rilke wasn't scared. There was something else in her expression: part fear, yes, but part sick, gleeful excitement too. It was utterly insane. She smiled at them, a grin that belonged in a madhouse. All the while the fire moved, chasing shadows as it hurled itself from wall to wall.

"Rilke," Cal said again, his voice an empty husk.

"Don't you see?" the girl called back. The shape dropped in front of her, the flames dulled now but still covering it like a flickering blue coat. It was a body, its arms wrapped around itself, its legs splayed out at unnatural angles, like they were broken. Its head was tucked into its chest, but Daisy had no difficulty working out who it was.

Schiller.

The boy arched his back, his mouth splitting open and unleashing another bone-shaking scream. The inferno raged, too bright to look at. He thrust himself from the ground so fast that he slammed into the ceiling. One of the panels snapped loose, crashing down beside Rilke. She didn't even notice it, her eyes locked on her brother as he flapped upside down against the top of the room, as if gravity had suddenly been reversed.

He slid out of sight, and Daisy found herself taking a step forward. Her terror was now so extreme that she could barely feel it, it could no longer register. She felt Cal's hand around hers, both of them walking through the door together because they had to see, they had to know what this thing was.

Schiller was rolling against the ceiling now, looking like he was trying to put out the flames that burned from his skin. That fire gave off no heat, and it didn't spread. It did the opposite, in fact, leaving sparkling crystals of ice wherever it touched. It was sucking the warmth from everything, feeding on heat and light, devouring it. He cried out again, ripped from left to right and slammed into the far wall.

Rilke's brother wasn't the only shape in the flames, Daisy realized. There was something else there, faint but unmistakable. Unmistakable but impossible. Impossible but real. It stretched out from Schiller's hunched shoulders, unfolding gracefully, longer than the boy's whole body. It swept down with incredible force, blasting debris from the floor and propelling him across the room. Schiller screamed again, the sound cut dead as he struck the other wall, hanging there like a rock climber as that shape beat frantically.

It was a wing. A single, flaming, beautiful, terrible wing.

"Don't you see?" Rilke said again, looking at them.

The flames flickered, fading again, and Schiller collapsed to the floor. He cried out, trying to crawl toward his sister before disappearing inside another inferno, that same swanlike wing pushing from his back, hauling him into the air. Rilke laughed as she watched him go, a sound like cut glass.

"Isn't it obvious what we are?" the girl went on. "What we're becoming? What we're meant to do?"

Nobody answered. How could they? Schiller flapped toward the window, tearing at the boards. Sunlight trickled in but it had no power here, cowering before the living flame. His single wing beat and he was hoisted up to the ceiling again, then slammed back to the floor with just as much force. Daisy didn't know how he could still be alive, but he was, his face knotted into a mask of pain, of confusion, as he tried to climb to the window again.

"You have to make a choice," said Rilke. "You have to embrace this, embrace our gift, or turn your back on it."

She got to her feet, walking unsteadily toward the door. Her hands were held out in front of her, no gun in sight. But she was still dangerous, Daisy knew, more dangerous than ever. Her brother railed behind her, drowning in fire.

"We are all changing," Rilke said. "We have been chosen. Look at what Schiller is becoming. It will happen to all of us, don't you see that, Daisy?"

And Daisy *did* see it. It was suddenly clear. Marcus had been right all along, and yet he'd been so wrong too. She looked at Cal, feeling the last of the warmth drain from her, snuffed out. Rilke was telling the truth, they were all going to change.

"The ferals, they're not the ones who are possessed," Daisy said, staggering back, wanting to cry but unable to remember how. Cal reached for her but she stepped out of the way, toward the stairs. "They're not the ones with the demons inside them."

Everyone but Schiller was now looking at her, waiting for her to finish, to state what they all knew.

"*We* are."

BRICK COULDN'T TAKE HIS EYES OFF RILKE'S BURNING BROTHER.

The boy was quiet again, those blue flames simmering from every pore. He lay on the floor, his head turned up. Even his eyes had ignited, pockets of impossible light.

Daisy was right. Schiller was possessed.

"Daisy, wait!" Cal was yelling after the girl but she was gone, her footsteps fading. The rest of them stood there, paralyzed by the cold fire from Schiller and the intensity of Rilke's gaze. Cal turned to her, his face gray. "You're mad; you're off your bloody head."

But she wasn't. What she was saying made a terrible kind of sense.

"You don't have to listen to me, Cal," said Rilke. She had to pause as Schiller erupted again, like somebody had flicked a gas burner from the lowest setting to the highest. The boy howled, that hideous wing punching out and launching him into another lopsided flight. "You just have to use your eyes. Look at what he is. Listen to your head and tell me you don't feel it too."

Don't listen, Brick ordered himself. But it was there, lodged in his brain, an inescapable truth that seared through everything else. There was something inside him the same way there was something inside Schiller, inside all of them, fighting its way to the surface. It had started with the headache, that maddening *thump-thump, thump-thump, thump-thump.* The noise *had* been something trying to get in, something knocking at his door. And it had succeeded. It was here.

"I don't know why we were chosen," Rilke went on, fixing her doll's eyes on them all in turn. "But we were. Give it time and you'll all see."

"It can't be," said Chris, crumpled against the banister.

The others too were shaking their heads. Brick could see it in their faces, though. He could see that they believed. Even Cal.

"Demons aren't real, Rilke," the boy said without conviction. "*This* isn't real, it's a . . . a . . ."

Schiller was clawing at the window again. He ripped away the board, hurling it across the room so hard that it impaled itself in the far wall. Sunlight streamed in, seeming to funnel around the burning shape. The effect was dizzying, making it look as though he was burning inside a pocket of darkness.

Rilke smiled.

"These aren't demons," she said. "I don't know why we're here, but it isn't for something evil. It is for something good. Something incredible."

"What?" asked Jade, her red-rimmed eyes swimming.

"Don't you see?" Rilke said. "After everything that's happened to you, isn't it clear?"

Brick screwed his eyes shut, fighting the swell of emotion that churned up from his gut. He saw the people at the station, grunting and howling and barking like mindless animals as they chased him. These were the people he had hated for so long, who had hated him. The idiotic, annoying masses who'd been making his life a misery since long before all this had started. Wasn't it right that they should be punished?

Not Lisa, though. Not her. She hadn't hated him.

"Don't fight it, Brick," said Rilke. "You know what we have to do."

He could feel her thoughts in his own, planting a seed in the flesh of his brain. People were bad, people did terrible things. Humanity needed to be purged.

He recoiled at the thought, his mind fighting it. That couldn't be right, that *wasn't* right. Rilke had made a mistake.

"Don't resist it," she said, her whisper detonating inside his head, a shock that swept away his reason. "You can't say no, Brick. It's why we're here, it's what we have to do."

He felt something warm and wet trickling from his nose, the taste of salt and copper on his tongue.

"Don't listen to me, listen to *them*," Rilke said. "Listen to what they're trying to tell you."

It *was* trying to tell him something, whatever it was that sat inside his soul. There were no words, just an instinctive feeling that burrowed upward. *We've been chosen, but not for this, for something else.*

"You're wrong," he said, his voice faint and distant like a muffled recording of himself. "That's not it."

"It *is*," she hissed. "If you don't see it, then you're no better than the rest of them. If you don't understand, then you'll *die* with the rest of them."

Schiller screamed, a pulse of sonic energy, the flames fading like a broken jet engine. He collapsed, his second skin flickering on and off, only the fiery sockets of his eyes still fierce.

"What we are is a miracle," Rilke said. "What lives inside us is holy, it is right. Those of you who accept it will be saved. Those of you too blind and too scared to comprehend what is happening will perish. You have to make a choice, right now, or it will be too late."

"But what *is* inside us, Rilke?" asked Jade, taking a step toward the other girl. Blood dripped from her nose, and her eyes were wide, innocent, trusting.

"Jade," said Cal. "Rilke, let her be."

"I want to know," Jade said. "Don't you? Isn't that—" She gestured into the restaurant but she could find no words to describe what she saw. "Isn't *that* proof enough?"

Cal wiped a hand across his face, smearing away crimson tears.

"What is it, this thing inside us?" Jade asked again.

"You already know," Rilke said. "You all do."

Jade smiled, like someone hypnotized. She glanced at Cal, then at Chris, and finally at Brick. He thought he could see right into her head, into the broken pieces of her mind. Then she walked into the restaurant, collapsing to her knees in the middle of the room.

"Come on," yelled Cal. He grabbed Adam's arm, dragging the boy toward the stairs. "Let's go."

Brick didn't move. He wanted nothing more than to be outside, to be away from this madness. But still Rilke's voice clamored inside his skull, utterly wrong and yet utterly convincing. He looked at Schiller, bathed in flames. Was this his fate too, if he stayed? Could he really walk away from such a gift?

"Last chance, Cal," said Rilke, calling down the sweeping stairs.

"Screw you, Rilke," he shouted back. "Go to hell."

Chris was already stumbling after him, but Marcus wasn't moving. His face wore the same look of rapture as Jade's had.

"Last chance, Harry," Rilke said to Brick, and the sound of his real name sent a surge of poisonous euphoria vomiting up his throat. He almost threw himself to his knees right there, ready to embrace her. "Listen to its call, make your choice."

He took a step toward her. Marcus was moving too, laughing softly to himself as he pushed into the restaurant and knelt down before Schiller.

"You know what it is," Rilke said. "How can you say no?"

Brick opened his mouth and let out a hoarse, desperate scream—a noise that seemed to come not from him but from the thing inside him. Then he turned, falling over himself and crawling backward toward the stairs, tumbling down the first few before he recovered. He slid down them, never taking his eyes off Rilke. She shook her head, her expression drenched in a profound sadness as she closed the restaurant door. He turned and ran, tearing through the foyer and down the corridor, pushing through the fire door so hard that the chains ripped out a lock of his hair.

He fell in the dirt, his whole body shivering in the blazing sun. And all the while the truth of it was a beacon inside his skull, burning with white heat, the thing inside him issuing a clarion call that he could not ignore.

No, not a *thing*. Not a ghost or a demon either.

It was an angel.

CAL / *Furyville, 4:42 p.m.*

CAL CAUGHT UP WITH DAISY BY THE CAROUSEL. When she looked around it was as though she didn't see him, as though the burning boy had blinded her.

"Daisy," he said, wrapping his arms around her.

She blinked, her eyes swimming in and out of focus and eventually finding him. He held her tight. He didn't know what to say.

After a moment or two he heard heavy footsteps on the gravel. Chris was walking down the path, Adam treading on his shadow. Daisy saw them too. She peeled away from Cal's grip and ran over to Adam, hugging him. He didn't react. He didn't even seem to notice she was there.

"Tell me Marcus and Brick didn't go in," Cal said. Chris shook his head.

"Marcus, yeah. Brick's over there puking his guts up."

Cal put his hands in his hair, clenching so hard it hurt.

"What happened in there, Cal?" Chris said. "What was wrong with that boy?"

He's not a boy, Cal thought. *Not anymore. He's something else.*

But he wouldn't let himself say what, even though the word flashed up before him like a signal flare in the darkness of his thoughts. He didn't need to speak, because Chris plucked it right out of his head.

"Angels?" the boy said. "That's insane, man."

"Forget it," spat Cal. *Ha, yeah, just forget it, forget that you just saw a boy covered in fire flying around the restaurant, it's not important.*

He ran back the way he'd come, turning the corner to see Brick on his hands and knees outside the door. He wasn't being sick, he was sobbing, which was a million times worse. Cal went to him, putting a hand on his back. Brick glanced up, his face so pale that his freckles looked like pen marks.

"Come on, mate," Cal said eventually, holding out his hand. Brick took it, hauling himself to his feet. They had taken a dozen steps back toward the carousel before he let go.

Cal collapsed on the steps, the same place they'd been sitting only a few minutes ago but which was now on the other side of time. Brick sat down next to him.

"What—"

"Don't," Cal interrupted Chris before he could say it. If they didn't talk about it, then maybe it might not have been real. "Don't say it, Chris, not now, not ever."

"But we have to—"

"We *don't*," Cal snapped, looking up. Chris was sitting on the path. Daisy and Adam were next to him, both of them staring at nothing. "Look, there's something weird going on, sure, something we don't understand. But I can promise you this, Rilke doesn't have a clue what it is either, she's just guessing, like us. Which is why everything she says is total bull."

Nobody argued, but nobody looked very convinced.

"Jade, Marcus, they'll see that soon enough. They'll be back. And we need to keep our heads screwed on straight, yeah? We can't afford to start falling apart now."

"So what do we do?" Chris asked after a moment.

"We're all exhausted. We've all been through more in a few days than anyone should have to go through in their whole life. None of us has eaten much, we're probably all bordering on crazy anyway."

"That was no hallucination," said Brick.

"I'm not saying it was. But it was dark in there, yeah, and, I don't know . . . We just need to stick to the plan, we need to get some food. We'll be able to think of something when we've had a chance to eat."

He looked around. Chris was nodding. Brick shrugged. The idea of going for food seemed alien to Cal. The idea of doing *anything* seemed alien to him now. Yet they had to do something or fall back into the madness of what they had just seen.

"Need to get the hell away from this place anyway," Brick croaked. "I never want to come back here again."

"Daisy?" Cal asked. She seemed to stir, her eyes drifting up.

"I want to go home," she said.

"I know. We all do. Just not yet. Not yet."

They sat there, listening to the ocean running its endless course against the shore.

"So what is the plan?" Chris asked.

"We get the car," Cal replied. "Your car. We go to the factory. We'll work out the rest when we get there."

THEY WERE OUT OF THE PARK IN FIVE MINUTES. As soon as Cal squeezed free from the laurel hedge he felt the warmth of the day settle back inside him. It was brighter out here, like the park had been drowned in shade, caught beneath the weight of a dirty big cloud. It was easier to forget.

He held up a branch so that the others could push through, Daisy and Adam first, then Chris and Brick. He could hear them all taking a sigh of relief when they stepped into the shimmering haze of the empty street.

He looked up, seeing Brick's graffiti on the Fursville sign. The glaring face looked down at him with its dead "x" eyes, making him shudder. What if they got to the factory and it was full of people? What if they got trapped? One mistake was all it would take for them all to die.

Yet the alternative was worse. The alternative was going back up to the restaurant and falling to their knees in front of Rilke and her burning brother.

They reached the parking lot and walked through the damaged section of fence. The Jag was rammed into the hedge behind the shed, its tail end glinting through a mask of branches, its trunk still open. Brick jogged ahead, pulling away the foliage.

"Got the keys?" he asked. Chris patted his pockets, pulling a face. "You *kidding* me?"

"Yeah, I'm kidding you," said Chris, pulling out the fob and unlocking the car. "Calm down."

Brick's expression was so sour that Cal couldn't help but laugh. Daisy too.

"Seriously?" Brick asked. "You think this is *funny*?"

"Just your face, mate," said Cal, and God did it feel good to smile again.

"Yeah? We'll see if you're still giggling when your face is under my backside," Brick stuttered, the stupid insult making them all laugh harder. "Just shut up," he said, but his eyes showed a glimmer of light. "You know what I mean."

"Come on," said Cal, pushing the trunk shut. "Before Brick sits on my face. Shall I drive?"

"Uh-uh," said Chris, jiggling toward the car and sliding behind the wheel. "My car, my rules."

"Shotgun!" Cal and Brick yelled together, both of them making a break for the passenger door. Brick got there first, ripping it open and diving in headfirst. He maneuvered his gangly body around, extending two middle fingers toward Cal.

"Looks like all the babies are in the back," he said with a grin as Cal kicked the door shut.

"Up yours," he said. He held the rear door open so that Daisy and Adam could clamber inside, getting in after them and planting his knees into Brick's seat. The bigger boy's response was to slide his chair all the way back. "Hey, no fair," Cal yelled. "Chris, tell him."

"Behave," he said, starting the engine. "I'm not going anywhere until you stop messing around. And put your seat belts on."

That did it, all of them doubled over with laughter—even Adam, caught up in the sudden surge, his eyes shining. It could go on forever, Cal thought, this golden light that melted up through every fiber of his body, that made every single particle in the car seem to glow. It wasn't coming from him, it was flowing from somewhere else, a current of warmth that spread from him to Daisy to Adam to Chris to Brick and back again. Whatever this thing was inside them, it was healing them. It would keep them strong and it would keep them safe.

Cal wiped the tears from his eyes, his cheeks aching. He looked at the others, and in that moment of quiet they seemed to know each other like they had been together for an eternity.

"You ready?" he asked.

They all nodded. Chris put the Jag in reverse, revving the engine. "Then let's do this."

RILKE / *Furyville, 5:15 p.m.*

RILKE COULD HEAR THE FAINT GROWL OF A CAR ENGINE, rising and then fading. She knew who it was, she could almost see it through Daisy's eyes—the five of them inside the big silver car, the fat boy driving. They were laughing. *Laughing.* The sound of it, echoing almost silently through her thoughts, made her blood boil.

She knew where they were going too. She could pluck that

thought out of the storm of emotions inside their minds. It was a sign that whatever was inside her was growing in strength. It had to be. Soon she'd be like Schiller, gripped with a holy fire and ready to burn down the world.

He sat before her now, and even though he was no longer alight, even though he was slumped and loose-limbed like a marionette with its strings cut, she could feel the energy pulsating from him. He was still cold, the carpet beneath him a lake of ice. He stared at the floor with two sets of eyes—the old eyes she knew so well, and two pits of fire that sat over them, shimmering gently.

Marcus and Jade were there too. They were both on their knees, gazing at Schiller as though they had just seen the face of God. It wasn't too far from the truth, she guessed, except they both had this same gift. It just hadn't been opened yet. They all had it. She'd seen it inside the man with the shotgun, the one she'd killed—the creature of flame that had died when he died. The ones who fled had it too. She was disappointed that so many had run from their responsibility. It was no surprise that Brick had gone, Cal too, blinded by his own self-righteousness. But she had wanted Daisy to stay. Of all of them—Schiller aside, of course—Daisy was closest to changing, to becoming what they were all destined to become.

Jade turned around. Her eyes were wide and wet, her copper-colored hair like a pyre in the sunlight from the broken window. She was the kind of weak creature that Rilke would usually hate. But she had been chosen too. She was her sister now, as much as Schiller was her brother.

"What are we, Rilke?" Jade asked.

"Angels," Rilke replied.

Jade cocked her head, her mouth hanging open. It seemed an age before she spoke again. "How can that be?"

"Because they have chosen us."

Rilke could feel a force inside her stirring as she spoke. It was so small, now, but it would grow.

"But *how* can it be?" Jade said. "How is it possible?"

"It doesn't matter. I don't think we're supposed to know. The only thing that's important is what we're being asked to do."

Schiller groaned. His left arm was hanging at a strange angle, it had been dislocated at the shoulder. *Don't fight it, little brother,* she told him, knowing that the words would get through. *You're going to be okay. Just don't fight it.*

"What are we being asked to do?" said Marcus. A trickle of blood was winding down from his ear and he wiped it away with the back of his hand. "I saw it in my head, I think. I saw people, the ones that tried to kill me."

"They tried to kill you for a reason," said Rilke. "Because they know how dangerous you are."

"But why would angels want to hurt people?" Jade said. She was glancing toward the door, frowning like she was stirring from a deep sleep. Now that Schiller had stilled, she seemed to be changing her mind. "They're supposed to be good, aren't they?"

Rilke spat out a laugh.

"What do you think they are? Little cherubs with harps and halos? No. They're soldiers. They are powerful, and they are cruel." She knew that much from church. "They can't exist here by themselves, they'd burn right through the skin of reality. They need a host, a vessel. They need *us.*"

Marcus and Jade looked at each other. If they bolted now, Rilke decided, she'd shoot them both dead before they reached the door. How could they be so ignorant?

"They're cruel?" said Marcus.

"No, that's the wrong word," Rilke said. "They're not cruel. But they're not kind either. They have no emotions. They are warriors. They have no love for us, they don't feel anything at all. They have been sent here before, to destroy cities. They've killed thousands. If I had a Bible I'd show you, there's proof. It says that the angels will cleanse the world of the wicked."

Even as she spoke she knew the creature inside her had nothing to do with the Bible. It was much, much older than any human stories. Rilke could feel the weight of its age on her soul. But they must have been here before, they must have *inspired* those stories.

"That's our job?" Jade said, shaking her head. "Killing people? It doesn't feel right."

"Just the bad ones. Don't you see? The world is a horrible place. People do terrible things to each other all the time. Would it be such a bad thing to purge all that . . . that rot?"

As she said it, a sudden doubt took hold of her. She thought back to what she'd seen with Daisy, the man in the storm that hung over the street and howled, that sucked in all that was warm and light and spat out only absence. If they were angels, then what had that thing been? One of them?

No, not one of us, it isn't one of us. That thing is the opposite of us, it's here to destroy everything. We have to fight it, we have to fight it. The words in her head were not hers, and she pushed them away. She had to believe that what she was doing was right. If she didn't believe it, then she was lost.

"You'll see," she said. "You won't doubt me for much longer."

None of them would. Something incredible was going to happen—even more incredible than Schiller's transformation—she could feel it the same way she could feel the tickle of a sneeze. She didn't know what, but it would involve fire. She wasn't sure if that premonition had been hers or Daisy's, but it was inevitable. There would be fire, and they would see the truth.

And she knew what she had to do to make it happen.

"I need a phone," she said. "Do either of you have one?"

"Mine's got no signal out here," said Jade. Marcus fished his from his jeans and examined it.

"Why d'you want it?" he said.

"Trust me."

He obviously did because he handed it to her.

"They're going to the factory, aren't they?" Rilke asked. "To look for food."

Jade nodded, her expression uncertain.

Rilke dialed and lifted it to her ear. Daisy and the others would soon understand exactly what they had to do—if they survived, that was.

DAISY / *Hemmingway, 5:34 p.m.*

BY THE TIME DAISY HAD FINALLY MANAGED to clip in her seat belt they were already slowing down.

The factory loomed up from the horizon, a cluster of black buildings and half a dozen towering chimneys that pierced the brilliant blue sky. There was nothing else nearby apart from a sign on the side of the road that said "Thank you for visiting Hemmingway and Fursville—Please Drive Safely!" The same bug-eyed squirrel grinned at them from it. Fursville itself now lay half a mile behind them.

"See anything?" Cal asked. The factory entrance was set just off the road, up a short, wide driveway. There was no gate, just a barrier. On either side of that were big walls topped with mean-looking spikes. There was a booth there too, a little one with a door and a window, attached to the main building.

"There's somebody in there," Daisy said, seeing a blurred shape behind the sun-drenched glass. "I think we should turn around."

"It might just be one person," Chris said, letting the engine idle.

"And he might have fifty mates out the back," Brick said. "A hundred."

Daisy felt her stomach complain. It was partly fear but mostly hunger. She wished they could just phone the factory people and ask them to bring out some food. Wouldn't they do that for a car full of kids?

"Yeah, we should call them," said Cal, scooping the thought out of her brain. "Look, the number's right there on the sign."

"And say what?" Brick asked. "Hi there, we're just wondering if there's anyone in today because we'd like to break in and steal some stuff?"

"No, idiot, we could just see if anyone answers."

Chris tapped a button in the center of the dashboard and a keypad appeared on the touch screen there.

"Nice," said Cal. "Does it have a signal?"

"Let's find out," he said, typing in the digits. There was a hum, then a flurry of numbers, then the sound of ringing through the car's speakers. Daisy tuned it out, gazing through the window and back toward Fursville. The whole park looked tiny, and shimmered in the baking heat. It didn't seem real, as though any minute now the view would just flicker and switch off. It was a crazy thought, but surely not anywhere near as crazy as having creatures *inside* them.

Angels.

And yet it felt so right, what Rilke had said. Well, *most* of what she'd said. What lived in them wasn't really angels, she didn't think. These weren't the same things her mum had pictures of in the house, the ones she'd become obsessed with when she was ill. Those had smiling faces and rosy cheeks and sat on fluffy clouds.

These . . . they were different. Daisy didn't have the right words to explain how, only that they weren't alive in the same sense that people were. They couldn't live here, in this world. That's why they'd chosen her and Cal and Brick and the others. They needed a body to ride around in, the same way that humans needed cars to get places.

They were good, though, these things. Not like nice people, more like a friendly animal, like a dog or a tiger. They wouldn't speak, but they would look after you. That's where the ice cubes in her head came from, those little glimpses of other people's lives. Only other people with angels in them, she realized. That's how they talked to each other.

The big question was why the angels were here. There was no way that angels would make them murder people. Rilke was wrong, *really* wrong. Daisy didn't blame her. It wasn't like they'd all been given a big instruction book or anything. None of them had any idea what they were supposed to do. But they weren't here to hurt people, Daisy was sure of it.

"Nobody's answering," said Brick as the ring tone continued to fill the car.

"Really?" said Cal. "I thought somebody had picked up and was just making phone impressions."

Brick had his mouth open to reply when a voice blasted out of the speakers.

"Welcome to Cavendish Agricultural Technologies. Our office hours are nine a.m. to five p.m., Monday to Friday. If you require emergency assistance or product advice outside office hours, please hold."

Music, something classical that reminded Daisy of her drama class. The memory of it was like somebody had slapped her around the face. The play! They would have done it by now. Emily Horton would have played Juliet, she would have kissed Fred. It should have been *her*. The hunger in her stomach turned into something much worse, like she was being crushed. Tears tickled down her cheek but she wiped them away before anyone could notice, taking a couple of deep, shuddering breaths until the weight lifted.

She couldn't worry about the play now. There were more important things. There had better be, anyway. There had to be a reason for this, something that made it all okay, otherwise she'd have lost everything—*everything*—for nothing.

It's the thing you saw, she thought. *The man in the storm. He's the reason you're here. You have to fight him.* And even though the memory of that creature was terrifying, the thought settled her.

They were here to stop him. Before he could eat the whole world.

That's what he wants to do. He wants to eat everything, until there's nothing left but darkness.

"Hello?" said a voice through the speakers, making Daisy jump.

"Oh, yeah, hello," said Chris, looking urgently at the others and mouthing *What do I say?* "Um . . . How are you?"

Cal was pointing at the booth, and they all squinted through the glass to see that the person inside was on the phone.

"This is an emergency number," the voice said. "We're closed. Call back tomorrow."

"Wait," said Cal, leaning between the front seats. "We need to speak with somebody urgently."

"Is it an emergency?"

"Yeah," Cal went on. "Er, we're outside and we think someone might be trying to break in."

"*What?*" hissed Brick. "You trying to get us caught?"

"Who is this?" the man repeated.

"Outside, on the road, a gang in a silver car. They look suspicious."

There was a clunk, a squeak, shuffling noises, then the door of the booth opened. Daisy ducked down, peeking as a man in a security guard's uniform appeared. He cupped a hand over his forehead, looking toward the Jag.

"What the hell are you doing?" Brick said.

"Trust me," said Cal. "He's going to come over. Chris, as soon as he gets close enough, move off, okay? Drive slowly, make him follow you back up to Fursville. There are plenty of places to turn around up there, just make sure you keep him hooked. And lock the doors, yeah?"

"Sure," said Chris, his voice a tremor. "No probs."

The guard reached into his booth for a cap, putting it on then walking out into the sun. Daisy could hear his footsteps crunching on the sandy track as he approached the road. He wasn't far away. Any second now he'd sense them. She took Adam's hand, squeezing it.

"If he gets too close then you just floor it," Cal went on,

doing his best to smile at Daisy. "Keep them safe, whatever happens."

He popped open his door, the car rocking as he got out.

"Come on, Brick, you're up."

"No way, man, I'm staying here," Brick said, snorting a laugh. "Why doesn't Chris go?"

"Can you drive?" Cal asked. The guard was walking fast, shouting something at them. Brick swore, slamming a hand down on the glove box. "Come on, mate, this is your chance to be a hero."

Brick grabbed the handle and shouldered open the door, almost knocking Cal over.

"Hey, stay where you are," the guard yelled. He was jogging now, a big belly swinging beneath his tight gray shirt.

"Good luck," said Daisy, putting her hand on the window. Cal pressed his against the other side as Brick slammed the door shut. "Be safe, Cal, please be safe."

"You too," he said. "We'll meet you at that car dealer, Soapy's, yeah?"

"Gotcha," said Chris, pressing a button to make the doors lock. "Good luck."

"Who arrrrrrr ooooo?" the guard's mouth was drooping out of shape. His eyes filling with a depthless rage. Daisy pushed herself away from the door as his steps became lurches, then bounds, propelling him down the last section of path.

"Go!" yelled Cal, running into the ocean of sea grass that grew by the side of the road. Brick followed him, both boys ducking out of sight as the guard careened toward the car.

"Oh crap, should have thought about this," said Chris. He spun the wheel, trying to turn around. The back of the Jaguar slammed against the guard rail as he reversed and the engine almost stalled. Daisy screamed as the guard threw himself against the window, thumping the glass. He butted his head against it, his nose bending at a weird angle. Blood gushed past his yellow teeth but he didn't notice. He didn't know anything except the Fury.

Chris revved hard. The front of the car scuffed the rail at the side of the road, swerved the other way, then they were clear. Remembering what he was supposed to be doing, he eased on the brakes. Daisy looked through the back window to see the guard tearing after them, his face a mask of cruelty and anger. Behind him, sneaking from their hiding place, Cal and Brick jogged across the road toward the factory.

"Be safe," Daisy said to them. "Good luck."

But she had an awful feeling that luck wasn't going to be enough.

CAL / *Cavendish Agricultural Technologies, 5:46 p.m.*

BRICK REACHED THE BOOTH FIRST, running through the open door so hard that he almost ripped it off its hinges. Cal skidded to a halt outside, casting a look back up the road. He could just about make out the glinting roof of the Jag, the guard's guttural shouts drifting back on the wind. His pulse was so fast and so hard in his throat that he felt like there were fingers there, squeezing.

"Cal, come on!" Brick was at the door, furiously waving his hand. Cal pushed past him into the small room. It was empty, just a desk, a control panel, a couple of security monitors, and a phone with the receiver out of the cradle. He lifted it to hear the roar of a car.

"Hello? Chris, you still there?"

"Cal?" Chris's voice was laced with panic.

"Yeah, we just got in. There's nobody else here. You guys all right?"

A pause, then Daisy's voice:

"He's catching up!"

"We're okay," Chris said. "Go on, get it done."

Cal dropped the phone back on the desk, keeping the line open. Brick was focusing on the monitors, clicking a switch that changed which camera was being shown.

"Looks dead," he said.

Cal walked across the booth to the other door, opening it a crack to see a short corridor. He stepped through, stopping when he heard Brick's voice.

"This might come in handy," the other boy said, pulling a sheet of paper from the wall and handing it to Cal. It was a plan of the factory, made up of fine lines and even smaller print. Cal recognized the booth in which they stood and, close by, a big rectangle marked STAFF.

"Gotta be it," he said, pointing. "Right?"

"One way to find out."

They walked through the door, Brick doubling back to pick up a giant Maglite flashlight from the desk. He held it like a bat as they ran down the corridor, past a big reception room and a toilet. There was another door at the far end, and Cal opened it up onto a sunlit courtyard. Two jeeps with the factory's logo sat there alongside a dented blue Rover. Cal glanced at the map, getting his bearings.

"That way," he said, setting off. They jogged past the cars, their ragged breathing the only sound in the entire place. The factory loomed over them, giant chimneys casting fingerlike shadows over the open ground. He increased his speed, making for a squat, low building dead ahead.

They'd almost reached it when another security guard appeared, a short woman who strolled out from between two huge, gleaming silos about thirty meters away, swinging a set of keys around her finger. She was whistling, the tune cutting out when she saw them. Cal skidded to a halt against the wall, Brick running into him, and for a second all three of them stood like statues.

"You Roger's kids?" the woman asked, dropping the keys into her pocket and reaching for her radio. "You can't be playing back here."

She was walking toward them, speaking into her handset. Her words dropped into a low, wet groan, the whine of a dying dog. Then she was running, her hat flying off. Cal ripped open the door, but Brick held his ground.

The woman reached him, her fingers hooked like talons, her teeth gnashing. Brick didn't hesitate, swinging the Maglite. It struck her in the jaw, the crack echoing between the buildings. The woman dropped. She twitched, then lay still. Brick stumbled away, throwing the flashlight on top of her like it was a poisonous snake.

"Get her radio," Cal yelled.

Brick snatched it up from the ground, running to the door. "Oh Christ," he was muttering. "I didn't mean to hit her so hard."

"She'll be okay," said Cal, grabbing the walkie-talkie from Brick's trembling fingers. "You didn't have a choice."

They were in another corridor, this one longer and darker. The only light was coming from a door up ahead on the left.

Cal grabbed Brick by the arm, dragging him toward the door. A glance inside revealed a big room lined with lockers and empty coat hooks. They jogged a little farther, past another toilet and a room packed with sofas. *Come on,* Cal thought. They were running out of corridor. *It has to be here.*

It was. The last door they reached led into a canteen with dozens of tables and chairs and a big silver counter. Cal ran past it, through a set of double doors, and he was grinning by the time Brick caught up.

"Whoa," said Brick.

"Whoa indeed."

They were in a kitchen similar to the one in Fursville, only this place was spotless. There was food everywhere, shelf after shelf of cans and jars and packets and tubs and bottles. Brick angled straight for a crate of bread, ripping open a brown loaf and wolfing down three slices. Cal was tempted to do the same, a pressure in his gut almost dragging him toward the mountain of snack boxes in the corner. But they might not have long. They had to take what they could.

"Bags," he said, dropping the radio on the floor and pointing toward a pile of sacks. He upturned one, releasing an avalanche of potatoes. Brick did the same, both of them working in silence as they looted. Cal stopped when he could barely lift what he had, spinning the sack around to seal up the top. He dragged it toward the door. "You nearly done?"

"Nearly," Brick spat through a mouthful of something. He dropped a tin of spaghetti into his sack then spun it closed, hefting it over his shoulder.

They were running back into the kitchen when the radio bleeped. The sound almost stopped Cal's heart dead and he lost his grip on the sack, a box of coconut wafers dropping to the floor. There was a burst of static, then a man's voice. "Roger? Susan? You there?"

They tore through the double doors into the canteen, but even from here they could hear the radio bleep again, the amplified voice chasing them back out into the corridor: "Guys, what's going on? The police are here."

DAISY / *Hemmingway, 6:05 p.m.*

THE SECURITY GUARD WAS GETTING TIRED, but he wasn't slowing down. He chased after the car with that same ferocious expression, his bloody teeth bared, his fingers stretched out toward them. His feet scuffed the road, and at one point he even tripped, falling flat on his face. Chris slammed on the brakes, waiting for the man to push himself up again. He teetered, looked for a second like he might be coming out of it, then caught scent of them again and stumbled forward.

It was horrible. The guard didn't know what he was doing, and they were going to kill him at this rate.

Chris slowed as he reached the end of the road, Fursville almost directly opposite them now.

"Left or right?" he said, glancing at Daisy in the rearview mirror. The guard almost caught them again, his fingers squeaking on the trunk as Chris made a decision and swung left. Daisy heard the man utter a soft mewl as he scuffed his way along the road after them, his shirt hanging out over his big belly and one foot shoeless.

The poor guy. She wished there was something she could do.

Surely there was a way to switch off whatever was making them so angry.

Chris pulled into the abandoned showroom across from the park, turning in a circle so they were pointing back the way they came. The man shuffled toward them in a pitiful, shambling run. He tripped, falling again, and this time Daisy heard the crack of a broken bone.

"That's enough," she said, watching the guard try to push himself up. A red nub of bone was sticking out of his forearm but there was still nothing in his narrow eyes but rage. "Please, Chris, he's going to die."

"I don't know what else to do," Chris said. "We can't let him catch us, and we can't leave him here because he'll go back to the factory."

The man had somehow made it back onto his feet. He stumble-ran across the forecourt, his good arm held out. He hit the window, slapping it with no real strength. Chris swore, moving the car out onto the road again.

The ambulance shot by so quickly that it made their car rock. Daisy screamed, watching in horror as the ambulance wobbled, clipping the high divider and spinning into a series of cartwheels. It disintegrated as it rolled, shedding glass and metal and plastic for what must have been fifty meters before lying still. The engine ignited with a soft puff, smoke drifting lazily into the flawless sky. Only the security guard was moving, still throwing weak punches at the side of the car.

Chris said something, his words drowned out by another siren. This one was a police car, catapulting past them and skidding to a halt beside the ruined ambulance. "Oh no, oh no, this is really bad."

Two policemen scrambled out of the car. One of them ran toward the ambulance, the other gazing at the Jaguar. He shouted something to them but the wind snatched it away. Chris spun the wheel around, accelerating to the left away from the accident. The security guard toppled over behind them, but Daisy was no longer watching him. She was gazing across the flat land toward the factory, and the flickering blue haze that surrounded it.

CAL / *Cavendish Agricultural Technologies, 6:11 p.m.*

IT WASN'T JUST THE POLICE. A fire engine was coming through the open barrier, its siren still blaring. There was already a cop car in the courtyard, and was that a bomb disposal van on the road?

Cal ducked back inside the door of the staff block.

"We've had it," he said.

"What happened?" Brick asked. "How'd they even get here so quickly? It's been, what, ten minutes since we broke in?"

They looked at each other, and the answer seemed to dangle in front of them in the gloom.

"Rilke," they both said together.

Brick threw his sack of food to the floor. "I'm going to kill her."

At this rate he wasn't going to get the chance. Cal could hear shouts among the sirens, dozens of them. Luckily nobody was close enough yet for the Fury to trigger. But it wouldn't be long. There were already people running this way through the shimmering blue light. He gently clicked the door closed, his thoughts wheeling.

"Is there another way out?" he asked.

"How would I know?" Brick said. "Left the map back there, didn't I."

They set off, dragging their bags of food. There had to be a back exit, surely. For fires and stuff. Cal glanced up, seeing the familiar green emergency signs with the running stick man on them. He followed them inside the canteen, crashing through the double doors. It took him a second to spot the fire exit at the rear of the kitchen.

They were halfway there when they heard a voice from outside, distorted by a loudspeaker.

"This is the police. We know you're inside. Return to the front of the facility immediately."

"Man, it's like a bank robbery or something," Brick said. "What are they worried about, that we're going to steal a big bag of horse manure?"

"It's fertilizer, isn't it," said Cal. "It's what you can make bombs out of."

"Out of horse crap?" said Brick as they reached the door. "Seriously?"

"Shut it, Brick, we need to be quiet."

Cal pushed the bar in the center of the door, nudging it open. There was a soft click, then the silence of the room was torn apart by a clanging alarm.

"Real quiet, Cal," said Brick, punching open the door and legging it outside. Cal ran after him. They were in another courtyard, smaller this time, with a squat, square building dead ahead and more massive industrial vats to the right. Right behind those was the wall, five meters high and crowned with black spikes.

"This is your last chance," said the loudspeaker man, muffled but still painfully clear. Cal thought he heard a bark, the sound making his skin grow cold. Ferals he could outrun. Dogs he couldn't.

"What now?" he said. There were footsteps close by. He glanced over his shoulder, imagining fifty cops tearing around the corner of the staff block. Brick was moving toward the shining metal vats, each of them four, maybe five times as high as the wall. The giant silos were held in a nest of white scaffolding, and it didn't take Cal long to work out what Brick was planning.

The barks were louder now, heading their way. And there was another sound too, the distant *whump-whump-whump* of a helicopter. Why the hell did it have to be a fertilizer factory? He had to force himself to start moving again, panic making his body feel twice as heavy as it actually was, filling his bones with lead. The sack didn't help, and he nearly dropped it. But if they left here empty-handed then they'd be right back where they started.

Brick was obviously thinking the same thing, because he was spinning his bag around like a hammer thrower at the Olympics. He let go of it, food spilling out in a tight circle as the sack rose up toward the top of the wall. It didn't quite make it, bouncing off the bricks and thumping back onto the dirt. He ran to it, picking up cans and cartons and lobbing them individually over the spikes. Cal tore open his own bag and started throwing too, a barrage of food sailing over the wall. He'd thrown seven or eight items when he heard voices, much closer now.

"That'll do," he yelled, throwing over the now nearly empty sack. "Let's go."

They both ran to the nearest silo. Brick went first, jumping and grabbing one of the thick diagonal struts of the scaffolding.

He grunted as he hauled himself up, his feet struggling for purchase on the smooth metal. He made it to the next one, and Cal followed. His fingers slipped on his first attempt, jarring his knee as he fell back onto the concrete. He ignored the pain, leaping up and grabbing hold just as the first policeman ran into sight.

The man started to call out, but the word never made it as the Fury took over. He threw himself across the courtyard, his mouth open too wide, his eyes black pebbles. Cal's heart almost juddered to a halt. He reached for the next pole, clutching it and pulling his feet up just as the cop slammed into the bottom of the scaffold. Fingernails raked at his ankles, the man's mouth a dark, gnashing pit.

Cal climbed, screaming, not caring that he was overtaking Brick. They pushed against each other, their frantic movements almost knocking them both loose. Two more uniformed figures skidded past the side of the staff block, changing into ferals without missing a step. They clustered at the base of the silo, clawing upward. A fourth appeared, slipping on a can and cracking his head open on the ground.

"Keep going!" Brick said, navigating his way up the side of the silo. Cal looped his arm around the next strut, almost slipping into the ocean of hands and teeth that swelled beneath him. He hung there, the terror almost too much for him, leaving him faint. Then Brick's hand was on his arm. "Don't you dare," the other boy said. "You're not leaving me on my own."

His feet found something solid and he pushed himself up to the next level. More and more police were piling into the courtyard, howling as the Fury overwhelmed them. There were dogs too, their tails between their legs as they watched their masters turn into beasts.

Brick was level with the wall now. He stretched out one arm, the spikes almost close enough to touch. But it was a long drop, and certain death lay in the surging, shrieking chaos below.

"Do it," Cal said. "You can make it."

Brick swore, then with a choked cry he pushed off the scaffold and flapped toward the wall. He hit hard, grunting, but he managed to hook his hand over the top and pull himself up. The bass thump was louder now; a helicopter flew overhead like a bloated bluebottle. Cal could imagine the pilot's face as he looked down, seeing his police mates baying like wolves.

"You coming or what?" said Brick, moving carefully to the side. Cal eased up another couple of struts, trying and failing not to look down. The courtyard was now a heaving mass of black uniforms and hate-filled faces.

He took a deep breath then threw himself at the wall, his stomach turning in wild circles as he reached out for one of the spikes. It sliced into his hand but he held on, hauling himself up until he was perched on the edge. A quick glance down the other side revealed a sheer drop into a patchy meadow, nothing but sand and sea grass and assorted items of food.

Together, they eased themselves around, hanging over the drop. The helicopter spun overhead, angling ever lower, battering them with a hurricane of wind and noise. Cal looked at Brick and smiled.

"This is insane. If we die, I just want you to know that you're an arsehole," he shouted.

Brick grinned back. "I know."

Then they both let go.

IT WAS LIKE WATCHING A DOZEN DIFFERENT FILMS at once on a television that flicked wildly and randomly between channels.

Rilke could make out snippets—a huge steel container that flashed brilliantly in the sun, a wall with spikes on it, a moving car, an ambulance in flames. But she couldn't make much sense of what she saw. All she knew was that her plan was working. The others, the ones who had turned their back on her, were now at the mercy of the Fury. They would either drown in an ocean of human rage, or they would be forced to take action, to do what it was they were here to do.

They would have to fight back.

She opened her eyes. Some of the madness outside was bleeding into the restaurant. Faint sirens faded in and out with the soft lull of the sea and the guttering roar of a fire. There was a helicopter out there too. She wondered how long it would hang in the sky before its pilot was consumed by the Fury.

"Shouldn't we go and help them?" whispered Jade. "They'll die out there."

"Not if they embrace their gift," Rilke replied.

Schiller had been quiet for a while now, but he was starting to stir. He tilted his head up, looking at her with eyes of fire. His left arm still hung oddly, a lump beneath his skin where the joint had popped out. He didn't seem to be in any pain, though. If anything, he was stronger than she'd ever known him to be, his gaze so intense that she had to look away.

"But what happens when the others are caught, or killed?" Marcus asked. "Won't the police come here? Won't they sense us?"

"Yes," she said, glancing at her brother again. "But we'll be ready for them. Won't we, Schill?"

Schiller lifted his good arm, studying his hand as if he'd never seen it before. It burst into flames, soft blue tongues that caressed his skin, darting between his fingers. He pressed the burning palm against his dislocated shoulder, those playful flames spreading. With a series of ugly, wet cracks his arm slotted back into place. He held both hands in front of him, radiating cold light. He was smiling.

"Oh yes," Rilke said, grinning back. "We'll be ready."

DAISY / *Hemmingway, 6:15 p.m.*

"Turn around, Chris, we can't leave them!"

Chris ignored her, the car accelerating hard, an invisible hand pushing her back into her seat. She cried out again, and this time he slammed on the brakes, tires squealing as they shuddered to a halt. It wasn't her pleas that had stopped him. Up ahead, blocking the road, was a police car, its blue lights flashing.

"No!" Chris yelled, wrestling with the gear stick and reversing. He swung the car around, gouging a chunk of dirt from the shoulder as he drove back the way they'd come. The police gave chase, pulling up close behind them. Daisy twisted, looking at the policewoman driver, seeing the exact moment that her face went from normal-angry to feral-angry. She let go of the wheel, reaching over it. The man next to her was doing the same, leaning forward in his seat, his cries misting up the windshield.

With nobody steering it, the police car slammed into the angled roadside embankment, flopping up then down, the windows shattering and the airbags deploying. Chris was going too fast for her to see what happened to the people inside. The burning ambulance was up ahead and Chris jerked the wheel, Daisy sliding across the leather seat into Adam as they reentered Soapy's car lot. Two policemen were waiting for them. One flashed past the window, too fast for the Fury to kick in. The other bounced off the hood, rolling over the car and hitting the ground limply.

"Chris, no!" Daisy wailed. "You're killing them."

He didn't answer her, his eyes bulging in the mirror. He kept his foot down as they plowed toward the rusty fence at the back of the forecourt. Daisy wrapped her arms around Adam—the boy still as quiet as a mouse—the impact bumping her into the air and cracking her head against the roof.

She blinked away the pain, seeing that they were in a huge, open field. The factory sat at the other end of it, its ugly bulk filling up the cracked windshield. She bit down on another cry as the car bounced over the uneven ground, her insides feeling like they were being shaken to pieces. At least they were going in the right direction again. They might be able to find Cal and Brick.

A fresh siren, another police car pushing through the loose flap of fence and giving chase. This one was bigger, one of those giant truck things. It hardly even seemed to notice the craters and hillocks of the field, looming up behind them like a shark in the ocean.

"Don't!" Daisy cried out to the policemen inside, her voice lost in the thunder of engines. "You'll get hurt!"

But they had already turned feral, nothing but glinting eyes and half-moons of teeth in the darkness of the four-wheel-drive. It shunted them, the back of their car jolting off the ground. The view through the windows lurched like a ship's wheelhouse in a stormy sea. She had time to see the ditch dead ahead of them, a deep scar that ran the width of the field.

Then the car plunged into it and her world flickered off.

CAL / *Cavendish Agricultural Technologies, 6:18 p.m.*

CAL CRIED OUT AS HE LANDED, his legs sinking into the soft, beachy soil. The pain in his knee was like a poisoned knife twisting into the cartilage. There was a thud as Brick dropped beside him, rolling clumsily away from the wall. He scrabbled to his feet and picked up the sack Cal had thrown over before running back and offering Cal a hand.

"You okay?" he asked, hauling him up. The pain flared as Cal pulled his foot free and he couldn't stop the moan tumbling from his lips.

"I'm fine," he said, limping across the rough ground. Brick ran off, frantically foraging for food in the short grass and throwing anything he found into the sack. From behind them came a nerve-shredding chorus of banshee wails and the thunder of fists against the wall. The cops would go back to normal as soon as he and Brick were out of range, then they'd start the chase again. The helicopter roared above them, flattening the strands of sea grass and making the field ripple like water. It was so loud that Cal didn't hear the growl of engines until there was an almighty crunch from the other side of the field.

He looked up to see a silver car flip end over end, its hood crumpled up like a fist, punching into the dirt, then collapsing onto its roof. A police Land Rover somersaulted gracefully over it, losing momentum midair and tumbling sideways. Smoke spewed from the wrecks, but through the billowing black curtain Cal recognized the driver.

"It's Chris," he said, pointing. He began to run, his twisted knee forgotten.

"Here they come," yelled Brick, slinging the half-empty sack over his shoulder. Cal glanced back to see four or five cops charging from the main road, all of them shouting and pointing. They were a hundred meters away, maybe, but they'd soon catch up once the Fury had them.

We're going to die, Cal thought, and he was surprised by the lack of emotion. It was a statement of fact, one that seemed to carry no weight. If anything, it filled him with a trace of relief. *No more running, no more hiding, no more not knowing.* Just death.

And then he thought of Daisy, upside down in the car, clawing at the window as gas fumes filled her lungs. He ran harder, putting his head down, overtaking Brick. In the distance, another Land Rover was emerging from Soapy's, the bulk of Fursville hanging over it like a dark cloud as it accelerated across the field. Incredibly, somebody was clambering out of the crashed one too, a broken shape whose police uniform had been all but torn away. The man staggered onto his feet, then seemed to collapse on the upturned Jag, kicking at the windows.

"What do we do?" Brick said, wheezing.

They were halfway between the factory and the car now, the sound of shouting behind them rising up even over the thunder of the chopper. There were barks too. It wouldn't be long before

Cal felt needled teeth in his legs, dragging him to the ground. Then it would be game over.

"Cal? What do we do?"

He didn't have a plan, only his instinct. If they could just get to the car, if they could just reach Daisy, if they could just get back to the park, they'd be okay.

"Keep running," he shouted as they closed the gap. The other Land Rover was going to beat them to it, but it didn't matter. "Keep running, and trust me."

DAISY / *Hemmingway, 6:20 p.m.*

SOMEBODY WAS SHAKING DAISY FROM A DREAM OF FIRE. She was glad, because in her dream the whole world was burning, but instead of heat there was cold—bodies freezing and buildings collapsing while ash-colored snow fell from the heavens.

She snapped open her eyes, thinking at first that her dream had come true. Everything was wrong, the world upside down, her head full of horrible, choking smoke. Her whole body ached, but there was a really bad slicing pain in her neck. When she reached up—no, *down*—she felt a noose there, digging into her skin. It took her a moment to understand it was her seat belt.

It took her another moment to realize that someone was next to her, crouching on the ceiling, which was now the floor. His small hands were on her shoulders, shaking her wildly, and his sooty face opened up like a flower when he saw that she had come around.

"Adam?" she wanted to ask, the word coming out as a hacking

cough. Something was banging, a bare foot crunching against the window, the toes bruised and bent unnaturally. Daisy's memories shone in the smoke, the police car that had chased them, then Chris driving into a ditch.

Chris. He too was suspended the wrong way up in the driving seat. Blood dripped freely from his nose, forming a little pool on the ceiling. She called his name between more coughs but he didn't respond.

Adam was fiddling with something on the seat, and she followed his hands to her seat-belt clip. The button was jammed, not budging no matter how hard she pressed it. A powerful wave of claustrophobia ripped through her and she cried out, tugging the belt in an attempt to free it. There was a funny smell in the air, behind the smoke. It was the way her dad smelled every time he put the barbecue on in summer. It was the horrible fuel stink that came right before a fire.

"Go," she said to Adam. "Get out."

She wasn't sure if they were words or just coughs. Either way Adam showed no sign of leaving. He pulled at her belt, making soft, scared whimpers, his face screwed up with the effort. She could hear another engine sound from outside, then their car rocked wildly as something thumped into it. The cramped space seemed to shrink and darken even further. There was a soft *whumping* noise, and the air flickered and glowed.

"Please, Adam, you have to go or you'll die in here."

He shook his head, still pulling at the belt. There was a shriek from outside, then the window right next to her shattered. A pair of rough, bloody hands reached in. She screamed, fingers like steel rods in her skull. Another crash, a cutthroat grin slithering in through the rear window and bloodied fingernails around Adam's throat.

Daisy's world was growing dark, the pain too much. And the worst of it was that as the shadows and the smoke crept into her head, turning everything to dusk, she could only hear Rilke's voice. *I told you,* it said. *Why didn't you listen?*

But if Rilke was right, and they were here to murder the world, then Daisy didn't really want to live anymore anyway. She would rather be with her mum and her dad, wherever they were. At least this way she could go home.

She let go of the claws that ripped at her scalp, and reached out to Adam.

"We're going together," she said. "And I'll always look after you."

Even though he was being dragged from the car, Adam seemed to hear her. He stuck out his hand, stretching his fingers toward her. And incredibly, he was smiling.

It's not such a bad way to leave, Daisy thought. *Looking at a smile.*

And offering him one back, she grabbed hold of his hand.

BRICK / *Hemmingway, 6:23 p.m.*

BRICK WAS ONLY TEN METERS AWAY WHEN THE CAR EXPLODED.

The upturned Jag was surrounded, five policemen kicking and punching it, trying to get inside. One of them had his hands through the back window and Brick could make out a familiar face in the billowing smoke. Daisy. Rage boiled up from his stomach, howled from his mouth as a ragged scream.

"Leave her alone!"

There was a flash of pure white light, a bubble that expanded from the car and blasted away the smoke. Brick threw himself to the ground, a hand over his face, waiting for the noise and heat of the blast.

It never came.

He looked up to see that searing white light engulf the police, burning through them. They crumbled into ash like sticks of dry wood, filling the air with a snowstorm of burning embers. The blinding orb flickered, then was sucked back into the car with lightning speed. A shock wave blasted across the field, a crack of thunder that almost knocked Brick's head off. Then an impossible silence.

He worked his way unsteadily to his feet, swaying. Beside him Cal was doing the same, wiggling his fingers in his ears as though he'd gone deaf. They peered back through the infinite quiet to see the surging mass of police still stampeding toward them from the road, not yet close enough for the Fury. In the other direction the Jag sat inside its blizzard of incandescent ash, no sign of life anywhere near it.

"What happened?" Cal's voice sounded a mile away. Brick flexed his jaw, sounds gradually easing their way back into the world. The helicopter had pulled back from the explosion, but it was hovering above them again, the downdraft making Cal's hair billow.

Brick didn't answer him, just started running again. It was only after a couple of steps that he realized he'd dropped the half-empty sack of food. Not that it mattered—as hungry as he was, it didn't look likely that any of them would live long enough to eat again. He reached the car in seconds and dropped to his knees beside it. Hot ash danced around his face, burning his skin where it landed. He brushed the falling flakes of dead people away, peering into the crushed darkness to see Chris there.

"Daisy?" Cal yelled, ducking down next to him. They both looked into the backseat. It was empty. "He must have dropped them somewhere. Come on, help me get him out."

"But I just saw her," Brick started, wondering if he'd only imagined her face in the churning chaos.

Cal tried the door but it was crumpled into itself. He stood back and kicked the splintered glass of the window, reaching through the gap and calling Chris's name. Brick looked up, the mob of cops maybe thirty meters away, close enough to make the ground shudder. There was an army of them.

He pushed in beside Cal, both of them trying to loosen the seat belt. There was a pool of blood in the bottom of the car, still dripping off the tip of Chris's nose. He was unconscious, his motionless bulk making it impossible to free him. Brick glanced up again. Twenty meters, and the ones at the front were already turning. He grabbed Cal's shoulders, pulling him out of the window.

"We can't leave him!" Cal shouted, throwing himself back, wrenching at the boy inside.

"We have to," Brick said. Fifteen meters, a line of witches' faces. "Cal, come on!" He grabbed Cal's arms and ripped him free, hauling him up. *"Look!"*

They stared at the wave of uniforms that surged toward them, the grunts and howls and shrieks and growls almost too much to bear. Cal looked back at Chris.

"I'm so sorry, mate," he said. Then they were both running again, bolting from the madness at their heels.

DAISY STOOD UP, REELING. She was standing in a field. The *same* field. But their upside-down silver car was all the way over *there*. She spun around to see the deserted showroom right next to her, and behind it the towering toothless grin of the big wheel inside Fursville.

We moved ourselves, she realized. *We touched hands and somehow got from over there to over here.*

The air was alive with fireflies, those same glowing embers that she'd seen back in the restaurant with Rilke.

She realized there was a hand in hers and she looked to see Adam there, a halo of ash circling his head, dropping onto his shoulders. He was still smiling.

Gradually pieces of reality were clicking back into place—the sound of sirens and the fat black fly that hovered over the distant car. Squinting into the sun, she could make out a swarm of people stampeding across the other side of the field, and two more sprinting toward her.

"Cal!" she shouted, recognizing them. "Brick!"

She tightened her grip on Adam's hand and started running, stumbling over the lumpy earth and through knotted traps of long grass until they were within earshot.

"Daisy?" Cal was calling.

The two boys galloped up to her, both of them drenched in sweat. They all looked back across the field. The car was invisible beneath a mass of writhing, black-suited forms, the helicopter hanging over them and making the whole horrible scene swim in dust.

"Chris," said Daisy, the tears bubbling up even though she didn't want them to. Whatever they'd done, she and Adam, they'd left him behind. She peered through the blur to see Cal shaking his head.

"I'm sorry, Daisy. We couldn't get him out."

There's still time. She didn't say it, though, because it was a lie.

"We should go," said Brick. "We might be able to hide inside the park. It's our only shot."

But none of them moved, watching as the horde tore their way into the upturned car. And they all felt it when Chris died, a sudden cold shadow in their heads as though something had been switched off. A burning shape seemed to claw its way out of the wreck, a flickering, insubstantial figure made of flame. It spread its huge, graceful wings, opened its mouth as if to howl, then evaporated into the heat and noise of the meadow.

That was Chris's angel, Daisy thought. *It died too.*

"Come on," said Brick. "We should go."

Daisy looked for a moment more, seeing the police seem to snap out of a trance. Some of them had red, glistening hands. She hated them so much. It didn't matter that they hadn't known what they were doing, that it wasn't really their fault. They'd still murdered him. Some of them were already turning to face her, pointing and shouting. The helicopter banked, sweeping toward the park.

They clambered over the broken fence that led back into Soapy's, running past the bodies of the security guard and the policeman. The ambulance lay to their right, just a smoking shell. But there was nobody else in sight. Daisy looked up as they jogged across the road, seeing the sign that Brick had painted over. FURYVILLE. Cal disappeared into the thick hedge and the rest of them followed. Only in the welcome coolness of the shade did Brick turn to her.

"What happened back there?" he asked. "In the car? I saw you inside it, then you vanished."

"It was the angels," she said. "Rilke was right. They moved us. They *saved* us."

"And what happens now?"

"Something bad, I think," she said, shaking her head. "I don't know."

She didn't know, yet hadn't she already seen it? The park drowning in flames, and Rilke standing in the middle of the inferno, laughing. What choice did they have, though? Outside there was only the Fury, there was only death. At least in here they were together.

Brick held her gaze for a moment more, then he took her hand and led her and Adam into the park.

RILKE / *Furyville, 6:30 p.m.*

THEY'RE HERE, SAID SCHILLER.

Rilke straightened at the sound of her brother's voice. The words seemed to be beamed right into the center of her head, and she couldn't work out if he was actually talking or just *thinking* them at her. He sounded the same, and yet different. There was a hidden depth to that familiar, whining tone. Something ageless that resonated inside her skull.

She stared at him. His hands were still alight, painting the room in a shimmering glow. As she watched, the fire spread up his arms, engulfing his torso and his neck and finally his face. His eyes were two raging suns, their light overwhelming. Rilke gazed into them, and it was like she was looking through her twin into a realm of pure being, a place of terrifying, mesmerizing power.

Schiller shrugged, and this time two translucent wings unfurled elegantly behind him, stretching over his head like twin sails. They seemed to shimmer in and out of being, as if they were made from nothing more than air, heat. He extended them, their tips almost bridging the gap between the restaurant walls, and when he folded them again they unleashed a hurricane of wind. It sent Marcus and Jade rolling across the room, tables and chairs crashing into the walls, but Rilke held her ground against the cold blast, kneeling before her brother like someone praying at an altar.

She had never loved him more.

"You know what you have to do," Rilke said to him. He cocked his head, unsure.

I think so, he said, or didn't say.

"You *know* so," Rilke said, standing and taking a step toward him. "Because I've told you why you're here. Don't disappoint me, Schiller. Don't disappoint *them*."

Schiller's fire flared, and he smiled at her.

I won't, sister. I promise.

Jade was crawling frantically back. She lay prostrate beside Rilke, laughing. Marcus huddled against the back wall, shaking his head. Schiller extended his wings again, and with a gentle effort he raised himself into the air. He began to move, not walking, just gliding a foot or so off the ground. Beneath him, things seemed to grow from the floor—tremulous shapes that looked like budding plants but which were made of flame, twisting and evaporating after a second or two.

"Where is he going?" asked Jade.

"To do what he was called here to do," Rilke said, watching her brother float ghostlike toward the doors. He pushed through them, and the wood evaporated at his touch, blossoming into a cloud of dust and ash that defied gravity, buoyed up by the energy streaming from him. Rilke followed him as he descended the stairs, Jade huddled against her, Marcus too, all of them treading carefully over the carpet of glowing tendrils in Schiller's wake. He gave off a subsonic hum, a sound that made the air tremble.

"To do what we were all called here to do," Rilke said. She was giddy with excitement, a surge of insane glee that rattled up her throat and exploded from her grinning lips. "He's going to start a war."

CAL / *Furyville, 6:35 p.m.*

BRICK LED THE WAY DOWN THE SIDE of the Boo Boo Station, his face a grimace of panic as the helicopter swept overhead. Daisy followed, pulling Adam along with her. A tornado of rubbish swirled in the narrow alley, the world shaken by the helicopter's relentless thunder. Cal screwed his eyes shut against the grit, trying to remember the way. His head was spinning—partly fear, partly a painful, gnawing hunger. He could hear Brick calling out.

"Where are we going?" At least that's what it sounded like. There was no air anymore, just the howling dust.

He opened his eyes as much as he dared, pointing up the path. "Pavilion," he shouted. It wouldn't exactly be safe there, but there was nowhere else to go. In seconds the park would be infested with police, all of them feral. If they could get inside then they might be able to barricade the doors, hole up until they thought of a plan. Brick shrugged, cupping a hand to his ear. "Pavilion!" Cal repeated, as loud as he could manage.

He didn't wait to see if Brick had understood, just led Adam and Daisy to the end of the path then up past the carousel. The chopper banked around the big wheel, the wind easing up. In the sudden lull Cal could make out voices behind them. He looked back in time to see the main gates balloon inward, spitting shrapnel. There was a growl of an engine, and with a massive crunch the chains snapped. A Land Rover barreled into the park, its hood smoking, and a river of police streamed after it.

"Do not move!" one of them shouted, pointing right at Cal. "Or we will be forced to open fire."

Open fire?

Three helmeted cops with automatic rifles ran to the front of the pack. They crouched, aiming the weapons down the path. Even from here Cal could see that their fingers were on the triggers. Who could blame them? They'd just seen their mates get blown into ash. He slung his hands up.

But there was nothing they could do. If they ran, the chances were they'd be mown down. If they stayed, they'd be torn to pieces as soon as the cops got close enough.

"We're just kids," Cal shouted. "Don't shoot."

"Stay where you are," shouted the same man as before. Some of the cops were moving cautiously forward.

"Please don't," Daisy said, Adam sobbing next to her. "If you come near us then bad things will happen. Please stay away."

"Yeah," said Brick, his voice cracked in a hundred places. "We've got a bomb."

The police hesitated.

"A bomb?" hissed Cal, looking at Brick. "They're definitely going to shoot us now."

"We need you to put the device on the ground," the man shouted, his words almost drowned out by the helicopter that circled overhead. "And step away. Do this now, or we will be forced to shoot."

"Now what?" Cal said.

"Hell do I know?" Brick answered. He took a step backward.

"Brick, stay still for God's sake," Cal said. But the boy wasn't listening, taking another step, and another. His body was tense, like he was going to bolt. "Brick, *don't*!"

As he spoke, he realized that the helicopter wasn't the loudest sound in the park anymore. There was something else, a hum inside his head, soft but deafening. It was like the noise an amp makes when you stick an electric guitar in it but don't play any notes, a dull buzz that was making his skull vibrate. Brick could obviously hear it too, because he clamped his hands to his ears, crying out.

A howling shriek erupted as one of the cops stepped past the invisible line of the Fury. His face shriveled into something that was only just human, white rage driving him on. Someone else, a policewoman, chased after him, turning feral, both of them hurling themselves down the path.

There was nothing else to do. Cal turned and ran, they all did, as the air behind them was torn apart by gunfire.

SOMETHING WHISTLED PAST BRICK'S EAR, sounding like a hornet, stinging his flesh. He ducked down, his arms and legs like pistons as he sprinted toward the pavilion. He didn't look back—not because of the fear but because of the guilt of leaving the others.

He made it halfway before he saw it, the sight stripping away every grain of strength and making him crash to his knees.

Schiller floated from the pavilion, bathed in flames, the building's walls literally peeling away from him like the edges of burning paper. His feet didn't touch the ground, an invisible force holding him up. Something extended from his back: a pair of wings made up of gossamer-thin flames. The boy's face wasn't his anymore—his eyes were twin furnaces that blazed out across the park, devoid of all emotion.

There was more gunfire, but distant now. It no longer seemed to matter. Brick heard screams, the cry of the Fury, but he couldn't quite remember how to be scared. He could only gaze at Schiller as the boy advanced. He would look at him forever, even if it burned his eyes from his sockets. Was it possible that a creature like this lived inside him too, dormant for now but ready to wake and embrace the same power? For the first time he believed it, he believed what Rilke had said.

Schiller reached him, making the path erupt into a forest of fiery plants that curled up and vanished as quickly as they appeared. The hum in the air was incredible, a current of pure energy. Brick shuffled around on his knees, watching the boy—the *angel*—as he glided toward the front of the park.

It was chaos back there. Cal was on the ground, pinned by two cops, his legs kicking out helplessly as they tore at him. Daisy and Adam were still running, both of them blinded by tears. Behind them was a seething wall of feral police. The three men with guns were still firing. A bullet punched through Daisy's shoulder, emerging from the other side and dragging a comet tail of dark red blood behind it. The impact threw her forward, rolling her over in the dirt until she slid to a halt, motionless.

"Daisy!" Brick shouted. He raced over, skidding down beside her and lifting her head. Her eyes were open, but they weren't seeing anything. Adam was there too, holding her hand in both of his, tugging on it like he was trying to wake her up. "No!" Brick shouted, the word as weak and as useless as he was, drowned out by the gunfire and the roar of the helicopter and that endless, nightmare hum.

Brick lifted Daisy up and pushed his hand against the wound, blood spilling through his fingers, so hot it felt like it was burning him. He held her, wanting it to be over, wanting it all to end. It was just too much.

Schiller turned his head, surveying the park with those soulless pockets of light. The men with guns had turned their weapons on him—aside from one, who had ripped off his helmet and was gouging at his own face in a fit of insanity. The bullets seemed to freeze when they reached the boy, hanging in the air in front of him and forming a shimmering curtain of lead. With a swipe of his hand, Schiller scattered the projectiles in all directions, a dozen cops thrown backward as their heads and chests exploded.

Kill them, Brick screamed silently. And he wanted it more than anything. These pathetic, murderous humans who had broken into his home, who had attacked his friends. They had given up their right to life. He clutched Daisy to him, firing out the message to the boy who hung in his cradle of flame. *Kill them all, kill them now.*

A hand dropped onto his shoulder and he looked up to see Rilke there. Jade and Marcus were behind her, both of them transfixed by the creature before them. Rilke smiled at him.

"He will," she said, turning her face up, bathed in her brother's golden glow. "Watch."

Schiller opened his arms, like he was about to hug someone. His eyes settled on the police. More and more of them were turning feral, running up the path toward the angel. Even the ones that had been stamping on Cal switched their target, throwing themselves at the floating boy.

They didn't even get close.

Without so much as touching them, Schiller lifted the two closest men into the air and turned them inside out—their bodies folding and refolding until they were nothing more than mangled meat. He flicked his hand and the ruined corpses sailed over the park, rising into the darkening sky as though launched by a catapult. The other ferals didn't notice and continued to charge mindlessly at him with bared teeth and clawed fingers.

Schiller cocked his head and another dozen cops were scooped up by the same invisible force. This time they were thrown at each other, crushed into a giant ball of flailing limbs. It spun wildly, growing smaller and smaller with a chorus of cracking bones until those twelve men and women were no bigger than a beach ball. The knotted lump of flesh slammed into the ground with enough force to shatter the concrete, a web of cracks stretching out from the crater.

This isn't right, something in Brick protested. He pushed it aside. He didn't want to hear it.

The helicopter was retreating, pulling up fast. Schiller pumped those vast wings and launched himself into the air. He rose alongside the machine, and even though he didn't lay a finger on it the rotors buckled and twisted, breaking free with an ear-shattering squeal. The rest of the chopper began to crumple, something red and wet blossoming behind the shattered windshield. Then the wreck jolted to the side with incredible force, plowing a hole through the pavilion and the fence beyond, carving a mile-long trench across the surface of the sea.

The ferals were still coming, but Schiller had only just started to experiment with his powers. He dropped back down, stopping just above the ground and stretching his arms out once again. The electrical hum grew louder, making Brick's eardrums feel like they were about to rupture. The flames around the boy were as bright as phosphorus, burning a hole in the very surface of reality. His mouth opened, a pocket of utter brilliance.

And he spoke.

His voice was wordless and world-ending. It was a roar that ripped through the air and shook the ground to dust. Everything before it fractured and disintegrated—the concrete and the stone beneath, the Land Rover, the bricks in the walls, the metal gates, the flesh and blood and bones of the ferals, the mud and grass in the field beyond—a tidal wave of broken matter that rose into the air, blotting out every last scrap of sunlight.

Brick cried out, teetering on the brink of madness as that cloud rose and rose into an endless, lightless night.

Then Schiller's voice died and the night died with it, a million tons of debris falling back to its resting place. Brick curled into himself, the noise impossible, utterly terrifying. The world shook, and shook, and shook.

And finally fell silent.

CAL / *Furyville, 6:59 p.m.*

FOR AS FAR AS HE COULD SEE, the world was an ocean of ruin; a landscape of rubble and plundered earth, rent and broken all the way to the distant factory. Even that hadn't escaped unscathed, pillars of smoke rising in front of the glowering sun like prison bars. Dust was still falling, a rain of dirt and blood and bone that pattered onto the vast grave that had once been Hemmingway.

Every part of Cal was in pain. He thought his nose might be broken, and there were welts over his face and neck where the ferals had torn at him. One of his fingers was bent at an odd angle, too sore to touch. He cradled it against his chest. He should be grateful, because he was alive. But he wasn't. The cost of his survival was too great. It wasn't just the town that was gone. Everything he knew had been irrevocably changed.

It took him a moment to find the courage to look around. The first thing he saw was Schiller. The boy sat on the path, his legs curled up to his chest, no trace of the flames or the wings or those star-burned eyes. He was shivering, and his sister crouched beside him, her arms locked around his shoulders. Jade and Marcus stood close by, holding each other.

Brick was on the other side of the path next to Adam. He was holding something, and when Cal realized it was Daisy he pushed himself up, stumbling over to them. The girl was deathly pale, an ugly, gaping wound in her shoulder. But she was alive. Her soft, shallow breathing filled him with such an overwhelming sense of relief that he didn't notice the ice until he touched her.

She was freezing.

He pulled his hand away like he'd had an electric shock. Her skin was pearled with frost, and the chill that emanated from her was like a winter breeze.

"Daisy?" he whispered, stroking her cheek. "Daisy? Can you hear me?"

"She isn't answering," said Brick, his teeth chattering. The tears had frozen in the corners of his eyes and on his cheeks, hanging there like glass beads. "It's just like Schiller."

"She's changing," said Rilke matter-of-factly.

"She didn't want this," said Cal. "Make it stop."

Rilke shook her head.

"None of us can make it stop. Didn't you *see* him? Don't you understand what we're capable of?" She laughed, a chuckle of amazement. "It was wonderful. Schiller saved you, Cal; he saved all of us."

He had. There was no doubt about it. Without him, they would all have been trampled into the dirt. Rilke's twisted logic battered against his mind. Was she right? Was this really why they were here? To uproot all of humankind, to purge their species from the face of the earth? He looked out across the wasteland that Schiller had created. Only it wasn't a wasteland. It looked more like a field that had been plowed and furrowed, which was ready for something new. And the peace that hung over it, free of shouts and screams and sirens—it was truly perfect.

Yet still that nagging doubt, the feeling that Rilke was wrong, that she was making an awful mistake.

"She'll be okay," said Rilke. She got to her feet, hooking an arm under her brother and hoisting him up. Schiller smiled at her, just a boy again. But that power was still there, his to call on. Cal knew this the same way he knew that he too would someday go cold, and that something terrible would break through his soul. "We'll all be okay. You'll see, Cal. It might take a day, it might take a week, but you'll see."

"It doesn't hurt," said Schiller, his voice weak and quiet, almost exactly the same pitch as his sister's. After seeing him burning through the sky, ravaging the earth, Cal could make no sense of the boy before him. "It's like . . . like there's something in your body, but it doesn't control you, it doesn't force you to do anything. It just makes you strong, it keeps you safe. Don't fight it, it's . . . it's . . ."

He obviously couldn't find the word, but his rapturous expression said everything.

"But it told you why we are here, didn't it," said Rilke. "To wage war with humanity."

Schiller's eyes fell, scouring the ground for a truth he couldn't quite find. Rilke's grip on him tightened, so hard that Cal saw the boy wince.

"Tell them, little brother."

"Yes, that's why we're here," he said, trying to break away. But for all his new power he couldn't find the strength to free himself from her. His eyes met Cal's and there was fear in them, fear and a terrible sadness. "That's why we're here."

Rilke started walking, her brother taking small, cautious steps like someone using his legs for the first time. Marcus ran to the boy's other side, looping Schiller's arm around his shoulder and taking his weight. Jade finished the procession, brushing her hair from her eyes and glancing nervously at Cal.

"You don't have a choice," said Rilke as she walked patiently by her stumbling brother's side. "No matter where you go, no matter what you do, the same thing will happen. People will try to hurt you, and you will fight back. They won't leave you alone. They can't. It's in their nature. And that rotten, violent, corrupt nature is why we're here. We got it wrong; it isn't their Fury that will change the world, it's ours. Just think about it. Try to imagine what this world will be like when our job is done."

Cal *could* imagine it, nothing but sunshine and peace.

No no no no no, the protest railed, a drumbeat in his skull.

"Look after her," Rilke said, stepping onto the ocean of dirt, her feet kicking up clouds of black dust that had once been buildings and cars and people. "It will be easier for you when she wakes."

"Where are you going?" Cal asked.

"Nowhere, and everywhere" was her answer. "When you're ready, you'll know how to find us."

Cal watched her walk into the reddening sky with her flock—Schiller, Jade, and Marcus—the dust of the world raining down at their feet.

"We need to go too," said Brick. "This place will be swarming soon. We should find somewhere safe."

Safe. Rilke was right. There was nowhere safe anymore. They would be hunted wherever they went. Cal looked down at Daisy, radiating coldness, her eyes iced over, her small face expressionless. He wondered where she was, and what she could see there. He wondered if she knew what she would become when she woke.

"Yeah," he said, getting up. "You're right. Let's go. My mum's car's still down the beach, by the toilets. We can use that. You want me to carry her?"

"I'm okay," Brick said, struggling to his feet with Daisy in his arms. He shuddered with the cold, his words billowing from blue lips. "You take him."

"Come on, little guy," said Cal, scooping up Adam, wincing as pain lanced up his finger. The boy didn't react, staring at something only he could see. "Don't worry, it's gonna be okay."

"No it's not," said Brick. "Whole planet's going to hell."

"Thanks. Way to make him feel better."

"Up yours," Brick said, but there was a glimmer of a smile in his eyes. It spread to Cal, and even though it had no place here it felt good.

"You really are an arsehole," he said through a grin as they staggered across the park.

Brick looked around, sighing. Then he turned back to Cal. "I know."

DAISY / *Furyville, 7:05 p.m.*

SHE HAD ALWAYS THOUGHT that death would be peaceful, a place of infinite calm and quiet.

But Daisy stood inside a kingdom of fire and ice, of relentless movement and noise. She was at the junction of a billion different lives, the joining place of worlds. From here, she could see everything.

She had been shot, she knew that much at least. They had been inside the park, Fursville, running from the police. Then she'd felt

like she had been struck by a sledgehammer. She couldn't remember hitting the ground. It had been more like she'd fallen
through it, through the skin of the real world and into what lay
beyond. She'd been like Alice tumbling down the rabbit hole,
only what she was looking at now was no Wonderland.

And there was no sign of her mum and dad. She'd hoped at the
very least they'd be here waiting for her.

It's because you're not dead, something said. Was that her own
voice? She couldn't be sure, everything was too chaotic.

"Who's there?" she called out. "Where am I?"

No answer. She focused on the wheeling shapes around her,
all inside ice cubes just like the ones in her head. They made
no sense, countless flickering images and muddled sounds in
each one.

"Daisy, can you hear me?"

The voice seemed to cut through the rest, and with it one of
the ice cubes grew larger, groaning and cracking like an iceberg
as it filled her vision. It was Brick, his copper hair glowing in the
sun, his clothes ripped to tatters and covered in blood. It seemed
like his chest was on fire, an orb of blue flame that sat where his
heart should be. It took her a moment to notice that he was holding something in his arms, a tiny shape whose head lolled, whose
eyes were open and unseeing. It was *her*, she realized. But she
wasn't scared, because she too had a smokeless inferno inside her
chest—one that burned even brighter.

It's them. That's where they live.

And with that thought the ice cube melted. Another rose in
its place, and through it she saw more people she knew. Rilke
was helping her brother, Schiller, walk across an endless field of
dust and dirt. Marcus and Jade staggered alongside them, their

shadows long in the setting sun. They all had flames in their chests too, except Schiller, whose whole body was alight. He seemed to have another shape laid over his own, a figure with blazing eyes and huge Sphinx-like wings, which left glowing trails where they dragged along the ground. Looking at them made Daisy feel scared and excited at the same time.

That's what they look like when they've . . . She paused until the word "hatched" popped into her head. *Yes, when they've hatched. They can't survive in our world, so they have to live inside us.*

The image changed again. Did that mean she was right? Was this a test, maybe? She swept toward Rilke, into the girl's head, the world unraveling and re-forming. This time she saw people, hundreds of them, maybe thousands. Schiller stood among them, his face emotionless as he spread his hands and turned those men and women and children to dust. She could just about see Rilke there too, grinning insanely, before the scene was lost in a billowing cloud of ash.

So this is why we're here? Daisy said, her heart dropping to her toes. *But I don't want to hurt anyone. People do sometimes do bad things, and some of them aren't very nice, but most are kind and funny and peaceful. They don't deserve to die.*

The same scene again, Schiiler slaughtering countless more innocents. Daisy seemed to understand what she was being shown.

That's what Rilke sees, she said. *But she's wrong, isn't she? We're not here to kill people, we're here to save them.*

The shadows of the last scene melted away, the ice cubes clinking. Even though she had no body in this place, no face, she still felt like she was grinning.

I knew it! she told the angel inside her. *I knew you weren't bad!*

Her happiness didn't last. Another image swelled, this one

even worse than the last. Daisy knew what she was going to see there, but she could not close her eyes. She felt herself pulled into the scene, battered by a wind that stank of flesh and smoke. The man in the storm stood inside a nest of fractured darkness, his mouth a churning, grinding whirlwind. That same horrid, deafening sound—the endless inward breath—made her skin crawl.

Daisy screamed without sound, struggling to escape. But there was nowhere to go. She could do nothing but watch as the man in the storm opened his arms and more of the world shattered like glass, falling into a bottomless, lightless abyss. It was impossible not to notice how similar he was to Schiller. But this thing was utter evil, the opposite of life. The man in the storm turned his dead eyes toward her and somewhere in that awful sound was a sickening, gleeful, howling laugh. He tilted his corpse hands and even from this distance, even though she was only seeing it inside her head, she could feel the light draining out of her, the happiness and the love. It was leaving her utterly empty.

He's why we're here, Daisy spat, squirming, praying that it was the right answer and that the scene would fade away like the others. *He's a bad man, and he's doing something terrible, and we have to stop him.*

Cracks began to appear in the view, a golden glow spilling through them until the man in the storm disappeared in the haze. Daisy walked into the heat, like she was stepping onto a beach in the middle of summer. There was nothing here but light.

Who are you? she asked. *Are you angels?*

No answer. The view didn't change. Did that mean she was right or wrong? Or maybe she was a little of both. Maybe they weren't angels, but something else—something that people had caught glimpses of over the centuries and which had been given that name. There were all sorts of things that people didn't know about yet. Who was to say that creatures like this couldn't exist?

Daisy realized that there was a face in the light, so faint that it almost wasn't there at all. It was devoid of all emotion and feeling, its eyes burning pockets. It seemed to constantly peel apart and repair itself, as though it couldn't hold its shape for longer than a few seconds. Those blazing eyes looked at Daisy, so much power there that she could hear it in the air like thunder.

This is my angel, she understood, her terror and her awe like a white heat inside her.

Then, just like that, the light fell apart, the face dissolving into the fading glow. Daisy felt herself pulled away, so fast she left her stomach behind. She landed somewhere dark and cold, but she could feel that creature in every cell of her body, its fire spreading.

Voices, ones she recognized, echoing in the shadows.

"Which way?"

"Any way, just get us out of here."

She would wake up soon enough, and when she did she would be something different, something more. But Cal and Brick and Adam would still be there. They'd look after her. She'd look after them too. That was her job now, at least until their angels hatched.

And when that happened, they'd all be ready.

Ready to fight the man in the storm.

THE OTHER (4)

Nature, in her indifference, makes no distinction between good and evil.
—*Anatole France,* The Revolt of the Angels

THE SOUND OF THE PHONE wormed its way into his dream, and for a moment he was floundering in an ocean full of bells. Then he was awake, switching on his lamp and groping in the dark for the phone beside his bed. He had it halfway to his ear before he noticed it wasn't making the noise, and that realization blasted the last few scraps of sleep away.

It was his other phone. The *bad things* phone.

He swore, tumbling out of bed and ignoring the murmured protests from his boyfriend. The ringtone cut through his head, its cry shrill and relentless. *Bad things bad things bad things,* his mind sang along as he rummaged through the suit trousers hanging on the wardrobe door. He ripped out the phone, the vibrations making it feel like a living thing trying to squirm free. He almost dropped it, better to let it go than to find out why it was ringing. Instead he flipped it open and put it to his ear.

"This is Hayling," he said, although the introduction was pointless. The caller knew he was Graham Hayling, chief officer of the army's counterterrorism division, otherwise he wouldn't have dialed this number. Because this number was for emergencies—not your average run-of-the-mill serial-killer or arson or train-crash or bank-robbery emergencies, but code-red, critical, end-of-the-world emergencies. *Bad things.*

"Sir . . ." The voice belonged to Erika Pierce, his second in command, only it sounded somehow hollow, dead. *Don't say it*, he prayed. *Please don't say it.* But she did: "Something's happened."

"An attack?" he asked, using his shoulder to pin the phone to his ear while he scrabbled into his trousers. Erika sighed, and he could picture her chewing her bottom lip. In the pause that followed he heard the echo of sirens on the line.

"I think so," she said eventually. "It's . . ."

Bad, he thought when she didn't finish. It couldn't be worse than 9/11, though, could it? Or 7/7, the last time he'd had to pick up this phone, only that time he'd been in Majorca and they'd flown him home in a VC-10. He glanced at the bed, David propped up on one elbow blinking at him.

"Where?" Graham asked Erika.

"London," she replied. "Somewhere on the M1. We can't be sure yet."

Can't be sure meant they couldn't get near, and that scared Graham so much he slumped onto the edge of the mattress. *Can't be sure* meant dirty bombs, or worse; it meant contamination.

"We sent two teams up," she went on. "Neither came back. There's something . . . It's not right."

"I'll be right there, Erika," he said. "Don't be scared." And that was just about the stupidest thing he ever could have said to Erika Pierce, who had come top of her academy class at just about everything, who had single-handedly uncovered a plot to smuggle liquid explosives onto a Navy carrier and once punched a suspect so hard that she'd broken his jaw. But the voice on the phone didn't sound like his partner; it sounded like a child, lost and frightened.

"No," she replied. "Don't. I wasn't calling you to get you here. I was calling you so you could get away."

"What?" he said. "Erika, what are you talking about? Listen, I'm leaving the house now, just hang on."

"I won't be here," she said, a ghost's whisper. "I'm sorry, Graham."

He said her name again before he realized she'd hung up. *What the hell?* He looked at the phone as if somehow it could tell him more, then tucked it into his pocket and tightened his belt.

"What's wrong?" said David, rubbing his eyes.

"Nothing," he lied, pulling yesterday's shirt over his head and throwing a jacket on top. He didn't bother searching for socks, just slipped his shoes on, the leather cold and unpleasant against his skin. "I've got to go. I'll call you when I know."

He took three steps toward the bedroom door when something stopped him, a pressure in his stomach. It felt like a rope, one that had wound itself around his guts and was anchoring them tight. *Fear*, he told himself. And that was true, but this was something else, something more. *I was calling you so you could get away*, Erika had said. *Get away. Get away. Get away.* He turned back to David, wanted nothing more than to take his hand and run, and keep running. Instead he walked out of the bedroom and down the landing to the apartment's front door.

Outside, dawn had failed. Where sunlight should have been pouring over the lip of the world there was only a muted haze. It hung in the air, rotten, the color of a dead man's skin. The sensation in Graham's gut intensified, his pulse racing, that same nervous chant—*bad things bad things bad things*—battering the inside of his skull like a trapped bird. There were too many people here. At this hour there should have been a sprinkling of delivery drivers and market sellers and the last dismal dregs of the drunken clubbers. But the street was full, cars gridlocked and honking all the way up to the store on the corner, where a white van straddled both lanes, engine smoking. He was amazed the noise hadn't woken him sooner. A crowd was moving up the street, weaving in between the motionless traffic as people made their way toward Gospel Oak Tube. Everyone was moving east, and when Graham turned his head to see where they were coming from he understood why.

Over the rooftops and the trees of Hampstead Heath, the sky was broken.

Smoke churned upward, a vortex so thick and so dark it could have been granite. It looked almost like a tornado, only it must have been two miles wide, maybe more. It rotated slowly, almost gracefully, forming a pool of oil-colored cloud overhead. Explosions detonated inside the column, but they had no light—whipcracks of black lightning that left traces on Graham's vision, dark spots when he blinked. Every time they flashed they rent the air apart, revealing what was inside the vortex. Or rather what *wasn't* inside it.

Nothing, Graham thought, feeling like he was teetering on the edge of some vast, awful madness. *There is nothing there.* It wasn't just empty, it was utterly, *utterly* devoid. He could make out slivers of sky that weren't dark and weren't light—that weren't anything at all. It looked as though a mirror had been smashed, shards shaken loose to reveal the truth behind.

Another blast of negative light sliced through the vortex, cutting a silhouette into the smoke. Was that a *person* in there? It was too big, surely, too high off the ground. Yet it was there, a figure in the very center of the maelstrom, a man in the storm. Graham was miles away from it, and yet he felt as though that man was looking right at him with eyes of inverted fire. They burned into him, the darkness seeming to expand in his vision until he was blind. *It doesn't matter,* he heard himself think. *It's better that I can't see, better that I just—*

Something thumped into him, sending him stumbling back into the door of his apartment block. A woman muttered an apology, dragging a screaming child down the road after her. Graham caught his breath, shaking some of the darkness out of his eyes. He almost looked up again before stopping, putting a hand up to shield himself from the skies. Whatever it was over there, it was a bad thing, a *really* bad thing. And it was his job to make sure bad things didn't happen. He turned away, flicked open his phone, and hit the first number of his address book. It rang just once before somebody answered, and Graham didn't give them a chance to speak.

"Get me General Stevens," he said. "And tell him we're under attack."

EARLY MONDAY MORNING

And where two raging fires meet together
They do consume the thing that feeds their fury.
—William Shakespeare,
The Taming of the Shrew

IT WAS DAWN AND ROLY HIGHLAND WAS STILL DRUNK.

He staggered down the beach, a nightful of cheap rum making the world reel with every step. At one point he missed his footing entirely and sprawled forward, landing on his face. For some reason he found it insanely funny, giggling into the soft, cool sand. If his mum could see him now she'd throw a fit. He was supposed to have been home by eleven, but the rum had made time fly by too fast for him to keep up. What felt like half a year later he pushed himself to his feet. He'd dropped his bottle somewhere. The faintest trace of light was creeping over the horizon. The rest of the sea was as dark and as flat as slate. He could hear it whispering, urging him toward it. He didn't like the sea, not since he'd almost drowned in it when he was eleven.

"Can't hurt me now, though," he slurred as he teetered back to his feet. " 'Cause I'm *drunk*!"

He gave up on the rum—there had only been a couple of mouthfuls of backwash anyway—and set off to his left. His best mates Lee and Connor were out here somewhere, plus Connor's new girl, Hayley. It was Connor's fault they were out so late; he'd dared them to stay up all night. Roly's thirteen-year-old brother Howie was around as well, although he'd wandered off an hour or so ago claiming he wasn't feeling too good. That was the rum, it did that to you. Roly's head had been thumping for most of the night too.

"Hey," he called out. Something erupted upward from nearby, the flap of its wings like somebody clapping. The silence it left behind, broken only by that same endless whisper of the waves, was almost spooky. "Whooooooo," he said, nearly falling flat on his face again, scuttling crablike on his hands until he found his feet.

The others were probably hiding, planning to jump out at him or something. But he wouldn't give them the satisfaction of seeing him flinch.

"Because I'm invincible!" he shouted, his words swallowed by the sea. He giggled again, thinking of how impressed they'd be when they failed to scare him. Connor was two years older, seventeen now, and there were times when Roly felt like a total baby in front of him. That's why he'd drunk so much tonight—he'd matched his friend drink for drink and was still standing. Connor had to be impressed by that, and Hayley too. She was proper fit, and maybe if he impressed her enough tonight, then she'd dump Connor and go out with him instead.

Only if he could find them. Where the hell were they?

"Oi!" he screamed, lobbing a few choice swear words into the sunrise. The beach had been pretty deserted all evening, which was weird considering it was a Sunday smack bang in the middle of summer. Probably something to do with whatever had happened along the coast earlier. There had been some kind of explosion north of here, apparently, somewhere up by the old Fursville theme park. Roly hadn't seen anything but he'd felt the tremors at about seven.

"Mines," Connor had said matter-of-factly. They'd been sitting in the older boy's flat and the blast had been so powerful that the windows had rattled.

"Huh?" Lee had said.

"Them old sea mines, from the war and stuff. They find them all the time, they probably just blew one up."

They had all nodded, and that had been that. Connor was seventeen now, and he was going to join the army. He knew about stuff like explosives.

God, that all seemed like *years* ago. Roly staggered onward, gulping down salted air and trying to remember what else had happened that night. Already some of it was fading away, like disappearing ink.

"Screw you guys," he called out, fed up with their games. "I'm going home."

He stopped, wheeling from side to side in an effort to work out which way led back to town. The sea lay to his right, vast and black and menacing, so he steered his stubborn legs left toward the dunes. A soft breeze kicked up grains of sand, carrying them into his mouth where they crunched between his teeth. He muttered curses as he struggled on the crumbling ground, grabbing ropelike strands of sea grass to help haul himself off the beach. Once he was over the hump of the dune the going was easier, and he stumble-ran down the other side, wondering if there was any way of getting another drink.

The first line of Hemsby's crappy wooden beach bungalows was in sight when he heard voices up ahead. Or *were* they voices? They sounded more like grunts and whimpers, dogs maybe. He wouldn't be surprised. People would be waking up soon, taking their mutts for a walk before going to work. He ducked down onto one knee, planting his hand in the earth to stop himself tumbling. Was it his imagination or was the air suddenly colder? He shivered, tilting his head and waiting to see if the noises came again.

They did, a distant, snorting squeal that belonged in the slaughterhouse up the road. There were footsteps too, fast and hard, coming this way. It had to be Connor and Lee. They were probably still trying to scare him—and it was working, his pulse tripping, the pleasant numbness of the rum starting to wear away.

Man up, Roly, he told himself. He couldn't look scared, not in front of the others. They'd never let him forget it. He rose unsteadily, creeping onto the tarmac road that seemed to sprout organically from the beach. It curled around to the right, widening into the beachside promenade up ahead. The streetlights were still on, forming puddles of sickly yellow light that seemed to make the shadowed parts of the street even darker. Another cry barked out from between two shuttered arcades fifty meters away, those hammered footsteps getting closer. Then somebody shouted, a voice so full of grief and terror that Roly didn't recognize it until a figure skidded out onto the road, slipping on the sandy tarmac and crumpling into a heap.

"Howie?" Roly said, watching his little brother scrabble for a footing. What the hell was he up to? Howie lifted his head. He was still some distance away, but there was something wrong with his face. His mouth hung open, surely too wide, his eyes huge and white and wild. Roly took a step forward, adrenaline stripping the last of the alcohol in his system and leaving him as sober as he had ever felt in his life. "Howie," he called out. "What's wrong?"

There were more footsteps coming from the same direction. His brother made it to his feet and started running toward him, his arms wheeling, just as Connor sprinted out from between the arcades. The older kid didn't even stop for breath as he turned up the street toward Roly. Hayley followed, then Lee, then some guy dressed in a milkman's uniform, all of them leg-ging it toward him at full pelt. Something really bad had to have happened, because they all looked like they were seething with anger.

Not anger, he thought. *Fury.*

His little brother had halved the gap between them now, foam spraying from his lips. Connor was closing on him fast, uttering the same guttural wet barks. The urge to turn and bolt was so strong that Roly almost went, but he couldn't leave his brother.

"Howie, what's wrong?" he asked. Howie didn't answer, just kept running, pounding down the street in the hand-me-down Nikes that Roly had given him last Christmas. They all kept run-ning, a tide of people surging along the promenade with nothing but hatred in their faces. "Howie?" he said again, his voice cracked and broken, *"Howie!"*

Howie seemed to see him for the first time, and his expression flooded with relief.

"Roly," he cried. "Help me!"

Even as the words left Howard's mouth Connor reached him, grabbing a handful of his T-shirt. They tripped on each other, falling hard in a tangle of limbs.

Roly ran at them, watching in disbelief as Connor drove his knuckles into Howie's cheek. Even twenty-five meters away he heard the dull thump. Howie cried out, his hands slapping at his attacker, his eyes locked on Roly silently screaming *Help me help me help me.*

"Hey!" Roly yelled, still sprinting, twenty meters away now. "Get off hi—"

His world turned inside out, a soft, dark explosion inside his head that seemed to burn every single thought into oblivion.

Every thought but one.

Kill it kill it kill it kill it kill it

The boy on the ground wasn't his brother. It wasn't even human. Disgust boiled inside his stomach, raging into a white-hot fury that drove him down the street. Time slowed, everything perfectly quiet compared to the sapper's fire that flared in the very center of his mind. Only one thing was important. There was only one thing in the entire world that he had to do

Kill it kill it kill it kill it kill it

because this thing was wrong, it was his enemy, it was something that shouldn't be, that couldn't be

Kill it kill it kill it kill it kill it

something there inside that bag of flesh that had to be obliterated

Kill it kill it kill it kill it kill it

He fell to his knees, driving his fists into the squirming shape, again and again, tearing at it with his nails, his teeth, with every weapon he had, wanting just to

Kill it kill it kill it kill it kill it

Wanting it to be gone, to be dead, to be dead, feeling like he wouldn't be able to breathe again until he had killed it, like he was drowning, his lungs screaming, and the only way he would ever be able to get to the surface again was to

Kill it kill it kill it kill it kill it

He punched and scratched and gouged and choked and fought and dreamed of the breath he could take when it was dead and raged and raged and raged

Kill it kill it

• • •

HOWIE COULDN'T FEEL THE PUNCHES ANYMORE. He couldn't feel anything. It was as if he was sinking into a grave, dark and numb and cool and peaceful. His thoughts were ravaged, torn to shreds, but in those pieces he saw what had happened: the headache he'd had for days now suddenly vanishing, and then they'd turned on him without warning—Lee, Hayley, and that idiot Connor—throwing themselves at him outside the hardware shop, howling like animals. He wasn't even sure how he'd gotten away the first time, he'd just put his head down and run. He was good at running, he always had been, but Connor had been faster.

And Roly, his brother. How could he be in on it? Howie felt his head snap to the side and for an instant he was out of his grave, back on the street. He wasn't sure if his eyes were open, or if he was just imagining it, but he could see Roly now, kneeling next to him, his knuckles red. *That's my blood on his hands,* Howie understood. *He's stealing it.*

He tried to call his brother's name but he was six feet under again, or at least it felt that way, worms as tough as fingers burrowing into his skin. *I don't want to die, Roly,* he thought, hoping the words would reach his brother even though they would never find their way out of his mouth. He was only thirteen, he hadn't even kissed a girl yet, or had a go on Lee's dad's quad bike like he'd been promised. *It's not my time yet, just stop, stop!*

At least he was numb down here. It was getting darker, like somebody was throwing spadefuls of soil onto him. The thought was terrifying, and the shock of adrenaline that followed brought him back for an instant, the street once again there in shades of yellow and gray and red. Fists and feet rose and fell like pistons, like he was stuck inside an engine, and somewhere in his shattered mind he fumbled at gears, trying to drive himself away.

His brother was still there, but he found he couldn't even remember his name. Howie lifted a hand, wondering why his skin sparkled like he was wearing a suit of ice. His brother slapped it aside, preparing for another strike.

It never came. His brother's hand disintegrated, becoming a cloud of ash that hung in the air for a moment before spiraling slowly to the street. The boy didn't even seem to notice, just attacked with the stump of his wrist and his other fist. The fingers of his left hand came apart, leaving trails of red and white in the air like streamers. Then the rest of his body came undone, dissolving like he was a sculpture of salt thrown into a hurricane.

Howie couldn't move his head, but in the corner of his vision he saw Connor melt away into the gloom. The soft breeze made the boy's ashes dance in looping circles. Two more soft pops followed and the air was a shimmering haze of dust.

"Is he alive?" the words seemed to come from a million miles away. Somebody crouched down beside him, a girl, brushing powdered bone from her skirt. She put her hand to his head, leaving it there for a moment. Howie tried to nuzzle against it, but she pulled her fingers away, wrapping them in her other hand.

"He's freezing," she said. "He's one of us."

Thank you, Howie wanted to say. The words were forgotten, though, when a boy appeared beside her. Where his eyes should have been there were pockets of fire, blue and gold and fierce. The inferno drenched his whole body, and from his back stretched two huge, perfect wings as pure and as bright as the sun. *An angel,* he thought, and he wondered if he had died.

Then the boy blinked, and the fires burned out.

"No, you're not dead," the angel boy said. "You'll be okay. We'll look after you."

"Get him up," said the girl. Howie felt hands under him, lifting him, and there was no pain. The girl ran her hand through his hair, saying, "My name is Rilke. This is Schiller. You're going away somewhere now, but it won't be for long. When you wake up again, well . . ." she smiled, but Howie couldn't quite work out what was in that smile. "You'll have fire too. Don't be scared, you've been chosen."

He wasn't scared, even though his vision was darkening, cotton wool in his ears. It didn't feel like he was sinking into a grave this time, it was more like he was lying in bed and drifting off to sleep, warm and comfy and safe.

The girl called Rilke placed her hand on the angel boy's cheek, offering him the same smile.

"You're getting good at this, little brother," she said.

"Thank you," he replied.

"Let's go," she went on. "Burn it all, don't leave anything except sand."

And that was the last thing Howie heard before sinking into sleep, already dreaming of the fire that would be his when he woke.

CAL / *Hemmingway, 6:01 a.m.*

PIECES OF BROKEN WORLD WERE STILL FALLING when Cal opened his eyes.

They drifted down onto the windshield of the Freelander,

forming a translucent layer that looked like snow but which he knew was actually rock and metal and powdered flesh. He sat up, his back numb from a night in the passenger seat, his feet full of needles. The entire car wore a jacket of dust, all except for the broken driver's side window. Through it, he saw that the land had turned the color of bone, blanketed in the same fine powder. It was like every single thing on earth had been erased.

Every single thing except us, he thought.

It had to be morning, because parchment-yellow light streamed into the car. And there were birds too, singing so loud and so hard he wondered if that's what had woken him. They had short memories, the birds, they had already forgotten what had happened. Not him, though. He had spent the night dreaming of it over and over and over again—the police, the Fury, and Schiller, the boy in the fire.

The angel.

Cal shook his head, easing his aching neck around to see Adam lying across the backseat. The little boy was out cold, shivering in his sleep. It was no wonder. Daisy lay in back behind the seats, smothered in coats and blankets and pretty much everything else they could find, but still ice-cold. *Literally* ice-cold. The chill coming off her had frosted the inside of the tailgate window, had turned the leather seats into crystal. The poor girl had been shot, had taken a bullet in the shoulder from one of the few policemen who hadn't gone feral. And now . . .

She was changing, Cal knew. Schiller had gone through the same thing, imprisoned in ice before he was gripped by fire. Daisy was in some kind of cocoon, and when she woke she'd be just like him. Sooner or later they all would.

No, he told himself. *Not like him, not killers.*

The memories were making him sweat despite the cold. He popped open the door, an avalanche of dust sliding free, filling his eyes and nose and mouth. He clambered out, spitting, ignoring the protests from his cramped back. At least his finger felt better—stiff but not painful. His nose too. He didn't think anything was broken. Winter had risen overnight, the world covered by the same snow-gray sheet. Dark clouds scarred the cold blue sky—not rain clouds, not storms, just earth and cars and trees and people blown to atoms, lighter than air. Clumps danced their way back to the land only to be kicked up again by the breeze that whispered in off the sea.

"We need to go." The voice didn't seem to have any place out here, and it made Cal jump. He turned, looking over the Freelander's hood to see Brick standing there. The older boy's red hair was the brightest thing in sight, glinting like copper. A trail of footprints spiraled out around him, curling around the boarded-up toilet block all the way up the dunes. Once upon a time this had been a parking lot, Cal remembered, the place where he and Daisy had first met Brick. How long ago had that been? Three days? It felt like forever. The entire universe had been turned upside down and shaken like a snow globe.

"Now," Brick said, his tone just as blunt and infuriating as always. "Been here too long."

"Morning to you too, mate," Cal replied, running his fingers down the hood and leaving grooves in the dust. Up close he could see the different colors there—brown and silver and red, so much red. Blood, muscle, brain, all reduced to powder by the power that had blazed from Schiller's new body. It couldn't have been possible, and yet here it was, all around him, life made dust by the blink of a burning eye.

Only it hadn't really been Schiller, had it? He was the one who had turned, but it was his sister who had forced him to kill so many.

"Rilke," he muttered, remembering some of the last words he'd heard her speak: *But it told you why we are here, didn't it? To wage war with humanity*. Schiller's eyes had burned, yes, but the insanity in Rilke's own gaze had scared Cal far more.

"What about her?" asked Brick. "Rilke's long gone, isn't she?"

Cal nodded. He wasn't sure how he knew, but she was miles away from Hemmingway. He could almost see her, walking with Schiller and Marcus and Jade, leaving a trail of death in her wake. Or maybe that was just his imagination. He wished Daisy would wake. She'd know for sure which way Rilke had headed. Daisy knew things like that, even when nobody told her. But Daisy was frozen, and when she woke she'd be something else entirely.

"We need to talk," Cal said, scuffing his sneaker on the ground. "About what happened. We need to think of a plan."

Brick snorted a humorless laugh, running a hand through his hair and giving himself a pale halo of powder. They hadn't spoken much at all last night, they'd been too exhausted. They had found the car, climbed inside, and fallen asleep.

"We don't need to talk," he said. "We just need to move. Been here too long, slept right through, though God knows how."

It *was* weird—they'd slept for almost twelve hours straight. Shock did that to you, Cal guessed. Knocked you out so the body could recover.

"But Rilke, Schiller, they're killing people," Cal said. "We need to tell someone at least, the police."

"They killed about a hundred cops last night," Brick said. "I think the police know. You saw what he did. How the hell can we stop it? I can't believe Rilke even let us go."

Because whatever Schiller was, they were too. *You'll see, Cal,* Rilke had said. *It might take a day, it might take a week, but you'll see.*

"We show up now, we get in her way, and she'll just set Schiller on us. One word from her and we're . . ." Brick scooped up a handful of ash from the hood of the car, letting it trail from his fingers. Then, disgusted, he rubbed his palm down his filthy jeans, glaring at Cal like everything was his fault. "I haven't gotten through all this just to get killed by her pet dog. We need to get out of here, and whichever direction she's gone, we go the other way."

"What about Daisy?" Cal asked. "She needs help."

Brick glanced at the back of the Freelander.

"She's going to be like Schiller, isn't she?" he said. Cal didn't reply. They both knew the answer to that. "She's got one of those *things* inside her."

"An angel."

Brick snorted. "That's what Rilke said they were."

But Daisy had said it too, thought Cal, and she had known the truth. She'd known other things too.

"But what if Daisy was right," Cal said. "What if there is a reason we're here—to fight whatever it was she saw." *The man in the storm,* she had called it.

"Yeah, Cal, sure. The world is in peril and it's you, me, and a couple of kids destined to save it. I'm tired. I just want all this to be over."

Cal nodded, looking up at the trees. Most of the needles had been blown off by the explosion and the birds had nowhere to hide, exposed like pinecones. They still sang, though. There was a message in there somewhere, he thought. He leaned against the Freelander, the metal frozen.

"Think it will still work?" Brick asked, sniffing.

Cal climbed back into the driver's seat, fishing the keys from his pocket. The Freelander had taken a proper battering on the way up here from London, but Schiller's onslaught didn't seem to have reached it. He mouthed a silent prayer, then flicked the ignition, grinning when the engine spluttered, whined, then finally caught. There was a cry from the back and he turned to see Adam there, sitting up in his seat and looking around with wide, wet eyes.

"It's okay, mate," he said, leaving the car in neutral so he could take his foot off the clutch and shuffle around. "You're safe. It's Cal, remember?"

Adam nodded, relaxing a little but still not blinking.

"You have nightmares?"

The kid nodded again, silent as always.

"Me too," Cal went on. "But they're just dreams, they can't hurt us. You're safe here, with me and Brick, Daisy too, she's sleeping just over there."

Adam glanced into the back, reaching down to touch Daisy's face. He quickly pulled his hand away, putting his fingers to his lips.

"She's . . . you know the story of Sleeping Beauty, right?" Cal said. "That's what's happened to Daisy. She'll wake up soon, I promise you. Will you put your seat belt on for me, Adam?"

He did as he was told, as meekly as a beaten dog. Brick opened the passenger door, angling his lanky body inside and slamming it behind him. It took a couple of attempts to get it shut, and by that time the car was full of dust, countless cremated dead swimming in their ears and mouths and noses. Cal lowered his window, stuck the car in gear, and steered it through the parking lot, leaving a perfect circle of tire tracks in the ash.

"You know where we're going?" Brick asked.

The car rocked down the potholed path that led through the trees, back to the coast road.

"Cal?" Brick said.

"I know where we're going," he replied as they reached the road, checking that the route was clear before heading south, away from Fursville. He thought about Daisy in her coffin of ice, and about the creature inside her. The angel. A hospital wouldn't help her, not the police, not the army either. There was only one place he could think of where they might find answers. He put his foot down, the car accelerating and dragging a flowing cloak behind it. Then he looked at Brick and said: "We need to find a church."

RILKE / Caister-on-Sea, 7:37 a.m.

THEY WERE VERMIN, ALL OF THEM.

Men and women and children teemed over the dead grass of the campground, their eyes black and small and empty, their teeth bared. They swarmed from caravans and chalets and cars, blind to anything but their own hate. Some tripped and were quickly drowned in the stampede. More thumped into each other, the slap of flesh against flesh almost as loud as the thunder of footsteps. Others shrieked and howled, the air alive with the cries of the damned. And they *were* damned, there was no doubt about that.

"Are you ready, little brother?" Rilke asked, turning to Schiller. He stood stooped next to her, pale and frightened and weak. He looked so tired, the flesh of his face loose, the corners of his mouth turned down like a crescent moon. The ground shook as the ferals flocked closer, the first of them—a huge, hairy ape of a man dressed in shorts and an undershirt—now ten meters away. Close enough to smell. Oh how she hated them, these parasites. Once upon a time she would have been scared, but not anymore. Now there was only fury—*her* fury, as white and as hot and as dangerous as their own. "Schiller," she said. "Do it."

"Please, Rilke," he started, but she cut him off, grabbing his arm and twisting hard. Behind him stood Jade and Marcus with faces like sheep. The new boy, the one they had found in Hemsby, lay between them, still frozen. Rilke turned back to her brother.

"Do it."

Schiller might have been reluctant, but the creature inside him was eager. Her brother's eyes blazed. In a heartbeat the flames had spread, a second skin that wrapped him in angry light, and he opened his mouth in a silent scream of fire. With a snap like a pistol shot his wings punched through his shoulders, blasting out a shock wave that kicked up dust and sand and sent the first line of ferals rolling back into the crowd. Those wings beat slowly, almost lazily, forged of flame and so bright that Rilke could feel it burning into her retinas. The sheer power there made the air tremble, a generator hum that seemed to pull reality apart. She had to bite her tongue and screw her eyes shut to stop the vertigo, and when she looked again Schiller was already at work.

There had to be a hundred of them, fast and hard and angry. They didn't seem scared by Schiller's transformation. If anything, it seemed to incense them even further. They threw themselves at the burning boy, hands like claws reaching for his throat, barking the same awful, guttural cries. A hundred of them, and they never stood a chance.

Schiller opened his arms, the air around him shimmering. He was hovering off the ground now, ripples spreading outward over the dirt like it was water. The hairy man came apart with a soft pop, his atomized body holding its shape for a fraction of a second before drifting apart. Others ran through his floating remains before disintegrating with the same speed, the sound like somebody playing with bubble wrap. But still they kept coming, until a churning cloud hung before Schiller, as dark and as thick as smoke.

"Rilke!" She turned to see Jade screaming as more ferals approached from behind them. A couple of teenage boys led this crowd. Both threw themselves on Marcus, tumbling into a tangle of limbs and teeth. Three more followed, piling onto the skinny boy until he was lost. Others ran for Jade, and more still turned toward Rilke. *Don't be afraid of them, they are rats,* she ordered herself, but the fear turned her legs to stone. She didn't have Schiller's powers, not yet. She was still a pathetic human, nine pints of blood in a paper shell. They would tear her apart as easily as pulling petals from a plant.

"Schill!" she cried. A woman leaped for her, tripping on one of Marcus's flailing arms and falling short. A man followed, raking nails across her face and making her stumble backward. Then she was falling, the man's other hand grabbing for her throat, his eyes black pits of utter hatred.

She never hit the ground. The air beneath her grew solid, holding her up. The man was moving, but impossibly slowly. His fingers were almost frozen in front of her neck, like a piece of film playing at one-tenth of the right speed. She could see the dirt beneath his nails, the tarnished wedding ring on his finger. Spittle flew from his lips, rising almost gracefully, hanging in the sun like dewdrops.

Everything seemed to have almost stopped, time grinding reluctantly along its axis. One of the ferals sitting on Marcus was lifting a fist, a pearl of dark blood suspended from her knuckles. Others were still approaching, their sprint now a snail crawl. Rilke found herself laughing, her own movements sluggish too, as though she were swimming in a lake of honey. She was still falling, she realized, but so slowly that it felt like she was still.

Only Schiller was immune. He floated through the crowds until he was standing next to Rilke, then he pressed a fiery hand against the man's chest. This one didn't explode into dust. He folded in half with a chorus of breaking bones, then folded again, and again, until he was no bigger than a matchbox. Schiller flicked him away, then turned his attention to the other ferals. Even if they hadn't been moving in slow motion they couldn't have fought him. All her brother did was turn his palms toward the sky and every feral man, woman, and child in sight jerked upward like a puppet on a string. They came apart as they rose, limbs popping loose, clothes and skin torn into patchwork, teeth and fingernails spinning free, all linked by spirals of blood—rising until they were as tiny as distant birds, then vanishing.

Time seemed to remember itself then, wrapping its fingers around Rilke and pulling her to the ground. Her ears popped, her heart juddering for a handful of beats before finding its rhythm. Marcus squirmed on the ground before noticing that his attackers were gone, while Jade sat in a heap, her eyes glazed, a little more of her sanity rubbed away. Rilke scrabbled to her feet, planting her hands on her knees to stop herself from falling again.

"All of it," she said. She coughed, said it again. "All of it, Schill. We don't want to leave anything."

He looked at her, those unblinking eyes portals to another world. Staring into them brought on a creeping kind of madness, one that made her sick to her stomach. The vibration in the air intensified, and she could feel a finger of blood wind its way down from her ear. But she didn't look away.

"Now, Schiller," she said again. And it was her brother who broke, his head dropping. He didn't even move this time, but all the same the landscape dismantled itself just like it had done in Hemmingway and in Hemsby. Trailers lifted off the ground, doors and windows flapping like agitated limbs as they shook themselves into dust. Chalets crumbled as though made from sand, dropping crumbs as they passed overhead. Cars and bikes and strollers broke apart with muffled clanks and rings. Rilke watched them go, a tide of matter that flowed above them like a river, heading over the dunes and out to sea.

Schiller nodded his head and the remains of the campground dropped with a roar like thunder, the water churning into a rage. Rilke felt the salt spray on her face and she wiped it away. She hated the smell of the sea. Maybe if Schiller dropped enough into it then it would dry up, earth and ocean both wiped clean. She turned to him when the echoes had died away, seeing the flames ebb from his skin, the wings folding and fading. As always, his eyes were the last to return to normal, the blazing orange giving way to watery blue. He reeled to one side and she only just reached him before he fell. She lowered him gently to the ground, brushing his hair out of his eyes.

"You did well, little brother," she whispered. "You kept us safe."

He looked half-dead, but her words drew a smile. Marcus crouched down beside them, pulling a bottle of water from his rucksack. They had gathered supplies back in Hemsby, before Schiller had razed the little town to the ground. Rilke took the bottle from him, unscrewing the cap and holding it to her brother's lips. He drank deep, as though trying to quench a fire that still burned inside him.

"Thanks, Schill," said Marcus. "I didn't think I was getting out of that one."

She took a sip of water herself then handed the bottle back to him.

"Nothing will happen to us," she said. "We're too important."

"I know," Marcus replied, but he was frowning.

"What?" she snapped. She was exhausted. They hadn't slept since Fursville. They had tried on the way to Hemsby, in a hollow between the dunes, but the police had found them after about half an hour and Schiller had been forced to take care of them. They'd been on the move since, and the police had apparently decided to leave them alone. Either that or there were no police left nearby—her brother had shown them absolutely no mercy.

"Nothing, Rilke," Marcus said. "It's just . . . there are so many of them, and some of them were kids."

Her anger boiled up her throat but she clamped her mouth shut before it could break free. She couldn't blame Marcus for having doubts, even with everything that he had seen. It wasn't like she hadn't had moments of denial as the crowds had disintegrated before her eyes, especially the children. There had been babies here too, newborns with wrinkled faces who had screamed with a fury they could never hope to understand.

Yet the truth was unmistakable and inescapable. They were here to humble the human race, to make it understand that there was a higher power, that the illusion of free rein, of impunity, was just that: an illusion. They were the angels of death, the great flood and the cleansing fire. People were bad. Rilke knew that better than anyone. *Deep down they all have secrets, they're all rotten.* Marcus was just having doubts because he hadn't turned yet, that was all. As soon as his angel hatched, then he'd see the truth. Schiller had turned, and he knew.

"We're doing the right thing, aren't we, little brother," she said, but it wasn't a question.

Schiller looked at her with those big, sad eyes, eventually nodding. "I think so," he said.

"You *know* so," she said, smoothing a hand over his head. When she lifted it there were clumps of his hair woven between her fingers like seaweed and she wiped them off on her skirt. "Trust me, Schiller."

He tried to push himself up but didn't have the strength, dropping onto his back. His forehead was slick with sweat, his skin gray. *It's just tiredness,* she told herself. But there was another thought there that she pushed aside. What Schiller had inside him was a miracle, something good. It made him strong, it kept him safe. It wouldn't do anything to hurt him.

"I see things," her brother said, looking up at the sky. "When it happens, when I turn, I see things."

"Like what?" Rilke asked.

"I don't know," he said after a moment. "It's something bad. It's like a man, but a bad man. I can't see his face, only . . . I don't know, it's like he's living inside a tornado or something. I keep seeing him, Rilke. He scares me."

"Forget about it, little brother," she said. But she had seen him too, in the quiet moments between sleep and waking, a creature even more powerful than her brother. The man in the storm. "It's one of us," she said. "It's here for the same reason we are. Don't worry about it, he's on our side."

This would be so much easier if she had turned too, but the angel inside her showed no sign of hatching. The only reason she even knew it was there was because of the headaches she had suffered—*thump-thump, thump-thump, thump-thump*—and then the Fury. It *was* there, though, and sooner or later she would be born again with the same powers as her brother.

And when that happened . . .

Rilke grinned, the thought blasting away the last scraps of exhaustion. She got to her feet, pulling Schiller up beside her. The world had never seemed so big, and they had so much work to do.

"One more town, little brother, can you do that?"

He sighed, then nodded.

"Good boy."

She waited for Marcus and Jade to hoist up the new kid, letting him hang between them. They were shivering, but they knew better than to argue with her. Rilke held her brother's arm, taking some of his weight, and together they set off across the ruined land, kicking up the dust of the dead behind them.

THE FREELANDER JUDDERED, looked for a moment like it might keep going, then conked out with a quiet wheeze.

"Dammit," said Cal, turning the key. The engine gave out a series of pathetic coughs, but no matter how hard he wished for it he couldn't get the gas gauge to lift. "Empty."

"Nice one," grunted Brick. "You didn't bring any extra with you?"

"Yeah, Brick, I popped into a gas station on my way out of London, fought off the ferals, and filled up a couple of spare tanks. Got myself a cup of coffee too. What do you think?"

Brick slammed his palm against the dashboard and opened his door. Cal took a deep breath then clambered out after him. The air was so much cleaner here, didn't taste like a crematorium. The journey had pretty much blown all of the powdered flesh from the car, leaving only pockets in the corners of the windows and the alloy wheels. Cal breathed deep as he took in the surroundings, nothing but fields, trees, and hedges in every direction. The only evidence of where they'd come from was a gray fuzz on the sky. At least it was warm, the dawning sun like a jacket thrown over Cal's shoulders.

"Where are we?" Brick said, hawking up a spitball and launching it at the side of the road.

"Not sure," Cal replied. "Been heading west pretty much, it's hard to tell." The satnav had been working, but he hadn't known what address to put in so he'd just used it as a guide, following the spiderweb of roads that led out from Norwich. He'd kept to the smallest ones, and so far they'd only passed three other vehicles— two cars that barreled past fast enough to rock the Freelander, and a tractor in front that they'd kept well behind until it turned off into a farm. They'd passed through a few villages, but they had largely been deserted. "Last sign I saw said something like Tuttenham."

"So where is that?" he snapped back.

"You're the local, you tell me."

For a moment they eyeballed each other, quietly fuming.

"Okay," Cal said, sighing. "Okay, so I guess we carry on by foot, yeah?"

Brick shrugged, looking a quarter of his eighteen years. He scuffed the ground with a dirty shoe, then combed his fingers through his hair.

"Probably a town or a village or something around here," he mumbled. "Maybe a farm, could steal some diesel."

"Freelander's gas," said Cal. "Worth a try. You want Adam or Daisy?"

Brick didn't answer, just started traipsing up the road, his powder-covered body looking like some strange, gangly ghost in the soft morning light. Cal opened up the back door to see Adam there, as wide-eyed as always. The little boy was shivering.

"You want to get out of the car?" Cal asked him. "Get some sun? It's freezing in here." Adam glanced nervously at the girl in the back. "Daisy's coming too. Maybe the warmth will help thaw her out. Come on."

Adam shuffled off his seat onto the road. Cal smiled at him, then walked to the back of the Freelander. The windows here were frosted over like it was Christmas, and when he tried to open the rear door he found it was iced shut. He kicked at it a couple of times, shaking loose flakes of crystal, and finally managed to work it free. Daisy lay cocooned inside a web of silk, her face as white and as fragile as bone china. She looked dead, but he knew she was just asleep. What was the word? *Metamorphosing.* Cal thought of Schiller, consumed by fire, and wondered if Daisy would be better off dead. If they all would be.

"Here we go," he said, easing his hands under Daisy's rigid body and lifting her out. She seemed lighter, despite the crusting of ice, and the way she sparkled was almost terrifying. Cal's skin burned from the cold, his hands already numb, but he held her close and tight. "Hang on in there, Dais, we're going to find help."

Adam was waiting by the front of the car, and he offered a glimmer of a smile when he saw Daisy.

"See, she's going to be fine," Cal said. "We all are."

He cast a look back at the empty Freelander, then set off along the lane. Brick had vanished, but after fifty meters or so his head popped up from the large, grassy bank that lined the tarmac.

"Better get off the road," he said. "Fury or no Fury, Norfolk drivers are all twats."

Cal waited for Adam to scramble up the divider, then staggered over, almost falling down the other side. He stumbled into a field of bright yellow plants, only just managing to keep his feet and twisting his ankle in the process. He bit back a curse, limping to Brick's side.

"Thanks for the help," he said, but the other boy was already walking away. Cal set off after him, taking a couple of deep, shivering breaths to calm himself down. Adam trotted by his side, occasionally breaking into a run to keep up. The only sound, other than the crunch of their feet on the dry earth, was the chattering of the birds. They'd sing right to the end, Cal thought, even as the world came apart around them.

Brick kicked at a stone, sending it tumbling into the shadows between the crops. They walked in silence, crossing a dry ditch and pushing through a hedge at the end of the field. The next stretch of land was bare, which made the going easier. They'd only walked a few paces before Cal felt Adam tugging on his tracksuit pants. The boy was pointing, and sure enough when Cal followed his finger he saw a steeple thrusting up.

"Well spotted," he said, smiling. Adam beamed back, brighter than the sun. "See that, mate?"

Brick glanced up, shielding his eyes even though the sun was behind them. It was hard to tell how far away the church was, maybe a mile or two.

"Still don't know why you want a church," Brick answered. "Fat lot of good it's going to do us."

"Well you haven't exactly been full of suggestions," Cal shot back, feeling like he was about to come down with a bout of the Fury himself. Brick had a way of doing that to people, driving them up a wall. "Just thought . . . I don't know, but if these things inside us really are angels—"

"Fine," he said. "We'll try the church. But it won't do any good."

Cal hoisted Daisy up to his chest, his teeth chattering. It took them ten minutes to reach the end of the field, and another five to work out a way past a barbed wire fence. Beyond was a dirt track that ran beside a pasture full of cows, the animals staring at them with those sad black eyes. At least they weren't trying to charge them down. Being trampled to death by a herd of furious cattle would not be a good way to go.

Brick kicked out at the track, scattering pebbles. He was

making such a racket that Cal almost didn't hear the sound of an engine up ahead, rising and fading. He slowed, cocking his head as another distant growl came and went.

"Must be a road," Brick said. "What should we do?"

"Get closer, see what happens, yeah?" That wasn't exactly the best plan in the world, but that was the trouble with the Fury, you only knew if it was there or not by getting up-close and personal. And by that time, chances were you had somebody's teeth in you.

Brick didn't reply, just stepped over the fence. He held out his hands and Cal passed Daisy to him. His arms were two blocks of cold stone, but somehow he managed to lift Adam over the fence before stepping over himself. The field was starting to rise above the track, and they walked up the hill in silence listening to the traffic ahead. Cal counted seven vehicles coming and going before they reached the end.

He hunkered down, peering through the fence to see a road below them. A sidewalk ran along both sides, and there were houses opposite—large ones, with thatched roofs and wide driveways. To the left, the road led toward a small town. Cal could make out what might have been a bakery, and a supermarket. Rising above it all was the church tower. There were people up there, six or seven of them, too far away to make out properly. Three disappeared into the supermarket, their laughter ghosting down the road.

"What do you think?" Cal asked.

"The hell should I know?" Brick replied, clutching Daisy to his chest and shivering. "We could go down there and get our faces ripped off."

Cal straightened, and offered Brick a nervous smile.

"I guess there's only one way to find out."

BRICK WATCHED CAL STUMBLE ACROSS THE FIELD, Adam teetering after him, but he couldn't bring himself to follow. Daisy was cradled in his arms, and the cold that blasted from her had turned his bones to ice, rooting him to the spot. He suddenly realized just how exhausted he was, his body and his mind running on fumes, ready to sputter out like the car. The thought of getting to his feet seemed like the most impossible thing in the world.

Adam staggered back, stumbling on the uneven ground. The little boy reached out and grabbed Brick's T-shirt, gently tugging on it. His eyes were pockets of sunlight, dazzlingly bright, and they seemed to lend a little warmth to Brick's body. He took a deep breath and pushed himself to his feet, a head rush making him feel like he was pirouetting across the field. When it had settled, he took a step, then another, following Cal toward the town.

"Maybe we should do the whole distraction thing again?" Cal said. "Like at the factory, yeah?"

Brick shrugged, even though he knew Cal wouldn't see it. At the factory there had only been one guard to distract, at first, and even that had gone wrong.

"I could lead them off, try to make a path for you to get Daisy and Adam into the church," Cal went on. "Or you're faster than me, you could do it."

Fat chance, Brick thought, saying, "What if the church is full of people?"

"On a Monday morning? It won't be."

"What if it's locked?"

Cal put both hands on his head, grabbing fistfuls of hair.

"Fine," Brick said. "Whatever, let's try it."

Cal hunkered low, moving quickly down the hill. Another car idled along the road, maybe thirty meters away, followed by a mail truck. For a village, this place looked pretty mobbed.

"You should go around the back," Cal said. "Those gardens, try to cut through." He was pointing to where the field joined the houses at the back of the village, a few small yards boxed in by fences.

"What about you?" Brick asked.

"I'll take the main street. If they've still got the Fury, I'll draw them off." He wiped a hand across his mouth. His fingers were trembling. Right now Cal didn't look like he could stagger another twenty meters, let alone outrun an entire village of ferals. "Maybe I'll get over there and no one'll notice me, yeah?"

Brick shrugged again. He hoisted Daisy up, the girl so light and yet somehow now the heaviest thing in the world.

"Stay with Brick, Adam, he'll look after you until I get back."

The little boy's mouth drooped, but still he didn't speak. Cal looked at Brick and nodded, then he was on the move again, heading down the hill toward the road. Brick watched him for another few seconds, swore, then set off in the direction of the houses. With Daisy in his arms and Adam clinging on to his T-shirt, the going was tough. Twice he tripped on the dry earth, and it seemed to take forever before he stopped beside the first fence.

There were no screams, no squealing brakes, no explosions.

The fence was a little shorter than him, and he stood on his tiptoes and peered over it. Beyond was a shoe box of a garden leading up to a terraced house. The house had a passage down the side of it, and Brick took a few paces to his left so he could see to the end. There was a gate there, probably locked. He stumbled to the next garden, this one surrounded by a thick hedge. The one past that had barbed wire coiled around the top of its fence, but the fourth house along was falling to pieces, its derelict wooden greenhouse missing several panes of glass. A quick glance down the passage revealed a straight path to the road beyond.

There was no gate, but the garden wasn't exactly Alcatraz. The fence was coming loose, and he kicked out at it in a hail of splinters. He tried again, and with a damp creak the panel tumbled into the overgrown grass. The house was blind, curtains pulled tight across every window.

"Come on," he said, traipsing through the garden and into the passageway. Their footsteps echoed off the walls, making it sound like there was somebody right behind them, and twice he checked over his shoulder to be sure. Sunlight spilled through the arch at the far end and he stepped cautiously into its heat, squinting until the light-bleached road came into focus. It was a residential street, small houses standing shoulder to shoulder like soldiers. He held his breath, once again listening for noise. The air was hot and silent, as if the whole town was imitating him, holding its breath too, waiting for the right moment to spring to life.

He swallowed hard, his throat like sandpaper, then he stepped out of the passageway onto the pavement. It was deserted, but wouldn't there be people inside the houses? Wouldn't they have sensed him by now, come streaming from their doors and windows? He angled his gaze up to see the church tower, close enough now that he could make out the weathered gargoyles on its steeple.

A distant car horn cut through the heavy quiet, making Brick jump so hard that Daisy almost slipped from his grip. He clamped her to his chest. *Wake up, Daisy,* he thought as he set off across the road, heading for the passageway opposite. *Please wake up, I can't carry you forever.*

Then he remembered what she'd be when she woke, and sucked the wish into the darkness of his thoughts.

The houses on this side had gates on their passageways, but a little farther up the terraced properties gave way to larger, semi-detached homes. He cut through a graveled driveway and down a long, perfectly manicured garden. The hum of traffic was louder here, and he thought he could hear voices too. He reached a wall and leaned against the crumbling brickwork, trying to catch his breath.

"Can you climb it?" he asked Adam. The little boy looked up at the wall—all six feet of it—and shook his head. Brick grunted in frustration, crouching down and gently laying Daisy on the ground. He shook his arms, trying to warm them up, then grabbed Adam under his armpits. His hands were so numb, and the boy so light, it felt like he was lifting air. He boosted him to the top of the wall and sat him there. "Just lower yourself down. It's not far."

Adam shook his head again, fear etched into his features.

"Do it," Brick snapped. "Unless you want me to push you off."

The kid wiped his arm over his face, smudging away tears. He eased himself around, clinging on with white-knuckled fingers as he dropped. Brick ducked to scoop up Daisy and it was as he was straightening that he heard the sound of a door opening. He glanced back, seeing a man step from the house.

"Hey, you, what the hell do you think you're doing?"

How far away was he? It was a big garden, maybe twenty meters between the back door and the wall, give or take. Brick didn't move, even his heart seeming to slow its mental beat, waiting. The man took a step forward. He *had* to be close enough for the Fury, didn't he?

"I'm talking to you," he yelled. "Get out of my garden before I call the police."

Another step. Brick retreated until the wall was against his back. The man had stopped, staring at him, both of them deadlocked. Maybe the guy'd just go back inside. Brick was tall, and he had one of *those* faces, the kind that made you think twice about picking a fight. Maybe he'd just back off, lock the door behind him and call the cops. Maybe things were different now that Schiller had changed. Maybe the Fury wasn't there anymore. Please God, please be true.

The man rubbed his unshaven face, frowning. He was looking at the bundle in Brick's arms.

"What have you got there?" he said. "What is that?"

Brick ignored him, turning to the wall and trying to lift Daisy. This time he managed to boost her to the top but he couldn't angle her body over. His muscles gave out and she tumbled to the ground by his feet like a rag doll, like a dead thing.

"Hey, get away from her," the man shouted, and Brick heard him start to run. He bent down, grabbing fistfuls of Daisy's clothes and flesh, not caring if he hurt her. He pulled her up, bracing her against the wall with his chest while he repositioned his arms.

"Ge aaay fom er," the man's voice was a wet slur, and Brick almost screamed when he heard it. He got his body under Daisy, pushing her up like an Olympic weight lifter. The man coughed out more words, his footsteps drumming the ground, louder, closer. He shunted Daisy with everything he had and she rolled over the top, flopping down the other side. Then he clutched the bricks, hauling himself up.

The man grabbed his leg, iron fingers gouging into his calf. Another hand took hold of his thigh, yanking. Brick cried out, digging his nails into the crumbling wall. He lashed back, his feet kicking at thin air. The man was howling, loud enough to bring the whole village down on them.

Brick kicked again and this time his foot met something soft. There was a crack, a gurgled cry of fury, and he was free. He tumbled over headfirst, doing a clumsy somersault in midair and landing on his back. The impact emptied his lungs, making him groan, but he forced himself up.

Daisy was lying in a heap, Adam crouched next to her. They were in another garden, this one filled with crates and old fridges rusted shut. There were noises from behind the wall, angry shouts and something scuffling. The man would be over in seconds.

"Move!" wheezed Brick, shoving Adam out of the way so he could get to Daisy. This time he lifted her onto his shoulder, staggering through the garden and down the side of the building. It was a shop, he realized as he drew level with the front, an electrical store. The front door was open, but there were no people inside. In fact, there were no people *anywhere* on the street, just shops and—up to his left—the church. He set off toward it, making it halfway before he heard the sound of someone screaming.

No, not just one person, a *load* of people.

He stopped, looking back. At the other end of the deserted road was a junction, and it was swarming. There must have been thirty people there, maybe more, all running in the same direction.

Cal.

Brick almost took a step toward them. Almost. *But you can't go, you have to look after Daisy.* And that was a good enough excuse to make him turn away, walk toward the church, gritting his teeth so hard he thought they might snap clean out of their gums. He wouldn't see it, he wouldn't see the moment that Cal died, the creature of flame that would rise from his corpse and evaporate into the summer air. He *would not see* the moment that he was left on his own.

He drowned out the screams, running the last few meters to the church gate and across the wide, tree-lined graveyard. The door was ancient oak, and heavy, but it was unlocked. He pushed his way in, Adam entering behind him. Then he threw his body against the door, shutting the madness and the guilt outside, sealing himself in the cool, quiet, secret dark.

CAL / *East Walsham, 8:37 a.m.*

THERE WAS NOWHERE TO RUN. Ahead, people were streaming out of a shop like an artery had been opened, all of them howling. They were coming from behind him too, the glass door of a bakery smashed into golden shards as seven, ten, fifteen people pushed out onto the street. Cal stumbled away, tripping off the curb. On the other side of the road two men were staggering out of an estate agent's, the Fury twisting their features into Halloween masks.

There were too many of them, all running, the first—a kid, maybe eleven or twelve with a broken arm in a cast—just seconds away. Cal staggered back. He thumped into a car, one of the ones parked along both sides of the road, and before he even acknowledged what he was doing he had scrambled underneath it.

There was barely enough room for him, the metal rib cage of the car on his back, pinning him against the road. *What the hell were you thinking?* he screamed at himself.

Something thumped against the car, turning day to dusk. Then it was as if the heavens had opened, hail thundering down all around him, plunging him into absolute night. The screams were so loud that he was drowning in them, he couldn't breathe, he couldn't move, he couldn't do anything but lie there and listen to that deafening, awful chorus.

People were flooding underneath, a torrent of limbs and teeth. Hands grabbed and pinched at him, trying to pull him out. Bodies wormed in beside him, crowding his coffin. The car rocked from side to side, its suspension groaning. They would roll it, then they would fall on him, and he would be no more.

He was dead.

No, Cal, fight them!

The voice didn't sound like his, but there was no doubt it was coming from his head. What did it want him to do? There was another car in front of him, he knew that much. There was a line of them running down the side of the street, parked almost nose to tail. Could he reach it?

He started to wriggle forward. Legs barred the way, forming a fence between his car and the next, but he pushed past them. There wasn't enough room for them to get a proper hold of him, their punches and kicks deflected by the bumpers, and just seconds later he was underneath the next car.

It didn't do any good. The crowd followed him, their radar tuned in to whatever it was inside him. He couldn't creep away because they didn't need their eyes to find him. They surrounded him, blotting out the sun, a hundred fingers working into his flesh.

Burn them.

That voice again. It wasn't his, but it was familiar.

Someone was crawling in beside him, a nightmare face with a distended jaw. Cal smashed his elbow into the woman's nose, knocking her out cold. That was good, because the other ferals couldn't reach past her. They were still squeezing in from every other angle, though, pinching and biting, all the while that same voice pleaded *Burn them burn them burn them*.

Fuel. That was it! He was under a car, and somewhere above him was the tube that fed gas into the engine.

He struggled onto his back, reached up, ignoring the pain as something bit his leg. There were dozens of tubes above him, huge pipes and smaller, softer lines. He grabbed one of the latter, pulling hard. It resisted, but he didn't let up, wrenching at it with everything he had until it tore loose. Fluid dripped from it, but it wasn't gas—he knew that from the smell. He scrabbled for another. It was too dark to see anything, and twice he felt a hand clutch at his fingers, only just managing to shake them free.

"Come on!" he said. "Where are you, you piece of—"

Another pipe, and this time when he tore it from its mount the pungent smell of fuel instantly punched up into his sinuses. He gagged, feeling the steady drip of gas onto his clothes, forming a pool beneath him. That was a problem, because even if he found a way to spark it up he'd be burned alive in the fireball.

You do have a way, said the voice. And Cal suddenly saw the restaurant back in Fursville, the candles. He reached down to his pocket, feeling the box there. Matches. He pulled them free. Something thumped his arm and they almost spilled, but he clutched the little box tight, sliding it open and taking a match from inside.

That still left the whole being-burned-alive problem.

"Think!" he yelled, his voice lost in the howls around him. He needed to move again, get under the next car. He grabbed hold of the underside of the vehicle, using it to pull himself backward. Once again there were ferals in the way, but the space between the cars was too tight for them to grab hold. He wiggled his way across, the crowd following, burrowing in next to him like maggots into old flesh.

He drew the match across the box, once, twice, three times before it sparked. Careful not to drop it on himself, he flicked the flaming stick back the way he'd come. It bounced off a tire, looked for a second like it was going out, then landed in the gutter in a puddle of fuel.

Darkness exploded into light, every scrap of metal beneath the car, every distorted face, every bloodied fingernail revealed in impossible detail. The flames spread fast, engulfing the people closest to the car. One of the men who was crawling underneath lost his face to the fire, but even through the inferno, even as his eyes melted, he raged.

Cal's shoes were on fire and he thrashed his legs to extinguish the flames. There was no air, his lungs full of smoke and smoldering flesh.

An explosion ripped through the car in front as the fuel tank ignited, the shock wave peeling away the crowd. This was his chance, now or never. He rolled to his side, lashing out at the people in his way, gouging at eyes and throats and everything else he could find until the sky opened up.

They were on him before he could stand, but he threw himself away, heading into the smoke so they wouldn't be able to see him. He collided with a flaming shape, shoving it as another blast shook the street. He was running now—a lumbering, unsteady shamble. He felt like a corpse that had been set free from its coffin. He put his head down, nothing quite working the way it should, but each clumsy step carrying him farther from the pack.

Only when he could no longer feel the heat of the fire on his back did he risk turning around. The street was a mess, at least four or five of the closely packed cars now engulfed. The smoke was too thick to really see much else, but Cal could make out a dozen shapes there, bodies dressed head to toe in fire, weaving in and around each other like ballroom dancers. Even now they were coming after him, and he was grateful for the Fury, because they would never know what happened to them, would never know the horror of their own deaths. One burning thing collapsed to its knees, and another, the dance coming to an end. Other shapes were emerging from the billowing black curtain, though, soot-black silhouettes that stumbled toward him.

They couldn't have him, though. Not now, not ever. Cal turned, began once again to run, while that same quiet voice rose up once again in his skull.

Burn them. Burn them. Burn them all.

"BURN WHO, LITTLE BROTHER?"

Schiller started, like he'd been woken from a dream. He licked his lips, as if to erase all trace of the words, looking at Rilke with big, sad eyes. They were still walking along the coast, south, leaving a vast blanket of dust in their wake. They hadn't seen more than a handful of people since the last little town, the trailer park. Word must be spreading—that something bad was coming.

No, something good, she thought. *Something wonderful.*

"I asked you a question, Schiller," she said. Her brother had started whispering those words a few minutes ago—*burn them, burn them*—as though reciting a mantra to himself. She assumed he was speaking about the humans—she had come to call them that, knowing she was no longer one of them—that the purpose of their mission was finally getting through to him. Yet there was something in the urgency of his speech, and in the way his eyes had flicked back and forth, seeing a world she could not see, that made her think he was hiding something. "Burn who?"

"Nobody," he said. "I mean *everybody.* Sorry, I didn't even know I was saying it."

She held his gaze until he broke away and peered out across the quiet, slate-colored water. He was chewing something over, she could tell. She knew her brother better than he knew himself, and there was something inside that little head of his that wanted out.

"Schill, I won't ask you again."

"I . . ." He kicked at the wet sand, clumps of it sticking to his shoe. Then he looked up at her. There was no fire in his eyes, but they seemed somehow brighter. "It's nothing, really. I'm just tired."

She opened her mouth to press him, but decided not to. They were all tired—exhausted, really—Schill, her, and Marcus and Jade, who traipsed behind with the new boy strung up between them. It was a wonder they hadn't all dropped dead from fatigue.

"There will be plenty of time to sleep," she said. "And a whole world to rest our heads on. Imagine it, Schiller, how quiet it will be. How empty."

He nodded, staring at his feet as he shuffled down the beach. It was infuriating, Rilke thought, that her brother went back to being his usual self. Why couldn't he be an angel all the time? Why should she have to put up with these bouts of sniveling misery in between his displays of God-like rage? She knew the reason—it was evident in the bald patch above his right ear, and the waxy sheen of his skin. Too much fire would kill him.

"One more," she said, looking up ahead. The wide, sandy beach led toward a town, a big one by the looks of things. A cluster of houses sprang up to their right, and past them a collection of piers and promenades blighted by towers. "This place, can you end it?"

Schiller seemed to shrink at the thought, his back stooped as though all the world rested on it. He looked ready to wither away into dust and sand. It was pathetic. Where was the creature inside him? Where was his angel? She felt a hot stew of anger rise from her gullet, and for a second she saw nothing but white. Schiller must have sensed it—he knew her temper well enough to fear it—because he gave her a sharp, hurried nod.

"Then end it," she said.

Somewhere, far away down the beach, a bright yellow kite nuzzled the sky like a hungry fish. Maybe the word hadn't spread as far as she thought. Maybe people hadn't heard about Hemsby, about Caister. Well, they'd know soon enough.

The world erupted into color as Schiller transformed, tongues of blue and orange fire licking at the beach, freezing the damp sand and spreading a web of silk-like ice all the way to the water's edge. It was getting easier for him, Rilke realized. He didn't even react as the wings unfurled from his back, sails of pure energy that emitted a ceaseless pulse, one that made her bones hum like a tuning fork that would not quiet. His red-rimmed eyes erupted, the light inside them like molten rock, spitting and spilling down his face.

Schiller began walking—floating—toward the sea, plant-like tendrils of light curling up from the ground as if to touch his feet. The water retreated from him like a feral cat, lurching back in desperate movements, hissing and steaming. His fire was cold, but it was something else he was trying, something new. *What is it like, little brother,* she thought, *to wish the world apart and watch it obey, to peek inside the very center of things, the spinning orbits that make us all, and to pull them inside out?*

Schiller opened his mouth, and once again spoke something wordless and world-ending. She didn't see it, but she heard it—or rather *felt* it, because the sound of his voice was so alien that her ears almost couldn't register it, like when a church organ plays a subsonic note. But it raged inside her head, inside her stomach, inside every single cell, forcing her to her knees.

The sea rose up, a wall of water as thick as rock, so immense and so sudden that Rilke screamed. Vertigo hit her like a punch to the gut—the sight of the ocean there, upended, the unbearable groan of a billion gallons of water held against its will, just too much. She had to look away, curl into herself, unable to stop the cries that spilled from her lips. The ground was trembling, and she expected it to split open, to disintegrate at Schiller's touch and plunge them all into darkness.

The wall of water made a noise like a million peals of thunder detonating at once, the sand so agitated that it leaped two feet into the air. Not seeing was worse than seeing, and Rilke peered through half-shut eyes to glimpse Schiller, her burning boy, standing before the wave. It towered above him—fifty meters, a hundred, she couldn't tell. Probing fingers of sunlight sluiced through it, turning the water a color she had never before seen in her life, a deep, angry green filled with flecks that could have been fish or boats or rocks or people. It churned and raged and howled with anger at the way he was treating it, but it could not refuse him.

Schiller turned, his mouth still open, still speaking in that voiceless, deafening, unbearable whisper. Then he raised his hands toward the town and let his new pet off its leash. The water surged past her, around her, over her, a tunnel of noise and movement that seemed as if it would never end.

But it did, the rush and thunder gradually fading, leaving only the ringing in her ears. She looked up to see the ruined beach, stripped of its sand to the bone-white stone beneath, and beyond that a roiling black line as the ocean did its work. It looked like a giant eraser, one that scrubbed the horizon clean in frantic, desperate motions, leaving trails of white foam that reached for the sky. There was another sound behind her, the sonic boom of the displaced ocean as it filled the space Schiller had created. It thrashed and spat toward them as if seeking revenge, but crashed to a halt against the invisible bubble of energy that surrounded them.

It felt like a thousand years before the sea grew quiet again, its outrage turning to a stunned, silent disbelief. Rilke tried to get to her feet, the unsettled ground spreading out beneath her, making her lose her footing. Schiller showed no sign of turning back into the boy, hovering before her, those twin portals watching the last of the tidal wave as it soaked back into the earth.

"Well done, Schiller," she said, and before she even knew it was coming a giggle tumbled out of her mouth. She glanced over her shoulder to make sure the others were still there. Marcus and Jade looked back, moon-eyed, and she wondered how much of them remained intact; whether there would be anything left inside their minds for their angels to possess. "Are you ready to move?"

Marcus nodded, slowly, as if each movement of his head required every ounce of his intelligence. Jade didn't reply at all.

"Let's get away from here," she said, finally managing to stand. "Find somewhere to rest. I think you deserve it, Schill."

He cocked his head, his molten eyes fixed on her. And she wondered just how much control he had. Not over the earth—that much was clear in what had just happened—but over her. She had trained him well over the years, the way you train a dog to know who is in charge. But how many dogs, if they knew they were faster, stronger, deadlier than their masters, would continue to tread by their heels? *Come on,* she thought, willing the message deep inside her, to whatever part of her soul her angel occupied. *You need to hurry up, because we can't control him forever.* And what would happen then? What would her fate be if Schiller turned against her?

She watched him float away, and once again she wondered who he had been talking to—*burn them*—and, more important, who he had been talking about. And in doing so she realized, for the first time in her life, that she was scared of her brother.

BRICK / *East Walsham, 9:03 a.m.*

IT WASN'T THE EXPLOSIONS THAT STIRRED HIM, but the softer sound of movement from inside the church. Brick shook the grogginess from his head, realizing that he had almost drifted off in the unnatural stillness of the vestibule. The noise came again, short, echoing taps that could have been footsteps. There was another door opposite the one they had entered through, this one just as old and just as solid. It stood an inch or two ajar, a current of cool air seeping through the crack.

A distant explosion rumbled through the ancient stone. *It's Cal,* he thought. *It's the noise of him dying.* But he hadn't *felt* the boy's death, not like he'd felt Chris's, back in the field beside Fursville—that sudden tearing inside him, like a piece of him had been wrenched loose.

He thought for a moment about leaving Daisy where she lay, in a heap against the door, but then decided not to. There was a chance he might have to make a quick getaway. He steeled himself for the cold, then squatted down and fumbled her into his arms. She looked so *dead*. Adam sat beside her, staring at Brick with an expression that was part fear and part hate.

He walked to the inner door, peering into the gloom beyond. He could make out some stone columns and the back row of wooden pews, but that was about it. There were huge stained-glass windows in there, but if anything they seemed to keep the day outside, only a trickle of sickly light making it through. The glass saints, or whatever they were, stared at Brick with lead eyes, and he half expected them to start hollering a warning. He used a knee to ease open the door, entering the church.

It was bigger than it looked from the outside, *way* bigger. There must have been fifteen rows of pews, leading up to an altar. It stank of the cold in here, of stone and damp and endless centuries. He wrinkled his nose, waiting to hear the screams, waiting for something to charge down the aisle baying for his blood.

Something moved up ahead, a dark shape in the space behind the altar. It lumbered to one side with the sound of feet sliding over stone, and Brick's stomach almost shot right up his throat and out of his mouth. The shape coughed, then, to Brick's utter relief, spoke.

"Hello?" The voice sounded as old as the church. "Can I help you?"

"Don't come any closer," Brick said. "Just stay where you are."

"Excuse me?" The shape stepped up to the altar, into a shaft of murky, multicolored light, revealing a priest's black suit and white collar. He was a plump, elderly man with a completely bald head and glasses, which he removed, wiped on his sleeve, then replaced.

"I mean it," Brick said. "Stay there."

"I don't know who you think you are, young man, but I don't appreciate being spoken to like that." The priest took a defiant step from the raised platform, and Brick hoisted Daisy against his chest.

"Take one more step and I swear to God I'll hurt her," he said, not sure what else to do. "Go on, test me, but it'll be on you if anything happens."

He could hear the trembling desperation in his voice, and the priest must have too because he raised his hands, retreating up the steps to the altar. There was a good twenty-five, thirty meters between them. So long as neither of them crossed the invisible line of the Fury, they should get on just fine.

"Sit down," Brick said.

The man wheezed as he lowered himself onto the top step. "Easier said than done for me these days," he said with a nervous laugh. "But it's getting up that's the real problem."

"Then don't get up," Brick spat back. "Is there anyone else here?"

"Just me," the priest replied, shaking his head. "Margaret has Mondays off, she goes into Norwich to see our daughter and our grandchildren."

The back row of pews was right in front of him, and Brick laid Daisy down there. In here, surrounded by stone, she seemed even colder than before.

"Sit there," he said to Adam, pointing to the space beside her. "Don't say anything." The little boy obeyed, and Brick wrapped his arms around himself, trying to hold in the shivers. If the old priest was telling the truth then at least they were safe in here, for the moment anyway.

"Is she okay?" the man asked. "The girl? She looks sick. If you like, I could take a look at her. I was a medic, many years ago, before I found the faith. In the army."

He spoke this last sentence with what felt like a warning, but Brick ignored it.

"Whatever the problem is," the priest said. "Let me help you."

"Shut up," Brick said, pointing to the decorative curtain that hung behind the altar, rope tassels dangling from either side. "I need you to tie yourself up. Use them."

"Please, son—"

"*Do it*, before I lose my temper." The man started to rise, and Brick shrieked at him. "I didn't say get up!"

Calm down, for God's sake, he's an old man, he's not going to hurt you. Unless he got too close, of course; then he'd be clawing at Brick with those wrinkled hands and gnawing at his throat with his dentures. Yes, he was being more of an arsehole than ever, but he couldn't take any chances. He watched the priest lean back and pull the ropes free, struggling to bind his wrists.

"Wait," Brick said. "Tie the rope to the altar first. To the banister there. Just one wrist will do, don't worry about the other one."

The man did as he was told, looping the rope around the wooden pole of the banister before knotting it tight around his left wrist. He gave it a tug, to show it was secure, then shrugged at Brick.

"Knot it again."

"If you're in trouble, there is always a way out," the man said as he followed orders. "Please, son, let me help you, help her, before things get out of hand."

"Out of hand?" Brick said, laughing bitterly.

"Is this to do with the attack? The one in London?"

"Attack?" Brick asked. "What are you talking about?"

"You haven't heard? It's been on the news all morning. There has been a terrorist attack in north London, some kind of bomb. A big one. They're still trying to figure out what it is. We're all frightened, but we'll get through this together."

It took Brick a second to understand. Not a bomb, a *storm*, and a man inside it who wanted to devour the world. He didn't reply, just waved the priest's words away. *Priorities*. The first thing he needed to do was eat something. Once he had some food in his belly, some water too, he'd be able to think straight.

"At least tell me your name," the priest said. "And the names of your friends. I'm Douglas, Doug."

"Got any food, *Doug*?" he said.

"Not in the church, no, Margaret doesn't allow it. But there is plenty in the rectory, just over the yard. If you let me go, I'd be happy to show you."

"You stay put," Brick said, grabbing the back of Adam's T-shirt and hoisting him to his feet. "I'm taking him, and if I come back and find you've moved I swear to God I'll do something bad. You understand me?"

"I won't move. I'm on your side, son, whatever you're trying to do. It's all in the kitchen, the front door's open, we never lock it."

Brick took one last look at Daisy, then set off, pulling Adam along beside him by the scruff of his neck. The little boy was trying halfheartedly to wriggle free, making so much noise that Brick didn't hear footsteps until the outer door of the church started to swing inward. He fell back, almost tripping over Adam. Sunlight streamed past a figure there, gleaming off the blood on his clothes and skin, turning him into yet another stained-glass saint with pockets of lead for eyes. The figure lurched into the church, dragging in the stench of smoke.

"*Cal?*"

The boy stumbled, started to fall, and Brick caught him clumsily beneath the arms. He dragged him into the body of the church, lowering him gently to a sitting position against the back wall. Scratch marks covered his face and neck and arms like veins, and his shoes were black and misshapen, like they'd been burned.

"Cal? Are you okay?"

It was a stupid question, but after a few seconds Cal's roving eyes finally landed on Brick and he nodded. He opened his mouth, uttering a percussion of dry, clacking notes from deep inside his throat.

"Okay . . . I'm okay. Cold?"

"Huh?"

"Am I cold?" Cal asked, his eyes dark with fear.

Brick understood what he was asking, laying his hand on Cal's forehead. The skin was hot.

"No, you're burning up."

Cal breathed a sigh of relief, bubbles of blood bursting on his chapped lips.

"Could do with some water, mate."

"Yeah, sure. Is it safe out there?"

Cal nodded.

"It better be" was all Brick could think of to say. He straightened, wondered if maybe he should just scoop a handful of water out of the font or something before deciding that was probably bad luck. And bad luck was the last thing he needed right now. He headed for the vestibule, pointing at the priest.

"I'll be back in a second. If you try to escape, he'll hurt you, understand?"

Cal didn't look in a state to hurt anything, but Brick sensed the old man seemed to have resigned himself to the fact he was here for the long haul. "Adam, sit down and don't move."

Brick made his way outside. Sunlight poured through the

swaying trees, forming golden disco lights on the grass and graves there, but the cemetery was deserted. There was nothing ahead but the street, so he set off to his right, hugging the lichen-slick wall of the church, turning the corner to see another building spitting distance away. It was made of stone too, with leaded windows and a thatched roof. It could have been something from a fairy tale.

Checking that the coast was clear, he dashed across the graveyard, turned the handle, and let himself in. It was almost as cold in here as in the church, but there was a smell in the air, some kind of soap. It made him think of his mum, long dead, buried in a church just like this out near King's Lynn where her folks had lived. It was too painful to think about, so he shut the thoughts out of his mind, using anger to batten down the hatches the way he always did.

The kitchen was small, but easy to find. There was a bread bin on the table and he pulled a loaf out from inside, white and fluffy and still warm from whatever oven it had come out of. While he chewed he opened the fridge, taking out a packet of ham and a hunk of cheddar. He scarfed it all, washing it down with a guzzle of milk. There was a bottle of Golden Badger ale knocking around at the back of the fridge and he swiped it, popping the cap on the edge of the counter. He'd never really been a big drinker—he'd seen what lager and cheap whiskey had done to his dad—but there were certain occasions that demanded alcohol. *Birthdays, weddings, and being possessed by angels who want you to save the world from a force of pure evil.*

He took two deep, long pulls, letting his mind grow still and quiet. *Christ*, how long had it been since he'd done that? The silence was so immense that it was unnerving, threatening even, and he straightened up, clearing his throat, taking another swig of sweet, frothy ale. He needed water.

He walked to the sink, noticing the portable television on the countertop. Maybe he should check the news. If this thing, this man in a storm, really was in London and they thought it was a terrorist attack then it would be all over the news, on every channel. He reached for the On button but froze halfway. Did he really want to see it?

He left his hand there for a moment more, then jabbed the On button. It was an old set, and it took a few seconds to warm up, the gray mush gradually giving way to a kids' show. A little penguin with a funny orange beak was scooting around an igloo, honking. That had to be good news, didn't it?

He pressed the channel Down button, and it was as if the television were a dam that had suddenly broken, a million tons of filthy water sluicing from the screen, blasting away the kitchen, the rectory, the cemetery, and everything else. He saw it there, amid the darkness, grainy footage of a vast, churning vortex of smoke and debris, suspended above the city, above the skyscrapers; saw the clouds of matter that spiraled toward it, all being sucked toward the center of the storm, toward . . .

There was a man there, only not a man. How could it be? It was too big, its body ballooned to the size of a building, and yet there it was, its mouth the very core of this abomination, the event horizon at the center of the black hole. Even from this distance, even on the small screen of the television, Brick could feel the force of the thing, the sheer, unrelenting power of it as it dismantled the world piece by piece.

He dropped to his knees, the bottle slipping from his hand, forgotten. And somehow, impossibly, the man in the storm seemed to see him there, cowering in this kitchen, because its dead eyes rolled in their sockets, filling with something that was not laughter, that was not madness, that was not glee but some combination of them. It looked at Brick and it spoke, a voice that was lost in the thunder of the tornado, drowned out by the roar of its fury; a voice speaking in no language Brick could recognize, no language that had any place here on earth; but a voice he could understand as easily as if it had crawled into his ear and breathed its needled words directly into his brain.

You are too late.

THE OTHER (5)

Your enemy the devil prowls around like a roaring lion looking for someone to devour. —1 Peter 5:8

THE WORST THING WAS THE NOISE. It was deafening—literally, he couldn't hear the people screaming, couldn't hear the revving engines or the wailing car alarms or the crash of metal as it folded into metal at the intersections, not even the explosions. There was only the storm, an endless roar that made the streets tremble, as if the city were a living thing that quaked in terror. It was so loud that Graham hadn't seen more than a handful of windows still intact on his way across town, glass ripped from frames by the immense, rolling sonic pulse that pounded the streets. It was doing the same to his skull, as though the sound was a solid, living thing seeking the right frequency to split open the bone and let his brains slop out onto the pavement.

He pushed past a crowd of tourists fleeing in the opposite direction, then turned onto Millbank. For a second the storm appeared in the gap between buildings, a vast, churning mass of matter that curled and spiraled around a core of darkness. He tried not to look at it—the same way he tried every time it came into view—and yet his eyes were drawn to it, as if they had no choice, as if they had to see this thing that turned everything he knew about the world into a joke. From here, ten miles away, it looked halfway between the cloud from an atom bomb and a storm, the sky impossibly dark, as though a section of night had fallen loose, dropped onto London. But in the gaps between the debris, between the flotsam and jetsam of his city, he saw something worse than darkness. He saw the places where the world had been rubbed away.

He wrenched his head forward, focused on where he was going. It had taken him—*how long?*—over four hours to get from his house to Millbank. He'd had to walk. The city was clogged with people trying to escape, nobody going in the same direction. All the main roads were frozen solid by accidents, the trains and the subway were shut down, which meant everybody was on foot. He felt as if he had battled past each and every one of London's eight million inhabitants just to get to Thames House. He'd headed over to Whitehall first, to the counterterrorism unit, but Erika Pierce hadn't been lying, the place had been deserted. MI5 was the next logical destination, but he had the awful feeling that he'd get there to find its rooms empty too.

Because they've all fled, and you should too, because it will eat you, that storm, it will devour you. And he knew that was the truth, knew that he should turn tail and run. He'd called David three hours ago, told him to go, to head south, get out of the country if he could. With any luck he'd have reached the coast by now, could head over the Channel into France. *Or maybe he went the other way, maybe he got caught up, carried toward the storm. Maybe now he's circling the pit, or lost inside it.* And the thought of him pulled into nothingness, snuffed out like a flame, the very essence of him extinguished, made Graham want to die. He could go, call him on the way, meet him in Calais and just survive. *Just go just go just go.*

He pushed the words away, turning the corner to see the river dead ahead. Even that was agitated, vibrations herding the water into white-lipped eddies and whirlpools, spitting dirty fountains and filling the air with the stench of sewage. The noise was louder here, echoing off the buildings back and forth over the embankment. It sounded like a vast turbine sucking every last scrap of air into its engine. And yet it sounded like something else too. It sounded like trumpets, like a million war horns were being blown in the skies above his head.

It was the sound of London being eaten alive.

He ran the last hundred yards to Thames House, finding the main doors open and deserted. There was nobody in the lobby, just a snowstorm of papers on the marble floor. At least the lights were on. Luckily the building had its own power source—several, in fact—because from what he could see half of London was dark.

He ducked into the first elevator, using his counterterrorism keycard to activate the control panel. If there was anybody left, they'd be in the emergency bunker control center, standard procedure for an attack. He counted down the seconds as the elevator descended, wondering how powerful the storm had to be for him to feel its voice so deep beneath the ground, in the rocking of the elevator, the vibrating whine of the metal cables.

The door slid open to reveal the huge, open-plan room. At first he mistook the constant movement for people, but he soon realized it was just the monitors that lined every wall and sat on every desk, displaying images of the city and the storm. He wiped the sweat from his brow, wondering how the hell he was supposed to handle this alone, when a woman stepped into view. She looked up from a sheaf of documents, frowned, then broke into a huge smile.

"Graham? Jesus, I thought nobody was coming."

He recognized her as Sam Holloway, one of the MI5 codebreakers. She'd done some work for him over at the CT unit last year.

"Sam, it's good to see you," he said, walking into the room. "Please tell me you're not here by yourself."

"No, Habib Rahman's over in comms trying to get a feed on what's happening. That's it, the rest of them either jumped ship when the RAF fleet went down or are over in Downing Street trying to evac the P.M. and the Cabinet. That's Priority One."

Yeah, save the idiots in government, definitely a priority. He didn't say it out loud, though.

"RAF fleet?" he asked, walking to the director's desk. On the monitor there more of the city was being sucked into the vast maw of the storm.

"The air force sent in an attack force, three Apache gunships and a squadron of Tornados. That thing swallowed every last one of them."

"Any idea what it is?"

"No," Sam replied. "But it's big. Everything from Edgware in the north down to Fortune Green is gone."

"Gone?"

"Yeah, gone. It just isn't there anymore." There was a tremor in her voice, nothing to do with the roar of the storm. "This footage is from a U.S. Black Hawk brought in from Mildenhall, positioned five miles from ground zero."

Five miles, but the picture was sharp enough to make out the vast gulf that had opened up beneath the tornado. It looked bottomless. More than bottomless. Somehow Graham had a hunch that if you were to step off the edge of it, you would simply cease to exist.

"Any other eyes on?" he asked.

Sam nodded, running her hands across the touchscreen monitor until the view changed.

"From a Sentinel," she said.

This shot was higher, making the storm look more like a tornado than ever, a looping coil of shadow that towered over the city, maybe three miles wide now. Even as he watched, Graham saw a chunk of land snap free from the earth, rising slowly, almost gracefully, into the maelstrom where it began to break apart. The entire room shook, dust raining down from the ceiling and several of the computer screens shutting off before rebooting. It was like he was back in the Gulf, bunkered up inside a cave while enemy RPGs pounded his hideout. That island of land had to have been five hundred meters across. *How many people?* he asked himself as it crumbled, caught in the howling spiral of the vortex, pulled toward the mouth of the storm. *How many more just died?*

"Theories?" He coughed the word out.

"None," Sam said. "No radioactive signature, no indication of a biological threat. But . . ."

He looked at her, at the way the color drained from her face, and felt a million icy fingers run up his back.

"But what?"

"The epicenter of the storm. There was something there when all this started."

"A bomb?"

"No, Graham, a man. A dead man." She chewed her bottom lip, loading another piece of footage onto her monitor. It showed a morgue table, one of the ones upstairs in this very building, he thought. Lying on it was the body of a man, pulled open by a coroner's tools to reveal the empty box of his torso. And yet even sitting here, watching it on a screen, it was obvious that there was some kind of life there, in the man's pale, quickening eyes, and in his endless, inward breath. *Oh Jesus, it's the same noise,* he realized. *It's the same sound as the storm.* "He came in on Friday, from Scotland Yard."

"Why wasn't I told?" Graham asked.

"It was blackbooked, no communication in or out. The plan was to get the . . . get *it* to Northwood, get it secure, then bring people in. But they never made it. Something happened on the way."

Graham wiped his mouth, staring at the screen, at the living corpse that lay there. That was the figure he had seen in the tornado, the shape that hung in the center of the chaos. *The man in the storm,* he thought, the words appearing from nowhere. And suddenly the overwhelming unreality of it hit him like a punch to the gut, a high-pitched whine popping in his eardrums. He leaned forward, hands on his knees, wondering if he was about to puke, swallowing the acid back down with noisy, gasping gulps.

Focus, Graham, he commanded himself. *It's your job, you need to get a hold of yourself.* He straightened, cleared the mess of his throat, spoke in a grating whisper: "So what do we know for sure?"

"That it's expanding fast," said Sam. "That's why this place is deserted. We're a good ten miles from the center of the attack"—*It's not an attack,* Graham thought, *it's something more than that, something so much worse*—"but at the rate that thing is growing we'll have to be out of here soon. Other than that, we don't know anything."

"We need satellites, Sam," he said.

"I'm attempting to task one now, but the only one close enough is an NSA bird, and the Yanks are being cagey."

"Do whatever you have to," he said, pushing himself to his feet. "Hack it if you can." He walked around a bank of screens to see Habib at his desk. He didn't know him personally, but the guy was pretty famous for writing unbreakable cyphers for the army. "Habib, anything from the general?"

"He's been alerted to the attack," he replied, shrugging. "Northwood has been evacuated, but he has given us full use of any tactical units, and is happy to discuss other options."

Other options? There were no options, not that Graham could see. They didn't even know what this thing was. Part of him wanted to believe it was a nuke, a big one. Yes, it would be awful. Yes, parts of the city would be destroyed, would be radioactive for decades, and hundreds of thousands would perish. But a nuke was still a nuke, a fission warhead, a neutron striking a concentrated mass of uranium 235 and starting a chain reaction of energy release. He *understood* a nuke, it was one of the first things they had taught him. The scenario was right at the top of the nightmare list—*what if somebody detonates an atomic weapon in a major British city*—and they had procedures to deal with it. Hell, during the Olympics they'd done nothing but prepare for a strike like this. No, he could handle a nuke.

This was different. *Because it isn't science. Whatever that thing is, it doesn't obey the rules of the universe, it destroys them.* And that's what was truly terrifying, because there were no instruction manuals dealing with this, no computer simulations, no emergency drills. This was unknowable.

He pressed the heels of his palms into his eye sockets, wishing he was back in bed, that this really was a nightmare. How many times had he had dreams like this? The *Bad Things* dreams, nothing more than stress or too much port and cheese before bed. Why couldn't he wake up?

"Sir, you need to take a look at this as well."

He opened his eyes, a solar storm of flashes filling the room. Sam was standing next to her desk, both hands clamped in her short hair. On her screen was a bulletin report from district command. He squinted, reading the message twice and still not quite believing it.

"Another attack?" he said. "Where exactly?"

"On the coast," said Sam. She sat, typing instructions into the console. The images on-screen disappeared to be replaced by a crude photograph. For a moment Graham couldn't quite make out what he was looking at: a beach, an angry gray sky. There was something wrong with it that he couldn't put his finger on.

"What is that?" he said.

"It's a wave."

He saw it even as she gave her answer. Only it wasn't a wave. It wasn't the right shape. This huge mass of water was scrunched into a fist, as if a vast explosion had been set off beneath the ocean. It hung above the horizon, and Graham only realized the sheer scale of the image when he noticed a town there—tower blocks and houses and cars and tiny specks of people dwarfed by the great dappled shadow of the water.

"Oh my God," he said, slumping into his chair. "When was this taken?"

"Half an hour ago," Sam said. "In Norfolk. Yarmouth."

"Half an hour!" he said. "Why are we just finding out?"

"It got logged by the local law enforcement, but everything's tied up with that," she said, nodding at Graham's screen where the storm still raged. "There's not enough of us here, I only just picked it up in the hourlies."

Graham swore, once again feeling the urge to get up and run.

"The city—or town, really—it got wiped out. There's nothing left."

"What caused it?" he asked, pushing his feelings away, rubbing his eyes again. Sam shook her head.

"We don't know. It's related to another attack last night, in the same area. An explosion—at least we think it was an explosion—destroyed a town called Hemmingway. Nothing there, nothing worth attacking anyway. But for some reason it was hit."

"Meteor strike?" he said. *Wishful thinking.*

"Uh-uh. The radar station up in Neatishead recorded no meteor activity. Nothing has come in from the skies."

Which ruled out missile strikes too. That was one good thing, it meant that someone like Iran or North Korea hadn't decided to lob a bunch of nukes at them. He took a deep breath, trying to shut out the white noise of fear, trying to arrange his thoughts into neat, logical patterns. One thing at a time, establish a clear chain of events.

"Is there any footage from the attack last night?" he asked. Sam fiddled with her touchscreen, loading up a video feed.

"There's this," she said. "Came in just now with the report. From local law enforcement, Norfolk Constab."

She pressed Play and they sat and watched it together. It was a night shot, everything green. A bunch of SWAT officers were jogging over what looked like a sand dune, the sea a huge slab of slate in front of them, the darkest thing on the screen. He could hear barked orders, the harsh, panting breaths of whoever was wearing the helmet cam. They reached the summit of the dune, and began to descend toward . . .

"Kids?" he said, seeing the group on the beach. Two girls and two boys, from the look of it, the fear in their expressions obvious even in shades of black and green. "What the hell do they want with children?"

There was a scream, the front row of police breaking into a run. They charged at the children, their howls of utter rage so loud, so clear, that Graham had to look over his shoulder to make sure there was nobody behind him. The flesh of his arms rippled into goose bumps as the police charged, trampling over each other, looking more like animals than people.

One of the children yelled something; a name, perhaps. *Schiller*.

"Did you catch that?" he asked. "Sounded like—"

The screen flared, the light so bright that Graham had to screw his eyes shut. When he looked again, a moment later, the scene was in chaos. The camera was shaking wildly, everything a blur, but that didn't stop him seeing one of the cops jerked up into the air like a fish on a hook. The man—or woman, Graham couldn't be sure—thrashed and shrieked then *popped*. Graham could think of no other way to describe it, the body just burst into specks of ash that drifted down through the shimmering green light, looking like fish food dropped in a tank of water. Another of the cops was pulled apart by invisible fingers, then another, all the while the man with the helmet cam sat on the beach shaking his head. He howled again, lumbered to his feet, then turned his head toward the sea.

It was only for an instant—before the picture lurched upward then fizzed into static—but it looked as if there was something on the beach, something where the kids had been standing, something *burning*.

"Go back," he barked, hearing the panic in his own voice. "Go back and freeze it."

Sam scanned back through the file, then played it forward, frame by frame, each expression caught with perfect clarity, the eyes of the cops shining like they were feral cats. Their expressions were like nothing Graham had ever seen, so full of anger—no, *fury*—that they didn't look real. He tried to ignore them, watching as the scene lurched up instant by instant, the beach coming into view, then a girl, then a white flare, burning like phosphorus. Sam paused it, and for a while they sat there and stared at the boy in the flames, two huge plumes of fire arcing up from his back, his eyes pockets of absolute brilliance that made Graham's retinas itch.

"They set him on fire?" Sam asked. Graham shook his head, but what else could it be? *The kid, he isn't human, look at him, he's something else.* Sam was edging the footage on, the burning boy visible for only a dozen more frames before the cameraman went airborne and the picture was lost.

"Get images of that over to the general," he said, feeling suddenly cold despite the heat of the room. "Tell him to send a squad out to the coast, try to find out what happened. Anything on the satellite?"

"I can get it," Sam said. "If you don't mind breaking the law."

"Do it," he replied. She brought up a new panel on her monitor and he watched as she broke the NSA satellite command code. It took all of thirty seconds.

"It's already in place," she said. "They're watching us."

Of course they were. The NSA would be monitoring London and the coast to make sure whatever was happening over here wasn't a threat to them over there. *Nice of them to share.* Sam loaded an image onto the screen. Fortunately the skies were flawless today—not counting the storm—and the view of the coast was perfect. It had been decimated, nothing but rubble and ruin still glistening in the sun.

"Can we go back to the time of the attack?" he asked. Sam shook her head.

"This is live, ish. Just got to hope we get lucky," she said.

He leaned forward, studying the images on-screen, the quagmire that had once been roads and buildings and people. Something else was there.

"You make any sense of that?" he asked, pointing. It looked like an island of land in the sea, and on it a ball of light, almost like a solar flare, too bright for the satellite cam to properly capture. Sam shrugged. "Can that be real? Is it a data transfer glitch?"

"From an NSA bird? No way. It's real."

Past the glare Graham could make out five black dots there, five people. There was no way of seeing who they were, the shot was too wide, too far away, but he had a hunch that they were the same kids as in the police video. After all, this was only a few miles away.

"Can we track them if they move?"

"Yeah, but the moment I do, NSA will know we've taken control of it. The last thing we want right now is to piss off the Yanks."

"Do it," he said, jabbing at the screen, at the little dots there. "Whatever happens, we need to maintain eyes on."

Sam sighed, typing in code until the image on-screen shifted.

On the other side of the room a phone started to ring. He ignored it; it would be somebody from the States, somebody very, very angry.

"They're attempting to regain control," said Sam.

"Fight them off as long as it takes," he said. "I'll have the general put together a team. We need to bring them in alive."

"Yes, sir," Sam said. The phone stopped ringing, then began again, sounding somehow even louder and more irate than before. Graham tuned it out, staring at the screen on his desk. It still showed the burning boy, those plumes of flame stretching up from his back. *They look like wings,* he thought with another sweeping rush of vertigo. It was impossible, and yet the cataclysm that raged not ten miles from where he sat was impossible too. He thought about the shape in the darkness, the man who hung in the storm. Wasn't there a likeness there, between him and the burning boy? A similarity? There was no way it could be a coincidence. Whatever was happening in London and on the coast, those events were connected.

If they could just find those kids, they'd find answers.

LATE MONDAY MORNING

And I saw another mighty angel come down from heaven, clothed with a cloud: and a rainbow was upon his head, and his face was as it were the sun, and his feet as pillars of fire. And he had in his hand a little book open: and he set his right foot upon the sea, and his left foot on the earth, and cried with a loud voice, as when a lion roareth: and when he had cried, seven thunders uttered their voices. —Revelations 10:1–3

THERE WAS SO MUCH VIOLENCE, and she didn't know how to turn it off.

It played out before her, inside the giant glaciers of her frozen world, each scene more horrific than the last. In one, she saw Cal beneath a car as the fire bit at his legs. She called to him, reached for him, but this place, wherever she was, had turned her into a ghost. It was okay, though, because he made it out, leaving a trail of charred corpses behind him. In another, she watched Schiller lift up the ocean and use it like a sledgehammer, pounding a town into oblivion, all those poor souls washed away. The scene was so insane that she wondered how it could be real, if maybe this was just an illusion in her head. But she could taste the salt water deep in her throat, could hear the awful sound of the sea as it rose up and ate the land. It was real. It was all real.

Schiller was growing more and more powerful, that was obvious, transforming from boy to angel with nothing more than a thought. But it was taking its toll. Daisy could see the fire in his chest, the place where his angel rested, and it was spreading, burning him from the inside out.

There was someone else with Rilke and Schiller now, not Marcus or Jade—although she could still see them there, could sense their terror and their awe—but another boy. She heard a voice, faint, as though traveling a long way on a high wind.

Howie, it said. *My name is Howie. Where am I?*

It was him, the new boy, speaking to her. Maybe he was here too, somewhere in this palace of ice and dreams.

"You're . . ." she started, wondering how best to explain it. "You were injured, I think."

My brother, the boy went on, and even in that soft whisper she could hear a heavy weight of sadness. *He killed me. Am I in heaven?*

"He didn't kill you. He . . . you're still alive, but you're changing."

Into what?

"An angel," she said. "But not really an angel. It's just what we call them. They're . . . I don't really know, Howie, but they're good, they're here to help us."

Is that what he is? He meant Schiller, Daisy understood. *I don't want to be like that. I don't want to kill people. I don't want to burn.*

"You don't have to," she said. "It's not him doing that, it's *her.*"

Rilke. Poor sad, angry, crazy Rilke. How could she have gotten it so wrong?

"These things, Howie, they don't want to hurt us. They're trying to help us. There's something we have to do."

The man in the storm raged inside the ice, clearer than ever. He hung above the city, churning everything into nothing. His mouth was huge, that same awful, endless inward breath sucking up buildings and cars and *people*—thousands and thousands of people. It was horrible.

Howie didn't respond. Daisy floated through the ice like she was in a hall of mirrors. And all the while her own angel sat in her chest. She knew it was hatching in there, like somebody waking from a deep sleep. Yes, that's what it was like. The angel had come from a place far away, she knew that much, somewhere even the fastest spaceship couldn't ever get to. It had been a long journey, and now the angel was waking up, remembering how to use its arms and legs the same way she sometimes needed to when she woke from a deep sleep. And once that happened . . .

"Howie?" she called, wondering where the boy had gone. Had Schiller heard him? Or Rilke? Were they keeping him quiet somehow? "If you can hear me, don't listen to Rilke. She's not a bad person, but she's got it all wrong. We're not here to hurt people, I know it. We're here to help them."

Still no answer. Her voice was just too quiet. But not for long. Her angel was nearly ready. Then she wouldn't be a ghost anymore, she wouldn't be a girl either. She'd be a voice, loud enough to blast away the storm.

CAL / *East Walsham, 9:29 a.m.*

ONLY NOW, IN THE QUIET STILLNESS OF THE CHURCH, did his body seem to remember what pain was. It started in his feet, pushing up into his abdomen. He could feel his heartbeat like a pulsing heat in his skin. But he was alive. Alive and safe—if anybody had followed him to the church they'd be here by now, howling up and down the aisles.

And he was *warm*. That was the main thing. He wasn't slipping into a pool of ice like Schiller and Daisy. That was good. It meant that whatever was inside him wasn't in a hurry to get out. He just wanted to drink something, lock the church door, and sleep for a hundred years.

But what to do about the priest? The old man sat on the altar, muttering something beneath his breath and occasionally smiling nervously at Cal. He kept taking off his glasses and cleaning them on his jacket, again and again and again. If he wasn't careful, there would be no glass left in them. He put them on his nose, coughed, then spoke in a soft voice that carried the length of the church.

"Your friend needs help. *You* need help. Look, let me free and I'll tend to your injuries. There's a first-aid kit in the rectory. I promise I'll do everything I can."

"No," Cal croaked. "You don't understand. If you come near me—come near any of us—you'll try to kill us."

"That's absurd," the priest said. "I would never hurt a child, I would never hurt anybody. Please believe me, I'm a man of God."

"I don't think God has anything to do with this," Cal said. "It's . . . it's older than that." He had no idea what he was saying. "Tell me what you know about angels."

"What?" the priest asked, cleaning his glasses. "Angels? Why?"

"Just humor me," Cal said. "Angels."

The man cleared the phlegm from his throat, a noise that might have been a laugh. Then he must have seen the look on Cal's face because his brow creased and he glanced at the floor.

"Angels, well, I don't know what you want to know. In the Bible, they are spiritual beings, they are the messengers of God—in fact, that's what the word means, messenger. It's Greek originally. Um . . ." He shrugged, the coil of rope rising then slapping on the floor. "Is that the sort of thing you want to know?"

Cal had no idea what he wanted to know.

"No." He struggled to think of the right question. "Can they possess people? You know, like demons. Can they come to earth?"

How insane did *that* sound? The priest was shaking his head.

"Look, son."

"Cal," said Cal.

"Cal, I'm Doug. I'm not sure what it is you want to know. I—"

There was a crunch of gravel from outside, then the squeal of the door. Brick pushed into the church carrying a glass of water in one hand and a loaf of bread in the other. He looked ashen, each freckle picked out like a pen mark against his pale skin, and when he held out the glass Cal could see that his hand was shaking—so much that most of the water had sloshed out over his arm. Cal took a sip that burned down like acid. It was cool in his stomach, though, and he instantly felt better.

"I thought I told you not to speak," Brick said, looking at the priest.

"You told me not to try to escape," the man replied.

Cal took another sip, bigger this time, before adding: "It's okay, Brick, I asked him a question. About angels."

Brick hissed through his nose, crashing down on the back pew next to Adam. He handed the boy a fistful of bread, and Adam tucked into it like a feral dog.

"Angels," snorted Brick, spitting out crumbs. "I'm telling you, that's bollocks."

"If you tell me why you want to know about them, I might be able to give you a better answer."

"Because . . ." Cal started, hesitating, wondering if saying it aloud inside a church might make it real in a way it hadn't been before. In front of him, Brick tore off another chunk of bread with his teeth, shaking his head. "Because I think we're possessed by them."

The priest didn't reply, just swallowed noisily and started eye-balling the church door.

"Doug, I know how insane this sounds. If we could prove it to you we would." He cocked his head, an idea floundering inside the sea of pain that was his thoughts. "Wait, do you have a camcorder?"

IT DIDN'T TAKE LONG TO FIND IT INSIDE THE RECTORY, Brick returning after five minutes with a small Flipcam. He crashed back into the pew, fiddling with the camera, snapping open the viewfinder.

"Please be careful with that," said Doug. "It's Margaret's. She would be very upset if it was damaged."

"It will be fine, we'll be careful," said Cal. "I need you to make sure that rope is secure, okay? It needs to be tight. Knot it again, just to be sure."

The priest did as he was told then tugged his arm, twice. It looked safe enough, but right now he was just an old fat guy. In a moment or two, when they crossed the line, he'd be something else, a creature of ancient, instinctive rage.

"Do it," said Cal.

"You do it," Brick replied. "No way I'm going over there."

"Look," said Doug, his voice an octave higher than it had been. "Whatever you're thinking of doing to me, don't."

"Brick, just do it."

The older boy pulled a face that made Cal want to kill him there and then. He looked as if he was going to try to hand the camcorder to Adam, then pushed himself to his feet and slid out into the aisle. He hovered for a moment, unsure, cast one glowering look back at Cal, then hesitantly made his way toward the altar. There was a soft chime as he started to record.

"Please, just stop there," Doug whined, starting to pick at the knot with his free hand.

"Leave it," Cal said. "We're not going to hurt you, I promise."

Brick took another short, shuffling step, and another, closing the gap between him and the priest. How far was it now? Twenty-five meters maybe? Cal couldn't be sure, but it wouldn't be—

The priest uttered a nasal whine, which curled up at the end into a snort. Even from the other end of the church Cal could see the man's eyes grow dark, his face slack, as though the meat was slowly sliding off the bone. His whole body lurched, bumping him down onto the next step, his arms gouging at the carpet, at the stone, like he was having a fit. Brick paused, and Cal could almost see the waves of fear pulsing from him, filling the building with a sour, unpleasant smell.

"Go on," he said. "You're not close enough."

Brick muttered something that Cal couldn't hear, then stepped over the invisible line of the Fury. The priest rocketed to his feet, a brittle scream grating from the black chasm of his mouth. He charged at Brick, making it all of three feet before the rope grew taut, locking him in place. Momentum caused his legs to fly up, his body thudding to the stone. He didn't care, thrashing, howling.

"That's enough, Brick," Cal said. Brick staggered back, almost tripping on his own feet. And just like that he was back over the line and the priest was just a priest again, a bundle of black cloth in the aisle, panting for breath and spitting blood. It took him several minutes to remember where he was, wheezing his way onto the lowest step of the altar, wiping the sheen of sweat from his bald head. He clutched his wrist, slick with blood, his cloudy eyes searching the church until they landed on Cal.

"What . . . what did you do to me?"

"Show him," said Cal. Brick flicked the camcorder closed and bowled it down the aisle. The little hunk of plastic skidded over the uneven stone, thudding into the wooden rail that the priest was tied to. He no longer seemed concerned about his camera. He didn't seem too concerned about anything anymore, as though the Fury had picked him up and shaken out anything that ever mattered, leaving him hollow.

"Watch it," said Cal.

Another silent age passed, then he reached down and picked up the camcorder. There were more quiet beeps, then Cal heard his own voice—*Go on, you're not close enough*—followed by the unmistakable soundtrack of the Fury. Even hearing it like this made his skin crawl. The priest's eyes were like golf balls, huge and white, as he watched himself on the tiny screen. What was it like, to see yourself like that? To know that, for a short while, you were not you, you were something else, something terrible. The man watched it again, then gently folded the screen into the camera and laid it by his feet.

"My God," he whispered, suddenly a child. "What happened to me?"

"We did," Cal said. "Now please, tell us what you know."

BRICK / *East Walsham, 9:52 a.m.*

"ANGELS ARE AGENTS OF GOD, MORE THAN MEN. They are messengers, mainly, bringers of revelation—like Gabriel and Mary, for instance. But they are warriors too."

Warriors, Brick thought as he listened to the priest, isn't that what Daisy said? That we are here to fight?

"What do you mean warriors?" he asked. "Aren't angels like goody-goody cherubs with fat faces and halos and stuff?"

"Well, no," the priest said with a shake of his head. He was still pale and trembling, and in the heavy shadows of the far end of the church he looked like a ghost. "Maybe now, perhaps, on Christmas cards. But originally they were more like an army, or . . . guardians is maybe a better word. They are usually depicted with flaming swords. Some stand by God's throne."

"Like an imperial guard or something," said Cal from the back wall. Brick could hear the exhaustion in the boy's voice, wondered how long either of them would stay awake. It was just so still in here, like time had decided to cut them a break, stop awhile. Adam was already curled up on the bench like a dog, eyes scrunched shut. "You know, like with the emperor out of *Star Wars*."

"Well, I'm not sure about that comparison," the priest said. "But yes, I suppose so. As for the others, they were mainly tasked with carrying messages to mankind. They're not just in the Bible, you know, they're found in almost every religion across the world."

"So what are they made of?" Cal asked.

"I don't understand why you think angels are responsible for this, for whatever is happening," the priest said. "It's . . . it has to be a chemical thing, a reaction of some kind. A disease maybe."

"Trust me," said Cal. "You haven't seen what we've seen. Go on."

"What are they made of?" The priest shuffled uncomfortably, cleaning his glasses once again. This time he didn't put them back on, just held them in his hands and examined them as if the answers were written there. "They are ethereal, I know that much.

They are spirits. Have you heard the question 'How many angels can you fit on the head of a pin?' The answer is an infinite number, because they are not creatures of this world. Scholastic theologians teach us that they are able to move between places instantly, which allows them to travel back and forth between here and heaven. Because of this they are often shown as being crafted from fire."

At this, Brick peered over his shoulder and met Cal's eyes.

"So no robes and little harps, then?" Brick said.

"No, I don't think so. I'm not one of these priests who believes God is an old man with a beard sitting on a cloud. That would be absurd, don't you think?" Doug pushed his glasses back on and blinked, seemingly unsure if the question was serious or not.

"What did you mean by guardians?" asked Cal.

"Um, they watch over us. Many people believe that, you must have heard the term guardian angel, yes?"

"But you get bad angels too, right?" Brick asked, thinking of what he had just seen on the TV, the man in the storm.

"Bad ones? Yes. According to the Bible, Lucifer was once an angel, an archangel really. He believed that he could be more powerful than God, and attempted to lead, well, a rebellion I guess, with his army of angels. Because of his sin of pride, God cast him down into the Lake of Fire, hell, along with his supporters. This is part of the scripture that I, personally, have difficulty with. It's always tempting to believe that human evil can be blamed on the devil, and yes, there are occasions where this is the case. But I think evil is also part of who we are. We have only ourselves to blame for the bad things of the world."

At one time, Brick would have believed that. But not now, not with everything he'd seen. The man in the storm, that wasn't human. It was the very opposite of human, the very opposite of all life.

"This isn't getting us anywhere," he said, just so there was noise.

"Yeah, I know," Cal replied. "I know. Look, Doug, some of the stuff in the Bible is probably based on real things, yeah? No offense, mate. I mean, I remember hearing that the great flood, the one with Noah and everything, might have been because of some massive tidal wave or something."

"Yes," Doug said. "I once attended a class on science in the Bible, back during my curacy in Oxford. You're talking about the Black Sea deluge theory, around 5600 B.C. Water from the Mediterranean Sea breached a sill in the, um, in the Bosporus Strait I think. It would have caused a terrible flood. There are other examples too. The story of Moses and the Red Sea. There are conditions where a strong wind could actually part the waters of a river. It's called a wind setdown. It has happened other times too, in the Nile Delta. It is quite astonishing."

"So religion isn't real then?" Brick said. "Stupid thing for a priest to say."

"No, you misunderstand me. Religion is about faith, and faith is a very different kind of knowledge. God is a scientific fact and there is a science that explains the nature of God. Of course there is. But we do not know what that science is yet. Perhaps one day, we will understand it, the same way that we now understand the science of gravity, of lightning, of some, uh, quantum particle behaviors. Perhaps one day we will know the scientific truth about God, and our creation. Then science and religion will be one and the same."

"So angels," Cal went on, and Brick realized he was talking to him. "Maybe this has happened before. Maybe, like thousands of years ago, people got possessed by . . . by whatever is inside us. Only they didn't know what they were, they just saw these things made of fire, with wings; creatures that could destroy a whole town with a single word. They saw them, and they called them angels, God's messengers, and they told their kids and so on and eventually it just became a part of religion. That makes sense, doesn't it?"

It did, but Brick didn't say anything.

"And the thing in London, the man in the storm. Maybe he's been here before. Maybe people saw him and thought he was just like us, like the angels I mean, but a bad version. They might have just made up a story about how he was cast down and wanted to take his revenge. It could have all happened before, Brick."

"So what?"

"So, it means they've fought him before, the angels," Cal said. "It means they stopped him doing whatever he is here to do. It means they won."

"How do you know that?"

"Because we wouldn't be here otherwise, would we? That thing wants to eat everything. It's like a black hole. It won't stop until we destroy it."

"Yeah?" Brick had to swallow a sour lump of bile that rose from the churning pit of his stomach. The image of the man in the storm appeared before him, seeming to fill the church with darkness. Trying to fight that would be like trying to stop a train with a toothpick. They would be torn apart, pulled into that raging mouth along with everything else. "How the hell do we do that, Cal?"

"We wait," the other boy said. "Until they hatch."

And that thought was equally terrifying, the idea that there was something in his chest—no, deeper than that, in his *soul*—that was waiting for the right moment to burst through in a fist of fire, to take control of his body.

"But why do people hate us?" Brick asked eventually. "That's the bit I really don't understand. If we're here to fight that thing, then surely people would be on our side, they'd help us, not try to kill us."

"I don't know," said Cal. "Doug, do you remember anything about what just happened, when we were filming?"

The priest went two shades paler, and shook his head.

"It's like . . . like that part of my memory, my life, just doesn't exist. One minute I was talking to you, then I black out, then everything's back to normal. Only . . . only it's not, is it, because I tried to kill you." He wiped a hand across his face and Brick realized the old man was crying. "It wasn't me. It wasn't me."

"Have you ever hated someone so much you lose your mind over it?" Brick said, the words out of his mouth before he even knew they were coming. "Hated them so much your whole vision just burns white and it's like you're somebody else?"

Nobody answered. He shuffled, uncomfortable to be sharing so much.

"I think that's what it's like. The Fury. You get so angry, so full of rage, that you just lose yourself. Only, times a million."

He swallowed noisily, blushing. For a while, the only sound was the rush of his pulse in his ears, then Cal spoke.

"Yeah, that makes sense. I guess in a way it's like what we talked about before, back in Fursville. But it's not a chemical thing, or an emotional one, it's *this*, the angels. People can't accept them, because they're so . . . what's the word?"

"Alien?" said Brick.

"Yeah, I guess. They're so alien that they make people lose themselves. People just have to kill them, kill *us*."

More silence, as deep as the ocean. Brick looked down the church and saw the hot-dog stand from Fursville, burning, and beyond that the pavilion. He snapped his eyes open, realizing that sleep had ambushed him.

"We should go," he said, wiping his eyes. When Cal didn't reply, he looked over his shoulder to see that he too had dropped off, his head resting on his knees. "Cal, we can't fall asleep."

"It's okay," said the priest. "You can. You have my word, I won't move. I know what will happen. I couldn't bear to be like that again."

Brick scowled at the man. He was a feral, he couldn't be trusted. *But just for a second, just to get your energy back.* He closed his eyes and looked past the pavilion, saw the ocean there. There was a boat on it, a boat that became an island, and then a house, and by the time Brick had swum to it, opened the door and walked inside, he no longer knew he was dreaming.

RILKE / *Great Yarmouth, 10:07 a.m.*

THEY STAGGERED IN SILENCE, the sea behind them as still and as quiet as a beaten dog. The further they went, the more they saw of the destruction Schiller had wrought. To their left was another ocean, this one made up of bricks and concrete and bod-ies, buoyed up on silt and seawater. Smoke rose from three or four places. She wondered if there was anyone left alive over there, then she thought of the wall of water that had crunched into the town. Nothing could have survived that. They wouldn't have even known it was happening.

"You did well, little brother," she told him for what must have been the tenth time. "You wiped it clean."

"Can we rest now?" was his response. "Please, Rilke, I don't feel very well."

Rest rest rest, it was all he ever said. They'd rested for what had to have been half an hour after the town had been destroyed, all of them too tired to move. What more did he want? He brushed a hand through his hair, coming away with strands between his fingers. His hair was no longer blond, she saw, but gray. *It's killing him, it's using him, it's eating him from the inside.*

"Okay," she said, suddenly full of panic. "But not here."

The land was perfectly flat, but there were a few landmarks. One, maybe half a mile away, stood tall over the wasteland. A windmill. She set off toward it, as fast as she could manage, dragging the others along behind her. It seemed to take forever. The door was locked, but it was old, and after a couple of kicks it wobbled open, releasing the stench of damp and rot. She let Jade and Marcus go first, carrying the new boy inside. Then she ushered Schiller in. She followed him into the stale darkness, closing the door behind her.

"I need to sleep," said Jade, collapsing in the dirt in the middle of the small, circular room. Marcus dropped next to her, his eyes already closed. Pathetic, both of them. Did she even need them? When her angel hatched she and Schiller could change the world by themselves.

"An hour," Rilke said. "No more. It isn't safe."

"Safe?" said Jade, her words slurred. "From who? The police?"

"Yes," said Rilke, watching as Schiller dropped instantly into sleep. She sat down beside him, part of her wondering where he would go in his dreams, and who he would talk to. "And others. The army."

Daisy too, she thought but didn't say. Because when the little girl woke she would come for them, bringing the fury of an angel with her. And when that happened, there would be nowhere for them to hide.

DAISY / *East Walsham, 11:09 a.m.*

THERE WERE MORE PEOPLE HERE NOW, in her kingdom of ice. She could sense their arrival, like birds alighting on a branch, making it sway almost imperceptibly. The ice cubes clinked, bouncing off each other, each one still full of other people's lives. The whole world swam with liquid movement, the constant burble and splash of a swimming pool.

"Hello?" she said. Was it the new kid, the one called Howie? He was still here somewhere, lost in the maze of icy mirrors. She'd heard him calling out, shouting for his mum and his brother. "Say something, please, I know you're there."

"Daisy?" The voice came from right behind her and she spun around. The creature she saw there was so beautiful, and yet so terrifying, that she didn't know whether to laugh or cry. It stood tall in robes of diamond-white flame, its wings curling overhead. It was so bright that she turned away, before realizing that she wasn't really staring at it, not with her eyes anyway. She looked back, seeing the creature's face, recognizing it.

"Schiller?" she said. It wasn't his face, and yet it was. It shimmered in the light, like a reflection in a sun-drenched, wind-rippled pool. But there was no doubt it was him, because as soon as she said his name he broke into a huge, blinding smile. "It *is* you. How are you here?"

"I don't know," he said, and even though he looked like his angel his voice was high and soft, so much like Rilke's. "The last thing I remember . . . we're inside a windmill, by the sea. I must have fallen asleep."

Of course. It had happened before, not with Schiller but with Brick and Cal. On their first night in Hemmingway they had shared a dream. It didn't seem like something that could actually happen, but then *nothing* that had happened was like something that could actually happen. Besides, if they all had angels inside them then why wouldn't they be able to communicate like this? There had to be some kind of link between them now, one that didn't bother with things like distance and time and space.

"Are you okay?" she said. "Tell me what it's like, the angel."

Schiller shrugged, his wings lurching up then down. This was the first time she had heard his voice, she realized. The first time she had met him, really, because he had been frozen for so long. *No, you heard his voice, remember,* a part of her brain said. *In Hemmingway, when he spoke and ended that place, a single word that smashed a hundred people into ash. You were unconscious, but you still heard it.*

"I didn't mean to do that," he said, reading her thoughts. "But they were going to hurt us, hurt my sister. I didn't know what else to do."

You didn't have a choice, she thought.

He shrugged again, but this time his mouth was turned so low that it looked drawn on, an upside-down smiley.

"Have you spoken to it?" Daisy asked.

"I think so," he said. "It doesn't really have words, just, I don't know, like feelings. It tries to show me things, but I don't always understand."

"Did it show you why it's here?"

"The man in the storm," he replied without hesitation. "That's what I keep seeing."

Daisy nodded. She was the same. How many times had she been pulled toward that particular ice cube, the one filled with furious darkness, the one where *he* lived? It loomed there even as she thought about it, cracking toward her with the sound of breaking glaciers. But she knew how to push it away now, and she did so gently, insistently.

"Rilke says it's because it's telling us what to do, the man in the storm, it's one of us. She thinks we have to follow its example, destroy things."

He was shaking his head as he spoke, and Daisy could sense his reluctance.

"Your sister is wrong," she said. "She's made a mistake. A terrible one. We're not here to join it, we're here to fight it."

As if in response, she felt something moving in her chest. Well, it wasn't so much her chest as something deeper, someplace she couldn't quite identify. It was like a pressure there, like her heart was about to burst, but in a good way, like waking up and remembering it's Christmas Day. It was her angel. It was close to hatching.

The space around her grew cooler, as if the ice cubes were leeching heat from the air. Then somebody else spoke, a voice just as cold. "I knew it."

Daisy turned to see another figure. This one was definitely human, although that same blue fire burned where her heart should be. Rilke didn't step so much as float toward them, her face so twisted by anger that she could have been a feral.

"I knew I'd find you here, little brother."

"Rilke, we were only talking," said Daisy. Rilke swept down on them like a bird of prey, glaring at her. She wasn't the girl that Daisy remembered, it was almost like a dream person, somebody that didn't look quite themselves but who was definitely them. *Of course, because she isn't really here, and neither am I, I'm with Cal and Brick and Adam.* That knowledge made her feel safer; surely Rilke couldn't hurt her in this not-real place.

"Don't listen to her, Schill," said Rilke. "She doesn't know what she's saying. She hasn't seen what we've seen."

Daisy saw it once again, in the ice, the wall of water that trembled across the land. For a moment she felt it too, that huge weight of darkness swallowing the sky, falling down on her, and she had to push herself out of the sensation before it made her scream.

"Oh, Schiller, no," she said. "All those people. You didn't have to hurt them, you didn't have to do that."

"You're wrong, Daisy," spat Rilke. "He did. Don't you see it yet? Hasn't it gotten into your stupid little head? You can protest all you like, but sooner or later you'll be forced to see the truth. He called us, the man in the storm. He wants us to join him, he wants us to help him cleanse the world."

"No," Daisy said. "You're *wrong*, Rilke. Please, why won't you see that?" She turned to Schiller, silently pleading for him to stand up to his sister. But even though he burned like a giant sentinel of molten glass, he could not look either of them in the eye. "Please." She felt so powerless, so small. Why couldn't she be like Schiller right now, why couldn't her angel do something to help her? If it had hatched, then Rilke would have to listen to her.

"Don't threaten me," said Rilke, even though Daisy didn't realize she had. "You will change soon, but don't even think about getting in my way. I won't hesitate to kill you. Schiller won't hesitate, isn't that right."

It wasn't a question, and after a moment of uncomfortable fidgeting Schiller nodded.

"And it isn't just him anymore. We've got another one, ready to turn."

"Howie," said Daisy, remembering the voice she'd heard. Rilke's expression flickered, unsure. She glanced around at the kaleidoscope of ice, as if she could see him there.

"He's ours," she hissed. "You hear me? And if you're listening, Howie, then remember this—if I think you're going to turn against me when you hatch, then I'll just smash in your skull before you wake up. Understand?"

How could she be so mean? The Fury—it had scratched away at the foundations of her mind and now everything was crumbling. Daisy could almost see it in the girl's face, the way her features seemed to grow and shrink like some hideous painting warping in the cold. She was falling apart from the inside.

"Leave her alone, Rilke." Another voice, and this one so, *so* welcome. Daisy turned to see Cal there, or at least a shimmering dream shape that looked like him. Brick was close behind, and Adam too, floating there, among the constantly shifting sea of ice.

"Oh and the *hero* returns," Rilke said. "As self-righteous and arrogant as ever. Go away, Cal, nobody wants you here."

"Yeah? I didn't see your name on the door, Rilke," he replied. "What do you want?"

"I want you to leave Schiller alone," she said. "Leave us all alone. Let us do what we're here to do. I don't care if you want to hide away, waiting out the end days cowering in each other's arms. But you *will not* stand between us and our duty. Do you hear me? I mean it, Daisy, if I find out you've been talking to Schiller again—any of us again—I'll finish you."

"But you're wrong!" Daisy shouted, and the movement of the ice grew more agitated, the giant cubes crashing against each other. "You're wrong wrong wrong wrong wrong!" As she spoke the pressure in her chest grew. She felt like a can of fizzy drink that had been shaken, one that was about to be opened.

"Am I?" Rilke seemed to chew on something, her dream face expanding, deflating, like a pair of lungs. "Then maybe it's time we found out for sure."

"What do you mean?" Daisy asked. Rilke's smile was loose and wet, a clown's smile. She looked at Schiller, then behind her to three more figures that Daisy hadn't even seen arrive. It was Jade and Marcus, and between them stood the new boy, Howie. They all had that same heatless fire blazing in their chests. Rilke turned back, her eyes small and black and full of something that Daisy didn't understand, something utterly human and yet completely alien. Daisy thought that the angel inside Rilke was probably screaming the truth at her, trying to make her understand, in a language that none of them could ever hope to hear. She felt sorry for it, felt its frustration. If only there was a way for them to know once and for all why they were here, and why they had been chosen.

"But there is," said Rilke, plucking her thoughts once again with icy fingers. "Don't you see, we just have to go there."

Go where? Daisy wondered, and once more it came for her, the storm in the ice, crashing through the floe in a hail of splinters. She looked and saw the man there, the beast, wrapped in a spiraling cloak of debris, its mouth open, devouring everything it could, turning substance into absence. It rolled its dead, scribble-black eyes toward her as if it knew she was there, and in the thunder of its voice she heard laughter. She shoved it away with the fingers of her mind, silently screaming *No no no no no.*

"Yes, Daisy. It's the only way for you to learn." Rilke's smile grew even wider, until it seemed too big even for her head. She began to retreat, pulling her burning brother along with her. "When we wake we go there, to the man in the storm, and we ask him."

RILKE / *Great Yarmouth, 11:43 p.m.*

THEY WOKE AS ONE, Rilke swimming up from sleep in time to see Schiller's watery eyes open, Jade groan and sit up, Marcus hunch against the wall as if he knew what was coming.

The dream-that-wasn't-really-a-dream was fading, but what Rilke had said in it was as clear as ever. There was only one way they would know for sure what the truth was. They had to find the man in the storm and listen to what he had to say. The thought was like a fist clenched tight in her stomach, but fear was just another reminder of her weakness, her despicable humanity, so she ignored it.

The question was, How did they get to him?

"I'm still tired, Rilke," said Schiller in that infuriating puppy whine of his. He pushed himself up with his elbows, everything about him loose and soft and disgusting.

"All you ever do is moan and sleep," she said. "Get up."

"But—"

"I said *get up*, brother." She stepped forward, hand raised, ready to beat the seriousness of her command into him. He flinched, scrabbling until he found his feet, standing stooped and frightened in the fingers of sticky light from the windmill's boarded window. She stared at Marcus and Jade, and they obeyed without her having to ask.

"I'm hungry," mumbled Jade. With her filthy face and hair she looked like an urchin, and this just angered Rilke further. Food was unnecessary now that they were made of fire.

She walked to the door, opening it a crack and peering out into the blazing heat of the day. The only blemish on the huge blue canvas of the sky was a dull haze over the town they had annihilated, a faint black cloud that reminded her of a funeral veil. Helixes of seagulls swooped through it, feasting on whatever was left. It looked so far away. How were they going to get all the way to the city, to where the man hung in his storm? She clenched her teeth together, her fists, nails chiseled into her palms. They would just have to set off on foot and see what luck brought them.

"Let's go," she said. She stepped out into the day, its warmth making her feel even more uncomfortable in her own flesh. She wanted to burn as fiercely as the sun, not feel its condescending touch on her. There was the scuffle of movement behind her, and a moment later Jade edged from the door with the new boy's arm over her shoulder, Marcus propping up his other side. Schiller was the last, looking three feet tall as he stooped from the windmill. "You're all stronger than you think now," she told them.

"You have angels inside you, they will keep you safe. The weakness is just a memory from your old life, ignore it and it will go away."

Even as she spoke she felt the blood drain from her head, the world spin like a giddy fool around her. There was a farmhouse fifty meters away, and beyond that nothing but fields until a line of distant trees. If they walked west for long enough they would surely find a road, wouldn't they? It just looked so *far*.

"Please, Rilke," said Jade. "There's a house there, can't we just ask them for some food or something?"

Rilke looked at the house and saw it, a flash of black behind one of the whitewashed walls.

"Schiller!" she yelled, turning to her brother, seeing more black shapes rise from the crops, wearing helmets and holding rifles. There were too many to count, all advancing on them. How had they found them?

"Don't move!" someone shouted. "We *will* open fire!"

They were approaching from all angles, streaming from behind the farmhouse, from the fields in both directions. She ran to Schiller, grabbing the collar of his shirt, shaking him so hard that more of his hair fell loose.

"Kill them!" she ordered, willing him to change. "Do it, little brother, *now*!"

"Stay where you are," the voice barked again.

Schiller wailed, no sign of fire in those big, wet, blinking blue eyes.

The soldiers charged, sunlight glinting from their visors, from their weapons. Jade was on her knees, screaming, Marcus was crawling back toward the windmill on his hands and knees. There was only poor, frightened, wretched, human Schiller.

"On the ground, now!" yelled the voice. "All of you!"

"Don't you *dare* fail me." Rilke's voice was a scream as she shook him. He exploded into light, a second skin of blue flame rippling across his body, a concussive thump blasting her backward, sending her tumbling head over feet. The air ruptured into that mind-numbing hum, so loud and so deep that it blotted out every other sound. Schiller hovered off the ground, the fire working its way up his neck, over his face, one wing pushing out of his back.

Something cracked. *It's gunfire,* she thought with a laugh, *you're too late, you can't hurt him now.* But Schiller's head jerked back, like he had been hit by an invisible sledgehammer. The flame flickered off and he dropped to the ground, shrieking, clutching his face.

"No!" Rilke screamed, clawing her way back over the ground. "Schiller!"

He looked at her, the flame erupting again, so fierce now that she had to bury her head in her arms. The world went dark and she looked again, saw him lying on his side, a gaping wound in his left temple.

A bullet kicked up the dirt inches from her brother, then something thudded into his chest, bursting from his back in a fan of brilliant red, so bright that it didn't seem real. Rilke screamed again, throwing herself over the last few feet, colliding with him, wrapping her hands around him, willing the creature inside him to find its strength, to fight. And it did, Schiller once again detonating into cold fire. This time she clung on, holding him tight, trying to feed herself into him, to pass him every last ounce of strength she possessed.

He spoke, the word a sonic pulse that tore outward, turning

the windmill to a storm of dust, mixing men with mud until the field looked like an artist's palette. But the cry faltered after a second, stuttering back into her brother's soft voice. He whined, blood pumping from his head wound, dripping on her. The flames rippled back and forth over his skin, unable to catch hold, his eyes blazing then black, blazing then black.

She held him to her as the soldiers advanced. The ones at the front were already turning, dropping their guns and reaching out for them, their faces slack, their minds broken by the Fury. Others were still shooting, the air alive with burning lead.

A bullet hit Schiller in the shoulder. This time he screamed with pain, the fire blazing back on. His wings punched from his back, sweeping down and lifting him up inside a tornado of dust. He spoke again, a tsunami of sound that tore across the field, unknitting the soldiers into clouds of ash that held their shapes for a moment, as if not quite understanding what had happened, before fading. But still they came, from every direction, shouting, shooting, too many to fight, just too many of them.

Like at the rave, she thought, remembering the first night that the Fury had almost taken them. *Our fingers touched and we knocked loose the stars.*

She looked at Schiller, and he seemed to know what she was thinking. The fire paled and he slumped back, falling out of life, but she held him to her, saw Jade next to them, reaching out, saw Marcus running back, the knowledge of what they were about to do somehow in his eyes—*Don't leave me*. He skidded into them, one hand on Rilke, one hand on the boy who burned, one hand on the frozen kid beside him; Jade clutched her arm; Schiller roared, engulfed them all in cold fire, and the world came apart.

This time she knew what to expect. A shock wave of energy

blasted outward from where they were standing, then the field was ripped away with such force that Rilke's scream didn't have a chance to leave her lungs.

An instant later, life found them again, wrapped them in its fist as if furious that they had found a way loose. The world re-formed with the sound of a million prison doors shutting at once, locking them back inside. Rilke leaned forward, a stream of milk-white vomit blasting from her mouth, jetting over tarmac. She wiped away tears with a trembling hand, seeing that they were on a narrow country road. Woodland shielded them on one side, a high grassy bank on the other, but she could hear the soft pop of distant gunfire. A rain of embers drifted down around them, dancing on the breeze.

She turned at the sound of retching, seeing Jade and Marcus spraying the road. Only Schiller was motionless, once again just a boy, just her brother. Blood pooled beneath him, looking black against the gray. She pressed her hand against the wound in his chest and it spilled through her fingers. She pushed down with her other hand, trying to clamp the wound shut. He didn't respond, he lay there and stared at the great big blue sky overhead, his pale eyes darting back and forth as if he read a truth there.

"What the hell just happened?" said Marcus, trying to get to his feet and falling on his rump. "Where are we?"

"Schiller?" said Rilke, ignoring the other boy. "Can you hear me?"

His body juddered, stalling, and the sobs escaped Rilke before she could stop them. "Little brother," she said, smoothing down his hair. "I know how to save you." That was a lie, of course, she didn't know anything. "I need you to take us somewhere, like you just did. I need you to take us to the man in the storm. I think he can fix you."

Schiller's body shook again, a soft tremor deep inside him like an earthquake beneath the ocean. He rolled his eyes toward her, their color almost totally drained, and his lips twitched into an almost word. ". . . can't . . ."

The gunfire in the distance had stopped, but she could make out the rumble of a helicopter. It wouldn't be long before the soldiers found them. She took Schiller's hand, kissing his fingers.

"Take us there. I know you can."

"She . . . she doesn't want me to," he said.

Daisy. The white heat inside her made her ears ring. "Ignore her, Schill, she doesn't love you like I do."

At this, Schiller's eyes brightened. He squeezed her hand as best as he was able. It was like being gripped by a bird claw, so brittle she worried his fingers might snap off.

"I *do* love you, little brother, more than anything."

"I love you too," he managed, coughing more blood.

"So do this for me."

She gripped him hard, then looked up at Marcus and Jade.

"I don't want to," said Jade, scuffling away on her backside and shaking her head. "I can't do it anymore."

"They'll kill you," Rilke said. It didn't matter, they didn't need her. Let her die, it would be one less sheep for Rilke to shepherd. Marcus placed a hand on Schiller, clutching her brother's shirt with white-knuckled fingers. He took hold of the new boy's arm, then nodded.

"You can do it, Schill," he said.

Rilke closed her eyes, pictured the storm that raged over London, and the creature who sucked out the rot of the world with that huge, unending breath. *Take us there,* she thought, directing the words into Schiller's head. *I know you will.* And she did. There was not a single doubt in her mind. The man would save Schiller, he would save all of them. He was their guardian angel.

Schiller nodded, then he spoke, and once again the universe— time and space and all the spinning orbits of life—had no choice but to let them go.

CAL / *East Walsham, 11:48 p.m.*

HE WOKE AND ASSUMED HE WAS STILL DREAMING, because Brick sat on the back pew of the church stroking Daisy's hair. Brick must have sensed Cal waking, because he stood up, wiping the back of his hand over his nose.

"You saw her too."

Not, *Was that a dream?* Or, *Did we really meet there?* Cal shook the last few scraps of sleep from his head, pushed himself up only to feel like he had been thrown into a pool of razors. "Ow," he said. *Understatement of the century.* "Don't suppose you saw any painkillers on your travels?"

"There is a first-aid kit in the rectory, like I said," said the priest. Doug. Cal had almost totally forgotten about him. He sat where he had promised to sit, rubbing his legs as if to keep the blood flowing. Cal nodded a thank-you at him, then looked at Brick.

"I went last time. You go." Brick glanced down at Daisy once more, and Cal could see how much he loved her. Brick did a good job of trying to hide his feelings, but he was an awful liar. "Where was that place?" Brick asked, crossing the aisle and sitting on the pew opposite. "All the ice and stuff."

"Dunno," said Cal, trying once again to get to his feet. He braced his back against the wall, sliding up an inch at a time until he was more or less vertical. He thought back to the place he'd visited when he was asleep and already it had almost faded. There had been ice there, yeah, but other things too. And other people. "Rilke," he said. "She was there."

Brick nodded, using one of his thumbnails to pick at the wood of the bench in front of him. "I don't think Rilke can do anything to her there, other than talk to her anyway."

"That's bad enough," said Cal. "Bitch is nuts."

At this, Brick almost smiled. He gave up on whatever he was scratching at.

"What now? Rilke said she's going there, to the storm. You think she was telling the truth?"

Cal took a tentative step toward the door. Now that he was up and moving the pain seemed to have dulled, as if it had grown bored with him. He took another step, gently shaking his arms. His backside felt like it had turned to the same rock as the church. His mum had always told him that sitting for too long on the ground would give him hemorrhoids. That's just what he needed on top of everything else, a bad case of the piles.

His mum. How had he gone for so long without thinking about her? She was right there in London, right in the heart of it. *Swallowed whole by now, devoured by the beast.* He shook the thought away, better not to think at all than think of that.

"To be honest, Brick, I don't care if she was telling the truth or not. You know what, if she goes over there, to whatever that thing is, then maybe we'll get lucky. Maybe it will just swallow her up, her and her brother. Do us all a favor."

Or maybe she's right, he thought. *Maybe the man in the storm is one of us, maybe she'll ask for its help and bring it here, right to where we're hiding.* And he saw the clouds grow dark, the roof of the church peel away into the churning, raging mess of the sky, the man there sucking the world into its mouth, obliterating everything. He shuddered so hard he almost fell, the church too dark, too cold, too quiet. He walked unsteadily to the door where a finger of sunlight beckoned him.

"Be right back," he said. Stepping into the day was like stepping into a warm bath, the light a liquid gold that washed over him. The sun was right over his head, which meant they'd been asleep for a little while; an hour maybe. There was still a whisper of smoke in the air, but there was nothing else to be heard in the little town, no sirens or shouts or screams.

It took him a while to find the rectory, as he set off down the wrong side of the church. The cemetery was large, and surrounded by a hedge of yew trees and something prickly, so dense that there might as well not have been a world beyond it. The little cottage was set among flower beds and more trees, almost sickeningly quaint. He pushed his way through the door, stopping when he heard voices up ahead.

". . . department claims up to a million people may already be dead, while many times more are missing."

The television, he recognized the formal tones of a news anchor. He crept forward nonetheless, ready to spring back the way he'd come if he needed to. Didn't the priest say he had a wife? The thought of her shrieking down the corridor ready to claw his eyes out made him feel like bolting. He didn't think his body could survive another attack, old lady or not. He pushed past his fears, through the door, into a kitchen. The television was in the corner, a man and a woman sitting at the news desk while the storm raged behind them. Cal looked away. He didn't want to see it. He listened, though, as he rummaged through a cupboard.

"We'll bring you more on that in a moment," said the man. "Meanwhile a statement from Downing Street confirms that the Prime Minister and the Cabinet have been evacuated from the city, amid criticism that they are not doing enough to help the people of London. With the death toll already in seven figures, and no indication yet that the threat has even been identified, the government faces increasing pressure from the international community to provide safeguards for the population."

He opened up a second door, seeing nothing but pots and pans. The third contained linen and, right at the back, a green case with a white cross on the front. He unzipped it, pulling out a bottle of aspirin, still listening to what was being said.

"Our London correspondent Lucy White is still on the scene. Lucy, can you tell us what the word is on the street?"

The woman's voice was almost blotted out by the grinding noise of the storm, the sound of a million trumpets blaring.

"As you can see, Wes, the word here is chaos, and understandably so. I'm standing south of the river, a stone's throw from the London Eye. Just yesterday there were thousands of people here, locals and tourists enjoying the city. Now the streets are jammed with crowds attempting to flee the attack taking place just fifteen miles from here. Over the river there you can probably see army vehicles. They are setting up a quarantine zone on the northern embankment. The bridges have been closed. Nobody is allowed back there, not even the press. Whatever happens next, we'll have to watch it from here."

"Can you describe the attack, Lucy?"

"Yes, it's a cloud, almost like a mushroom cloud from an atomic blast. Only . . ." She gulped for words. "It's moving, like a tornado. It's huge, estimated at five miles in diameter, and it's growing. Everything that gets close, and we have reliable information that this includes some air force aircraft, is what you might say vacuumed up, buildings and cars and even whole streets."

Cal popped open the bottle and swallowed a couple of aspirin. After a second, he took two more, using his hands to splash tap water into his mouth and over his face.

"There have been some reports of a figure inside the cloud," the woman continued, and at this Cal turned back to the television. "A man. We believe it is some kind of optical illusion, but . . . but we just don't know."

On-screen, the reporter was pushed out of the way by an angry foreign guy who shouted something at the camera before running off. There were so many people there, hundreds of them in this one shot alone, most fleeing in the same direction. Over her head it might as well have been a winter's night, the sky as black as pitch. The screen was too small to really make out what hung there, but it swirled and thrashed, a squirming coil of vipers. She was right, it was *huge*.

"The defense secretary has announced that he is bringing in a panel of experts to attempt to identify the threat," the woman went on. "But until that report is made public we have literally nothing to go on."

A soldier jogged into shot, shoving the woman and gesturing to the camera. She struggled to speak as she was roughhoused off the screen.

"We're being told the quarantine line is being moved south. Back to you, Wes."

Static, then the studio again. The man shuffled his papers, his mouth open like a goldfish. He coughed and Cal turned away. It was always a bad sign when the newsreaders lost their tongues; that's how you knew you were really in trouble. Cal rubbed his temples, seeing the phone next to the television, and his thoughts turned back to his mum. She'd be worried sick about him, she would have left countless messages on his phone, but he'd had no signal out in Fursville, and his mobile had been lost somewhere in between the raid at the factory and Schiller's destruction of Hemmingway. He picked up the cordless handset and racked his head, trying to remember her mobile number, typing it in. It started ringing. *Please be okay,* he thought. And she would be, right? They lived in Oakminster, it was way east of the city, miles away from the storm. *Unless she'd gone into London,* he wondered. *Maybe she was there looking for you.*

"Hello?"

The single, simple word took him utterly by surprise, a crack in the dam. Before he even knew it he was sobbing, the cries flooding up with so much strength that he couldn't get a word out. He collapsed against the counter, the tears streaming down his face, salty on his tongue, his whole body juddering with the force of it.

"Callum? Cal is that you? Jesus, where are you? Are you okay?"

He spluttered out a handful of not-quite-words, taking a deep breath and trying again.

"I'm okay, Mum," he moaned, the sobs ebbing into soft hiccups. He wiped the tears away, his eyes feeling like they were stuffed with cotton wool, his throat aching. "I'm okay."

"Oh God." She was crying too. "I was so worried, Cal, I thought . . . I thought something terrible had happened. Where are you?"

"I'm safe," he said. "I'm out of the city. You need to get out too, Mum, something really bad is going on."

Scuffling, like she was unlocking a door or something. He could hear voices.

"I'm okay," she said, sniffing. There was a steeliness to her voice now. Cal knew it well, once the tears were gone there was always anger. "Do you know how worried I've been? You just took off with the car. I'm assuming it was you who took the car?"

"Yeah, sorry, I—"

"Cal, I've had the police out looking for you, the neighbors, nobody could think why you'd up and run away. Was it because of what happened at school, the stampede? Your friends are scared, Cal, and furious too, they think you've abandoned them. Poor Georgia is still in the hospital. Why, Cal? You better have a good explanation."

I've got something inside me, a creature that's waiting to hatch and turn me into a weapon so that we can fight the man in the storm, but it's so powerful and so alien that people can't stand to be near it, so they try to kill me. The thought was so ludicrous in his head that he snorted a bitter laugh.

"This isn't funny, Cal. Your dad is flying back tomorrow, he's gonna be so angry."

"Sorry, I wasn't laughing. Look, Mum, I can't tell you everything, not yet. I just wanted you to know that I'm safe, that I'm okay. I'll come home soon if I can, I promise, there's just something I've got to do first."

Was that true? Would he ever be able to go home? What happened if they did fight the man in the storm, if they somehow managed to defeat him? Would the angels just go? Or were they there for good?

"Don't go home," said his mum. "I'm not there. I'm at your Auntie Kate's. Haven't you seen the news?"

"Yeah." He offered a silent thanks that she was safe, or out of the city at least. Kate lived over in Southend, right by the ocean.

If they needed to, they could always get on a boat and head into Europe. "Yeah, it's really bad, Mum."

"They're saying millions are going to die, or are already dead. God, Cal, can you get here? Where are you? I promise I won't be angry with you if you just drive to Kate's right now."

"I . . . I can't, Mum, not just yet. But I will, yeah?" The sobs were pounding at his chest again and he locked them in. "Look, I gotta go, but I love you."

"Cal, please, just tell me where you are, I'll come get you."

"I love you, Mum."

It took her a moment to hear him, not his words but the truth inside them, the understanding that it might be the last time they spoke. She began to weep again.

"I love you, Cal," she said, her voice just a whisper. "I love you so much. Tell me it's going to be okay?"

"It's going to be okay," he said. "I promise, it's going to be okay." He felt like he had a rock in his throat, he almost couldn't force the air past it. "I gotta go, Mum."

"Cal, don't."

But he did, thumbing off the call, standing there in a pool of sunshine feeling too exhausted even to cry. He let the phone tumble from his fingers and it clattered off the counter onto the stone floor, the battery flap spinning loose.

It's going to be okay, it's going to be okay, maybe if he kept saying it, it would be true. And he'd almost managed to convince himself of this when he heard a change in sound on the television, a chorus of screams carried over the airwaves. He looked back, saw the storm, somehow still vast even on the tiny screen, heard the reporter cry out: "It's true, we've just had confirmation, it's *moving.*"

THE OTHER (6)

The weight of this sad time we must obey,
Speak what we feel, not what we ought to say.
The oldest have borne most; we that are young
Shall never see so much, nor live so long.
　　　—William Shakespeare, King Lear

"IT'S MOVING."

Graham looked up from his screen, blinking the spots of light from his vision. The video footage from the field op in Norfolk had come in a few minutes ago, and he'd already watched it four times. The soldiers had been wearing helmet cams—standard procedure now for any offensive action—but what they had recorded just didn't make any sense. The kids had come out of the windmill and the boy, the same one as before, had somehow *changed*. They didn't have any decent footage, the light that he had been pumping out was simply too bright for the cameras, saturating them, bleeding white. But somewhere in the blur he swore he could make out a creature of flame, with two huge, burning wings.

Then, in an instant, they vanished. He had flicked back and forth from one frame to the next, just a thirtieth of a second between them. In one, four normal kids and the boy in the inferno; in the next an empty circle of fire, like when you took a photograph of a moving sparkler. And after that there was just a hail of ash and burning embers. What he was looking at was unbelievable, utterly impossible. It had to be some kind of camera glitch, only every single piece of footage they had, half a dozen different cams, all showed the same thing.

The worst of it was they'd also lost over thirty men. Graham didn't have the full report yet, but from what he'd heard in his brief call to General Stevens there weren't even any bodies, the soldiers had simply been vaporized along with the windmill and a field of beet. *There's just dust,* the man had told him. The other soldiers were all being treated for shock. Apparently two had tried to scratch out their own eyes.

"Graham, did you hear me?" It was Sam, sitting next to him.

"Huh? Sorry, what?"

"It's moving." She jabbed her hand at the screen and he followed the rough arc of her chewed fingernail to see the satellite footage of the city. It showed everything from Watling Park in the north to Fortune Green in the south, and most of that was solid inkblot black. It was like watching a weather forecast and seeing the unmistakable spiral of a hurricane. This too had an eye in the center, a pocket of absolute night that showed up black and blank on visible, infrared, UV, and every other lens they had. It was as though beyond that event horizon was nothing, no heat, no matter, no air, just a hole where the world should be. And Sam was right, the storm seemed to be shifting south, engulfing the train lines of West Hampstead. He saw a chunk of something huge lift up into the maelstrom, a warehouse, maybe the Homebase store they had up there. It crumbled as it went, shedding pieces of itself as it vanished into the churning current.

"We're—"

And that was as far as Sam got before the entire room lurched. Graham almost screamed, grabbing his chair so hard he thought he'd broken half his fingers. Every single monitor in the room went dark, the lights strobing as the emergency systems fought to regain control. When they booted back on Graham saw that a crack had opened up in the thirty-meter-thick solid concrete ceiling of the bunker. *Not good.*

"What the hell was that?" he asked. There was still a tremor running through the room, making his teeth chatter.

Sam's monitor flashed back on, the satellite feed still in place. The storm's movement had increased, sliding south like a patch of oil slowly dripping toward the bottom of the screen. In its wake it left an ocean of pitch, an empty trench where once there had been a city. Graham's jaw dropped. He could taste the dust of the room on his tongue, in his dry throat. *It's coming this way, it's heading right for us.*

"There's nothing left," said Sam. "Oh God, it's . . . it's destroyed everything."

But "destroyed" was the wrong word. Destruction left ruin, left rubble, left corpses. This thing left nothing, no bodies, no wrecks, no ash. It devoured it all. Graham knew that if he was standing there, on the lip of that trench, he would see only darkness. The room shook again, the very earth around them seeming to groan in outrage like a helpless beast suffering some dreadful torture.

"There's nothing we can do," shouted a voice behind them. Graham looked to see Habib, heading for the elevator. He shrugged an apology. "You should go too. If you're still here when it arrives . . ."

He didn't need to say it. Graham understood that if the beast— *The beast, where did that come from? It's an attack, just an attack*—hit Thames House then being underground wouldn't save them. It would reach down with fingers of storm, pull them up to the gaping hole of its mouth, and everything he had ever been would be eradicated. He turned back to the screen, hearing the soft chime of the elevator door.

"He's right, you know," he said. "You should get out of here."

"Yeah, and leave you in charge?" said Sam. "No way. I don't trust a man to get us out of this."

She smiled gently, squeezing his shoulder, and he placed his hand on hers for a moment. If the storm continued south then they'd leave, but there was still time. A muffled explosion rippled through the ceiling above them, more dust raining down, making such a racket that Graham almost didn't hear the phone on his desk. He picked it up.

"Yeah, this is Hayling."

"Graham, it's Stevens." His years of military service made him sit up straight in his chair when he heard the general's voice.

"Sir," he said. "It's on the move."

"We know," said the general. "We're out of options."

"Sir?"

"We launched another air assault fifteen minutes ago, but the bastard swallows everything we throw at it. Whatever is at the heart of this, it's not letting us close. You any closer to working out what we're dealing with?"

"No," Graham said. "You know what we know. It's not atomic, it's not meteorological, it's not geological, and it's not biological. But now we know it's mobile."

"If it carries on in its current trajectory it will hit the City in half an hour." The general's voice, usually so strong, was like a little boy's. "It's almost like . . . like it knows where it's going. You make any sense of that?"

It's going where there are people, Graham thought.

"No, sir," he said.

"And the other incident, the one by the coast, any more leads?"

"No, sir."

"Graham, I need you to be honest with me." Stevens cleared his throat, something bad coming. "Do you think your team can identify this threat before it reaches the center of London?"

"My team?" he replied, looking at Sam, at the empty room beyond her. He chewed on it for a moment, then said, "No, sir. I don't think we can."

A pause, and a rattling sigh.

"Then lock yourself in good and tight, Graham, because we're going to nuke it."

"Sir?" That must have been a mistake, surely. Graham almost laughed at the insanity of it. "Can you please repeat that?"

"You heard me," the older man said. "We're out of options. We don't do something now then there's no telling what will happen. It's growing, it's getting stronger, and it's moving. Contain the threat, Graham, neutralize it, worry about the collateral damage later. It's our policy overseas, gotta be our policy at home."

"But you can't," he stuttered. "You can't authorize a nuclear strike on U.K. soil, on *London*."

"It's done, P.M. gave the green light five minutes ago. We're doing our best to get everyone out, but we have to do this quick. That's why I'm calling, Graham. You seal that bunker until this is over. Either that or you bolt, but I can't guarantee you'll get out of the blast zone, not now. Dragon 1 is airborne as we speak."

"How long have we got?" he asked.

"Ninety minutes max, almost definitely less. I'm sorry, Graham, batten the hatches, hunker down. With any luck we'll knock this thing clear into next week and get a hazmat team to you ASAP."

"And if not?"

The general snorted down the phone, not quite a laugh. "If not, then God help us all. Good luck."

"And you, sir," Graham said, but it was to an empty line. He gently placed the phone back in its cradle, staring at it as if waiting to hear it ring again, waiting to hear the general say *Ha! Got you, Graham, this is revenge for that time you rubbed chilies into the latrine bog roll out in Iraq.* But of course it didn't. It wouldn't ring again. He turned to Sam.

"You hear that?"

She had, he could see it in the parchment-gray sheen of her skin, her vacant stare.

"They're nuking London," she said, shaking her head. A tear wound down her cheek, tracing a path through the dust that had settled there. "Oh God, Graham. It's actually happening."

He looked at the screen, at the city there. *His* city. If the attack—*No, the beast, deep down you know it*—didn't devour it then an atomic blast would wipe it clean, leave it a ruin that nobody would be able to set foot inside for decades. There had to be another way, but his mind was an empty bowl. He swore and thumped the desk in frustration.

"You want to lock it down?" Sam asked. "There's enough supplies here to keep a hundred people for a month, we'd be okay."

Hide away, shut the door behind them, let the city burn. No, how could he live with himself if he did that? But what were the options? Make a run for it, head south to where the general was running the operation? At least he'd have a good view of the mushroom cloud as it curled up over Big Ben. He thought of David, prayed that he had gotten out of the city, that he hadn't waited for Graham to come home.

"I—" he started, then the satellite feed flashed, somewhere around Maida Vale. A tiny spot of flickering color beneath the raging storm, as if something were burning through the screen from the other side. He craned forward, his nose practically against the glass. "What is that?"

The footage was too wide to make out the source of the light, and after a second or two it vanished.

"Can we zoom in there?" he said, pointing at the location where the flame had guttered out. Sam nodded, typing in a string of code. The satellite blurred, zoomed in, sharpened, blurred, zoomed in, sharpened, three more times until the view was a handful of crescent-shaped streets and box-shaped houses. The storm was no longer visible, but it was close because its shadow stained the top half of the picture like a bruise. There was no sign of life apart from four little dots, undistinguishable, but unmistakable. "It's them," he said, ramming the screen with his finger.

"Who?" Sam asked.

"The kids, from the coast." It sounded ludicrous, impossible, but then so did everything else that had happened today. Somehow he was sure of it, he would have bet everything on it, he would have bet his life on it. In fact, that was exactly what he was willing to do. He pushed himself up. "Lock yourself in, Sam, stay safe."

"No way. You go, I go," she said, pushing up from her chair.

"Sam—"

"Sam nothing, it's my job to look after this city. Whatever you've got planned, I'm with you."

He nodded, walking into the elevator. Ninety minutes till detonation, give or take. That was enough time if he could locate a motorcycle and hotwire it. He had no idea what they'd find if they got there, but at least they'd be doing something. If those kids were somehow good, at least he could warn them. And if not, he'd have the satisfaction of seeing them burn. The elevator closed, and Sam grabbed his hand as they headed up into the storm.

MONDAY MIDDAY

Whoever battles with monsters had better see that it does not turn him into a monster. And if you gaze long into an abyss, the abyss will gaze back into you.
　　　　　　　　　　　　　　　　—Friedrich Nietzsche

IT SEEMED TO TAKE LONGER, THIS TIME, for life to catch them.

The world snapped into place around her, and with it came a noise like no other, a roar so loud, so terrifying, that it felt as if it were pushing her into the earth, grinding her down like a giant boot. She clamped her hands to her ears as the same jet of milky vomit erupted from between her lips.

She forced herself to open her eyes, already knowing what she would see there. The sky was alive, a madness of movement that boiled overhead like an upturned cauldron of oil. Vast clouds of matter circled in slow, almost graceful orbits. In them she could see scraps of things, the glint of a truck, the outline of a tree or a church spire, and countless smaller objects—*people*, she realized— that could have been leaves kicked up by the wind. The tornado was so dense that the sun was a copper penny in the sky, forgotten, the streets around her as dark as dusk.

And in the center of it all was *him*, the man in the storm. Rilke couldn't see him past the chaos of the clouds, but he was there. She could feel him, like she could feel gravity, pulling on her, calling to her with that ageless, endless inward breath. He was the ghost inside the machine, inside that engine of darkness and dust that raged over her, and his voice was the cry of a million horns.

A lunatic cackle escaped her, drowned out by the storm. She was still on her knees, she realized, Schiller lying before her. Beads of blood hung over his wounds, just floating there like they hadn't quite remembered what they should be doing. He blinked up at her, his left eye a crimson pool. Part of his skull was cracked where he had been shot, chipped loose like a flake of flint. What lay beneath was slick and dark and matted. She cupped her hand to it, as if to hold in his brain.

You did it, Schiller, she thought to him, knowing that her real voice would not carry here, that there simply was not room for it in the screaming air. *You brought us to him, I'm so proud of you.*

He smiled at her, and his eyes rolled back in their sockets. She shook his head gently until he focused again, then she looked up.

The storm thrashed in its own fury, the sweeping clouds like the tentacles of a hundred creatures writhing and coiling. Rilke looked around, past Marcus, whose face was a portrait of pure horror, past the new boy, Howie, still locked inside his casket of ice, seeing a street, houses on both sides. Everything was covered in dirt and ash, a fine rain that still fell from the ruined sky. There was nobody else in sight. How did they talk to him?

Schiller had to change. It was the only way. If he was an angel again then the man in the storm *had* to notice him. She placed her other hand on Schiller's cheek, lifting his head off the ground. *Once more, little brother,* she told him. *Let it out, and the storm will see you.*

He shook his head, just the slightest of movements that she could feel in her fingers.

He'll make you better, and you won't have to be weak ever again. Let it out.

Her brother's eyes emptied and for a moment she thought she'd lost him. But he must have caught a glimpse of death there, of something worse than pain, worse than the Fury, worse even than the storm, because his whole body suddenly lurched up like he'd been woken from a nightmare. And with the motion came the fire, erupting in the furnaces of his eyes, flooding over his body, turning him into a phantom of blue and red and yellow. His wings unfolded, so bright against the brooding clouds. He screamed a word at the storm, a word that cut across the street, that pushed its way through house after house, demolishing them.

And the man in the storm heard him.

Something detonated in the middle of the tornado, an almighty crack that could have been the earth splitting. A shock wave ripped outward, sending a cloud of debris surging up into the sky and out across the city, stripping away the clouds, revealing what lay beneath.

He hung there, too big to be human—so much bigger than the tower blocks he soared above—and yet somehow still a man. He shimmered in the unsettled atmosphere, like a heat haze, a mirage, his body made up of shifting shapes and shadow, his hands held out to his sides. His face was not really a face, just a spinning vortex that reminded her of those huge drills that carved tunnels into mountains, an endless, seething gyre that sucked in everything around it.

But it was his eyes . . . two gaping sockets in his head, so dead and yet so full of rancid glee. It was impossible to tell how far away the man was, a mile or two maybe, but Rilke knew those eyes had seen her, she felt them crawling over her face like corpse fingers, working their way into her head, into her thoughts. Her mind was suddenly a clockwork toy, a clumsy mess of tin and spring, peeled apart and broken by its touch. *It's a bad thing a bad thing a bad thing,* something in her railed, but she fought it, *He's not, he's going to save Schill, he has to save him because nothing else can, please please please.*

Schiller was standing now—or hovering, a foot above the road—that atomic pulse making the concrete vibrate. He spoke again, a rippling surge of energy that opened up a trench in the earth, channeling toward the man in the storm. And the man answered, whatever he was. That inward breath never so much as paused, but those eyes beamed their message directly into her head; not words, not even images, just the awful silence and stillness of the end of all things. The sheer weight of it, of eternal, infinite nothingness, sent her reeling. She tripped over Howie, falling onto her back, the wind knocked from her lungs. *That's all it will leave,* she thought. *A gaping hole where the world once sat.*

"No!" she screamed, the word sucked out of her mouth by the snapping wind, by the endless roar of the storm. She *would not* believe that. *Go to him, Schiller, kneel down at his feet, show him that you are here to serve.* He would surely open his arms and welcome them as his children, wouldn't he? He would skin the flesh from their souls, fillet their bones, leave them as pure fire. The two halves of her waged war, and she felt the little clockwork engine of her mind come apart even further.

Schiller rose, a fish on a hook, the brightest thing in the sky. The man watched him, vast tidal waves of matter still flooding across London, engulfing everything they touched. Whipcracks of black lightning lashed out from the ground beneath the storm. Only there was no ground there, Rilke realized, just a void. It had simply been erased. The man watched her brother the way a lizard tracks a bug, its black eyes full of greed, of hunger. But there was a spark of recognition there. It understood who Schiller was.

It knows you, she told her brother, looking up to where he blazed against the unnatural night, a star that had been knocked loose from the firmament. Her heart seemed to lift alongside him, the knowledge that she had been right, that they were here to serve the man in the storm. She grinned, the euphoria a flood of sunlight inside her arteries, making her feel like she was already nothing but heat and light.

It didn't last.

The man in the storm twitched its fingers and turned the world inside out.

The ground ripped away beneath her, the air suddenly full of rock and stone and houses. She opened her mouth to scream but it never came as she tumbled into darkness, like she was falling into a bottomless grave. Schiller still burned high above her, and she reached out for him, knowing that if she did not then she would fall forever. Her brother's eyes raged, a flicker of emotion deep inside the fire, and she felt his arms wrap around her—not his flesh but something else. He wrenched her from the pit, pulling her up to his side along with Marcus and the other boy, holding her to him with a thought while the city crumbled around them. There was no ground between her and the storm anymore, just the void, an ocean of emptiness.

The man gestured with his hands again, pulling up the earth like he was lifting a blanket. On either side of him a billion tons of matter rose into the air, hurled toward them. The air roared, Rilke's ears popping as a concussive wave of pressure reached them first. She lifted her hands to her face, knowing that they would offer her no protection, that she would be crushed into dust. But even though the world shook and shook and shook there was no impact, no pain.

She peeked between her fingers, seeing a bubble of flickering firelight around them. House-size pieces of concrete smashed against the emptiness like waves against the rocks, cars and trucks and trees and people too, bursting into liquid as they struck. The tide was endless, flooding into the darkness beneath them, pressing against them, gushing overhead, making her feel as though she were inside a cave, her brother burning like a campfire. There was nothing written on his face, no sign of Schiller's human weakness, everything blazing at full strength as he fought to keep them alive.

The torrent stopped, the sky opening up once again, still full of smoke, a waterfall of matter dropping into the darkness. Ahead of them, the man hung in his storm, and there was something else in those eyes now—not so much *in* them, she understood, as being channeled *through* them. It was hate, pure and simple. It wanted to kill them.

What have I done? she asked, panicking, seeing the gulf beneath her feet, an open mouth just waiting for her to fall. Schiller's power was the only thing keeping them up, and how much longer would it last? She grabbed her brother, the flames cold against her skin, tickling her. He beat his wings, the bubble of fire around them guttering out, spirals of dust dancing off in all directions. Marcus hung beside her, held by invisible fingers, the new kid too, the four of them locked in the fury of the man's eyes. *Oh what have I done, Schiller? I was wrong, wasn't I? I was so wrong.*

The howl of the man's endless breath increased, black streaks slicing through the air as if life were a canvas being torn. The storm once again began to funnel into his gaping maw, debris pulled from the air, sucked inside. Rilke too, her stomach doing loop-the-loops as she hurtled toward him. She held on to her brother with everything she had, even though she knew she didn't need to, feeling him being pulled through the air like a boat into a whirlpool.

"Fight it!" she yelled into his ear, barely able to hear herself. His answer fluttered into her thoughts.

I can't, I can't, Rilke, he's so strong.

The current was too powerful, dragging them toward the churning blades of his mouth. They were speeding up, the man looming before them, so big, a colossus. His eyes burned. He was going to eat them, and then what? *Then nothing, you will never have been and will never be again.*

"Schiller!" she pleaded.

Her brother spoke, the word like a missile detonating in the middle of the storm. The man didn't even seem to feel it, reeling them in faster, faster, until there was only his mouth, only that boundless, lightless throat. Schiller spoke again, but his voice was human, a kitten's mewl. His coat of flames vanished and he flailed in midair, caught in the flow. It was done, it was over, it was lost.

Rilke closed her eyes, took a deep breath that stank of flesh and smoke, and screamed, *"Daisy!"*

DAISY / *East Walsham, 12:24 p.m.*

"Daisy!"

Daisy looked up at the sound of her name. The ice cubes had grown agitated. They were all retreating, all except for one, *his* one, where the man in the storm still hung. She didn't want to look but how could she stop herself? The view it contained was different now, the city rubbed away beneath him the way she would sometimes rub away a piece of a drawing she didn't like.

Everything around him was still being vacuumed into his mouth.

"Daisy!"

Her name again, and this time she recognized the voice. It was Rilke. And sure enough, wasn't that her and her brother and Marcus and Howie right there, like insects drowning in dust as they were funneled into the storm? *Oh, Rilke, you went to him, just like you said,* she thought, the sadness like a pressure in her chest. And now the girl was going to die. Why hadn't Rilke listened to her? Why hadn't she believed her? She was so *stupid*!

That pressure shifted, growing, and Daisy's heart gave a painful thump. It wasn't sadness, it was something else. She put a hand—the one she didn't really have in this place—against her chest, feeling the coldness there, and when she looked down tongues of flame licked between her fingers.

Oh no, she said. *It's happening.*

Her angel was hatching.

"Daisy?" Another voice this time, from somewhere close by. She peered between the huge, grinding ice cubes to see the new boy there, Howie—not his physical body, that was with Rilke, in the storm, this was just the other part of him. *His soul,* she guessed. He was the same age as she was, maybe a little older. A pocket of fire sat in his chest too, spreading up toward his shoulders and down to his tummy like he was made of straw. He looked terrified, his eyes wide and white, staring at himself like a boy who had seen spiders burst from his skin.

"Don't worry," she said to him, trying to hide her own fear. She held out her hands and in an instant he was next to her, hugging her, his not-real-head buried into her not-real-shoulder. Already the icy touch of the flames had reached her neck, now her chin. She held Howie and he held her, both of them going up in flames together. Something was chiming inside her head, a tune almost like the one her little music box had played when she was a kid. There were no words there, and yet she knew that this was a voice, that it was *its* voice.

"Can you hear that?" she asked, feeling Howie nod against her. "It's not scary, is it?"

The tune in her head grew louder as her angel found its voice, and even though she could not understand it she still knew what it was showing her—the billion years of its life laid out in a single second. There was no time to process it before she felt herself pulled up, the same way she sometimes rose from dreams, like a diver being winched from the ocean on a rope. She screwed her eyes shut against the sudden rush of vertigo.

Howie vanished, heading back to his body in the real world. He would be an angel now, she knew.

She breached the surface of the dream ocean, the real world knitting itself around her—a church, stained-glass windows, wooden pews—but nothing looking like it had before. She felt as though she could peer into the very heart of things, see the building blocks there, the little atoms and their orbits. If she wanted, she could pull them apart with just a thought. Her fire was the brightest thing here, blazing forth from her, kicking out a bass hum that seemed to make everything tremble.

It wasn't so bad, was it? It was—

And then it hit her, a sudden panic, the awful knowledge of what she was. She looked at herself, at the inferno of her skin, the way her hands seemed translucent, tiny blots of energy surging up and down her fingers. Something was pushing at her back too, as if her ribs were trying to claw their way free—not pain, just a maddening itch. And when she realized what it was—*My wings oh God oh God*—she shrieked, the noise that of a monstrous baby bird pushing from its shell.

She turned, trying to see them, but the motion carried too much force, launching her across the room. She flew into a wall, her wings twitching, out of her control, sending her spinning back across the church. Somewhere in the wheeling chaos she saw Brick and Cal and little Adam, all of them diving for cover. There was another man too, a priest by the look of things, screaming at her, lost to the Fury. She held out her hands to the man, trying to tell him not to be scared, but to her horror he detonated into a cloud of ash, hanging ghostlike in the air until he remembered to drift apart.

Her wings twitched once more, hurling her up into the rafters. *Stop it please stop it.* But the angel would not hear her, making her thrash against the ceiling, her huge, beating wings loosing an avalanche of ancient wood and stone. She pushed herself away, dropping back to the floor but not hitting it, just hovering above it like there was an invisible cushion there.

"Daisy!" Her name again, but this time it was Cal. She saw him run down the aisle toward her, stumbling on the wreckage of a pew. She held out her hands to him but the movement sent her tumbling back, cartwheeling down the church. She shrieked again, the sound exploding a stained-glass window, flooding darkness with sunlight.

Stay still, stay still, she ordered her body. She froze, listening to the dizzying thrum of the angel—*That's what its heart sounds like*—hearing the patter of footsteps. Cal skidded down beside her, squinting against her brightness. It looked just like him, but when she focused hard enough she could see the bits and pieces he was made of: the slick, butcher-shop organs, the pores in his skin, and deeper than that the cells that swam in his blood and the firework show of sparks inside his brain. She didn't like it, she didn't like seeing that people were just engines of flesh. But she didn't turn away in case she hurt him.

"Daisy, can you hear me?" he asked. He lifted a hand—a constellation of atoms—as if to place it on her, then seemed to change his mind.

She didn't dare reply. Her voice was something else now, a weapon.

"Is she alive?" It was Brick this time, standing at the back of the church with his hands in his copper hair. His face was a mask of concern and she did her best to smile. It didn't do much to calm him, which wasn't really a surprise. If she looked anything like Schiller had then her eyes were made of molten steel.

"I think so," said Cal. "Daisy, can you hear me?"

Yes, she said, speaking to them inside her head, somehow beaming the words out. This voice couldn't hurt them. *I'm here, Cal, don't be frightened.*

Cal grinned, looking over his shoulder. "You hear her?" he asked, and Brick nodded. The bigger boy took a few steps down the aisle and Daisy noticed that he was holding Adam's hand.

Hello, Adam, it's only me, Daisy. I know I look different but I'm still your friend, okay?

The boy nodded, a shiver of a smile darting over his lips. Daisy took a deep breath—though she didn't think she needed air the way she was right now—and pushed herself off the ground. Slow, considered movements, that was the trick. Nothing too dramatic. She clambered onto her knees then gave her wings an experimental flex. It felt so strange being up here, taller even than

Brick now. She felt like an adult, which was kind of exciting, and kind of sad too. She didn't want to be grown up just yet.

She remembered the priest—*Doug*, she thought. That had been the man's name—clamping a hand to her mouth as she turned to the far side of the church. All that remained of the man was a little puddle of burning ash. A halo of glowing embers floated in a circle around it, as if they didn't want to stop living yet, as if they could keep death away with a dance.

Oh no, what did I do? she said. *I killed him.*

Yet the stew of emotion she was expecting, that unbearable flood of sadness, didn't come.

You're protecting me from it, she said to her angel, *like a shield.* And with that knowledge came the understanding that it could not last forever, that as soon as she went back to being normal that awful sadness would suddenly be there again.

"You didn't mean to," Cal said, using a pew to pull himself to his feet. "It wasn't your fault, Daisy."

I know, she replied. She would mourn him later, but now there was something else she needed to do. *Cal, we have to save them, Rilke and Schiller, they need us.* She saw the image in her head, the man in the storm sucking them into his churning mouth, and she knew that Cal and Brick and Adam saw it too. *They're going to die.*

At the back of the church, Brick spat out a laugh. "Why should we help her? She's done this to herself."

"Kind of got a point there," said Cal, shrugging. "She did ask for it."

It's not about her, said Daisy. *We need her, we need all of them, if we're going to fight it. I don't think we can do it by ourselves.* They didn't have any time, it might already be too late. *Please, Cal, we have to go.*

The thought of it, of cutting a hole in space and climbing through, finding herself in the shadow of the man in the storm, should have been terrifying. But this too was numbed by the angel. It felt more like an echo of fear, something she couldn't quite remember. *It's keeping me strong,* she thought to herself. *Keeping me brave.*

Cal looked back at Brick, the two boys sharing a thought that Daisy couldn't quite read. Then Cal turned to her and nodded his head. His fear pumped out of him in big, black waves but his expression was firm. He swallowed noisily, then took her hand. She held him gently, careful not to hurt him. Adam pulled himself free from Brick and raced down the aisle, hugging her around the waist.

Brick? she asked. The older boy stood there, shuffling his feet, chewing his lip. She saw the lightning show inside his skull, saw the thoughts there racing back and forth, fighting with each other, and the moment where his decision was made. She didn't even wait for him to nod. She just used her mind to open up a hole in the air, reality burning away around her like the skin of the world had caught fire. Behind it was the city and the storm, and with a beat of her wings she pulled them all toward it.

BRICK / *London, 12:32 p.m.*

DAISY DIDN'T EVEN GIVE HIM A CHANCE TO REPLY. One second he was standing in the church, wondering how the hell he was going to get out of this one. The next he felt like a spinning top set in motion.

He somersaulted upward, everything a blur, his stomach scrunching to the size of an acorn. Then his senses snapped back on and he was somewhere else, lying on his back. He opened his mouth to cry out, but all that emerged was a jet of white vomit. The air was full of embers, landing on his tongue and leaving their bitter taste. He spat them out, wiping puke from his lips, then struggled into a sitting position.

Daisy was a few meters in front of him. Only it wasn't Daisy, not anymore. The creature she was now, the one that had stolen her body, hovered above the ground, still engulfed in flame. Her wings were like the sails of a burning ship, twice as tall as she was. And the noise she was pumping out was an electrical charge, pulsing through the air, through the ground, making his fingers tingle and his hair stand on end. It made no sense, that the little girl he had been carrying just a few hours ago, that bundle of sticks and bones, could now be this. He had to look away.

But what he saw there was infinitely worse.

The sky above the horizon was like an upturned ocean, a roiling sea of darkness whose waves carried the city—*Is this London? It can't be, it can't be, there's nothing left*—into their depths. And in the middle of the ocean was a shape, illuminated by bolts of black lightning that lashed through the chaos. He hung there like a leviathan, a vast, bloated sea beast who churned up the water. The sight was so awful that a groan rose up from Brick's stomach, feeble and wretched, spilling from his mouth. And before he could stop himself he was sobbing, scrabbling back, screaming, "Why did you bring me here? *Why?*"

Because we need you, Brick. Daisy's voice was so loud in his head, so clear, that she could have been standing there in the flesh of his brain. He even thumped a hand to his temple as if to shake her out. But no, she still hovered there above the pavement, framed by the rubble of a dozen houses, her eyes boiling, spitting flecks of fire, her mouth hanging open to reveal a throat of pure white light, as if she had swallowed the sun. *I need you Brick, I can't do this by myself.*

"But what the hell can I do?" he cried back. Beneath the storm the ground had been erased, a pit that must have been ten miles wide. How could he stand up to a creature that could do that? It would turn him inside out with just a look.

Believe in me, Daisy said. *That's all I need.*

A deafening clap of thunder detonated from the center of the storm and Brick looked to see lightning there—not dark this time but bright. A shock wave of scalding air blasted across the city, almost hard enough to knock him backward, and in the heart of the tornado he thought he saw a huge, gaping maw. There was a burning shape right next to it, so small that it could have been plankton about to be devoured by a whale. He knew who it was, and he spoke the boy's name aloud: "Schiller."

I have to go to him, Daisy said inside his head, her voice half hers and half her angel's. *They'll die if I don't.*

She looked at Cal, then at Brick. *Be strong. Look after Adam.*

"Daisy, wait!" Cal yelled, but it was too late. She flexed her wings, their tips seeming to set fire to the air like it was paper. There was a flash of light, a gaping hole in the sky, then she was gone. Reality flooded back into the space like water, a pistol crack echoing around the ruined street as the vacuum was filled. Adam staggered forward, almost falling before Brick caught him, both of them standing there in a snowstorm of ash.

Another crack, and Brick looked into the storm to see a flash of light there, right in the heart of its darkness. Daisy, burning bright. *She's just a little girl,* he thought, suddenly furious. He smashed himself on the chest with his fist, calling to the creature that slept there. *Are you happy now? She's just a little girl and you've killed her.*

He took a step toward the storm then stopped. He needed to help her but what could he do? Never in his life had he felt so small, so pathetic. He caught Cal's eye, saw the frustration there, the powerlessness, mirroring his own.

"We have to do something," Brick said. "She'll die."

Cal cocked his head to the side.

"What?" asked Brick.

"Don't you hear that?"

It was a few more seconds until he did, a soft whine rising up over the ceaseless thunder of the storm. An engine, coming this way.

"Daisy can handle herself," said Cal, pointing as a motorbike skidded around a pile of debris at the end of the demolished street, accelerating their way. "We've got our own problems."

DAISY / *London, 12:38 p.m.*

IT WAS LIKE THROWING HERSELF into a fast-flowing river, the current sweeping her up, pulling her along against her will, so fast and so strong that she didn't even know which way was up. She spun in midair, seeing storm and sky, storm and sky, then him, his mouth so big it could have been a volcano she was hurtling toward. She could see his eyes too, like two inverse suns in the sky, radiating darkness, *huge*, and staring right at her.

She snapped out her limbs, all six of them—arms, legs, and wings. It was like opening a parachute, slowing her sideways fall. The wind was a living thing that buffeted her, huge chunks of stuff flying past, sucked into the vortex. She felt like Dorothy in the tornado, seeing whole houses there and people too, everything being devoured.

A flash of light up ahead, in the middle of the man's mouth. *Schiller,* she called. *I'm coming.*

Daisy! The voice was his, broadcast right into her head. *Help us!*

Ahead she could make out not one angel but two. *Howie, of course, he hatched too.* He and Schiller were hovering inside a bubble of orange fire, the pair of them so bright that at first Daisy didn't even notice Rilke and Marcus beside them, held up by invisible string. There was no sign of Jade.

Hang on, she thought to them. In an instant she was there, right on the edge of the vortex. She snapped out her wings again, locking herself in place. Schiller and Howie were doing the same. It was taking everything they had to stop themselves disappearing down the drain of his mouth.

Daisy cracked her wings, lifting herself up to where the man's eyes blazed. She wasn't even sure if they were eyes, because other than them and his mouth the man didn't really have a face, just a whirling gyre of smoke and storm. And yet they seemed to study her, his hate like a living thing that thrashed and writhed there. She opened her mouth, felt fire burning up from her stomach, scorching her throat, blasting from her mouth.

What she had wanted to say was "Leave us alone," but what came out was a word that she didn't know, a word that wasn't human. It was like she had spat out a rocket, a pulse of energy escaping her lips with such force that it flipped her backward. She righted herself in time to see the shock wave strike the man in his left eye, a wave of fire that ate into the rippling black flesh like water through snow.

She hadn't wanted to hurt him, she just wanted him to go away. She opened her mouth to tell him that but another word cannoned out, this one carving its way into his other eye, ripping loose chunks of flickering dark matter that swept down toward his mouth.

The monster's head rocked backward, and that gasping, inward breath guttered out. It was like gravity had suddenly been switched on again, everything falling toward the void below. Daisy punched out her wings, seeing Schiller and Howie do the same. She flew to them through a monsoon of dust and debris.

Schiller, she yelled. The two angels were so alike that she almost couldn't tell them apart, but somehow she still knew which one he was. He looked at her with the twin suns of his eyes, and even past the fire she could see that he was injured. Rilke clung on to him like a baby monkey. Marcus hung beside them, buoyed up by some invisible force. They both looked so weak, so vulnerable. *Go, get them out of here.*

I don't want to leave you, Schiller replied in her head.

Daisy reached out to him, her hand made of fire, looking seethrough, a ghost's hand. She brushed it over his ghost-face, their flames overlapping, joining. When she pulled away she drew dewdrops of golden light from his skin.

Go.

He nodded, closed his eyes, and burned himself and the others out of existence. Air rushed in to fill the space they had just occupied, making the glowing embers bob and play. Daisy looked through them to see Howie there, his face both a boy's and an angel's, all in one. She felt like she had known him for so long that it was hard to believe this was the first time they had actually met.

The man in the storm was recovering, the engine of his mouth starting up again, sucking Daisy in. The noise was so loud that it felt like a fist pummeling her brain. She screamed, her voice almost as loud, a physical thing that cut upward into the churning sky, blasting away clouds so that—for just a second—the sun shone through.

She flapped her wings, imagining she was a bird, darting away. Another huge piece of building spun toward her but she passed right through it, ripping it to pieces. Howie was beside her, his wings pumping.

We have to fight it, Daisy said. *Just speak, the angels know what to do.*

They turned together, facing the man. Daisy opened her mouth, the word halfway up her throat before a bolt of black lightning snapped out from the storm and lashed across her chest. She felt as if everything inside her had been pulled loose, the blow sending her hurtling through the air. She extended her wings but it only seemed to make her spin faster. Another whipcrack, then a shout that could only have been Howie fighting back.

Daisy pushed her wings out with every ounce of strength she had, controlling her fall. She looked back at the storm—it seemed miles away now—patting the flames of her body to make sure everything was okay. Her human heart thumped, her angel heart thrummed, but that awful feeling sat in her stomach. It was the same feeling she'd had when she had found her mum and dad, dead in the bed, only so much worse. It was the storm, that's how it wanted the whole world to feel.

The thought made her furious, dwarfing the tickle of fear. She flicked her wings, propelling herself into the heaving mass of the tornado. Howie was there, a blur of fire against the darkness, his shouts crashing against the skin of the beast. More jagged thorns of black lightning tore up toward him, unleashing a fountain of sparks when they snapped against his burning armor.

Daisy opened her mouth and let the angel speak, the word boiling through the air, smashing into the beast. It fired another shard of broken black light her way and she dodged it with a twist of her wing, speaking again, then again, Howie joining her, forcing the storm back. Its sucking breath snapped off again, the turbine of its gullet stalling. She didn't let up, screaming another word out, seeing it eat into the skin of his face.

The man's mouth opened even wider, seeming to take up the whole sky. This time he didn't breathe in, but *out*, a monstrous fog horn that punched her backward. She blacked out for a moment, like her brain was a computer that was restarting, and when she came to she realized she was falling. She screamed, and the voice was hers. When she tried to move her wings they did not obey. She looked down at herself, the flames gone, just her own body there, her school uniform, one shoe missing. She tumbled toward the abyss below, calling out to her angel, *Where are you? Come back!*

The beast was still pumping out its call, a word that seemed endless. The air was full of movement, a million pieces of debris churning toward her like a wave. Something struck her, the pain unbelievable, filling her whole body as the pit rose up to greet her.

CAL WATCHED THE MOTORBIKE GLIDE TO A STOP in the middle of the street, beside the ruin of a house. There were two people on it, a man and a woman, neither of them wearing helmets.

"We should go," said Brick. He had let go of Adam and was stumbling over a mound of broken stone. The little kid didn't even seem to notice, wide-eyed as he watched the skies. Above them the storm still raged, and Cal could see where Daisy hung, a burning moon orbiting the core of darkness. *Be safe*, he told her, turning back.

The man clambered off the bike and held up his hands as if to show that he wasn't armed. The woman followed, taking a couple of steps toward them. They turned and spoke to each other, the man shrugging.

"Who the hell are these guys?" Cal asked. Brick didn't answer, still retreating, leaving Adam in between him and the newcomers. *Unbelievable,* Cal thought, stretching out his hand to the boy. "Adam, mate, come here."

The man shouted something, but the roar of the storm was just too loud.

". . . don't want to . . . you . . . questions," the man tried again, his shout reduced to a whisper.

"What?" Cal called back. Something detonated inside the storm, a pop of thunder. The woman moved forward and Cal waved her back. "No, stay there, don't come any closer."

She couldn't hear him, taking another step their way. Brick

was half running, half tripping over the cracked asphalt. Cal moved toward Adam, ready to pick him up and carry him away.

"Wait!" the bike man was yelling, ". . . back . . ."

The woman took another step, and just like that she turned, charging forward. Cal swore, breaking into a sprint. The woman lunged at Adam, her lips pulled back over her teeth. She was fast, half pouncing, half falling on the boy, grabbing fistfuls of his hair.

"Get off him!" Cal slammed into her like he was playing rugby, the impact sending them both sprawling across the ground. They rolled, her mouth a cobra's, snapping at his arms, his throat, her teeth clacking. He managed to pin her down, aimed a punch only to be bucked off by her writhing body. He grabbed flesh, locking himself in place, trying again. His fist connected with her nose in an eruption of blood, but she didn't even seem to feel it, scraping at him with broken fingernails.

Brick! Cal tried to shout, but there wasn't enough air in his lungs. He glanced over to see the bigger boy hanging back behind a car, just watching. *You selfish bastard,* he thought. A look in the other direction told him that at least the man wasn't moving any closer. The woman—the *thing*—beneath him grabbed his face in an iron fist, her thumb in his eye socket. Cal spat out a guttural cry, batting her away, lashing out again, hearing something crack beneath his fist. He wedged his elbow into her throat, putting all his weight on it, trying to deflect her flailing arms with his free hand. She groaned, choking, the most horrific sound Cal had heard in his life, but the murder never left her bulging eyes.

"I'm sorry!" he screamed. "I'm sorry."

A gunshot ripped across the street. Cal looked back, blinded by fire, realizing that it hadn't been a gunshot at all. Schiller stood there, a statue of flame, his wings the tallest thing in the demolished street. Rilke and Marcus were on their knees beside him.

Schiller looked over with his molten eyes and the woman beneath Cal popped. He fell into the mess of her, suddenly drowning inside a cloud of multicolored ash. He coughed, rolling away, lying on his back for as long as it took him to remember the man. When he glanced over again, though, he saw that the man had fallen onto his backside, his mouth hanging open.

Rilke pointed to him.

"Kill him too," she said, her voice perfectly clear. The storm had grown quiet, and Cal looked up to see that it was no longer sucking in air. The twin flames of Daisy and the other boy hung beside its mouth, emitting barking shouts that seemed to detonate against the darkness like anti-aircraft fire. *They're winning,* he thought, the relief like sunlight inside him.

Then the beast opened his jaws and a fist of noise erupted from his mouth. He vomited a cloud of dust, a whole city reduced to rubble and blasted outward, engulfing the light, making the day grow even darker. Schiller spread his wings, took a deep breath, then vanished with such speed that his sister fell through him. She scuttled on her hands and knees like a crab until she found her balance.

"Schiller, no!" she screamed at the storm, holding her hands out to it.

The man in the storm breathed out his cloud of poison, the ground shaking so much that Cal had to crouch down to stop from falling. A spark ignited in the maelstrom—it was Schiller, fighting against the tide.

Cal scrambled up, running across the street, stopping twenty-five, thirty meters away from the motorbike man.

"Who are you?" he yelled. He had to repeat himself twice

before the man could hear him over the sound of the storm. He stepped forward but Cal held up his hand. "Come any closer and you'll die," he said. "Just tell me what you want."

"My name is Graham Hayling," he yelled back. "And I want to help."

DAISY / *London, 12:46 p.m.*

SHE WAS LIKE A STONE THROWN INTO THE OCEAN, plummeting into the cold, lightless depths. On either side of her she could see distant walls of sheer rock where the city had been torn in half, waterfalls of debris tumbling from the top of them. Beneath her was nothing but the pit.

"Please!" she called out to her angel, but it did not answer.

She fell, somersaulting head over feet, the world above growing darker and quieter with every thrashing beat of her pulse. Any second now she'd hit the bottom and that would be it. It was the worst thought in the world until another one occurred to her—that the pit might simply go on forever, that she might never stop falling.

Fire erupted, and for a second she thought her angel had returned. Then she felt arms around her and saw Schiller there, falling alongside her. He extended his wings, the flames impossibly bright against the shadows, then came the familiar stomach-churning rush as he carried them out of the pit. They reappeared in the middle of the storm, in the center of the beast's raging howl, and Daisy had flexed her wings before she realized her angel was back.

Thank you, she said to them both, breaking free of Schiller in order to avoid a hail of concrete and metal that ripped past. Something else was hurtling toward her—a building, still intact. She opened her mouth and let her angel speak, the word hitting the building like a missile, demolishing it in midair. She soared through the dust, through the million pieces of debris that still streamed from the beast's mouth, heading for a distant flame that had to be Howie. He was still shouting, still fighting.

Schiller appeared next to her, weaving in and out of the storm, his eyes like beams searing into the gloom. The beast was up ahead, his mouth the biggest thing Daisy had ever seen, a mountain-size hole in the sky. She screamed a shock wave of sound that vaporized a path through the chaos, striking him between the eyes. Beside her, Schiller called out, his voice a canon shot. Daisy ducked and wove until she hung beside Howie, the three of them punching out word after word, until the man's face was a nest of burning black worms.

The beast shook its giant head, so big that it looked like it was moving in slow motion. A noise like machine gun fire rose up from inside him, followed by a bolt of black lightning, so dark that it burned its shape into Daisy's eyes. It grazed her, knocking her back, but it was Schiller who took the brunt of it. The lightning hit his face with a whipcrack, another one snaking up and punching through his torso like a harpoon, gone as quickly as it appeared. The boy's fire flickered off and he began to fall.

"No!" Daisy cried, the word twinned with one of the angel's, burning from her lips, hitting the beast like a huge invisible hammer. Howie screamed as well, his cry detonating in the middle of the storm. Daisy tucked in her wings, diving after Schiller. She reached out to him with her mind, wrapping phantom hands around him, using the same thought to shield him from the flying rubble. She reeled him in, holding him next to her as another fork of lightless lightning lashed across the sky, close enough that she could feel its icy touch on her skin. He wasn't moving. She couldn't even be sure he was breathing, and when she peered into his skull she could see none of the little flickering thoughts there.

Her anger was accelerating up her throat, exploding as another shout. The noise it made as it left her lips was like a crack of thunder, and when it struck the man it stripped the storm away to reveal the pasty white skin of his bloated face. The flesh seemed to melt, dripping down into his eyes like candlewax. She didn't hesitate, screaming again and again and again, her words and the angel's combined, "Die! Die! Die!"

It uttered a deafening groan, the sound of a huge ship sinking. The storm from its mouth had all but stopped, and the rage in its eyes had been replaced with something else, something that might have been fear. It looked at her, at Schiller, at Howie, like it was studying them, remembering their faces. Then the sky went black, as if it had pulled night over itself.

Daisy couldn't quite work out what had happened until she looked up and saw them. Wings, two of them, crafted from flame so dark that it looked as if somebody had cut their shape out of the world with a giant pair of scissors. They radiated their black light across what remained of the city, and she thought that if fire could rot then this was what it would look like. It was horrible, and yet hanging there before it, her own wings spread and her own eyes blazing, there was no way to ignore the similarity.

The beast swept its vast wings down. The storm ripped outward, the creature's fire spreading, burning up its body and over its face. Daisy understood what it was doing and shouted out another word, but it was too late. With a thunderous crack and another flash of blinding darkness the beast vanished. Air rushed into the space it had occupied, buffeting her, everything that had been held up by the storm now dropping into the pit. Something huge missed her by millimeters and she grabbed Schiller, pulling him close.

Let's go, she said to Howie. He nodded at her, his eyes burning, and together they blinked out of existence.

RILKE / *London, 12:57 p.m.*

THERE WAS NO LONDON ANYMORE, just a hole, as if somebody had simply ripped the city out of a giant map. Buildings still clung to the edge of the pit—Rilke thought she could see the London Eye teetering over the brink in the distance, and the Shard too, although it was missing its top—but everything else was gone. All that was left was absence and ruin, an abyss ringed by a wasteland. She felt as if her mind was the same, a gaping chasm where her sanity should have been. At least the storm had disappeared. Whatever Schiller had done it had worked. Other than the ceaseless rain of dust and rubble that streamed into the pit, the sky was empty.

There was a flash of light to her side, making her flinch, but when she turned it was Daisy materializing. She held a limp figure in her arms, a heap of empty sack that couldn't be her brother. It couldn't be.

Rilke scrabbled across the ground, skidding onto her knees next to Schiller. There was a gaping wound in his stomach, the wetness there as dark as ink but flecked with streaks of blood. She hugged him to her, smoothing down his hair. There were only a few wisps left, his scalp bald and wrinkled. In fact his whole face looked like an old man's, his eyes two puffy bags and his mouth loose.

Beside her, Daisy took a breath and her fire whispered off, her wings fading and folding until she was just a little girl again. She teetered and Cal ran to her, catching her as she fell. Her nose was bleeding, and the boy gently smeared the blood away. She too could have been a hundred years old.

Cal lowered Daisy to the ground and Adam ran to her, taking hold of her hand as if it were a butterfly. Rilke hated her, she hated all of them. And she hated herself most of all. How could she have been so stupid?

The emotion was pounding at her chest with iron fists, screaming to be let out, but she locked it down, the pain in her throat like she had swallowed glass.

"Is it dead?" came a voice from behind her. She turned to see Brick emerging from the shell of a building.

"No," said Daisy. She sat up, leaning her head on Cal's chest, taking deep, rattling breaths, some color returning to her cheeks. There was another flash of light and suddenly the other boy was with them, his arms wheeling as he fought to catch his balance. He failed, plopping down onto his knees, looking around in shock. Daisy smiled at him, saying, "Howie, are you okay?"

"Not really," he said after a moment, shuffling onto his backside. "I think I may have drunk too much rum."

Rilke grabbed a handful of her brother's shirt, clutching it so hard that she thought her fingers would break. How dare he make jokes when her brother lay dying.

"So what, then?" Brick went on.

"I think the storm just moved," Daisy said. The little girl

wiped the back of her hand across her face, smudging blood into a Zorro mask. "The same way we do. It transported."

"Where?" asked Brick.

"California," shouted the man, the one who had shown up on a motorbike, still standing farther down the street. He clipped his phone shut. He was covered in dust, looking like a phantom in the weird orange light of the broken day. "It's appeared in the States, it's just been confirmed."

"Cal, who's he?" asked Daisy.

"He's a friend, I think," Cal replied. "Everyone, this is Graham. Graham, everyone."

The man nodded a greeting, his brow furrowed. "Who are you people?"

"Just kids," said Daisy. "But something else too."

Schiller seemed to be sinking into himself, deflating. Rilke pulled him to her, the sobs finally breaking out of the prison of her throat. She couldn't stop them, couldn't breathe, forcing herself to suck in great big lungfuls of air between her strangled cries. She couldn't bear it, to be so *weak*.

"Help him," she said to nobody, to everybody. "I don't know what to do. He's going to die."

She wiped away her tears but they kept flowing, and she pushed her face into the wetness of Schiller's stomach so that nobody would see them. "Don't be scared, Schiller," said Daisy. Her voice was close, and when Rilke looked up she saw the girl there, her hand resting on Schiller's forehead. She didn't want her to touch him, but she could not find the strength to object. "They'll look after you."

"What are you talking about?" Rilke said. "I'm going to look after him, me and no one else, do you hear me?"

Daisy didn't take her eyes off Schiller. The boy coughed again, and his milky eyes cleared. He looked at Daisy, then at Rilke.

You will do what I say, Rilke told him in her head. He had always done as she said, always.

He smiled weakly at her. She could almost see the life draining from him, more of that oil-black fluid pumping from his stomach, as if his blood had been poisoned. He opened his mouth to speak but retched instead, a fountain of ink gushing over his cheek. His body was a huge, broken thing that he could no longer control, that *she* could no longer control.

"I'm not scared," he said in a liquid whisper. "It doesn't hurt."

"But I need you, little brother," said Rilke. "I love you."

His reply wasn't a word, but a thought. It was golden, and bright, and full of the smell of lavender and old books like in the library back in their house—*their* place, where nothing could ever hurt them. Why couldn't they be there now?

Schiller managed to lift a hand, placing it on the back of her neck, his skin so cold it was like he was frozen again.

"I'm sorry," she sobbed. "I'm so sorry."

Don't be, he said, and she knew it would be the last time she heard his voice. Schiller's body trembled, his hand slipping loose, slapping against the ground. He gasped in one last breath, but there was no fear in his eyes, no sadness either, just a flicker of relief and then nothing at all. A trickle of flame burned up through his chest, rising, growing, until with a sudden rush his angel clawed its way free from his flesh, soaring upward with its wings spread, howling as it faded into the light. It seemed to rip the rage from her belly as it went, because Rilke found herself on her feet, screaming after it.

"This is your fault! You did this to him! You bastard! You *bastard*!"

But it was gone. She turned to Daisy, then to Cal, then to Brick, wanting to murder them all, to beat them into their graves for their part in Schiller's death. But without him she was just a half person, a half soul, and she could not keep her balance. She staggered, falling down beside her brother, clutching him to her as if she could reattach him, shivering as the warmth of her twin chased up after the angel into the clearing skies.

CAL / *London, 1:12 p.m.*

IT SEEMED LIKE AN ETERNITY BEFORE ANYONE SPOKE. Cal stood and stared at Rilke as she sobbed against her dead brother. The only other noise was the hail-like patter of debris as the heavens cast back the broken earth.

"What now?" asked Brick. He kicked at scraps of stone on the ground, his hands wedged in his pockets. "It's over, right. For all of us, I mean."

"No," said Daisy, wiping her eyes. "We have to go after the man in the storm. He isn't dead."

Brick's eyes bulged and he shook his head.

"There is no one else, Brick," she replied. "There's just us."

"But who are you?" asked the motorbike guy, Graham. He still stood on the other side of the street, just past that invisible threshold. He kept glancing nervously at the sky, his phone open in his hand. "I don't understand."

"You wouldn't believe us if we told you," said Cal. The man snorted a laugh, looking at Daisy.

"Wouldn't believe that I saw you on fire, with wings, flying up there fighting the . . . the whatever that thing was? Try me, I'm more open-minded than I was this morning."

"It doesn't matter what we are," said Daisy. "It's what we're here to do. We're here to stop it."

"But what *is* it?"

"Evil," said Marcus from where he crouched on the ground.

But evil was the wrong word, thought Cal. It was more like a black hole, mindless, mechanical, devouring matter and light until there was nothing left.

Graham shook his head. "So you're telling me you're the good guys?" he asked.

Cal looked out over the city, the pit that had been sunk into the middle of it—ten, fifteen miles wide and God only knew how deep—opened up in the battle. How many people had died as a result? A million? And how many of those had the angels killed?

"Yes," Daisy said. "We are."

Graham seemed to chew on this for a moment, then he nodded. He put his phone to his ear, talking too quietly for Cal to listen.

"Seriously," whined Brick. "It's gone. It's not our problem."

Graham was shouting now, his cheeks red with anger. "This might be our only chance," he said. "Are you willing to bet every-thing on that? General? General?"

He snapped the phone closed, pacing back and forth. He looked up at the sky, shielding his eyes from the ever-brightening sun.

"Okay. We've got a problem. We've got to get underground."

"I don't think the storm is coming back," said Daisy.

"Not the storm," said Graham. "A missile."

"A *what?*" said Cal.

"A tactical nuclear strike on the city. The main target was the storm, but they're betting against you guys too. They think you're part of this."

"But why?" said Daisy, pulling loose from Cal.

"Because of what happened on the coast. You took out a whole town up there."

"That wasn't us," said Daisy, looking at Rilke, shaking her head. "I mean, it wasn't our fault, it was an accident."

"Not my call," he said. "It's already been launched. We've got minutes. Come on."

He set off back the way he'd come but nobody followed him.

"What did you do, Rilke?" Cal asked. "You killed a whole town?"

"I'm serious," said Graham, looking back over his shoulder. "You can have this conversation when we're underground, but if you don't start moving then you're all going to die."

"No," said Rilke. "We're not."

She stood slowly, running a hand down her top to brush away the blood and dirt that caked it. She turned to Daisy.

"Can you find it?" she asked.

"The storm?" Daisy scuffed her feet in the dirt. She was missing a shoe, Cal noticed. "I think so. Why?"

"Because I'm going to kill it," she said. "It's going to die for what it did to my brother."

"Listen," said Graham. "There's a Tube station nearby, but if we don't leave now we're not going to make it."

"He's right," said Brick, stumbling toward the motorbike guy. "We should go with him."

"And then what?" said Cal. "Hide? And what are you going to do when he starts trying to rip your face off?"

Brick stopped, uncertain.

Something growled overhead, a distant peal of thunder. Cal's heart seemed to forget what to do for an instant as he thought the man in the storm had returned. It grew louder, searing a path through the sky.

"Last chance," said Graham.

Rilke looked at Cal, her expression full of a feral fury. There was a question there, as clear as if she had spoken it. *Are you coming?* What choice did he really have? If they didn't stand up to the storm then sooner or later the whole world would look like this. He nodded. Rilke turned to Marcus, who smiled weakly.

They all turned to look at Brick.

"Fine," he said. "Have it your way."

"You should go," Daisy said to Graham. "Before it's too late."

"What about you?" he replied. "You need to get underground, somewhere safe."

Daisy closed her eyes, the flames spreading slowly out from her chest, her wings unfolding like those of a waking swan. "Just tell them we're on their side," she said, cold fire crawling up her neck. "Tell them we're trying to help."

The inferno engulfed her, and when she opened her eyes it was as if they were portholes on the side of a burning ship. The air shook with the strength of her, that same mind-numbing hum, but behind it the growl of a plane grew louder.

"You sure about this?" asked Brick. "I mean, we could just—"

Daisy didn't let him finish, just lifted her arms and pulled the world up over their heads. Cal's stomach lurched. He saw Marcus vanish, then Adam, then Howie. Rilke too, with one final, heartbreaking glance at the body of her brother. The man, Graham, was pulled up alongside them. Even as they went something exploded overhead, a pure light that seemed even brighter than

Daisy, a noiseless explosion that turned the sky silver. Cal saw the damage the nuke did as it exploded, a chain reaction that ripped things apart at their core. Would an angel have been able to stand up to that? Would they have lived if they hadn't been warned?

Then there was nothing but the rush and tumble of the ether, and the awful knowledge of what awaited them on the other side.

THE OTHER (7)

If I should die, think only this of me:
That there's some corner of a foreign field
That is for ever England.
       —*Rupert Brooke, "The Soldier"*

"IT'S CLEAR."

Reiko Stone spoke the words into her collar radio, knowing they'd be fed straight to her commanding officer on the other side of the field. She ducked out from under the hedgerow, using her free hand to brush spiderwebs from her visor. In her other hand she held her Sharpshooter rifle. She had her finger on the trigger, which breached just about every safety protocol the army had ever taught her, but she wasn't ever going to let her guard down. She'd been part of the assault group at the windmill. Through the scope of her rifle she'd seen the men and women in her squadron blown into dust and vapor by the creature in the fire. The *demon*. She didn't have any other word for it. It had killed them all with a word.

"Roger," said the CO. She glanced across the field, seeing a row of soldiers dressed in black, just like her. They'd been searching the area since the attack, looking for the demon and the kids that had been with it, all of whom had vanished in a storm of embers. *They're not kids, though,* she told herself. *They're monsters, all of them.*

The unit advanced, leaving no stone unturned. Behind them sat the ruin of a town. The whole place had been destroyed by the demon, tens of thousands murdered. There were other reports, too, of an attack in London. Another beast in a storm. She was scared, yes, but she was ready. That's why she had joined the army, to protect her country, her people. If she saw those kids again she'd execute them on the spot.

There was another hedge up ahead where the field ended, and Reiko squeezed through it, emerging onto a small country road. On the other side was a dense patch of woodland, so dark after the brightness of the day that she could barely see past the first line of trees. She put the stock of the gun against her shoulder, squinting down the barrel. The rest of her unit melted through the hedge beside her with barely a whisper.

"Proceed," came the order. "Maintain a five-meter spread, be alert."

She crossed the road, her booted feet kicking up what looked like ash from the tarmac. A few steps later and she was inside the cool gloom of the woods. Her eyes adjusted quickly, revealing the maze of trunks and branches, trickles of light seeping through. She scanned them, her whole body jumping every time she saw a leaf move or heard the soft thud of a falling acorn.

Crack.

Something breaking up ahead to her left, a branch beneath a foot. She dropped down onto one knee instinctively, seeing the rest of her unit do the same. She could hear a voice, too weak to make out. It was a girl, though, she was sure of it. A child.

"Cranston, Williams, flank left," her commanding officer's voice was urgent. "The rest of you, provide currrr . . ."

Do what? She put her hand to her ear, cupping the radio unit.

"Proooo currrr," he said again, his words breaking off into a wet snarl.

She looked at him, ready to inform him that there was a transmission problem, and saw him suddenly get to his feet and stumble forward. He dropped his gun, thumping into a tree and spinning in a clumsy circle, almost falling. Another member of the unit, Cranston, was screaming as he charged into the forest.

Reiko got to her feet, chasing after them, trying to make sense of it. Then she saw her, through the trees, a skinny girl with red hair. It was one of the kids from the windmill. She stood in a small clearing maybe thirty meters away, drenched in sunlight as thick and as orange as sap. Her eyes were too big, her mouth drooping. She didn't look real, more like a fairy, something out of a picture book.

Not a fairy. A demon.

Her commander was running right toward the girl, his hands bent into claws. Cranston was close behind, followed by Williams and Donoghue. They were like dogs, Reiko thought, closing in on a rabbit. They would tear her to ribbons.

She got down on one knee again, looked through the scope of her rifle, her finger tight on the trigger. The girl was sobbing, her freckled face covered in dirt. Why didn't she turn into a monster like the boy? Why didn't she erupt into fire? All she did was look up at Reiko, sunlight glinting in her eyes, and speak. Reiko couldn't hear her over the howls of her unit, but she could read her lips.

Save me.

She hesitated, swallowing, her throat dry. The girl vanished beneath the bulk of her CO and Reiko had to adjust the scope to see what was happening. The man was scraping his fingers over the girl's face, leaving great big ugly welts on her pale skin. She was screaming, but still she looked at Reiko, mouthing those same words. *Save me, save me.*

Reiko understood what she wanted. Not rescue, just peace. She lined up the crosshairs with the girl's forehead, took a deep breath, steadied herself.

Thank you, mouthed the girl.

Then she pulled the trigger.

There was a sudden flare of light, so bright that Reiko yelped as she pulled her head away. She held up a hand, peeking through her fingers to see a shape rise through the trees, a writhing plume of fire that howled as it burned itself away. A blast ripped through the forest, knocking her backward into the bracken, and for a moment she saw nothing but black.

Reiko lifted her head, struggling to put her thoughts in order. She used a tree to pull herself to her feet, staggering toward an armored shape half-hidden in the undergrowth. Ahead the forest was smoldering, full of smoke. The girl—the demon—was gone, but her commanding officer was there, on his knees.

"Sir," she called out to him. He didn't respond. She crouched down beside the body beside her—Donoghue—shaking him until he stirred. His visor was covered in soot.

"Christ," he said as she pulled him up. He coughed out coal-colored spit. "Were we hit?"

She didn't have time to explain before the forest lit up, as if the sun was rising in the middle of the afternoon. *Oh god, it's here, it's come for us,* she thought, thinking of the demon. Her first instinct was to turn and run, but she'd been trained to ignore the fear. She steeled herself, moving forward in a crouch, her rifle once again braced against her shoulder. The edge of the forest was only a few seconds away, that light rising slowly into the canopy. She emerged onto the road, expecting to see it there with its wings, its depthless eyes, nearly squeezing off a shot in anticipation.

But the fire wasn't coming from the demon. It was a glowing bubble beyond the horizon, a supernova of light that darkened into a cloud as it rose. Reiko recognized it immediately, and the bolt of terror it unleashed inside her stomach was worse than the one she'd had back at the windmill. She let her rifle drop, suddenly a child again, sobbing into the summer air as the atomic blast burned its way into the atmosphere. Something was whispering to her, and she realized that her earpiece had been knocked loose in the forest. She put it back in, hearing a voice.

"London has been hit, repeat, London has been hit."

DMITRI / *International Space Station, the Thermosphere, 1:24 p.m.*

DMITRI IVANOV HAD BEEN FLOATING IN THE CUPOLA of the International Space Station when the bomb went off. He'd been there for hours, staring through the seven windows at the planet below, marveling, as he always did, that he was inside a hunk of metal the size of a football field moving at 17,500 miles per hour through the thermosphere. At this speed they orbited the planet every 92 minutes. An hour and a half for eight billion people to pass beneath him. It made his head spin.

He'd been taking photos to show his sons when he finally got home to Moscow. He'd already snapped thousands—images of the world at night, lit up by the glow of countless cities; of thunderstorms raging; of the aurora borealis swimming over the world like schools of luminous fish; of the planet's ghostlike atmosphere, the bubble that kept everyone alive; of oceans and deserts and mountains, giants that he could cup in the palm of his hand. And photos in the other direction, too, of space.

Although not so many of these, because it scared him a little to look at it, at the sheer, unimaginable infinity of it. When he'd first arrived he'd felt as if he was an insect on the edge of an endless waterfall, that one slip and he would fall into the silent depths, lost forever. He'd never really managed to shake off that gut-churning sense of vertigo.

As he'd lined up his camera to capture the flawless curve of the horizon, the planet had erupted. It had been more like a volcano than an explosion, liquid fire spilling out into the atmosphere. He'd recognized the shape of the cloud and his camera had fallen from his trembling grip, floating calmly into the wall. They were too far over Russia for him to see exactly where the bomb had gone off, but he guessed western Europe somewhere, maybe England.

When he finally found his voice he'd radioed the other astronauts, and now all six of them were cramped inside the Cupola trying to work out what had happened. The explosion was nothing more than a faint halo, a sickly glow, but there was no doubt what it had been. An atomic bomb. A *big* one. He knew enough about physics to understand that it had been detonated above the surface. They floated there, in silence, waiting for the rocket plumes from Russia, China, America—*please God no, not now, not my sons*—that would signal the beginning of World War III. But there had been nothing else. This, Dmitri figured, meant one of two things: either the explosion was a terrorist attack, or a country had somehow launched a nuclear weapon against *itself.*

They were over the Pacific now, heading toward America. The world beneath them was engulfed in night, so dark that it looked less like a globe than a bowl, scooped out and hollow. *Come on,* he said, willing the station to fly faster so that they could see what had happened. It would be another hour before they were back over the UK. *Come on come on co—*

"Hey, what the hell is that?" It was Sally Phillips, the American flight engineer, and she had pressed her finger right up against the glass of the central window. Ahead the world was emerging from night as if the shadow was a blanket, so bright and full of color that Dmitri sputtered out a breath he didn't even notice he'd been holding.

His relief didn't last, though. He followed Sally's finger, seeing the west coast of the United States. It took him a moment to get his bearings, identifying the long, thin Baja peninsula first, then working his way up past the still-shining light clusters of San Diego, LA . . .

He stopped when he reached San Francisco. Something was happening to the ocean there, roiled into a fever. He swore in Russian, leaning in to get a closer look. It was as if the water was consuming the land, taking great big chunks out of it. He could see parts of the shore collapsing into the maelstrom, sections that had to be a mile wide. *An earthquake,* he thought. *It's causing a tsunami.* Only he'd never seen nature do anything like this. This was something else, something impossible.

"Oh God," said somebody else. Dmitri didn't look to see who. He couldn't take his eyes off what was happening 250 miles beneath him. The ocean was parting, as if a plug had been pulled at the bottom of the Pacific. The pattern it was making was almost like the clouds of a hurricane, a spiral of raging white water. And in the eye of it Dmitri thought he saw a storm crawling out of the earth, a writhing shape of smoke and shadow that looked larger than a city.

It's swallowing the earth, he thought. *It's going to eat it all.*

"Somebody, call this in," Sally was saying. "Christ, we've got to warn them."

Dmitri didn't move, just stared, wishing that he could open the hatch and let himself drift off into the endless darkness of space forever and ever and ever.

MONDAY AFTERNOON

Theirs not to reason why,
Theirs but to do and die:
Into the valley of Death
Rode the six hundred.
—Alfred Lord Tennyson,
  "The Charge of the Light Brigade"

THIS TIME, SHE KEPT HER EYES OPEN.

It was like the world was made of colored sand, pulled apart by a hurricane. Even as she rose up and out of time—Cal and Brick and poor, lost Rilke and everyone else rising beside her—the landscape was scrubbed clean. The white light she had seen, the one that burned in the sky, brighter than the sun, brighter even than the angels, was a bomb, she realized. She peered into the very heart of it with her new eyes, saw the atoms colliding, the power that burst from each one as the reaction spread. The explosion reached for them, but they had already slipped through the cracks, stepped into a place where nothing, not even a nuclear blast, could ever hurt them. Gradually the light faded, the ruined city disappeared, leaving them hanging in an empty, quiet place.

There was nothing around her now but darkness, and yet it was a strange kind of darkness that was also light—she could see the others floating alongside her, as if they were all sinking into an ocean. They all had their eyes closed, but even if they hadn't she didn't think they'd have been able to see her. *It's not the same for them,* she thought. *This is just a blink of the eye, a single beat of the heart.*

She felt a sudden loss. *Jade,* she thought, seeing the girl for an instant, in a forest, surrounded by soldiers. Then the crack of a gunshot and nothing. *I'm sorry,* she said, her angel once again numbing the sadness.

The world around her was vibrating ever so slightly, just the smallest tickle in the air, in her skin. The tremor was growing stronger, though, more insistent. It was the universe, she understood; they were in danger of breaking it. The little wheels and cogs and spinning things of reality just weren't designed to hold them here. What would happen if she resisted for much longer? Maybe time and space would simply close up behind her, shutting them out forever, locking them tight inside this pocket of nothingness. The thought frightened her, and she started to relax her mind, ready to let life reel her back in.

Only . . . something stopped her, another thought. She reached into her head, into her soul, to the thing that now lived there. It didn't react, didn't seem to notice her, which wasn't surprising. These angels, they weren't really angels at all, not the angels she'd been brought up to believe in. They were more like, like animals or something. No, more like *machines*. They didn't know how to communicate, she thought. Maybe they didn't know that communication was even a possibility. They were utterly single-minded, built for one purpose: to fight the man in the storm whenever and wherever he appeared. Everything else was alien to them, unknowable. They were programmed to defend life, and yet they didn't even know the magic, the wonder, of what they were fighting for. If that was true, she thought, it was awful.

The vibrations around her were growing worse, making her teeth chatter even though she was pretty sure that here, in this place, she didn't have teeth. The others were jiggling around where they hung in midair, looking like sheets left out to dry in a strong wind, their faces growing distorted and strange. Daisy relaxed her grip on the ether, letting herself slide back toward the world, only anchoring herself again when she felt something move inside her chest. The angel, was it trying to tell her something?

There was suddenly a thought inside her head, a sensation.

This was uncomfortable too, scratchy feathers bristling in the flesh of her brain, but she seemed to understand its translation. This place, this awful, empty, shaking, freezing, groaning place lost behind time, was home. This was where they lived, the angels, until they were called to fight, and this was where they returned once the war was over. There was no life, not here, no happiness or fun or family or friendship, just flashes of duty drowned in aeons of nothingness.

You poor things. You poor, lonely things. I wish there was something I could do. I wish I could help you. You could stay with me forever if you want. I promise I'd never send you back here.

And as soon as she'd thought the words she wished she could take them back, because she didn't mean it, not really.

She pushed the thoughts away, hoping that the angel hadn't heard her offer, or at least hadn't understood it. Pulling the hooks of her mind from the world, she let herself fall. The others fell with her, those little blue flames burning in their chests. All except for Brick, that was. His flame had grown, spreading out across his shoulders and down toward his stomach.

He's next, Daisy thought as their descent increased, the roar of wind in her ears, the thunder of the fall making her bones rattle. She closed her eyes against the rush, doing her best not to scream. It was terrifying, and yet she felt something else too, something different. Whatever it was inside her—alien or angel or some piece of timeless cosmic machinery designed to keep the world in balance—it was eager, it was keen, it wanted to be away from here.

As the tumble ended, the world re-forming itself around her, Daisy wished once again that she hadn't said what she'd said. Because what if, when all was said and done, the angel didn't want to leave?

BRICK / *San Francisco, 1:26 p.m.*

ALMOST AS SOON AS THE SMOKING, GAPING WRECK of London had vanished, another landscape appeared, wrapping itself around Brick with enough force to send him reeling. He staggered back, tripping on his own feet, sunlight like a fist pounding at his face. His stomach lurched, puke pooling in his mouth as he fell. He thumped onto his backside, spitting, groaning through his wet lips and trying to see past the moisture in his eyes.

They were in a forest, a pine forest, which at first looked so similar to the one back in Hemmingway that he had a sudden rush of nostalgia. It didn't take him long to notice that the trees here were bigger, though, swaying wildly from the shock wave Daisy had created as they arrived. Branches snapped free, crashing to the ground, thirty seconds passing before everything was still. A breeze drifted through the quiet shade, carrying the smell of conifers. Through the trees he saw the sun was lower, like it was morning, and he wondered how far Daisy had brought them. The other guys were scattered over the forest floor, all of them except Daisy and the new boy, Howie, wiping vomit from their lips.

Brick stood up, ignoring the way the world seemed to spin. He didn't understand a single thing about what was going on, but he was pretty sure that getting repeatedly ripped apart into atoms and then reconstituted wasn't good for you. The truth was, he didn't actually feel that great. There was something wrong with his stomach. He put a hand to it, feeling almost as if a piece of him was missing, had been left behind in London. It wasn't painful, just *weird*. The thought of it, of being damaged, made him angry. Or at least it should have. But he felt strangely calm about the whole thing.

"Where are we?" asked Cal, staggering to his feet. Daisy, just a girl again, shrugged her shoulders, taking in the forest with a look of confusion. Adam ran to her and she gathered him in her arms.

"I'll take a look," said Daisy. She eased herself free from Adam, and Brick heard the *whoomph* of fire as she turned, followed by the slow, powerful beat of her wings. He peeked over the filthy, freckled skin of his arm to see her burning up through the branches. It was like watching the sun rise, and within seconds she hung against the blue, the brightest thing in the sky.

"What happened to that man?" Cal asked. "Graham. Didn't he come with us?"

"Yeah," said Marcus. "He did. I think that's him."

The gangly kid was pointing between two trees, and when Cal turned and looked he slammed a hand to his mouth, gagging. Brick walked over to them, curious, peering into the shadows to see a lump of something small and red and wet, like a butcher's parcel. Only this one had what looked like half a face, a ridge of teeth pushed up into an empty eye socket. He turned away, clamping his eyes shut.

"He wasn't one of us," said Rilke, whispering her words into the dirt. "He couldn't survive it, and he fell to pieces."

"I'll cover it up," said Marcus, rooting around until he found a loose branch, hefting it over the man's mangled corpse. He stood back, wiping his hands on his trousers. The man's face was out of sight, but Brick could still see it in his head, as clear as day. He figured he probably always would, right up until the end. There it was again, not a sensation but an absence of one, something he couldn't quite put his finger on. Something, a piece of him that had been there for as long as he could remember, was now gone. This time he actually lifted up his dirt-caked T-shirt, prodding his belly.

"Hungry?" asked Howie, the new kid. Brick dropped his T-shirt and looked at him. The kid was fourteen, maybe younger, and even though he'd turned, his skin was still mottled with bruises and cuts. "I could eat a plate of something right about now. Think there's somewhere around here we can get some food?"

"How can you be hungry?" Cal asked.

"Man's gotta eat," said Howie.

The forest grew brighter as Daisy returned, her fire sucked back into her pores as she touched down. She shook her head, the engine of her eyes sputtering out.

"We're on the top of a big slope," she said, pointing to her left. "There's a city over there, with loads of hills and a pointy tower thing. And the sea. And a big orange bridge. I can't see any sign of the man in the storm."

"Still say you've scared the bastard away," said Brick, shivering. "You tore his face off, he's not coming back after that, right?"

Nobody answered, and he glanced up to see that they were all looking at him. Daisy's head was cocked, a soft smile on her lips. He frowned at her, ready for that stew of anger to bubble up from his gut, almost disappointed when it didn't. There was only that same lull in his stomach, that absence. That's what it was, he suddenly understood, the anger, it wasn't there anymore. He slapped a hand to his belly, as if somebody had taken a kidney. His rage was so much a part of him that it was almost frightening not to feel it there.

"What?" he said, everyone still looking at him. "What is it?"

"You," said Cal. "Look."

He didn't want to, but what choice did he have? He lifted his T-shirt once more, the skin there blue. It could have been dirt, except for its soft sheen, a subtle sparkle when it caught the light. He put his hand to it, feeling the cold there. He scrubbed his skin, shaking loose flakes of ice, like he was dusting off his motorbike after a winter's night.

"No," he said, waiting for the fear, for the anger, for anything. But his stomach was empty, his head was empty. That was even worse than the ice, which crept slowly up over his ribs, which stretched down from his fingertips like an infection, turning his hands to stone, because he didn't care about his body, not really. He'd never liked it, too tall, his face too blunt. But his anger, that was who he was, that's what made him Brick. Take that away and what was left?

"Just let it happen," said Daisy, taking a step toward him. "I know it's scary, but they're here to help. They'll look after you, keep you safe."

"Like they did with Schiller?" he spat, his lips too cold to shape the words properly. It felt like he'd been out in a blizzard, his skin frozen, as rigid as plastic. He staggered, stumbling into a tree, trying to lift his hands to his face, to turn his head. The others were growing faint, the world turning gray as his eyes iced over. Why was it happening like this? Didn't you have to be injured first? Like Schiller, like Howie?

He felt himself fall, no pain as he landed in the needled undergrowth of the forest. He couldn't even be sure if he was facing up or down. A bolt of panic thudded into his heart, the briefest flare of dull anger quickly swallowed up by the same overwhelming calm.

Don't fight it, said Daisy.

He fought it, trying to ignite his rage, like a pilot in free fall trying to fire up a stalled engine. Another dull explosion, too soft, too short to fight the paralysis. He tried again, and this time he managed to wrench open his eyes. He struggled to his feet, stumbling toward the light, not caring where he was going, just wanting to move, to get away. He made it three paces before he noticed he wasn't in the forest anymore. He made it another two before noticing that he didn't even have feet to pace with. He hung inside a palace of ice, the walls constantly shifting and full of other people's lives. It was the same place he'd visited in his dreams, when he'd fallen asleep in the church.

He spun around, searching for a way out, finding himself face-to-face with Daisy. She was engulfed in fire, her body a shimmering web of light, her face something from a dream, not quite real, not quite able to hold its form. Her wings arched over her head, towering up like a fountain of flame, spitting molten sparks of blue and red and gold. She reached out to him with a hand that was not really a hand, cold against his cheek.

Something was starting to burn in him, as if a taper had been lit. This thing, this creature, was trying to smother the fear and the anger. *Just let it happen, please,* Daisy said. *It needs your help.*

It needed him, and he needed it too. He relaxed, taking a deep breath of air that didn't really exist, trying to switch off the rage. For now, at least. This creature, it didn't know him, didn't understand that he was made of anger. Nothing could extinguish it. He would just pretend to be calm, he would go along with it, but his fury would still be there. It would *always* be there. Even with a being like this inside him, he would be able to find it. He smiled at Daisy with his nonexistent lips.

"I'm ready."

DAISY / *San Francisco, 1:38 p.m.*

Daisy SLIPPED BACK INTO THE REAL WORLD in time to see Brick's angel hatch. Fire burned through the eggshell-thin fabric of his skin, starting in his chest and quickly spreading. He opened his mouth to scream, white light blazing up his throat, his eyes erupting into twin supernovas. His back split, his wings unfurling with enough strength to crack the trunk of the tree behind him, filling the forest with gunshots and groans as it fell. He struggled against the transformation, launching himself off the ground and into the branches overhead, his cry pistoning out of his mouth, loud enough to make the ground tremble. Birds scattered from the trees, so many that they darkened the sky.

Don't be angry. That's why they numb you, because it's easier when you aren't angry or scared. Honestly, Brick, you have to believe me.

Brick turned to her, the infernos of his eyes meeting hers. He was fighting it, trying to hang on to his rage. But that was a bad thing. It wasn't what the angels wanted.

It's what I want, he said. *I didn't ask for this, didn't have a choice. So if I'm going to do it, then this angel—whatever you want to call it—needs to do something for me too.*

What? But she had a feeling she already knew. Brick's girlfriend, Lisa, trapped in the basement at Fursville, cornered like a rat by Rilke, then shot in cold blood. Daisy turned to the others, seeing Rilke still crouched on the ground, glaring up at Brick with cold, dark, frightened eyes.

Don't, Daisy said. *Brick, please, she didn't know what she was doing.*

Yes. She did.

Brick sailed into the clearing like a man-of-war, his wings full, twice as tall as he was. That sound radiated from him, from her too, churning up the ground, making pebbles dance and shaking pinecones from the trees. He stopped beside them, his eyes burning across the clearing, never leaving Rilke. She must have understood, because she scrabbled unsteadily to her feet, backing off.

I just want to show her what it's like.

He stretched out his hand again and even though he didn't touch her, Rilke's head snapped back. She screamed, her fingers clawing at her forehead.

Please! Daisy yelled. She looked at Cal, at the others, but nobody moved. Even Howie, bathed in flame, was rooted to the spot. Why wasn't anybody doing anything?

"She was one of them!" Rilke said, choking on her own words. "She was one of the ferals, she had to die."

Brick moved closer, his fingers playing with the air. Even through the shimmering haze that covered him it was obvious that he was grinning. He held out a finger, pointing it right at Rilke's face.

She didn't have to die. She wasn't hurting anyone down there. You should have left her alone, she'd have gotten better. But you killed her, you shot her in the head.

"She would have hurt us," Rilke said. "I had to . . ."

How does it feel, huh?

He twitched his fingers and Rilke lurched into the air. She squirmed against his invisible grip but there was nothing she could do.

That's enough! Daisy reached out with her mind, her thoughts becoming a physical force that slammed into Brick, knocking him away. He spun, two, three times, his wings tangling in each other, kicking up a whirlwind of dust. Only for a moment, though, then he fired them out again, turning to face Daisy. The smile was gone, his eyes two blazing pits of fury.

Stay out of this, Daisy, he said, the words somehow carried inside the thrum of his angel's heart, halfway between spoken and thought. *I don't want to hurt you too.*

He wouldn't, would he?

I said, How does it feel, Rilke?

He jabbed his finger forward. Half a dozen meters away Rilke's head snapped back, her skull splitting. Blood gushed out of her wounded forehead, running over her nose and into her mouth, turning her screams into wretched, awful gargles.

Brick, no! Daisy shouted. Brick hung there, drenched in flame, his finger still out. It was hard to see the expression on his face. He dropped his hand, turned to Daisy.

I . . . I didn't mean to . . .

Rilke was staggering away, blinded by blood. Her foot hit a tree root and she went down, her head thudding against the dirt so hard that it splashed a crimson halo in the soil. The girl groaned, trying to crawl forward.

Rilke? said Daisy, moving after her.

I was just trying to scare her, said Brick, his voice a little boy's inside her head. *I'm sorry.*

He reached out again and the world lurched, scattering Cal

and the others like bowling pins. The air trembled, a shock wave that pushed Daisy back so hard that she had to stretch out her wings to root herself in place. Thunder ripped across the clearing, not just in the sky but from the ground too, as if an explosion had been detonated down there. Even Brick was rattled by it, his flames flickering, his eyes wide and fearful for a moment before the inferno erupted again. He stared at his hands, as if he couldn't believe what he had done.

Daisy almost didn't dare look at Rilke. Yet when she turned, she saw that the girl was still alive, writhing on the ground, her hands over her face. Daisy looked back at Brick, asking *What did you—*

Another roar, everything moving, as if the forest was a vast creature that had decided to pick itself up and walk away with them on its back. The ground tilted, Cal and Adam rolling between the trees in each other's arms, Rilke sliding underneath the tail of the conifer.

It wasn't me! Brick shouted, his mind-voice stripped of anger, full of terror. *It wasn't me, I swear.*

That same awful, endless groan rose up, the howling roar of a billion trumpets in the sky, a noise that seemed as if it could shake the universe to pieces. Daisy flexed her wings, propelling herself out of the forest, rising once again above the shuddering trees. In the distance was the same city she'd seen before, now being shaken into dust by the force of the tremors. Beyond it the ocean was white, worked into a frenzy.

It wasn't me, she heard Brick say again, fainter now. Of course it wasn't. This was something so much worse.

It was the man in the storm.

BRICK FOLLOWED DAISY, using his wings to propel himself out of the forest. He burst from the canopy, the sky opening up around him, vertigo gripping his stomach in an iron fist. He'd never been fond of heights, and now here he was hovering a hundred meters up with nothing to stop him falling except a pair of flaming wings. The thought was so absurd, so terrifying, that he laughed—an insane, screeching giggle that lasted less than a second before he looked to the horizon and saw the city disappear.

It came apart like a sand sculpture, the tower blocks vanishing first, then the hills—solid mounds of rock—dissolving into puddles. The ground had become an ocean, a vast whirlpool that churned in a slow circle. The actual ocean was so white that it could have been made of snow, groaning as it was sucked into the vortex. Brick saw a bridge—a huge, great red thing—snap apart as if it were made of matchsticks, pulled into the flow. The edge of the whirlpool was spreading out from the city with unbearable speed, everything crumbling into dust and smoke. The earth seemed to cry out, a scream of pure anguish that made Brick's ears hurt.

It's him, said Daisy from his side, her voice full of grief. *Oh, Brick, he's killed them all.*

How many people? A hundred thousand? A million? They wouldn't have even known about it, sucked into his gullet so fast they'd have been dead before they could draw breath.

We have to fight him, Daisy went on. Howie had risen to her side, his angel form so similar to hers that they could have been twins. *Where is he? I don't understand.*

It was different from London. There was no storm, for one. Back there he had hung in the air, sucking everything into that pit of a mouth, the skies full of darkness. Here there was no sign of him, just the drowning city.

He's underground, Brick said, suddenly comprehending.

The epicenter of the destruction was now nothing but a gaping hole, a mile wide and growing fast. Land and sea alike poured into the pit, throwing rainbows against the cloudless sky, the effect dizzying. Something else was happening too, vast, snaking cracks radiating out from the destruction, pulling the earth to pieces. One was making its way up toward the wooded hill beneath them, carving a trench through the streets, through houses. Everything was falling apart.

Wait, Brick said. *Where are we? Didn't that man say it had reappeared in San Francisco?*

I think so, Daisy replied. *Why?*

Because of the fault, Howie answered before Brick had a chance. *The San Andreas line.*

The what? Daisy asked, looking at Brick with her burning eyes.

It's a crack in the earth, a weak spot.

It was like the man in the storm was ripping out the foundations, the skeleton that held the earth together. Break enough bones and the whole continent would collapse.

So what do we do? Daisy asked. *How do we get down there?*

Brick looked at her, at Howie, knowing the answer but refusing to say it—because saying it would make it real. Not that there was any point hiding things anymore, Daisy could see inside his mind as easily as if it were her own.

We go down there, she said.

Brick shook his head. The only thing he wanted to do was turn around and get the hell away from here.

Until the man in the storm finds you, Daisy said. *Because he will. You think he's going to stop here? He's going to ruin everything, Brick, the whole world. He's going to swallow it up. Don't you get it? There will be nothing left.*

He turned away from the roaring void to a horizon bathed in gold. It would be so easy to go, to not look back.

Please, Daisy said, reaching out to him, the flames of her hand curling around his own, interlocking like fingers, trying to root him in place. He pulled away, flapping his wings once, carving a path through the sky, flexing them again, the madness and chaos shrinking, Daisy's pleas growing fainter, the rumble of the ruined city fading behind the rush of air as he soared, so good to be moving, moving, always moving.

CAL / *San Francisco, 1:56 p.m.*

THE GROUND WAS SHAKING SO MUCH he couldn't stand up. Every time he tried the soil beneath him would pitch like a ship in a storm, sending him sprawling. He held on to Adam with everything he had, his hand clenched around the little boy's T-shirt. It was too dark to see anything, the trees collapsing all around him, cutting out the sun.

"Daisy!" he cried, the air full of the stench of pine. There was no way she could hear him over the rumble of the earth, the crack and creak of the trees, but she didn't need her ears, she would *sense* him.

The ground lurched downward, so fast that for a moment Cal was suspended in midair. He landed on his back, winded. Adam rolled next to him, the kid not making the slightest sound, his eyes liquid with panic. Cal grabbed him, hugged him hard. A shaft of light cut through the branches, revealing a cliff face that hadn't been there before. Tree roots poked from the earth like earthworms, an avalanche of soil drumming against the ground. He waited for another quake, waited for the world to open up beneath him and finish the job, but there was nothing but quiet.

Relative quiet, that was. He could still hear the distant groan, the noise of some monstrous leviathan in the deep. He wasn't sure exactly what it was but he could hazard a guess: the man in the storm, hanging over some city, swallowing it whole. He pushed himself up on his elbows, waiting for the agony of a broken bone or sprained limb, finding only bruises.

He stood, the sloping ground making him feel drunk as he hoisted Adam to his feet. He'd lost all sense of direction, other than up and down. He glanced through the branches, seeing the glare of the sun—or maybe an angel, he couldn't be sure.

"Daisy!" he yelled again, his voice making Adam jump. "Where are you?"

"Cal?"

He recognized Marcus, the sound coming from above him. He wondered if the other boy had transformed, was hovering in the air, then he spotted his skinny face peeking over the top of the cliff. He was grinning.

"You see Daisy anywhere?" Cal asked. "Brick or the other guy?"

Marcus glanced behind him and shrugged.

"Just me up here. You guys okay?"

Cal nodded absently, trying to see a way up the cliff face. The earth was still trembling, the tremors vibrating up through his shoes and making the bones in his legs ache. He'd always trusted solid ground, but now he couldn't help but think about how thin the crust of the planet was, how fragile, and the bottomless ocean of molten rock that it floated on. This would be so much easier if one of them had turned, they could just spread their wings and fly the hell out of here.

But there was no sign that his angel was anywhere near to hatching. Typical, he got the lazy one. He snorted a humorless laugh.

"You see a path, anything?" he asked. Marcus shook his head.

"Like this as far as I can see, on the other side too. I can't budge, gonna have to wait for a lift. You might be able to get out that way, though." He pointed to his right. "Could be a break in the trees there."

"I'll go take a look," Cal said, setting off. Progress was slow because the ground was broken up by smaller cracks, his feet sinking into the soil. Every time he took a step he gritted his teeth, waiting for a pothole to open, for darkness to take him. Twice Adam shook free because Cal was holding the boy's hand too hard. "Sorry, mate, maybe you'd be better off staying here." Adam shook his head, gripping Cal's fingers just as hard. They pressed on, pushing through clumps of broken branches, sticky with sap. There was no sign of a break in the trees, as Marcus had said, but after what had to be five minutes Cal heard something. He stopped and cocked his head, listening to what could have been the grunts of a wild animal. For the first time he wondered where exactly they were, and what kinds of things might live in the woods.

He squeezed between two trees, scanning the gloom ahead, eventually seeing a shape there. Two huge white eyes sat bodiless in the shadows, ghost eyes. Then the shape shuffled around and he realized it was Rilke. Her face was so drenched in blood that it was almost invisible. She was muttering something in between those guttural breaths, although Cal was too far away to make out words. He pulled Adam through the trees, dropping onto a knee by the girl's side.

This close he could see the hole in her forehead, the one Brick had made. How the hell could she still be alive?

Rilke was still mumbling, occasional flashes of white teeth brilliantly bright against the red. Cal leaned in closer, his pulse pounding in his ears.

"Rilke," he said again. "Can you hear me?"

"Schill, is that you?" Her voice was an old woman's, broken into a million pieces. "Little brother? I can't see you."

"It's Cal," he said. He waved a hand in front of her face but she showed no sign of seeing it. What had Brick done to her? He swore under his breath, looking at Adam, then at the forest. She needed a hospital, but even if she lived long enough to get to one the doctors would tear her to pieces as soon as she walked in the door.

The clearing suddenly brightened for a split second, then fell dark again. Cal looked, expecting to see Daisy or Brick descend through the trees. There was no sign of them, and when the light flared up again he realized it was coming from Rilke. Cal scrabbled back as a wave of fire washed over her, quickly guttering out. It happened again, the flames squeezed from her pores, trying to get hold, burning themselves out in a heartbeat. Rilke was oblivious to it, still muttering nonsense words, her eyes big and white and blind.

"Adam, come away," Cal said, holding out his hand to the boy. Adam took a hesitant step back as the girl erupted again, flames curling up from her torso, flickering over her neck and face then dying away. This time Rilke seemed to feel them, her lips freezing mid-word. She placed a hand to her chest, snatching in a weak, wet breath. Tongues of fire licked between her fingers, stronger now.

"I'll keep you safe, little brother, I'm here for you."

The flames were holding, burning up from her chest, spreading out to her limbs, the chill coming off them unbelievable. That same thrumming purr rose up in the air, growing louder then dimming, an engine trying to ignite. It faded, then came back with a vengeance, the flames burning up so violently that this time Adam ran to Cal's side. It didn't look like what had happened to Brick, to Daisy. This was different, the fire more urgent, raging from head to toe, as if it were attacking her. It roared like a thousand gas burners at full strength, fighting to stay alive, to catch. Cal could almost see it there, the angel, the shape of it writhing inside the flames.

"Come on," Cal said, taking hold of Adam. He wasn't sure what was going to happen, but whatever it was, it couldn't be good. Rilke was blasting out cold air as the angel sucked in the heat of the forest, that noise rising in pitch, like she was going to blow. Even if she didn't, even if she transformed, her mind was broken into pieces. She wouldn't be able to control her power, she'd end up being as dangerous as the man in the storm. For a fleeting second Cal thought about grabbing a branch, staving her head in before she could turn. But her angel seemed to read his mind, thrashing harder, the noise of its heart like a physical force pushing Cal back.

The inferno blazed, jetting from her eyes and from the hole in her head, as if there was a flare burning inside her skull. Cal covered his eyes with his arm. When he looked again Rilke was airborne, a single, half-formed wing propelling her upward at an angle. It vanished and she plummeted, then it fired up again, both wings curling out, pulling her into the sky where she faded into the glare of the sun.

Cal turned away, blinking the spots of light from his vision. He clutched Adam's hand, leading him through the trees, hoping that there was enough of Rilke left to remember what to do, enough of her left to know how to fight, but not so much that she remembered what Brick had done to her.

DAISY / *San Francisco, 2:17 p.m.*

DAISY WAS TORN. In one direction lay the city, now nothing more than a smoking void, ten, twenty miles across. It looked like pictures she'd seen of the Grand Canyon, only this one had a floor of roiling, coiling smoke. She could just about make out a shape in the darkness down there, the man in the storm, looking like a monstrous spider in its web. And the pit was still growing, the edges crumbling like sand, pulled into the spiraling tide of matter that circled his mouth. The ocean poured into it, a waterfall that stretched as far as she could see, unleashing clouds of steam.

Behind her, Brick was little more than a speck in the sky, a shooting star. She couldn't believe he'd gone. He was such a *coward*. She was terrified, even with the angel inside her. But they couldn't run away, because there was nobody else. If they didn't fight him, if they didn't *win*, then there would be nothing left.

She could hear Cal too, from the forest, calling her name. At least they were safe down there. Safer than they would be up here anyway. She'd get to them when she could, *if* she could. Right now she had bigger problems.

Howie was at her side. The morning sun was behind him, the light shining through the burning, gossamer-thin fabric of his outstretched wings. They were beautiful. She could have stared at them for hours. *We hurt it once,* he said. *We can do it again.*

Daisy wasn't sure. There had been three of them before, and now the man in the storm was underground. Why hadn't Brick just stayed? They could have beaten it if they'd stuck together.

Something rose from the forest beneath her, searing a path through the sky. It dropped, lifted again, the light blinking on and off, struggling.

Rilke! Daisy called to her.

There was no reply, and Daisy tried to tune in to the girl's thoughts, pulling away quickly when she saw the chaos in there, the darkness—something had happened, something terrible, something even worse than the madness she'd had before.

Rilke, please, listen to me!

Rilke spun in midair, focusing on the distant, fading light that was Brick. Then she vanished, blasting out a sonic boom that rippled through the air, knocking Daisy backward. She used her wings to right herself, staring at the space where Rilke had been, the embers that dripped back to earth. *No!* It wasn't fair, why did they have to be like this? They were going to kill each other. Daisy opened her mouth and let loose a sob that rocked through the sky.

She had to focus, the way her mum had taught her to when she was really scared.

Come on, she said. *I can do this.*

We can do this, said Howie. He nodded at her, and she returned it. Then she put her head down, burning through the skin of reality. She reappeared above the heart of the canyon, buffeted by the winds that howled into the vortex beneath her. It was huge, so much bigger than it had looked from a distance, a raging sea of rock and water. Bolts of lightning—black and white—lashed upward, clawing at the walls, sparking monstrous dark fires wherever they touched.

And there it was, the beast. She couldn't make him out, not with her eyes, but she used the angel's to see him, suspended there in the heart of the storm, breathing in that same endless inward breath. He saw her too, because he stopped breathing in for long enough to bellow out that same earth-shattering foghorn cry, one that vomited up a ruined city, a cloud of dark matter that punched toward her.

She put her head down, feeling the angel powering up inside every cell of her body, the noise of its heartbeat even louder than the roar of a billion tons of rock and water. Howie flew beside her, both of them diving straight down, meeting the attack head-on. Daisy opened her mouth, a word firing out of her lips, cleaving a path through the debris. Their angels spoke, a language of pure power, opening up a channel into the storm. The world darkened as she plunged, her fire revealing every chunk of rock, every glinting scrap of metal, every mangled corpse that rushed up beside her. She ignored it all, plummeting, shouting word after word after word until finally she saw him there.

He was somehow still a man—bloated and monstrous, yes, but

with two arms and two legs and a head. His body was the size of a building, a skyscraper, the skin stretched out, broken in places, held together by a net of poisoned black strands that might once have been veins. Darkness churned inside the gaps, as if he had been emptied out and filled with smoke. Those wings, those horrible, dark wings that were so similar to her own, and yet so different, stretched out behind him like a spiderweb of shadow.

Nothing human remained above the neck. There was just that mouth, that gaping hole where his face should be, looking more like a whirlpool or a tornado than ever. She couldn't see his eyes but she could feel them watching her, hooks embedded in her skin.

She opened her mouth again, feeling the energy blaze a path up her throat, surging from her lips. It struck the man in the bulk of his torso, pulling away strips of old, dead flesh. Howie shouted too, the word carving through the air and ripping a chunk of darkness from the storm. She fired again, both of them calling out together, screaming, throwing everything they had at him.

Something was happening to the man's mouth. It was starting to turn, like an engine, a turbine, no longer blowing out but inhaling again, like before.

She felt the current in the air change, sucking her down. The void of his mouth grew closer, bigger, the sound of it like thunder rocking through her mind. She screamed at him, her voice and the angel's lost in the madness. Something lashed out from his throat, a blade of darkness that sliced scalpel-like through the air beside her. Another followed, this one coiling around her body, a piece of liquid night that gripped her like a fist.

Daisy panicked, trying to stretch out her wings but finding

them bound tight. Her angel sparked violently, fighting the darkness, and she twisted her body in an effort to get loose. She spun deeper into the pit, her mind unable to make sense of the thing that held her. There was nothing there, just a strand of complete and utter absence that seemed to eat into her, like it was trying to scrub her out of existence.

No! she yelled, screaming at it again and again until the piece of night began to unravel, dissolving in the cold fire of her angel. But it was too late, the current had her, reeling her into the clouds of smoke and dust that circled the beast's throat.

The roar of the vortex grew even louder, and there was a sudden rush of movement, like she was being sucked down the drain. She closed her eyes, then realized that not seeing was infinitely worse than seeing. When she opened them again she saw it up ahead, the end—a point of utter blackness into which everything was being pulled. It was the tiniest of holes, surely too small to hold all this *stuff.* But it breathed in every last scrap of matter, bolts of not-quite-lightning cracking up from it, dozens every second. There was no sound, here, and she wondered if maybe she'd gone deaf.

Another flutter of liquid night, but she twisted out of the way, feeling the unbearable nothing of it brush past her. She opened her mouth, fighting back. Something odd was happening as she closed in on the flickering hole. Things were slowing down—or maybe not slowing down but breaking apart, as if even time couldn't hold itself here. Time, sound, matter, life, the man in the storm hated it all, he hated *everything.* She could almost see its story in the immense quiet that surrounded his throat. This thing, whatever it was, it came from a place where there was nothing. This thing was what had existed before life, before the first stars, before the Big Bang. It was the emptiness before the universe, and the emptiness that would follow it.

The awful sense of loneliness that washed over her was too much. She couldn't bear it. This thing was a black hole, it would devour everything, just feed and feed and feed until there was nothing left—no warmth, no laughter, no love. Just silence, forever and ever. There was nothing they could do against this. It was hopeless.

She heard Howie calling to her but she ignored him. She took one last look at the beast, then flexed her wings and burned herself out of its reach.

RILKE / San Francisco, 2:32 p.m.

THERE WAS SOMETHING WRONG WITH HER HEAD, but she couldn't work out what. It hurt, for one, a throbbing needle of agony right in the center of her brain. Noise seemed to radiate out from it, the sound of cathedral bells ringing, and there was a whistling, maddening itch in her ears. She couldn't think straight, couldn't seem to hold a thought up there. All she knew was that *he* had done it, the tall boy. Brick, was that his name? Rilke tried to remember, but the images and memories in her brain were like jigsaw pieces in a box, they didn't make any sense.

She couldn't see too well either. In fact, she couldn't really see at all. Something else was seeing for her, the world a web of golden strands that made up trees and fields and hills and sky. There was something inside her, something made of fire. But why?

Revenge. Someone had died. *Schiller*. Someone had broken

him. The tall boy, the tall boy with wings. The engine of her brain stalled, the whistle rising in pitch, like people were screaming right into her ears. She felt her body shake, a fit that made every muscle spasm.

She looked around with her new eyes, seeing the world laid out before her, bare and vulnerable. Were they atoms she could see, the building blocks that made up every stone, every cloud, every chirping bird, every mouthful of air she took in? There were so many of them, galaxies of them, but they seemed to make sense to her. She could see a glowing trail in the sky where someone like her had been, like a ship's wake. The tall boy, he had come this way.

She beat her wings. Had she always had them? She couldn't be sure. The noise was too much, she couldn't see anything past it.

Her brain screamed. She ignored it as best she could, following the trail, the world passing by beneath her like she was being carried, like something had her under its arm, something old and terrible and full of fire. She could almost hear it, behind the chaos, howling at her with words she could never hope to understand, trying to tell her something.

It's okay, she said. *I know what you want me to do.* She thought of Schiller, and she thought of the tall boy. *I'll break him, I'll break him, I'll break him.*

CAL STOPPED WALKING, aware of a growing darkness in his head. The air was shuddering, gusts of wind snapping between the trees carrying the stench of smoke and blood. The ground felt like a living thing, shaking so hard it made his teeth chatter. Adam hung on to the pocket of his jeans, staring at him.

"Daisy," Cal said, sensing her terror.

She was *dying*, he realized. He swore, his voice so human, so pathetic and small against the undying roar of the end of the world. He thumped himself in the chest, hard enough to hurt.

"Come on then," he yelled to the thing inside him, the creature. He knew it was there, because it had made his friends try to murder him, his mum too, what felt like a million years ago.

He hit himself again, and again, but the angel didn't respond. Maybe his didn't work. Maybe it had died on the journey over from wherever it had come from. Was it lying inside Cal now, a collection of weightless, broken parts rattling around inside his soul? The thought made him want to open himself up and pull everything out just to get rid of it.

And what could he do without his angel? Walk up to the man in the storm and ask him nicely to just piss off? All the man would have to do was think it and Cal's body, the body he'd had his whole life, every single cell of it, would simply be erased. Nine pints of blood, a few bones, all wrapped up in the thinnest coat of leather.

"Dammit!" he said, shaking the darkness away, taking another step. Adam held on, dragged along beside him. He didn't show any sign of changing either. If anything he looked younger and more feeble than ever. The new kid, Howie, had gone with Daisy, hadn't he? And Brick? Cal couldn't be sure. Rilke, poor lost Rilke, had turned too. Maybe all four of them were fighting. Surely that was enough, wasn't it? They'd scared the beast away when it was just three of them, back in London. It *had* to be enough.

Only it wasn't. He knew it, and his helplessness, his exhaustion, his fear, was suddenly a fury that boiled up from his belly.

He charged through the trees, running now, heading for a band of sunlight that sat ahead. He burst free, sunlight blinding him, so much so that he almost didn't see the trench that ran parallel to the forest, a sheer cliff that dropped off meters from his feet. He skidded to a halt, kicking pebbles into the crack. There were footsteps behind him and he held out an arm so that Adam wouldn't topple off.

"Jesus," Cal said, creeping to the edge, leaning over. Below— maybe thirty, forty meters—was the ground that had once been joined to the forest. Between him and it was a ravine that had been opened up in the shaking earth, stretching as far as he could see in both directions. He felt his head spin and took a step away, looking to the horizon. Dominating it was a black hole that stretched north to south, land and ocean boiling into it as it continued to grow. He was on a hill, near the top, and could see for miles—but all there was against the sky was the pit, a halo of dark cloud suspended over it.

The man in the storm was eating everything, every rock, every drop of seawater. He was devouring it.

He collapsed to his knees. It was over. Daisy would die, the others would follow, and the world would end. He closed his eyes, hearing the relentless grind of the storm, the deafening crack as the bones of the world snapped deep beneath him.

Something touched his shoulder, and he flinched. He looked, saw Adam right next to him, the little boy's face as expressionless as always.

"Sorry," Cal said. "It's over, I think. There's nothing we can do."

Adam took Cal's head, holding it against his chest. Cal rested there, hearing the beat of the boy's heart, as fast as a rabbit's. It should be the other way around, he thought. He should be comforting the kid. He pulled away, wrapped his hands around Adam's waist, hugging him.

"You've been so brave," he said. "I'm sorry this had to happen to you."

Adam looked up to the horizon and Cal followed his gaze, seeing more of the world slip down the throat of the beast. The sea was making a noise the like of which he'd never heard, a sonic groan that sounded almost human, as if the ocean couldn't believe what was happening to it.

Please, he said to his angel. *I'm begging you. I need you.* He put a hand to his chest. Maybe pleading with it was the wrong way to go. Maybe it needed a different kind of encouragement—like a gun to its head.

"I need you to wait here," he said. "Promise you won't follow me, yeah?"

Cal rested both hands on the boy's face, holding him.

"It will be okay. If you don't see me again, go back into the trees. Someone will find you. Pretend it's a game, like hide-and-seek. Go back in the forest, find a place to hide. Just for a while, then . . ." He swallowed, tried to cough out the lump in his throat. "You miss your mum? Your dad?"

Adam turned those big eyes to Cal.

"I miss my mum so much," Cal said. "I think . . . I think we'll see them again soon. It won't be long, yeah?"

He let go of the boy, and turned back toward the ravine. From up here it looked bottomless, like it led right to the very center of the earth. This was so stupid, it was insane, but what choice did he have?

He took a deep breath, leaned forward, and let himself go.

BRICK / *Clear Lake, California, 2:42 p.m.*

HIS LANDING WAS MESSY, his wings getting in the way as he materialized, tripping him up. The ground rose up too quickly and he covered his head with his hands, crying out, the sound tearing its way through grass and then rock and then water. He tumbled head over heels, hearing the crack of ice as it formed around him, momentum carrying him across the surface of a lake then throwing him up the other side where he eventually rolled to a halt.

There was no pain. He didn't think he could feel pain in this state. There was relief, though. He'd gotten away. He didn't have to fight. He sat up, the world a shifting myriad of atoms and molecules that should have been dizzying but which somehow made sense. Holding up a hand he could see the things he was made of, the cells of skin and bone and muscle and fat, the shifting current of his blood, and the fire that burned, somehow inside him and outside at the same time, making him look transparent. There was a dark stain against his burning skin, and it took him a moment to understand that he was seeing it *through* his hand. He dropped it to his side, seeing a cloud of smoke in the sky over the distant hills. He hadn't gone far enough.

He got to his feet, lifting himself up by just thinking about it. How many times in his life had he wished for power like this? The power to do whatever the hell he wanted.

That made him think of Rilke, and he shuddered. *She deserved it,* he told himself. *She had it coming, ever since she killed Lisa.* But the words made his gut churn.

He tried to forget about it, reaching deep into his head and switching off the angel. That was the best way to think about it, as a machine, a suit. The angel was the powerful one, but it didn't have any control. It could only do what he told it to. He wasn't quite sure why, but it made sense in a way. They couldn't survive here, in this reality, by themselves. They had to live inside you, like a parasite in a host. And once there they didn't have any choice but to go along with what you wanted. He was pretty sure his angel was trying to communicate with him, was probably trying to tell him to go back, to fight the beast. Well, tough.

The flames flickered out, and he felt a moment of discomfort as his wings folded themselves back into his spine. Being human again wasn't pleasant. He felt too real, nothing but meat and gristle. His teeth felt awkward inside his mouth, big and blunt and loose. He was tired too, and when he ran a hand over his hair he came away with strands of copper between his fingers. He shook them away.

Seeing with his old eyes was good, though. He was in a field. No, a valley maybe. There were no crops here, just wildflowers. The lake he'd hit on the way down was huge, stretching all the way to the horizon, the surface still agitated from the impact.

Along the closest bank were a few houses. Maybe he'd be able to get some food there. He was starving.

He set off, the sun like a second skin, making him itch. The heat reminded him of home, of Hemmingway, and that in turn made him think of Daisy. *You left her, all by herself, left her to die.* He carried on, forcing himself to forget. The first house was close, a big, wooden thing that might have been a ranch or something. There were horses in the garden, a few of them looking up at him with big black eyes, their tails swishing. What was he going to do? Knock on the door and ask for a sandwich? Just go in and help himself? It's not like anyone could stop him, not now.

He'd taken another few steps when a door opened in the house, an old woman stepping out. She was holding a basket of something, washing maybe, and was so focused on getting down the porch steps that it took her a while to notice Brick. When she did, she flinched.

"Hello?" she said in an American accent. "Can I help you?"

"I'm hungry," he said, not sure what else to say. "I haven't eaten in a while."

"Oh . . ." The woman backed up toward the door as Brick kept on walking. "I'm afraid you'll have to go. We don't feed migrants here. There's a town around the lake where you might be able to find a . . . a . . ."

Brick cocked his head, trying to make out what she was saying. Her words were long and wet, shapeless, and one side of her face had sloped, like she was having a stroke. The basket slipped from her fingers, spilling laundry over the ground. Then she was running, coming straight for him, her eyes two blisters of hate almost bursting from her face. Brick swore, retreating. How the hell could he have forgotten about the Fury?

"Wait," he said, turning, tripping on his own legs. He fell, landing awkwardly, a bolt of lightning-sharp pain firing up his left wrist. He pushed himself up but it was too late, the old lady's hands around his neck, her nails digging into the skin of his throat. He gagged on the sudden stench of BO and perfume, crying out as her fingers gouged a path up his cheek.

Panic ignited the force inside him, the *whump* of flames filling his ears, followed by the thrum of the angel. He launched himself upward.

"Go away!" he said, the words causing the old woman to erupt into a red mist, blasting the wooden house into splinters. The force of it knocked him back and he cried out again, a sound that hit the lake like a rocket, the water splashing. *Calm down,* he ordered himself, not daring to move, just hovering there above the frozen grass. There was movement from the other houses now, people brought out by the sound of the explosion.

Time to go. He rose up, ready to fire himself away from this place, feeling the air around him twitch and wobble as the angel started to pull reality apart. He was on the verge of transporting, the world beginning to melt away, when he spotted the shape in the sky—another flame, just like his. He stopped, peering into the sun as the angel got closer. It would be Daisy, coming to plead with him. It wouldn't work. He'd made up his mind.

Leave me alone, he said, keeping his words inside his head this time where they wouldn't do any harm, knowing she'd hear them anyway. *Just go away, Daisy, I'm tired of all this.*

She replied, but he couldn't make any sense of it, catching snippets of words—

Rilke, he realized, and by the time he'd thought her name she was on him, a scream ripping across the valley hard enough to create a tsunami of dirt. The shock wave punched him backward, through the wreckage of the farmhouse and the one behind it. He curled his wings around himself, the fire protecting him, but there was no time to recover before she attacked again. He felt himself lifted off the ground, and *now* there was pain, like his spine was being ripped out. Rilke swam up before him, her burning fingers dancing in the air, pulling invisible wires in his skin.

Here he is, she said, her words echoing around the dome of Brick's skull. *Here he is, Schiller, the tall boy. Shall we break him? Shall we pull off his wings like a butterfly? Mother will be so proud.*

Her face was an angel's, her eyes two pockets of rancid sunlight, and yet past the fire, barely visible, he could see the girl's true expression—and it terrified him. It was loose, slack, like a badly painted doll. There was still a hole in her head, the one he had made. She had always been mad, but he'd done this to her. Anything good left in her had leaked out of that hole, dribbled away. It had left her a broken, empty thing.

No! he said, struggling against her. *I'm sorry, I didn't mean to!*

She wrenched his head up, like she was trying to pull the cork from a bottle. He spat out a gargled cry, his arms cartwheeling. Something popped, a vertebra, and this time he fought back, shouting at Rilke, letting his angel speak. The word fired upward, rumbling across the valley like thunder. It missed her and he tried again, screaming this time, his ears ringing with the strength of it. It struck her like a sledgehammer, but he didn't wait to see what would happen. He closed his eyes, burned a hole in the world, and stepped through.

HE FELL, THE RUSH OF WIND STEALING EVERY BREATH from his body. He crunched off the side of the ravine, the pain lost in the roar of adrenaline. Then he was spinning, hitting the wall again, everything going black. There was no indication that the angel was waking. But it was *so* cold down here, freezing. He felt like he was plummeting into the heart of a glacier. That had to mean he was changing, right?

Another impact, although there was no pain this time. *Come on, you bastard, it's now or never.* If he hit the bottom of the ravine before transforming, then both he and his angel would die. The chill was spreading, seeming to radiate from his chest. He tried to look at his hands but it was too dark and he was falling too fast, spinning in wild circles, feeling like a skydiver whose parachute had to be opened by someone else. Something burst from his skin, a flicker of flame that was blown out instantly by the wind.

That's it!

Another trembling flame swept over his body, fading as fast as it had appeared. In the flash of light he could see the walls of the ravine narrowing. He was going to hit the bottom, he was going to—

He felt it surge up from inside him, a cold shape that clawed its way free from his soul, that screamed like a newborn baby as it erupted into fire. He balked at the horror of it, fighting it, suddenly wanting to die rather than be host to the creature inside him. He thrashed, the movement jerking him sideways *through* the rock, detonating it into splinters. He opened his mouth and unleashed a howl that cracked open the earth, splitting it like an ax through wood. He cried out again, feeling two impossible shapes fold themselves out of his spine, sails of pure energy that cleaved through everything around him, carrying him upward until he burst from the ground.

He forced himself to stop, to hang there, a hundred meters up, the land laid out below him. His horror was gone, replaced by an excitement that roiled inside his gut. The angel thrummed, its fire in every cell, the sonic pulse of its heartbeat making the air sing. He'd never imagined it would feel like this, like he could take the whole world in his fist and crush it. He'd never imagined it would feel so *good*. Every other emotion—the fear, the helplessness he'd felt just minutes before—was gone.

"About—" he said, the word rocketing from his mouth so hard that he did a backflip. He thrust out his wings like he'd had them all his life, steadying himself.

"Whoa," he said, his lips tingling. He finished inside his head, thinking, *About time. I didn't think you were ever going to show up*.

If the angel understood him it showed no sign of it. He felt no glimmer of humanity there, nothing familiar at all. He pulled in his wings, starting to dive. The roar of wind in his ears reminded him of playing football, the sheer joy of running as fast as he could. The world rushed up to meet him, a constellation of golden particles, billions upon billions of them, each moving in its own little orbit, every single one connected in some way. He could dive right through them if he wanted, part reality like a swimmer through water. He laughed, the exhilaration bubbling up his throat as he extended his wings again and came to a halt, remembered *why* the angel was here.

Ahead of him, the horizon was broken. It looked different now, through his angel's eyes. It wasn't just that the earth had collapsed there, it had been *erased*. There were pockets of complete emptiness, none of those subatomic cogs and wheels that he could make out everywhere else. The man in the storm had eaten them. He'd left absolutely nothing.

And he was still down there.

Daisy, he thought, wondering how he could have forgotten her, even for an instant.

He focused, pulling himself free of the world again, tracking her. He materialized instantly, life locking the door behind him with a clang that made his head hurt. When the halo of embers cleared he was back in the forest. Daisy was a bundle of rags sitting up against a tree.

Cal switched off the engine of his angel and dropped down beside her. He couldn't believe how old she looked, bright white streaks in her hair. Her eyes were dark and full of sadness.

"Daisy," he said, walking to her. Specks of dust drifted upward from her body, defying gravity, as if she were disintegrating. He kneeled down beside her and put a hand on her face. She was so cold.

She put her hand on top of his. The whole forest shook with the rage of the distant storm, even the birds quiet now.

"Adam?" she asked. Cal looked over his shoulder, trying to work out where they were, where he'd left the boy. He opened his mouth to tell Daisy what had happened, only to see her vanish in a pillar of flame. The air popped as it filled the space where she had just been, barely having time to settle before she reappeared in a storm of glowing ash, Adam clamped to her chest. The boy's eyes bulged, and he sprayed milky vomit over her shirt.

"Sorry," she said to him, wiping his mouth. Adam was shaking, but Cal wasn't sure if it was because he was scared or if it was just the tremors from the ground.

"What happened?" Cal asked. "Did you see him down there? The man in the storm, I mean."

Daisy nodded, swallowing noisily.

"He's even more powerful than before," she said. "He almost ate me. I . . . think I saw . . ."

She sighed, her whole body juddering.

"Saw what?" Cal asked.

"Where he comes from," she replied. "What he is."

He sat down next to her on the soft, wet ground, put his hand on her shoulder. He didn't push her, just waited for her to find her words.

"Do you know about black holes?" she asked eventually.

Cal nodded. "Collapsed stars or something."

"I don't know," she said. "But they eat stuff, don't they? Like, everything. Light. They just eat until there's nothing left."

"Daisy," he started, realizing he had nothing to follow it with.

"The man in the storm, he's like a black hole," she said, smudging a tear from her eye. "Because he'll never stop, not until . . ." She swung her arms up. "Not until everything is gone."

"It's not a black hole, it can't be," he said.

But maybe something like it, he thought, something just as powerful. Was she right? Would it keep eating and eating until the whole planet was just dust? Would it stop then or would it swallow the moon, too, and the sun, turn this little pocket of the universe inside out?

Daisy looked up at him, sniffing, just that little girl he'd picked up in his car a million years ago. It was eating her, too. The fear, the doubt. The storm had sucked up everything else. He saw the question in her expression.

"We *can* beat it, Dais. We have to."

She nodded, taking a deep breath, seeming to steady herself.

"We need all of us," she said, her voice little more than a whisper.

"All of us? You mean Brick? Wasn't he in there with you?"

"He ran away," she said. He opened his mouth, ready to vent, but she beat him to it. "He's just scared, Cal, it's not his fault. He'll come back, I know he will."

Don't count on it, he thought. This was Brick, after all. He'd let the whole world burn if it meant saving his own ass.

"Where's the new guy?" Cal asked. "Was he with you or did he run away too?"

"Howie. He was there. I . . . I don't know where he went."

Cal hadn't felt another death, not like when Chris had been killed back at Fursville.

"Rilke's gone after Brick," Daisy said. "I tried to talk to her, but . . ."

"But she's Rilke," he said.

"And she's broken, Cal. Brick hurt her too much, I don't think she can be fixed. We need her back, though. We need everyone, or we won't be able to fight him."

Schiller was dead. And Chris. Jade too, he'd felt her go, snuffed out like a candle flame. And maybe Howie as well. What about the others? The man with the gun, back in Fursville, the one that Rilke had shot. He'd had an angel inside him. The person in the burning car, the one he'd passed when he was driving out of London. The people that Marcus had traveled with. They had been killed on the way. How many more?

There might have been dozens of us. Hundreds. But they never stood a chance, not with the Fury. It didn't make any sense. Why hadn't the angels just picked a hundred people in the same room?

"I don't think they had a choice," Daisy said, coughing again. "When they cross over from their world they have to get inside the first person they see, or they won't survive."

How did she know that?

Daisy shrugged. "I just think it, that's all. And there aren't hundreds of us. I don't think there is anyone left, only us."

Cal shook his head, staring between the trees. The sky was darker now, over the pit.

"Only us," Daisy said. "But it's enough, Cal. We're enough. You're right, we can beat him."

"So how do we do it?" he asked. She didn't have time to reply before there was a clatter of branches. A skinny figure ducked under a tree and skidded to a halt beside them. Marcus grinned, his face crisscrossed with scratches.

"Thought you could hide from me, eh?" he said. Daisy laughed, the sound somehow louder than the thundering earth.

"You okay, mate?" said Cal. "Found a way down?"

"No, you found a way up," he said. "So what's the plan? Fly home, kick back, take it easy?"

Cal smiled despite himself. How could he be so relaxed? He didn't understand why they weren't all curled up in a corner somewhere, screaming and sobbing and pulling out their hair. Wasn't this enough to drive a person crazy, leave them a gibbering wreck? It could still be the shock of it, he guessed, a delayed reaction. If they got through this, they might all end up in the loony bin.

"It's the angels, silly," said Daisy, once again plucking the thoughts from his head. "They're keeping us safe in more ways than one."

"You need to stay out of my brain, Daisy," he said. "I'm a teenage boy. There are things in there you don't want to see."

"Like Georgia?"

"Shut up," he said, reaching into her head, seeing a boy there, onstage, the image so clear it could have been his own memory. "Or I'll start going on about Fred."

"Hey!" she said, backhanding him gently. "Don't go there, mister."

They laughed quietly, then sat in silence listening to the distant storm.

"First things first," said Daisy. "We find Brick and the others. We can't do this without them."

"Easier said than . . ." Cal stopped, cocked his head. His ears were ringing, like the morning after a concert. "Hey, you hear that?"

"It's stopped," said Daisy.

That's what it was. The storm had grown quiet, so suddenly and so completely that the silence in the forest was almost unnerving. He stuck a finger in his ear, flexing his jaw like he'd gone deaf.

"You think it's gone?" Marcus asked.

"No," said Daisy, sitting forward, her eyes darting back and forth as she listened. "I don't think so. It's just moved."

"Moved where?" Cal asked.

The ringing in his ears grew louder, and the forest lit up, full of fire. A shape crashed between the trees, thudding into the soil, glowing with such strength that Cal couldn't make out the form inside until the flames guttered out. He blinked the spots of light from his vision, seeing the new kid crouching on the ground.

"Howie!" said Daisy.

"Got lost when I transported, or whatever it is. Somewhere dark, cold. Thought I was never gonna get back. What about you, saw you get sucked in."

"I got out," she said.

Howie rolled onto his backside, looking exhausted. He looked frightened too. "I think he saw me."

"Saw you?" Cal asked. "What do you mean?"

"The man in the storm," Howie said. "I think he knows where I went. I think he's coming."

BRICK / *Rio de Janeiro, 2:52 p.m.*

HE BURST FROM THE SKY LIKE LIGHTNING, unleashing a peal of thunder as the world re-formed around him. Disoriented, he stumbled, crashing into a sheet of corrugated iron. It was a house of some kind, or a shed, his cold fire reflected in the dull metal. He whirled around, his wings slicing through it, blowing it to dust. There were similar buildings everywhere, hundreds of them, stretching down a hillside. In the distance was another city, and another ocean. He saw a mountain with a huge statue on top that he half recognized from TV.

Where the hell was he?

A noise behind him, somebody shrieking. He turned again, seeing a face appear between two of the buildings. It was a kid, but the expression belonged to an animal, full of wild rage. Others took up the boy's cry until the place sounded like a zoo at feeding time. Footsteps pounded the dirt as they came for him, swarming from all directions, their eyes bulging, their hands twisted into claws.

Go away! he yelled, trying to hold his words in his throat where they couldn't cause any harm. Even so, the thought seemed to have power of its own, rippling over the buildings and turning the first line of ferals to ash. *No, I'm sorry, I'm sorry!* he said, flapping his wings, the sheer size of them kicking the cloud of powdered flesh and bone into whirlwinds that darted playfully between the buildings. He soared, seeing the ferals below, hundreds of them now, trampling each other to reach him.

Something detonated in the sky, a shock wave blasting over the favela, flattening the tin houses and everything else. Brick held up his hands to shield himself from it, and through his fingers he saw Rilke cannon earthward. She was on him in a split second, the impact punching him down through metal and soil and rock, like he was being slammed into his grave by a freight train. He felt the fingers of her mind worm into his head, into his heart, trying to undo him, and he swore at her, each word a hammer blow that forced her back.

Brick squirmed loose, his angel burning at full strength, its electrical hum the loudest thing in the world. He rocketed up the channel that he'd carved in the rock, escaping into sunlight. Rilke was waiting for him, hovering, so bright it was as if the sun had fallen out of the sky. All around her was a crater of destruction. People were still streaming across the wreckage, stumbling over the corpses of their friends and neighbors, blinded by their own instinctive hate.

He stretched out his wings, ready to flee again, but Rilke grabbed him with invisible hands, holding him there. She clamped something over his mouth, a fist of air wedged down his throat. How could she be so strong when she was so broken?

I'm sorry, Rilke, he said.

Look at him, Schill, he heard her say. *Look at him beg, like a dog. What shall we do with him? Shall we do to him what he did to you?*

Brick struggled, unable to prize himself loose. He couldn't even force a word up his blocked windpipe.

You killed him, Rilke screeched, a witch's cackle between his ears. *You killed my brother.*

No was as far as he got before Rilke opened her mouth and spat out a sound. It wasn't quite a word, just a wet, gargled noise, but it came from her angel, and when it struck him he thought the entire universe had been turned upside down. He hit the ground again, rolling through steel and rock. Even past the chill of the fire he could feel the agony of it, like he was in a giant tumble dryer with hundreds of pins and needles.

It seemed like forever before he finally stopped moving. He pushed himself up from the ground, his angel no longer burning. Liquid dripped from his face, impossibly hot against his skin, and when he put his fingers to it they came away red.

No, he thought, his ears ringing so much that he didn't hear the ferals until the first one had him by the throat. He grunted, trying to work the fingers loose, only to feel something collide with his cheek, a fist or a boot. Colorless fireworks danced against the sky, gouging holes in his vision. He tried to kick-start his angel the way he used to kick-start his motorbike, but he didn't know how. A long, dirty nail jabbed into his eye and he screamed.

More ferals were on him, so many that they blocked out the sun. Not so many that they hid Rilke as she sailed through the air, her wings unfurled. He could hear a noise over the pounding thrum of her angel, high-pitched and ugly, like a nail against glass. She was laughing.

His anger clawed up from his stomach, an inferno erupting from every pore. It incinerated the crowd, shunting Rilke backward, letting him push himself from the ground.

He didn't give her a chance to recover. He swung his arms like this was a bar brawl, each strike lobbing great gobs of energy through the air. Most of them missed her, carving trenches down the hill, through the city, lashing across the distant ocean. He shouted too, not caring what he was saying, letting the angel speak for him. Rilke fought back, bolts of lightning crackling in all directions as the air between them was churned into a fever.

One of his assaults must have landed, because suddenly Rilke was cartwheeling, burning like a Catherine wheel as she vanished into a sea of debris. Brick swiped his hand through the air, invisible fingers lifting up a thousand tons of metal and wood and people, crunching it into a ball. He flicked it out into the water.

She had to be dead, that had to have finished her.

The ocean exploded, Rilke blazing up from it like a missile fired from a submarine. She vanished, reappearing instantly in the sky above him. Her fire flared up and she disappeared again, then again, filling the air with embers. He could hear her voice fading in and out, still laced with insanity.

She pulled herself out of reality again, and this time when she re-formed she was right behind him, her fire casting his golden shadow out over the land. She wrapped her arms around him, hers *and* the angel's, locking his own against his sides. The sound their angels made together was unbelievable, the thrum so loud that he could see rocks dancing on the ground below, everything solid turned to liquid. Sparks hissed and cracked around them, as if the world couldn't take it, as if it was about to explode.

"Should have left him alone," she said, her lips against his ear, the words ricocheting off his armor of fire in every direction. The air was growing more agitated, groaning against the force of them. In the distance the city was crumbling, tower blocks blown to dust. The immense statue snapped in two and toppled, half of the hillside collapsing after it.

He fought her, trying to pry himself loose, but he just couldn't budge. The earth beneath them was being pushed away, like a helicopter hovering over water, forming an immense crater. The sonic pulse of the angels grew louder, rising in pitch. Still those flashes of light—white and gold and blue and orange—snapped out like whips, each one making the sky shake. He could barely hear Rilke past the roar of it.

"You shouldn't have broken us."

I didn't! he yelled at her. "I didn't! It was the man in the storm! He killed your brother!"

His words must have rung true, because he felt her grip loosen. He took his chance, burrowing out of her arms. The moment he broke contact something detonated in the space between them. It was like another nuclear explosion, propelling him upward on a wave of light. It took him a moment to find his wings, stretching them out and bringing himself to a halt, his eyes bulging at the sight of what they'd done.

The force of their explosion had left nothing—no buildings, no people, no water—just a desert of sandy-colored dust from horizon to horizon. The ocean bubbled across the distant land as it tried to level itself, the roar of it audible even from up here. The air rose and fell around him, the planet catching its breath, the odd crackling spark darting up toward the sky.

I didn't do that, he told himself, his own heart pounding almost as hard as the angel's. *It was her, she did it, she killed them, not me.*

There was no sign of Rilke anywhere. Maybe she'd blown herself up, ripped herself into atoms, scattered them over the boundless grave below. A murder-suicide. It was just as well, as Brick had never felt so weak, so tired, even with the fire coursing through his veins.

Something drew his attention to the sun and he turned his head up, seeing it split in two. Rilke dropped toward him, her scream kicking up the dust of the dead, churning the ash into dunes. He lifted his arms, ready to defend himself, realizing even as he did so that he couldn't beat her, not by himself.

He cast his mind out, opening up the fabric of time and space and stepping through. This time, he knew exactly where he was going.

DAISY / *San Francisco, 3:01 p.m.*

"HE'S COMING."

Howie had barely finished speaking when Daisy heard a pistol crack in the air above the forest. She looked up through the branches as a streak of black lightning split the sky in two, so dark that it scarred her retinas. A second followed, clouds of darkness seeping from the broken air like ink spilled in water.

Thunder dripped down from the ruptured sky, filling the forest with noise.

"Get ready," said Cal. "Whatever happens, stay together, yeah?"

The sky was now filthy with smoke, gouts of ugly black fire spraying from the center of the chaos like poisoned solar flares. A shape was forming in the churning madness, two huge wings that beat with enough strength to crack the trunks of the trees, strip them of every single needle. The beast roared as it pulled itself free, an *inward* roar, like a deafening asthmatic breath. Its face was hidden by smoke but Daisy could see the silhouette of its mouth there, the darkest thing in the sky.

"Stay together," Cal said again, shouting now. "How do we do this?"

Daisy glanced at him, then at Howie, then at Marcus, who held Adam in his skinny arms. They were all staring at her, waiting for an answer. But why? Why did they think she knew what to do?

Only . . . she *did*. The truth was somewhere deep inside her, yelling as loud as it could, telling her that if they stood their ground here and tried to fight the man in the storm then they would all die.

The beast was hauling itself from the emptiness behind the world, tearing reality to shreds. That same horrid feeling seeped out with it, sucking all the warmth from the day, all the goodness, making Daisy feel like she could just cry and cry and cry and never stop. There was nothing above her but an upside-down ocean of boiling tar, the sun a faint halo. It was like night had fallen, suddenly and without warning. The man's eyes were dark spotlights that scoured the forest, searching for them. Its gasping breath sucked up trees and roots and rocks. It hadn't seen them yet, though.

She felt it before she saw it, Cal's transformation pumping out a vibration across the clearing.

"Wait!" she shouted, but he had already shed his human skin, a blast furnace erupting in the hollows of his eyes, spreading out over his body. His wings thrust up from his back, a burning beacon that turned night into day once again. The beast shifted his lightless gaze to where they stood, and she could almost sense the rancid joy there as he realized he had caught them.

Daisy dived into her head, unlocking the door and letting her angel out. Howie did the same, erupting into flame. She looked up with her angel's eyes and saw the man attack with a fist of smoke, knuckles of liquid night thrashing at the ground, exploding trees into splinters. It hammered down like a meteor, impossibly fast.

She reached out with her mind and grabbed time in her burning fingers. It was like trying to hold back a Doberman on its leash; she could feel herself being dragged along behind it. But she dug her heels in, hearing the aching groan of the universe as its rules were broken, every single atom shuddering in protest.

I can't hold it, she said, seeing the sky fall in slow motion, waiting for the moment it struck her and everything ended. Cal knew what to do, though, opening a door and pulling them through—first Marcus and Adam, then Howie, then her—letting it slam shut behind them.

Daisy looked back as reality closed, seeing the fist of storm strike the ground where they had been, cleaving a giant hole in the world. Then time shook itself free from her grasp, her stomach doing a dance as they burned themselves back. Through the flurry of glowing embers she could see the others, two angels who glowed like molten steel, plus Adam and Marcus wrapped in each other's arms, a blue fire burning beneath the skin of their chests.

The world lurched back into place, fluttering for a moment like a piece of stage scenery about to topple. When it had settled she made out a landscape of ice and snow, a ridge of mountains jutting from the horizon like teeth. It was almost dark.

Daisy lowered herself to the ground, switching off her angel to let it rest. As soon as she had she regretted it; it was *freezing* here, the wind like a dead person's fingers running up and down her back.

"Little warning?" said Marcus, wiping puke from his mouth. He and Adam were doubled over, a pool of white sick beneath them. "I don't mind being dragged all around the world, but give me a chance to prepare, yeah? Never mind the puke, I think I might have just cacked myself."

Daisy laughed through a shiver. Adam ran to her and she wrapped her arms around him.

"Could have brought us somewhere warmer too," said Marcus, his teeth chattering.

"Sorry," Cal replied. "I haven't exactly got the hang of this, yet. Besides, it's quiet, nobody around to try and kill us."

"Should've fought," said Howie, shaking his head. "Now it knows we're scared."

"We couldn't have won," said Daisy. "It would have been suicide." The word caught in her throat, images of her mum lying dead in the bed. *We would have hurt you.* "We weren't strong enough."

"How do you know?" Howie spat.

"Mate," said Cal. "That's enough. None of us have any idea what's going on, but Daisy, she knows things. She has right from the start. You can do what you like, but I trust her."

Cal flashed her a smile and she returned it, although it was quite difficult because the muscles in her face were frozen. Howie just swiped an arm through the air, dismissing them, turning away to study the distant mountains, nestled in twilight.

"We *can* beat him," Daisy said. "But we need everyone. Brick and Rilke."

"Rilke?" said Marcus. "She has to be dead by now, after what he did to her."

"You and Adam too," Daisy went on. "We need your angels to hatch."

"Yeah, I've been trying," said Marcus, prodding himself in the chest. "Bloody thing isn't paying the slightest bit of attention to me. I must have got the laziest angel in the whole . . . I don't know, angel place."

"Why do you call them angels?" Howie said over his shoulder.

"You know," said Cal. "Fire, wings, flying, beating the crap out of a big, bad devil in the sky. Pretty obvious really."

"You sure?" said Howie. "What if they're on his side, what if we're supposed to be helping the man in the storm?"

"Don't you bloody start with all that," said Cal. "Heard it from Rilke, and look where it got her."

Howie held up his hands in surrender. "Just trying to cover all the bases, is all. Not easy going from walking around drunk on a beach to being possessed by a not-quite-angel who wants to save the world from certain destruction."

"You were drunk?" asked Daisy. "How old are you?"

"Thirteen," he said. "Plenty old enough."

"You *still* drunk?" said Cal. Howie smiled.

"No, unfortunately. Think a bottle of rum might make all this a bit easier to cope with."

"Ew," said Daisy. They were silent for a while, and she turned inward, speaking to her angel. *Is he right? Are you good? Have you been here before?* It gave no answer, sitting there like a statue in her soul.

"So, how do we do it?" Marcus asked. "Might take days for my angel to wake up. By then there won't be anything left to save."

"Not necessarily," said Cal. "There's a way of . . . of motivating them."

"Yeah?"

Cal nodded, but instead of speaking he seemed to beam out an image of it. Daisy saw him standing on the edge of a cliff, then tumbling over it. If his angel hadn't woken then it would have died, Cal too. That had been a huge gamble.

"Whoa, dude, no way!" Marcus said. "You're insane. No way I'm making a leap of faith like that."

"Just an idea," Cal said. "Got a better one?"

"I might," said Daisy.

She smiled at Marcus, firing up her angel, looking at the blue flame in his chest, the way it strained out, trying to reach her. He backed off, squinting against the brightness of her eyes, muttering, "Why do I think I might not like this?"

CAL / *Manang, Nepal, 3:15 p.m.*

Trust me, Daisy said. *It doesn't hurt.*

Cal watched as she floated toward Marcus, her fire blazing but giving off no heat. Fingers of light reached up from the snow, crumbling away almost instantly. The air drummed with the strength of her, sounding like a dozen guitar amps racked up to full volume. Her eyes were like pools of liquid sunlight and Cal still felt the fear tickle his spine, the unreality of it.

"Yeah?" Marcus replied, taking an uncertain step back. "I gotta take your word for that?"

Daisy didn't answer, just stretched out her hand and reached toward Marcus's chest. Cal couldn't see anything there until he flicked the psychic switch and fired up his angel. Suddenly Marcus was an engine of parts, his chest filled with blue fire. Those flames seemed to stretch out toward Daisy, reaching for her. Her fingers were pure fire, ghosting through Marcus's shirt and into his skin.

"Whoa whoa *whoa*!" Marcus yelled, stepping back, his path blocked by Howie. "That's not cool, Dais, just—"

It will be okay, she persisted. The blade of her flattened hand sliced into him like a surgeon's scalpel, her fingertips touching the fire that burned in his chest. As soon as she made contact there was a sharp crack, and Daisy flew back, as if she'd stuck her finger in an electrical socket. She was grinning, though, because Marcus's fire was spreading out from his chest, through his veins and out of his pores. He fought it, slapping his skin, dancing on the spot like he'd been doused in lighter fluid. He was yelping out swear words, cursing Daisy with every breath.

Don't fight it, she said. *See, it doesn't hurt, does it?*

He didn't answer, just pranced about kicking up drifts of snow. Those cold blue flames flickered up and down, trying to find purchase, until suddenly they roared to life, red and orange and gold. Marcus screamed into the air, the noise echoing off the distant mountains. His eyes filled with firelight, spitting out sparks. He dropped onto all fours as a wing broke free of his back, sweeping down, pulling him up at an angle. He turned awkwardly in midair, crashing back among them. Cal had to launch himself out of the way as Marcus squirmed on the ground, ripping out chunks of rock with his new hands.

Only when his other wing slid free did he seem to calm down, hovering a meter or so off the ground. His chest was heaving, even though Cal was pretty sure they didn't actually need to breathe when they were this way. Marcus spun upright and lifted his hands to his face, studying his new skin.

"Coo—" The syllable ricocheted between them and Marcus clamped a hand to his mouth.

Indoor voice, said Daisy.

This one? he replied, his words in Cal's head, weak but growing stronger. *Whoa, I . . . This . . . It's insane, man. It's got to be a dream.*

If it is, we're all having it, said Cal.

Daisy knelt down beside Adam, her burning hand resting on his shoulder. The little boy didn't look scared, didn't look much of anything, really. But his big eyes were full of trust as he gazed at her.

You don't have to do it if you don't want to. But it's not scary, Adam, they're here to look after us.

Just leave him, said Howie as he shrugged on his angel. *He's a kid, he won't be any good in a fight anyway.*

That was probably true, but even if he didn't fight at least the angel would keep him safe. The little flame in his chest was straining out toward Daisy, and she gently pushed her hand toward it.

She made contact, releasing another supernova of light and sound. Cal had to turn away this time, and when he looked back he saw Daisy and Adam in the air, leaving a trail of billowing flame in their wake. The little boy was struggling—Cal didn't so much see this as feel it—but Daisy held on to him, refusing to let go. Thunder ripped across the sky, then a flash of lightning as Adam turned. After a minute or two, both angels descended, not quite touching down on the snow.

You okay? Cal asked. Adam nodded, his eyes two pools of molten ore, unblinking.

He was such a brave boy, said Daisy. *I knew he would be.*

Adam smiled up at her, his wings twitching above his head.

Cal waited, wondering if he would speak now that he didn't have to open his mouth. There was no sign of him, though, in the jumble of voices in his head. Whatever the boy had been through when the Fury began, it had broken more than just his voice.

Give him a chance, Daisy said, collecting Cal's thoughts like butterflies in a net. *He'll speak soon, I know he will.*

Cal nodded, and for a moment they hung there, all five of them, their wings arching up into the fading day, the tips almost touching. Their angels scattered light and sound across the snow, making everything seem like it was dancing. Even the mountains rumbled against the horizon, trembling like they were afraid. *And they should be,* Cal thought. *Because we're ready now.*

Just one thing, Daisy replied, staring past Cal, past the mountains, over continents and oceans. *We need to find Brick, Rilke too.*

He isn't coming back, said Cal. *I know you have faith in him, Dais, but trust me, right now Brick is about as far away from the man in the storm as it's possible to get, and we're the last people he wants to see.*

BRICK / *San Francisco, 3:18 p.m.*

THEY HAD TO STILL BE THERE, THEY HAD TO HELP HIM.

Brick followed the path he'd made just minutes before, on autopilot, letting his angel guide him through the space behind the universe. When he was spat back into the real world, it was night instead of day, and where the forest had once stood was now a featureless expanse of dirt that stretched all the way to the broken horizon. Wind thumped against him as he tried to land, like fists, the hum of his angel's heart so loud that it took him a moment to notice the rumble of thunder overhead.

The man in the storm hung in the sky, looking like a giant crow in a nest of darkness. His wings towered out to either side of him, made of a fire the color of smoke and oil. Between them was a gyre that turned and turned, a tornado that sucked up everything in sight. Brick felt its cold touch on his skin, wrenching him up along with the fracturing rock of the hillside. He tumbled in midair, calling out with his mind and his voice together, barely able to hear himself.

Where the hell were they? They'd flown away, left him. The selfish *bastards*. They'd left him to die. He fought to control his wings, beating them to try to pull free of the current. It was too strong, its pull relentless, dragging Brick up into the man's mouth. He swore, the word breaking free of his lips like a cannonball of light, slicing across the land in completely the wrong direction.

"Help!" he screamed, trying to burn himself away like he had with Rilke. Rilke, she'd been a puppy compared to this.

He tried to hear Daisy's voice, Cal's, anyone's, but it was like his ears had been pounded into mush. The entire universe turned around him, growing darker and colder, closing around his head. He was spinning too fast even to see where he was going, the man's vast, grinding maw appearing then disappearing with impossible speed.

He unfurled his wings to steady himself, swiping a hand through the air and lobbing a gout of energy at the thing above him. He opened his mouth and cursed it, howling his fury at the beast. The man in the storm didn't even seem to feel it, that relentless turbine breath still sucking him upward. Brick spun around, the earth so far beneath him now he could see the curve of the horizon. He pumped his wings, his legs, his hands, like he was swimming, desperately trying to get purchase. But the current of air was merciless.

"No! I won't let you!" he screamed. The world was growing dark as he was pulled into the storm clouds, the noise of the man's mouth pummeling his brain. "I won't!"

He felt so small, so powerless, so pathetic, so *angry*. All his life he'd been furious with the world. He'd carried that anger around with him everywhere he went, never able to let it go. His anger was the reason he'd been where he was when the Fury struck. It was why all this had happened to him. And now it was going to kill him.

No. It didn't have to be that way. He didn't have to be angry. Maybe that's how they functioned, the angels, maybe that's why they tried to numb everything in your head. Maybe they only worked if you weren't angry—weren't sad, weren't happy, weren't afraid. Emotions, they were so *human*, they just got in the way.

He closed his eyes, trying to ignore the rush of wind in his ears, the cold, damp air that clung to his body like soil, like he was in a grave. *Be calm,* he said. His heart didn't obey, drumming a frantic rhythm in his chest, feeling as if it was about to pop under the pressure. *Let it go.* He forced himself to think about the beach back at Hemmingway, the beautiful ocean, as flat and brilliant as tinfoil, nothing there but warmth and silence and stillness.

Sure enough the boiling rage in his gut began to soothe, the flare in the center of his brain fizzling out. In its absence he could sense the angel there, occupying every cell of his body, waiting for him to understand, to do the right thing. There was still something unpleasant coiled around his gut, but he figured this was as close as he was going to get.

Adjusting his wings, he turned to face the storm. He could feel something else burning up from inside him, from inside the angel, a surge of cold heat. It sliced up his windpipe and launched from his lips, so powerful that it set fire to the air. The word carved a path of flame, leaving a trail like a missile as it vanished into the smoke. He waited for the explosion, for the man's face to melt, for him to bellow out a cry of defeat.

Nothing happened.

Brick opened his mouth, waiting for his angel to reload. That tickle of fear was still there, the growing rage.

A barb of black lightning flashed from the vortex, so dark that it was like a tear in reality. It snapped down toward Brick, too fast for him to avoid, cracking as it impacted with his left wing. The pain was so severe, so unlike anything he had ever felt, that at first it didn't even register. Then it hit him, an agony that rocked him to his very core, that seemed to emanate not from his body but from the angel's.

They screamed together as another whipcrack snaked down, punching through his back. Brick looked over his shoulder, saw a darkness latch onto his other wing, gripping it like a kid with a mayfly. He reached behind him, trying to grab hold of it, but he was spinning too fast, rising up and up and up toward the tornado. There was a tearing sound, another bolt of white-hot pain, and when he looked again he saw his wing flutter past him, a sheet of pale fire that bucked and curled on the wind, fading.

His angel screamed again, no power in its voice this time. And, wingless, Brick tumbled up into the storm.

COME OUT, COME OUT, WHEREVER YOU ARE.

Rilke peeked behind the skin of the world, trying to find the boy with wings. Was that what she was doing now? Hide-and-seek? Playing hide-and-seek with Schiller?

No, he's dead, remember? something told her. She reached up with a hand made from glowing ether and touched her forehead. There was a hole there, like a third eye, about the size of her finger. She couldn't for the life of her remember how she'd gotten it. *A boy with wings, a boy with fire for hair, the same boy who killed your brother.*

And she almost saw him in the confusion of her thoughts, a tall boy called Brick. But why was she playing hide-and-seek with *him*? It didn't make any sense, and when she tried to think about it her head pulsed with waves of discomfort, her thoughts jamming like somebody had thrust a stick between two cogs. She let it go. It would come back to her soon enough, she was probably just tired, and . . . and . . .

She looked around, seeing a desert, almost like a beach only the sand beneath her was all different colors—gold and white and gray and red. Little coils of firelight snaked up toward her feet, like fingers reaching for her, only to collapse again after a second or two. She could see every single grain there, and inside them all were little cities of light and matter. It was mesmerizing.

Focus, Rilke, she told herself. *Find the boy. Don't you remember? He broke you?*

That was it! He'd broken her, like she was a doll. And he'd

broken Schiller too. That should have made her angry, but there was nothing inside her other than an infuriating numbness, like she was packed head to toe with cotton wool. That was what happened to broken dolls, wasn't it? Packed up and boxed away, or thrown in the bin.

Something buzzed overhead, a fly, and she reached out with a hand that wasn't really her hand, her invisible fingers plucking the object out of the sky and crushing it. The fly fell to the ground, hitting the sand with a mechanical crash and bursting into flames. There were more of them up there now, hovering overhead making a dull *thud-thud-thud* sound, and she swatted at them, bringing down two more before the rest hovered away. *Great,* now she'd totally forgotten what she was supposed to be doing.

She peeled open the world again, just like opening a door. Something had disturbed the air here, leaving a kind of golden ripple, almost like the wake a boat makes in water. The tall boy obviously wasn't very good at hiding, he'd left a trail for her to follow.

Got you! she said as she stepped through the door. Her body blasted into atoms, a sudden rush like she was going over the top of a waterfall, then she was whole again, the world locking back into place around her. She swiped a hand through the air to clear away the embers, trying to make sense of the chaos.

The sky was alive, a storm in the shape of a man. He thrashed inside a roiling ocean of dark cloud, almost like he was drowning up there. Something about him was familiar, but Rilke didn't know what. The wind here was incredible, a hurricane that did its best to suck her up. It looked like a vast field, one that had just been plowed. In the distance was a hole in the world, like something huge had burrowed up and crawled out of it. She stretched out her wings, locking herself in place, scouring the land to try to find him.

A gunshot, overhead. Was that a shotgun? No, it was too loud. A million shotguns couldn't make a sound like that. She glanced up, into the upturned ocean, seeing a speck of flame against the spiraling dark. *It's him!* She knew it, the boy made of fire. He was disappearing into the smoke, trying to hide from her.

Don't let him go, her brain said. *He broke you, he broke you.* She wouldn't let him hide, not now, not ever. She pushed herself up from the ground, pumping her wings, ascending toward the fire. The tall boy was struggling, tongues of black light wrapping themselves around him. One of them punched through his wings, ripping one away, and she could hear his scream over the ear-pounding clatter of the moving sky. He vanished into the spinning vortex of cloud and she increased her speed. More of those forks of black lightning snapped past her but she wove through them, focusing on the only thing that mattered.

Come out, come out, wherever you are, she said again, giggling as she followed the burning boy into the darkness.

DAISY / *Manang, Nepal, 3:25 p.m.*

YOU READY?

Cal asked the question, staring at her with his angel's eyes. All five of them stood in a circle, drenched in fire. The noise of their hearts was almost liquid, filling her ears, making her head feel funny. She was finding it hard to move as well, like they were all magnets pushing against each other. She wondered what would happen if they all touched, whether it would be too much for this little world. She had a feeling they might just burn a hole clean through it.

Daisy?

She nodded, but it was a lie. She didn't feel ready at all. How could you ever be ready for something like this?

Cal turned to the others, saying, *You guys?*

Marcus shrugged. *Not like I got anything else I need to be doing right now.*

Daisy reached out to Adam, her fingers throwing off bursts of static where they touched his face. He didn't seem to mind, smiling at her. His eyes seemed bottomless. She felt as if she could tumble into those twin pits of fire and never get out again.

We'll keep you safe. But you don't have to fight. As soon as we land just stay hidden.

What do we do about Brick? Cal asked.

He'll be waiting for us, she said. She wasn't sure how she knew that, but she could almost see him there, drowning in darkness. He'd changed his mind, come back to help them, and now he was fighting the beast on his own. She took a deep breath of air she didn't really need, felt both her heartbeats drumming. The angel was doing a good job of keeping her calm, but she was still scared, she could feel it tickling her stomach. It made her feel weak, uncertain, and that made her wonder something else.

I think, she started, then stopped, trying to make sense of her thoughts.

What? asked Cal.

She chewed on it a moment more, then spat it out. *I think we're supposed to be calm,* she said.

Oh, sure, said Howie. *I always feel calm when I'm about to pick a fight with a creature that's trying to eat the world.*

No, Daisy said. *I'm serious. The angels keep us calm, stop the emotions getting in. That's how they fight, maybe. They can only do it if our emotions don't get in the way.*

Yeah? said Cal. When he shrugged, his wings bobbled up and down. *I guess that makes sense.*

Daisy shook her head. All she had was her instinct, and what she'd just said felt right.

So keep the emotions under control, said Marcus. *Cool, check.*

Any other bits of advice? Cal said.

She wished she had some, but there was nothing.

Cal blew out a spluttered breath that made the air tremble.

It all seemed so simple, back in Fursville, he said. *All we had to do there was survive.*

It seemed like months ago that they'd been inside the amusement park. But they had left Hemmingway that morning, less than twelve hours before. It didn't make any sense to Daisy, except she understood that somehow time was different for the angels, different for them now too. For what seemed like forever they all stood in silence.

The tickle of fear had become something else, a wedge of rock in her throat. Even past the dam the angel had built inside her she could feel the tears about to break. *Nice one, Daisy, way to forget about your emotions,* she said to herself, hoping the others wouldn't hear her. They must have, though, because Cal laughed.

Come on, he said. *Before we all start bawling like babies.*

Speak for yourself, said Howie. He spread his wings, flexing them in front of the sun and turning its light into twists of amber.

You doing the honors? Cal asked. Daisy nodded, taking Adam's hand, the air between their fingers crackling like a bonfire. She closed her eyes and opened up the world, a big enough hole to pull everyone through.

Good luck, she said. Then they were gone.

IN THE SPLIT SECOND THEY WERE MOVING he tried to prepare himself, tried to steady his nerves. Then they were there, reality clamping shut around him like a bear trap, sinking its jaws into him to try to lock him in place. They were back where they'd been before, the vast, empty canyon that had once been a city off to his left, the ocean still emptying into it. The whole sky seemed to vibrate for a moment, a crack of thunder echoing across the land as physics adjusted to fit them in. The noise didn't last for long, swallowed up by the storm that raged overhead.

The beast sat there on a throne of smoke, his wings spreading from horizon to horizon, his mouth resembling some immense, diseased moon that hung over the world. There was almost nothing else left of him, just strands of loose, dead flesh stretched impossibly long, fluttering out to his sides like torn flags. His eyes were pockets of night.

Those inverse searchlights scoured the ground, finding them in seconds. As soon as that sickly not-light washed over him Cal felt as if he'd been punched in his stomach, in his *soul*, like the impact had knocked every last drop of life from him. He groaned at the horror of it, the complete and utter emptiness, knowing that this was what he would feel forever if the man in the storm swallowed him up.

Cal felt a sudden gust of wind take hold of him, pulling him up, the beast's mouth like a vacuum cleaner. He spread his wings,

trying to clamp down on the emotions, shouting for his angel to
fight back. He didn't need to tell it what to do, a sound barreling
up his throat, fired from his mouth like a mortar shell. It ripped
upward, scorching a path through the angry clouds until it detonated against the creature's face.

More shouts followed his own. Daisy hung in the air to his
side, screaming in her voice and the angel's. Marcus and Howie
were to his right, their heads recoiling like pistol barrels every
time they barked out a shot. The air between them and the storm
turned to liquid fire, boiling and hissing like a living thing. The
beast unleashed another cry, this one like some deep-sea leviathan.

It's working! Even though Daisy's voice was in his head he
still had trouble hearing it. *Keep going!*

Cal beat his wings, rising up through the boiling skies. He
opened his mouth, letting his angel hurl out another word. This
one slammed into the beast's mouth, tearing out a chunk of
smoke and dark matter the size of an office building. It was instantly sucked into the spinning void, like the creature was eating itself. The motion of its swirling face stuttered and slowed,
the bone-shaking rumble dimming for a second before powering up again.

Something whipped out of the darkness, a barbed flail of
black lightning that cracked the air right in front of Cal's face.
He tumbled down, blinded by the black scar it had left on his retinas. He heard another pistol shot, twisting his body to avoid it,
blinking the world back into view.

Daisy and the others were above him, darting back and forth
like fireflies as they unleashed blow after blow. They were aiming
for the man's eyes, a barrage of explosions tearing at those

searchlights. The man squirmed in his storm, that inward breath guttering out and restarting, again and again. He was panicking. He was afraid.

Cal pumped his wings, tearing up toward Daisy. They were so tiny compared to the man in the storm, but that was working in their favor. Every time he snapped out a fork of lightning they would dart out of the way, his attacks too slow, too clumsy. Cal swept his arms forward, punching out with invisible fists, hammer blows that thudded into the beast. It was like watching a battleship fire off every single weapon in its arsenal.

The sky moved, the whole thing falling earthward, the impossibility of it making Cal scream. He threw his hands up in front of his face as a shock wave of energy smacked into him, spinning him away like a ball. He hit the ground, plowing through tree roots and rocks, exploding everything into dust until he came to a halt.

Even past the angel he could feel the pain. He sat up, seeing the man in the storm against the horizon, so far away. The sky was still falling, only it wasn't the sky, it was the creature's wings. Those enormous plumes of rancid fire swept down, unleashing a hurricane. He couldn't see Daisy anywhere, or the others. Everyone had been blown away.

He sat up, giving his angel a moment to find its strength. Then he pushed himself off the ground, throwing himself back into the melee. It was too late. Those wings rushed down a third time and the man in the storm vanished in a blizzard of black embers.

IT WAS LIKE BEING INSIDE A WASHING MACHINE at full spin, and he had nothing left to fight with.

His angel was dying, it had been too badly injured. Brick tried to stretch out his wings but one was missing, the other like a torn parachute, useless. Fortunately his armored skin still burned, although the fire was weaker now, barely strong enough to illuminate the funnel of smoke and cloud around him. Even if he'd still had his wings they wouldn't have done him any good. He could no longer see where he'd come from, or where he was going.

Something loomed up in the darkness, too fast to avoid. He curled up, punching through it, seeing chunks of masonry explode into dust. There were other things here, caught like scraps of food in the man's gullet. People, or what was left of them, pieces of gristle that still had human faces, snagged on the edge of the throat. They flashed past him, hundreds of them, thousands maybe. These were just the dregs. How many millions more had been swallowed?

And he was one of them. Stupid, angry, pathetic Brick. It wasn't like anyone would miss him anyway.

Don't think it, he told himself, feeling his emotions cut through the heart of the angel. *It'll make you weak.*

He flailed, thumping through a vast, floating mountain of rock. On the other side of it he suddenly saw where the tunnel narrowed, ending in a point that radiated utter darkness. Clouds of smoke and atomized matter spiraled around it, sparking off bolts of lightning. The roar of the storm was fading, the silence that pulsed from the hole the most terrifying thing Brick had ever heard. Everything was wrong here, time seemed to be breaking, everything slowing down as it circled the drain.

It wasn't death in there, it could never be anything so simple. It was eternity, infinity, an ageless gulf of nothing that he would never, ever be able to escape. It was a black hole, a pinprick in reality that would eat until there was nothing left.

"No!" he shouted, the angel's voice swallowed up without so much as a tremor, like he had been muted. Brick shrieked, his arms cartwheeling, his stunted wing flapping. He managed to flip himself over, looking back the way he'd come, the walls of the tunnel corkscrewing relentlessly, dragging more and more of the world toward its end. There was something else up there, a flicker of fire against the madness. *Oh God please please please,* Brick said. The shape grew closer, exploding through chunks of floating debris. It had to be Daisy, or Cal. *It has to be, please God.*

Come out, come out, wherever you are, said Rilke. She swept toward him, her wings opening at the last second, like a dragon's. She gazed at him with the molten pools of her eyes, grinning. That third eye still blazed in her forehead, the one he'd made, gunks of fire dropping from it as if her brain were melting.

There you are, she said. *I found you.*

Please, Rilke, Brick said. The contrast of silence in one ear and thunder in the other was making him feel sick. *Please, help me, pull me free.*

Rilke cocked her head, her grin sliding away, slack and loose.

Help you? she said, her voice scratching across the surface of his brain. *Why?*

Because I'm dying! he yelled, clawing at the air, trying to reach her. *It's going to kill me!*

But you killed me, she said, beating her wings to fight the current of air. *You snapped me in half.*

I'm sorry, he said. She was mad, she was broken. *I'm sorry, Rilke, I didn't mean to.*

And Schiller, you broke him too.

No, I didn't! he said, feeling himself slip closer to the hole. He felt as if he was being stretched, like he would be pulled into ribbons. *I didn't, it was him, the man in the storm. You have to believe me.*

No, it was you, the boy with wings, she said, studying him with those blazing orbs.

No, I . . . I don't have wings, he shouted, trying to twist around, to show her his back. *It wasn't me, look. How could it be me?*

She frowned, the hum of her angel making the whole tunnel shake.

He broke me too, Brick stuttered. *The man with wings, with huge wings. He's broken me, and now he wants to kill me. We have to fight him, Rilke, together, please.*

Where is he? Rilke said, flying closer, almost close enough for him to touch. He reached out, not with his arms but with his mind, trying to latch on to her, to anchor himself, but he couldn't work out how.

We're inside him, he said. *He's trying to eat us.*

Don't be silly, she said, giggling. *He can't eat us.*

He will, Brick said. Bolts of white light were detonating in his vision, fireworks. His fire was fading, fast. His angel was dying. *He hates us, he's going to break us all, unless we fight back. Please, Rilke, don't let me die. I'm . . . I'm your brother.*

Schiller? she said. *Is that you? I can't see so well.*

Brick felt something curl around his waist, an invisible tentacle that reeled him toward the burning girl. The black hole didn't want to let him go, clinging on to every cell in his body. It was like he was coming undone, a piece of paper in water, dissolving. Rilke hauled him in, back into the roar and thunder of the storm, and he fell against her, holding her like a child with a parent. She hugged him for a moment, then recoiled.

You're not my brother, she said, her voice as cold as the inferno around her. *You lied to me.*

I am, he said, praying she was crazy enough to believe him. *Don't you recognize me, sister?*

She looked lost, the fire of her eyes flickering as the busted gears of her mind clanked and shook and tried to turn. The storm trembled, clouds of debris spilling from the walls of the tunnel. An almighty groan rose up all around them, then another explosion, like somebody was lobbing artillery shells at them. What the hell was going on out there?

Rilke, please, you have to get us out of here, before it's too late.

Her whole body trembled, like she was having a fit, great waves of energy pulsing from her. When it was over she grabbed him with the fingers of her mind, towing him along beside her as she pumped her wings and pulled away. The current attempted to suck them back but she was too strong, cutting a path upriver. All around them the storm shook, rocked by thunder. He could sense something, voices in his head—Daisy, Cal, the others too. Was it them? Were they attacking the storm? *Please please be true,* he thought as the clouds parted ahead, a shaft of weak, murky sunlight trickling through.

That's it, sis, you're beating him.

She stopped, spinning him around in the air, her eyes blazing.

You're not him, she said. *You're not Schiller.* Her shriek pummeled his brain, her grip on him growing stronger. He slapped at it with his hands but there was nothing there to fight. His fire burned, but nowhere near as bright as Rilke's. *It is you, I knew it, you lied to me, you broke him, you broke us both.*

Brick lashed out, an arrow of translucent flame slicing into the girl. Her hold on him loosened and he peeled open the world, ready to flee into the absence there.

The man in the storm bellowed, every single particle in the storm howling. Something was happening, black lightning bursting from the walls, churning up the smoke. Then the world disintegrated around Brick, his scream guttering out as he was blasted into atoms and sucked into the void.

DAISY / *San Francisco, 3:44 p.m.*

"WE CAN'T LET HIM GET AWAY!" Daisy heard Cal yell. His voice boomed across the deserted land, vibrating as the agitated air rushed into the space where the man in the storm had just been. The sky was full of flakes of smoldering ash, like Christmas but tainted, poisoned. Past them, the sun was starting to break through the thinning clouds. Its light spread almost nervously across the blackened earth, as if it were studying the damage that had been caused, feeling for survivors. There were none. How could there be? From up here in the sky Daisy could see for miles in every direction, every scrap of life scrubbed away by the beast.

The pit was still growing, straining against the flood of seawater that cascaded into it. Huge sections of land crumbled into the growing void. She wondered if the man in the storm had moved himself back underground, but she couldn't sense him there. No, it was more like he'd carved away so much of the world that it couldn't hold itself up anymore.

She could sense him, though, a long way away from here. He had left a trail, one that vanished in midair, almost like a mouse's tail beneath a rug. If she lifted up the world there she'd be able to see where he'd gone.

Cal flew to her side. Howie and Marcus were there too, scanning the horizon. She looked down, panicking when she couldn't see Adam. The blast of relief when he hovered up behind her almost made her cry. She wrapped her arms around him for a second, the air between them sparking in protest, then let him go.

We scared him, Cal, we must have, to have made him run away like that.

Guy's a chicken, said Howie.

Come on, said Cal. *Before he has a chance to recover.*

He didn't wait for her this time, his body exploding into incandescent dust. Daisy followed, using her mind to lift up the carpet, chasing the mouse's tail into the emptiness there. It was like she'd been able to do this all her life, as natural as walking.

A heartbeat later the world shaped itself around them with a protest of cracks and rumbles. The embers tore free from the dispossessed air—that's what they were, she realized, the parts of the world that were burned away to make room for the angels. Through them she saw the beast. He was hanging over another city, this one like something out of a fairy tale, full of old buildings and towers. A huge, dirty-looking river wound through it. There were people there, thousands of them, all staring and screaming at the storm, and the thing that lived in it.

Cal was a speck of flame against the brooding night, his angel's voice punching into it, echoing across the city below.

Daisy hurled herself after him, feeling the others by her side. Even Adam was there this time—she understood that he didn't want to be by himself. The turbine of the beast's mouth was starting up again, the buildings below starting to disintegrate, rising in pieces. The river was like an upturned rainstorm, draining against gravity. The people too were being sucked up. Daisy reached out for them with her mind, trying to hold them down, but there were too many, too fragile, and they came to pieces under her touch. *I'm sorry,* she said, the horror of it swelling inside her chest.

Focus, Daisy, said Cal. *Switch your emotions off.*

She tried, swallowing them down. Opening her mouth, she unleashed a cry that tore through the clouds, slicing into the man's face. Cal was attacking the eyes again, Marcus and Howie unleashing shot after shot at the tattered remains of the monster's body. The wind was a fist, grabbing them and shaking them as it swept into the cavernous mouth. It took everything she had not to be carried away by it.

The beast was fighting back, vomiting more of that horrible black lightning. The air was alive with it, none of the bolts coming close. Most were hitting the ground, blowing up like bombs, reducing the city to rubble. That endless breath was like a howling cry, full of rage, so loud that it made every bone in her body tremble.

Keep firing!

They didn't need her to tell them. Cal had pretty much demolished the beast's face, chunks of dark matter pulling loose from its eyes, sucked into its mouth. It seemed to be rebuilding itself, though, smoke filling the gaps and solidifying there. Daisy burned through the sky, letting her angel speak. The word was like a giant bullet cracking open the storm's skull, the force of it knocking her back. She flipped in midair, feeling another attack bubble up her throat and out of her mouth. There were so many explosions detonating against the storm that the man was more fire than smoke. There was no way he could survive much more of this, no *way*.

And yet his fury was growing, boiling from him in huge black waves, healing the wounds they made. She loosed another cry and this one was met by a whipcrack of utter darkness, the two forces crackling as they canceled each other out. It was using the lightning to block Cal's cries too, like a force field.

Daisy dived, avoiding a finger of inverse light that snapped out to meet her. The ground rushed up, close enough for her to see the ruined city, the stains that had once been people. She turned at the last minute, the earth beneath her exploding as the man in the storm lashed out again. She pumped her wings, hurtling up through the roiling smoke, pausing when she saw a burst of fire *inside* the beast's mouth. The man in the storm howled again, that awful, inward, sucking cry. Something was happening in there.

Brick, she realized, sensing him, and as soon as she called his name she heard his reply, a brittle scream for help.

You hear that? Cal said, appearing beside her. He looked exhausted but his angel burned fiercely. *That's Brick.*

Daisy lurched away from him as another sliver of lightning slashed the air between them. Cal opened his mouth and fired a word at it, the sound disappearing into the clouds around the beast, not even leaving a scar.

It's not working, he said. *It's too strong.*

He was right, they were hurting it but not killing it, like wasps stinging the hide of an elephant. But they were doing everything they could, weren't they? Switching off their emotions, giving the angels everything they needed. What was she missing? What were they doing wrong?

Over the howl of the storm she heard Brick shout again.

What's he doing in there? Cal asked.

Daisy didn't know, only that he wasn't alone. Cal shook his head and she heard him call out, *I'm coming, Brick, hang on!*

Wait, Cal! She chased after him. Before she could reach him, though, the world grew dark. A fist of smoke swung from the storm, so big that it blotted out the last of the sunlight. Daisy screamed, burning herself out of the world before the smoke could hit her. She fizzled back into existence on the other side of the storm, the sudden shift of perspective making her dizzy. That immense bulk of darkness was dropping toward the ruined city, like somebody was pouring a billion gallons of oil from the sky. Cal swept out of the way with Adam, Howie bursting into embers as he fled.

Marcus wasn't so lucky. He looked up too late, loosed a cry that vanished in the smoke. Then it hit him, punching him into the ground, the fist bigger than the city that had once stood there. It didn't stop, funneling into the earth, pushing the boy deeper and deeper with a series of booming cracks. Daisy called out his name, but there was only a gaping absence where the boy's thoughts had once been.

No! She lifted herself up, the anger like a living thing inside her. She opened her mouth and this time the cry that broke free was powerful enough to blister the air, carving a path of fire right into the heart of the storm. There was a second where she thought her attack had died away, then an explosion detonated inside the beast. Huge clouds of gunk jettisoned from the sky, trails of poisonous smoke trailing earthward.

She reached out with her mind, slicing into the wound she had made, grabbing anything she could find in there and ripping it out. Her angel's invisible hands wrenched and mauled, the beast above her bellowing like a million wounded bulls. The rage boiled inside her and this time she didn't hold it back, letting it fuel her.

She'd been wrong, so wrong. They weren't supposed to hide their emotions, they were supposed to *use* them.

She unlocked the door she'd closed against them, a hundred different feelings sluicing up inside her. It was like a volcano, the fire raging, spewing out of her. She cried out again and the whole sky seemed to shake. The hole it punched in the storm was huge and perfectly round, daylight pouring through it. The beast groaned, flexing its wings, a forest of lightning sprouting from its tattered flesh. It was going to vanish again.

It swept its wings down, blasting out a wave of dust. But it didn't disappear. Instead it lifted itself up, rising slowly, gaining speed with each clumsy stroke.

Where is it going? she asked, sensing Cal swoop up beside her. A rain of dust and ash was falling, like black snow.

It's running, Cal said, smiling. *Let's hunt this bastard down.*

CAL / *The Thermosphere, 3:58 p.m.*

IT ROSE LIKE A ROCKET, trailing a plume of impossibly dark smoke, the air trembling in its wake. Cal darted to one side as part of the city fell past him, disintegrating as it went. There were buildings there, office blocks that crumbled as they rose, screaming faces visible inside. Cal tucked his arms in, burning up through the sky, seeing the world shrink. The horizon was bent into a curve, the sky growing dark, stars appearing even in the middle of the day.

Howie flew up beside him. Daisy was there too, on the offensive again, her shouts impossibly loud and bright as they slammed into the body of the beast. Marcus was gone, smashed into the earth so hard that even his angel couldn't save him. Cal had felt the moment that the boy died, a split second of agony, then nothing.

Stay calm, don't think about it.

He put his head down, rising faster, slowing only when he heard Daisy's voice inside his head.

Cal!

He looked to see her there, her wings outstretched. It was like she was made of burning magnesium, a flare, so bright that even with his angel's eyes he had to look away.

I was wrong, she said. She stopped next to him and he risked looking again, feeling as if he was hovering next to the sun. *Cal, we have to let go. The angels want us to use our emotions, it's the only way to make them strong enough.*

What? How do you know?

I just do, she said. *It's okay to be scared.*

No, she was wrong. Fear would only make him weak. He'd learned that over and over again in his martial arts classes—stay focused, never get angry, never get scared, or you were guaranteed to lose. Center yourself, let everything wash over you, focus, then strike.

Wait here, he said. *Look after Adam.*

He ignored her protests, blasting up until the spinning chasm of the man's mouth was overhead. From here it looked big enough to swallow the world whole. Those same flashes of fire erupted inside the smoky flesh of its throat, and flickers of sound kept breaking through the deafening weight of silence, mind-voices that might have belonged to Brick and Rilke. Cal felt like he was in a boat floating on the lip of a whirlpool, but he clenched his teeth against the terror of it.

He folded everything in, feeling himself sucked upward so violently that he thought he'd left his stomach behind. He tumbled in the churning air, smelling air and ocean in the vapor around him. The world beneath him shrank away, so small, so vulnerable in its bed of boundless night. Then it too vanished as the storm swallowed him.

As soon as he was inside it he thrust out his wings, turbulence making his head spin. It was like being inside a cave, only one made of roiling smoke. Chunks of earth and city spiraled around him in a silent dance, disintegrating as they collided. Everything here was moving toward a distant point, a speck of absolute darkness. *She was right,* he thought. *It is a black hole.* Between him and it, caught up in the flow of churning matter, was a flickering orb of fire that had to be Brick or Rilke. *Or both of them*, he realized, seeing the two forms inside that thrashed and fought.

Brick! he called out, sailing toward them. The wind blistered past his ears, trying to grab hold of him, and it was all he could do to resist. *Brick! Rilke!*

Help me! Brick screamed. Jagged bolts of electricity were sparking from them, pumping out a cold, prickling energy that Cal could feel against his skin. He let himself slide closer and lost his grip, suddenly lurching toward the throat. The pull was just too strong. He couldn't hold himself here; if he got any nearer he risked being ripped away.

Brick would have to wait. Cal cried out. Here, beneath the armor of the storm, his attack was like a rocket-propelled grenade, sinking deep into the wall before erupting. He opened his mouth again, letting his angel speak, an onslaught of power that cut a path toward the event horizon ahead.

The storm shook, a sinking battleship, but the endless inward breath was as strong as ever. Cal felt himself caught up in it, his angel burning at full strength but still unable to resist the pull. It wasn't enough. *He* wasn't enough.

You are, Cal, he heard Daisy say, a whisper in the middle of his brain. *But you have to use them, you have to be you.*

Use what? His emotions? He'd seen what that had done to Brick, to Rilke. It had driven them both mad. Even now he could see it, in the way they scratched and bit and wrestled in the ether. *Clear your mind, focus, strike.*

Trust me, Cal.

And he did. More than anything. He took a deep breath, then set it free—all the fear, all the misery, all the confusion, and all the fury, *his* fury. It ignited in his stomach, in his heart, in his head, a pure, white fire that blazed out from his mouth. The air roared, a shaft of light puncturing the man in the storm, cutting out through the skin of cloud, through the tattered flesh. Cal screamed until he thought he would turn himself inside out, his cry eventually fading. The emotion still boiled there, though, an infinite supply of it, a lifetime of it, giving him strength, giving his angel power. He opened his mouth and cried out again, the world around him igniting.

RILKE HAD TO CLOSE HER EYES against the sudden brightness of the explosions, but there was no sound, no thunder, just the pathetic cries of the burning boy.

Please, please, just let me go.

Not that he was really burning anymore, just the thinnest shimmer covering his skin, and even that was flickering on and off like a candle in the wind. She held him before her, using the hands that weren't really hands. The world was nothing but smoke and shadow—no ground, no sky, just a tunnel of roiling darkness pockmarked by detonations. It was trying to pull them in, but her wings held them both in place. She was so tired, and so confused, that she couldn't remember if it had ever been different. Almost everything inside her was used up now, but that was okay. She only had one more job to do, then she could go home and be with her brother again.

But the burning boy just would not die.

She reached out with her not-hands, squeezing the boy's head. His fire blazed where she touched him, crackling and spitting. It was like a second skin, armored. She couldn't get past it. But every doll could be broken. She swung him to the side, smashing him against a floating island of rock, breaking it into splinters.

Please, I'm not who you think I am, the boy screamed inside her head, his buzzing voice so annoying. Why wouldn't he just *stop*? She pulled him back toward her, holding him there, studying the molten glow of his eyes.

He held out a hand to her. *I didn't hurt him, it wasn't me.*

Maybe he wouldn't die because he was telling the truth. Could she break him if he was innocent? But Schiller had been innocent, and he had been broken. Everything was so confusing. She pictured her brother, his beautiful face, so like her own and yet so different. His blond hair, those big, round blue eyes. The wings of fire that had stretched from his back.

Wait, that couldn't be right, could it? Her brother wasn't the boy with wings.

She reached up with her hand, the one that had always been hers, feeling the hole in her head, the ache that pulsed there. How had she gotten it? Who had done this to her? She had a memory of a blazing figure, an angel with wings, burning through her head with just a thought. The thing before her, the sniveling wreck, was nothing like that.

What was she doing?

Her last reserves of strength drained away. It was too much. All she wanted was to be with Schiller, back in the library at home, in the big bay window seat, drenched in sun, breathing in the heavy, dusty air. She loosened the grip of her mind, the boy there already half forgotten as he spun away. *I'm coming,* she said. *Wait for me.*

She didn't know where to go, but surely if she just relaxed then she'd get there. She folded in her wings, feeling the current of air wrap a cold hand around her, pulling her along. Wasn't this what happened when you died? A tunnel? A light at the end? There was nothing at the end of this one, nothing she could see anyway, but she could sense death there, as real and as certain as anything she'd felt in her life.

Help me! It was the burning boy again, floating alongside her, scrabbling at the air. She ignored him, smiling as she floated gently down the stream, toward the end of it all, toward her brother, into the arms of death. Let it have her. She was done.

DAISY / *The Thermosphere, 4:07 p.m.*

SHE LET LOOSE ANOTHER SHOT from the cannon of her mouth, a missile fueled by the emotions inside her. It needled into the face of the man in the storm, erupting in the smoky flesh. There was almost nothing left of him now, just that gaping mouth, a hole in the sky that kept turning, gulping down everything it could.

Cal was inside there somewhere. Brick and Rilke too. They were all still alive, she knew that much, but she couldn't tell whether they were winning or not. Silent explosions threw out webs of light that ebbed into the darkness, and tongues of fire were poking through the skin of cloud, like he was burning up from the inside.

She stared down at the blue bowl of her planet. It had always seemed so big, vast, such a long way to go to get anywhere. Now, though, she could stretch out her arms and hold it between them. It looked so fragile.

You can't have it! she screamed, turning back, opening her mouth and uttering another cry, one made up of rage. It erupted inside the storm, echoed by another three or four blasts from its throat. Cal. There was no sign of Howie but she could hear him shouting. Adam was close, a speck of light hanging below her. She almost called out to him, to ask if he was okay, before remembering that he couldn't answer her.

No, not couldn't. *Wouldn't.*

She paused, closing her mouth, remembering the day that Adam had arrived at Fursville. They'd been sitting around the table, trying to make sense of what was going on, just a few days—*a few million years*—ago. It had been Brick, that was it, going *thump-thump, thump-thump*, scaring the boy. And Adam had screamed, the sound of it tearing across the table, smashing glass, blowing out the candlelight. Fear had done that to him, the cry of his unhatched angel. The only sound he'd made in all the time they'd known him.

Adam! she called out, diving down to him. He looked so scared, his legs curled up to his chest, his face tucked into his folded arms. He reminded her of a little tortoise, but with a shell made from fire. Only his glowing wings were outstretched, holding him in orbit. They were huge and bright.

She pulled him close with her mind, then wrapped her arms around him. The space between them crackled and spat, an invisible force trying to separate them like she was holding a float underwater, but she held on.

I know you're scared. It's just me, Adam, it's Daisy. Look at me.

He tilted his head up, those big, burning eyes never blinking. Daisy smiled at him, aching with the effort of holding him close. She wouldn't let go, though.

I know this is all crazy. But trust me. I'll look after you, Adam, always. I promise. Is that okay?

He nodded. Daisy glanced over her shoulder, seeing something forming in the chaos of the storm.

I know it's scary, but it's okay to be afraid. We all are. Me, Cal, the new boy, we're all frightened. I think we're meant to be.

He frowned up at her, his own face like a ghost's beneath the skin of fire.

It's like . . . She struggled, trying to think of the right words.

Like you know when something really bad happens and you just want to scream? But you don't, because you don't want to get told off. Do you know what I mean? Did your mum and dad ever tell you off for shouting and screaming?

He nodded, and she thought she could see a picture there, beamed from his head into hers, a tiny house, packed with junk—not a scrap of floor visible beneath the mess. A living room, full of nasty cigarette smoke and the smell of wine—but not the nice wine her mum and dad sometimes bought, this was something stronger and older. A bedroom, too, full of broken toys. There was no noise allowed here, she understood, even though the television was blaring from the other room, even though she could feel a hunger in her belly that wasn't really hers, even though she was cold and tired. To make a noise in here would bring *him* in, a man she couldn't see but who smelled just as old and rotten as the house. Better to stay quiet, to hold it in, to never cry.

Oh, Adam, she said. *Were they really like that, your mum and dad? Were they really so horrid?*

He squirmed away, like he was embarrassed, but she held on to him, even though it felt like the space between them was about to explode. Another memory—Adam crying in the dark after a nightmare, a figure slamming open the bedroom door, storming across the room, lashing out so hard that there were stars. She felt the pain as if it was her own, the blood in her mouth, the anger too, like she'd swallowed a beehive into her stomach.

He hit you? she said, incredulous. This wasn't the Fury, this had been going on for years. She had to shut it out, it was so awful. She felt Adam do the same, stuff it deep down where it couldn't hurt him.

No, she said. *Don't run away from it. Use it. All that stuff down there, you need to get it out. It's like the bad bit in a peach, the rotten bit. If you cut it out it's fine, but if you leave it there too long it poisons the whole thing.* She shook her head, trying to think of a better way of putting it. *You need to think about it all, all the anger and sadness and fear. Let it out, Adam, please. Just scream and scream and scream.*

Adam's mouth opened and she could almost feel it bubbling up inside him, so many years of sadness and silence, a dam about to break.

That's it! she said. *I knew you could do it, I knew it.*

It was so nearly there, so nearly out of him.

Adam's eyes widened, his face screwing into a mask of horror. Daisy looked up, seeing it too late, a guillotine of smoke that dropped right toward her. She reached out before she even knew what she was doing, opening the door in the world, pushing Adam through it.

You can do this, Adam. I love you.

The air between them exploded like a bomb as they parted, an inferno of white light that sent her spinning out into space.

CAL / *The Thermosphere, 4:13 p.m.*

JUST LIKE THAT SHE WAS GONE.

Cal twisted around, looking back through the churning smoke. One minute Daisy had been there, the next she'd been wrapped in darkness, ripped away. He searched for her in his head but he couldn't tell if it was her voice he heard or just the echo of it.

Daisy? he called out. No reply. He beat his wings, pulling against the current, thrashing his way out of the storm. The air beside him erupted into ash, a figure appearing there. Adam flinched when he saw Cal, his wings spasming as he tried to control them.

What happened? Cal said. The answer was in the little boy's face as he stared out into oblivion. She was gone. The rage inside Cal was white hot, a supernova that burned in his core. He looked up at the storm, the man who sat fat in his bed of cloud, who gorged on the world. *She was just a girl! You bastard, she was just a girl!* The grief was too much, like it was burning him out from the inside.

He looked at Adam, saw his eyes narrow with the same outrage. The little boy didn't know how to handle it, the fear, the anger.

But his angel did. Cal could almost see the emotion there, past the transparent haze of his skin. It was like nothing else in the world, no atoms spinning in their orbits, no electrical sparks, just a ball of light, brighter than the sun, rising up the boy's throat.

Do it, Cal said. *Please.*

Adam opened his mouth and screamed Daisy's name.

It cut its way free from him like a flamethrower, blasting out with a jet engine roar, bright enough that it bleached all the color from the world. The shock wave hit Cal like a hammer, sending him reeling. He spread his wings, seeing the boy's fire punch into the storm, slicing its way across the face of the beast. It seemed to go on forever. He could have no air left in his lungs, but still he screamed, an inferno that set the sky alight.

Cal felt the cogs of his mind slip at the sight of it, the *impossibility* of it. It was too much. The angel inside him seemed to feed on the frenzy of his emotion, drawing it from his soul, pulling it up his throat. Cal choked on it, gagging as every single bad thing in his life was suddenly regurgitated. He thought of Daisy, always smiling, always brave, always ready to hug him with those stick-thin arms. Never again, though. She was gone.

He howled at the storm, vomiting an inferno of light and flame, purging himself. The air shook with the power of it, the world beneath him groaning as the physics it rested upon began to fracture. Their voices blazed relentlessly—their fury without end, without mercy. They would scream the world away if they had to, if that's what it took to stop the beast. They would scream him into dust to make him pay for what he had done.

Their fire was stripping the clouds away from the storm, revealing the pale ribbons of stretched flesh beneath. The engine of its mouth was stalling, spinning then stopping, spinning then stopping. Darkness washed from it, like it was vomiting out the emptiness behind the universe.

Still Cal screamed, even though it felt as if he was drowning, even though his brain pleaded with him to stop. He didn't think he could even if he wanted to. He felt like a ghost, like he no longer belonged inside the flesh and bone of his body. If he died now it wouldn't matter, because his angel was here. It had slipped on his skin like an anorak. It had found a way to make itself real.

That thought was terrifying, and his fear was just more fuel for the fire. It flared out between his lips and he screamed and screamed and screamed.

DAISY / *Space, 4:19 p.m.*

THIS WAS HER GRAVE, AND IT WAS BOUNDLESS.

The fist of smoke wrapped itself around her, the same way it had done back in the pit. Only this time it didn't pull her toward the man in the storm, it thumped her outward, hurling her away from him, from the planet, from her friends. The coil of liquid night ate into her, spreading across her mouth and her face, smothering her, blinding her. Her angel was working at full strength, fighting it. But it couldn't last much longer. She could feel its pain in every cell, its exhaustion. They would die together, in the cold, dark void of space.

No, it was too horrible. She didn't want it all to end here, where there was no sunshine and no birds and no flowers. How would she find her mum and dad? She cried out, her voice muffled by the cushion of smoke against her face. She ripped at it with her fingers, tearing at the shroud, peeling it back in time to see a huge silver medallion in the sky ahead. It took her panicked mind a moment to understand that it was the moon, and a heartbeat later she hit it, punching through white rock. She detonated out again in a shower of debris, still not slowing. She felt like a fish, hooked by a dark barb, being reeled out of the ocean.

It was getting colder, and something was happening to her head—her vision flickering. The smoke wrapped itself around her and it was as if death already had her, everything so dark, so quiet, apart from the thrashing hum of her angel's heart. The filthy, living smog was eating into her, dissolving her. When she tore at it again there was no sign of the earth, no sign of anything other than the stars.

No! she screamed. This time she thought she heard a reply, somewhere deep down inside her. It was a voice she knew, but she had to wait for it to come again before she believed it. *Mum? Is that you?*

It wasn't. How could it be? It was just a piece of her brain trying to keep her calm. She didn't care. It was so nice to see them, her mum and her dad, in the stuttering light of her imagination. Pain clawed up her back as the smoke continued to burrow into her, her fire ebbing. Once it was gone she would have no more defense against the universe. At least it would be quick.

She closed her eyes. Her parents were there, and she smiled at them. It felt like so long. She took herself to them, back to the day they'd had a picnic in the garden. Her mum had been too weak to go any distance, but she'd made it outside with their help, lying on the blanket in the shade of the next-door neighbor's trees. One of Mrs. Baird's cats had tried to run off with her dad's lunch while he was in the kitchen making tea. Daisy had chased it halfway back to the fence, picking up the chicken drumstick from the flower bed and dusting it off.

"He'll never notice," she'd told her mum. He'd come back and taken a bite out of it, and she and her mum had rolled around on the ground like monkeys, giggling so hard she hadn't been able to breathe—especially when he'd pulled a clump of cat hair from between his teeth.

Daisy laughed now, the feeling like the bubbles in the wine they'd had that day, fizzing up from her stomach. The hum of her angel heart grew louder and she could feel the sudden roar of her fire as it flared up.

It's laughing too, she realized. The sensation of it was like nothing she had ever felt, like her whole body was made of sound. Even though she was surely too far away to find her way back, even though the smoke meant to bury her in the endless nothing of the universe, she was smiling.

What else was there? The time they'd gone to a salmon farm in Scotland, and her dad had tried to ride the aerial slide over the lake. He'd sat on the wrong bit and ended up waist deep in water— even though he'd spent the whole day telling her not to get wet. They'd had to send out a little boat to rescue him. She giggled, her stomach aching, the fire blazing like she'd turned the gas burner to its highest setting.

She didn't understand where they came from, these memories, but her head was suddenly full of them, each one brighter than the last. Her angel was like a child hearing music for the first time, blazing inside and out. Its own laughter pulsed from every pore, so alien and yet utterly familiar too. It was a not-sound in her skull, a chime like bells. It chiseled against the smoke like a physical thing, splitting it, casting off squirming ribbons of night.

You're pathetic! she said, talking to the man in the storm, to the beast who raged in the sky so far behind her. It could eat all it wanted, but it could never win, not really. How could it ever triumph when there was laughter in the world? *I'm not scared of you, you're a joke, a big fat stupid joke!*

Her laughter—her *angel's* laughter—detonated against the smoke, breaking it into wisps. Beyond them was an expanse of starlight so immense that she couldn't take it all in. It was as if she hung in the center of a vast, hollow planet whose crust had been speckled with diamonds. There were millions of them, billions, all different colors, all so far away. She spun, mesmerized, terrified, thinking *which one is mine? Oh, God, which one is it?* Even with her angel's eyes the stars all looked the same. She could fly to any one of them with just a thought, but it would take her the rest of time to find her way home. She was going to die out here, but she didn't have to die alone.

She folded her wings around herself, letting the memories pour through her like daylight. The angel lapped them up, feeding on them, growing stronger, its fire so bright that she felt like she had to take a step back in her own head. It wanted more, she understood.

She thought back, searching for them. The time Chloe's chair had broken beneath her in English one day and she'd pretty much rolled right out the door. Daisy had almost peed herself because she was laughing so much.

Despite the fear, Daisy laughed, her angel laughed, the sound of it blasting away the last of the smoke. This time, even the vacuum of space permitted it, the sound echoing in her ears. It had never heard laughter. All the way out here there was only absence. There had only ever been absence, infinite and unbearable. This place, the emptiness between the stars, was what *he* liked, the man in the storm. He wanted to wipe everything else away so this was all that was left.

Well, she wouldn't let him, she *wouldn't*. She would fill it all up with laughter.

Fursville this time, riding the horses of the carousel with Adam and Jade. Then playing tag, chasing each other over the sun-drenched ground, Brick's gangly legs slipping on the gravel, his giggles high-pitched and surprising. The Fury hadn't mattered. Nothing had mattered. Right then she'd been just about the happiest person on the planet.

She laughed, the angel blazed, swept up by the wonder of it. It emanated a silent chime that cut across the void, which found an echo in the other angels, a call that led the way home.

Daisy stretched her wings, tuned in, burned out.

BRICK / *The Thermosphere, 4:27 p.m.*

BRICK SWAM AGAINST A CURRENT that was way too strong for him, his arms and legs useless against the flow of air. He was still burning, but he didn't have the energy to transport himself. Rilke had done her best to kill him and she must have come close; everything ached, everything felt wrong. His angel had taken the brunt of it, and now it was running on fumes.

The storm raged around him, sucking him into its throat, back toward the hole at the end of the world. Pieces of planet floated past, breaking up as they went, and through the debris he caught glimpses of *her*, Rilke, burning as bright as the sun but refusing to fight. He didn't understand what she was doing. It was like she'd given up. If she wanted, she could pull them both out of here. She was injured, yes, but only her human body. Her angel was still running at full strength.

Rilke! he called again, for what must have been the hundredth time. *Please, don't do this!*

The storm shook, those same ear-pounding artillery shells detonating somewhere outside.

There was something else now as well, something that roared even louder than the hurricane. Whatever it was, it had to be working, because the clouds were spinning more slowly, the current weaker.

Not weak enough. He slid down the gullet of the beast, unable to find purchase. It was going to swallow him whole, into the empty infinity of its stomach. The thought of it—an eternity of nothing, an eternity alone—made him howl, the noise coming as much from his angel as from him. He didn't want to die alone. He'd been by himself for so long, not letting anybody in, not even Lisa. His anger had always filled him up, he'd never made room for anything else.

Rilke, wait! he called to her. If she heard him she made no sign of it, floating downstream in her web of fire. He scrabbled in midair, feeling like a parachutist in free fall. Beating the current was one thing, but crossing it was another. She was slightly ahead of him, and he wheeled his arms and legs, steering closer— *Hold on, for Christ's sake*—maybe ten meters, then five.

The air between them began to spark, like somebody was letting off firecrackers. Invisible fingers pushed him back, and he thought it might be her, trying to shunt him away. She was smiling, like she was in the middle of a waking dream.

Rilke! he said, using the last of his strength to push himself toward her. Bolts of energy fizzled up his arm as he grabbed her foot. He climbed her like a ladder, too frightened to let go. Just like before, when they'd been fighting, the hum of their hearts rose in pitch, sounding like they were about to explode. He hugged her, just grateful to have somebody next to him as he spun toward the end.

What do you want? Rilke asked, staring blindly, like her body was a shell. What was he supposed to say? That he didn't want to be on his own when the beast devoured him? He didn't reply, just clung on. It couldn't be much longer now, the event horizon dead ahead, clouds of matter spiraling around it as they were crushed into dust and sucked inside. Even sound was being pulled in, leaving nothing but silence.

It's not too late, he said, his voice impossibly loud against the quiet. *You can get us out of here.*

I'm tired, she replied. *I just want to go home. I want to see Schiller.*

The storm rocked again, pieces of it crumbling away as the attack continued outside. He clung to Rilke with trembling arms, feeling the pressure build between them. He couldn't hold on for much longer, but he didn't need to. In seconds he would simply disintegrate, as if he had never existed.

We don't want you here, Rilke said. Finally her eyes turned to him, two pools of molten lead and a third in the middle of her forehead, the one he'd made. She lifted her arms and pushed him, but he held on as best he could. *It's just me and my brother. Go away.*

No, he said.

Go away!

She shunted him hard, almost slipping out of his hands. They were deep into the deafening silence now, sliding toward the black hole. Rilke was already coming apart, pieces of her crumbling loose like she was made of sand. Her angel blazed, trying to hold her together. Brick pulled her close again, his terror so intense that it almost didn't register at all. The air between them pulsed, spitting liquid fire, but he fought it. He would not let go, he would not face the end by himself.

A blinding flash, and suddenly he was inside a room, a library, watching motes of dust drift lazily between the shelves. Schiller sat on a window seat opposite him, his breath misting up the glass. There was nothing out there but gold, as if the room floated in an ocean of sunshine. Brick was crying, but he understood that these weren't his tears, they belonged to someone else, to *Rilke.*

"He's gone," said Schiller, turning to Rilke—to Brick. "I won't let him hurt you again, I promise."

"I know, little brother, I know," he heard himself say. "We'll keep each other safe, forever. I love you."

Schiller leaned forward and hugged him and the memory— *Was that what it had been?*—faded. It had been so real that Brick had almost forgotten about the man in the storm, about the black hole at the bottom of its throat. He looked at Rilke, seeing her life as if it had been his own—her dad long gone, her mum insane, and the man, the *bad* man. His face loomed up, his breath stinking of coffee and alcohol, his nails long and dirty. Brick almost screamed, forcing the memory away, the pain that came with it.

He scrabbled, trying to keep hold of Rilke, knowing that she needed him as much as he needed her.

I don't, she said. *I have Schiller. I'll always have him.*

He's not in there, Brick said, both of them dissolving in the dark light of the black hole. *There's nothing in there, it's empty. Schiller's gone.*

Their eyes met, and he realized that deep down, past the madness, past the exhaustion, she knew the truth.

It doesn't matter, she said. *I'll find him.*

She smiled, her lips bursting into ash. Brick felt his fingers slip as her body fell apart, tried to scoop her up in his hands, to hold her together. As soon as they parted the air between them ignited, the same nuclear detonation as before, blowing him back up the throat of the beast. He rolled like a spinning top, pushed on by a rippling wave of energy. He called Rilke's name, reaching back for her with his hands, with his mind, trying to pull her along with him.

But it was too late. She was gone.

CAL / *The Thermosphere, 4:29 p.m.*

HE SPAT FIRE, AND THE STORM BURNED.

The beast was coming apart, its body blown to smoke, just its mouth still open wide. Even that was losing power, its inward breath nothing more than a whistle. Clumps of half-eaten debris were falling from it, along with flickering strands of dark light. It was almost as if the man in the storm was turning himself inside out.

Adam hung in the air like a dragon, the same unbroken plume

of fire roaring from his lips. Howie too, hurling bolts of magma from his mouth. Each one made the sky shiver. Cal never stopped thinking about Daisy, the sadness and anger fueling the inferno inside him. He would never stop thinking about her.

That's very sweet, said a voice, *her* voice. The shock of it silenced his angel and Cal looked out into the heavens. One of the stars was moving, falling toward earth. It was emanating a sound, and it took him a moment to understand that it was laughter.

Daisy? How?!

I don't know, she said, flickering out of sight before reappearing next to him in a halo of incandescent ash. He stared at her, open-mouthed, and she laughed even harder.

You'll catch flies if you keep your mouth open like that.

Then she threw herself into his arms, the air between them blistering in protest. He grinned, holding her as tight as he was able. The relief was like a river bursting in his soul.

Use it, she said, pulling loose, looking up at the beast.

What?

That, she said, pointing at his chest. *Use it.*

He did, laughing out a bolt of fire that lashed up into the fading darkness of the storm. Daisy was doing the same, the sound of her giggles like birdsong. Adam had stopped for breath, and when he saw Daisy he too started to laugh. Not just him but his angel too. Each burst of sound was a weapon, tearing into the void over their heads.

The man in the storm was trying to burn himself away, but his wings were in tatters. The stumps twitched like an injured crow, lightning rippling over the surface. The air was full of movement, a hail of black feathers that drifted down toward the planet below. He was no longer making any sound at all, just the pitiful wheeze of a dying thing. A last, desperate breath.

A pearl of white light appeared in the heart of the darkness, hanging there for a moment like a dewdrop. It expanded in a heartbeat, a silent supernova. Cal buried his head in his arm. When he looked again the beast was lost in fire. A lone figure hurtled from the cold inferno, spinning through the air like a burning rag doll.

Brick, he said. But Daisy was already chasing him, snapping out of existence with a pop, appearing again almost instantly with the other boy in her arms. He was alive, but only just, his angel's fire stripped away from every part of him except his eyes. He had lost his wings, one gone completely and the other like a scarf of candlelight that hung from his shoulder.

You okay, mate? Cal asked.

Rilke, he said. Cal searched for her in his head, but she was nowhere. He glanced at Daisy, met her eyes, and she knew it too. Rilke was gone, but she'd taken half of the storm with her.

Come on, said Cal. There was barely anything left of him, his mind and body emptied, packed with cotton wool. But there was enough. He flexed his wings, carrying himself up toward the storm. The clouds were dissipating now, like rats deserting a sinking ship. Behind them was a scarecrow of old flesh, his throat an open wound that blazed black light. It was done. It was dead. It was over. *Let's finish this.*

THE FURY / *The Thermosphere, 4:32 p.m.*

CAL FOUGHT IT. He lashed out with every last piece of himself, every dreg of emotion. The angel did what it was supposed to, converting it into energy, into fire, hurling it at the beast. The man in the storm was now neither of those things. Everything about him had been ripped away, leaving just that spinning core, that black orb, like an obsidian marble in the sky. Even this was shrinking, its dark light guttering out. Like the angels, it could not survive here on its own, Cal thought. Without its host it was nothing. It pumped out waves of deafening silence, each one like an inverted scream. Cal no longer even felt like his body was his own. He felt clumsy inside it, as if he were operating an unfamiliar machine. It didn't matter, though. He felt the joy of it blister up his throat and burn from his mouth. None of it mattered anymore, because they'd beaten it, they'd won.

BRICK FOUGHT IT, even though he couldn't hold his own weight. Daisy kept him afloat in the trembling air, her mind like a harness around him. He could barely see, his mind a mess of white noise. But he knew what to do, sweeping his arms through the ether, somehow finding the energy to attack what was left of the storm. All he could think about was Rilke. The girl who had killed Lisa, who had tried to kill him; the girl whose brother had been murdered; the girl whose mind he had ruined, whose sanity he had ripped right out of the hole in her head; the girl who had been so sad, so angry, who had refused to talk about it to anyone, not even her own brother—so much like Brick, *so much* like him. He couldn't make sense of her, of what had happened, but her rage was now his to use, and he did, screaming the beast into oblivion. *This is for you, Rilke, I'm sorry, I hope you find your brother, I really do, I'm sorry, I'm sorry, I'm sorry* . . .

HOWIE FOUGHT IT, the fire inside him so natural that he wondered if it had always been this way, if he had just woken from a dream of a normal life, a dream of a family by the sea, of friends, of nights on the beach drinking rum. How could any of *that* have been real? It felt so artificial, like he'd watched it on TV. This was the truth—he was a creature of energy who could pull the world apart with just a word. The storm was now a quivering speck of shadow against the brilliant canvas of space. It flickered, poisonous roots of lightning growing from it, fading almost instantly. Howie attacked it, stamping down with his mind like he was crushing a beetle, again and again and again. The sound of it was like thunder. He never wanted to fall asleep, never wanted to go back to the dream life, to the place where he had no power. And his angel didn't want it either, he realized, because if it left him then the only place it could go was somewhere dark and cold and timeless. He clung on to it, feeling its freezing fire flare up inside his soul, laughing.

ADAM FOUGHT IT, screaming at it, seeing his mother's face in the sky, his father's too. He was so angry with them, he *hated* them. All these years they'd told him to shut his mouth, to keep quiet, to stop moaning, stop crying. But not anymore. "I'm talking now!" he yelled, and his voice was even louder than his mum and dad's when they were shouting, louder even than the man in the storm. It was the loudest thing in the world and it was *his*. "I'm talking and there's nothing you can do!" He wouldn't let them hurt him anymore, he wouldn't put up with it. He never wanted to see them again and he didn't have to if he didn't want to. He'd live with Daisy, and Cal, and maybe even Brick, even though the tall boy was always grumpy. He looked at them now, glittering in the sun like Christmas tree ornaments. They were all made of fire, just like him. They were his brothers and his sister, and he loved them so much it made his heart hurt. They shouted at the sky and he did too, all of them together, the way it would always be.

DAISY FOUGHT IT. It didn't feel like fighting, because all she was doing was laughing. It bubbled up inside her as if it had been buried for a million years, finally set free. She couldn't stop it even if she wanted to. Each giggle was a golden flame that swept from her mouth, reminding her of breaths on a cold day. They rose up to the man in the storm, covering him. Not that there was much left anyway, just a circle of darkness, like somebody had used a hole punch on the sky. It was getting smaller and paler, the universe healing. She opened her wings and flew to it, still laughing at the relief of it. Her angel laughed too, the hum of a tuning fork, making every cell in her body feel lighter than air. The storm shrank away from her, and she almost felt sorry for it because it could never know what she was feeling. The beast— although it wasn't really a beast, it wasn't really alive like an animal or a person—roamed through the cold, dark emptiness of space looking for life, because it couldn't stand it. All it knew was nothing, absence. To it, this world was *wrong*, a horrible blip in the rules, something that couldn't be tolerated, that had to be rebalanced, set right. But it hadn't counted on the angels, hadn't counted on the people either. And it certainly hadn't counted on laughter. If there was an exact opposite to emptiness, to that infinite nothing it loved so much, it had to be laughter, didn't it? There was nothing more human. She fought it, reaching out, the storm now a speck of dust that she could trap between two fingers, then smaller than the little atoms that made up the air, then so small that even her angel's eyes could no longer make it out, tiny enough to fall between the cracks in the world. A single spark of black lightning flickered across the sky, then she felt it end, everything that it was erupting from it in a rippling explosion. The shock wave knocked her back and she burned herself out of time and space, taking the others with her, riding the sound of their laughter all the way home.

MONDAY EVENING

Courage is resistance to fear, mastery of fear—not absence of fear.
—Mark Twain, The Tragedy of Pudd'nhead Wilson

AT FIRST HE WASN'T SURE WHERE THEY WERE. Then the world caught up, wrapping its fist around them, and through the swirling halo of embers he recognized it. To his right was the sea, still unsettled even after all this time. To his left was a parking lot, and a little squat building with its doors boarded up. Ashes still coated the ground—fewer now, but enough for him to see the footprints there, the tire tracks too, from when they'd left that morning. It all looked different through the eyes of his angel, but when he reached into his head to try to turn off the fire nothing happened.

Is it over? The voice was Brick's, and Cal looked around to see him lying on the ground, propped up against the dune. His fire still burned too, although weakly, and the boy shuffled uncomfortably in it. His big, bright eyes blinked.

Better be, said Howie, floating above the ground beside the toilet block, his wings half-folded. *I am proper knackered.*

It is, I think, said Daisy. She and Adam stood side by side, their angels humming loud enough to lift the sand and ash in a dance around them. It made the whole parking lot look like it was formed of liquid. There was another noise coming from her, a crystal chime that made Cal's head feel weird. *The man in the storm is dead.*

You sure? Brick asked. Daisy cocked her head, as if she was listening for something. After a moment or two she nodded.

I'm sure. Can't you feel it? He's gone.

Cal *could* feel it, the sensation like he'd eaten something bad, something that had made him feel sick for days and days, and he'd finally puked it up. He wondered if his angel was relieved too, because it felt different up there. It was as if Cal were a hitchhiker inside his own skull, pushed to one side by the chill of the creature. He couldn't work out if the sensation was the result of an injury, something that had happened during the battle, but when he patted his head, his body, nothing seemed to be missing.

I can't turn it off, said Brick. The bigger boy was writhing in the sand and ash, his single wing flopping beneath him like a mangled limb. *It won't go away.*

Cal tried again, flicking that invisible switch that would put him back in control of his body. Nothing happened, and he felt the briefest glimmer of panic in his gut. The angel seemed to relish it, his second skin flaring up, pumping out that same mind-numbing sonic pulse. *Keep calm, keep calm,* he told himself, but suddenly the suit of flames felt wrong, like he was wearing somebody else's flesh. He didn't want to see through its eyes anymore, didn't want to see the secret mechanisms of the world, the little atomic engines that turned relentlessly; didn't want to feel the immense, gaping emptiness that waited just beyond the paper-thin shell of reality. He shrugged his shoulders, trying to shake himself free, but the angel sat right in the middle of his head, smothering his thoughts.

What's going on? he said.

Make it go away, Brick yelled, on his feet now, swiping at the air in front of his face like he'd wandered into a swarm of bees. The boy's fear was contagious, Howie starting to scratch at the inferno around him, his wings cutting through the wall of the toilet block and blasting it into dust. Adam was whimpering, each one making the air tremble as it spilled from his lips.

Wait, it's okay, Daisy said. *Don't be scared.*

"Piss off!" Brick was screaming now, his words punching through the dunes, sending chunks of sand into the white foam of the sea. "Just go away, we're done, we don't need you anymore."

Brick! That's enough! Daisy insisted.

Cal bit down on the rising panic, watching Daisy float through the air, pulling Brick into her arms. It was like watching a mother with a child, and he soon calmed down, even though the space between them kicked off a firework show of light. She let go of him, a thumping pulse of energy escaping, kicking up whirlwinds of dust.

But I can't turn it off, Brick said, his hands clenching his temples. *It won't get out of my head.*

They're . . . She looked like she was struggling for words. *They don't want to go back to where they came from. It's cold there, and dark.*

They can't stay here, Brick said, punching himself now. *It's my head, you hear me? Get out!*

That's enough, Daisy said, taking hold of his hand. *The more emotional you get, the worse it will be. That's what they want, emotions. All that anger, they're feeding on it.*

You told us that's what we should do, he said, his burning eyes fixed on her. *You told us to use them. It's your fault.*

Lay off, mate, said Cal. *If she hadn't told us that we'd be dead, yeah? Give her a break.*

Go to hell, Cal, Brick spat back. *I didn't ask for any of this to happen.* He screwed his face up, groaning. *I can feel it in there, get out get out GET OUT!*

Daisy looked at Cal, her face full of sadness. That chiming noise was gone, and the air felt heavier for it.

They're so lonely up there, she said. *They hate it. Can't they stay?*

If they stay, we die, he replied. *It's the Fury, Dais, as soon as anyone comes near us they'll tear us into pieces. We can't hide forever, it's only a matter of time.* He thought about the creature inside him, the thing that had kept him alive, and felt inexplicably guilty when he said, *Tell them to leave, it's the only way. Can you do it?*

Daisy stared out across the sea, but she was looking at something else. Cal tried to peer into her thoughts but what he felt there—a pressure on his chest, in his throat—was unbearable.

Daisy? he said. She looked at him and smiled, just about the saddest smile he had ever seen.

I think I know what I have to do.

DAISY / *Hemmingway, 4:59 p.m.*

SHE WASN'T SURE WHY she had brought them back here, to Hemmingway. It was home, she guessed, the only one she had now. The only one she needed. It had been a lifetime ago when she and Cal had driven into this parking lot, a lifetime ago when they had driven out again. It felt like she had spent years here, by the sea, in the sun, with Cal and Brick and Adam and the others. But years—and seconds, minutes, hours, days—they were different now. Time was a broken thing.

Home. She had been happy here. Not all the time, of course. She had been sick and scared and angry too, at Rilke and Brick and all the ferals and most of all at the man in the storm. But to have found even a little bit of happiness in the middle of all that was like when the sun breaks through the heaviest of clouds, painting the world gold. Yes, she had been happy here. She would always be happy here.

They could be happy here too, the angels. Why did they have to go back to where they came from just because their job was done? It wasn't like they were machines ready to be stuffed back in the cupboard. She remembered thinking they were like robots, soulless weapons to be used in the war against the beast. But that was wrong. They were more like babies learning to use their emotions for the first time, discovering all the wonderful things that they could feel. They didn't have any of their own, she was pretty sure about that, but that didn't mean they couldn't feel what she was feeling.

And who would want to go back to a horrid dark empty place forever if they could stay here and have laughter and love and all the nice things? Even as she thought it she felt her angel laugh, that tuning-fork ring filling the air, so unlike human laughter and yet so unmistakable. It made her giggle too.

What do you mean? Cal asked. *What do you have to do?*

She smiled at him again, looking at the angel that sat inside his soul. She still didn't truly understand what they were, or where they came from. How could she? These things were older than time, older than the universe. They'd been here forever, always existing. So had the man in the storm. He *was* the forever, the ageless, empty aeons. It made her brain hurt just trying to think about it, so she stopped. None of it mattered, not now they'd found a home. She was tired, the angels were tired. It was time to rest.

She made her way to Brick, the boy squirming in his suit of fire. He was such a *baby*.

Brick, she said. He ignored her, his arms wheeling as if he could somehow pull himself out of his own body. *Brick!* she said again, touching his shoulder. He flinched, glaring up at her.

Just get it out! he said.

I want you to listen to me, she replied. *I want you to be less angry. And less selfish too.* He started to argue but there must have been something in her expression that stopped him. *Everything is easier when you're nice, and it doesn't take much, does it? It doesn't cost anything.*

What are you talking about? he said. *It's got nothing to do with you, Daisy.*

Just try, she said. *You think everyone hates you, but that's not true. Don't you see, we love you, Brick. We always will. Be nice, promise me.*

His mouth dropped open and he nodded slowly. She giggled again—the laughter was so easy now, for her and her angel—then she moved her hand to his chest, pushing her fingers into the fire. It was like putting down a leaf in front of a ladybird, watching it crawl on. Brick's fire shot out with enough force to catapult him backward, rolling him across the parking lot. It ebbed along her arm, making its way toward the sound of bells that rang from the very center of her. She felt the moment where it joined her angel, the two of them sitting in her chest, chiming so hard her teeth rattled.

Brick cried out, writhing on the sandy concrete where he'd landed, thirty meters or so away. He stared back at her with his own wide, wet, human eyes. When he tried to push himself to his feet Daisy held out her hand.

Don't. You're human now, remember. You can't come near me.

He stood but stayed where he was.

"What did you do?" he croaked, his words weak and stuttered, like this was the first time he had spoken.

Daisy turned to Howie, who backed away into the wreckage of the toilets. He held his hands up to her.

Wait, what if I want to keep mine? he said.

It will kill you, sooner or later, she replied. *Then it will die too.*

But what about you?

I'm offering them something else, I think, she said, floating to him, reaching into his chest. *I wish I'd had time to get to know you.*

His angel came willingly, burning up her arm and into her soul. The force of it sent Howie spinning backward almost to the tree line. After a second or two he lifted his head, putting his hands to his ears. It was no wonder, the hum emanating from her was deafening, three angel hearts beating in the same place. She felt so cold now, and heavy too. But she couldn't stop. She looked at Adam, smiled at him.

Are you ready? she asked him.

But I want to stay with you, he replied, and it was so good to hear his voice. She floated to him, pulling him to her, feeling that same electric charge build up between them.

I'll always be here, she said. *I need you to be a brave boy, Adam. I need you to be strong. Promise me you'll never be afraid to use your voice again, okay?*

She let him go and he blinked up at her with his burning eyes.

Promise me.

I do, I promise.

This doesn't hurt.

She pressed her fingers to his chest, his angel freeing itself faster than the others. It seared a trail along her skin, diving into her. It was like she'd eaten too much food, like she was about to pop. The sudden current of energy swept Adam away, depositing him softly at Brick's feet. The bigger boy bent down, helped him up, holding him tight when Adam tried to run toward her again.

She almost wasn't able to turn to face Cal, her body too heavy, too full of ice and fire.

How did you know it wouldn't kill you? he asked. *How did you know any of this?*

I didn't, she replied. *But they did.*

What happens now?

She shrugged. *We live.*

She straightened her arm, reaching for his chest, but he hovered away.

Thank you, he said. *We would never have made it without you.*

I know, she said, giggling again. *Promise me you'll look after Adam. Never let him go.*

Cal looked over, smiled at the boy.

Sure, I'll try, Dais, but I don't know what will happen—

Cal . . .

Okay, sure, I promise. I'll never let him go.

She tried again, but he backed away even more.

I don't know what else to say, he said.

Then don't say anything. She reached out a third time, her fingers pushing into his chest. There was a flash, like an electric shock, a bolt of pure energy crackling into her body. Cal flew back, rolling through the dirt. When he looked up his face was covered in ash. He looked like a ghost, and that just made her laugh even harder. The angels laughed too, like her body was hollow and filled with chimes. The hum coming off her sounded loud enough to split the earth.

"Daisy?" somebody shouted, but she could barely hear them. She couldn't see very well either, the inferno blazing from her so brightly that even her angel's eyes were struggling. It was too much, the world trembling to hold her, the skin of reality stretching to fit her in. The angels were agitated, she could feel them inside her thoughts, her blood, her soul. It felt like she was about to blow and take the whole universe with her.

She blinked, seeing Cal and Brick and Adam through the haze, looking so small, so human. She remembered the first time she had met them—Cal, when he saved her, in the car, telling her about the grumpy lady like she'd never heard of a satnav before; Adam, when he had arrived with the others, so quiet, so afraid, until they'd ridden the horses of the carousel, Angie and Geoffrey and Wonky-Butt the Wonder Horse, and his face had opened up like a flower; and Brick, poor, sad, angry Brick who'd met them right here on this very spot, who'd taken them to Fursville, whose laughter was like a bird's when he had finally forgotten to be mad at the world. How was it possible to love people so much, so *hard*?

You should go, she said. *I think something is about to happen.*

"Daisy, no, don't leave!" said Adam. He started toward her but Brick held him back.

"Goodbye, Daisy," Cal said. He smiled at her.

It's not such a bad way to leave, Daisy thought. *Looking at a smile.*

She offered him one back, turning away before her laughter could become tears. She'd see them again, she was sure of it. Maybe not in the same way, but that was okay. This wasn't the end. She drifted across the dunes, the world peeling open at her feet, the sea hissing as she flew over it. Even though she felt heavy she rose like a balloon, heading up into the brilliant blue. The movement of the angels was growing more frenzied, like they were cats trapped together in a basket. She hushed them, but they didn't understand. The thrum of their hearts was rising in pitch. How much longer did she have before the world simply couldn't hold her anymore? Seconds? Minutes? Hours?

But time is broken, she said to herself. *It can never catch us.*

She turned back and looked down, saw the boys walking away into the leafless trees. Beneath her the sea had been stripped away, the ground too, the energy that poured from her carving a crater in the earth. The air shook as it tried to escape, like it knew what was coming. Time ground past, trying to snatch her up in its fingers, but she was too heavy for it now, it couldn't carry her.

She held on until she couldn't see them anymore—Brick the last one to go, raising a trembling hand, his tears like crystals on his dirty face as he disappeared. *Go,* she told him. *Nothing bad will happen now*—then the universe broke beneath the weight of the angels.

They seemed to burn up inside her, an explosion that started in her soul, expanding outward. It got as far as the edge of the forest before she reached out with her mind and took hold of time, pulling herself free of it. Something groaned, the noise like a giant foghorn in the center of the world. Everything was shaking, reality threatening to come to pieces, the explosion desperate to finish what it had started. But she would not let go. The angels worked with her, holding on to the reins of time.

In her head she clung to that memory in her garden just as tightly, lying in the shade of the trees, watching beads of sunlight chase each other across the grass. She rested her head on her mum's leg, smelling linen and dewberry. Her dad waved at her from inside the kitchen window, looking a hundred years younger than he had before, looking like himself again. She'd been so happy, *so* happy, and she would always be, because she never had to leave that garden, she never had to say goodbye. She would lie there with the breeze on her face, with her mum's hand on her arm, with the neighbor's cat weaving in and out of her feet, purring like a steam train, forever and ever and ever.

She laughed, and outside the world moved on without her.

Slowly at first—she saw people there, down below, crowds of them—but quickly speeding up. Day became night became day became night. The faces changed, but she saw people she knew, Cal and Brick and Adam, moving too fast for her to see what they were doing. There was rain, and snow. The forest disappeared, replaced by buildings, then they too vanished, the coastline changing with every beat of her heart. But still she saw them, her friends, her brothers, standing there by the sea, watching her for the blink of an eye. Every time they appeared they seemed older, until they were gray and stooped, but she always knew them.

The world went on without her, years passing, decades, centuries, and she watched the land recede, the ocean rise. She saw cities in the sky, and rockets, she saw the sun grow big and red, all while that same laugh rang out of her, just a single breath that held all of time at bay. At some point she would have to let go, she knew, when the man in the storm appeared again, or something else like him. At some point the angels would pull their way free from her so they could fight another battle. But until then there was just the garden, and the sun, and her mum and dad—*I love you guys so, so much*—and a laughter that pealed out across the ages.

BRICK / *Hemmingway, 5:23 p.m.*

BRICK COULDN'T BEAR TO LEAVE HER THERE ALONE, but what choice did he have? He could hear the sonic pulse of the angels inside her, growing all the time, like she was about to explode.

"We should go," said Cal, taking Adam by the hand and leading him away from the sea. The little kid resisted, trying to pull loose, but Cal was holding on to him. "Mate," he said to Brick. "Seriously, that doesn't sound good."

It didn't look good either. The world was coming apart around Daisy, the land and water boiling as she floated up into the sky. He could feel the tremble through his feet, the ground trying to shake itself to pieces. He could barely see the girl anymore through the orb of fire that surrounded her. She looked like a bird in a burning cage.

"I don't want to go," said Adam, sobbing. "I want Daisy."

"She's going to be fine," Cal said. "Can't you hear her?"

Incredibly she was still laughing, the sound crystal clear, rising even above the hum of the angels. Cal bent down, slinging the boy over his shoulder. He started to run toward the tree line and Brick followed, that pulse chasing him, growling against his back. Howie had already vanished. Brick slipped on the ash, on the sandy concrete of the parking lot, so tired he could barely put one foot in front of the other. It felt like he was learning how to use his body from scratch again, now that his angel was gone. He felt too light, too brittle, as if he might break into splinters at the slightest touch. But it was a miracle he was moving at all. His angel must have healed the most serious wounds; it had patched him up from the inside.

He hobbled into the trees, looking back through the bare branches. Daisy hung over the sea, burning as brightly as the sun. The water steamed beneath her, freezing and then boiling, again and again, forming statues of ice that lasted just seconds before melting away. It was mesmerizing, and he almost forgot himself in the kaleidoscopic wonder of it. He held out a hand to her, realizing that he was crying. And even though he no longer had his angel, he heard her voice in his head, like she was standing right next to him, whispering in his ear.

Go. Nothing bad will happen now.

He stepped between the trees and the world behind him turned white and silent. A noiseless wave picked him up, carrying him through the air, so fast that he couldn't even scream. Then he fell onto the soft, sandy ground, and life went dark.

HE DIDN'T KNOW HOW MUCH LATER IT WAS when he opened his eyes. He lay there on his back, staring up at a sky that was halfway between day and night. His ears were ringing, like he'd been at a concert all night, but past the annoying whine he could hear voices. He tried to sit up, feeling like every single cell in his body had been brutalized. Even his eyeballs were sore, his vision watery. He tilted his head to the side, blinking away the tears. Something was moving over there, maybe several somethings. He couldn't be sure.

He pushed himself up onto one elbow, running his other hand across his eyes. When he looked again the shapes had solidified into figures, people, one running in his direction. A bolt of adrenaline rocked through his exhausted body. *The Fury.*

It's gone, he tried to tell them, his mouth refusing to form the words. *The angel, it's gone.*

The shape thundered toward him and he clambered to his feet, managing one step before stumbling down again. Were they screams he could hear? Choked, feral cries? After everything that had happened, after all he'd done to fight the man in the storm, was this how it was going to end? Teeth in his throat, fingernails in his eyes? He tried again but there was nothing left inside him. Hands grabbed him, rolling him over, insect eyes burning into his, the black hole of a mouth dropping toward him. He prayed it would be quick. It was the very least he deserved.

"You okay?"

He almost couldn't hear the words over the whine in his ears.

"Mate? Can you hear me?"

Brick lay still, his heart trying to beat its way out of his chest. He blinked until the face above him came into focus.

"Cal?" Brick grunted. The other boy grinned, looking bruised and tired but otherwise intact.

"You okay?" Cal said again. Why did he keep asking? It was pretty bloody obvious that he wasn't. Brick struggled to sit up, trying to recall how he'd gotten here. Everything in his head was white noise, but he remembered running with Cal and Adam, remembered Daisy floating out over the ocean. What had happened to her? Had she *exploded*? He grabbed hold of Cal's arm, hauling himself to his feet.

"Daisy," he said. *Please let her be okay, please don't let her be dead.*

"She's there," said Cal, pointing. Brick hung on to the other boy, the world spinning. He could have been standing in the middle of the desert. Only the sand here was a million different colors, and dead ahead was the ocean, so foamy somebody could have poured a thousand tons of detergent into it. The sun sat on the horizon, high over the water, but when Brick turned back around it also hung over Cal's head. The impossibility of it made him reel.

"You need to sit down," said Cal.

Brick shrugged himself free, staggering across the beach toward the first sun, *her* sun. There were more people ahead, silhouetted by the glow. He had to get closer before his watering eyes could identify them as Adam and Howie. They were both filthy, their clothes in tatters, but their angels had looked after them well, repairing the worst wounds before jumping ship. They were smiling.

"Hey," said Howie, his voice like sandpaper. "You look like crap."

Brick laughed, even though it hurt to do so. Howie was black and blue, his hair silver.

"Don't look so good yourself," he said. "You look like my granddad."

"He must be a very handsome man," said Howie, making Adam laugh.

Brick looked back toward the sun. It was forged of light, of colors he had never seen before, waves of energy shimmering back and forth over the surface. He couldn't see anything inside it, but a crystal chime emanated from the sphere, the sound unmistakable.

"She's laughing," said Adam. "She's happy."

"You think?" Brick said. But the kid was right, there was no doubt about it. How many times had he heard that laugh, had it pulled him out of his anger, made him human again?

"Daisy," he said, and the thought of her there, trapped inside that bubble of fire, made him angry. Why did it have to be her? She was just a girl, it should have been someone else. She should have been allowed to go home, to live her life. It wasn't fair, it just wasn't—

He felt a hand on his shoulder, looked to see Cal there.

"You made her a promise," he said.

Brick realized his fists were clenched, his nails digging into the flesh of his palms. He *had* promised her something, he'd promised not to be angry. But how the hell was he supposed to keep *that*?

"Seriously, mate," said Cal, nodding out over the water. "You really want to risk her coming after you? She'll fry your ass."

He laughed again, despite himself, letting his body relax. The truth was he was just too tired to be angry. The deep breath he took was full of the smell of the sea, the smell of home. He could try, for Daisy. She had saved them, after all, time and time again. He owed her that much.

"Fine," he said. "You're looking at the new me, one chirpy arsehole coming up."

Cal laughed, and for a while they stood there, squinting into the brilliance of the second sun. It seemed impossible that less than a week ago he had sat on this very beach worrying about money, gas, Lisa. How could so much change in such a small space of time? The thought of it made his legs shudder and he almost fell, Cal's hands holding him up.

"Hey!" The voice came from behind them, and they all spun around together to see a man in a police uniform walking over the dunes. Brick took a step back, calculating the distance between them. Thirty meters. *Please don't,* he thought. *Please don't turn.* The man—not a cop, a fireman—was running now, pointing up at the new sun. "What are you guys doing?"

Twenty-five meters. Twenty. The man stumbled, groaning. *Oh no, it can't be.* Fifteen meters, and Brick had almost turned, almost started running, before the fireman found his feet again.

"You kids need to get out of here," he said, running right past them, kicking up sand. "Go on, get home."

Brick remembered to breathe, watching the fireman as he ran into the woods, yelling something into a radio. *Thank you,* he said, to Daisy, to the angels, to anything else that was listening.

"We should go," Cal said.

"Go where?" Brick asked. "What are we supposed to do after

that? Pretend it never happened? Pretend it might not happen again?"

Cal shrugged. "The only thing I know is that I'm desperate for a can of Dr Pepper. Everything else can wait."

"You know that stuff is poisonous," said Brick. "Nothing but sugar and chemicals."

"I know," said Cal. He turned, walking up the beach, away from the sea. The others followed, each of them carrying two shadows from the two suns. "But if I can survive today, I can survive a can of fizz."

Brick shook his head, then found that he was smiling so hard his cheeks ached. Cal was right. It didn't really matter what happened next. Right now they were safe, they had survived. He glanced back toward Daisy, hidden inside her bubble of light. Was she watching him now? He raised his hand and waved to her.

"Goodbye, Daisy," he said. "I'll see you soon. Be safe."

Then he turned, running after the others, hearing her laughter fill the air behind him as he chased his shadow into the sun.